The Glass Cocoon

by

Serena F. Holder &
Christopher J. Jarmick

Published by Flibbertigibbet Promulgations, Mesa, AZ
Produced by Five Star Publications, Incorporated, Chandler, AZ

This novel is a work of fiction and as such, the names, characters, places, and incidents are either creations of the authors' imaginations or are used fictitiously. Any resemblance to actual persons living or dead, specific events, or locales is entirely coincidental.

Flibbertigibbet Promulgations
P.O. Box 31894
Mesa, Arizona 85275-1894
Toll-free 1-877-91FPPUB

Library of Congress Cataloging-in-Publication Data

Holder, Serena F., 1948–
The glass cocoon/by Serena F. Holder and Christopher J. Jarmick. -- 1st ed.
p. cm.
ISBN 0-9702078-0-8
I. Jarmick, Christopher J., 1958– II. Title.

PS3558.O347755 G58 2001
813'.6--dc21

00-065436

Published by Flibbertigibbet Promulgations
Electronic version: www.eBookery.com

Produced by Five Star Publications, Inc.
P.O. Box 6698
Chandler, AZ 85246-6698
(480) 940-8182 • Fax (480) 940-8787
website: www.BookProducer.com • email: info@FiveStarSupport.com

Publishing Consultant: Linda F. Radke
Editor: Paul M. Howey
Cover Design: Jeff Yesh
Interior Design and Typesetting: Kim Scott
Proofreader: Sue DeFabis

Printed in the United States of America

I believe because it is impossible.

Tertullian

Words are only painted fire; a look is the fire itself.

Mark Twain

PROLOGUE

A common thread

A golden cord

A delicate string

Of hearts and souls

Strung on a line

So fragile

It can be severed by

The touch

of an

Eyelash

Chapter One

"Phillip? Phillip is that you?" Patricia was unable to control the desperation in her voice.

"Trisha? What's wrong?" Phillip asked, immediately regretting his question. He heard her sigh before she began to explain.

Later that same evening, KTAO, a local Taos, New Mexico radio station, interrupted its regular programming lineup with a news bulletin. The smooth-voiced reporter said that a one-vehicle accident on State Highway 64, near the town of Eagle Nest, had claimed the life of Taos resident Mack Shaw.

"No!" Patricia gasped out loud. She stared at the radio while the announcer continued.

"Details are sketchy, but eyewitnesses report that Mr. Shaw was traveling at a high rate of speed and apparently failed to negotiate a turn onto State Highway 38." The reporter continued, "Mr. Shaw, an employee of the Taos Floral and Design Shop, was apparently en route to Red River on a scheduled delivery at the time of the accident.

"According to authorities, evidence at the scene also indicates that more than one vehicle may have been involved in this tragic accident. A search is currently underway for a second vehicle. Several witnesses told police that they saw the van near the Angel Fire turnoff in the minutes just prior to the accident and that a late-model dark sedan accelerated and pulled alongside the van.

"Barbara Ortega, owner of the Taos Floral and Design Shop, has declined any comment other than to verify to authorities that Mack Shaw had been in her employ for approximately two years. KTAO will bring you further details as they become available."

For Patricia, there was no longer any doubt. Tragically, the coincidences were all too clear.

Earlier that day Mack Shaw slowly removed the coffee-stained paperwork from his lap, placed it on the seat next to him, and checked the address on the delivery slip one more time to make sure it matched the numbers on the old adobe house. He let out a bit of a groan as he opened the van door. Though not old by today's standards, Mack lived each day with a few more aches and pains than he'd like to.

Mack winced as he pulled a large floral arrangement toward him and lifted it from the carpeted floor of the van. The walk up the uneven flagstone path was a slow one. He'd been completely unaware of the car that had parked directly in front of his delivery truck. Nor had he seen the well-dressed man step from it and stare directly at him. Mack had been too preoccupied with making sure he had the right address.

The young man nervously adjusted his designer sunglasses. He couldn't be certain that the delivery man hadn't spotted him. *Damn it! Why didn't you just circle the block and wait for him to leave? You're really brilliant sometimes!* He didn't stop beating himself up until he saw the driver go about his job without even glancing his way. He briefly considered the possible repercussions of his lapse in judgment, and then made up his mind. Moving briskly in the direction of the well-kept territorial home on Pond Street, it was only a few seconds before he'd crossed the yard and disappeared behind the row of cottonwood trees that lined the bank of the irrigation canal.

The canal, which had been flowing for hundreds of years, was said to have been built by the ancient Anasazis, ancestors of the Indians who still lived in the Taos Pueblo just north of town. Once much longer, the canal now just meandered quietly through the fields and pastures surrounding the Ridgeway house and past the majestic old cottonwoods that were just now beginning to turn brilliant yellow-gold as early fall began to embrace the valley.

Upon reaching the front portico of the grand old house, Mack leaned forward and managed to press the button with his elbow. A smile slowly stretched across his aging but pleasant face. He listened as the magnificent chimes finished their melody. Perhaps most men would never have noticed the doorbell. Mack, however, was not like most men. His thirty odd years of work as an air traffic controller had taught him the value of being cautiously alert at all times. But the job had also taken its toll on him, both mentally and physically.

His decision a little over two years ago to take an early retirement and relocate to the quiet, remote mountains of northern New Mexico had been a good one for him. It had changed his life in many ways. It had even crossed his mind that maybe it wasn't too late for him to find a good woman with whom he could spend the rest of his life. He had been devoted to his career and had known that he had neither the time nor energy it took to build a strong marriage and at the same time concentrate on such a demanding job.

So far, however, Mack hadn't met anyone that he thought would tolerate his old, annoying habits.

The door chimes first startled and then annoyed the lone occupant of the house. Patricia Ridgeway slammed her pencil down on her glass-topped desk, regretting the gesture almost as soon as she'd done it. "Damn! It's been one small irritation after another all morning!" It had started with Sylvia, her much too curious and garrulous friend who had kept her on the phone longer than she would have liked. No sooner had she concluded her conversation with Sylvia than there began an annoying series of phone calls. Each time, the caller—whoever it was—had hung up on her. Then there was that noisy garbage truck clamoring through her normally quiet neighborhood. These had all worked together to break her concentration to the point where she'd taken an unplanned break. She picked up a leather-bound book and smiled as she ran her fingers over the gold embossed lettering which spelled out "Daily Journal" in a beautiful script across the cover. She wished that she were disciplined enough to write down her thoughts and dreams on a daily basis instead of waiting and then trying to retrieve them from the recesses of her mind. She wondered if, a hundred years from now, the impact of the words would be as strong and mean as much to anyone as they did to her now.

On the quietest and most cooperative of days, trying to concentrate on the balance sheets from her bookstore was certainly one of Patricia's least favorite activities. And now, especially after the events of the last few weeks, trying to get back into the task at hand was nearly impossible. In all honesty, she seldom did it correctly, distractions or not. She had been doing it for thirteen months and it simply shouldn't be this hard! But it was.

"Damn it all," she said in total frustration. She jerked her gold rimmed reading glasses off and tossed them on the desk, starting a small chain reaction that ended with the pencil rolling to the edge of the desk and falling to the floor at her feet.

"Great! That's just great!" she declared. Rising up from her bent position, she arched her back against her fists. She was unaware that she must do this a dozen times a day, trying desperately to ease the dull ache in her back caused by too much sitting at her desk and too much fretting over those damned figures.

Patricia glanced down at the pencil and chuckled at her own ineptness. Her foul mood was already beginning to mellow out a bit. Patricia kicked the pencil aside as she made her way toward the door of her office. "Move, you lazy ol' fool," she hissed as she stepped over the cat sprawled across the floor of the hallway.

"Well, whoever the hell this is, it better be important!" Patricia walked across the oxblood sealed dirt floor of her old hacienda. The Ridgeway home was a combination of unique design and colorful architectural innovations that made it a charming and comfortable home for Patricia and her husband Trent since moving to Taos in the mid-1970s. Now, twenty-five years later and childless, Patricia still managed to smile as she counted her many other blessings. She quickened her pace as she neared the front door.

Counting her blessings is something that Patricia had always done following one of her emotional outbursts. Something from her childhood always brought out the worst in her whenever and wherever numbers were involved. She could laugh now because she could always count on herself to react in exactly the same manner to these simple, minor interruptions and annoyances. With the need to balance out the figures of her rather lucrative bookstore, it was at the very least a monthly occurrence.

"If I weren't making so damned much money," she once told her husband, "you can bet your sweet ass I wouldn't be doing *this* right now!"

"Well, if you are making so much money," he'd countered, "why don't you just hire it done?"

She had to admit that she really didn't have an answer. Secretly, she knew she wanted to learn every aspect of the bookstore and to learn to do all of the tedious jobs and do them well, even the ones she loathed.

Patricia placed her hand on the brass handle on the front door and peered through the glass panel. She was able to see the white van with its colorful and familiar logo of the Taos Floral and Design Shop parked directly in front of an unfamiliar black sedan.

Patricia and Trent had been semi-happily married for a long time. All of that had changed recently and so it was not likely that the flowers were from her husband. Even in the best of times, flowers were simply not something Trent had ever given much thought to. He'd always given her beautiful gifts, saying that he preferred to give her things she could touch, feel and cherish. Patricia loved him for that, and their home was filled with his presents and other special treasures they'd collected together over the years.

As she turned the handle of the door, Patricia was suddenly and inexplicably reminded of a long forgotten memory. There *had* been a time when Trent did send her flowers—a dozen, long-stemmed, yellow roses to be exact—to commemorate their first date. They'd met in Texas. Patricia was a senior in high school and Trent was a shy college sophomore. Embarrassingly enough, she hadn't even remembered the exact date herself. But being so touched by his gentle gesture, she'd begun to cry as she read the card that accompanied the roses. Crying was definitely something that

Trent could not stand for her to do. Patricia realized that was the last time he'd ever given her flowers. She was still caught up in her thoughts as she opened the door.

"Hello. May I help you?" she inquired. Patricia eyed the jolly-faced, portly gentleman standing just beyond her threshold. She tried desperately to hold a smile in check as she watched him juggling the monstrous floral arrangement. As Mack peered cautiously from behind the foliage, Patricia quickly recognized him from other deliveries he'd made—not to her home, but to her bookstore. He was in the Take Another Look Bookstore several times during its grand opening week. A few loyal patrons and a secret admirer or two still sent flowers occasionally. Sometimes, instead of flowers, a colorful balloon bouquet would arrive. The cards were always unsigned, of course. Patricia assumed that this was just a way for grateful patrons to thank her for some kindness she might have shown them. She was rather good at locating hard-to-find first editions, and often went the extra mile in helping people research special projects. Little did her customers realize that she was actually using them as an excuse to do that which she enjoyed most.

The deliveryman was still holding the large fall arrangement that nearly obscured him from Patricia's view. The voice from behind the earth-toned chrysanthemum blossoms announced simply, "Delivery for Patricia Ridgeway. Are you Mrs. Ridgeway, ma'am?"

"Well...yes...I mean, are these for me?"

"If you're Patricia Ridgeway, they are, ma'am," Mack answered with a chuckle. Mack waited for a response but received none. "Say, would you mind taking these while I get the delivery slip for you to sign?"

Still slightly stunned by the massiveness of the arrangement, Patricia finally reached out to take the basket from him. It was even heavier than she anticipated. She stepped inside and carefully placed it on the dark oak library table behind her. She turned back toward the door and accepted the two-page form and pen that Mack offered her. Just as she reached for them, a movement in the yard caught her eye. She glanced over Mack's right shoulder to see an unfamiliar man step from the curb and onto the street directly in front of her house. He was rather smallish and very well-dressed. She wondered where he had come from and why. The Ridgeways had lived on Pond Street for quite a while and, other than the regular delivery people, rarely saw anyone who didn't either live nearby or knew someone who did.

Taos was a teeming tourist town, both in the summer and in the winter. However, during this lazy Indian Summer time of year, the streets always seemed almost eerily deserted. Seeing the stranger in the street created an uneasiness in Patricia. Too many horrible and unbelievable things had occurred in the last few weeks.

Mack turned to see what she was looking at. He spotted the young man standing by the driver's side door of the black car looking up and down the street and occasionally glancing in their direction. Mack suddenly felt an almost forgotten but quickly recognized sensation of dread. It was the same feeling he'd experienced years ago when a plane's signal had suddenly disappeared from the radar screen in front of him.

"Hmm, now who is that?" asked Patricia when she realized that Mack was also looking at the man in the street.

"Dunno, Mrs. Ridgeway. Not a friend of yours? Maybe someone from the store looking for you?" Sensing Patricia's concern, Mack quickly changed the subject without waiting for an answer. "Gosh, Mrs. Ridgeway, I can't tell you how glad I am that I found you at home. I'd hate like heck to leave a beautiful arrangement like this outside in this sun. They sure can wilt in a hurry."

Still distracted, Patricia handed the paperwork back to Mack without taking her eyes off the young man as he got into his car. As he took the pen, Mack noticed that her hand was trembling. As soon as she let go of the pen, Patricia began absent-mindedly rubbing her hands together the way someone would for warmth on a cold winter day.

"I see you've got arthritis too, Mrs. Ridgeway. That's sure a shame at your age."

"Oh, I'm sorry. What was it you were saying…uh, Mack?" She tried not to appear as though she were reading the brightly embroidered name sewn over the left breast pocket of his shirt.

"Just commenting on your arthritis, ma'am. I have a time with it myself, especially this time of year. S'pose it's the change of seasons. That's what those old Indians out at the pueblo say, anyway." It only took him a second to realize that Patricia once again wasn't listening to a word he was saying.

"Well, I'm sure glad I was home, too, Mack. Thank you so much. Oh, and by the way, please tell Barb that these flowers are absolutely beautiful!" She looked back at the arrangement and added, "You don't happen to know who they're from, do you, Mack?

"No, ma'am, I sure don't. But I know there's a card with them somewhere in there. Saw it as I was carrying 'em up the walk." Mack couldn't help but notice the obvious anxiousness in her manner now, despite her attempt to appear unconcerned.

"Oh, right. Well, thanks, Mack." Patricia had the door closed before he had an opportunity to reply.

Patricia stood in the foyer and stared at the arrangement for a moment before noticing the small, white envelope with her name printed on it. It had been carefully inserted into a clear plastic holder which was attached to a small tree branch and pushed deep inside the arrangement. She opted to leave it there for the time being.

An almost overwhelming feeling of anxiety enveloped her. She stared at the flowers almost as though she expected them to speak. Then she hurried back to her office, leaving the flowers and the card untouched on the antique table.

As Mack hobbled back down the walk to his van, he saw that the black car had pulled away from the curb and traveled slowly east before turning around and coming back toward him from the rear. He pulled himself up into the van with more than a little effort. As he started to turn the key in the ignition, he glanced in the rearview mirror and saw the car approaching and also that he'd forgotten to close the back doors of the van. Cursing the so-called "golden years," he got out and went around and closed the doors. Once back in the driver's seat, he put the truck in gear and pulled away, completely unaware of the approaching vehicle until it startled him by pulling up beside him on his right. The window of the car was down slightly, just enough for Mack to see the driver remove his sunglasses for a moment. Without the least bit of guilt on his part, Mack thought to himself, *As if we don't have enough problems here with all these damned tree huggers, don't tell me we have to start dealing with the damned boat people, too!* The dark sedan pulled in front of the van and accelerated as it turned south toward the downtown plaza.

Chapter Two

Phillip Craven had only recently begun feeling good about himself again. So why was he depressed now? Things were going well. He felt alive again. Motivated. At times—and after a long absence from such emotions—he even felt passionate about his life, his work, his future.

In all honesty, he knew why, of course. He needed to have that conversation with Mary that he'd been putting off for nearly two months now. Or was it three? Whatever it was, it was too long, he told himself. He was in love with someone else. He had to tell her. He owed her that much at least. Not that Mary and he were ever going to wind up getting too serious with each other. Still, if she had deeper feelings for him than he had for her—well, it was an awkward situation and Phillip didn't want it to get any more complicated. Maybe it wouldn't change a thing between them. He hoped secretly it wouldn't. It was just time to make sure she understood.

As he gripped his mug of hot coffee in both hands and stood on the deck of his home located on the scenic banks of the Tenaway River in Cle Elum, Washington, he knew he had little right to be depressed. How many people had the pleasure of waking up at their own leisure and strolling out onto their deck and breathing in the crisp, clear mountain air and listening to the refreshing sound of the river running just a few yards away? How many people would exchange their lives for his? Quite a few, he figured. No, he had little right to be depressed. But yet…

Phillip took a sip of his coffee and watched a red-tailed hawk soar high above him in search of its morning meal. Staring off in the direction of the circling bird, his mind drifted back to another brisk fall morning, five years and fully another lifetime ago. It was an October morning in the Los Angeles suburb of Woodland Hills when Sarah and he, barely speaking to one another at that point, had looked without emotion into each other's eyes.

"I *do* still love you," Sarah had said blandly. Phillip had a million things to say in reply, but all he could do was turn away. It was painful then and was still painful now, and no less so for knowing the right decision was made by both of them. They just needed to get away from one another. And so here he was, certainly not living a playboy's lifestyle, yet still thinking of Sarah, a woman he never could get close enough to then and was never far enough away from now.

The two of them had met in college, and drifted in and out of each other's lives for a few years before deciding that a writer and photographer were a reasonably good match. Okay, so he fancied himself a writer, too, but not the journalist she was. After a while, they separated for several months only to stumble into each other while both were on separate assignments at the pyramids outside Mitla, Mexico, in the fall of 1974. It certainly seemed that fate was telling them to stop playing games and admit they needed one other. So the handsome young man from New York City and the quiet, disarming girl from Fresno got married.

It was all downhill from there. Well, not *all* down hill. Granted, for fifteen years their marriage sputtered, stalled, and disintegrated until they became little more than roommates. But there were those moments filled with passion and lust and desire and a love that was nearer to perfection than either of them had ever experienced. Such moments, however, got fewer and fewer. Phillip supposed that's what made it all the more painful in retrospect. He was emotionally mature enough to know, even then, that a marriage is like a prized rose bush that constantly needs attention. Pruning, feeding, and caring is what a marriage needs to survive and certainly to flourish. Sarah and Phillip had allowed their love to die and whither away. It was only after three years of avoiding the inevitable that they realized it was time to officially cut the legal strings that insisted they were married. Yet, even as they were severing the relationship, it almost came back together with the force of a tropical storm recapturing the love and passion from years earlier. But, alas and inevitably, it was short-lived. They both knew the old pattern would return in time and that was simply unacceptable now. *All or nothing* they had once said they wanted—*it had to be all or nothing.*

"Nothing, huh?" Phillip mused as he drank down his last bit of lukewarm coffee. Certainly what was happening in his life *now* was a great deal more than nothing. Though there wasn't anyone he could actually hold in his arms. Nor was there anyone he could say was particularly special. Still, there was a recent development. One, which he knew, held great promise.

Phillip tried not to think of his career. He'd basically kissed that off a long time ago. A photojournalist without a Pulitzer after fifteen years had better be content with the grind of the job and some occasionally rewarding moments. That or find another line of work. Well, that is if he weren't already operating as a photo editor. There are always younger, hungrier ladder crawlers willing to put themselves at risk, willing to take a veteran's place for a lot less salary and at a moment's notice.

His brief experience as an entertainment critic wasn't satisfying either and the PBS documentary which he'd produced certainly hadn't led to the job security he'd hoped it would. Politics were everywhere in this business and he hated playing competitive games and kissing ass instead of doing his job the best way he knew how.

With Sarah gone now, Los Angeles had looked even worse to him. So when an acquaintance suggested that he move to Seattle and work for an alternative newspaper, Phillip took very little time to consider the opportunity and left almost immediately. Desperate times called for desperate actions, didn't they?

Phillip took a side job working as a forensic photographer for the King County coroner's office. At times, he even felt that his pictures of autopsied body parts and the occasional run-of-the-mill crime scene was more important than anything he had ever done! Fuck, now how scary can that be?

Of course, that was because he was sleepwalking through life. Sleepwalking to cope with his loss. He had shut down part of himself. The biggest part of himself, actually. To replace it, he pretended to be busier. When feelings had begun threatening to rise too close to the surface, he took that job in order to be too busy to think. Then he woke up. That was nearly two years ago now. Woke up, overreacted, and ran away again. This time to Cle Elum, a little over a hundred miles east of Seattle.

Phillip had lived modestly for most of his life. He had wisely invested regularly in a mutual fund which—fortunately—had done very well. There had been a little split equity in the Woodland Hills house which was sold as part of the divorce settlement. He and Sarah never had any children.

He'd wanted children, but he didn't dare. He was haunted by that. What if it was genetic, he thought. He'd read that children of alcoholics often wind up alcoholics, and children of abusers often grow up to be abusers.

The hawk was gone now. And he hadn't seen the small deer that often passed near his deck. He'd been hoping for that moment. Something simple and natural might help to take him away from his complicated thoughts.

Phillip sighed. It was time to get some work done. Time to sit in front of his computer and explore, research, and write his syndicated weekly article bylined Internet Phil: *Helping Consumers and Parents Understand and Cope With the Internet.*

There were five sources of income in Phillip's life. His syndicated weekly column, a few dollars from his book, the part-time work he did for the coroner's office, and his freelance photography sales at galleries and from his photo library. His stock photos, which had been earning a little money for him for over twenty years, were now earning him almost enough to live on, especially after he was discovered by a major magazine publisher. You could find a "From the Phillip Craven Archive" photo in about two well-known magazines almost every month, if you looked hard enough. The photos might be of an interesting face, a landscape, a twisted tree, an old barn, a country road, an abandoned building. And he loved to see his signature seascapes. They had always been his favorite photo shots. Who knows why. Maybe it was because he loved the sea himself, or maybe it's just that unexplained, age-old lure of the sea. Then there were the ruins. He had always longed to go back to Mexico and visit the ruins.

Phillip was feeling a bit sorry for himself now, although that was not really his style at all. Besides, he'd had a great showing at an art gallery in Seattle just a few months ago. His book was selling reasonably well, and there was some interest in him doing another one. This time, he might actually get more than a token advance from the publisher. That would be nice. Maybe with that he would break down and buy himself a DVD player and a few dozen films. Maybe he'd do a lot of things he'd been thinking about lately.

The local sheriff's office and the daily newspaper also called on him occasionally to do some crime scene or journalistic photography. He'd even done some portrait shots of a neighbor woman who was running for a local council seat. In fact, that was how he'd met Mary Foreston. She was a friend of the wannabe politician. Mary had helped her knock on doors, get signatures, raise a few dollars, and had easily convinced Phillip to take some pictures of her friend—at no charge, of course. Mary told her friend that she and Phillip had worked out "an arrangement" to cover his normal fee for campaign flyers. Mary was an attractive woman, just past the prime of her life. Lonely. Too lonely. She missed the city and no longer enjoyed the quiet of the country. She was restless.

Phillip felt an almost immediate attraction to Mary. She had sad eyes, but she had a wonderfully warm smile that she used to hide her pain. She had a certain way of starting to say something, a bit too directly, and then quickly softening her almost harsh words as if she were embarrassed; afraid of being too honest, too blunt. And her hazel eyes were full of the spark of life. He hadn't slept with a woman in months, and her looks and her demeanor reignited his dozing libido.

Phillip didn't act on the impulse. But he didn't forget it either. He'd had a few fantasies about Mary and being intimate with her. Once, he thought he'd spotted her grocery shopping in the Ellensburg IGA Market and had clumsily raced his shopping cart over to her only to discover that it wasn't her at all.

The next time he saw her was in the Cle Elum drugstore. She'd flirted with him and told him that he had the most wonderful blue eyes. "Someone should photograph *you*, Mr. Craven," she'd said.

"Would you like to have a cup of coffee sometime, Mary?" he'd asked in reply.

"I would. But, honestly, if you want a good cup of coffee around here, you'd best make it yourself."

"I make very good coffee," he answered without hesitating, "and I could even fix you a helluva lunch, if you would like!"

Phillip had known it would be more than coffee and lunch. He really wasn't fantasizing about it. And he actually wasn't hoping for it. No, he just knew that he and Mary would begin a torrid affair. Two days after meeting in the drugstore, Mary invited Phillip out to her secluded cabin to let him show off his prowess as a chef.

And what a lunch it was! Phillip smiled as he remembered that day. He was beginning to feel a familiar stirring as he thought of running his hand over the smooth, warm flesh of Mary's hips…

The phone was ringing. Phillip suddenly realized that he was completely caught up in his thoughts. It was at least the second ring. Moving swiftly through the hot tub room, Phillip entered the main part of his home and picked up the receiver.

"Hello!" he said a little too loudly.

Silence.

"Hello?" Phillip repeated.

"Phillip Craven?" asked a quiet voice with what sounded like an exaggerated nasal tone.

"Yes, this is Phillip Craven."

"You're easy to find."

"Who's looking for me?" Phillip wondered if some friend was poorly disguising his voice.

"Well, no one is, right now." The voice reminded Phillip of a poor Peter Lorre imitation.

"I give up. Who is this?" Phillip chuckled.

"Oh, don't give up. It's not any fun if you just give up."

"Well, I'm not *having* any fun right now and I've got to get back to work."

"Aww… Don't lose your head. Don't go yet."

Suddenly Phillip realized he had an idea of who this was on the phone. "What do you want?" As he waited for an answer, he recalled the three phantom phone calls he'd received right before his trip.

"I think you know."

"If you answer a question, I won't go right away," growled Phillip.

"Okay."

"Did you call and hang up a few times last week?"

Silence.

"Yes," said the strange voice finally.

"And I know you?"

"Kind of."

"Were you the person who was in my house recently?" Phillip asked.

Again silence. Phillip waited. He knew in his gut that it was probably the person who had erased some files from his computer. It wasn't someone he had been face-to-face with, but it was someone he knew. Someone he very much wished he didn't know at all.

"Where are you calling from? Seattle?"

"Oh, you ask too many questions."

Phillip was worried the caller knew how tense he was feeling. He forced himself to say with a chuckle, "Well, you said I could ask you a question."

"I'm playing a game with you, but I assure you it's not a joke, Phillip Craven."

"Oh, is that right?" The caller never heard these words. A loud click indicated the other party had hung up.

Phillip put the phone down. *Who the hell was that?* He quickly dialed star 69. The phone rang and rang. Without a digital readout, however, he had no way of knowing what number he was ringing back.

"Son of a bitch!" As he began to move toward the coffeepot, the phone began to ring again.

"You gotta be kidding me," Phillip actually said aloud.

Phillip picked the receiver up too quickly and almost dropped it. As he brought it to his ear, he heard a familiar voice.

"Phil, this is Sheriff Conway."

"Hi, Leo, what's up?"

"I need you to take some photos for me in the next hour or so, if you can." Leo Conway never asked favors, he just politely demanded them. Phillip pictured the six-foot, two-inch, beer-bellied, shoulda-been-a-Texas Ranger, Leonard Conway. Conway always seemed to be decked out in a heavily starched khaki shirt, dark brown polyester stretch pants, and shiny black patent leather highway patrolmen boots. He looked every inch the part.

"Sure, I can help you out," Phillip answered. "What do we have? An accident?"

Leo recalled when Phillip first moved to this area a couple of years ago from the Seattle area. As a matter of fact, Leo's brother-in-law Mark Murphy had known Phillip. Former brother-in-law actually. Mark had divorced Leo's sister several years earlier. He didn't blame Mark for it though. His sister was not an easy lady to get along with and she wasn't the type of woman an officer of the law should have married.

As a Seattle police officer, Mark had first met Phillip when he was taking pictures of a shooting which had taken place during an authorized drug bust. Mark's partner had shot and killed a suspect and Phillip arrived a little over an hour after the shooting to take pictures for the coroner's office. Mark quickly realized from a knowing look that Phillip had given him that Phillip most certainly suspected that the gun lying by the side of the victim was a plant. It was.

Mark's partner had thought that what the suspect had held in his hand was a gun, and not a chrome-colored crack pipe. It was a tense situation and Mark probably would have been cleared of any wrongdoing in the incident, even without the planted gun. Without the gun, however, there would have been a long suspension for Mark's partner and a much longer investigation into the incident.

Phillip drew Mark aside at his first opportunity and spoke quietly while looking down at his feet. "You know, a guy like this would have had a much bigger piece than that." Phillip turned to go and then stopped, turned, and looked directly at Mark this time. "Oh, and remember to turn the safety off in the future."

Mark was nervous about the encounter with Phillip for a while. Somehow discovering Phillip was a freelancer for the coroner's office made him feel a little better. When the investigation ran its course after about six weeks without any problems or questions arising, Mark concluded that Phillip Craven was a man to be trusted. A few months later, Mark got a promotion to detective.

A year or so later, Leo mentioned to Mark that a guy from Seattle had bought Nancy and Otto Etts' place. Nancy and Otto's oldest daughter had gone to college with Leo's sister, Mark's former wife, Connie. Mark remembered Phillip talking about looking at some property outside of Seattle. Mark told Leo that Phillip was "good people" and had worked as a freelancer for the coroner's office down there.

"Fact is, if you paid him a few bucks to photograph crime scenes for you, it might save you some grief in the courtroom," Mark had said. This time Mark was referring to an embarrassing set of circumstances that led to an acquittal of a suspect because of a lawyer who made Leo Conway look like an oaf with a badge in the courtroom. Leo made it a point to make Phillip Craven's acquaintance.

Phillip was forty-three years old, but looked young enough to pass as someone in his early thirties. He was five feet, eleven inches tall. Short-cut, medium brown hair, blue eyes, and a good physique with perhaps fifteen extra pounds on him. He seemed easy going, friendly, and sharp. He didn't flaunt it or look down his nose at you, but you could just tell he was very intelligent. He also had a wicked sense of humor.

"It's one of the forks at the end of..." Leo Conway started to say. "Oh, hell, you'll never find it. I'll meet you at Canyon Road and you can follow me here. It's bad, Phil, and there's gonna be media coverage on this one."

"You're east of Tommy's place?" Phillip asked quickly.

"Yeah. Well, southeast. I'll meet you on Canyon Road, near where the old barn with the collapsed roof is."

Phillip knew it well. He'd photographed it several times. In fact, that wasn't too far from Mary's place. But Mary and he carried on quietly. No reason giving the gossips more things to talk about.

"Okay, I'll see you in half an hour."

"Prepare yourself for this one, Phil. It's bad."

"Jesus, for you to say something like that, you must mean it," Phillip said.

"Yeah. Don't have to tell you we don't see this kind of thing here unless a piece of farm equipment is involved or it's an accident on the main highway. The victim was decapitated."

Phillip was quiet. He hadn't photographed anything really gory for almost two years. There was the nasty accident on the main highway halfway to Ellensburg last year, but that kind of carnage was a lot different than a brutal crime scene. Phillip barely had the stomach for even the accidents anymore. He didn't like the sound of this. Then something the strange caller had said ran through his mind: *Don't lose your head over it.* Phillip felt the blood drain from his face and his mouth suddenly got very dry again.

"You there, Phillip?" Leo asked.

"Yeah. Glad you told me what I was in for. I can kind of mentally prepare myself, I guess."

"Well, yeah, you better be prepared."

"Regular Boy Scouts we are, huh?"

Leo chuckled. "Appreciate your help on such short notice, Phil."

"Glad to do it."

A few moments later as Phillip was refilling his coffee mug for the third time, the phone rang again.

He seldom got three phone calls in a row like that. Phillip looked at the phone for a moment before answering.

"Hello?"

"Phillip?" It was a nervous, recognizable female voice. "Phillip, is that you?"

Phillip instantly knew Trisha's voice. She was upset about something. No, not just upset. She was scared.

"Trish? What's wrong?"

"Oh god, Phillip!"

Chapter Three

Phillip knew the fear in Patricia's voice was genuine. After all, this was not the first time he'd heard it.

"He's here!"

Her voice was a near whisper now, her panic barely controlled. "God, Phillip, I'm scared."

"Who's there, Trish? Tell me who's there!"

"Jordan! Jordan's here!"

"Stop this, Patricia! What do you mean, Jordan's there?"

"I saw him! I'm *sure* it was him. I didn't realize it right away, but it was him. From that picture you had..."

Patricia's heart was pounding and she was finding it difficult to catch her breath.

"Trisha, that's impossible! We both know that's impossible! He wouldn't dare do anything now. He has to know we're onto him." He couldn't tell Patricia that Jordan was at his place last night, making it highly unlikely Patricia could have seen him.

"Trish, are you in any danger right this minute? He isn't in the house, is he?"

"I don't know. I don't know, Phillip! Shit, I mean *no*, he isn't in the house! He was outside by the street when I went to the door. I think he's gone now. I'm sure it was him, Phillip! What's he doing here? How did he find me?"

No matter how hard she tried to stop them, she could feel the tears welling up in her eyes. God, how she hated this helpless feeling.

"Sh...it's okay, baby. We're going to be okay."

Patricia wondered how Phillip could sound so calm when he could clearly hear the fear in her voice. She wished that he was there with her and could put his arms around her and hold her. Yet, even if he could, Patricia wasn't so sure everything would be all right. Especially now, after the truth was known. It would all be resolved soon. Or so she foolishly believed until a few minutes ago. Finally, her heart no longer felt like it was going to burst from her chest.

"I wish you were here, Phillip." She paused to weigh her words before continuing, "Can't you please come, Phillip? Please?"

"I will, as soon as I can. You know that." Phillip wished he had never left.

Patricia could almost feel his strong arms giving her the hug she wanted so badly. Phillip's voice was soft and seemingly without fear. She remembered the brief time they had spent together and his deep blue-gray eyes filled with tears as he looked at her a moment before they embraced that final time, holding each other so tightly. Too quickly he ended the embrace and before she realized it, he was leaving. She knew it would have been best to turn and walk away. She told him that's what she would do. But she couldn't. She stood there watching him. He smiled and then was gone.

She tried to remember exactly how it felt to hold his hand in hers. She almost could and that was good, but it wasn't good enough. She could hear Phillip breathing. She envisioned him leaning against the wall, cradling the phone against his ear with his left shoulder.

"Okay, baby," he said softly, "now tell me what's going on."

As the deep, rich sound of his voice enveloped her, Patricia felt herself relaxing, her thoughts becoming clear. She needed so badly to explain everything that had just happened and what she had seen. She needed to sound rational, not frightened and disjointed. So many thoughts were running through her mind now. Standing out amid all of them, however, was the measured dispassion in Phillip's voice. Only seconds before, that serenity had annoyed her and forced her to scramble all of her words together. She had been trying as quickly as possible to tell him everything he needed to know. That had been a mistake.

She needed him to know how scared she was. But now, even with all the turmoil in her mind, she found herself smiling, reminding herself that it was his quiet strength that she needed most. It was this same combination of power and quietness that had gotten them safely to where they were now, or where she thought they had been until twenty minutes ago. Now Patricia had to be strong for him. She had to trust him again. There was no one else who would understand the danger, and certainly there was no one else left to trust or who could trust her.

Before Patricia could go on, she took a deep breath and whispered, "I love you, Phillip. I love you so much." After a long pause, Patricia heard him sigh like he always did. He never replied or even acknowledged that he heard her. But she knew he did. Her heart was quiet now. It would be all right. He was right. He was always right. They would be okay. He'd said that, hadn't he?

Phillip listened as she told him about Mack and the strange car in front of her house, about the flower delivery, and seeing who she thought was Jordan emerge from beyond the row of trees that separated her property from Sylvia's, and about the card and the mulberry branch. Phillip stopped her suddenly.

"What was that, sweetheart? What did you just say?" Phillip had heard her. He'd heard her just fine.

"The mulberry branch, Phil. We don't have mulberries around here, and nobody would put something like that in an arrangement, don't you see?"

She was starting to sound impatient, annoyed, and nervous again.

There was a long pause. She was sure he wanted to say something to her. Then after waiting a little too long, Phillip said softly, "What did the card say?" Phillip shut his eyes tightly and rubbed his knuckles hard against his forehead as he waited for the reply he knew he didn't want to hear.

"Phillip, I told you. I ran in here to call you before I opened the card. I don't know what it says. Aren't you listening to me?"

"Of course I am, Trisha. I am. Really." His voice faded away at the end and was now less than convincing. She heard him clear his throat.

"Sweetheart, go get the card, okay? Then come back and read it to me."

Patricia laid the phone down on her desk and started for the foyer. As he waited for her to return, Phillip thought about how everything was careening out of control. Last year started out so well, maybe too well. He'd met Patricia and then, like some lovesick teenager, he was writing poetry again. Poetry that he thought was pretty good, and he was his own harshest critic. And there was the poem Patricia suggested he use in connection with his gallery show. What was he thinking? He must be going insane.

And then there was Mary. He'd have to make sure she wasn't too serious about him. She was a wonderful lady, and he enjoyed her company. He especially liked making love to her, sometimes tenderly and slowly, sometimes wildly passionate—almost too passionately—as it was that time a few months ago.

He'd gone to her house, but she didn't seem to be anywhere around. He worried about it for just a moment and then smiled when he remembered that she'd said she was going to do something a little different and surprise him the next time she saw him. He'd bounded up the stairs two at a time and entered the bedroom. He fully expected to see her there, perhaps in that sexy negligee she'd worn a few times for him. She wasn't there. There was a candle burning on the dresser and another on the nightstand. He smiled. Yes, she was indeed playing a game. Then he felt her behind him, felt her even before she touched him. The aroma of her perfume—not too sweet, not too strong, just sexy—confirmed her presence in a most intoxicating way.

He'd remained motionless as she slid her arms under his and began to caress his chest. He could feel her through his thin sweater, her soft breasts pressed against his back. She was naked or nearly so. Her hands moved slowly and sensuously down his body. She moaned softly and her knees buckled slightly when she felt his growing hardness. He wanted to turn toward her and kiss her passionately, but he waited. Her small hands were smooth and warm.

"Oh, baby…that's so nice," Phillip moaned softly.

"I want to drive you crazy and then I don't want you to make love to me."

"Huh?"

"No, I don't want you to make love to me. I want you to fuck me, Phillip." She spoke the words slowly, her voice a lustful whisper.

She released him from his slacks and slipped her hands under the waistband of his briefs and began slowly stroking him. Feeling the explosion of lust and desire building, he began yielding to the long-awaited excitement. Her fingers somehow knowing where to touch him, how to hold him. Mary remained behind him, her body pressed into his, her magical hands alternately stroking and squeezing him. He was out of his mind with passion. God, he'd needed this!

"Phillip? Phillip, are you still there?"

"Yeah. Yeah, Patricia, I'm here." He felt guilty about allowing his thoughts to drift to such an intense memory at a time like this. What the hell was the matter with him?

"I'm going to read the card to you now, okay?"

"Yes. Go on, Patricia."

"But I'm scared, baby."

"I know, honey. Just read it to me."

"Okay. It says, *Remember the spoils of Sleepy Hollow*, and it's signed *Ichabod Crane*.

Phillip heard Patricia gasp. He was suddenly aware of his heart pounding.

"He's playing with us, Trisha." He tried to sound as calm as he could, but he was feeling dizzy.

"Oh god, Phillip, you need to get here." He could hear the desperation in her voice. "He knows about us, Phillip."

"Yes, but he's just playing with us, trying to scare us. We've got to be strong, Patricia. You've got to hold yourself together and be strong. We've got some time or he wouldn't have sent you the flowers. He's not going to do anything right now because if he did, then his sick game would be over."

Phillip paused. "Trisha, did you hear me?"

"Yes." Although he was trying to hide it, Patricia could tell Phillip was upset and nervous.

One of Patricia's earliest childhood memories was one shrouded in the eeriness of the foggy predawn hours, the quiet periodically shattered by the distant sound of rifle fire. It was a dreary October morning in the Black Hills of South Dakota, opening day of antelope season. She was four years old then, and a day alone with her father was something she had been looking forward to since he'd told her a few weeks before that she could go hunting with him.

Patricia's father was Cherokee by birth, a dedicated military man by choice. Her mother was very young and beautiful; English mostly. She was the oldest child of five, born to a hard driving ranching family from Texas that eventually made its way north to Colorado where she ultimately met and married Patricia's father. Her father was well over thirty years old now and still working hard to put behind him the horrors he had endured for forty-two months as a Japanese prisoner of war. He was pursuing the great American dream, the same dream he knew had sustained him through those long, trying years.

Despite the dampness and cold, these rare days spent alone with her father meant the world to Patricia. Everything they did together and everywhere they went became an adventure for her. It was just after dawn now and she remembered looking up at her handsome father and then being startled as an unexpected shot rang out nearby. It's odd, when you think about it, how some memories never seem to fade and special moments stay etched in our minds, not unlike yellowing snapshots in a priceless family album.

Right now she was remembering how her father had paused and winked down at her where she was crouched behind a large, fallen log. She remembered that he was wearing gloves, and that he held two fingers against his lips and quietly shook his head. Patricia knew this meant for her to be very still and quiet. She shrugged her shoulders in reply and put two of her mittened fingers to her lips. Her father smiled, then turned his coal black eyes back toward the east and scanned the vast emptiness of the Badlands.

Patricia felt like a character in one of her treasured books that he was always bringing to her when he returned from his long flights away from home. Patricia had no brothers or sisters and often retreated to her room to study the beautiful pictures in the books. She was a precocious child, but well behaved. Being raised in an era where "good children" were seen and not heard was just a bit of a challenge for her.

The dew crystallized in the freezing temperature and she watched as little streams of water fell from one leaf to another, one blade of grass to another and slowly melted from the warmth her body provided. Beneath her lay a silent world where only minuscule insects lived, labored, and played.

Patricia's imagination took her beneath the frozen blades of buffalo grass into the world that existed there. Hundreds of bugs scurried about as she smiled down on them, pretending that it was just like Thanksgiving morning and she was skipping and dancing along on her way to her grandmother's house for dinner. Even at four, she knew that Grandma was someone to cherish. Someone who cherished her, as well. Cherished her even when she threw the best laying hen in the coop into the irrigation ditch because Grandma had refused to fry it for her dinner!

Patricia's brows furrowed as she watched the smallest of the ants trying to lug an enormous clump of dirt up a limber green weed stalk. Just as the ant was almost to the top, his weight caused it and him to crash down to the ground in a silent calamity! Dozens of nearby ants hurried madly to the scene. After apparently evaluating the situation, they left him alone to struggle unaided with his heavy load. Patricia continued to watch as the insects dashed madly to and fro, wondering to herself about the fairness of things even then.

She questioned why some people are born destined to be helpless and forever children, perpetually ordered about and never allowed to make a decision or voice an opinion. She wondered how some people were so special that they were born grandmas and grandpas. Of course, being a grandma or a grandpa was far better than being a king or a queen or a fairy godmother in her opinion! Grandparents just had to be the most wonderful people in the entire world.

Grandma lived in a cozy blue house way out in the country away from everybody else in the world. Green fields surrounded her house and garden where Patricia would go and help her pick things that she actually cooked for supper! And beside the house flowed her grandparents' very own sparkly little river. She didn't understand why, but Grandma always called it a ditch and warned her about playing too near it. To Patricia, it was a river, one that carried the crisp fall leaves on a long, slow voyage to somewhere over the edge of the world. She would watch the leaves as they floated idly past the fields of corn as far as she could see. It flowed past the battered old mailbox that leaned against a pine tree at the end of the rough and rutted narrow dirt lane that led up to the house from the main road. Then the river veered a bit to the left and disappeared into the tunnel that ran under another old road that nobody ever used anymore. Well, she *had* seen her uncle and the old man who lived next door use the abandoned road to drive their tractors on as they moved from field to field. Then the crystal clear cold water began its downhill descent until it was totally out of sight.

She knew that the little river ended abruptly at the foot of the rugged rock outcropping that loomed in the distance because that's where the world ended, of course. She had never been allowed to go that far from the farm, but Patricia always wondered what glorious wonders might lie at the base of those rocks. How many priceless treasures like the gaily-colored leaves had the river carried down there and deposited at the base of the mighty rock that held up the sky?

A sudden and deafening rifle shot startled Patricia, and she looked up just in time to see her father lower the long gun from his shoulder. Squinting against the sunlight, he looked intently in the direction in which he had fired, sure by the sound of the solid thud that the bullet had hit its intended mark. The sun was just beginning to peek above the crest of the mountains to the east and it was impossible for her to see anything beyond the edge of the small thicket which hid them. As her father struggled to get up from the cold ground, he pushed against the log that sheltered her secret insect city. Patricia smiled up at her father as he offered his hand to her, pulling her gently up from her frosty nest. He smiled back and gave her one of his famous "thumbs up" gestures that told her very soon they could be back to the big, warm truck and they could talk again and sing along with the radio as they drove the bumpy roads back into Rapid City. They'd be anxious to share their adventures with her mother and begin the process of getting the winter-kill processed and in the freezer.

Patricia wondered what other kids ate when their daddies didn't go hunting. Not once did she ever remember being sad or upset over the killing of a game animal. That was the way of things as she knew them. She did remember, though, being really sad for having to leave the tiny world beneath the log. Years later, she would recall that memory again and wonder if the little ant ever found another route or if he just continued to walk up the stalk, only to fall to the ground again just as his goal was in sight. She'd watched people she loved do the same thing over and over again. Something within her, however, told her that ants were much smarter than most people. Lessons like that came easily to Patricia.

She was five years old when her paternal grandmother died. That was the first time that she can recall ever being called an Indian. In the dingy and peculiar smelling hospital where she sat alone quietly and unattended, she listened to a small group of old ladies who stood clutching their plastic handbags to their chests, glancing in her direction every now and then.

Their voices were barely above a whisper but carried clearly across the corridor. Occasionally, one of the ladies would look her way and smile sort of a sad smile and then turn back to the huddled group and they'd all begin to talk at once. Two different times, however, while Patricia was looking at the tattered pages of an old *Readers Digest*, she overheard one of them whisper something about *that* little girl being Mutt's girl. She didn't have to look up to know they were talking about her. Mutt was what everyone who knew her father very well called him. Mutt was a funny name for a man, Patricia thought. She would ask her grandmother why she named him that when she got to go into see her. Then she heard a different lady who had just joined the group say, "Sh, Stella. That little Indian girl over there is Sugar's granddaughter. Yes, Mutt's girl."

Patricia wondered why there were so many of her grandmother's lady friends there. And she wondered how that lady she'd never seen before knew her grandmother's name was Sugar. That's the only name Patricia ever knew her grandmother to be called because when she would ask her mother or father a question about Grandma, they could be counted on to quickly ask, "Which grandma?" Patricia would roll her eyes even then and say impatiently, "The grandma who always wants me to call her Sugar." So Sugar it was to all who knew Mable.

The red and white flowers that adorned Mable's casket a few days later had a white satin banner woven through them on which shiny, gold letters spelled out: *In Loving Memory of our Wife, Mother, and Grandmother... Sugar.*

The very same wrinkly, old women who had gathered at the hospital now filled two pews at the front of the small chapel. They looked sad as they glanced over at Mable's family. Patricia wasn't really sure what the word "family" meant, but she'd heard it several times already that day. When she was older, Patricia learned that "si da ne lv hi" means "family" in the Cherokee tongue. Traditions would hold a special place in Patricia's life, once she learned of the uniqueness of the People. Most importantly, she would learn that tradition would also hold true about the People's belief that a common thread links all times, places, and people together forever.

Hushed voices that whispered a little too loudly kept announcing the arrival of "the family." There was a young man in a suit that looked way too big for him and who kept his hands clasped together tightly behind his back. He seemed to be in charge of "the family," and he had the palest skin Patricia had ever seen. He stayed very close to all of them and somberly pointed the newcomers to the area where "the family" was sitting. Now all of this seemed very odd, Patricia thought, as "the family" could easily see and hear the other people entering and greeting one another. She watched them all find seats in the softly lit room.

Lying so very quietly was Sugar, sound asleep in a shiny silver box. All around her were flowers and plants stuck onto wire stands that held them up in the air. Sugar looked very pretty lying there. Patricia told herself that "being asleep with God" must be quite different than going to bed and saying your prayers every night. She knew right then and there that she never wanted to be "asleep with God" though, because she would *never* take a nap in front of all these people! A lot of the people were whispering and some of them were even crying. She was confused.

Patricia had a cousin named Wayne. She didn't know him very well and frankly, she didn't like him very well, either. He was sitting directly behind her and she heard her aunt telling him that Sugar was going to sleep forever. Patricia sighed audibly and rolled her eyes. People had always told her to stop doing that. She never understood why and she never could understand the explanation she always got when she asked why she was being yelled at. "Just because, Patricia. Just because."

Just because, my hind leg. That was her favorite thing to say, although she usually just thought it to herself. Her other grandma always used that expression when she didn't agree with something that her grandpa said. When her grandma said it, everyone would laugh. Everything about her other grandmother made people laugh. Even Grandpa, but especially Patricia. *My hind leg, indeed!* When Patricia began laughing quietly to herself, her father leaned over and reminded her that it was time to be quiet.

Patricia was still confused by this entire event unfolding before her. Why was "the family" all behind the dark curtain and by themselves now while everyone else was sitting in the other room? She would ask the pale young man that very thing—whenever Sugar was finished with her nap, of course. She began squirming and fidgeting in her chair. How long was Sugar going to sleep, anyhow?

At that moment, a man appeared at the tall wooden box that was placed near Sugar's silver bed. Just as he looked like he was about to say something, eerie sounding music came from the organ in the corner of the room. A pretty lady who Patricia recognized as Sugar's next door neighbor began to sing.

Patricia loved music and loved to sing. She knew all the words to "The Old Rugged Cross," and when it seemed clear to her that the lady was having trouble remembering the words, she began to sing along with her. Though barely above a whisper, everyone in the room turned in her direction and listened as she softly continued singing. It never occurred to her that she and Sugar's neighbor were the only ones in the room singing.

The rest of the memories from that day escaped Patricia now as they had the last time she tried to remember them over a bubbling glass of champagne at the last New Year's Eve party. Patricia and the same annoying cousin Wayne, who had chattered and shuffled his feet in the chair behind her that day so many years ago, tried to recall certain events that must have taken place. Neither one of them could remember. Perhaps there was simply no need to remember.

Five-years-olds have a way of dispensing with things that don't appeal to them or things that frighten or annoy them. It was good to be five, back when only special people were born grandmas and some people just stayed little kids forever. Why couldn't that have been the way of things now?

She pushed those thoughts from her mind as she placed the Waterford "Millennium Edition" champagne glass gingerly on the marble table in front of them and waited for her cousin to speak. Wayne was a well-known and well-respected West Texas attorney now, and Patricia had sought out his advice a few times in the past. He had assisted her with the legal documents she needed when she purchased the bookstore from Butch Killen the year before. Butch had insisted that a handshake would seal the deal. Honorable as he was, however, and as much as she loved the dear man, Patricia knew that a handshake would not bind a contract if problems ever arose.

Despite the fact that their fathers had been brothers, the two families had never been particularly close and he and Patricia had only in the past five or six years renewed their childhood friendship and had quickly and easily grown quite close. Fairly late in life, Wayne had married a charming West Texas belle. She had been a breath of fresh air for the entire family. At forty-eight years of age he'd become a father for the first time, and Patricia had been with them at the birth of their son which she knew would have meant a great deal to her father. It meant a great deal to her, too.

Wayne could see that she was lost in thought. Being born of the same Indian blood as Patricia, he knew things about her that others didn't and never would. He knew that to speak to her now would be useless. And in a moment, when she returned to him, she wouldn't even realize that she'd been gone. Wayne was glad that they shared that same magic world, that unseen world just beyond the veil of the moment. Wayne's brother, the only other direct descendant of their Cherokee grandfather, didn't possess any of the same personality traits and characteristics they had. Patricia and Wayne were unique in this way and spoke of it often when they were alone.

Wayne bit on his upper lip as he thought about what Patricia had just said to him. As calloused as lawyers get sometimes, even the best of them are shocked by some of the wild tales told them by their clients. Quite frankly, what Patricia had just shared with him took him more than just a little by surprise.

As he watched her expression change, Wayne knew that Patricia was slowly returning to the present and he knew that when she did, she would have a renewed spirit and her thoughts would be clearly in place. She would need that strength and organization now, especially after what she had told him.

"Patricia, if what you have told me is true—and I'm certainly not implying that it isn't—are you aware that you could be in a great deal of danger?"

She reached across the table and put her hands on his. Wayne's hands were shaking and she was sure he wasn't even aware of it. "Yes, I am all too aware of the implications." She made the statement flatly and with little emotion.

The room full of friends and family surrounding them came to life. Patricia spotted her husband making the rounds and refilling glasses with champagne. When Trent stopped at the table where Wayne and Patricia were sitting, he leaned down and kissed her on the cheek. Only half-teasingly, he told them to quit being party poopers and that they could re-live the "good old days" tomorrow over honey-baked ham and football games.

The three of them laughed as Trent helped Patricia to her feet. With his arm around Patricia, he smiled as everyone began the countdown along with the announcer on television as the crystal ball began to click slowly down the rod toward the New Millennium. Trent whispered in Patricia's ear, "You cold, sweetheart? You're shivering." His arm tightened around her. His question went unanswered.

Seven. Six. Five. Four. Three. Two. One.

Tonight, unlike all the previous years when this same group loudly and heartily welcomed in the new year, they all stood reverently quiet. The television announcer, however, was anything but silent as he shouted to be heard above the raucous crowd of people who had crammed into Times Square in New York.

Trent reached out and set the near-empty bottle of champagne on the hearth in front of him and pulled Patricia close to him. He wrapped his arms around her, burying his face in her hair. She thought she heard him whisper, "I love you." At that same instant, their family and friends began blowing their cheap party horns which they'd been given earlier in the evening.

In keeping with her New Year's tradition, Patricia had furnished them all with English "crackers." Everyone suddenly remembered them and started popping them open. They all foolishly began donning the tacky tissue paper crowns and comparing their treasures which had been hidden inside the colorful little packages. Everyone got a small plastic animal of some kind—hippos, lions, elephants. Those seemed to be the dominant animals for the New Millennium. Patricia finally opened her cracker. She'd been enjoying watching everyone else giggle and squeal over theirs. She laughed as she unfolded her torn and pitifully wrinkled paper crown. Chartreuse! Oh lord, she hated chartreuse! She'd dropped her cracker as she'd popped it and when she bent down to retrieve it from the floor, she stared for a moment at her small plastic toy. Lying at her feet atop a piece of the wrinkled, torn party hat was a little brown snake.

For an instant, Patricia was frozen in place. Trent and the others in the group were going from one to another, sharing hugs and kisses and wishing each other a Happy New Year. Wayne stepped in front of Patricia. "Is something wrong?" he asked. He reached out and touched her arm and repeated his question. Her silence was beginning to make him uncomfortable.

"It's nothing, Wayne," she said finally. "Nothing at all. Really."

"What's nothing at all?"

"Oh, that stupid snake. That's all." She kicked it to the side and quickly regained her composure. She threw her arms around Wayne's neck and pulled him close to her, holding him there for a long moment.

"What about the snake, Patti?" he insisted on knowing. "You've got to tell me everything eventually, if I am ever going to be able to help you." He paused and waited for the answer which didn't come. "Please, Patti. Tell me about the snake, okay?"

The tears filled her eyes now and she hid her face in Wayne's soft, cashmere sweater. "I can't explain it, it just reminded me of a silkworm on a leaf, Wayne. When I was a little girl in Japan, I knew this lady who had a silkworm farm. Oh, never mind. You wouldn't understand." Things and events happened too quickly in Patricia's life following that memorable evening for there to be an opportunity to share anything else with Wayne.

Chapter Four

Phillip forced himself to breathe deeply and slowly. *Take it easy, old boy. Everything'll be fine.*

He was within a few miles of Canyon Road where he was to meet Sheriff Leo Conway. He started going through his mental checklist. "Damn!" He couldn't remember if he'd replaced the batteries in the flash unit for his old Pentax he affectionately called "Piggie" because when the leather case was closed over the camera, it resembled the silhouette of a pig's snout.

He took one more long, cleansing breath to alleviate the stress which understandably had made his entire body tense. *I must keep calm. Being upset does no one any good.* Under the circumstances, it was normal to be scared, but it wasn't okay to feel helpless. He was still alive. Patricia was still alive. And even if the game were suddenly turning even more deadly...well, there was still time.

But how much time, Phillip? How much time do you have now? How much time do you really think you have? It's in your own home, in Patricia's home, too. It was as if...well, it was as if he was inside your own head. He seems to know as much about you as you know about yourself. Only he uses what he knows to play games with you. Maybe worse. Huh-uh, you son of a bitch! Nope. You don't get the satisfaction.

Phillip smiled, knowing he had more strength than he'd ever imagined. Besides, now someone really loved him. He would be strong for both of them. He knew Patricia really did love him. She loved him like no one else had ever loved him before. And it was not just based on passion; it was a deep and ageless love that he knew would last until the day he died. There was passion, of course. But it was the type of passion one might think belongs only to the young—the type of passion that people write embarrassing love songs and poetry about—the type of passion most of us gradually outgrow and leave behind believing there are more important and responsible things to do.

Although Cle Elum had seen its population quadruple in the last ten years, it remained mostly a quiet community, a surprisingly congenial mix of local farmers and those who lived there only part of the time, a place of farmhouses, log cabins, and A-frames. Here the Tenaway River broke off into smaller streams. Phillip's house was on one called the South Fork. During the spring thaw, the river rose several feet and flushed down the mountain with an unstoppable force. Some people insisted on building their cabins too close to the river and every few years, some of these homes would be completely washed away.

While his cabin was set back far enough as to be out of harm's way, Phillip's life often teetered on the edge, his innate sense of balance of people and issues often barely enough to keep him safe. He could see now that Sarah had been an integral part of that balance, keeping him from being too reckless or from foolishly telling people what he really thought. When they became disconnected from one other, no more than strangers sharing the same living space, his balance faltered. He fell one day and was swept away from the life he once had and away from Sarah. It all had happened so quickly.

Sometimes he was sorry, but most of the time he was thankful. Grateful for what had happened and for the full life he was leading now and for the changes—changes that kept him from getting too old and too set in his ways, too dull.

But in the process, his emotional side had shriveled. It was Patricia who'd made him see how he'd shut down a major part of himself in order to cope with the loss of Sarah. He'd become withdrawn into an inner part of him that was vulnerable and, in his opinion, too soft.

He was older now, and it was time to put away foolish things and to get strong. Hell, he didn't need anyone. In fact, he hadn't needed anyone for a long time, and it was perhaps just as important that he wasn't needed by anyone either. That way, he could concentrate on his work, on things *he* really wanted to do. Though his work didn't give him the satisfaction or make him feel as complete as it once seemed to, he would simply put more effort into it until it did.

He felt this little plan was working pretty well, until Patricia had opened him back up again. She had touched him as deeply as anyone ever had and made him realize what had been missing from his life.

And so the plan was modified. It would somehow have to include Trisha now. Despite all the complications, it would involve this angel who had entered his world and made him realize how precious life really could be. Somehow, he would have Trisha and stay completely out of harm's way in Cle Elum.

But the danger was bearing down on them now as sure as come spring thaw, the river would rise and sweep everything in its path down to the sea.

The false hope, which he had so tenaciously been clinging to, that they were not in any serious jeopardy, had been obliterated in that one phone call from Patricia. He knew Jordan wouldn't stop, at least not until he was made to stop. Maybe his mental state was such that the bastard couldn't stop until he'd completed what he'd started. For a couple of minutes, Phillip believed that, while Patricia seemed to be in imminent danger, she would be spared any direct attack. Perhaps, he thought, this could be used to their advantage. Maybe it would give them a chance to devise a workable plan. Jordan, of course, would pick on whomever he perceived to be the weakest. Patricia could hardly be considered weak. For someone from the outside looking in, however, she might appear to be so. Perhaps Jordan would make just such a misassumption and, in the process, commit a fatal mistake.

"*You have no idea who the fuck you're dealing with. No fucking idea*!" Phillip had shouted after hanging up the phone when he was done talking with Patricia. The prank phone call he'd received just before she'd called him was childish. Though it had taken him by surprise, it hadn't scared him. It just made him angry. He was dealing with a prankster who was acting like an idiot. An idiot trying to be a bully. But playing with Patricia, perhaps coming out of hiding to scare her, meant something more.

Phillip would be meeting Sheriff Conway in a few minutes. Maybe now it was time to tell him his story, especially since it looked like someone had been in his house last night. When the opportunity arose, Phillip would try to explain what he thought was going on.

Most would assume that Leo Conway and Phillip Craven were friends. Leo wasn't a friend. Phillip didn't call neighbors or acquaintances "friends" even as a shortcut in conversation with someone else. It wasn't that Leo wasn't a decent man. He was. Phillip respected him, too. It was just that Phillip didn't like too many people in law enforcement. Never had. This was partially rooted in the 1960s, of course, but later on he'd met scores of working police officers and their bosses whom Phillip had nicknamed "Little Napoleons." They were too impatient or maybe just too dumb to play politics very well. For the most part, they kept their noses clean, but they loved to step on the fingers of the officers who were trying to get detectives' gold shields of their own. They were sadistic in their little brutalities. Little things, like making an officer assist with some work which would require officers to put in for overtime which, in turn, would upset their superiors. It often meant the officers would miss having dinner with their families. It wouldn't be an exaggeration to say that the detectives did it for the perverse pleasure they'd get from creating tension in the officers' marriages.

Sheriff Conway, however, was different. Leo stepped up to the plate when he was needed many years ago. He hit a few singles, never struck out, and wouldn't think of taking a walk. So, twenty years after filling in for a sheriff who had not so graciously retired, he seemed as much a part of the town now as the Tenaway River. He was always fair, always pleasant to deal with, and only once did someone try to run against him in an election.

Leo had actually organized a few people to help Phillip move into his house and worked really hard to make him feel welcome. At first, Phillip was edgy about the attention, but he soon realized that Leo actually knew a little about him from his ex-brother-in-law Mark, someone Phillip actually did consider a friend. Later, after Phillip was settled in, Leo had helped Phillip turn half of his garage into a darkroom. And before long, Leo had convinced Phillip that occasionally the Sheriff's Office might need his photography services.

* * * * *

Last night, Phillip had left his 1998 Subaru Outback in the driveway as usual. There was room to pull it into the garage and keep it cleaner, but he rarely bothered to do so. As he walked outside on his way to his darkroom—or office, as he called it—he stopped. The garage door was up. He hadn't left it like that, he was reasonably sure of that. Most of the time, he used the small side door to go in and out of the garage. While he often left the main garage door unlocked, he always kept it down. Deer, free range cows, the occasional bobcat, coyote, raccoon, timber wolf, or bear weren't welcome in there.

As he walked toward the garage, his boots crunched noisily over the gravel driveway. He stepped into the garage and as he waited for his eyes to become accustomed to the low light, he could hear the sound of horseflies. And there was that musky animal smell. It was almost overpowering. His eyes quickly scanned the dark, windowless room.

Phillip jumped back. A mutilated deer lay in the middle of the floor! A young, headless deer. Perhaps it was the same deer he eagerly waited to watch in the early morning hours and late afternoons while he sipped his coffee on the deck. Phillip stumbled to his darkroom and grabbed a camera. As if by instinct, he clicked nearly a dozen pictures of the deer. This had to have happened very recently, as the blood had just stopped pooling. If the deer had been dragged in here after it was dead, there should be a trail of blood, he thought. Why hadn't he heard anything and where was the deer's head?

* * * * *

Phillip realized his mind had drifted again into the recent past. His right hand hurt from gripping the steering wheel too tightly. There, on his left, was the collapsed barn and about a hundred yards farther up, he saw Sheriff Conway's pale yellow Cadillac. Phillip slowed his SUV to a crawl.

He didn't know the history of Cle Elum very well and had never bothered to find out much about it. He did, however, remember Leo telling him that in the late 1970s and early 1980s, three or four of the locals split up their twenty or so one-acre parcels along the South Fork of the Tenaway and let real estate broker and former used car salesman Willie Martin sell quarter-acre and half-acre plots to city folk. It didn't take him long to sell all the land. Most of it was sold to people from the Seattle area who wanted a little piece of recreational land where they could camp, build small cabins, or park their mobile homes. But some of the land was sold to people who wanted to live permanently in Cle Elum. People, who perhaps like Phillip, wanted to be a few hours outside of Seattle but a world apart from the noise, the overcrowding, and the bright lights.

Bright lights. That's what had inspired him to write a poem a few months ago; a poem he'd never shared with Patricia, but would some day soon. She would know almost everything there was to know about him in time, or at least he hoped she would.

A Conversation with Mary

"You like this?
This quiet?"
she sighed.
"Where your thoughts
scream?
And you can't run away
or hide?"

"Yes,"
he said.
"I like a place
just beyond the city limits.
Few lights.
I can see the stars
at night.
Look at all the stars!
So many.
So bright."

"There's a place
in the city,"
she smiled.
"You can see all
the lights.
So many lights.
Spread below,
like the stars,
for miles and miles.
That's where
I go
or used to.
Where I belong,
you know."

"Then why are we here?"
he asked,
touching her face.
"What is it that
drew you to this place,
keeps you in
this place.
To Run?
To Hide?
To Forget?
Or was it,
or is it
a change of pace?"

"I don't know why.
Sometimes I can forget.
Sometimes there's some satisfaction,"
she said, about to cry.
"But then I realize
this isn't me.
I like distractions.
Maybe that's why."

"Because it was
a distraction…"
he said,

his voice afar,
"...from where you
were.
I can see that.
And I'm here
because I'm a distraction
from who
you are."

"Let's talk of something else,"
she said with a sigh.
"Just be with me tonight,
hold me,
love me just right,
and we'll stare
into your sky."

Phillip pulled up behind Leo's Cadillac. Leo got out of his car and walked over to Phillip. "A lot of roads are still not clearly marked, and I figured you might get lost if I didn't meet you out here on the main road."

"Yeah, it's hard to spot some of these roads, that's for sure."

Phillip, however, did know this particular road pretty well. It was the one he took that led to Mary's house. Somehow, Leo—who seemed to know a lot of everyone's business in Cle Elum—didn't realize that Phillip and Mary had been having an affair for over a year. Well, they were pretty discreet about it, rarely going anywhere except to each other's homes.

"Just follow me up this road and when it forks, I'll be going left and...well, you'll see." Then Leo added, "Thanks for doing this, Phil. I appreciate it."

"Don't worry about it, Leo. Always glad to help out. You know that."

"This one you won't be glad about," replied Leo. "It's not a pretty sight." Leo tapped the hood of the car and walked back to his Cadillac, grunting loudly enough for Phillip to hear him.

Phillip's heart began beating faster as they drove forward slowly. He'd had a horrible thought. The moment it occurred to him, he tried to ignore it. It couldn't be true, he reasoned. This was just some kind of macabre coincidence and besides, he was just unnerved by the other disturbing events of the day.

Everything began to seem surrealistic. Phillip's senses were alternately overly keen and then totally numb as Leo's car turned off the road and crept into a large clearing in front of the modified A-frame house. Phillip began to pray silently. *Please tell me this is some horrible movie or a nightmare.* He didn't want to believe he saw the bright yellow crime scene tape stretched across the steps of the small front porch he knew so well.

Phillip sat in his car, desperately trying to regain his composure. He needed something to steady him, something to give him back some sense of control. He listened to the sound of his own breathing. *This couldn't be happening! There must be some mistake.* Phillip badly needed a drink of water.

Leo had gotten out of his car and was waiting for him. Phillip had to get it together and join him. He reached over on the seat beside him and grabbed his two camera cases. He willed his legs to be steady as he stepped out of the car and stood up. He slung the camera straps around his neck and began to walk slowly toward Leo.

"You okay, Phil?"

Phillip nodded, unable to speak. Fortunately, Leo didn't notice, but instead turned and started walking toward the house, talking quickly as he went.

"I'm pretty sure it's Mary Foreston," Leo said. "You've met her a few times, haven't you? I think you did those pictures of her friend when she was running for the city council, didn't you? She kept pretty much to herself. She's a widow. Pretty woman, though, as you probably noticed."

Leo pulled the police tape off the porch railing and climbed up the five short steps. Phillip felt his knees begin to buckle, but managed to grasp the railing and steady himself.

"Whoa, watch your step there!" Leo said to him.

Phillip climbed up the steps but paused on the porch railing and looked out over the field of tall grass instead of following Leo inside the house. Leo turned around to see where Phillip was. "Hey, you all right, buddy?"

"Yeah, just kind of preparing myself, Leo," Phillip said quickly, hoping his voice sounded strong. *How could he do this?* In a moment, Phillip pretty much knew what he would be seeing. It was difficult enough when it was someone you didn't know.

"Yeah, okay, take your time."

"Who discovered her?" Phillip asked partially out of curiosity, partially to stall for time.

"George did. He found her a few hours ago. Mary was suppose to pick up Emma. They were going to go to the beauty parlor. When she was late, George decided he would drive Emma into town, but they swung by here to see if Mary wanted to go with them or drive in herself. Guess the door was wide open. George said he hollered for her and then went inside. Poor George nearly had a coronary...rushed outside and got sick...right about where you're standing now." Phillip looked down at where his hands held the railing and was suddenly aware of the rotten cheese smell.

"George rushed home then and called me. I told him and Emma to stay put and not talk to anyone. I think they listened to me so far. Before long, though, this place will be getting crowded. County is sending the coroner down. And some detectives are on their way, too, so be sure you don't touch anything. Well, hell's bells, you know the drill."

Yeah, I know the drill. My secret lover has just been brutally murdered and I'm about to take pictures of her body.

"Ready then?"

Phillip made a point of looking at Leo's eyes when he answered quietly, "Yeah, let's do it."

He followed Leo through the house and into the kitchen where Mary's body lay on the floor. There was blood…a lot of blood. It was splattered on the counters, the white porcelain sink, the oak cabinets, and on the yellow walls.

"Pretty sure that's Mary." Leo said after a moment.

Phillip got his camera out of the bag and was trying to steady his shaking hands so he could change lenses.

"…haven't found her head," Leo continued.

Phillip remained silent as he began taking pictures. It wasn't Mary he was focusing on through the viewfinder, he told himself. Mary was long gone. This was just a body, an empty carcass. He hoped that she hadn't suffered, that it was as quick and painless as possible.

He finished one roll of film and then grabbed the other camera and took several more pictures as a backup. Then he began taking pictures of the kitchen and hallway. After about half an hour, he was back on the porch and fighting back the tears.

This was my fault! I had no idea something like this would happen, but it's still my fault!

"Never saw anything like this." Phillip hadn't heard Leo come up behind him. "You ever seen anything like this before, Phil?"

"It's pretty gruesome all right."

"Sorry there, buddy. You okay?"

Phillip nodded. There were a lot of things to tell Leo, but he couldn't do it now. He wasn't strong enough for that at the moment. Pretty soon, he would tell Leo about the last strange year of his life and the headless deer in his garage. He would tell him about Patricia and the possible connection. But not now.

Chapter Five

After Patricia hung up the phone, she realized so much was left unsaid. Letting Phillip slip away from her like that was always so difficult. On the one hand, she hoped she'd not caused him to worry too much. In all honesty, however, what she really wanted was for him to head straight for the airport and come to her.

She knew he didn't really want to end the conversation, but he was on his way to an appointment. *What did he say? Someone was waiting for him? Did he say who?* She hadn't asked. That was selfish of her. She knew he sounded rather distant when they first began talking. Now, as she tried to recall parts of the conversation, she thought about how many times he didn't seem to be listening to her; not ignoring her exactly, more like he was just preoccupied. That was so unlike Phillip.

She tried to remember if she'd told Phillip how much she loved him. Everything was so muddled in her mind right now. She was almost sure she had. Almost was not good enough where Phillip was concerned. Saying "I love you" had become such a habit now that if a phone call went by where they didn't exchange those words, Patricia felt oddly empty. She didn't like that. Phillip was too important to her. Their love for one another was undeniable, regardless of how unexplainable. Patricia knew that a love like this deserved her utmost attention and not a single aspect of it could she dare leave to chance. She picked up the phone and held the redial button down until the message on the lighted screen indicated it was dialing. An instant after the fourth ring, she heard Phillip's voice: "You have reached the home of Phillip Craven…" After a series of beeps, Patricia took a deep breath and spoke quietly into the receiver, "Phil, it's me. I'm not sure if I told you that I loved you before we hung up, sweetie. I just wanted that to be the first thing you heard when you got home. Call me when you get back in. It doesn't matter how late it is. I love you, and I miss you so much."

Just as she was about to hang up, she remembered one more thing and added, "You mentioned you were on your way to an appointment. I realized I didn't ask where you were going. Call me soon and tell me, okay?"

Patricia knew the message was getting long and tedious, not to mention the fact, that given the circumstances, she was sounding foolishly chipper. But for some reason, just talking to his answering machine was reassuring to her at this point. Patricia needed Phillip with her, in her arms, safe and warm. They would be together again soon, she knew. It was their future.

Sometimes the thought of a "future" left Patricia feeling confused. Patricia put her head down on her desk and closed her eyes. Unable to walk away from a memory that flooded over her now, she wanted to take a moment to daydream and remember.

As imaginary stars danced behind her closed lids, Patricia recalled that special night a few months ago when she and Phillip were together near the banks of Blue Lake. She had led him to a small patch of ground in front of a towering pine tree. She told him some of the legends passed among the local pueblos, stories about this magical place she loved so much. She told him how the ancients believed they had originally came from the depths of the lake in what they called the "Emergence of the People." It is the cornerstone of their time-honored Anasazi beliefs. Phillip listened intently as she recounted the legend of First Man and First Woman and how they were followed by a multitude of other beings from the crystal blue lake. Four sacred mountains surrounded the lake and she and Phillip had traveled there together in their hearts and minds just as surely as the Indians go there now to perform their mysterious, spirit-filled rituals.

That night was the first time that they both had finally accepted their incredible and undeniable connection to one another. It was also the first night that they made love. It was then that Patricia realized that no matter what else happened, her life would never again be the same.

She sat up and stared at the phone. She wished she had said in her message to Phillip that she was going next door to Sylvia's to visit for a bit and have some coffee. Patricia knew that returning to her balance sheets would be useless now. Some lighthearted human contact was what she needed most. Besides, she'd promised Sylvia she wouldn't stay alone in the house for too long. Sylvia had been so worried about leaving her alone. Bill had promised Phillip that he'd keep Patricia safe.

Sylvia had finally relented and let Patricia go back over to her own house, but not until after Sylvia's son, Carlos, had gotten her computer up and running again. Even then, she called Patricia less than an hour after she'd left that morning, having spent the night in Patty's guest room, and insisted that she come over for some coffee. Sylvia sounded like a teenager in love and said that she had something she wanted to talk to her about. Sylvia was so full of enthusiasm and sounded so happy. Patricia knew it was because of Bill. She smiled to herself, knowing all too well what it felt like to have someone in your life whom you love and who loves you back. Patricia thought that perhaps Bill had finally asked her the question.

Patricia was feeling better now, although she felt a twinge of guilt over her shortness with Sylvia when she'd called earlier. Now was a good time to wrap up some of her homemade pumpkin bread and go make a peace call. It would be good for her to get away from the house and her dark thoughts. Besides, she was anxious to hear the news Sylvia was so eager to share. Sylvia and Bill Conner made such a great couple.

Bill was a newcomer to Taos, but Patricia had a good feeling about him. He was pleasant, sincere, and always a perfect gentleman—a quality which was all too rare these days. And beneath all of this, she also sensed a very sensual man. Patricia chuckled aloud and thought to herself that in matters of the heart it seemed each of us was in search of the same things. Such simple things really. *Why then did they seem so hard to find? Or to grasp? Or especially to hold on to?*

Patricia had known Sylvia Mondragon since she'd moved next door seventeen years earlier. Patricia had seen Sylvia through her difficult pregnancies—her son Carlos, over sixteen years ago and the daughter she had lost to her husband's clan at the end of their marriage. After Sylvia's husband walked out on her to return to the Isleta Pueblo, the home of his ancestors, Patricia watched her friend go through the motions of life without ever really living it at all. Whenever it seemed appropriate, Patricia encouraged her to get out and enjoy herself. She wanted her to meet people, especially men, and to try and start a new life for herself. Sylvia was thirty-nine when her husband left. She was still very beautiful and vibrant ten years later.

When Patricia had first gotten to know Bill Conner after he moved to Taos a couple of years ago, she couldn't help but see that he and Sylvia had a lot in common and could be good for one another. Bill was an avid reader and Patricia first met him at the library where she worked. He often went there three or four times a week. Occasionally, he would sit in one of the comfortable chairs and read. Other times, he would sit at one of the old hardwood tables and write. He wrote a lot. Letters, she suspected; probably to his children who lived with their mother in Texas. He had told her on more than one occasion how much he missed them. A time or two, she had detected a hoarseness in his voice and she had quickly looked away so he could wipe away the tears that threatened to spill from his eyes as he spoke about his children.

When Patricia made the decision to buy the Take Another Look Bookstore from Butch Killen, Bill was one of the first people in town she told. She could tell Bill was touched that she had taken the time to personally tell him of her plans, and he quickly promised her he would be a regular customer. They shared a soft, casual friendship and Patricia enjoyed his company and even their discussions about Texas and her love/hate relationship with the state.

Patricia had moved to west Texas to finish high school. That's where she'd met Trent, but that's where her passion for the Lone Star State ended. Whenever the topic arose, Trent always reminded her that she hadn't really lost anything in Texas. He understood her completely and secretly admired her courage for standing up to the prying relatives who often questioned their long absences.

After Patricia took over the bookshop, Bill began to drop by. Forever the secret matchmaker, Patricia had mischievously started sending Bill across the plaza to the deli where Sylvia worked. She would think up any reason for him to run over there for her or for one of her employees in hopes that he and Sylvia would strike up a friendly conversation. Bill always returned smiling, with the goods in hand, but never a mention of the pretty little Indian woman at the deli.

"Dang men!" she would say to her staff after he left. "They just don't get it, do they?" The women in the shop would all laugh, while the two men who worked there would look at Patricia as if she were speaking in tongues.

The hiring of Bill Conner as Sheriff Frank Garrett's new Deputy Sheriff had raised a few eyebrows in town, to say the least. Taos was a close-knit community. It most often catered to its own. To bring in an "outsider" when there were a number of qualified officers already on the force didn't set too well with the locals. It didn't take Bill long to establish himself in the community, though, and win the trust and respect of the citizens of Taos. The hard feelings over his appointment were quickly replaced by well-deserved accolades and commendations for his work both as a law enforcement official and for his dedication to community service.

Frank and Bill had met one another at college in Texas in the mid 1970's. Frank had chosen a hometown college because of an athletic scholarship in football and because that way he could stay in town and continue working in the family's refrigeration business. That kept him in spending money and a family car.

Bill grew up just outside of a small town in northern Texas and had followed his high school sweetheart to the mid-sized university. Bill and Frank ended up roommates on the third floor of an old, cold and drafty building. The dorm was bleak and the Texas winters even bleaker. The one bright spot was that theirs was the only dorm room that overlooked the field where the school cheerleaders practiced!

Bill had brought freshness and a dignity to the Sheriff's Office that it hadn't possessed in a long time. Bill was a master in negotiations and was often sent out on domestic calls that called for a firm but understanding hand. Frank was a good sheriff, but he sometimes lacked the tact needed to defuse those types of situations. He was much better at standing between two neighbors when they fought over ditch rights or whose pig was whose when it was found trotting down a public road. Taos was quaint in its own amusing way. Distanced from any large community, it existed in a time all its own. So removed from the present was Taos that it was easy to get caught up in its uniqueness and forget that there was a "real world" beyond the city limits.

Bill liked that, the insulation from the real world of heartbreak and loss, of coming home and finding the only woman he had ever loved in bed with one of the new rookies on the force. He often recalled how his mind just went blank. The days that followed ran one into another without meaning. People talked to him, consoled him, gave him advice, and told him that worse things could happen (though he couldn't possibly imagine what).

The hurt in his children's eyes was more than he wanted to remember. They loved him. He loved them. And they loved their mother, too. The decision was the judge's because, quite frankly, Bill was in no condition to make a decision; not one as important as the future of his children. His wife might have done some stupid and selfish things, but that didn't alter the fact that she was a good mother. He had no doubt that for now at least, the children needed to stay with their mother. They needed to remain in the home they loved, near their friends, and in their schools. Bill knew he had to leave. It would be impossible to stay on the force now. Even though the rookie was dismissed immediately, the stares and whispers, though probably imagined, would haunt him incessantly. Bill didn't want to owe anyone anything. He just wanted to get away and start all over again.

One night while sitting alone in his newly rented room that he'd acquired soon after he'd moved out of his home, Bill began thinking over the remnants of his life. Somewhere in the course of his thoughts, he thought of Frank. *Gosh, how long had it been since they had talked? Ten, maybe fifteen years?* They had run into one another on a ski trip to Red River one year, and in a matter of minutes their lives had picked up where they had left off, talking about the old days as if they had been the week before. He recalled how Frank had lamented his fractured knee which had ended his college football career. Then Bill remembered the day Carol told him after Zoology 101 that she was pregnant. By the end of their junior years, both he and Frank had left school and gone their separate ways.

When Bill swallowed his pride and phoned, he was relieved to hear the compassion in Frank's voice and his offer of a job. Only weeks before,

Frank's Deputy Sheriff had been pirated away by a larger police department in the southern part of the state. Frank had never gotten along with Manny and was not the least bit saddened by his untimely departure. Frank was surprised to hear from his old friend Bill, but then things always just seem to happen for a purpose they said to each other as they closed their phone conversation that evening. Bill told Frank that he would be in Taos by the following Sunday evening. Everything Bill owned would fit easily into the back of his Isuzu Trooper. The vehicle was the only asset Bill got from the marriage. Well, the kids, of course. But he considered them more blessings than assets.

Patricia picked up the bread. You could smell the aroma through the holes she'd poked in the plastic wrap so the bread wouldn't sweat. She loved fall and the smells that accompanied it. The smells and the colors of autumn. The October skies in the high mountains always seemed to be filled with streaks of muted grays and blues that would slowly be replaced by lavenders and deep velvet purples as evening approached. The sky seemed acutely aware of the changing of the seasons. It was dusk when Patricia stepped out the back door. Somewhere just beyond the row of cottonwoods, an owl called out and another answered. It was the time of day when peace settles over the winter wheat planted in the nearby fields.

Patricia had made a study once of the famous sayings of some of our country's most admired Indian chiefs and had used it as the basis for a thesis. The great Chief Seattle had been one of her favorites. As she made her way through the trees toward Sylvia's house, she recalled one of the most famous of his quotes: *Today is fair. Tomorrow may be overcast with clouds. My words are like the stars that never change.*

What made her think of such odd things at times like this? That was a good question, and one day she would take the time to see if she could come up with a logical explanation. She doubted that there was one. Phillip had asked her that same question recently. She smiled as she thought of him now. Thinking of him always made her smile. She carefully stepped onto the footbridge Trent had built years ago so that she and Sylvia wouldn't have to jump the ditch.

Sylvia's house looked a bit dark for this late in the afternoon, and Patricia hoped that she hadn't waited too long and missed her. She would have hated that. Patricia wanted to atone for her earlier behavior. Also, the smell of the bread reminded her that she hadn't eaten all day and she hated to eat alone. She was looking forward to sharing the bread with her friend and finding out what giddy little secret she had to share. Patricia would not spoil the mood by mentioning her unnerving day.

Actually, those events were thankfully becoming a more distant memory now. Only the words on the card haunted her a bit as she knocked on Sylvia's back door. Neither she nor Phillip seemed to understand their significance. That's what each of them thought, anyway.

* * * * *

Trying desperately to shake the images of the past five hours, Phillip fumbled with the car radio, trying to find a station with the evening news, when he recalled the words. *Beware the spoils of Sleepy Hollow.*

Phillip froze. He didn't know whether to pull over and use his cell phone or continue the short distance home. He was only about three minutes from his turnoff now. Phillip had to concentrate just to keep the vehicle on the road.

"Oh god, no!" Phillip found himself repeating to himself over and over. "My god, Trisha…"

As soon as he got home, he rushed through the front door and went straight for the telephone. The light on his answering machine was blinking. He would attend to that later. First, he had to call Trisha. He had to warn her to get out of the house, to get somewhere safe. And he had to call Leo right away and get some protection.

"Goddamn it! Where are you Trisha? Answer the goddamned phone!"

He was shaking now. He held the phone to his ear as continued to listen to Trish's phone ring and began punching in Leo's number on the cell phone in his other hand.

* * * * *

Patricia could swear she almost heard Phillip calling out to her. When a strong feeling like this had come over her in the past, she had been overwhelmed by it. She now recognized it as a strong connection that was so symbolic of their relationship. While she never took it for granted, it was not such an uncommon occurrence as to cause her to become completely unbalanced and unsteady. She felt the familiar warmth, knowing he was thinking of her.

Patricia knocked on the wooden screen door several times. There was no answer and as she feared, Sylvia was not at home. Before she left to return home, however, she decided to try the door to see if it was unlocked. It usually was. She had decided that she would just leave the friendship bread on the counter where Sylvia would find it when she returned home. Patricia turned the unlocked knob, and stepped inside. She was surprised at how dark it was. Although there was some daylight left, the row of trees cast long shadows over Sylvia's house.

For a moment she wondered where her neighbor might be. It was too early for her to take her son to Bill's martial arts class. Maybe she'd just gone to the store. She flipped on the kitchen light so she could find a pen and a piece of paper to leave Sylvia a note. She scribbled a quick message and started to place it on the loaf when she noticed the smell of burning coffee. She found that the coffeepot was on and had gone dry. She reached over and flipped off the switch. Sylvia was usually very meticulous and leaving a coffeepot on like that seemed a bit out of character for her. Then Patricia smiled as she recalled the giddiness in Sylvia's voice earlier that morning. Knowing the signs of a woman in love, Patricia found it all too amusing that she had gone off on a little adventure and left the coffeepot burning. Although it was dangerous, Patricia wouldn't mention it to her. That would only embarrass her. *Love, indeed!* She could almost hear Sylvia's giggling voice.

As she closed the door behind her, she saw that Sylvia's car was still in the garage. Patricia stood on the porch a moment, trying to decide whether or not to go back inside. If Bill had come by and picked up Sylvia, it was doubtful that she would have left the garage door up nor the back door unlocked. Besides, she would have called and told her of the change in plans. After all, it was Sylvia who had called and invited her over in the first place. Patricia decided to go back inside.

She turned on the overhead fluorescent light in the kitchen and called out Sylvia's name. Receiving no answer, Patricia walked through the kitchen to the adjoining dining room. She turned on the light switch on the dining room wall and looked around. The room was tidy and smelled of fresh pine cones. She could see partway into the L-shaped family room. Everything seemed in order there, too, but she had to go into the room and turn left in order to reach the light switch. When she turned on the light, she saw Sylvia near the front door.

The oddest thoughts go through people's minds when they're under extreme stress. For Patricia, she suddenly recalled a filmstrip she'd seen in a women's Bible study group years before entitled "The Silent Scream," a graphic documentary on abortion. She remembered being sickened and saddened and angry all at once, just as she was now. She stared at Sylvia for what seemed like an eternity. Then she tried to scream but the sound got caught in her throat.

Chapter Six

When Bill walked in and found Patricia standing there, he was confused. She had her hands pressed against her mouth and was just staring toward the door. He called out to her, but Patricia didn't answer. Then he saw what she was looking at. He began to scream, but his was anything but silent. The sound of it would live in Patricia's mind for the rest of her life.

Nearly an hour had passed since they'd stumbled over to Patricia's house and called the police. Sgt. Brenda Riley, of the Taos Sheriff's Office, had arrived quickly and said something about the crime scene being contained and not to talk to anyone. She told them to try and relax. At times, Patricia could focus and hear what was being said to her, but then her mind would drift someplace else, a vacuum where everything was still and dark. An image would sift through and then slowly fade away before it could be grasped.

Why was Sgt. Riley here. Where was Frank? Sheriff Garrett should be there. He should be the one containing the crime scene, shouldn't he? Patricia reached out and held onto Bill's arm. Then she remembered that Frank had disappeared again. There was a rumor that Bud Richards and Brenda Riley were going to arrest him again. Frank obviously didn't want to go through the turmoil of another arrest and the prospect of dealing with a suspicious public who'd elected him sheriff and then stood by him during the horrible ordeal five months ago. It was likely Bill knew where he was, but he wasn't talking. Patricia felt Bill gently squeeze her hand. "Are you going to be all right?" she asked.

There was a flurry of activity. Was it Sylvia's son Carlos? She didn't know. Bill had left. Maybe it was fifteen minutes later—Patricia couldn't be sure—she and Sgt. Brenda Riley were standing at the back door that looked west toward the large irrigation ditch and the golden cottonwoods that stood between Patricia's home and the Mondragon's house. During the summer, the dense foliage of the trees obscured the homes from one another. By this time of the fall, most of the golden leaves were usually gone, leaving skeletons a hundred feet tall lining the banks. This year, however, most were still dense with dying leaves that refused to drop.

From where they stood, the women could see the flurry of activity at Sylvia's. Floodlights had been placed around the property, and close to a dozen people could be seen wandering around the house. It looked as though all the lights were on, and they could see movement and shadows beyond the three large picture windows on that side of the house. It seemed as though there were at least as many people in the house as were outside on the lawn.

Patricia shivered. Brenda reached out and touched her hand. "Your hands are like ice. Can I get you something? A sweater or something?"

Patricia shook her head. "Is Bill okay?"

"He's with Carlos," Brenda said softly.

"Oh." Patricia felt a horrible ache within her. She knew that Sylvia's son Carlos would be devastated.

Patricia didn't hear the faint knock on the front door, nor did she hear Sgt. Riley speaking to the individual just beyond the threshold. Riley was leading someone up to her.

"Patricia, you remember Detective Richards."

Patricia was still in somewhat of a daze and wasn't certain at first who the middle-aged, craggy faced man in baggy khakis and corduroy jacket was. He just seemed to have materialized, and was now standing in front of Brenda muttering something. His slightly graying hair was dirty and oily and he had about him a musky, medicinal aroma. He spoke in a voice that evidenced a lifetime of smoking unfiltered cigarettes.

"Ms. Ridgeway? Bud Richards, New Mexico State Police, Albuquerque. Are you listening to me?"

Oh, so that's who this unpleasant fellow was. Of course, she knew who Bud Richards was. One of the last people she wanted to talk to was Detective Bud Richards from the State Police in Albuquerque. Earlier in the week, she'd stormed away from him when he was asking her questions. Now here he was standing in her own home.

"Yes, I guess I am."

"Patricia," he said forcing a slight smile on his face and in a manner that showed no signs of sympathy, "we need to start answering some questions around here. Sgt. Riley, don't you agree?" He didn't wait for an answer.

"You discovered the body at about what time, Ms. Ridgeway?"

"Four-thirty. Maybe five."

"Do you make it a practice of walking into your neighbors' houses without being invited, Ms. Ridgeway?"

"Yes, as a matter of fact, I do, *Detective* Richards," Patricia answered impatiently.

"Mrs. Ridgeway brought over the pumpkin bread that was on the counter," Brenda said.

"Sgt. Riley, please don't interrupt when I'm interviewing a suspect."

"Suspect?" asked Brenda.

"I meant witness."

"Bud, go grab a smoke, okay?" Until a few days ago, Brenda would never have spoken to him like that. Now, however, she viewed him entirely differently.

Richards wasn't sure what to say. He glared at Brenda, but could see that she was not about to be intimidated.

"If we could have a word, sir?" asked Pete Baker, the Taos County Coroner. He had just entered and was now standing directly behind Richards. He was beyond middle-age, and looked to be at least half Hispanic. He was short, severely obese, and wore a blood-spattered lab coat over his suit. "I need this authorization signed and…"

Detective Richards glared directly at Pete and, in a voice much louder than necessary, barked, "If you will just hold on a minute, Baker, I will decide if we are even in a position to sign that fuckin' authorization yet or not. Oh, and for your information and anyone else who happens to ask, I'm formally advising you that this investigation has been turned over to the State Police effective right now. So if you have any questions, have any answers, or just need to take a piss, you ask me first. That clear?"

Pete didn't respond. He just turned and made his way sluggishly toward the front door. A light softly illuminated a beautiful painting of Taos Mountain with a stunning full moon brilliantly lighting its crests and the flickering lights of town dotting the shadowy snowscape below. Beneath the painting on a long, carved table was a magnificent flower arrangement. As he stopped to admire it, he spotted the small envelope from the Taos Floral and Design Shop lying on the table near the vase.

Perhaps it was because Pete's nerves were on edge due to the horrific scene next door. Perhaps it was because he was fed up to his eyeballs with arrogant shitheads like Richards. Whatever the reason, he physically jumped and pulled his hand back away from the card.

Earlier in the day, he had stood vigil as a team of emergency personnel and paramedics extracted the charred remains of Mack Shaw from a burned out van several miles northeast of Taos. Pete and Mack had been casual friends from Lions Club and less than four hours ago, he had stood stoically as Mack, or what was left of him, was placed in a black plastic bag and taken to the county morgue in Cimmaron. Mack's van had flipped over several times and suffered a ruptured gas tank which then exploded in flames. Mack had apparently failed to negotiate the sharp turn near Eagle Nest. Pete had wanted Mack's remains brought back to Taos, but since the accident occurred in Colfax County, the country coroner in Raton had requested he be taken to a makeshift morgue located in the small regional hospital in Cimmaron. After he'd had a chance to get over and perform a preliminary examination of the remains, then Pete was free to transfer them to Taos. Now just hours later, Pete found himself witness to one of the bloodiest crime scenes he'd ever been called in on, and the coincidences were beginning to spook him just a little.

Pete was glad that Richards had offhandedly dismissed him. He felt certain there was more to the accident that took Mack's life and to the scene next door than he had first allowed himself to imagine. He looked back at the trio huddled in the dim hallway and then retreated to the front porch. As he stood there in the darkness, he rubbed his hand along his puffy jawline and tried to recall details of the sensational decapitation murder that had occurred in late May. Although that crime and this one were similar at first glance, there were some disturbing differences.

Pete walked back over the footbridge to the Mondragon house. This time, he was going to enter the scene as if he had never seen a crime of this nature before. Because he realized now that he hadn't. There were only a few people left now, but the floodlights were still in place. Over by the side of the house under one of the large windows, he saw a man and a woman, both dressed in dark blue overalls, pouring plaster into what were probably footprints in the soft dirt. Pete met a couple of uniformed officers coming out the back door as he ascended the steps. They were the same ones he'd seen earlier in the day when he went in for coffee at a small café in Eagle Nest before heading back to Taos. The two ignored him as they held the door open for him and continued their animated conversation, something about the upcoming Packers-Cowboys game on Monday night.

He'd never been a football fan, himself. Pete lived with his sister and they usually played Scrabble in the evenings. On Sundays, they listened to tapes that they bought from the Santa Fe Opera. He wasn't much of an opera fan either, but Sheila enjoyed it and it seemed to calm her a great deal, making it easier to get her to bed after their games. He saw no reason to change their habits.

Pete walked back into the family room. He was a bit surprised to find no one there. A sheet covered Sylvia Mondragon's mutilated body, but it did little to disguise the carnage that had taken place in that room. Pete was still amazed by the amount of blood pooled about her body and splattered around the room. The widespread blood patterns told him clearly that a tremendous struggle had taken place. Oddly, however, there was not a single thing out of order in the room. Even the pillows on the couch and in the two overstuffed chairs were in place. The wall that ran perpendicular to the front door was completely spattered with blood, as was the ceiling over half of the room. Although the furniture was undisturbed, there was a lot of blood and matter on the upholstered sofa and on the wood and glass pieces as well. Even the drapes in the front window and the glass had a great deal of blood on them, and they were rather far removed from where the body lay sprawled at the front door.

Pete stopped at the hallway entrance for a moment, then continued walking toward the back of the house. He followed the traces of blood on the light colored Berber carpeting and midway up the walls. There was very little blood actually, in comparison to the family room.

The first room on Pete's right was obviously Sylvia's son's room. The lights were on and the room was incredibly orderly, he thought, for a teenage boy. To the left and directly across the hall was a large bathroom. If it were her son's, he did as good a job keeping it up as he did his room. In fact, it was almost too tidy, except for the black smears on all the flat surfaces where the fingerprint experts had been working for over five hours now. The room at the end of the hall was obviously Sylvia's. It was large and airy and smelled of roses and expensive perfume. Both seemed out of the ordinary for her background. She was not at all like the Pueblo Indians Pete had encountered over the years. By all accounts, Sylvia had lived a rather "Anglo-cized" lifestyle. And everyone knew that she and Bill Conner had been seeing one another for several months.

Pete didn't know much about women. He'd never dated, and the only two women he really knew were his aunt who had raised him and his sister Sheila. Sheila was six years his senior and mildly retarded. He had taken care of her since their aunt died five years ago. Pete wondered what it would be like to be in love and to give someone expensive perfume. He walked over to Sylvia's dresser and looked at the various little bottles. All unique and rather sensuously designed. There was a framed photograph of a man and a woman sitting near a river and laughing so hard they seemed to be almost falling backwards. The man was Bill Conner. Pete tried not to envy him his physique and good looks, but he couldn't help it. The woman must have been Sylvia. It would be hard for Pete to make that determination based on the corpse.

Pete looked around the room, trying to get a sense of the person who had lived here. As he glanced toward the bed, he saw the roses for the first time. A beautiful arrangement of bright red roses, beyond buds but not yet fully open. Their fragrance filled the room. He guessed that women must love flowers. Mrs. Ridgeway had that beautiful bunch, and now this lady.

He'd never sent anyone flowers before. He didn't even send flowers to his aunt's funeral. How do men learn the right things to do, he wondered somewhat wistfully?

Pete walked over to the arrangement and leaned down to inhale the aroma. Then he saw the envelope from the Taos Floral and Design Shop and a small white card lying on the white, crocheted doily. Pete picked up the card and read it: *Sylvia—If you say yes…I will live my life to make your dreams come true…OUR dreams come true. I love you so much, baby… Bill*

Taos Floral and Design Shop. Pete placed the card gently back on the table as though it were a piece of delicate china. He felt a little like a peeping Tom, like he'd seen more than he should. Still, he was glad he'd looked. That lady who owned that flower shop sure must have had a good couple of days. He also wondered what she would do now that Mack was dead. Pete touched a rose with just the tip of his finger, and smelled them one last time. The tears that appeared in his eyes and threatened to spill down on his cheeks surprised him. *I bet she said yes, he thought to himself.* Then he wondered what it would feel like to have someone want to marry him.

Pete walked over to the shrouded body and stared down at it for a moment before bending down with a grunt and pulling the sheet back from the top half of Sylvia Mondragon's body. He knew what sight awaited him, and held his breath for several seconds before exhaling loudly.

He forced himself to make the mental comparisons he had gone over in his mind earlier. The most extraordinary difference was, of course, that Sylvia Mondragon was not completely decapitated, as had been the earlier victim. It took the authorities several days to unearth the previous victim's head which turned out to be buried near where the body was discovered. It had been overlooked by the swarms of investigators and dogs that had scoured the area. There was still some speculation that the head was brought back to the site and buried at some point after the murder. The answer to that question might never be known.

In that crime, the decapitation had been executed neatly and precisely with an extremely sharp and powerfully wielded blade. It's no easy task to decapitate someone. Pete surmised that it had been done by someone large, rather strong, and skilled with the proper weapon. Pete recalled everyone's amazement at the lack of blood at the scene of that murder. And then again, being outdoors, it didn't have the dramatic impact that this murder had.

When the head was recovered and brought into the coroner's office, an immediate order of exhumation was secured and authorities were amazed at how the two body parts would have fit almost exactly back together. The head, wrapped in a plain white towel and placed in the damp earth, had maintained its original size remarkably well. That fact had only added to the speculation that the head had been stored somewhere, perhaps in a refrigerated container of some sort, before being brought back and interred at the site.

What Pete saw before him now, however, showed few, if any, similarities. The main wound was jagged and irregular and placed too far down the neck to have been the decapitating cut. Upon closer examination, Pete noted that the cut began at the front of the neck near the base of her throat, but stopped short of the spinal column. At this point, he could not conclusively say that the blade used was a serrated one, but it certainly appeared so. The evidence indicated something more like a dull hacksaw than a smooth, sharp blade. The lack of a weapon always made something like this little more than an educated guessing game, at this point anyway. Pete was sure that a forensic pathologist and a coroner appointed by the state would be sent up immediately. He remembered what a pain in the ass they had been the last time.

Sylvia Mondragon had over fifty deep gashes along her face, in her scalp, and on her upper arms. There were no injuries on her back except blunt force trauma contusions and two unexplained abrasions. Her chest and stomach area showed similar signs of blunt force trauma and abrasions, but again no cuts of any kind.

The earlier victim, who had been discovered at a campground, had one small contusion on her left shoulder. That was the only visible mark except for the abrasions on the left side of her body where she had obviously been dragged back into the forested area and covered with leaves and branches.

This was not the same "doer" as they say. He felt certain Richards had brushed this off too quickly earlier in the evening as being another attack by the same person. In fact, the phrase "serial killer" had already been used. Pete was certain that couldn't be further from the truth. This might be a copycat murder, but it was definitely not the work of the same killer. Pete was certain of that, and would try to convince the authorities who were being brought in.

The odor in the room was getting repugnant now and Pete was beginning to get edgy and slightly nauseated. Still, he was able to shut his mind to it and treat the scene in front of him like an everyday occurrence. He cursed himself under his breath for having mastered the ability to separate himself from the soul of someone like Sylvia Mondragon. Prior to tonight, it had been something he prided himself on. But this was different. As he struggled to his feet, he made some life-changing decisions that would affect not only his career dramatically, but also his life. These weren't new feelings, but he'd let them pass before. He didn't intend to do that this time.

He wanted to experience the kind of happiness he'd seen in the faces of the two people in the photograph. He wanted to have someone to love so badly that losing her would be unbearable. He wanted to be someone so well liked that another person would be compelled to lavish him with incredible gifts like the flowers he'd seen today. And he wanted to send a woman flowers. He wanted all the things he'd denied himself in the past. And he would. Or least he would truly try for the first time in his life. But first, he wanted to find whoever it was that possessed enough hatred to have done this to so beautiful and harmless a creature. *What could possibly spark that kind of violence? How could a person like that live with himself?* He knew there were answers. He'd always left that part up to someone else. This time, however, his instincts were telling him it was time he pulled his head out of the sand and got involved. He didn't want it to go unsolved like the one in May. One last look at the bloodied body before him reconfirmed his decision. Pete bent down and put the sheet back over Sylvia Mondragon.

Grasping the back of a chair, he pulled himself to a standing position. With his right hand, he crossed himself, turned and then walked through the house and out into the cold, juniper scented night air.

PART I

Faceless oceans still in motion

Drift before my eyes.

The stabbing sounds, another's found

Briefly laughs then dies

How far must you go before you find out where you are?

The golden road

Its pleasures loathed

Memories explode.

Chapter Seven

Frank and Bill were sitting across the table from Phillip in a small, poorly lit room in the Taos Police Station. Phillip was explaining to them that he'd come there to help them in any way he could.

"And I appreciate that," the sheriff replied with a slight Texan accent. "I should say, *we* appreciate it." He glanced over at Bill Conner. Bill was the acting sheriff now, and Frank was merely an appointed deputy, at least for the time being. It had all come about through the bizarre series of events that eventually brought Phillip to New Mexico.

"Let me ask *you* a question, Frank," Phillip said slowly. Patricia had told him a lot about Frank Garrett. A decent man, she said, but one with a few too many secrets. Phillip knew a lot more about these two men than they did about him. He'd have to remember that. But why were they trying make him feel as though he were a suspect instead of a consultant anyway? Maybe they were just trying to show him who was in control. Hadn't Bill explained to Frank that he was there to cooperate and help them? Phillip knew that Bill's part in this was mostly a very good act. He was impressed up to this point and had to keep reminding himself that they were all on the same side.

"I was just wondering..." Phillip paused.

"Yes, what is it?"

"Well, not to be disrespectful, but you working on this case and all. It's a bit odd. I mean, Alma was your wife and it must be very difficult for you." He was uncomfortable asking the question, but felt a need to throw Frank off balance and perhaps get some respect. Phillip knew a lot about how law enforcement people think, and he could tell that Frank Garrett was examining him like he would a bug under a microscope.

Garrett glared at Phillip as he answered. "Know what? I'm going to see that justice is done here, whether I'm officially on the case or not. Is that perfectly clear, Mr. Craven? I don't sleep much at night, if you want to know the truth, and I never stop thinking about her. I also never stop thinking about getting the son of a bitch who killed her." His eyes finally blinked and he sighed, relaxing his stiff shoulders slightly, his jaw muscles unclenching.

He paused for a moment, and his demeanor seemed to change. He appeared a bit more relaxed somehow. "I really appreciate your help, Phil," Frank said. "When Bill first told me about this, I mean about what you were saying about all of this...well, I've got to be very honest with you. I thought it was a bunch of bullshit, if you want to know the God's honest truth. I mean, I know we live in a crazy world and things are getting crazier all the time...well, you know. Then it turns out you aren't some nut after all, but someone who just might know what he's talking about. I mean you write about this stuff. You're an expert in a way."

"Well, I wouldn't say that..." Phillip started to say modestly.

"Oh, cut the crap, Craven. You get paid a decent amount of money to know this kind of stuff, so that makes you an expert, right? That's the way it works, you know. If someone pays you money to write or talk about something, you're an expert. From what I hear, you're a goddamn, fuckin' expert, Phillip. I *can* call you Phillip?"

"Yes. Phil would be better. Don't call me Craven."

"Good. Fine then. And you can call me Frank. And Bill...well, you already know Bill."

Phillip had indeed talked to Bill on the phone several times and had even met him and his fiancée Sylvia, though apparently Garrett didn't know that. And Patricia had already let Phillip know that the police departments in both Albuquerque and Santa Fe were investigating the homicide, and that there was a detective with a grudge against Frank Garrett who was convinced Frank had been involved in the brutal murder of his own wife.

"Well, Phil, I know a lot of experts. And some of them don't seem to know shit." Frank Garrett was beginning to get excited, although Phillip wasn't exactly sure why. Phillip didn't know him well enough to know that he was acting, daring not to let anyone know all that he knew. He knew that the more people kept secrets, the less chance there was for a case to be solved. But Frank couldn't possibly be completely honest—especially now. He had only recently been reinstated after proving his own innocence in the death of his wife. "So just because you aren't some nut, doesn't mean a lot to me, if you know what I mean."

"I think so," responded Phillip.

"But then it turns out, or so Bill here was telling me the other day—it turns out that you used to work for the coroner's office in Los Angeles, and then up in Seattle. So, I'm thinking you ain't some slick Mick. Excuse the expression if you will. So I guess I have to listen to what you said. I mean, you just might know what the hell you are talking about, now isn't that true?"

Phillip smiled, not sure if Frank was joking or dead serious. Frank had no idea how much Phillip knew. And he wasn't going to tell him right now either.

"I am starting to believe an awful lot of what I write," Phillip said lightly.

"Now *that* sounds dangerous, Phil. Hell, pretty soon you'll be goin' on with that nice lady and her talk show. Rosie Donnelly or somethin' like that. You know who I mean. Maybe you're right, Phil. You seem to have some friends in the right places on the LAPD and up there in Seattle, too.

"Now this *stuff* you're talking to Bill about... I'd like to know more about it. I mean it's all *way* over my head and doesn't make much sense to me. But, Bill here... Well, he knows a hell of a lot more about it than me and he says you know much more than he does. Hell, I barely know how to switch the damn thing on, myself."

Phillip nodded with a smile. He knew Frank was lying, maybe he needed to, maybe he had to.

Then Bill jumped in, "The whole thing is rather new to most people, even me, really. About two years ago, I was in the dark about it as well. Haven't you been writing about it for over two years, Phil?"

"Yeah, I figured, why not get paid as I learn this stuff?" Phillip joked. "Not to change the subject or anything, but where is Patricia?"

"She's down the hall. We're talking to her about all this as well," answered Frank. "You've known her a while?"

"Oh, a little over a year now."

"*She* said you were *old* friends," Frank countered.

Phillip smiled. "We *are* old friends. We've *become* old friends in the year or so we've known each other. We've discovered we have a lot in common and...well, you know how it is."

Frank studied Phillip's face a moment. He learned a long time ago you could learn a lot the moment after someone stops speaking. You just have to be quiet and watch. Phillip seemed to know a lot more about things than what he was saying. For a moment Frank felt like he might even know about him. But surely that wasn't possible, no one *really* knew.

Phillip had been around a lot of cops and knew what Frank was doing. He was not casually being asked for information. He was being questioned.

"Guys," Phillip said with a forced smile, "I gotta tell you, I came here today to help out, and being interviewed like this is making me awful nervous."

"That was my idea, Mr. Craven," said Bill.

"What?!"

Phillip had gone into this liking Bill Conner from everything Patricia had said about him. He realized now that the feeling wasn't mutual. Of course, Bill didn't know much about him. But why should he? Patricia wouldn't have told him too much. How could she without being put in a very awkward position? And the few conversations he had with Bill himself, while seemingly lighthearted and friendly, were hardly long enough or serious enough for the two of them to form any type of bond or trust.

"Well, it was some things you said on the phone. I was concerned," Bill said trying to explain. His eyes turned cold and professional.

"Are you telling me I'm a suspect?"

"A suspect? Oh, no. Well, at least not directly," Bill replied.

Frank chimed in, "Let's just say that you are a person of interest to us, Phil."

"Gentlemen, maybe we should end this conversation. I'm not feeling comfortable here. What do you say we go grab a couple of beers or something?" Phillip pushed his chair away from the table.

"Sure. A couple of beers would be nice," Frank said. "When we're finished here, that is. Now sit down."

Phillip begrudgingly complied. "Look, guys, I came here to help you out."

"Maybe you did, Phil," Frank interrupted. "Maybe you flew down here just to help us out. But fact is, you came here three days ago, Phil. You came here three days early, so that gives us another problem now, doesn't it…Craven?"

"I see," Phillip said. His suspicions were confirmed.

"Phil, let's do this the easy way, okay?" Frank had raised his voice now but remained calm.

"Do *what* the easy way? What? You going to read me my Miranda rights now?"

"Phil, why did you come to Taos three days ago and fail to check in with us until just a couple of hours ago?" Bill asked.

Phillip sighed. Now he understood what was going on. Of course, Bill knew he had been in town, but Frank did not and Bill had to play dumb. They *were* right. It *did* look very suspicious. He had arrived more than three days before he was supposed to and had not let them know he was in town. He could see their point clearly enough.

"What have you been doing for these past three days, Phillip?" Frank asked the question this time.

Phillip was beginning to feel boxed in. If he told them the truth, and they asked more questions, it would all seem absurd. Hell, from all perspectives it *was* absurd. In many ways, the last year or so had been a completely new experience. He would tell them the truth. He had to. If they were to work together, he had little choice. He just wished he could make sure it was okay with Patricia. If they were to solve this homicide, the four of them would have to work closely together and learn to trust one other. That had to start with being honest. "Gentlemen, simply said…love is why I came here three days ago."

The two men seemed a bit stunned. He knew that Bill's reaction was an act. Phillip realized they must think he was off his rocker and he chuckled, which didn't help matters any.

"Gentlemen, I am a man in love and I took advantage of an opportunity to spend a few days with the woman I'm in love with."

"Patricia?" Frank asked with some surprise.

"Yes, Patricia."

"Well, uh…" Frank was flustered. "She's a fine looking lady and all." Frank hadn't even considered this as a reason for Phillip's early arrival. "And she seems nice. Actually, she was my wife's best friend. Alma worked for Patricia for years. But…well, I thought she was happily married and…"

He looked nervously over at Bill who now was smiling. Then he glanced back to Phillip.

Phillip grinned. "You boys thought of all kinds of scenarios, but not the most obvious one, huh?"

Frank started to laugh loudly and it was infectious.

"Please, let me apologize, Phil," Frank said, extending his hand. "Let me offer you my *sincerest* apology. When Bill told me that you had been in town a few days already, and you didn't get in touch with us, and we couldn't reach you at the hotel… well, we just started assuming, I guess."

Phillip put up his hands and laughed. "It's understandable. I realize how it must look. If I were in your shoes I'd wonder if I was an accessory too! Especially after my conversation with Bill, which must have seemed pretty weird."

They all laughed together for a few brief moments, and then Frank said to Bill, "Give Phillip here the five-minute tour and make him a fresh pot of coffee if he wants one."

"So, she's being questioned, also?" Phillip tried to mask his concern.

Frank stood up. "Yeah. I mean, we knew you two were friends, we just didn't realize…"

"… that it was more serious," Bill added tactfully. Phillip winked at Bill, who already had learned how close Patricia and Phillip were.

"Yeah," Frank said. "Yeah, that's right. Hell, I'm still a suspect, myself. Would've been nice to get the heat off of me. I mean I've been cleared officially, of course, or I wouldn't be here. But…" He paused. "Sorry, you don't know what I'm talking about do you?"

"Actually, I do, Frank," Phillip said. "I understand a lot of things that you don't realize I do."

Frank nodded and a moment later his eyes closed and he chuckled at Bill, because it was clear that Phillip and Patricia had talked many times about what was occurring and part of the conversation was about Frank Garrett.

Frank sighed. "Now I feel very stupid, Phil. I hope you'll accept my apology for being such an ass."

"Part of the job," Phillip smiled.

Bill and Frank laughed. They liked Phillip and knew he was someone they could trust.

"Well, we'll try this again in a few minutes. Maybe over some beers, as you suggested," Frank added.

"At this point, a scotch might be better. Though it's a bit early. Maybe just breakfast."

Later, that phrase—*might be better*—came flooding back into his consciousness along with a myriad of associated memories.

And as Phillip drifted back within his memories, he recalled reading a story that Albert Einstein had written about how people regarded time. He broke it down into mechanical time and body time. Mechanical time was defined as being rigid, never ending, traveling as if in a straight line from A to B, always moving forward, never looking back, never stopping. Body time was defined as time which made up its own mind, undisciplined and as difficult to hold and control as carrying water in your hands.

* * * * *

Sarah's hands were beautiful, he remembered. Graceful, soft, delicate, and with long fingers.

"It *will be* much better this way," Sarah had said to him. "We should have done this a long time ago."

After all the time they had been together. After everything they had been through together, it was over. Phillip realized he had been holding onto some sort of hope that their passion would somehow be reborn. He was so sure as they made the breakup official, something inside Sarah would go off and make her realize that she couldn't live without him, that she would want him like she hadn't wanted anyone, ever before in her life. Then they would wrap their arms around each other, and their kisses would be deep and passionate. They would end up forgiving each other and become the team they always said they would be yet never really were. Yet that was not happening. Sarah seemed to be accepting this so calmly, without protest, as though she were almost relieved it was over.

The loud honking startled Phillip and he realized the traffic light had turned green. As soon as he crossed through the intersection, he was once again lost in his thoughts.

Shit, that was nearly five years ago. *Five years!* How long would it be before he stopped thinking about her like this? What they had was never particularly passionate. For the last several years, in fact, they'd lived more like roommates. Sometimes, they didn't speak to each other for days at a time. They rarely kissed, rarely made love, and almost never said "I love you" to one another. Their relationship ended the way it had begun. As friends.

Old friends. Friends who sent each other birthday and Christmas cards and caught up, during the year, with a couple of long, pleasant phone calls. Calls which only served to underscore how disconnected they'd become from each other's lives.

Phillip turned his car into the left lane, planning on taking Union down to Fifteenth over to Cherry and wind down to Lake Washington Boulevard for a drive by one of his old stomping grounds.

He had spent three years in Seattle, before buying his place in Cle Elum. He liked living out in the middle of nowhere with the timber and the cows. He connected somehow with the hawks, the deer, and the river. He should have moved there long before.

He had enjoyed Seattle, though the traffic was getting so bad it was beginning to remind him a little too much of Los Angeles. He didn't care at all for LA and would have moved much sooner if it hadn't been for Sarah and his work. Now, he was doing mostly what he wanted to do, but he was alone. Although Phillip wanted someone special in his life, he refused to force things. When it's meant to happen it will happen, he had decided. In the meantime, he wouldn't worry about it. Well, he wouldn't worry too much anyway. Actually, he would *pretend* he wasn't worrying at all and then almost convince himself that this was the truth. He was quite good at *pretending not to worry.*

Nope, it wasn't working very well at all, Phil admitted to himself. He smiled; switching his thoughts like a remote control changed TV stations. Tomorrow night he would be attending the opening of a new exhibit of his photos at a small gallery on First Avenue right near the Seattle Art Museum. He was going to add one more piece to the show. It was the first one he had done like this. It was a picture of a raindrop about to fall from the underside of a Victorian porch railing. And around the picture he had placed a poem he had written, a poem Patricia had inspired.

First Autumn Storm
by Phillip Craven

Sleepless dreams
passing through
like a cloudburst
in the desert,
flooding my mind
with images

Flashing
like
a lightning
bolt.
striking
reality.

Stop making sense.
Then,
when the storm
has passed…

the birds
sing praises
for
predictable
changes.

…you notice
a single rain drop
clinging under
the porch
rail
like
Hope.

The poem was written in a silvery text wrapped around the picture of the raindrop. The picture was digitally altered to appear in a sepia tone fashion, but the raindrop was like a prism and there was a small, colorful rainbow within the drop. The idea of combining the poetry texture with the picture was Patricia's. It was a piece he was anxious to put in the gallery and see if it got favorable reaction. He hoped it would, so he could tell Patricia about it.

Patricia was new. He hadn't known her very long at all. Just a few months. And he couldn't believe he felt so close to her so quickly. And it was a long distance romance. She was in New Mexico where she owned a bookstore and he was in Washington. But, in the few short months they'd known each other, their relationship had grown. Phillip was in love with her—an idea that was absurd upon any reasonable analysis. He smiled when he recalled their last phone conversation.

"You're really going to do it?" The excitement in her voice gave Phillip renewed confidence.

"I am!" he said excitedly. "And if it doesn't go over…well, I can say it was all this crazy woman's idea."

"Yes, but you *listened* to the crazy woman."

"I can't be *blamed* for such things."

"Why not?"

"Oh, I'm a fickle artist type don't you know," Phillip teased. "I'm downright Bohemian."

"Oh, then you're in the wrong place, my friend."

"You mean I should be there in *your* warm embrace?"

"Oh, you *are* a naughty man, sir."

"And *you* wouldn't have it any other way, my dear."

"I'll have it any way you want to give it to me," Patricia said softly.

"Mmm, now what are *you* thinking?"

"Oh, only very good thoughts," Patricia said with a chuckle.

Remembering almost any conversation they had on the phone brought a smile to Phillip's face. They had clicked together from the start, and it kept getting better and better.

Chapter Eight

Butch Killen always got a bit of a knot in his stomach whenever he pulled into his familiar parking place behind the Taos Plaza. For so many years, he and Angie, along with that scruffy old, lazy Abby dog, parked in that very same spot and finished the last bit of coffee that they'd brought with them from home. The three of them would sit and talk about what the day might have in store. Every day was a good one for the Killens and their sheepdog, which they'd acquired soon after arriving in the area.

Angela had studied art in New York, and had always dreamed of coming to the Southwest and losing herself in the splendor of the mountains and the high deserts. As a young girl she had listened to the old western radio programs and fallen in love with Gene Autry, the singing cowboy. She really wasn't much of a reader back then, but devoured the radio stories and dreamed little girl dreams of handsome cowboys, beautiful horses, wide-open spaces and guitar serenades under starry western skies.

She had been raised in a small, rural Iowa community. The farthest her family ventured from their home was to travel the forty-five miles east to her grandparents' farm. She and her older brother, Ted, would count the days till those visits, not realizing the seriousness of the situation. They were elated when they were told that they would move onto the farm permanently. Angela was nine years old then.

The old couple should have moved to town years ago. It was something everyone in the family knew, but didn't talk about. Her grandfather had suffered an unexpected stroke, and could no longer manage the simple, everyday chores required to keep the farm working and producing, as it should. Although the sudden change in his personality saddened her, Angie was overjoyed at being able to move to the farm. Then there was Angie's grandmother.

Angie's grandmother was totally blind, and had been since she was thirty-four years old. She had survived a near fatal bout of scarlet fever when she was younger; but just as she was beginning to feel like her old self, she'd noticed her vision was deteriorating. After consulting a number of doctors in the area, her grandmother was forced to face the fact that gradually her vision would worsen until eventually she would be completely blind. The high fevers she had endured during the peak of the illness had taken their toll. With some time to prepare, Angie's grandparents were able to devise ways for Miss Mary, as her grandmother liked to be called, to maneuver around the house and the property. She would actually blindfold herself and "practice" being blind. She learned to count the steps between certain key areas in the house and in the yard. She could easily manipulate around the kitchen and accomplish the cooking with what seemed like astounding ease. She could clean her home, and even prune her beloved rose bushes in the fall. By the time she was totally blind, Miss Mary could manage as well as any sighted person. She was an inspiration to everyone who knew her.

Miss Mary was a remarkable woman and Angela Killen found great comfort in remembering her now. She seemed to be nursing a bit of nostalgia today. Whenever she came to the bookshop with Butch, her grandmother was never far from her thoughts. She always took a moment to pay Miss Mary a bit of earned homage when she thought of her and then went on her way knowing that some constants in life never change. Like treasured memories, leather-bound books, classic love songs, and the golden threads that bind people forever.

Miss Mary had been a rapacious reader before she went blind, so as she was making her many other preparations, she began collecting hundreds of books that were written in Braille. That adjustment came as easily as everything else did. Angie wondered sometimes what it was that gave some people the courage and the fortitude to carve a new life out of some of life's bittersweet offerings.

Angela Louise Killen had been very fortunate in her life. She had grown up in a pleasant, comfortable home. She had loved and been loved, and her life was rather remarkable by most standards.

When she was young and found herself alone, Angela would scrounge around for something to read or some paper and a charcoal pencil. She loved to draw and would sit and sketch just about anything that pleased her. One remarkably cold night, while alone on the farm, Angela ran across a book that she'd seen her brother reading earlier in the day. In fact, he had an entire collection of these books, but she had never paid much attention to them. He was always reading and daydreaming, and she didn't have the forbearance for that. This particular night, feeling a bit melancholy, probably because of being alone she supposed, she picked up the thin, worn book and remembers studying what was left of the gold, embossed lettering on the hand-tooled binding: The *Lost Pueblo* by Zane Grey.

Several hours later, Angie closed the book, the last words etched in her mind. With the radio stories to listen to and the books to devour at will, thus began her lifelong love affair with the American West.

Angie Killen knew she was destined to be right where she was that morning. Sitting in the shamefully old Subaru, sipping lukewarm coffee with Butch. Butch Killen was the only man she had ever given a second glance to in her entire life. She sat there quietly, watching him out of the corner of her eye, idly scratching Abby behind the ears, as the aged dog leaned over the back of the seat.

Butch was glancing over an inventory list that he needed to tackle first thing when he opened the shop this morning. That's one reason Angie had agreed to come in to work for a few hours. She had quit painting a few months back. She had developed a painfully sore shoulder, and it finally reached the point where even maneuvering a paintbrush was now unbearable.

Theirs was a comfortable life, she was thinking. She had loved the quietness and solitude of living up Taos Canyon. It was a wonderful place for her to have spent these past twenty years. Quiet and as idyllic as it sounds, almost trouble-free years of painting and drawing and enjoying one another, and watching the splendor of the seasons unfold year after year. Quietly and predictably, one followed another in an enormous display of light and color. They both relished the mystique of the world that surrounded them there in the quiet canyon. Music played and echoed around the canyon walls, and Angela sang along, sometimes dancing alone to the priceless old tunes she grew up with. It was not unusual to find Angie and Butch dancing together in the twilight of the day. Theirs was a life of composed passion for one another and for the loves they shared.

When Butch had bought the Take Another Look bookstore three years before, he held an open house to welcome the townspeople and merchants. He was anxious for them to get acquainted with some of the changes he had made and to reintroduce a lost era in book selling. He'd smiled when he'd said that to Angie as they were setting up for the event.

The store possessed an eclectic variety of books and furnishings, its ambiance begging you to come in and curl up with a good book by one of the potbellied wood stoves. To sit in the filtered sunlight beneath a lace draped window. To sink deep into a scuffed, broken down leather chair. To sip aromatic tea and expect a lap visit from a lazy cat, if you were lucky enough to be honored with such a tribute.

It was a chilly autumn evening when Butch and Angela hosted the open house. Following a toast to the shop's success given by the mayor, Angie presented Butch with her brother's collection of all of Zane Grey's original works. The gesture was touching, even to a casual observer, but it was touching beyond description to Butch. Many of the books were still blackened from the fire that had taken her brother Ted's life. Fire investigators determined that the house had been struck by lightning. The fire had started in the attic where the books were stored. Ted managed to get the Zane Grey books and his grandmother's collection of Braille books downstairs before he succumbed to the heat and smoke. Precious little else was salvaged from the fire. The books and the memories were all Angela carried away from that day. Memories of a softer time and the encapsulation of the exact moment in time, when a little girl gently closed the covers of a worn book, and planned her destiny.

Some people realize early on in life that destinies are made and not born. Lives are too priceless to be left to chance or to fate. We have a dream, we design a map, we plan a path, and we construct a road. That was what her grandmother had so skillfully done, and that was what she would do. Simple truths, attainable desire. Nothing left to chance. Appreciation of life's pleasures: love, music, art, words, nature, dreams, fantasies, constants, and fundamental trust. Where was the difficulty in life, she often wondered?

When days were dark and sadness tried to creep into her world, Angie often found herself at the river's edge. Watching the tumbling waters always brought an indefinable peace to her. Then in a gesture of her hands, she tossed the imaginary troubles into the water and asked that they flow away until they were so diluted as to not exist at all. Then she would rise from the bank, brush her hands together as though dusting unwanted dirt from them, and walk through the meadow toward her home. Her sanctuary.

That is what she would do later this day. After Butch was finished with his inventory and she was free to leave the bookstore and go back up the canyon. She and Abby would walk to the riverbank and cast away the gloom of the day, and prepare to tell Butch what a pleasure her life had been with him.

With her eyes closed and the soft drone of the radio in the background, she basked in the aroma of the coffee mixed with the stale air in the closed car. The softness of Abby beneath her fingers, and the fragrance of lingering cigar smoke and drug store aftershave which was "trademark Butch" casually assaulting her senses. Angie smiled and secretly longed for the day when she would be with her grandmother and her brother again. And they could talk of things she longed to share. Talk of days remembered and days to come. Theirs would be a good place to die.

She would have to tell Butch soon. Maybe not today though. The summer days were so beautiful here in the shadow of the mountain. Too beautiful to spoil with news that Butch would never really accept. Angela had known for several days that the lump she had discovered on her right shoulder a few weeks ago was malignant. The cancer had already spread to the bone and, after weighing the pros and cons of the various treatment options presented to her, she chose what many would consider a foolish approach. She opted to spend her remaining days in the comfort of her home, declining any treatment. She would languish amid the tranquility of the mountains and valleys, watching as the vibrant colors of the day came to rest. Sitting on her back lawn with Butch and Abby, and listening to the faint sounds that a slow moving river makes.

Sometimes there are no words to capture the essence of a feeling. Of the serenity and placidity that most people rarely experience. The running of a quiet river gently rolling over the smooth, polished rocks and then tumbling into crystal clear pools where rainbow and brown trout congregate. In time, the trout would join others on a journey down the Rio Grande. It must be nice to be a fish. Or an eagle, perhaps.

A family of wolves had taken up residence across the river in the past few years. One of Angie's fondest memories is of catching a glimpse of the mother wolf as she brought her pups down to the riverside one spring evening. Frantic to keep the litter together, the mother wolf eventually got into the water and corralled the pups against the bank. The father wolf stood back a fair distance and just observed. Angela named him Pointman. She watched this twice-a-day sojourn till the first snowfall. Then she didn't see the family again for many months.

She wondered what it would have been like to have been a mother. To have given Butch the opportunity to be a father. She didn't think about that much, really—or at least she tried not to. No use thinking about things that might have been, she always told folks. But that was one thought that sneaked in every now and again. She would look at Abby sometimes, however, and know that every woman is a mother to something. It's the way of things.

Angela's memories were good ones and her regrets were few. She cared not to spoil what she had earned in her life by falling prey to the medical skullduggery that would most assuredly ensue if she chose to prolong this inevitable process of dying. No, Angie was sure that she had come into this world honorably. She had lived an enviable life filled with happiness, talent, love, and great comfort. As a tribute to her life and to the man who had brought her more happiness than she dared dream existed, she would leave quietly by the same door through which she had entered. She would recall this day later, as she dozed quietly on the porch, and she would consider it one of the best days of her life.

Abby stirred as Butch leaned forward and shut off the engine. Taking one last sip of his coffee and placing the cup on the stained dashboard, he turned and touched Angela on the arm. "You ready to face the day?"

"You bet!" she said enthusiastically, clapping her hands together. Abby responded by leaping over the seat and upsetting the coffee cup balanced on Angie's knee. Neither one of them noticed as they laughed at the usual clumsiness of the dog they loved so. They didn't need to exchange words or even make eye contact to know what the other was thinking at that moment. As if on cue, followed by natural laughter, they both said. "I know. I know. She's a natural born klutz!" Anyone who was nearby would have sworn that the dog laughed out loud. It did as far as Angie and Butch were concerned.

Butch gathered his paperwork together and stuffed it into a worn leather briefcase and stepped out of the car. He drank in the pine-scented air and strode around to the passenger side of the car and opened the door for Angela and Abby. He held his knee up to keep Abby from bounding out too quickly and leaned forward and offered Angie his hand. She stepped out, turned back to shut the door, but bent forward instead to pick up the coffee cup from the floor of the car and place it on the dashboard next to Butch's. When she stretched to do so, the pain in her shoulder caught her by surprise and she winced. Butch noticed.

"Are you okay, honey?"

"Oh, sure! It's nothing that another cup of coffee won't cure!" She closed her eyes against the pain and knew that she probably would have to talk to Butch tonight. It was hard to prevent the tears. She felt Butch as he casually tugged at her sweater sleeve, moving to lead her away from the car. Abby bounded ahead in her usual comical fashion toward the back door of the bookstore. She was sitting on the worn mat, panting as they approached. Angela loved this store.

"It's odd, isn't it," she said to Butch, "how books can become closer to you than old friends?" They *were* old friends she thought. The best old friends, she quickly concluded. Butch had the door open and was waiting for her to come in. Abby had already lumbered in and found her place on the faded hooked rug near the front desk. She would post sentinel there until it was time to go home. It would have been easier if Abby had chosen somewhere else to lie other than in the main traffic path. That, too, made Angie smile. Of course, she knew that Abby would indeed, choose that particular spot to take up residence. That's what she loved about the old dog. Everything has its own special way of capturing what attention it needs. Abby simply needed to be stepped over and have her ears rubbed to feel whole and know that she was loved. If only that were enough for everyone. But that is not the way of things for most of us.

It would be nice to be a sheepdog, Angela thought. Then turned to smile as a young mother came through the door. Abby never acknowledged the camel bells as they clanged away and barely responded to the two little towheaded boys who ran in to pet her. The boys knew from experience that it was a false show of dispassion on Abby's part. They had to eventually move to keep from being beaten half to death by Abby's wagging tail.

Butch climbed the stairs to his office, which he had carved out amid the shelves of rare books and his private collections. Setting his briefcase down on the floor beside the old swivel chair, he fell heavily into it. He rested his chin on his fist, closed his eyes, and basked in the aroma of the dust and yellowing pages that embraced him there.

He would miss the store, he thought to himself. Miss it as much as he would miss Angela. But in a different way, of course. He knew about her cancer, and he also knew of her decision. He knew she would tell him in her own time. Somehow knowing but not *being told* made the entire nightmare seem to be just a very bad dream. Certainly not reality. This couldn't be happening to him. Not to his special angel. Who would rub Abby's ears? Butch loved the scroungy old dog, but had never shown it much affection. He would have to do that he kept telling himself. He would have to learn to do that.

Nightmares, illusions, bad dreams, x-rays, diagnoses—these were new realities to Butch. He had learned them all in a few short days following the phone call from the doctor in Santa Fe, the phone call he shouldn't have overheard. He had stood at the top of the stairs and listened. When Angie slowly hung up the receiver, he watched her through the upstairs window, as she walked across the meadow that spread out lazily between the house and the river. They had always kept two old, peeling Adirondack chairs down along the bank and he cried as he saw her sit down in hers and hold her head in her hands until the long shadows of evening almost hid her from his sight.

It was dusk before she came back up to the house. She was cold. He had started a fire, even though it was nearing summer. Darkness fell early in the canyon, and the temperatures dropped into the thirties at night. He handed her a shawl and a hot cup of coffee as she came through the door. If he hadn't known it, he would have hardly seen the evidence of the tears that had been falling for the past couple of hours. He admired her. He loved her. And he was so angry with her that he wanted to scream. How dare she do this to him!

Chapter Nine

It had been less than three years ago that Butch Killen had called Patricia into his office at the Taos County Library, and sat silently for a while before leaning forward on his cluttered desk and telling her about his decision to purchase the most popular bookstore in Taos.

Patricia sat quietly as the rumpled, former hippie she'd come to love and respect over the past twenty years, told her about his plans and dreams. They talked almost endlessly that day, reminiscing a little, laughing a great deal, and they occasionally shed a tear or two over a couple of their worst horror stories from the past two decades of working so closely together.

One of their favorite experiences, which they had often laughed over, had taken place a few years earlier. A popular book about the relationships between men and women had taken the country by storm and had become an overnight sensation. It was a book that started a new "relationship" craze and ultimately gave women even more unnecessary ammunition with which to win the war between the sexes. The new handbook on men and women aliens from opposing planets had offered Butch and Patricia a great deal of conversation and laughter. It had also helped forge a strong bond between the two of them as they began to share and discuss their own personal philosophies on the age-old subject.

Butch had ordered five copies of the book for the library when it first hit *The New York Times* bestseller list, and had added an additional twenty copies in the years that followed. Patricia kept a compilation of the library's most requested books, and that particular one stayed at the top of the list for several years in a row. Approximately half of the volumes had disappeared completely from the shelves, and the others had all been dog-eared, highlighted, and underlined, and most had some very comical cryptic notes in the margin. Its popularity both amused and confounded the two of them. The local Literary Book Club, which held its monthly meeting in the library's media room, had used the book for discussion several times. She and Butch had both sat in on a couple of those sessions, and had to graciously excuse themselves before they disrupted the somber group with their snickers and laughter!

They would retreat to Butch's office, share a cup of hot tea, and have their own discussion on love and the separate but combined roles of men and women in a relationship. None of these observations even began to resemble what was chronicled between the pages of the most popular and taunted "relationship bible" of all time.

Patricia and Butch had long ago outgrown the ideals that the difference between the mindset of men and women was what caused the normal problems within a relationship. Collectively, they had reached the same conclusion that it was *because* of these inherent differences that men and women *could* actually coexist as well as they did. Although their conclusions were the same, they were worlds apart in their origins. Patricia's was more from an innate philosophy gleaned from her culture and background and from some valuable teachings passed along in the wise words of the Elders. Butch's was from a long line of relationships and disappointments that finally culminated into a true love which, to all observers, seemed to defy the rules of reasonable compatibility.

Both of them had learned, through various life lessons, that there appeared to be only one true and simple rule to follow in life and love and that rule seemed to them, at least to offer an almost foolproof approach to lasting compatibility. Together they had queried one another why it didn't seem abundantly apparent to everyone. Their unpretentious philosophy was simple: Never take anyone or anything for granted, and treat all those you love with the utmost respect so long as they earn it honestly and graciously. This all seemed so very uncomplicated to them. And was the long and short of their entire shared philosophies.

"Patricia, how much do you think *Harper's Bazaar* would pay us for a one-page volume of our wisdom?" Butch quipped.

"One page? One page, you say? Oh, surely you jest. There would be four, at the very least!"

"Four? Oh, no way! We could never come up with four!"

"Oh sure, we could! Let's see...um...I know! There would be a cover page! And then an acknowledgment page, of course! Oh, and then the main text of the book and there would be...let's see...yes, there would have to be an epilogue. That's it!"

"An epilogue, my hind leg!" Butch said, repeating one of Patricia's trademark statements. "What the heck would the epilogue say, Miss Priss?"

"Well, for pity sakes, you disappoint me, you ol' reprobate!" Patricia loved teasing Butch and it was one of the primary reasons she had stayed at the Library as his assistant for so many years. One of these days she intended to tell him that. "It would say exactly the same thing the text said, of course! What else?"

Butch kicked back in his chair, threw his feet up on the desk, lit an unfiltered cigarette, and shook his head and smiled. He enjoyed the casual, uncompromising relationship he had with Patricia and she had made his years at the library some of the most enjoyable of his life. He watched her affectionately as she gathered some papers and folders up then rose from the chair, trying to look totally annoyed and disgusted.

"You know I *hate* those damn cigarettes! Why do you always do that? As if I didn't know that it was my signal to get my butt back to work. You could just say so and spare me *and* the rest of the world your pollutants!" She glanced up and smiled at him as he blew a smoke ring in her direction. Butch always wondered if she knew how much he admired her and that he winked at her every time she turned her back on him. One day he would have to tell her that.

Patricia was listening, though somewhat distracted from Butch's dialogue, as she sat recalling a number of moments like that one. Butch was saying that there would be a variety of reasons he would give the Library Board and the staff about his resignation, but the truth would most likely not be among them. He'd always harbored a dream to own his own bookstore. He had been waiting since the moment he had accepted the position at the library nearly twenty-three years ago for an opportunity to buy an existing shop or save enough money to open his own. He also knew it was something that he and Angela could do together. They were getting older and Butch worried about Angela a great deal. He wanted to spend as much time as he could with her.

By the end of the day Butch had written a letter of resignation and called a special meeting of the Library Board for the following week. He had also written a letter recommending that Patricia Ridgeway replace him as head librarian. He knew that her appointment went without saying, but as unconventional as he was on most issues, he stood on protocol when it mattered the most. Patricia took the helm at the library sixty days later. The Board was never disappointed in their decision to honor Butch Killen's recommendation.

Barely a year later, on a brisk fall morning in October, Butch strolled into Patricia's office and asked if she had any hot tea for an old friend. Four hours later, he walked out of her office looking more sorrowful and beaten than Patricia had ever seen him.

A few minutes later, Patricia told her staff that she had some errands to run about town and would see them in the morning. In the year they had worked under her direction, this was the first time that Patricia had ever left before everyone else.

Patricia walked slowly out of the back door to her designated parking place behind the library. She checked the back seat of her truck to make sure there was an extra jacket, and then got in. She headed for Blue Lake. The lake had always been her destination when she had a heavy heart and just needed to be alone with herself.

An hour later, she was parked beneath an old pine tree that years before she had fondly named *Amigo Viejo*—Old Friend. Patricia sat for a few minutes, the motor idling, while she listened to the last bit of an old Bobby Vinton cassette and observed the splendor of the lake and the surrounding area. For an odd moment, she felt safe here. Drifting back with the melodies to a time when life was simple and carefree and the thought of death was as foreign as the prospect for global peace. After the final strains of "Blue Velvet" faded, Patricia grabbed her heavy coat from the seat behind her and jumped down out of the truck. The late afternoon air was brisk, and the breeze from across the lake was almost cold. The fragrance of the fall forest conjured memories from somewhere in her past. She thought of her father and smiled. She spotted tiny birds flitting here and there among the trees. Two squirrels ran in front of her and dashed toward the trunk of a tree on her right. They stopped and chattered nervously, fussing at her for trespassing in their kingdom, then ran up the trunk of the tree and disappeared.

After a brisk walk around the lake, stopping here and there to gather a few golden aspen coins, Patricia felt like her thoughts had been spoken in her heart and sent on the wind where they would be carried and held by the invisible guardians of the spirit. Her tears had quenched the dryness of her heart, and what little mourning she felt she had to do was done now. The time for strength would come soon. She had to be ready for the friend who had given to her so much of himself for so many years. Patricia would miss Angela.

Now Patricia was faced with the same decisions as Butch had been such a short time ago. Her letter of resignation to the Board would be much the same as his had been. She would submit her recommendation for a replacement and would feel equally as confident about her choice as Butch had. She would give them only a two-week notice, however. Once it's time to cross a bridge, it's not wise to wait for the water to rise.

Tonight, Patricia would tell Trent about her decision and she was certain that he would share in her enthusiasm to purchase the bookshop from the Killens. Owning a business was a new adventure for Patricia, but her self-confidence helped buoy her waning enthusiasm as she pondered the various pitfalls she was sure to encounter. Butch had assured her that he would be available to assist her in any way that he could and would waltz her through the computer programs that were actually the brains of the operation. That was the scariest part to Patricia. For all the years at the Library and all the computer technology that had been introduced and the classes that the staff had attended regularly, Patricia had managed to avoid much personal contact with computers. She should have listened to Butch's advice when he told her that one day she might be sorry that she had so skillfully dodged the inevitable.

Chapter Ten

Phillip had a sudden and unpleasant Los Angeles flashback of never-ending traffic jams, stop-and-go traffic, everyone tailgating. Maybe there was an accident that had caused this snarling, crawling mess he found himself in. An Asian driver perhaps, refusing to tailgate, causing someone to stop, as they merged onto the freeway. Or maybe it was a slow-driving old man or a blue-haired elderly lady whose eyes barely peered over the dashboard, all petrified of freeway driving. It could have been a woman, probably paying too much attention to putting on her makeup, who might have smashed into a guy busy placing bets with his bookie via a cell phone. BAM! He'd hit the stalled twenty-year-old, low-riding, oil-spewing Chevy driven by a forged green card-carrying Mexican. The Chevy perhaps stalled out when its driver had to slam on his brakes to avoid an accident with the ten-year-old Cadillac that had illegally changed lanes suddenly when its African-American driver decided to switch stations on the radio.

Usually, however, the traffic jams weren't created by accidents or bad drivers, but by too many cars wanting to get from here to there at the same time. It's a pity the traffic jams created road rage, rather than ballot box rage, since the problem had much to do with poor urban planning by politicians in bed with greedy developers.

Phillip wasn't in Los Angeles though, and for that he was grateful.

He listened as the announcer on the radio told him that the New York Yankees were looking to easily trounce the Atlanta Braves. That would make them world champions yet again. Phillip smiled. Actually, he wasn't much of a sports fan. Hell, he barely followed baseball, which was his favorite of any sport! He didn't follow football, hockey, golf, or basketball unless a team he cared about was in a tight championship race. He didn't care much for boxing either, unless a friend invited him over for a pay-per-view fight night. The teams he cared about now would be the New York Yankees or the Seattle Mariners. He'd pick the Seattle Sonics for basketball, and if he were going to talk to his old friend in the next few days, he'd read an article or two about his friend's team, the Pittsburgh Steelers. He'd only do this so as not to look like he was completely out of the loop.

The Yankees' imminent World Series victory gave Phillip a deep warm feeling of satisfaction. He was instantly transported back to Yankee Stadium. Phillip saw himself sitting there behind the Yankee dugout with his grandfather, Pop-Pop. Pop-Pop was his father's father. Phillip was learning how to score the game on the tiny little squares on the scorecard. He learned that a "K" meant a strikeout, and "4-3" was probably a ground ball to the second baseman who'd tossed it to the first baseman for an out. He would keep track of all the outs, all the hits, and all the strikeouts and walks as the game progressed.

Since the Seattle Mariners were long out of the race now, the Yankees' impending World Series victory was particularly sweet at the end of the century. Phillip smiled, knowing his Pop-Pop would be happy.

Phillip was in the land of the past, not sitting in bumper-to-bumper traffic but rather in Yankee stadium with his Pop-Pop! Smiling and watching those boys in pinstripe blue bash baseballs in Yonkers on a sweltering mid-summer afternoon. Scoring the game, munching on peanuts in the shell, and hanging out with a very cool old man. The gruff looking old man would walk proudly with his grandson and wave to people, like he knew them.

"This is my grandson!" he'd boast. "Ain't he somethin?" Occasionally someone even waved back and called out his first name.

"Hi ya, John! Good looking kid you got yourself there." And Phillip would be amazed. Wow! Lots of people *really* do know my Pop-Pop! He's somebody *really* special and he wants to hang out with *me* at the game. *Yeah!*

It had been nearly six months since the last time Phillip was in Seattle. Most of the time, he preferred to stay close to his home in Cle Elum. He was in Seattle just overnight to attend the opening of an exhibit, which included many of his photos. He would get an opportunity to meet the media, talk to some collectors, and sign some copies of a book he'd published several months ago. There had been some coverage of the event and it was expected that as many as fifty or sixty people might attend. He knew that the gallery seemed crowded with just twenty people.

Phillip had just had lunch with Mark, a Seattle friend of his. A homicide detective. A good friend who'd accepted him almost immediately several years ago. They'd met at a time when Phillip began freelancing for the King County Coroner's office.

Phillip had grown up being a liberal, and was nervous about cops and most authority figures until he was into his late thirties. And then he found himself working with them, and they were *trusting* him, and *inviting* him to drink with them in cop bars. Interesting the turns and twists a life can take.

He and Mark would sometimes catch a movie together and passionately argue about it. Over lunch at a small Mercer Island Thai food restaurant, they talked about a lot of things, including movies. Mark had never met anyone who knew as much about films and filmmakers as Phillip did. And he'd never met anyone who could talk about it with such passion for hours. It was that passion that Mark noticed most about Phillip now. Mark wondered just what it was that sparked that enthusiasm in his friend today.

"That's right, Spacey was in *The Negotiator* with Jackson wasn't he?" asked Mark.

"Yeah," answered Phillip as he shoveled a mouthful of rice and garlic pepper pork into his mouth.

"So how are you doing, really, Phil?"

Phillip delayed a long moment before looking up at Mark and replying. "I'm a little lonely, but I'm doing really good. Actually, I'm very happy. I'm doing some good work that I'm proud of. Of course, I'm a little bit out of the loop, but usually it's okay. People are more interested than ever in my stuff, and I feel pretty good."

"Good! You deserve to be happy, Phillip. Hell, I deserve it, too. I guess everyone deserves it, huh?"

"Aren't you happy?" Phillip asked, genuinely concerned about his friend's statement.

"Yeah, I'm pretty damn happy, actually. The job's sometimes a pain in the ass, but usually it's okay. I keep thinking it's an *important* job. I keep reading maybe it's *not so important*. But hell, wasn't it you who told me not to believe what you read?"

"Sounds like good advice. Especially don't believe what you read if *my name* is on it!"

"Oh, yeah. I read your stuff every week or so."

"Oh, you're so full of shit."

"No, no, I do! Really! I read the thing you wrote about the kids that ran off to meet the guys...."

Phillip laughed. "That was months ago!"

"Well, I've been busy!"

"Still juggling a couple girlfriends, are you? The one you met at Hooters?"

"Oh, Rachel, yes. Well, actually, Rachel wasn't around for too long. But she had her charms. I'm still mostly with Judy."

"Mostly?"

"Well, I can't quite let Karen go. She's so much fun. But I will soon. I have to. Gotta propose to Judy and get it over with."

"Sheesh! Get it over with? Damn, Mark, you're quite the romantic!"

"You know how it is, for God's sakes! I've been running around like a tomcat in heat for five years now. It's time to settle down. And I love Judy very much."

"Yeah, I think you do," Phillip said.

"How about you, pal?"

Phillip didn't say anything for a moment.

"Okay, so who is she?" Mark asked.

"Someone I've been in love with for a long time and have never actually met." Phillip sighed. "It's very hard to explain."

"You're in love with someone you haven't met? You pulling my leg, Phil?"

"Kind of…" Phillip allowed his words to trail off along with his thoughts. He quickly caught himself and said, "But, hey! You gotta go, pardner."

Mark looked at his watch. "Son of a bitch. It's already 1:30? Well, hopefully I'll get a chance to come out your way soon."

"You'd better, my friend. You'd better."

Mark thought of one last question. "Hey, how's my ex-brother-in-law Sheriff Leo doing these days?"

"Nice people. Not a lot of work in the boonies, but I've done a few things for him. Gives me a chance to write and take more artistic pictures."

Mark grabbed the tab from Phillip's hand and they argued their way to the cashier. Their lunch and visit was too quickly at an end.

Phillip was back in the traffic again, headed for his old neighborhood. He was going to his ex-neighbor's house. He was actually Phillip's only other friend with whom he cared to keep in contact. Bob had been a good neighbor, a quiet shoulder for Phillip to lean on when leaving Sarah and Los Angeles behind. And someone who supported his decision when Phillip picked up his stakes again and left town.

He would sleep in the spare bedroom of Bob's house after the gallery opening that evening, and return home after morning rush hour was over.

A Cat Stevens song began playing on the radio. Phillip hadn't heard them play many Cat Stevens songs on the radio. And "Oh Very Young" was one of Sarah's favorites. He could almost hear Sarah's slightly off-pitch voice singing along. It was okay, these lapses into the past. It was finally okay, because he knew they were coming to an end. New love was in the air, and he was finally at peace with the past.

He remembered the first poem he'd ever written for Sarah, and now he finally had the courage to send her the last one he would ever write to her. Phillip had written poetry since he was very young. He had even published one when he was just thirteen years old. There were a couple that he genuinely liked and thought were good. But most of his work he considered treacle.

A few months ago he had come across a poem he had written when he was seventeen years old. It was not a poem you would expect a teenager to write.

Nineteen Summers from Birth
by Phillip Craven

Ain't it just like the boy
To play the man's game
Before he's learned
The child's game?
And ain't is just like the girl
To act like the woman
Before she's felt
The pain?
Ain't is just like the Earth
To swallow up all the things that we believed?
And ain't it just like my hands
To remember her touch
After she's left?

But who could speak of evil
When the day made the world look so pure?
And who could speak of love
When the time had placed tomorrow at our door?
Ain't it just like her smile,
To penetrate so deep in my mind?
And ain't it just like love
To hit so hard
At such a bad time?

Ain't it hard to see,
How little all your dreams seem to be?
And ain't it just like me,
To hang around after I've been freed?
Ain't it just like today,
To keep wanting to be yesterday?
And ain't it just like love
To show it's face
And have nothing say?

He had stopped writing poems before he ever met Sarah. And the first poem he wrote for Sarah wasn't really a poem at all, actually. And it was something he wrote as their relationship was ending. The relationship was stagnant and dying by this time. It had been for a while. And it was time to make sure there was nothing worth saving.

Surprisingly, Sarah had become more obsessed about her career than he was about his. She took on more and more freelance magazine work, and continued working as a copy editor for the *Los Angeles Times*. She had little time for him and he stopped expecting that she would.

Phillip still held onto a little hope that Sarah would find a way to accompany him on his upcoming photo shoot. He was going up to Washington state to photograph a group of endangered pelicans, and would be there for over a week. It would be a wonderful opportunity to relax with each other, and see if there was any love or passion left in their relationship. Sarah, however, was in the middle of writing an article and decided she couldn't go with him. Phillip realized how far they were drifting apart. So he wrote a note, as poetry, for her and put it on the refrigerator.

Hi hon,
Not much time,
Gotta Run

If you could stop
Hating me so
much

I know you would love
me.

Not that it would do you
any good
But perhaps to me
it would.

But now I'm done
Don't have too much fun
Before I feel
or pause to think,
I've got to run.

Sarah never mentioned it to Phillip. He shouldn't have expected her to.

Though he felt hurt she hadn't. Two weeks later after he returned from his trip, he found the note in a stack of papers she had left to recycle. He wasn't really surprised. And he knew, for sure now, what he feared most. They would not spend the rest of their lives together.

It was four and half years later that Phillip had written another poem for Sarah. For several weeks he looked at it, intending to send it to her. But he never did. Six months passed by. Yesterday, he wrote a quick note with the poem, put it into an envelope, and mailed it off to Sarah. It was time.

Hi, honey:

I wrote this six months ago. As I leave for Seattle, I decided it was time I shared it with you. I hope you…well like it, I guess. But it's important you read it.

Thanks. Good luck on the writing award. I'm crossing my fingers you'll get another to add to your collection. Heck, the Pulitzer can't be too far away you know.

Take care,
Phillip

For Sarah
by Phillip Craven

I reach out to touch your face,
In the photograph,
From another time,
Another place.
It hurts that I can't
Really look into your
Eyes,
Wake up to
Your face.

The how-have-you-been calls
Are pleasant.
At Christmas,
I really liked your present.
You would have liked
The moon tonight
It's crescent.

I'm in my
New place,
Mostly far enough
from the
Rat race.
But I look
Sometimes
At this
Face.

Will you let yourself
remember
My kiss?
Those too few
Moments of
Bliss?
There must be
Some you sometimes
Miss.

We left the scene of our
Love
as slowly
as we could
Did you
Look back?
Think some of it was
Right?
Sneak a peak
In the rearview
Mirror of
Hindsight?

Oh we had
Plenty of chances
We never took
Wonder sometimes
If we should have…
No that's not
Fair.

I really don't mean
To go there.
It's just sometimes
I catch myself
Realizing
I still care.

Oh, but you sounded so
Happy, so good
Last week.
And it made
Me smile.
Some.
What wonderful
Friends,
Wonderful strangers
We've become.

After your
Last call
I wished
I could look
At your face
In this photograph
And it didn't mean
Anything to me
At all.

Then in a lightning flash moment
I hold you so tight
And believe
How it could
Still be
All right.

I guess what I'm trying to say
I liked how it felt with you so
And I hated letting it go.
Letting us go.

Usually I
Can sleep.

I know
It had to be.
And I want you
To know
That you have
A piece of me,
I'd like you
To keep.

And know that
Sometimes,
Still.
I think of us
From long
Ago
Another lifetime

So
Understand
and
Forgive me

For not completely
Letting
Go.

Chapter Eleven

Frank sat at the dining room table, his fingers tracing the scars and gouges in the old pine that reflected nearly a hundred years of Trujillo family history. He could feel Alma's eyes on him as she questioned him. "Why are you doing this to us, Frank? Why don't you tell me what's going on?"

He didn't dare look up at Alma. When he ignored her for the second time, Alma rose from the chair, slamming her open palms down on the table. Standing for a moment, with both hands still braced on the table, she stared at Frank in total disgust, shaking her head in disbelief at his behavior. Without speaking, Alma turned and stalked angrily out of the kitchen.

Frank heard the heavy front door slam behind her, followed by the sound of Alma's new Mustang. He figured she was heading downtown to the bookshop which her friend Patricia owned. Maybe he'd drop by there later in the afternoon and see if she wanted to go talk over a cup of coffee. He owed her something. He just didn't know exactly what it was right now.

Right now though, he knew he had to leave for the station. He looked around at the cluttered kitchen. He wondered when it was that Alma stopped caring. Just as important, he wondered when it was that he stopped noticing. He couldn't believe how he'd allowed himself to get into the position he found himself in. Certainly, he was afraid that he knew the answers to all these questions. He was even more terrified that Alma did too.

Alma was confused and with reason, of course. And she was angry and scared, as well. She had been so confident that the world she had lived in for so long with Frank was strong and safe. Her confidence lay shattered. She realized now that her wonderfully happy and surprisingly passionate marriage of twenty-three years was in danger of going places she never dreamed possible. They had loved one another from the day they met. They had fought against family foes and cultural differences to prove their love and protect their world from the centuries' old prejudices that existed in the region. They had triumphed over substantial obstacles, and eventually earned the respect of her fiercely traditional Spanish-Catholic family.

Frank's reputation for being fair and honest also grew in the community, and he was elected Sheriff of Taos County by an overwhelming margin in 1996. The Trujillo family was old, strong and powerful. Things had a way of going in their favor, when they needed them to.

Frank placed his well-worn hat on his head, put on his sunglasses, walked out of the kitchen, and headed for his patrol car. Remembering that he'd left his computer on-line, he hurried back inside.

A familiar blinking icon on the monitor caught his eye when he entered his office. He smiled, knowing who the e-mail message was probably from. He was wrong. He didn't recognize the name of the sender. Frank thought he had blocked all unsolicited or unauthorized messages, but he wasn't very good at this thing yet. He opened the e-mail and began to read:

> HEY TOPCOP! MEMORIAL DAY WEEKEND, RIGHT? MAN, I BET YOU'LL HAVE YOUR WORK CUT OUT FOR YOU! START OF THE TOURIST SEASON, I THINK YOU TOLD ME. YOU SAID ALL KINDS OF CRAZIES COME OUT OF THE WOODWORK. THAT'S A SHAME, TOO. SOUNDS LIKE SUCH A NICE PLACE YOU HAVE THERE. DON'T LET THE HOLIDAY GET YOU DOWN, PAL. YOU KNOW WHAT THEY SAY...LOSE YOUR COOL AND HEADS WILL ROLL. LATER,
>
> ICHABOD.

"Ichabod? Who the hell is Ichabod?" He didn't have time to worry about this. He'd block that person when he got off shift tomorrow. Right now he was running late. He shut off the computer and headed for work. He got all the way to the office before he realized he hadn't even turned on his police radio. He'd been so lost in thought, he could recall nothing of the entire fifteen-minute drive.

Goddamn it, Garrett! Pull yourself together, you fucking idiot! He slammed his fists against the steering wheel a couple of times, and then just sat there.

"You okay, Sheriff Garrett?" It was Lucas Tafoya from the City Manager's office. He was a cocky young man who'd graduated from the academy but wasn't particularly suited for law enforcement.

"Yeah, I'm fine. Thanks."

"Do you want me to go get someone for you, Sheriff? I'd be glad to, you know."

"No! I'm fine, really. Just a sudden headache. I'll be okay in a minute." He watched Lucas reenter the office complex. *How many more times you gonna screw up today, asshole?* His days had been going like this for several weeks now, and people around town were beginning to notice. This whole thing was affecting every aspect of his life, yet he felt powerless to do anything to stop it. He'd have to make some decisions and soon. He would talk to Silky tomorrow night. After that, he'd talk to Alma and tell her everything. He saw no other way out of this.

Under Frank's leadership, the Sheriff's Department had grown in the past four years and now had sixteen full-time deputies and Bill Conner, an old college friend, had joined him as Under Sheriff two years ago. The two made a good team and Taos, though still plagued with all the crimes and problems that come with any community of its nature, rallied behind Frank when he went "out of district" to petition Bill to join him on the force.

Since Bill's appointment, Frank had been able to sit back and take a breather of sorts. He allowed himself more time to enjoy Alma. They had even taken a wonderful long vacation to the West Coast together the summer before. Frank had also enrolled in Bill's martial arts class, and had even taken a computer literacy class at the local community college. He particularly enjoyed the computer class, and was amazed at the knowledge he'd gained so quickly. He never imagined that he would have enjoyed his time on the computer so much. He was often startled to glance up at the clock and see that several hours had passed since he'd sat down and started surfing the Internet.

* * * * *

Alma and Frank got married after having known each other a mere two weeks. Frank and some friends had gone on a weekend ski trip to the Taos Ski Valley. Frank hadn't been skiing very long, but he and his buddies had heard about the infamous "Al's Run" which was one of the most challenging vertical drops in the Rockies. They were all young and fearless and more than just a little anxious to prove themselves. So, on a sunny Friday afternoon in March, they headed for the mountains in northern New Mexico.

While winding northeast up an icy State Highway 230 out of Taos, however, their '65 Chevy coughed, choked, and then took its last breath. A few hours later, they were having their car towed to the nearest shop which was located in Arroyo Seco, a small town just eight miles north of Taos. It was almost dark now, and the prospects of a blown engine coupled with the fact that the temperature was clearly below freezing worked to dampen the spirits of the once exuberant group. Some days just never worked out the way you planned them.

They rode in the cab of the tow truck with the cheerful Mexican driver who talked and laughed with them as he carefully negotiated the snow-covered road. Jose dropped them off in front of a dimly lit café. Frank finished up with the driver, and then watched as he drove another block up the street and pulled into the Trujillo Automotive and Repair Shop. Frank smiled as he opened the door to the diner. His friends were already settled into a large corner booth, coffee in front of them, listening to some terrific Mexican music on the jukebox. "God, am I hungry!" he exclaimed as he slid into the booth and joined his friends.

He looked up to see a delicate, olive-skinned hand offering him a menu. When he looked higher up, he saw the prettiest eyes he had ever seen. For a long and awkward moment, he just stared at the waitress. A cliché says it best. The rest was history.

Alma's brother, Rico, owned the café and she worked for him on busy weekends during the ski season. Anyone coming to the Taos Ski Valley from Taos proper drove right through Arroyo Seco. The town was settled by families from the Basque area of northern Spain. A couple of families eventually ended up with the largest portions of a settlement of lands, two centuries before, known as the 1745 Land Grant. Alma was a descendant of one of those families. Hers was a traditional Spanish colonial family, steeped in age-old traditions and rituals.

Alma appeared shy in a charming sort of way. She was articulate and conscientious as she waited on the table of newcomers, as well as taking care of several other tables that were filled with regulars. All Frank could see was the most beautiful girl he'd ever seen.

She spoke perfect English but had a rather unusual accent, much like what the tow truck driver had. Frank asked her if she was from the area when she returned with some coffee. After she hesitantly answered that she was, they continued to chat. His other four buddies watched as the conversation unfolded. None of them had ever seen this side of Frank before. He'd been a jock in high school, then briefly in college, and now just worked in his family's business. They had never even known him to date much.

As Alma spoke, she had leaned closer to Frank, and briefly laid her hand on his shoulder. He wondered whether or not her touch had been intentional. A sidelong glance her way confirmed his suspicions, as he caught her smiling and looking at him from under her long, black lashes. When she stepped away from the table, Frank let his eyes move down her body and then slowly back up again. He had an immediate feeling that he wanted to get to know this New Mexican beauty better. He shifted uncomfortably in the booth, thankful for the security the table afforded him.

Frank didn't go home with his buddies when they left a couple of days later. As a matter of fact, he didn't go home for another two weeks. And when he did, he left with Alma in the truck belonging to her brother. They headed for Texas where he introduced her to his mother and two older sisters as his new wife.

He seldom returned home after that day. Once, for his mother's funeral a few years later, and another time to sign some papers relinquishing any rights to the family business to his brother-in-law. He didn't see his sisters that second time. He did call his oldest sister, because her phone number was in the book. A kid answered the phone, asked him who he was, and then told him to hang on. When he returned to the phone, he told Frank that his mother was out of town and he'd forgotten that. Frank never bothered to try and locate his other sister. He'd heard from one of the old buddies that she'd moved to Austin a few months earlier. Some places are best just to drive away from and never look back.

Alma's family handled the marriage only slightly better. She was young and very traditionally Spanish. They had aspirations for her. Frank was young and very Anglo and appeared to have no aspirations whatsoever. In fact, he didn't even have a job. The two of them had no money, except what Alma made at the café, and they had no place to live. They didn't even own a vehicle between them. They were just about as ill-prepared to get married as any two people could possibly be.

One thing they did have, however, was a love for one another that shone and glittered like the high mountain night sky. No one could deny that, not even Alma's family. It took a bit of persuasion, mostly by Rico, to convince their parents to allow the young couple temporary quarters. Flora and Diego ultimately relented. After settling in, Frank went down to the Trujillo Automotive and Repair Shop and met with Jose. He was not only the tow truck driver, he was also the treasurer of the Trinidad Church Restoration Project, caretaker of the church's cemetery, and Alma's favorite uncle. He offered Frank a job, starting at fifty dollars a week, keeping the garage cleaned up, answering the phone when Jose was busy, and driving the tow truck on late night runs and on Sundays.

Each day, Frank and Alma grew closer and more in love. Frank was almost afraid to close his eyes at night for fear that when he awoke it would all have been a dream. He'd not had a lot of experience. Most of the girls he'd dated had, for the most part, left him cold and more alone than when they'd started. As a result, Frank and Alma's first attempts at lovemaking were clumsy and wrought with the nervousness and inexperience they both shared. One night, trying desperately to be very quiet in the family's hacienda, they held one another close. The nearly full moon shone through the window and cast a subtle light in the room that had been Alma's since she was born. The moon was just bright enough to illuminate the Sangre de Cristo mountain range in the distance. Although it still got a bit chilly during the night, they had the window open wide to enjoy all there was beyond their small world within the adobe walls. Frank's fingers were idly tickling Alma's cheek and he leaned close and asked her if she were still awake. She had been lying very still, her breathing slow and steady. She had been curling the hair on his chest with the tip of her fingernail, but now her hand lay still against his chest.

"Yes," she whispered, never moving. "I'm awake, love."

Frank wanted so desperately to say the right words. He felt foolish and more than a little inept. He wanted to be all that Alma could have ever possibly dreamed of, but he couldn't find the words. Alma looked up at him. In the moonlight, her features were soft and childlike, and her hair a mass of disheveled curls around her face. She pressed her fingertips to his lips and shook her head. "It's okay, my darling," she assured him. "It's okay."

She leaned close to his ear. "Can you see the snowpack still on the high peaks? See how it sparkles in the moonlight?"

For a Texas boy who had hardly ventured beyond the state line in any direction, this place was absolutely enchanted. He wondered if the legends he had heard about the Sangre de Cristos were true. All colorful tales about the "Mother of the Mountain" who was believed to dwell there. According to the myths, she was a caretaker, nurturer, and inspirer of all who lived in her shadow. It was also said that the "Mother of the Mountain" was responsible for the population control of the area. The enchanted land had an almost magnetic draw for thousands of people who come here yearly and then quickly left again. Most found the life too hard, winters too long, the people too clannish, modern conveniences too scarce, and money too hard to come by. She saw to it that only the blessed were allowed to remain beneath her magical mountain.

When Frank didn't answer, Alma turned her head toward his. He was overcome with his love for her, his eyes misty with tears of the soul pouring out itself to the keeper of the stars. "What is it, sweetheart? Why are you crying?" She ran her fingers over his eyes, wiping the tears away. Frank hugged her so tightly he was afraid he would crush them both. With his face buried in her hair and his lips against her ear, he talked to her until the sun began to crest over the peaks. They made love several times that night, and then lay contented and utterly exhausted as the morning sun shone brightly in on them.

A few weeks later, as they walked along the banks of the Rio Hondo, Alma told Frank that she was going to have a baby. Even after all of the happiness that the two of them had shared in such a short time, this moment eclipsed all others. That happiness would not last. Sadly, four months later, Alma lost the child that they'd created together. After several unsuccessful attempts to carry a child to term, Frank and Alma gave up their dream of having a family.

However, the entire community admired the Garretts as a couple and seemed to secretly share in their passion and zest for one another, for theirs was a contagious and visible love. However, when their lives began to unravel like an unskilled weaver unwinding a cocoon, the townspeople slowly split and began to choose up sides. Nothing can tear a close-knit society apart faster than the collapse of one of its supporting pillars. The battle lines would be drawn in concrete instead of sand.

* * * * *

It was a year ago that Frank's life began to change. Things started happening that he knows now he could have controlled but didn't. A month ago, his dream became a nightmare. He was faced with making decisions no man should have to contemplate. Now he sat at his desk and wondered what Alma would do once he told her about Silky.

Chapter Twelve

Patricia answered the phone on a last-minute impulse, not really wanting to since it was well after closing time. Her hands were full and she was juggling an armload of books, papers, her left over lunch in a bag and a cell phone. As she started to say hello, it occurred to her that her truck keys were between her teeth, making it nearly impossible to speak. Thankfully, before she had to, Alma's familiar voice chirped in pleasantly.

"Hi, Patty, it's me. Did I catch you at a bad time?"

Patricia had set down one armload of books and papers and quickly removed the keys from between her teeth. "No, not at all. What's up?"

"Sylvia just told me that Trent is in Santa Fe until tomorrow, so we were wondering if you'd like to join us and take a drive up and have dinner at the Alpine Lodge? Whaddya say?" Alma sounded excited and Patricia glanced down at the pile of work she was planning on lugging home. The decision was an easy one.

"Oh, wow, Alma, you have no idea how good that sounds to me right now! What time are you guys going up?"

"Sylvia is wrapping up things here at the deli right now. I need to run some lunch meat and stuff home for Frank, and change clothes. So how does around 6:30 sound?"

Patricia glanced at the clock behind the counter. She knew she'd have about an hour to get home, prop up her feet and rest her back for a second, make sure Kitty Gato was taken care of, and get freshened up. "Sure! That'll work great for me! What are you wearing *now* that makes you think you need to go home and change clothes?"

"Oh, Syl and I will both have on jeans, but I just left my pottery class! Trust me, you don't want to be caught dead in public with me the way I look right now! Jeez Louise, I had a huge vase that I was throwing blow clear off the wheel just as I was almost done with it!"

"Oh, no, Al! That's *too* funny!" Patricia could just imagine her cherished friend covered in wet clay.

"Fine! Easy for you to say, 'Miss Never Gets Messed Up!' It was awful, and the vase was almost perfect, too! I was furious! I probably would still be mad if the guy sitting next to me hadn't looked over to gawk at me and then lost his pot, too! It really was funny now that I think about it. He acted really pissed off, like it was my fault or something. Hell, I don't like the guy anyway, so it almost made screwing mine up worthwhile."

Patricia was enormously happy to hear that old spark back in Alma's voice. It had been gone a long time, and Patricia had missed it.

"By the way, Al, are you coming in to work tomorrow? I have a stack of stuff here I really should work on tonight. But if I can get you to help me with it tomorrow, I think we'll be okay."

"Yep, I'll be there. Uh-oh, Syl's ready. Gotta go. I'll pick you up about 6:30 then. Bye, Trish!"

It was wonderful to hear Alma acting like her old self, but Patricia was also selfishly thinking what a wonderful diversion this all-girl outing would be for her tonight. Trent was in Santa Fe, wining and dining some clients, and Phillip had gone to Seattle for his gallery showing and wouldn't be home until late tomorrow evening. Of course, it would have been a perfect opportunity to get some much-needed work done, but something in the back of her mind told her that she'd never get to it anyway.

When Patricia got home, the first thing she saw was the blinking light on her answering machine. She pressed the button and walked across the kitchen to fix some coffee, expecting to hear a message from Trent.

"Hi! Couldn't help it. It had to be done. Excuse me for calling, ma'am, but I was wondering if you might be interested in some aluminum siding for your adobe home. I'll get back to you tomorrow evening, at which time I will help you select a color and style. Goodbye and thank you for your time!"

Patricia was grateful that she didn't have a mouthful of coffee, because she would have likely spit it across the kitchen as she listened to Phillip's voice on her machine. Good lord, he had *never* dared call her home before and leave a message! That scamp! Patricia rewound the message and played it again before she erased it. She laughed again as she finished her coffee and headed for the bedroom.

Patricia was just putting her long brown hair up in a ponytail when she heard Alma pull up. Kitty Gato had been perched up on the bathroom counter, rubbing against her and begging for attention ever since Patricia had come in to wash up. She leaned down and hugged the nuisance of a cat, tickled her under her chin a couple of times, and told her to get down and go pester someone else. She took one last look at herself, grabbed a tube of lipstick, and flipped the light off as she dashed out of the bathroom. She remembered to set the alarm, and then locked the door behind her.

Patricia opened the door and literally fell into the low sports car that

Alma had gotten just a few weeks prior. "Damn, this car is a killer! Why didn't you consider all your old decrepit friends before you bought something like this?"

"Oh, hush! You have to admit it's damn cute, huh? It's our menopause car!"

"Oh, sure! It's cute all right...if you're a dwarf!"

Patricia turned and looked at Sylvia crammed in the backseat and began to laugh at her, too. "Hi, girlfriend! How was your day? I suppose you've already heard about Al's mud bath!"

"Oh, gawd, don't ask! Where do all these damn tourists come from anyway? It was a madhouse at the deli today!"

"Gosh, the bookshop was busy today, too!" Patricia interjected. "I wish that *someone* could have been at work today instead of out playing in the *mud*!"

"It was my day off, damn it! Don't you whine at me! Nobody twisted your arm to buy that dang shop. I could have refused to come to work for you, you know; then where would you be? Up a creek, that's where!"

The evening was feeling good already. It had been a long time since they'd had the opportunity to be out by themselves like this, and it was sort of intoxicating for the close little group. Sylvia and Alma weren't really that close to one another; what they did share was their friendship with Patricia. Patricia's relationship with Alma grew out of a working relationship at the library for so many years, and then they actually became much closer after Patricia bought the bookshop and Alma came to work for her part-time. And the unusual events of the past several months had done even more to bond the two of them, but in a much different way.

Sylvia had been Patricia's next-door neighbor for longer than either cared to remember. They had house sat for one another, and their husbands enjoyed an "over the ditch" friendship. Although Carlos was a bit more reserved than Trent, the two men had a great deal of respect for one another. Several times they had volunteered for fund raising events and attended town meetings together. Trent missed Carlos after he'd left his family and gone back to his Pueblo. Through the years, Patricia and Sylvia had gone through most of the major events of adult life, things that tend to draw people closely together.

"Who's idea was tonight, anyway?" Patricia asked. She wanted to get a conversation going so she'd keep her mind off of Phillip and the gallery show. She had glanced at the clock on Alma's dash and knew that the show was well underway. She would have given *anything* to be there with him. Before either of them spoke up, Patricia continued, "Well, whose ever idea it was, it was a great one! And I'm starving, too! Have either of you ever had the curried chicken up here? It's to die for!"

"I have!" Sylvia exclaimed. "And you're right. It's absolutely delicious! I might even have it tonight, as a matter of fact!"

"*You might*?" the other two women blurted out in unison. Then all three of them burst out laughing at the fact of how much they really knew about one another. It was well-known that Sylvia wasn't usually too adventurous with her choice of foods, so she'd really surprised the other two. Something about their recognition of closeness silenced the group for a few minutes, and they all just rode quietly, enjoying the scenery as the evening was bathed in the last light of day. *The Indians knew what they had here when they settled in this incredible part of the country! The entire area was steeped in physical and spiritual magic…it truly was the Land of Enchantment.*

As Patricia looked out the window at the river that ran along beside the road, it caused her to recall a word from her past. It was a Cherokee word that her Grandmother Sugar had taught her—*agowhtvhdi*, which meant "sight." "Sight" to the Cherokee means what we "see" when we touch something of beauty. They not only feel it, but they see into it. Both seeing and sensing the sweetness and gentleness of something. It can work the opposite way, too, in that they can touch and feel something's harshness and the reality of darkness and evil. The Cherokee believe that one is never really blind, except if they choose to close their minds or themselves and deny life to the Spirit, which dwells within all us.

This land was brimming with a life all its own; an undeniable Spirit filled the canyons, the valleys and dwelled within the mountains. A song of life and love, of death and peace played among the stars and drifted on the winds that swept down from the sacred mountains and blessed this land. A land which over the years had become home to a myriad of incredibly talented artists, writers, poets, and just eclectic people who enjoyed life for the sheer pleasure of enjoying it. This was a good place.

Riding along with her two dear friends, Patricia was also reminded of the fragility of the threads that connect one to another. She was grateful that the three of them had these kinds of adventures together that should never be taken lightly nor for granted.

Patricia had been helping Alma battle a private demon in her life for the past several months, and it had almost gotten the best of Alma. Patricia knew more than she had shared with Alma, and wrestled with what to do with the knowledge. As close as the three of them were, Sylvia was completely unaware of all this. Sometimes that was difficult for Patricia, but for the sake of everyone concerned, her undercover work with Alma was something that she simply could not share. The fact that Sylvia had become romantically involved with Bill Conner made it impossible for Patricia to ever say anything to her about it.

Patricia had told Phillip a little bit about what was going on with Alma, but she hadn't been totally honest with him either. What she didn't tell him was that the problem she was helping Alma with lurked right under his nose, too. It was a developing relationship in the same chatroom where she and Phillip had met over a year ago. Phillip knew none of the people involved, and there was not the remotest chance that he would ever come in contact with them. Heck, she believed in the small world theory, but you had to draw the line somewhere. She chuckled out loud and didn't even realize it.

"Patricia? Did you hear me?" Alma had leaned over and was touching Patricia's shoulder as she pulled into the parking lot of the resort.

"Excuse me, Al, what did you say? I'm sorry, I guess my mind was somewhere else!"

"Good lord, I guess!" Sylvia said as she struggled to lift herself out of the tiny red go-kart of a car. "Alma, how could you do this to us? This isn't nice!" Sylvia groaned.

"For heaven sakes, you two! You act as if you were a hundred years old!

Sylvia and Patricia were laughing loudly at the same shared thought.

"Alma, dawwwwling," Patricia stared in an exaggerated voice.

"We *are* a hundred years old, don't you know?!" Sylvia finished by imitating the voice of Valerie Harper on TV's *Rhoda*.

Alma rolled her eyes. "Oh, all right. I'll turn this little tuna can back in tomorrow and buy some damn huge limo to cart you two nursing home rejects around in! God, if this is what it's like to turn fifty, I got a lot of livin' to do in the next eighteen months!"

They hugged and laughed as they made their way up the steps and into the beautiful old lodge. They were seated promptly and their waiter took their drink orders as they settled in to study the elaborate menu. Patricia glanced up over her half-rimmed gold reading glasses and watched her friends for a moment. They were nothing alike. In fact, none of the three of them really had very much in common at all with the others. Yet, Patricia felt a kinship with them that defied description. Recently, during her new relationship with Phillip, things of this nature had taken on a new perspective. She and Phillip had often discussed the lack of words for some of our deepest feelings. The love of friends is just as important and vital as the love of family or mates, just in a different sense. But the words were no less hard to find in either case.

Perhaps the Japanese language offered her the most choices for defining love. Their language is compiled of several different words for love, intrinsic for a particular circumstance. For instance, *koi* is a word that translates the meaning of love as a "romantic attachment," as a girlfriend and boyfriend would speak of one another. *Ai* is more of a word used for a "passionate attachment," but still hardly more than an affectionate sort of love. *Seiai* is an intense word for a "sexual attachment," an extremely emotional and concentrated sort of love, as between ardent lovers. *Koibito* is a soft, casual, and carefree love. It would be one shared by close friends, as well as one shared by compassionate, controlled lovers. *Koibito* is a word often used by old lovers that have mellowed into a fondness for one another, as with longtime married couples. Then there is *ai suru*, which is a term of endearment meaning to have a great deal of love or affection or a strong liking that might not quite be love, but very close. And then there is *neru*. This is the strong Japanese word for "making love."

She had shared very little of her knowledge of Japan with Phillip, however she was really enjoying her other chatroom friend, Bishamon, of whom she had become quite fond. He was Japanese and had opened that part of her up again. She felt guilty that she had asked him to keep their casual friendship to himself, not wanting to do anything to jeopardize the relationship between her and Phillip. Although she didn't feel like Phillip was particularly the jealous type, there was just not a reason to give him the slightest cause for concern.

Patricia's smile grew as she turned her attention away from watching her friends and pretended to study her menu. She'd only recently shared bits and pieces of her early childhood spent in Japan with Bishamon. He'd been wildly fascinated and had listened as she'd shared things with him. Their talking brought back good memories of a time so long ago that were still vivid. She'd forgotten the words of love that she'd learned and would have to remember to share them with Phillip when they got the opportunity again.

"Excuse me ma'am, have you decided what you'd like for dinner yet?" It was obvious by the look on the waiter's face as well as the inquisitive expressions on her friends' faces that it wasn't the first time he'd asked her for her order. Patricia hadn't even looked at a single thing on the extensive menu, but quickly responded to the gentleman's question.

"Oh, yes of course. I'd like the Indian curried chicken, please."

"Well, ladies, you sure make it easy. Curried chicken times three. Can I get you any appetizers before dinner? Anything else to drink?" They all politely declined.

"Patricia, what in the *world* were you thinking about? Is everything okay? It's something at the store, isn't it?" Sylvia always worried about the store, she knew that there was nothing wrong in Patricia's private life that would ever cause her any undue stress. Everyone knew that she and Trent were the all-around, all-American couple whom everyone envied.

"Oh, sheesh, if I told you two what I was thinking about, you'd laugh me right out those doors!"

They all laughed much too loudly, and ducked their heads and tried to appear more dignified. They enjoyed the next few hours talking, reminiscing, and sharing one or two private jokes that not all of them had been aware of. They ended their dinner by promising to do this sort of thing more often, and then ordering one last glass of wine to toast to all of their good fortunes.

Chapter Thirteen

"Phillip, are you sure you don't want to sell it?" Linda asked quietly. The two of them had retreated to a small room in the back of the gallery.

"Yes. I told you that particular one isn't for sale. I will make up a limited number for you to sell, but the original belongs to someone else."

She arched her eyebrow and stared at him.

"Linda, stop that!" he chuckled. "I'm trying to find the right words. I'm mean I'm flattered with the offers. Humbled and touched, actually. But that one is not for sale. You negotiate a lower price and sell limited editions, and you'll make plenty."

"Oh, we'll both make a small fortune, Phillip. But you're very sure about this?"

"Quite," Phillip said with a smile.

Linda studied him for several moments, until Phillip looked at her and sighed. "What?!" he demanded.

"You're going to have to tell me about her sometime, Phillip."

"Tell you about who?"

"This special lady who gets the original."

"Oh, is that what you think?"

"Think?" Linda asked. "More than think, Phillip. Does she know how lucky she is?"

"How lucky *she* is?" Phillip asked quickly. "If I believed in luck, I'd say *I* was the lucky one."

"Aha! I knew it! Now that wasn't so hard, was it?" She grinned. "Well, Mr. Popular, you'd better get back out there. Your public impatiently awaits."

"Thanks, Linda. This entire evening has exceeded my wildest expectations."

"I told you!"

"Yes, you did. But my optimistic side is always tempered by my New York cynic side."

The gallery opening was indeed a big success. When Linda had hosted the gallery show and book signing about a year ago, Phillip was quite pleased that over one hundred and fifty people had attended and had purchased seventy-five books and five framed pieces. Tonight was another story entirely. The event, which was scheduled for three hours, brought several hundred people to the small gallery. There was still a line of people stretched outside and up the block waiting to get inside to sneak a peak at Phillip Craven's work. Linda had schmoozed the arts editor of the *Seattle Times* to interview Phillip for a major article which had appeared on the front page of the Arts section the preceding Sunday. And the paper had sent three people to the show—the art critic, the entertainment editor, and a photographer.

Phillip had signed over fifty copies of his book. *Emeralds* was a ninety-page photographic collection of the landscapes and people of western Washington. There were twenty-eight photographs in the gallery, including eight from the book. Three, however, seemed to be getting the most attention. One was of a mother and her three daughters sitting on the ground in a garden and leaning against some railroad ties. It exuded a warmth that seemed to be touching nearly everyone who saw it. Then there was the one of a panoramic view of Lake Washington, with Mount Rainier rising majestically in the background. In the foreground was a large blue heron perched atop the post of what appeared to be an abandoned dock. The colors were so vibrant that they rendered the scene nearly surreal. The other picture which got people's attention was the one he created at Patricia's suggestion. It was the one of a raindrop clinging to a porch rail and reflecting a rainbow, and his poem, *The Autumn Storm*, seemingly part of the photograph itself.

Several people insisted on buying *The Autumn Storm*, and a bidding war broke out amongst a group of people who worked together at Microsoft. Phillip kept laughing and insisting this particular piece wasn't for sale, but he would make others available. It was uncommon for people to bid out loud for a piece in a gallery, but these were the nouveau riche, most barely thirty years old. One, a Japanese man by the name of Toji was clearly ten years older than the others.

After one of the group doubled the bid to $6,000, Toji quietly doubled it again. For a split second, Phillip saw no one but Toji. He had a slight build, this programming genius, and was dressed almost formally—a rarity for Microsoft employees. And he appeared to be slightly inebriated.

"I think he likes it," said one of his friends.

"Phillip?" Linda was trying to get his attention.

"Wow, thank you," Phillip laughed, "but honestly, this piece is not for sale."

The group groaned, and then moved on to another picture. Toji remained behind, staring at the photograph. He looked at Phillip and nodded in knowing appreciation.

Phillip's attention was diverted again, this time by a local politician who was making his way to him, book in hand. A half-hour later, Linda whispered into Phillip's ear, "I've just gotten an offer of twelve grand for the "Autumn Storm" photo, Phillip. We should sell it."

When Phillip did a double take, Linda verified that he had indeed heard her right. His mouth dropped open, but only for a second. He looked at her and shook his head. Linda pouted, but she couldn't dissuade him. Phillip had turned down $12,000, the highest amount of money anyone had ever offered for one of his pieces. Most had been selling from $800 to $3,500.

By the end of the evening, Linda announced to Phillip that she had orders for twenty-five of the "Autumn Storm" piece at $2,500 per print. And though he enjoyed it, he wasn't completely comfortable with the idea of being in the spotlight, the person people wanted to meet, shake hands with, and spend money on.

Phillip wanted to send Patricia a note and let her know how the evening had gone! It had been Patricia, after all, who had given him a boost of encouragement and confidence. It was Patricia who had made him believe in himself again. When Phillip had expressed a desire to include some poetry in his next book, it was she who had suggested he integrate it somehow into one of his photos.

As he drove to his old neighbor's house to spend the night, Phillip's thoughts again turned to Patricia.

* * * * *

"You know how crazy this is?" he was saying to her on the phone not long ago. "I mean it's wonderful, but it makes absolutely no sense."

"I know," Patricia said chuckling.

"No one would understand this. Hell, I don't think I understand this. I feel so close to you and…" Phillip laughed nervously at himself for not being able to come up with words that described what he was feeling.

"It was meant to be." Patricia said softly, using words Phillip had said to her a few nights earlier.

"I know," he said soberly. "I know with all my heart. Though I don't think anyone would understand this."

"We understand." Patricia said.

Phillip let the words hang between them so they could mean as much and more than such simple words often mean.

"Six months ago, I would never have believed anything like this could be possible. I don't believe in luck or coincidences."

"I remember you saying that," she said.

Phillip had overanalyzed his feelings, as was his tendency to do even as he was falling in love with Patricia. It was ironic how it had all happened.

He had written a story about how the Internet was becoming the singles bars of the late 1990s. He knew he had to write about it, not from the perspective of some prudish, guilt-obsessed religious zealot, nor from a perspective of some defender of freedom and liberty at all costs. It was awareness that Phillip wanted to convey by writing about what he was seeing and discovering. He wasn't calling for censorship. He just wanted people to know as much as they could about what was going on so that they could make their own decisions, and make them safely and wisely. So if he could write about this Internet phenomenon to raise awareness and offer some different perspectives, then he would get some satisfaction from it. And so he made it a mission to learn as much about the Internet as possible.

He knew little about computers and the Internet when he first talked to the editor of *Rain City Weekly*, a small arts and entertainment paper in Seattle. The editor encouraged Phillip, and bought Phillip's first attempts for fifty dollars a piece. A few months later he was writing a syndicated column, distributed to over thirty major newspapers across the country. He was now making a few thousand a month for his efforts.

Internet Phil Explores the Internet

I just got wired, turned on, tuned in and am plugged into this wild and crazy world of the Internet. Okay, most of you are ahead of me, have had a computer for a few years, remember the days of bulletin board services (BBS), and are veterans of the Net.

You're probably slapping your foreheads right now saying, "Oh, no, why do they always get some dweeb who doesn't know anything about the web to write about the web?"

You know, I'm not gonna take the time to explain it, except to say that I asked for the job. And if you'll bear with me, I'll grow into it and maybe even impress you. So let this newbie get a few columns under his belt before you hand out report cards. Maybe we'll all learn a few new things.

Now that I have access to this unending, incredible vast resource which is larger than all of the libraries in the world combined, I also understand why WWW often stands for World Wide

Wait. Waiting for information to download is a lot like being put on hold on the telephone. A second feels like a minute, a minute like an hour.

This net thing is a very good thing...and I suppose, it's also a bad thing...

And so went Internet Phil's first syndicated column. Several weeks later, mostly positive responses were pouring in, and several more papers began carrying Phillip's column.

The Darker Side of Internet Chatrooms
by Internet Phil

Soon after turning on the Internet, I was directed by some acquaintances and friends to discover the world of chatrooms. The first few I stumbled across were filled with teenagers who were swearing a lot, acting out, and talking about movies, music, fashion, how school sucks, and occasionally demanding cybersex from someone. At first, I didn't understand what the big deal was with this.

Were all my friends and acquaintances really give up watching the latest Adam Sandler and Shannon Tweed movies on cable for this?

But a little more stumbling around and I found out what they were talking about. People were talking about s-e-x—pretending to have sex, being lewd, crude, wild, funny, romantic, and falling in love on the Internet in chatrooms. The were becoming the singles bars, the "meet" markets of the 1990s.

Usually the worst chatrooms get is like a bad day in high school. Especially if you were the kid being verbally abused in the school cafeteria.

There are chatrooms for every conceivable interest. From art, to home and garden, to wine, to movies, to books...to sex. Well, of course, sex. That's the secret reason the Internet is catching on so quickly you know. Sex. The promise of the forbidden, the promise of free sex.

Sex chatrooms can deliver, folks. Well they can deliver what is called cybersex anyway. A safe non-toxic, non-contact, only-in-the-imagination sort of sex. Well, it's interactive at least. You type something down and wait for a response from someone else. There are chatrooms devoted to every single fetish you can imagine.

> I suspect a good many husbands and wives are neglecting their responsibilities and sneaking cybersex on the Internet. Some chatrooms are full of women—bored housewives at home at the computer and bored secretaries at work.
>
> There's no chance of catching a disease from cybersex. And besides, you can pretend you are sleeping with your ultimate fantasy partner if you want. People can type back comments which will remind you of the dirtiest parts of Henry Miller and Harold Robbins, or the most hard-core porno film you'll never admit to seeing.
>
> That's the good news. There is a dark side, however. There are people who prey on others and lurk dangerously in the shadows of anonymity which the Internet gives them.

And as Phillip began researching chatrooms, he spent more time in them, getting to know the various personalities of the people who played, fought, hung out, and became addicted to the chatrooms. Phillip soon stopped appearing in chatrooms as Phil and instead adopted a couple of distinct personalities. "Diabolique" was a bit of a prankster, and pretty close to Phillip's own personality. Diabolique quickly got a reputation as a very nice person who flirted, but didn't seem to have a steady cyber girlfriend. Phillip, as Diabolique, would have some very personal, one-on-one discussions with people in the chatroom. But these personal conversations were not about having cybersex, but rather learning about people's personal problems and offering them some hope and occasionally advice. There were people going through traumatic events, who came to escape reality and find some semblance of friends in the chatrooms. Diabolique tried to be that friend to many people.

> **Chatroom Etiquette**
> by Internet Phil
>
> There really is, of course, no such thing as chatroom etiquette. Oh sure, some chatrooms are monitored…or at least they say they are monitored, and the use of foul language will get you "booted" or kicked out of the chatroom. At least under the nickname you are using and with more advanced software, chatroom administrators (cops) can keep someone out of a chatroom for 24 hours or so. Well, most people anyway. But lots of adults and lots of teenagers want forbidden fruit and seek out chatrooms where rules are very lax or non-existent. So perhaps "chatroom etiquette" is an

oxymoron. If you're the biggest and most obnoxious jerk you can possibly imagine being, there will still be people who will pretend to enjoy what you are doing.

I have seen characters come into romance chatrooms, and spout beautiful poetry, and I have seen people come into romance chatrooms and call all the women prostitutes in the most graphic of terms and naturally call the poet spouting individual a geek and homosexual. And the obnoxious individual will get all the attention he or she wants. Much of it will be negative, leading to more verbal abuse thrown about, and surprisingly some of it will be positive. And while some of the more sensitive chatters will quietly leave the chatroom at such a point, many will quietly observe with rapt attention, not unlike slowing down to view a car accident.

The world of the chatrooms is not for the faint of heart, my friends. It is an exciting, and interesting place. It is a growing subculture with its own rules (or lack of them), its own morals (or lack of them), and its own language.

The New Culture of Chat

by Internet Phil.

There are cyber marriages occurring in chatrooms. That's right. People who are probably already married, are venturing into chatrooms and pretending to get married in mock cyber ceremonies. Cybersex apparently is not enough for these folks. They want cyber intimacy, cyber headaches, cyber go sleep on the couch you bum, moments. Can cyber divorces and cyber divorce lawyers be far behind? Well, I'm stocking up on my cyber dollars just in case.

There is a whole new subculture out there. A whole new diversion occurring in cyber chatrooms across this great nation…I mean the entire world.

And one can enter the chatroom, make friends, exchange gossip and ideas, and jokes and talk about common interests. One can send private and secret messages to one another while in the chatrooms. You can comment on other people in the chatroom, you can flirt, you can have cybersex. Users will set up meetings with people in chatrooms, not unlike having a date.

And people begin to trust each other via chatrooms, too. Once that happens real friendships can develop, and sometimes people decide to meet in real life as well.

There are many stories, many successful stories of people

meeting online in chatrooms, talking and getting to know each other's thoughts and feelings, before ever laying eyes on each other. That's not a bad way to get to know someone actually. You get a sense of what they are like and how they think...or at least how they want you to think they think, before any physical contact whatsoever takes place. Heck you can even have cybersex and perhaps get a clue to what kind of lovers you would make in real life.

There are, of course, dangers involved and adults should take precautions before doing something like this. You would be surprised how many predators are out there on the Internet.

Be careful.

Chatrooms Are Not for Kids!!

by Internet Phil

If you have Internet access at your home and allow your young children to have access to chatrooms, it is virtually impossible for them not to be bombarded by pornography, X-rated ads for websites, and worse. Much worse.

In just the past few months, dozens of men, and a few women have been arrested around the country for using the Internet to sexually prey on young boys and girls. A few of these arrests involved men trying to "buy" a 12-year-old girl for sex. Another man was arrested for trying to set up a network of child kidnappers to grab young girls and boys to provide to pedophiles for sexual pleasure.

Just a few weeks ago, a 35-year-old male, an ex-con, a rapist, drove from the Hudson Valley in New York to a small town near Rutland, Vermont. In a chatroom, he had pretended to be an 18-year-old who was running away from home and had convinced a 15-year-old girl to runaway with him to California where he said he had a friend in the entertainment business who would help them get settled. They could run away together and have fun and sex. The girl's father saw his daughter sneaking out the door with her suitcase and was able to stop her just as she was getting in the suspect's truck. The suspect was later apprehended. He had been released from prison just four days earlier. The prison had provided him with access to a computer.

These cases are not as unusual as we would like to believe.

In Albuquerque, New Mexico, Sgt. Tom Delaney had a case involving a 14-year-old girl who ran away from home. Delaney located her in a suburb of Chicago where a 44-year-old man she had met on the Internet had put her up in a sleazy motel.

"This is a serious concern for parents everywhere," said Delaney. Pedophiles and child molesters frequent Internet chatrooms, often the teen chatrooms where children are likely to be. Sometimes they pose as kids, sometimes they pretend to be people they are not, and after getting the child's trust, they set up meetings with the children that can have horrific consequences."

A couple of weeks ago, as part of a team of journalists working from the Seattle area, I set up an on-line account, and pretended to be a 15-year-old girl named April.

Within fifteen minutes, I received an ad for a website offering live sex videos. Over the next two weeks, at least a hundred other ads and pornographic e-mails came in. None of it was e-mail I requested.

After visiting some of these sites, and clicking a few buttons with a mouse, I was able to see hard-core pornographic pictures and sign up for dozens of adult newsletters that were absolutely free. I was also able to sign up for and log onto 36 adult chatrooms.

When I logged on as April in a teen chatroom, almost immediately messages arrived on my computer screen. Messages from men who wanted to meet April. Messages that propositioned April for cybersex, for real world sex, and messages in which men said they wanted to send April pornographic pictures. Kids who use the Internet verified that my experience as April was common. Chatrooms can be very scary places indeed.

Phillip's articles varied, some were very cautionary, offering solutions and advice to parents to restrict the Internet usage, others were light, reviewing chatrooms and even talking about some of their most frequent visitors.

Friends in All the Chat Places
by Internet Phil

Melissa is from Encino, California, from an upper middle class family. She is 17 and has been a chatroom addict since she was 12. She's met five or six boyfriends online. One was from out of state, and they met and dated several times. She has run across many "perverted and probably dangerous" (her description) people online.

"First these guys will talk to you about general things, and then they will ask some personal questions. What do you look like and where you are from and what town you live in and what school you go to and even some questions about your parents and what they do for a living," she related. "Then they ask about what you like doing, and then they usually bring up sex. I was curious about this and when I was 13, I had my first cybersex encounter. I was still a virgin in real life, too. I had a girlfriend who had a cyber relationship with a guy who said he was 18, but he turned out to be in his late 30s and had a criminal record."

Jennifer is from Ohio. She uses the name Horny, or HOTMama, is 45 years old in real life, but 34 in cyber land. Sometimes she'll admit she's a large woman with a weight problem, but other times she'll pretend she's built like a Barbie doll. Sometimes she'll admit she's a mom with four kids, and other times claims she's not married but single, wild, and living near the beach in California. Jennifer is in the chatroom, to flirt, tease, joke and have cybersex.

"I can be the total slut," she explained. "I can fulfill my fantasies and the fantasies of anyone I want to. There's a tremendous amount of power I feel knowing I'm making men excited. And the way I do it. Besides, it's safe and without risk."

Phillip decided to explore the seamiest side of the Internet. He called himself Rave and entered a world he barely knew existed and now realized was thriving on the Net. He assumed the nickname Rave as he made his way through the world of the misogynists, the sadomasochists, the slave masters, the fetishists, and much more. Many of the players, of course, wouldn't dream of doing in real life what they pretended to be doing in cyber land. Some, however, *were* looking for people to meet in real life. And these people could be dangerous.

Catching Internet Sharks

by Internet Phil

Sgt. Tom Delaney says police and federal agencies are sharing information and setting up online sting operations to catch child molesters and perverts, but admits resources and manpower are limited.

"We need to train more people to specialize in this area, and we need a multi-jurisdictional task force to really start doing something and have some impact," Delaney says. "That doesn't exist now, and won't for a few years at least."

"The Internet is very much a part of our lives now. It's a wonderful thing and a great resource in so many ways, but parents need to be aware that it can also be a dangerous place. Parents should never hand over a computer and modem to their kids. There are many online safety issues to put into place before unsupervised Internet usage should be allowed," he says.

Here's some advice on what parents can do:

1. Communication is the most important thing. You as a parent should understand how e-mail works and how instant messaging works, and you should know a little about the Internet sites and chatrooms that are easily accessible. Talk to your kids about the dangers of the Internet, and about sharing personal information with anyone online.

2. Keep the computer in a high traffic area of your home so adults can see what is happening on the screen. Don't give children Internet access in their rooms.

3. Restrict younger children from chatrooms, no matter how innocent they sound. Children under 16 should be restricted from any chatrooms, unless you are sitting with them at a terminal and are at a children's site like Disney. Predators lurk in these chatrooms as well, posing as children. There are too many sick people in our society today ready to take advantage.

4. Install filtering software like Net Nanny, Surfwatch, and Cybersitter, and use all the parental controls you can with your Internet service provider which will block access to most (but not all) access to X-rated websites. Be aware that the best programs are not 100 percent effective. Don't forget to block your child's screen name from receiving any e-mail from strangers.

5. Never ever give out personal information on the Internet. No addresses, no telephone numbers, no Social Security numbers. Try to avoid using your last name and the exact town you live in. Remember to change your passwords frequently. Monthly would be best.

Within a year, Internet Phil was a well-known, respected, and trusted columnist. Police and private detectives had consulted with him searching for missing persons and trying to catch criminals. And then one day, Phillip met Patricia. The owner of a bookstore in Taos New Mexico, a place Phillip had never visited. She had never spent any time in a chatroom before and ventured in, out of a deep curiosity created by her friend Alma.

"Do you remember the first time we talked in the room?" Phillip asked, pressing the phone a little too tightly into his ear. "You were telling me where you lived and your real name and..."

Patricia laughed. "I had no idea what I was doing. I told you that."

"Yes, I remember. You were telling people you ran the bookstore and being very nice and pleasant to everyone in the room."

"And you came to my rescue, warning me about telling too much too quickly to strangers. I was so dumb."

"You were new, that's all! Lots of new people make the same mistake. I've seen it before and I know there are some strange people out there." Phillip said.

"Very strange people," Patricia said quietly.

Phillip chuckled. "The strangest people you'd ever meet."

"I remember you telling me about some of the people in the room. Who they were, a little bit about what they were like. Who was nice and who wasn't."

"And before the conversation was over, I knew you were someone I wanted to get to know," Phillip said. "You were someone very special and I wanted you in my life."

"And I was somehow attracted to you and thought how silly it was to be conversing with you on the computer and feeling attracted to you." Patricia admitted.

"Most people certainly wouldn't understand."

"I love you, Phillip." Patricia said.

"I love you, too, Patricia, very much. And I don't understand what is happening to us exactly, but I like it and I don't want it to stop and I want to meet you very much."

"I know we will have to meet in person soon, Phillip," Patricia said with a forced calmness. "But it scares me, you know? I mean, it isn't right what we are doing now, and meeting would be..."

Phillip sighed. "I know, Patricia, I don't mean to scare you. We'll take this one step at a time. We're grownups, we know what's at stake."

"Phillip, sometimes I want so much to be in your arms, for real, in real life, and have you hold me and kiss me and..." Patricia was quiet again.

"You okay?" Phillip asked.

"Oh, I'm *more* than okay, Phillip. I'm so much in love with you. I don't want it to ever end."

"Then it won't. We'll figure this thing out, and we'll hold onto each other until we get through this."

* * * * *

It was nearly 10:30 P.M. when Phillip found a parking place on the small suburban street in the Mt. Baker neighborhood of Seattle. It was a quiet dead end street. He looked at the house he used to own. He could see through the kitchen windows. The new owner had redone the kitchen. For just a moment, Phillip allowed himself to pretend to wander through the house he hadn't been in for over two years. He knew everything about that house—where all the light switches were, even the spot in the living room where the floorboards always creaked. Feeling a bit too nostalgic, he stopped the emotional exercise and went up the walk to his former neighbor's house. This was really nice of Bob, but Phillip wanted to get home to Cle Elum. He decided to go on in, have some tea and a nice brief chat with Bob and his wife, then leave for home. He could be on the road toward his house by 11:00 P.M.

Chapter Fourteen

As the last day of the three-day Memorial weekend was beginning to wind down, everyone connected with any of the various law enforcement agencies in and around the Taos area were almost in a celebratory mood. Traditionally, the area was plagued with more than its share of troublesome events in addition to the run-of-the-mill things that everyone was trained to expect.

The local hospital and clinics always put on extra medical and emergency staff, and most of the law enforcement agencies were manned at full strength. Some things, you just came to expect, like careless holiday visitors to the high mountains. People not used to the steep climbs and hairpin curves who often found themselves resting at the bottom of a canyon or top down in a shallow river. This always seemed ironic to Frank. Holidays should be happy and carefree times for everybody, yet the law enforcement agencies and hospitals had to gear up like they were expecting a natural disaster.

Frank glanced at his watch. It was almost four o'clock. He picked up the phone and called the bookstore. Chad answered. Patricia had hired the high school student who worked every afternoon not for money, but for school credit in the work/study program. Frank asked to speak with Alma.

"You know, I need to go upstairs and check with Mrs. Ridgeway. I haven't seen Mrs. Garrett today. She could be working upstairs, though. I haven't been up there yet. Do you mind holding on for a minute, sir?"

"Of course not. Go right ahead." Frank's mind drifted back to the confrontation he and Alma had had earlier in the day. He was beating himself up for not stopping her when she stormed out.

"Mr. Garrett, if you don't mind, sir, Mrs. Ridgeway would like to talk to you. She's on another line right now, but will be right with you."

"That's fine, Chad. I'll hold."

Damn! Frank knew that if Alma hadn't gone to work, she'd probably gone out to Arroyo Seco to her uncle's place. By now, that pack of her renegade cousins were probably rounding up a lynch mob! A few of them were less than upstanding citizens of the community and had found themselves on the wrong side of Frank's jail cell bars more than once. There was no love lost between most of them and Frank. He'd actually had a couple of threats made against him in the past, but that had been a few years ago. Since then, they'd all managed to be fairly civil at family functions and during the holidays. Frank was getting nervous waiting for Patricia to answer the phone. Just as he was about to hang up and call back, Patricia came on the line.

"Hi Frank, sorry to have kept you." Her voice was pleasant, but it had that air of "let's talk business" to it.

"Oh, no problem, Patricia. Say, I was just calling to see if Alma might have time to run over to the deli for a quick cup of coffee. I was going to take my dinner break a little early. Lucky for all of us it is unusually quiet around here."

"Frank, I'm sorry. Alma called me shortly past noon and said she was going for a drive. I was fairly certain that something wasn't quite right, and I might have pried a little too much. When you see her, apologize for me, will you, please?" Patricia waited for some acknowledgment from Frank. When she received none, she continued.

"Excuse me for being forward, Frank, but for some reason, I got the impression that she was crying when she called. She told me that you two had had a fight and she was just upset. I let it go at that, but was tempted to tell her that I really expected her to be at work. We are really swamped with the holiday, and...well, to be perfectly honest, I just wanted to see her come in so I could get her to talk to me a little bit. But she said she just had to go up in the mountains and walk off a few things."

When Frank did not respond to her lengthy explanation, Patricia thought they might have been disconnected.

"Frank? Are you there?"

Finally, Frank came back on the line. "Patricia, I'm sorry, but it looks like I need to go. Bill just stepped in and said we have a problem up in one of the campgrounds. Why is it I'm always fooled by thinking we could *ever* have a quiet holiday around here? Oh, well. Say, thanks, Patricia. Oh, and if Alma comes in would you ask her to call me?" Before she could say anything else, Frank rushed a quick goodbye and then she heard him telling someone that he was talking to Patricia Ridgeway. She was just about to hang up when another familiar voice broke in hurriedly.

"Trish, this is Bill. We've got a real problem down here. A really big problem." There was more background noises and she could hear a number of loud voices.

"Patricia. I'm not sure, but this might involve you somehow. Could you come down here right away?"

"Bill, what is it? Tell me!"

Bill didn't answer. Patricia had risen from her desk and was reaching for her sweater and purse, straining to understand the voices on the phone. She was certain that she could hear Frank's over the others, but she couldn't make anything out that was being said.

Bill came back on the line. "I'm sorry. You don't mind coming down here, do you? I think you'd better. I have to go now. Just come around to the back door and press the bell. Someone will let you right in."

Suddenly her blood ran cold as she thought about Trent. Good god, that had never even occurred to her! Something's happened to Trent! As she grabbed her purse, she could hear a number of sirens drawing closer. She looked out the window just as two Forest Service patrol vehicles and several local police department squad cars sped by going north.

When she got to the Sheriff's Department, she rang the bell by the back door as instructed. Almost immediately, it opened and she was ushered in by someone she didn't recognize. The lobby was deserted except for the young woman who had hurriedly opened the door and then quickly walked away to answer one of a number of ringing phones. Patricia had just started down a hallway toward where she heard some voices when someone grabbed her by the elbow. Startled, she turned to find Bill Conner standing beside her. His face drawn and serious.

"Thanks for coming so quickly, Patricia. Follow me. I think there's an empty conference room down here where I can fill you in on what's going on."

When they were inside the room, he closed the door, and motioned for Patricia to sit down. "Patricia..." There was a long pause, during which time Bill did not look up. He walked slowly toward the table and sat down on a chair directly in front of her. The pause seemed interminable as she waited for Bill to tell her whatever horrible news he had about Trent.

"Patricia, I am so sorry to be the one to tell you this. But there are going to be a lot of questions and a lot of people are going to be talking to you. You were her closest friend and she worked for you. That's the only reason they'll be doing that, okay?"

"Talking to me about what, Bill? Who?" She was utterly confused.

"About Alma."

"Where is Trent?" Patricia could almost hear herself speak, but it sounded like an echo in a very long tunnel.

"Trent?" Bill was the one confused now. Then he realized that Patricia must not have heard what he'd said to her. "Patricia, this isn't about Trent. Alma is dead, Patricia. The New Mexico State Police called us just a little while ago. Some Forest Service maintenance workers found her about an hour ago in a campground up near Questa."

Just as Patricia looked up to speak, the door of the room flew open and several uniformed and non-uniformed men and women entered. In the midst of them was Frank Garrett. He was deathly pale. He stared at Bill and Patricia as though searching for an answer.

Without thinking, Patricia rose to her feet and approached him. After looking at him for a minute, she spoke slowly and clearly. "Why did you do this, Frank? How could you do this?"

Everyone in the room was stunned into silence. One of the officers quietly closed the door. As soon as Frank could regain a bit of composure, he shouted, "Do what? What in the hell are you talking about, Patricia?!"

Patricia answered him. Her voice still strong and steady. "How could you let her do this? How could you just stand by and let her kill herself because of you?"

Bill moved swiftly when he realized that Patricia's sudden movement was a step toward Frank Garrett. He grabbed her wrist just as she was raising it to strike out at Frank where he stood paralyzed.

"Don't, Trish! Stop this! Stop!" He was leading her away from the group and back toward the chair where she had been sitting earlier. She looked at him, as if to ask what he was doing. Her eyes were blank and lifeless.

"Alma didn't kill herself, Patricia," Bill informed her. "Someone else killed her. She was murdered." The words hung in the air for several seconds. "We have no idea who might have done it, yet." Bill was holding both of her wrists in front of her now, slowly pushing her down into the chair as he continued to speak. The group of people in the room was ghostly quiet. "It's all right, Patricia. You heard what I said now, didn't you? You understand?"

Patricia looked up, her face red and her eyes flooded with tears. She nodded without saying a word. Then she heard someone a million miles away telling Frank to sit down. And then the voice demanding, "Call 911! Quick, someone call the paramedics!"

She could see Frank sprawled on the floor and someone was talking loudly to him and opening his shirt. She stared and then looked up at Bill, who had leaped up and was headed toward Frank. Someone stopped him and whispered to him, nudging him back toward her.

She needed to go now. Needed to get home and check on her cat. See if Trent had left any messages. Start supper and call Sylvia and tell her that they were still on for lunch tomorrow. *This was all so stupid and ludicrous*. She needed to wake up and get busy. She hated afternoon naps. She never could snap out of them very quickly. Patricia stared at Bill. He was talking to her with the mute on again. *Why was he doing that*? Why did he look so real and this dream have such dimension? This was all very confusing to her.

She had looked away for a moment and when she looked back at Bill, she saw he was standing and talking to someone she couldn't see, someone who was standing in front of him. This time she heard sounds but couldn't understand them. But they were becoming clearer. She could hear frenzied words from the group huddled near Frank, and she watched as he struggled, trying to get up from the floor. Suddenly the sounds became clear and audible. She was shivering and the room was cold and blindingly bright. The light was bothering her eyes and when she reached up to rub them, she felt the tears and her wet face. Bill turned back to her and smiled briefly, and then returned to continue his conversation with the person in front of him.

"Yes, I need to be going." Patricia said out loud. When Bill turned and stepped aside, she was jerked back to reality when she saw Trent standing there. The room was noisy now and frightening to her. Trent stepped forward, the concern etched on his face. He knelt down on one knee in front of her and took her hands in his.

"Oh, Patricia. I came as soon as they called me. I am so sorry. So, so sorry. C'mon, sweetheart. Bill says you can go home now and they will call you later when they need to talk to you." Patricia was staring at Frank, lying on the floor a few feet away. "Frank is going to be okay," Trent tried to assure her.

"You'd better take her on home, Trent," Bill said. "I've already had someone call the bookstore and they're handling things there, so you don't need to worry about anything right now."

Trent nodded and thanked him as he and Bill led Patricia out of the crowded room and down the hall. When they reached the door, Bill paused and said, "You two gonna be okay? Need anything?"

Trent reassured him that they would be all right, and thanked him for his concern. Before they stepped out onto the back parking lot, Trent turned and extended his hand to Bill. "Thanks," he said. "I know that you and Frank are really good friends, Bill. This has got to be hard on you. On everyone in here. I really am sorry."

Once in Trent's truck, Patricia noticed that the sun was low in the sky now and casting brilliant red shadows on the valley. The holiday weekend was nearly over, and Patricia thought about all the work piled up on her desk to do tomorrow.

When Trent started the engine, a song on the radio was cut short by a news announcement.

"The body of a woman found earlier this afternoon in a campground near Questa has been tentatively identified by the New Mexico State Police as that of Taos resident Alma Trujillo Garrett. Early reports indicate that the forty-eight-year-old woman was the apparent victim of a homicide. The victim is the wife of Taos County Sheriff Frank Garrett. Stay tuned for further information. At this time, the Sheriff's office has declined any comment. The New Mexico State Patrol has indicated that they have no immediate suspects and have no one in custody at this time. Once more, updating an earlier report, the body of..." Trent leaned forward and turned off the radio. He reached over and placed his hand on her knee. Neither spoke as they drove the short distance home.

As soon as they were inside the house, Trent got a sweater and put it around Patricia's shoulders.

"What do I tell them when they ask me, Trent?"

"Ask?" Trent was genuinely puzzled. "Ask you what, Patricia? What are you talking about?"

"I don't know. Whatever it is they will ask." There was an absence of emotion in her voice.

"You aren't making any sense. Ask you about what?"

Patricia never answered him. The look in her eyes told him that any attempt to get an answer now would somehow be futile. She needed to talk to Phillip. Phillip would understand.

"Trent, can you get yourself something to eat? I need to go into my office for a little while."

"Sure, but you need to eat. Whatever it is can wait."

"I'll eat in a little bit. I just need to take care of a couple of things. I won't be long, okay?"

Trent watched her until she turned down the hall toward her office. The day seemed like a dull series of unbelievable events, and he was having trouble getting his arms around it. He needed to call Emily and explain to her what had happened and hope she understood, instead he fell into his recliner and clicked on the television with the remote control. An Albuquerque channel was airing a special bulletin. A reporter was telling viewers that he was on the scene of a gruesome homicide near Taos. In the background, Trent could see a number of men and women and several paramedics, in dark blue T-shirts emerging from the dense trees with a stretcher. A white sheet covered a body. The newscaster continued, "At this time the local authorities have no suspects and no leads. Anyone with information concerning this crime is urged to call the Taos Sheriff's office, the New Mexico State Police, or the 800 number listed on the bottom of your screen."

Trent flipped off the TV. He could hear Patricia typing on her computer. He'd leave her alone for now. He knew that's what she would want. She'd wanted that a lot lately, and Trent was growing increasingly more worried about them everyday.

Chapter Fifteen

Subject: Phil are you there?
From: "Patricia Ridgeway" <PatriciaRidge@earthangel.net>
To: "Phillip Craven" <PhilCraven@foxnet.com>

I'm in the room and I desperately need to talk to you. Please! Something terrible has happened. I don't know how to even begin to tell you or prepare you for it. I really don't, Phil… I'm in shock. I don't know what I'm doing. I keep pinching myself hoping & praying it's just a nightmare.

You remember Alma, my good friend, the reason we met? The one who is married to the sheriff and works in my store? Phil she's dead…murdered. I just can't believe it; I don't want to believe it! God, Phillip, for a minute I even thought it might have been Frank who'd killed her! I'm so upset, I don't know what to do and I need you so bad, baby…you need to tell me what to do. What to say!

I'm okay, but this is such a shock…she was my best friend and I just can't believe this. I just saw her LAST NIGHT Phillip!

Please if you can just talk to me! I don't know what to do and just talking to you for a few minutes would mean so much to me.

xoxox Trisha

His first impulse was to pick up the phone and call Patricia. But he couldn't call her on her office phone because that was the line she used when she was on the Internet. If he called her other number, then her husband Trent might answer and that would make Patricia too nervous and she wouldn't be able to talk freely. He considered calling her cell phone, but he had no way of knowing if she'd be alone or not. The last thing Patricia needed now was more complications!

Phillip quickly logged onto the Lovemining.com chatroom and waited for the computer to download the site. A few more clicks with the mouse, and he would be there. While he waited, his mind was trying to grasp what he knew from Patricia's notes. Okay, he was thinking to himself, let's get this straight. First, her friend Alma had been murdered. Patricia was obviously and understandably distraught. Alma was the reason why Patricia had become interested in the Internet, and actually the reason he and Patricia had even met. A million questions were flooding his mind now. Was the murder random? A despicable act committed by a total stranger? Was someone trying to rob or rape Alma, and in the struggle killed her? Was it an accidental murder, a stray bullet meant for someone else? Was it someone she knew? Was it someone Patricia knew? From her note Phillip could safely assume it wasn't Alma's husband who'd killed her. Then who the hell was it and why?

The last few hours of Phillip's day flashed through his mind as he impatiently waited for the Internet connection to get established. He'd arrived home just three hours ago from Seattle. He'd driven much too fast after leaving Bob's house. He'd been anxious to get home and tell Patricia all about his gallery show. The first thing he'd done after getting home was to check his e-mail. He was delighted to see the message from Patricia.

Subject: Warm hugs
From: "Patricia Ridgeway" <PatriciaRidge@earthangel.net>
To: "Phillip Craven" <PhilCraven@foxnet.com>

Sweetie,
I know you probably won't be home till later but I can't wait to hear all about the wonderful gallery opening, the newspaper interview, and all the compliments I know you have been getting!! I just KNOW it was a wonderful success!

I felt you sooo strongly last night and I hope you could feel me sending you hugs, standing next to you, squeezing your hand so tight, baby. I went out last night with my girlfriends, Sylvia and Alma, and we had oodles of fun! Just girl stuff, mostly. Talking and joking and I told them about your gallery opening and how wonderful it was to have met such an interesting person on the COMPUTER, of all places!

Oh, don't worry... they don't know anything about us and they ESPECIALLY don't know how deeply I care for you and love you of course, but they teased me about it. I think Sylvia suspects I've understated our relationship slightly. She's very sensitive to people's emotions.

I'm so VERY proud of you, Mr. Craven, and I smile thinking somehow that you had even the smallest doubt that the show wouldn't be a complete success! I feel so proud and so fortunate to be a part of your life....And I love you so much.

Okay...I'm off to the store now. I know it's Sunday, but starting today we will be open on Sundays until after Labor Day. Gotta strike while the iron's hot, like THEY say! (And, of course, we all know who THEY are, right? Heeheehee). It was pretty busy yesterday, and I even talked with a young couple from Seattle, which made me think of you, of course! Small world, huh?

I can hardly believe how close I feel to you, how much I miss talking to you, being with you. I've never felt like this before...

Now...before I make a complete fool of myself, and make myself late, I better get going. Congratulations and don't forget your biggest fan is thinking of you, cutie!

Always,
Trisha

He ignored his other messages and quickly logged onto the chatroom, knowing she probably wouldn't be there, but hoping that just maybe there'd be no customers in the store and she could take a break and log on anyway. He decided not to log in as Diabolique. He was in a silly mood, and quickly typed in "**Pinocchio**." He was hoping against hope that Patricia was in the room so he could surprise her by coming in under a name she didn't recognize.

Boobalicious: Hi Pinocchio
fembot: Hi Pin
MagicTongue: Hey there Pinocchio
NastyOlGeezer: Hey wood boy.
Pinocchio: Hi there.

Phillip looked over at the names of the people currently in the room. About a dozen names were listed. His heart dropped a bit when he saw that "Looker"—Patricia's nickname—wasn't listed. A few familiar names were there: MiLady was someone he knew pretty well, as was MrHiBall. Boobalicious was very friendly to him, and they flirted a lot in the room, though never took it any further than that. He suspected that NastyOlGeezer was a mean spirited jerk whose real name might be Lane. Lane often changed his name but usually remained rude and crude and was easily recognizable. Then again, in real life, Lane could be just a mild milquetoast who allowed his dark side to flourish while he hid behind various nasty sounding names and vented his frustrations and acted out in near anonymity.

MrHiBall: Hey where's Gepetto?
fembot: Can I sit on your face Pinocchio?
Pinocchio: Oh that would be horrible! Ugh!
Pinocchio: Uh oh...
MagicTongue: He lied again, his nose is growing.
Pinocchio: Oh but it's not my NOSE that is growing. (heeheeheehee)
MiLady: Oh my.
fembot: lol
Boobalicious: Might say things are looking up?
Pinocchio: definitely Boobalicious.
Boobalicious: cum lie to me P.
NastyOlGeezer: WATCH OUT THAT THING WILL GIVE YA SPLINTERS.
fembot: No one believes anything you say Nasty.
Pinocchio: Ironwood won't give you splinters.
MiLady: Does Gepetto know your in this room little boy?
Pinocchio: Oh of course he does, MiLady, he likes me to come in here and talk to all you wonderful, well behaved people.
Pinocchio: Oh... Yikes...
fembot: I think he's growing again.
NastyOlGeezer: So any of you sluts want to stop playing with puppets and play with the real thing?
MiLady: Mmm I've had old men before! I'm in the mood to be a puppet master.
Pinocchio: Oh yes, MiLady pull my strings.

And so Phillip played in the room for a few minutes before he left saying he had to save Gepetto who was at that very moment trapped in the belly of a whale! No one realized that Pinocchio was really Diabolique, and few knew Diabolique's real name was Phillip Craven.

After checking his e-mail messages, Phillip logged off his computer. He would make a pot of coffee and get something to eat. Trisha would probably get home around seven that evening. He would have to wait and talk to her then.

An hour later, Phillip was sipping hot coffee on his deck as the enormous sun was quickly setting, and the mountain air was rapidly cooling down. He put his thoughts on hold for a moment and looked at the beauty that surrounded him—several different varieties of evergreen trees which were proudly showing an incredible array of no fewer than a million shades of green. There were muted oranges, bright yellows, deep burgundies, and browns all painting a picture he knew that he could never accurately capture on film. It was that magnificent warm glow of the setting sun casting a warm yellow-orange glow on the panoramic beauty surrounding him that couldn't be captured or held for long. And, as if perfection hadn't already been reached with the sound of the river flowing, the odor of a symphony of moist earth smells assaulted his senses. Suddenly, he turned to his right as another familiar, comforting movement rustled the leaves on the low juniper bushes below the house. There, almost hidden in the brush, was one of the most pleasant sights of his day...the almost calculated appearance of the alert, skittish deer which he had almost claimed as a pet. Actually, he'd almost considered claiming it a friend. And friends were something that Phillip was pretty particular about. Maybe too particular, which accounted for too much loneliness in his life sometimes. He watched the young deer, remembering the night a long time ago that he'd started telling Trisha about it in the chatroom and almost everyone in the room got caught up in his little tale. Phillip had learned through the years that animals and children have a way of captivating an audience.

This was a place where Phillip could experience a moment of peace and tranquility, where obligations, where neither the past nor the future existed. And then, just as the moment was felt, it passed and he longed to share this feeling. Communicate this feeling. Capture this feeling. Yet, just in considering capturing the moment, the impossibility of doing so created such a sense of frustration that it filled his mind with thoughts that removed him from the pureness of the scene. Perhaps he could convey it to Patricia someday soon, though. Yet thinking of sharing a moment like this with Patricia made him think of all the complications actually doing so would create.

He sighed. A deep, long sigh.

The rules which one insists on living by only dull our ultimate appreciation of the most important aspects of it. The need to control, to communicate, to understand, to be accepted by others is always balanced with the need to be selfish, possessive, secure, and content.

A smile grew naturally on Phil's face. Foolish to listen for answers to such things when they were already within. Phillip stared into the large glass-like brown eyes of the magnificent deer. Frozen, exposed, smelling; sensing the human presence. Then dismissing it, lowering its head to eat the leaves and berries from the bush for a moment...only to pop its head up again, listening and watching. Phil decided not to sip his coffee, not to make a movement that might alarm the skittish creature. Waiting for it to nibble on the bush again before moving at all.

Poetic words were taking form in his thoughts. A need, perhaps a jealous need, to show himself that he was capable of creating beauty with the clumsy, awkward tools of his species—language, words.

He smiled at his arrogant thought now. Accepting that it was a part of him, hoping that it would not prevent him from the honesty and pureness of thought and emotion that he was mostly too scared to ever allow himself.

He turned to watch three Steller's jays. So deeply blue, they were an incredible contrast to the rapidly dimming orange-yellow light of the last deep rays of the dying sun, the rustic fence built out of large branches from nearby poplar trees, and the river rock scattered about the edges of his property. Beyond the birds to the left was a large meadow of tall field grass which he allowed to grow wild, very much in contrast to his neighbor's neatly manicured lawn. And somehow Phil drew strength from the appreciation of this beauty and its contrasts. But, most of all, Phillip was beginning to understand and appreciate his ability to take it all in and cherish it. It had no specific meaning really, yet it meant everything to him. He chuckled as the thought hit him.

"What I need is a strong drink!"

He pretended that he didn't suddenly feel himself being drawn into his house, over to the computer, knowing somehow that Patricia needed to talk to him. When he logged on and saw the e-mail, he reread it, as if he did not believe it at all. Alma murdered? What was she talking about?

Over two hours ago, Patricia had written that to him! Where was she now and how badly was she needing him? She was scared, she was frightened, and she was turning not to Trent, to someone who was near her...but to him. And he wasn't there for her.

After several aggravating delays, he was finally logged into the chatroom. Patricia was there! He said a quick "hi" to the others in the room and began writing a private message to Looker.

(Private Message from Diabolique): Hey, just got your note...
(Private Message from Looker): Oh god, Phillip, Alma was murdered
(Private Message from Diabolique): Can I call you? Please?
(Private Message from Looker): No!
(Private Message from Diabolique): You sure you don't need me to call you?
(Private Message from Looker): YES!!! I NEED you to call me, but, Trent's home. Baby... maybe later.
(Private Message from Diabolique): Okay... now tell me what happened.

Over the next few minutes Patricia recounted what had transpired. She told him about accusing Frank of driving Alma to the point of suicide. She expressed her embarrassment at having done such a thing to Frank. Many thoughts and feelings washed over Phillip. The thing he most needed to be right now was calm and strong for Patricia.

(Private Message from Diabolique): I can't tell you how sorry I am, Trish. I can't imagine what you're going through right now...and I'm, so sorry I can't put my arms around you and just hold you and tell you somehow it is going to be all right.
(Private Message from Looker): Oh I wish you could too, Phillip.
(Private Message from Diabolique): I don't know why this happened, but it has and if it's a test of some kind, than be strong and don't be afraid, Patricia. What would Alma want you to do right now? That's what you need to do. What can be done to help? Does Frank need you? What do you need to do? You need to keep busy. Feel my arms around you baby. You're not alone. I love you, Trisha.
(Private Message from Looker): I'm so scared and so sad, Phil. Oh, I love you too, so much.
(Private Message from Diabolique): Of course you're scared. You've every right to be scared. I know you must be going crazy right now...but hold on, hold on and be strong. And baby...it's okay to be sad. All right?

Phillip wasn't sure what else to say to her. He couldn't know exactly what she was feeling. The death of a friend was a tragic loss, but the *murder* of a friend was positively frightening. An act of violence, of such finality, striking so close to home was hard for anyone to comprehend, really. Phillip had lost a few friends in his life. One of his friends drowned in a lake the summer before he was to start college. His death had made Phillip stop and assess what he was doing with his own life. Life could be taken from you at any moment. All those times you hesitated, all those chances you didn't take...

You remember the times you didn't come through for your friend. Things you had almost forgotten. Like when he wanted to go have a couple of drinks, and you didn't feel like it. When he needed to borrow a few dollars to pay for fixing his car, and you told him you didn't have the money but you really did. He asked if you thought he'd have a chance of going out with a certain great looking girl, and you didn't boost his confidence because you secretly wanted to try and go out with her first. It's now when you remember all the little betrayals, all the times you were selfish.

(Private Message from Diabolique): I have an idea what you are going through, Trisha. You're probably thinking of the times you should have done things with and for Alma, but you didn't. Don't beat yourself up over things like that, okay? If she was seeing you right now, what would she say to you about all that? I bet you know the answer! You were a great friend to Alma, one of her best. Maybe part of her wanted to go someplace else, and now she is there.

(Private Message from Looker): I know, Phillip. I love you more than you can ever know.

(Private Message from Diabolique): And I love you. We'll get through this.

(Private Message from Looker): I know we will now. I haven't had much time to think about it really and I need to do that.

(Private Message from Diabolique): Of course. Go for a walk, baby. Find that spot you were telling me about and just calm down and feel me. I'm always with you now Trisha.

(Private Message from Looker): I will. You know me so well.

(Private Message from Diabolique): I've known you for a very long time, Trish. I'm just glad I've found you again.

(Private Message from Looker): Yes.

(Private Message from Looker): Your gallery show went well didn't it? I was right about that; it went very well didn't it? I was smiling so much last night and I knew it was because you were...

(Private Message from Diabolique): Yes Trisha, it went better than anyone was expecting. More than 400 people showed up! At one point, people were actually bidding on The Autumn Storm piece. One guy wanted to pay $12,000 for it! Can you believe that??

(Private Message from Looker): Wow!!. You sold it for $12,000.?

(Private Message from Diabolique): NO! I didn't sell the piece. I took orders for limited editions of it. Linda sold at least 25 of them for about $2,500 each. It was pretty incredible.

(Private Message from Looker): Wait a minute. You didn't sell it for $12,000 and you took orders for limited editions?

(Private Message from Diabolique): I told you I wasn't going to sell it. It belongs to you.

(Private Message from Looker): Oh my! I don't know what to say! You should've sold it!

(Private Message from Diabolique): No I shouldn't have. I couldn't. You know that.

(Private Message from Looker): You're crazy, you know that?

(Private Message from Diabolique): Yeah and what does that make you?

(Private Message from Looker): It makes me smile.

(Private Message from Diabolique): Are you sure I can't call you?

(Private Message from Looker): Not now. I'm a little better now. I'll go for a walk like you suggested. Thank you! You have no idea what this means to me.

(Private Message from Diabolique): It's the least I can do. I wish I could do more.

(Private Message from Looker): Shush now. Hurry up and go so I can go for my walk.

(Private Message from Diabolique): Okay. I'll talk to you later tonight or tomorrow. Kisses and warm hugs.

(Private Message from Looker): Thank you...

Phillip logged off from the chatroom and stared at the computer screen. He felt she must be able to feel the hug he was sending her. He got up and poured another cup of coffee and then returned to the computer to compose an e-mail to Patricia:

Subject: Secret Spots
From: "Phillip Craven" <PhilCraven@foxnet.com>
To: "Patricia Ridgeway" <PatriciaRidge@earthangel.net>

Dear Patricia,

A few years ago, when I was still in Seattle, I had a place I would go to sit and think and relax. Just like the place I imagine you are now. Just like I do when I go out to my deck and look around me. The words seem to be coming out now, Trisha, so I will write a poem for you. I will imagine that I am going to that spot to write and think of our past few months together.

Secret Spot

There are few people
Around.
Listening
to the moored boats
As sail rigs tap
The aluminum masts
With a muffled wind-chime

A kayaker slides
Across the water
To my right
As I watch
From my Secret Spot
Sitting on the ground.

The snow capped peaks
Of Mount Rainier
Rising through the purplish haze
As it should
From the secret place
I've found.

The floating bridge
In the distance

I'm sitting in my secret spot
The cars look like toys
Scurrying around

But most important of all
Like the light reflecting

Off the dark glassy water
Of the lake.
On this beautiful day of Fall
I reflect on you.
Sip my coffee
Hot.
As I sit and watch
From my secret
Spot.

Love,
Phil

Chapter Sixteen

It was times like this that Patricia had learned to draw on the strength of the things she had been taught as a child. She thanked God she'd been taught well and hadn't forgotten many of the valuable life lessons. Patricia had taken these bits and pieces of shared knowledge and forged a philosophy that she had built on throughout her life. The people who shared her life and comprised her small world *allowed* her the privilege to do that. Someone new and wonderful in her life *demanded* that she do it. Often it is difficult to comprehend that someone can actually love you enough to *demand* that you do whatever it takes to keep yourself centered and whole. Demanding difficult things of people, Patricia had only recently learned, is done primarily out of love. That had been a hard lesson and admission for her in the beginning of this incredulous relationship with Phillip. He did that for her. He insisted that she do that which he instinctively knew she needed to do because he required the same things of himself.

Phillip encouraged her in subtle, casual ways. Sometimes by the words he said or by words that moved her as if they were a gentle touch of his hand. But more often than not, he did it merely with a *di ka nv to di*, meaning—Cherokee for "a silent touch." Along with these touches placed so quietly and so softly comes great strength. And not unlike a spider's delicate web or the fragile thread spun from a silk cocoon, these gossamer remnants possess the strength of forged steel. The Cherokee words for "silent touch" are often used synonymously with the word "love." Caresses that speak silently and allow us the ability to slip past the boundaries of human conception that guide and contain us when we haven't the strength nor the willingness to do it for ourselves.

Phillip had given Patricia permission to go and be with herself. To escape to her "place of renewal" and find the energy and power to regain and rejuvenate that spirit which had been stolen from her yesterday. Find it and replace it with the energy that she would need to cope with this incredible new loss.

Patricia needed to have a solid grasp on the suspicions she had concerning Frank and his possible link to Alma's death before investigators began questioning her. The fact that they would question her seemed to be a foregone conclusion. But what she chose to tell them was completely in her control. There were only two other people who knew what she knew about Frank Garrett. Alma was dead now. And Patricia sensed that Phillip, the only person she had dared share her suspicions with, no doubt believed her, though he'd been skeptical for a long time. Patricia was not altogether sure he wasn't still suspicious of her claims, and he certainly wasn't comfortable with the means by which she reached her somewhat illogical conclusions.

Patricia had been Alma's best friend for over fifteen years. Perhaps there was no one, since the death of Alma's mother years prior, who knew as much about her as she did. Alma had possessed a childlike charm that fascinated Patricia. In a way, Patricia was envious of Alma's innocence. Alma had shared almost every facet of her life with Patricia throughout those years. Patricia would have liked to be able to do the same thing, to be comfortable sharing such intimate things with another person. But something had kept her from being able to do that… until she met Phillip.

Right now, however, Patricia was frightened and just a little sorry that she knew as much as she did about Alma and Frank. But since she did, it was her responsibility to do the right thing with the knowledge she had. She owed that to Alma. At the very least, she owed it to the memory of her friend.

Patricia had expected the State Police or somebody to have contacted her by now. But it was nearly noon, and no one had called. She was growing restless, and wanted to take Phillip's advice and seek out her "secret spot." She was sure Phillip had expected her to go last night after they'd finished talking to one another. However, when she tried to move from her chair it was as if she were cemented in place. She sat there alone, in the deepening evening shadows, until well after she was sure that Trent was asleep. Then she crept silently into her bed and lay awake most of the night.

Since getting up very early, Patricia had been trying to reach Phillip, both by computer and by phone. He wasn't at home, and that was unusual. Patricia finally resorted to calling his cell phone, and even that failed to reach him. Phillip never failed to let her know his schedule. He always told her where he would be and when to expect to hear from him. His thoughtfulness greeted her like a warm, soft kiss every morning when she flipped on her computer. The fact that he hadn't left her a message today was highly irregular. Although he had sounded sympathetic when they'd spoken the night before, she understood that it was unfair to expect him to feel the same sort of grief that she was experiencing.

But where *was he* now? She nearly said this aloud as she bent down to pet Kitty Gato who was curled up in her favorite rocker near the door. "Where do you suppose he is, Miss Gato?" she whispered. "Why does he insist on worrying me like this? That's what I'd like to know!"

Patricia grabbed a jacket and went outside. She opened the door again, reached down into a basket on the floor, took two apples, and closed and locked the door. She polished them on her jeans and then quickly stuffed them into the pockets of her Navajo print jacket. She got in her pickup, already quite sure of her destination.

It was only then that the harsh reality of the circumstances surrounding Alma's death hit her full force. God only knows why the details of the murder had somehow completely skirted her. The instant she turned the key in the ignition, the local news station had just started its midday report. Evan Estaban, the station's owner/news reporter, was speaking.

"Recapping the latest developments on the continuing investigation into the murder of lifelong area resident, Alma Trujillo Garrett, wife of Taos County Sheriff Frank Garrett: Local and state authorities are still declining to release any further information on the grisly discovery of Mrs. Garrett's body found decapitated and partially buried near the Ponderosa Campground southeast of Questa late yesterday afternoon. A U.S. Forest Service recreation maintenance crew discovered the body. It is not known at this time how long the body had been at the site, and officials are awaiting the results of a state-ordered autopsy to determine the exact cause of death. The investigation continues at this time into a possible motive and clues to the identity of the killer or killers. The search for evidence in and around the area has been ongoing since the stunning discovery. The U.S. Forest Service law enforcement officials immediately contacted the New Mexico State Police who will continue to be in charge of the investigation. Due to the unusual circumstances surrounding this homicide, the Taos County Sheriff's department has offered to cooperate with the NMSP, though their involvement will be limited. Sheriff Garrett has been unavailable for comment. However, Deputy Sheriff Bill Conner has informed this station that Sheriff Garrett was placed on paid administrative leave, effective immediately, while the case is under investigation."

Patricia listened to the broadcast in stunned silence. *Decapitated? What was he talking about?*

She had already shifted into reverse when she realized she should leave a note for Trent. He'd been reluctant to leave that morning. He'd lingered, sitting on the edge of her bed much longer than usual, holding her and almost pleading for her to tell him what he could do. Finally, she simply told him that he should go meet with his client in Santa Fe. She'd be fine, she assured him. She could almost feel the relief in him when she told him that. Like Alma, Trent also seemed to dwell in a rose-colored world. Any disturbance that rippled his otherwise calm waters made Trent extremely uncomfortable.

Patricia left the motor running, and dashed back into the house where she scribbled a short note and leaned it up against the coffeepot. It would be the first place he went.

It's been said that you never really lose someone once you have had them. That's an easy statement to make. Not as easy to accept. Alma was gone, and Patricia would never have the comfort of that friendship again. She was very angry about that. Still, as pleasant as life had been for so many years for the two of them, Patricia and Alma's last few months together had been clouded with sadness and suspicions.

* * * * *

It had all started the morning that Alma came into work at Take Another Look, her eyes red and swollen, and asked to talk with Patricia. They talked for the better part of the morning, and the things Alma shared with Patricia were almost incomprehensible. Somehow, at the end of that grueling morning, when she finally stopped and hugged Alma and reassured her that everything would work out, she knew it really wouldn't.

Driving up the sparsely traveled road now to the summit of Taos Mountain, Patricia found herself recalling some of her travels as a young child. Most notably, Japan held a fascination for her. She had found it exceedingly extraordinary that she had found a friend in the chatroom who was actually Japanese. He was an older gentleman, who went under the nickname of Bishamon in the chatroom, but whose real name she didn't know. They'd stuck up quite a friendship and had been exchanging e-mails for quite a while now. He was charming and articulate, though sometimes Patricia felt he appeared to be a bit too naïve for his years. She attributed that to his background and didn't really think much about it. Her one real misgiving about their friendship was that she had never shared it with Phillip. She was sure that he would understand, and probably even give the relationship his blessing, but the timing had never been right, she supposed. Now, suddenly, too much of what she had shared with Bishamon was starting to haunt her. *Whoa*, Patricia said to herself, *one hurdle at a time here!*

The story that Alma shared with Patricia just a few months earlier contained some pretty unbelievable things. Had anyone but Alma confided these things to her, she might have been compelled to laugh at them. But these were the words of a very good friend whom Patricia loved and admired. Patricia had found herself totally willing to aid her friend in helping to untangle this web. She had no idea how she could accomplish that, but Alma was scared, and above all, she was deeply hurt. She *had* to help her.

Patricia was nearly at her destination now. The hour-long drive was hardly more than a blur. She slowed down to creep over the first in a series of rough cattle guards that led up to the secluded lake. It was the first day of June, but in the high country of northern New Mexico, that can mean a variety of things. This day the ground was still very soft from the snowpack that has been melting gradually over the course of the past two or three weeks. Some of the larger pines still had dirty drifts of snow lying against them. Soon, she would be at her "secret spot."

There were so many things for her to sort out in her mind. So many issues to try to bring together to form some sort of coherent scenario that she could present to the authorities. They would be quick to dismiss the fragmented ramblings of a woman under emotional stress. More than likely, the authorities she would have to contend with would be men. Men found it far too convenient to blame convoluted or non-sensory female rationalizations on women's innate emotional instability. *Instability indeed*, Patricia thought to herself. As far as she was concerned, women had allowed themselves to be stereotyped for way too long!

She had learned through experience that she must present a purely objective and justifiable case when she was questioned. She had failed at this many times in the past. She could ill afford to fail this time. Someone very dear to her was dead. Patricia sensed that she alone held the key to something. The problem was, she didn't know what the "something" was exactly. It might be the key to Alma's killer, or it might be the key to the reason why someone would want her dead. An even more horrifying thought was that it might be the key to something even larger.

Patricia pulled her truck off of the road next to a dead pine tree. It was sunny there, she thought, and the truck would stay warm. The lake was directly in front of her, the blue gray water shimmering in the afternoon sun. Across the lake, was a large mesa that ascended majestically upward and crowned out as flat as a giant's banquet table. She looked up and spotted two large birds soaring high above her. Hawks or eagles, she couldn't be certain. But their flight was smooth, almost synchronized.

Patricia was obviously experiencing difficulty in concentrating on her reason for being here. Perhaps that was the magic of the place. Perhaps that's exactly why she'd come. She leaned back against the smooth leather seat and in an extraordinary concession on her part, gave herself permission to drift in the whimsy that was consuming her thoughts now, part of the ethereal mystery of her "secret spot." It was, she was beginning to realize, precisely why Phillip had asked her to go there.

* * * * *

Very early in their relationship Phillip had taken Patricia with him to one of *his* favorite places. High on a cliff overlooking the crashing waves, the two of them stood on the balcony of a quaint old hotel in Big Sur and watched the sun fall into the sea as it cast a glow over their surreal world. She had never been there before, and Phillip told her a few stories about the area. As they talked, a giant condor seemed to materialize out of the wisp of white fog that had began to shroud the landscape below them. Phillip had gone to a great deal of trouble to set the stage for this meeting. Behind them, in the small, freshly scented room, soft music played and drifted almost in a whisper out to where they stood. Patricia's back was pressed against Phillips chest, his arms wrapped tightly around her, his face buried in her hair. His words were muffled as he spoke softly, almost reverently, of this place. Describing it as almost a "paradise lost" along this rugged coast of central California.

"There is a magic here, Trisha." He had told her as they stood swaying to the melody drifting on the wind.

"What magic, love?" she asked quizzically.

Phillip was quiet for a very long time. When he finally spoke, his words were well thought out, almost practiced and measured. They sounded as if what he said had the potential to last a lifetime.

"The Indians who lived north of here, called the Ohlone, I think…they have a phrase for Big Sur. Some say its been said and sung about for hundreds, maybe even thousands of years. They call this place 'Dancing on the edge of the world.'"

The two of them remained quiet. Phillip thinking how he had stunned himself by saying that to her. He had never talked like that to a woman before. To anyone before, for that matter. No woman he had ever known would have been even casually interested or even begun to remotely sense his admiration for this land. But Patricia wasn't just any other woman.

Patricia had closed her eyes when Phillip first began to speak, enjoying the sound of his voice. What he said to her almost took her by surprise. What an odd point of conversation at such an intimate time, she thought. She smiled and thought to herself that this was truly a remarkable man. She knew that this experience would be one of the most cherished moments in her life.

"This is a good place, Trisha. Can you feel it?"

"It's a very good place, Phillip. A very good place. Yes, I can feel it." Patricia wondered if this were really the proper time to tell him that she shared an almost similar world of her own, hundreds of miles and worlds apart from this place. No, this was not the time. In time, he would know more than she would even share. It would be the way of things with them.

"What's that odd smell, Phillip?" she asked in a dreamlike tone.

"I think you must mean the kelp. The odor travels up on the back of the fog as it settles. It's an interesting odor, isn't it?"

"Yes. Somewhere I've smelled it before, but I don't know where. It's unusual, that's all." Patricia said this almost apologetically not knowing exactly why she brought it up. Nervousness she supposed, because she knew it was a smell from her childhood. Thoughts of Japan and the sea and magnificent dragon kites flooded her mind for a moment.

"You're getting cold, aren't you?" Phillip tightened his arms around her, leaning to kiss her neck. He'd felt her shiver. Several seconds passed before she confirmed his thoughts. "No, I'm not cold at all, baby."

Patricia turned, her arms circling his neck. She drew him close to her and they kissed deeply and hungrily for a very long time before Phillip took her hand and led her into the small, candlelit room. In the glow of evening, the room had taken on a new personality as it bathed itself in the pale yellow light reflected from the sea. The sun had gone for the day and the fog had actually drifted in around them, crept into the room and caused a dozen or so of the candles to burn so low that they barely flickered in the semi-darkness. Others had gone out completely. There was a musky, herbal scent in the room that mingled with the fog and the yerba buena that was blooming beneath the balcony. It created a heady aroma. It was sensual and provocative. The stage was set too perfectly.

Phillip and Patricia fell into a slow, unrehearsed night of passion and lovemaking. In the beginning, they had been slow and deliberate, almost too careful with one another. As the evening turned to night, the two of them abandoned any preconceived notions of propriety and let their feelings carry them. They made love, long and passionately. It had been the most incredible experience for both of them. Instinctively, they each knew when to be still with one another for a time. To let themselves absorb some of this. Some of one another. It was the most beautiful blending, a coming together. When one of them would begin speaking, it was as though it was the continuation of a conversation they had started a very long time ago.

Sometime in the early morning hours, as a sliver of yellow-orange sunlight crept into the room, Phillip rolled toward her, his arm draped over her stomach and his lips pressed to her ear.

"Look, sweetheart, over the railing, you can still see the moon in the morning sky."

Smiling, Trisha turned where he directed and indeed saw the faintest image of the near full moon dangling there. "That has always amazed me.

Hasn't it you?"

"What, baby?" He really wasn't quite sure what she was referring to.

"When you can see the moon in the daytime. What in the world are the Chinese doing for light right now?" She said this quite seriously, but Phillip thought it an amusing statement and began to laugh. Patricia laid quietly and motionless, and in time Phillip realized that the innocent absurdity of her statement was a serious consideration for her. Just as he was trying desperately in his mind to find a way out of his self-induced predicament, Patricia was caught up in the infectiousness of his laughter and rolled toward him, playfully poking his stomach with her fingernail.

"You stop that right now," she demanded teasingly. That only heightened Phillip's raucous giggles and he grabbed her wrists and rolled her on top of him, holding her slightly above his face as he kissed the tip of her nose.

"You were serious, weren't you, Trisha?"

"Yes, I was. Why were you laughing at me?" She didn't give him time to answer before she continued. " Don't you ever think thoughts like that?" She was frowning, and her features were soft in the hazy morning light. Her frown saddened him when he realized how serious she was with that question. Never before, as far as he could ever remember, had anyone ever asked him what he thought about things that most assuredly would seem like nonsense to most. At that very moment, his love for her became an overwhelming thing and he pulled her tightly to his chest, needing to have her as close to him as he possibly dared to.

"The moon is a very important thing, Mr. Craven." She broke the tension with another playful poke. The statement came out of the blue, but it was not simply a statement, he was sure of that. It had profound meaning to her and in time it would to him as well. But right now, he sensed her playfulness and never wanted the moment to end.

"Oh, is it now? Well, tell me Einstein, just how important can a silly old moon be anyway? I mean...isn't it just a useless, old, over-rated chunk of moldy green cheese?" He heard her stifle a giggle and cover it up with an exaggerated cough.

"No, Sherlock. It isn't. Haven't you ever investigated the moon and its influence over...well, let's say for instance, lovers?" She was tapping her fingers on his chest as she waited for a response.

"Oh! Oh, yeah! You mean like in all those stupid things that poets write about and songwriters write dumb words about. That kind of foolishness?"

"Yes! That kind of foolishness! And, I caution you to be careful when you speak of poets and songwriters. They have written some very fine things, you know! Oh no, how stupid of me! How in the world would you know? You don't even know about the moon and love! What in the world could you know about inspiration and the things that dreams are made of?" She was smiling broadly in the slim light of day and her long, tangled dark hair fell over her shoulders and tickled against his chest when she moved. Phillip felt his pulse quicken and a sudden feeling of arousal as her fingers played on his chest. Patricia felt and sensed the quick change in him and leaned forward and kissed him lightly, then settled comfortably on him and they lay quietly for a time. In a few moments, Phillip began humming a tune.

At first, she didn't recognize it. "Moon River," she finally said in a whisper.

"Huh-uh," he replied, his fingers brushing the hair from her face.

"Blue Moon," Phillip said casually. The memory of a game she played as a child came back to her then, and she smiled another knowing smile. *How did he know?*

"Moon Over Miami." She giggled and raised her head to look into Phillip's eyes. He touched a finger to the end of her nose.

"Moonglow." His face was glowing from the beginning colors of day as it began to filter into the room.

"In the Misty Moonlight." The look on her face never changed as she smiled and quickly said, " By the Light of the Silvery Moon!"

Phillip reacted quickly and took her face in both of his hands. "Well how about Honeymoon Hotel.?"

"Mmmm, Moonlight in Vermont?" she whispered.

"Well, Sister Moon, why not Moonlight over Paris?"

"Oh a double huh?" she laughed.

"That's right! You give up?"

"I'll give up When the Moon comes over the Mountain, or..." She thought a moment. "There's a Moon Out Tonight."

They both laughed at their own foolishness, and Phillip caught her off guard as he quipped, "It's Only a Paper Moon."

It took only a split second for her to recover, "Polka Dots and Moonbeams" came her response and without a pause, "Blue Moon of Kentucky!"

"Oh, that's low! So you want to play dirty, huh? Okay, how about this one, "Here Comes the Moon and Boy With a Moon and Star On His Head."

"Boy with a Moon and Star on His Head?"

"Cat Stevens, yeah, don't know it? You know, Moonshadow?"

"Hey now! Talk about low! Okay, okay, Mr. Marvelous night for a Moondance! Two can play this game, you know! Try this one on for size! 'Moon's too bright, chair's too tight, the beast won't go to sleep!"

Before Phillip could respond Patricia leaned down and kissed his nose again and then broke into a very poor Dean Martin lounge show rendition of 'When the moon hits your eye like a big pizza pie, it's amore!' He laughed out loud for a minute and then lay there smiling up at her. For a very long moment, they watched one another, not speaking.

"Fly me to the moon, you." The quietness in her voice mixed with the quietness of the early morning enveloped them as Phillip gathered her in his arms and in a slow, quiet, and melodic voice began singing.

"...and lét me play among the stars. Let me see what spring is like on Jupiter and Mars. In other words, hold my hand. In other words, darling kiss me... fill my heart with song and let me..." His words drifted off and he rolled them to their sides and began kissing her neck with soft, light baby kisses, his tongue tracing its way as he did so. He began to hum again and she moved easily to the rhythm and into his embrace. Patricia's body shifted against him and his responded quickly. The passion welled up inside of both of them again. These were strong and powerful emotions for the two of them, not just animal responses. Lust had been infrequent visitors to both of them. Phillip had not led a celibate life since his divorce, not by any stretch of the imagination, but his liaisons and sexual encounters had been few and mostly unrewarding.

They made love again and lay for a long time afterward never speaking, drifting in and out of sleep. Very softly at first, Patricia began to sing something that Phillip had to strain to hear. He hadn't heard the tune in years, but it was one of his favorites and he never moved as she sang barely above a whisper, "'Til the moon deserts the sky. 'Til all the seas run dry. 'Til then I'll worship you. 'Til the tropic sun grows cold. 'Til this young world grows old..." Phillip let his fingertips lightly brush against her arm as she sang, amazed that what he'd struggled for so many years to keep buried within himself, she had managed to unlock so easily.

* * * * *

The memory of the words they shared that night gently jolted Patricia from her daydream. Their meeting had not really taken place at all, but yet it had, most assuredly as much or more than anything she'd ever experienced in real life. Not long ago she would have spent time contemplating how it possibly could be like this.

She was startled to see how quickly the evening had descended on the mountain. The truck was cold now, but she didn't want to start the engine. She watched for a moment as two chipmunks scurried across the ground in front of her. She smiled in spite of herself as she reached into her pocket and retrieved an apple along with a folded piece of paper. She knew immediately what it was. She carefully unfolded it and began to read as tears welled up in her eyes.

ANGELA BERNARD KILLEN
BORN: May 6, 1923 in Ames, Iowa
DIED: May 22, 1999 in Taos, New Mexico
INTERMENT: St. Anthony Cemetery, Taos, New Mexico May 25, 1999 AT 10:00 A.M.
Father Romero Torres officiating
In lieu of flowers, donations may be made to the Baca Grande Art Association and the Taos County Library

Angie had been buried less than a week before. Patricia had stood apart from the small crowd that had assembled beside the open grave. She stepped forward, as Butch motioned her to stand beside him. As she took her place, he handed her a sheet of paper. It was neatly folded and written in Angela's distinctive script.

The day following Angie's death, Butch had come into Patricia's office and sat among the memories that were his and Angela's and were now part of Patricia as well. He handed her the same folded piece of paper, explaining that it was something that Angela had written herself and asked if Patricia might read it aloud at her burial. She was going to ask Patricia herself, but time ran out too quickly.

It was a beautiful day to be laid to rest, Father Torres was saying. He concluded his part far too quickly as far as Patricia was concerned. All too soon, she found herself stepping hesitantly closer to the open grave, glancing toward Butch for confirmation that it was time for her to read what Angie had painstakingly written. Butch placed his arm around her shoulder as she began to read Angela's final words:

Don't miss me when I'm gone
When spring is done and summer's drawing nigh
And the sun is setting brightly
In God's
Grand and glorious sky

Smile and say you loved me
But please…don't miss me when I die

Don't fret and fuss and ask God why…

Why he left you all alone
You'll grow tired from looking upward
So once again I'll ask you nicely,
Please don't miss me when I'm gone.

For my weary feet have wandered
To a better land, I'm told
Where I'll rest and wait for you,
My love,
When you stroll in strong and bold.

So don't miss me for a moment
Too many moments
Rust a soul.
Don't hurry, please my love
You must tarry, linger still.
You must drink in another season
Hear another whippoorwill.

See, there's no reason to ever miss me
You see, I am here and with you still
Pause for just a moment…hear the words of the whippoorwill.

Vaya con dios, my darling
Vaya con dios, my love.

Patricia refolded the sheet of paper and put it back in her pocket along with the apple. The chipmunks were gone, and soon too would be the sun. Another day was done in Patricia's world. But all the days of their lives were over now for Angela and Alma. In the space of a week, Patricia had lost two very important people in her life, both of them poles apart and yet singularly a part of her. One having lived beautifully and died honorably. One living just as beautifully and dying tragically.

The "secret spot" had done its job today, providing the balm to soothe Patricia's wounded heart and offering her the strength to honor Alma the same way she was privileged to honor Angela.

She would contact Phillip as soon as she returned home and tell him of her decision. And she would ask him to come to Taos to help substantiate the allegations she was about to make. She realized they hadn't been prepared for any of this. But it was time for them to finally meet.

Chapter Seventeen

Phillip was finding it hard to concentrate. How many times in the past months had he wanted to just call Patricia on the phone and tell her that he had bought a plane ticket and was coming to see her? He had to look in her eyes, had to touch her, had to kiss her and to make love with her—and not just with thoughts and words. Sometimes, like now, it made it harder to focus on accomplishing all the mundane tasks that had to be done.

As his mind tried to comprehend the whirlwind of events exploding around him, his thoughts kept coming back to Patricia. Somehow not being with her was making less and less sense. The futility of denying his true feelings created knots in his stomach. Still, he was fully aware that Patricia had a comfortable life. She was doing what she wanted, and she appeared to be pretty happily married. That is, until he'd entered her life and screwed it all up.

He knew he'd gotten through to her, even though she had convinced herself that she didn't need anyone to do that. She was perfectly willing to accept that the little bit of emptiness and loneliness she felt was merely an important part of her and everything was just fine the way it was. Yet he'd opened in her an excitement, an extraordinary passion.

Most people walk around feeling like something is missing from their lives, don't they, Phillip rationalized. *Perhaps we all contemplate whether there exists somewhere a great love especially for us, one we've simply not found yet. Phillip the sentimentalist, the romantic, the fool perhaps? No, damn it. That's not me and I'm not going to kid myself. I told myself that I would compromise, I would conform and tow the line. But I also told myself that I would never stop looking. That would mean to stop living, and what is the point of that?*

He didn't have to change his life; he was pretty proud of himself and what he was doing right now. Often he even felt he was doing the right things, for a change. And since he was having some degree of success, it would be hard for him to argue otherwise. Yet, he knew that Patricia was someone he had known all his life, and probably long before that. Part of him believed in spirits and souls or life forces that continued after the human body was worn out and buried. There were some logical explanations for feelings and emotions and there was conditioning and all of that, but there were some things in which all the explanations came up short. These were things you simply accepted. He had to laugh to himself. *So this must be what they call faith!*

Still, there was something definitive, a line that would be crossed forever were they to take the next step, break more rules. He knew that taking the next step would only make things more intense and more real, and remove forever the possibility of choosing between what he thought must be and what should be.

For even if Patricia and he belonged to each other, were part of each other already, their current situations dictated otherwise. Even if there had been past lives when they were together, or lives in which they pledged to each other that they would never go through another life apart—these were merely words of love and devotion. Dangerous words. Words that were perhaps being twisted so that they could break through barriers and make it acceptable to break rules. After all, justifying is what illicit lovers do.

Illicit lovers? Hell, I've never touched her, kissed, looked into her eyes, or even held her hand. Few people ever have a love like this and fewer still dare to hold onto one if it ever comes their way. For when people get a rare glimpse of such love, they succumb to all the reasons, the logical reasons that exist, to deny themselves the folly of such emotions. But damn it, if I don't walk away now, then it's going to go too far and it will be utterly impossible to stop it!

Yet he knew that if he had doubts before today that he could not possibly turn his back on her now. To do so would be to abandon her, and possibly put her life at even greater risk.

Phillip suddenly felt cold. He knew there was great truth in the words coming from inside of himself. Alma's death wasn't an accident. Instinct told him that much. A conversation he'd had, actually several conversations recently, made him suspect there was a dark side to some of the people he thought he knew. It was foolish of him perhaps to have waited this long. Who could be certain about anything anymore? In trying to make sense of it all, he allowed himself some time to reflect on how it had all started.

He had just begun writing his regular Internet Phil columns and was relating to Internet users in chatrooms, places where he could go and hide his true identity, and then charm and argue, tease and even seduce other Internet users. He realized there was a bit of a sense of power in this. The anonymity was almost intoxicating in its security. He need never fear real rejection, because in the chatrooms, the playing field was almost level. Well, nearly so. A fast typist with a quick wit and some intelligence made him just a cut above most of the people who were in the chatrooms. He enjoyed helping other people have fun and momentarily escape their own lives, be they dull lives or ones filled with chaos and pain. He could help people escape into a type of alternate universe, and he could join them there.

It had been a gray, snowy February day when Phillip logged into the chatroom, choosing the nickname Diabolique that most knew him by.

SexxyThang: Hey Mr. Diabolique...

DaPuss: There he is. Hey Diabolique, just wondering about you. Long time no see.

They and others greeted him upon his arrival. It was as if he were a regular customer walking into a bar full of regulars. Soon the banter was in full swing. People having fun, killing time.

In the chatroom, SexxyThang was a voluptuous, slutty woman in her late thirties who teased and flirted and occasionally had cybersex with various people she flirted with. This was a fantasy world where anything was possible. SexxyThang had once told Phillip privately that she was actually in her mid-forties, weighed 210 pounds, was the wife of an alcoholic insurance salesman, and lived outside of Madison Wisconsin. Her nineteen-year-old son had gone to jail for stealing cars, and her sixteen-year-old daughter was pregnant, unmarried, and keeping the baby, which SexxyThang, whose real name was Margaret, would wind up raising. Her husband would disappear for several days on drinking binges, but he wasn't cruel or mean to her or the kids and sex was a once a month, five minute affair, that did nothing for her. It was amazing to Phillip how much people were willing to divulge sometimes.

In the room, SexxyThang was a sassy, oversexed flirt who was very popular with the male visitors to the room. She would admit to masturbating occasionally while typing naughty messages to her fantasy sex partners, whom she imagined were doing likewise. SexxyThang had never had cybersex with Diabolique, but considered him a friend.

Diabolique was a friend to many in the chatroom, someone they could turn to for guidance and advice. People knew he wouldn't judge them. He would simply listen and offer kind, helpful words.

Phillip didn't know much about DaPuss, but he imagined she was a bored housewife with a couple of kids, probably in her mid-thirties. She said that she'd married the captain of the football team, who ultimately became a junior executive at an accounting firm. She wanted a little more excitement in life than she was getting, but she didn't want to take any risks to get it. Several times a week, however, she would let her hair down and be the wild vixen she dreamed of being at times.

Another regular of the room was Boobalicious. Her real name, she said, was Carla. She claimed to have extraordinarily large breasts and to have worked as an exotic dancer somewhere near Miami. Supposedly, she was in her late thirties and happily married to an electrician who worked too hard and left her alone way too much. She usually displayed an extremely upbeat, fun-loving attitude in the chatroom and had a "steady" cyber boyfriend who called himself DeepLick.

Phillip didn't know too much about the males in the room. What he knew about them was what they said and how they acted in the open area of the chatroom. DeepLick didn't socialize much with the other people in the room, but was polite when he logged on and would then enter into an extended private conversation with Boobalicious, and then quickly say goodbye and leave.

Fembot acted like a wild uninhibited woman, often performing fantasy stripteases for the men in the chatroom. She rarely talked to anyone in private, however. Phillip had learned she was a widow, living on a generous insurance settlement. She pretended to be in her mid-twenties, but he guessed her to be much older.

Silky acted like a quietly sexy woman. She told everyone she was in her mid-thirties. But for all of her sultriness, she appeared to Phillip to be quite naïve. He wondered if she might be a young college student. Everyone who frequented the room knew that Silky appeared to be obsessed with ManInBlue. He came in quite frequently, as well, and claimed to be a police officer somewhere in the Southwest. It seemed Silky wanted the relationship with ManInBlue to cross over into real life. But the reserved ManInBlue, who was probably happily married, had not yet been willing to oblige.

Some of the characters who frequented the room, people like NastyOlGeezer, seemed to be there only to be as rude and mean as they possibly could be. Occasionally they made the room extremely unpleasant by intentionally causing fights and tempers to flare.

All in all, Phillip found the chatroom to be almost entertaining and a valuable source of material for his Internet Phil columns, and at times it was actually very educational and somewhat enlightening. Sometimes, however, trying to figure out who was talking to who could be quite a challenge, not unlike trying to follow a television soap opera. And yes, Diabolique would, on occasion, talk privately with a female and have cybersex himself.

SexxyThang: So why don't you whisper sweet nothings in my ear, Diabolique.

Diabolique: Oh my Sexxy...I wish I had more time to take you up on that offer

SexxyThang: Uh-huh... you're just scared you might like me too much.

Diabolique: That could be true Sexxy. That could be true.

Boobalicious: ooh Di... you're playing hard to get makes me hot. Mmmm I'd like to smother you in my...

Diabolique: Now now boob, behave yourself... Your man will be here soon enough to take care of you.

Boobalicious: Oh what he doesn't know won't hurt him!

SILKY: So what kind of woman do you want Di? What turns you on?

Diabolique: Oh, a lot of things turn me on, Silky.

DaPussy: Well, you make me wet, baby. I'd love to rub against you till you can't stand it anymore.

Boobalicious: Whoa Pussy...

SexxyThang: You go, girl!

GUYwithPIC: So who wants to see my new picture...

SexxyThang: Oh baby, you get brave and let it all hang out?

GUYwithPIC: Just about Sexxy...

DaPussy: Oh I just got it Guy... thank you very much.

GUYwithPIC: You liked that Pussy?

DaPussy: Oh yes.... I'm getting a couple of pictures myself and will make sure you get one.

GUYwithPIC: Oh I can't wait.

DaPussy: Silky just asked me to forward your picture to her Guy.

GUYwithPIC: Give me your e-mail address in private Silky and I'll send you one.

SILKY: I'd like that.

Boobalicious: Watch out for those quiet ones Guy....

GUYwithPIC: I've heard Silky is quite the lady.

SILKY: Have you now, Guy?

SexxyThang: Hey hung, where you been?

HungOne: Oh havin' fun.

LairBitch: Mmmm havin lotsa fun.

Boobalicious: Eeek it's the **LairBitch**... she's back.

Diabolique: lol... great name.

Boobalicious: OH you haven't met Lair yet Di?

LairBitch: I've been coming in here for a few weeks now Diabolique, usually pretty late at night. Hi there.

Diabolique: Did you like that movie?

LairBitch: Actually the jerky camera made me kind of sick...

but it was scary, yeah.
GUYwithPIC: That was a terrible movie...
SexxyThang: Yeah, maybe if you saw it before you knew what it was about it was better.

Often the conversation would continue like this for hours on end. At one point in this particular conversation, Diabolique left his computer to make a pot of coffee. When he returned, a recent newcomer had arrived in the room.

Diabolique: I'm back.
SexxyThang: Got your coffee?
Looker: hi there, Diabolique.
Diabolique: Oh hi, Looker... you snuck in when I was making coffee.
Looker: You remember me from the other night?
Boobalicious: Oh this sounds good.
DaPussy: Something you want to share with the class?
Diabolique: Now calm down, you animals. Looker is new to our room. She wandered in a couple of days ago.
GUYwithPIC: And so you showed her the ropes and some other things.
DaPussy: Ooh a rope... that sounds so very good...
SexxyThang: Uh oh...
Looker: I just thought I'd hang around for a little while.
GUYwithPIC: I've got something you can hang onto...
DaPussy: Well I'm ready for you to show me Guy.
SexxyThang: Sounds like it's time for you to get busy Guy.
GUYwithPIC: You think?
Boobalicious: Would you like a cozy room with a view, or the hot tub room, you two?
DaPussy: Hmm, hot tub sounds nice.
GUYwithPIC: tiny bubbles <singing> tiny bubbles...
Diabolique: And off they go
Looker: Off they go?
Diabolique: yeah, to have a private conversation.
Looker: Oh I see, I think (?).
Diabolique: You highlight the name on your screen... you know where all the names are on the right side of your screen? You highlight the one you want to send a private message to and click on the private message box, type in your message and then

hit enter.

Looker: And it sends a private message.

SexxyThang: Oh you are brand new aren't you?

Looker: Yes. I was in here for about an hour the other night. A friend of mine told me about this place.

Boobalicious: Oh a friend of yours that comes here?

Looker: I think so, yes.

(Private Message from Diabolique): Hey, this is one of those private messages I was telling you about. Only you can see it.

Looker: Oh, I see.

SexxyThang: Huh?

SILKY: I think Diabolique is talking to her privately...

Boobalicious: Oh of course. Watch out for him Looker...heeheehee

(Private Message from Diabolique): I just wanted to tell you that you should not tell people too much. I mean about who your friend is for instance. Most of the people here are very nice, but you never know.

Looker: Huh?

Looker: Oh let me try this...

(Private Message from Looker): I see...well thanks for the warning I guess. Yeah my friend told me to use a phony name, she does too,

(Private Message from Diabolique): Oh good. Well it's pretty safe here and all but some people play games.

(Private Message from Looker): I see. So who are you, if I can ask? You come here often?

(Private Message from Diabolique): Often enough. Several times a week. Nice place to relax.

(Private Message from Looker): Wow... do you work?

(Private Message from Diabolique): Yeah, but I'm self-employed so I can set my own hours and stuff. How about you?

(Private Message from Looker): I have my own business, a bookstore here in Taos.

(Private Message from Diabolique): Taos, New Mexico?

(Private Message from Looker): Yeah...

(Private Message from Diabolique): Oh that's a wonderful place. I have a few people I know who have spent a lot of time there, taking some really beautiful pictures.

(Private Message from Looker): It's a beautiful place that's for sure.

(Private Message from Diabolique): I should tell you that you need to be more careful. I mean I'm not someone you have to worry about but you've already told me you own a bookstore in Taos...

(Private Message from Looker): I guess I shouldn't do that. Not very smart is it?

(Private Message from Diabolique): Well I'm in the Northwest, pretty far from you but some of these people might be close to you...

(Private Message from Looker): Oh yes I see what you mean. I read an article about some guy who showed up at some women's doorstep after meeting her on the Internet.

(Private Message from Diabolique): Yeah, I've done some research on things like that. There are some predators on the Internet who have kidnapped people, who have caused trouble for people and you want to be careful. I don't mean to scare you, because it's a pretty safe place but you never know.

(Private Message from Looker): Damn you are scaring me a little.

(Private Message from Diabolique): Sorry about that...

(Private Message from Looker): You did some research you said?

(Private Message from Diabolique): Yes, I have written some things about the Internet.

(Private Message from Looker): Oh you're a journalist?

(Private Message from Diabolique): Yes that's right.

(Private Message from Looker): That's wonderful.

(Private Message from Diabolique): Also a photographer...

(Private Message from Looker): Oh I see.

(Private Message from Diabolique): Do you mind talking to me in private or should we go back into the main room.

(Private Message from Looker): No. I mean it's much quieter talking to you like this.

(Private Message from Diabolique): Yes, it is.

(Private Message from Looker): So have you published any of your things?

(Private Message from Diabolique): Yes, quite a few.

(Private Message from Looker): Oh, maybe I've seen them.

(Private Message from Diabolique): My pictures have been in several magazines, and there's a book that's published...

(Private Message from Looker): I really do own a bookstore, I have got lots of magazines and might even have the book that has your photographs in it.

(Private Message from Diabolique): LOL! Small world. So what's a polite bookstore owner in Taos doing talking to strangers in an adult chatroom on the Internet?
(Private Message from Looker): Truthfully?
(Private Message from Diabolique): That would be nice. Yes.
(Private Message from Looker): My friend told me about it.
(Private Message from Diabolique): Oh yes, you mentioned that earlier.
(Private Message from Looker): sometimes it gets very slow in the bookstore and.
(Private Message from Diabolique): You're bored, a little curious...?
(Private Message from Looker): Yes that's true.
(Private Message from Diabolique): Well that's why I'm here. I mean I discovered this place because I was writing an article about Internet chatrooms and I found it to be fun. There are some interesting and fun people here.
(Private Message from Looker): Yes that's what my friend said. My friend's husband left the computer on once and I guess he had been talking in the room and she wondered what he had been doing.
(Private Message from Diabolique): Uh oh
(Private Message from Looker): Well she really wasn't that upset. Just curious.
(Private Message from Diabolique): Well a lot of husbands and wives think having cybersex with other people is cheating.
(Private Message from Looker): Cybersex?
(Private Message from Diabolique): yes Cybersex, that's what people do here you know...
(Private Message from Looker): Oh...yes...of course.
(Private Message from Diabolique): LOL you don't know what I'm talking about do you?
(Private Message from Looker): I have a vague idea what you're talking about but...
(Private Message from Diabolique): People seduce each other and have sex with words.
(Private Message from Looker): And that's exciting?
(Private Message from Diabolique): Sure it can be...
(Private Message from Looker): Have you done that?
(Private Message from Diabolique): Of course!
(Private Message from Looker): I'm pretty naïve.

(Private Message from Diabolique): Really?
(Private Message from Looker): Well I can barely turn on and off the computer... and I've had to learn some software programs to place orders with, and my friend, well she's been helping me learn the computer and find books for people sometimes...
(Private Message from Diabolique): Oh... the friend who told you about this place.
(Private Message from Looker): Yes.
(Private Message from Looker): Sure, I see.
(Private Message from Looker): Hey, this is kind of fun.
(Private Message from Diabolique): Yes, it can be a lot of fun.
(Private Message from Looker): It's easy to talk to you, you know that?
(Private Message from Diabolique): Well thank you... you're easy to talk to as well.
(Private Message from Looker): Thanks...
(Private Message from Diabolique): I'm 41 years old, 5 foot 11 inches tall, blue eyes, brown hair, I'm in pretty good shape, weigh 175, live about 100 miles outside of Seattle in a pretty quiet area. And you?
(Private Message from Looker): I'm 39 years old, I'm five foot two inches tall, brown eyes, very long black hair, a few pounds heavier than I want to be....
(Private Message from Diabolique): 39 as in 39 or...
(Private Message from Looker): Okay, I'm 49, but I'm a young 49!
(Private Message from Diabolique): And you're married with a few kids and you own a bookstore in Taos?
(Private Message from Looker): No kids...
(Private Message from Diabolique): Oh. Married?
(Private Message from Looker): Yeah almost 30 years.
(Private Message from Diabolique): Happily married?
(Private Message from Looker): Oh yes. I have a wonderful husband, very supportive.
(Private Message from Diabolique): Well that's wonderful.
(Private Message from Looker): You married? Kids?
(Private Message from Diabolique): Divorced, no kids.
(Private Message from Looker): Were you divorced recently? I'm sorry...that's pretty personal.
(Private Message from Diabolique): No it's been a while. And

yes you have to be careful about being too personal here but...well, I don't know what it is but I feel very comfortable with you Looker.

(Private Message from Looker): Well, thank you. I was told that a lot of people here could be quite crude and rude...

(Private Message from Diabolique): Oh that's very true...

(Private Message from Looker): So I'm lucky I guess that I'm talking to a gentlemen like yourself.

(Private Message from Diabolique): Are you flirting with me, Looker?

(Private Message from Looker): Oh, maybe just a little bit. Hell if I know...lol!

(Private Message from Diabolique): Hmmm

(Private Message from Looker): Hmmm?

(Private Message from Diabolique): Yes, just thinking.

(Private Message from Looker): What about?

(Private Message from Diabolique): Oh I'm thinking about... Well to be honest. I'm thinking about when I first stumbled into this place and fumbled into a private conversation with a woman and first had cybersex.

(Private Message from Looker): Oh my!

(Private Message from Diabolique): It was very interesting.

(Private Message from Looker): I'm not sure I'm quite ready for that.

(Private Message from Diabolique): Oh, probably not, and that's okay.

(Private Message from Looker): I mean you probably came here to meet with someone, right?

(Private Message from Diabolique): No not really. I don't really hang out here just to meet someone to have cybersex with.

(Private Message from Looker): I see.

(Private Message from Diabolique): I'm a guy and that can be very nice, don't get me wrong.

(Private Message from Looker): Aha...

(Private Message from Diabolique): Oh, it must sound quite silly to you...

(Private Message from Looker): Yeah, it does actually.

(Private Message from Diabolique): It is rather silly actually. And it's hard to believe it can be quite erotic.

(Private Message from Looker): Well, I've read some pretty sexy

things in books...
(Private Message from Diabolique): It's very much like that.
(Private Message from Looker): I would imagine so...
(Private Message from Diabolique): It depends of course on whom you are talking with... Some people are not very good typists or not very good with words and it's rather...
(Private Message from Looker): rather what?
(Private Message from Diabolique): well crude and silly. I mean it can be almost funny... actually, though I don't laugh AT people and make them feel bad.
(Private Message from Looker): Well that's nice of you.
(Private Message from Diabolique): yes isn't it?
(Private Message from Looker): You're making me smile... you're very charming Mr. Diabolique.
(Private Message from Diabolique): Thank you, Mrs. Looker.
(Private Message from Looker): How's the weather where you are today?
(Private Message from Diabolique): Very gray, rather cold, it was snowing earlier but it's stopped now.
(Private Message from Looker): Ah, good fireplace weather?
(Private Message from Diabolique): Yes. I would love to have someone to snuggle with by the fireplace.
(Private Message from Looker): Sounds very cozy.
(Private Message from Diabolique): May I give you a kiss?
(Private Message from Looker): Give me a kiss?
(Private Message from Diabolique): yes... A bit forward of me, I know but...
(Private Message from Looker): Sure why not... I've not been kissed over the Internet.
(Private Message from Diabolique): I smile gently as I look deeply into your brown eyes.
(Private Message from Looker): Oh I see.
(Private Message from Diabolique): I wait for you to look into my eyes
(Private Message from Looker): Blue eyes right?
(Private Message from Diabolique): yes thank you for remembering.
(Private Message from Looker): I love blue eyes.
(Private Message from Diabolique): I'm glad you do. I lean closer toward you.
(Private Message from Looker): yes...

(Private Message from Diabolique): You move toward me, letting me know it's all right.
(Private Message from Looker): yes...I'd like a kiss from you.
(Private Message from Diabolique): And I barely touch your soft warm lips with mine. It almost tickles to touch our lips together. And after a moment I press just a little harder, our lips touching now, feeling how soft and warm your lips are. You push a little harder against mine and I lightly touch your upper lip with my tongue. Tracing it with my tongue ever so lightly.
(Private Message from Looker): That tickles.
(Private Message from Diabolique): Yes it does tickle a little...and then I move slightly back from you to look into your eyes again.
(Private Message from Looker): Wow! Thank you, sir.
(Private Message from Diabolique): Thank you!
(Private Message from Looker): that was kind of sexy.
(Private Message from Diabolique): Yes, it can be if you want it to be. So much of sex is in our head anyway... this can work very well.
(Private Message from Looker): I'm a little bit... nervous...
(Private Message from Diabolique): nervous?
(Private Message from Looker): yeah it's hard to explain... well maybe a little bit excited. This is kind of naughty.
(Private Message from Diabolique): Oh sure. This can be very naughty if you would like.
(Private Message from Looker): I am sure it can be.
(Private Message from Diabolique): And it can be fun.
(Private Message from Looker): I can see that it could be a lot of fun.
(Private Message from Diabolique): Are you flirting with me?
(Private Message from Looker): I think so...
(Private Message from Diabolique): Shall I give you another kiss?
(Private Message from Looker): I think you should.
(Private Message from Diabolique): I move closer to you. Your eyes begin to close.
(Private Message from Looker): Yes, anticipating your gentle kiss
(Private Message from Diabolique): Our lips touch. Warm, soft.
(Private Message from Looker): I press a little harder against

your lips.
(Private Message from Diabolique): And your lips part slightly. My tongue carefully touches the tip of your moist warm tongue. Just for a moment and then retreats. I give you a baby kiss. But I stay against your lips. My tongue touches your lips again and I feel you begin to melt. Our tongues touch and then glide over one another, softly sensuously.
(Private Message from Looker): my hands find the back of your head and hold you.
(Private Message from Diabolique): Mmm and our kiss become more passionate, hungrier. Our tongues rubbing against one another, finding a rhythm... I explore your mouth.
(Private Message from Looker): And I suck on your tongue gently.
(Private Message from Diabolique): Yes, and my arms move around you hugging you closer to me, kissing you even deeper, even more passionately. Our hearts racing almost too fast. When I gasp for breath I suck air from inside your mouth, ending our kiss tenderly moving back from you slightly.
(Private Message from Looker): Oh my...
(Private Message from Diabolique): Did you like that?
(Private Message from Looker): Of course I did. Wow.
(Private Message from Diabolique): I liked it to.
(Private Message from Looker): I'll bet you're a very good kisser.
(Private Message from Diabolique): Well, I like to kiss.
(Private Message from Looker): I do too. I haven't kissed someone passionately like that for a long time.
(Private Message from Diabolique): Really?
(Private Message from Looker): Really.
(Private Message from Diabolique): Well, I should let you go get back to work, we've been here for a while.
(Private Message from Looker): Yes, I should get back to work.
(Private Message from Diabolique): Me, too.
(Private Message from Looker): Thank you, Mr. Diabolique.
(Private Message from Diabolique): Phillip. My real name is Phillip. Most people don't know that, so never call me Phillip except in private.
(Private Message from Looker): Okay, mine is Patricia.
(Private Message from Diabolique): Patricia who owns a bookstore in Taos, New Mexico.

(Private Message from Looker): Phillip the journalist and photographer who lives in Seattle, or was it Portland?
(Private Message from Diabolique): Seattle. I hope we get a chance to talk to each other again soon, Patricia.
(Private Message to Diabolique): I do too, Phillip. This has been very nice.
(Private Message from Diabolique): Yes, I've got a wonderful feeling about you... If you don't mind me saying so.
(Private Message from Looker): That's very nice of you, Phillip. You're a very nice man, I would bet.
(Private Message from Diabolique): I try to be.
(Private Message from Looker): Can I talk to you more maybe later tonight?
(Private Message from Diabolique): Well of course you can. I would like that very much Patricia. I enjoyed spending some time with you.
(Private Message from Looker): Maybe around 10 tonight?
(Private Message from Diabolique): Ten your time...?
(Private Message from Looker): yes what is that 9:00 o'clock your time?
(Private Message from Diabolique): I think so, yes... I will meet you here tonight.
(Private Message from Looker): Wow that would be great, Phillip. You can tell me more about yourself.
(Private Message from Diabolique): Only if you tell me more about yourself.
(Private Message from Looker): Yes...
(Private Message from Diabolique): Then until 10 o'clock your time, I say goodbye.

Phillip smiled, remembering most of the details of their first kiss. Almost capturing the excitement he felt when he made that first connection. He felt something very strong, but of course was full of doubts over what he was feeling and felt some awkwardness.

Now he hoped that perhaps by writing her a poem that he could reassure her that she had nothing to fear. This time the words flowed fairly easily. It was a poem he was meant to write.

Perfectly
by Phillip Craven

It's all perfectly understandable
Perfectly arranged
Perfectly normal
Perfectly explained

Like the stars in the clear sky
Perfectly aligned
Perfectly in orbit
Perfectly explained

Like the dreams in our hearts
Perfectly attained
Perfectly in reach
Perfectly explained

Yet you don't want to meet
Perfectly afraid
Perfectly safe
Perfectly explained

You want me to believe
You're perfectly arranged
Perfectly beautiful
Perfectly explained.

I need your imperfections
Perfectly vain
Perfectly unique
Perfectly explained

Chapter Eighteen

The traffic was light when Patricia pulled onto the state highway from the gravel logging road leading away from the lake. The late afternoon air was starting to chill, and a slight breeze began to whistle softly through the pines and aspen. A light gray-blue smoky haze was just beginning to settle over the valley below. Patricia smiled when she thought how capriciously she'd spent the past couple of hours. She hadn't concentrated at all on the things she'd hoped to try and sort through during her visit to her "secret spot."

Today, as so often in the past no matter where her mind wandered or what vows she made to herself, the problems at hand somehow gently and without issue seemed to mesh into the fabric of the moment. Even though she hadn't really dealt with anything that was directly on her mind, somehow everything just became clearer.

Patricia remained both amazed and stunned that the horrors of yesterday hadn't totally consumed her thoughts today. Subconsciously, she probably *wanted* to feel guilty, considering her close relationship with Alma and the incomprehensible gruesomeness of her murder. But for some odd reason, she didn't.

Of course, talking to Phillip last night had helped her cope with some of that. She certainly wouldn't call it an hypnotic hold that he had over her, but his words always seemed to take her gently and hold her in a secure and comforting way. Yes, they were just words, but they were always articulately spoken and genuinely consoling.

While driving back toward Taos, Patricia finally began piecing together the events of the past several months, mental snapshots of past conversations. They began to take on a recognizable shape. A pattern? That was it! Very early on, Patricia had sensed a pattern emerging, but she didn't realize the significance of her feelings until it was too late, especially too late for Alma.

Although Patricia was admittedly skeptical of Alma's wild suspicions about Frank, she reluctantly succumbed to Alma's repeated pleas for help. Very quickly, however, Patricia began enjoying her amateur sleuthing attempts to help prove or disprove her friend's theories. Many times, she had felt guilty about not sharing with Alma her own activities within the chatroom. In some ways, Patricia wasn't ready to admit them to herself.

Patricia was mildly amused at first, which is primarily the reason she chose not to tell Alma about her attraction to a certain gentleman in the room. As time went by, however, she began to realize that the emotional and psychological pull was more than just a silly plaything. It was just as Alma had feared about Frank's involvement. When it began happening to her, Patricia realized her own world could just as easily be destroyed. That should have been enough, but there were other fears gnawing at her. Fears about things which she had no business being part of; but like it or not, she was totally enmeshed in them now. If her suspicions proved to be even remotely founded on truth, she and Phillip may, indeed, be as deeply involved as Frank.

Would she ever get used to her heart skipping a beat when she thought of him? She trusted him, didn't she? Of course. He'd never given her a reason not to, not since they'd set down the ground rules governing their relationship. Phillip had never violated their agreement or even remotely attempted to step over the line.

Their love had grown quickly and spontaneously, and that had frightened her in the beginning. Phillip claimed it hadn't scared him at all. Patricia somehow doubted that. But she also realized that he really had nothing at stake if their relationship moved beyond their agreed upon parameters. For one thing, he wasn't married, whereas Patricia was and therefore controlled by the restraints of guilt, reserve, and commitment. She felt she had everything to lose. On the other hand, she also felt she had everything to gain, as well. How could she rationalize that kind of thinking? There was no way, logically, to justify her involvement with Phillip. She only knew that everything in her life had led her to the place where she was right now. That was the way of things.

Alma's murder. The only way Patricia knew to pursue her suspicions about that would mean making her relationship with Phillip at least semi-public. She needed to convince him of that so they could involve others as necessary in order to gain the evidence to either prove or disprove her developing theories. The truth was, however, she didn't even know where to start. Still, someone directly involved in the investigation of Alma's death had said something yesterday that troubled her. *What was it? Why can't I remember? Damn! Was it a name, a word? And who was it?* Bits and pieces of yesterday were flashing through her mind like the rays of light now flashing from between the trees as she drove along the aspen thicket bordering the road. *And what the hell prompted me to lash out at Frank like that?*

The more she thought about everything, the more concrete became her suspicions. As soon as she got home, she would call Phillip. She knew the hardest part would be confessing to him that she'd developed a friendship with another man in the chatroom. It was time to be totally honest with Phillip, and pray that he would understand. He would have to if he were to see the possible truth in her fears. Otherwise, he would end up trying to convince her that she was being ridiculous and that what she was asserting was totally absurd.

When had all this craziness actually started? As she pondered possible answers to that question, she allowed her truck to drift to the other side of the road. "Jesus!" she screamed out loud as a fully loaded logging truck came around the curve and headed straight for her. The driver was blasting his horn and she could see the panic in his eyes. He was trying desperately to avoid hitting her. Patricia yanked the steering wheel to the right, and the front bumper of her truck hit the guardrail with a wrenching steel against steel sound. Her truck glanced off the railing and then hit it again. She pumped the brakes and brought her vehicle to a stop.

Her heart was still pounding as she looked over the guardrail to the river three hundred feet below. She looked in her rearview mirror at the logging truck as it disappeared around another curve. *You stupid, stupid idiot! You're gonna get yourself killed!* As soon as she'd calmed down a little, she pulled slowly back out onto the road.

At that moment, her cell phone rang. As her heart was still racing, she thought about not answering it, but changed her mind by the third ring.

"Patricia, where are you?"

She thought it was Phillip's voice, but she couldn't be certain. "Why? Who is this?"

"I'm sorry, Patricia. This is Bill. Bill Conner. I'm sorry; it's just that Sylvia called me a couple of times because she doesn't know where you are. She was worried about you."

"I'm fine, Bill. I guess I've been gone longer than I expected to be. Is everything okay? Sylvia okay?"

"In a way, yes, Patricia. Well, I don't mean to sound neurotic, but we just didn't think your taking off like that was a very smart thing to do, considering the circumstances. Where are you, anyway?"

Patricia started to lie to him, fearful there might have been some sort of report about the logging truck, but changed her mind. "I'm coming into town from Blue Lake, Bill, why?"

Bill became angry with her when he thought about how isolated that area was. "I'm not even going to ask you why you were up there, Patricia. Are you headed home?"

"Yes. Yes I am, actually. Is there anything wrong, Bill?"

"No, not really, Patricia. I'm sorry to sound edgy, but it's been a hell of a twenty-four hours! I haven't had any sleep, and the department is upside down right now and crawling with all sorts of outside investigators and experts. Frankly, it's a royal mess in here." He paused, then continued in a hushed voice. "The State Attorney General has asked Frank to take an immediate leave of absence, Patricia. That puts me in charge of handling things. You wanna know the truth? Quite frankly, I don't want the responsibility. I don't have the experience for this type of thing, I guess is what I am trying to say. Our department has been asked to step back and turn the entire thing over to the state guys. I hate to admit it, but I'm glad they did. The only thing is I'm afraid of what direction they are looking. There's already talk of Frank being a primary suspect. I guess I'm not surprised..." his voice trailed off.

She wasn't exactly sure why Bill was telling her all of this. Perhaps he just didn't know where else to turn to vent a little frustration. "Bill, can I help? Have you needed to talk to me today and couldn't find me? Is that it?"

"Not really. I'm surprised that the big guns haven't gotten around to you yet, though. They're talking to everyone who seems to be breathing. I'm not quite sure what's going on at the moment, but I do know someone's head's gonna roll." He hesitated when he said that, wondering what possessed that particular statement to come out of his mouth. *Damn!*

"You still there, Bill?" Patricia wasn't sure if they had been cut off or not. "Bill?"

"Yeah, I'm here. Sorry. Anyway, someone should have told you yesterday, probably me, that you needed to stick close to home in case anyone needed to talk to you." He sounded irritated.

"Bill? What is it?"

"Patricia, listen to me, okay? There's someone still out there. A killer, Patricia. We don't know who it is, why he did what he did, or if he'll do it again. Do you understand? I should have warned you yesterday when...well, when I realized you didn't seem to comprehend this whole thing. You do know what we're dealing with here, don't you?"

"I think so. Yes, I think I do."

"Okay, just do me a favor and call Sylvia as soon as you get home, okay?"

"Of course, Bill. I promise."

Patricia pulled up to the back door of her house and got out to check the damage to her truck. Then she went inside, flipped on the lights, checked the answering machine, and went to office and turned on her computer. While she waited for it to boot up, she placed a call.

"Hi, Syl, its Patricia."

"I figured it was, girl. Bill and I just saw you drive in. Thanks for calling. Bill's afraid you might be mad at him for coming on so..."

Patricia cut her off. "No, not at all. Gosh, I actually appreciated it. Please tell him that I should have been thinking. It was fine that he called. Especially since he called right after I'd pulled one of my dumber driving mistakes!"

"What do you mean?"

"I was just daydreaming and ran off of the road, that's all. No big deal, honestly. Just a little scrape on the bumper."

"Daydreaming? You sure you're okay?"

"I'm fine. Listen, I know Bill's there. I need to let you go. Tell Tex to relax and that I promise to behave and stick around town from now on. If I plan anything, I'll let both of you know, okay? I've got some things to catch up on around here. I need to get in touch with Alma's Uncle Jose and somehow get up the nerve to call Frank, or maybe I should just go by and see him. Ask Bill what he thinks is the best thing to do, would you? I'm not going to do anything one way or the other tonight, so tell him to give me a call whenever he thinks about it in the morning, okay?"

"Will do, cutie! You going to be okay tonight?"

"Sure, sure! I have a lot to do to keep me busy. Now go and take care of Bill. He didn't sound too good when I talked to him, Syl. Just hold him, okay? That's probably the best thing to do." Patricia clicked down the receiver before Sylvia had a chance to respond. She sat down at her computer and went straight to the chatroom. Her heart sank when she saw that Diabolique wasn't there.

Sin-Dee: Hi Looker

NastyOlGeezer: Well you're a fag then, pal.

WellHung: Takes one to know one.

NastyOlGeezer: Oh I'm laughing so hard, my penis is now soft.

LairBitch: Hi there, Looker!

Boobalicious: Looker, Diabol has been looking for you on and off all day!

WellHung: You still hanging around with that loser? Why? When you could have ME?

Looker: Hi room.

NastyOlGeezer: Wanna suck my cock, Looker?

Looker: Thanks, but no thanks, Nasty. But I'll keep you in mind. When was the last time Diabol was in here?
NastyOlGeezer: Oh, haven't you heard? He committed suicide. Left a note on the bulletin Board. Note said..."in case of suicide, NASTY Gets Looker,"
Looker: That's not funny, Nasty. I'm not in the mood for you today.
LairBitch: that's the way to tell 'em, Looker! Fuck you, NASTY!
NastyOlGeezer: Damn lesbos!
WellHung: You ruined another one NASTY?
NastyOlGeezer: Oh you're real funny today. Too bad nobody will have cybersex with you and help you get off.
LairBitch: How come you're such a jerk Nasty?
Boobalicious: Aw, NASTY is okay...
NastyOlGeezer: Mmm let me nuzzle my face in your tits booby.
WellHung: Hey where you from Sin-Dee?
Sin-Dee: Pennsylvania, Hung. Where you from?
WellHung: Texas... where big things that count cum from.
Sin-Dee: Mmmm I like big things.
Looker: Has anyone seen ManInBlue today?
LairBitch: Not me.
GUYwithPIC: Not me, either.
fembot: I did earlier, Looker.
(Private Message from Bishamon): Why are you looking for ManInBlue?

She was about to reply, when someone called "Shutterbug" logged into the room. She thought it might be Phillip, but she wondered why he would be using a different name.

(Private Message from Bishamon): Didn't you see my message?!
(Private Message from Shutterbug): Trisha, it's ME! Shhh...
(Private Message from Looker): yes, Bishamon, I saw your message. Can you hold on a second?
(Private Message from Looker): Phillip!! Why are you using Shutterbug as a nick? Are you hiding from someone?
(Private Message from Bishamon): I asked you why you asked about ManInBlue...
(Private Message from Looker): Phillip, Bishamon is asking me questions about ManInBlue...what should I do???
(Private Message from Shutterbug): Trisha, are you here? Talk

to me!
(Private Message from Looker): Phillip, didn't you get my message about Bishamon?
(Private Message from Shutterbug): No! What's going on? Where were you today? Did you get my e-mail?
(Private Message from Looker): NO, I didn't get your e-mail! Look, Phillip, log off and call me right away okay?
(Private Message from Shutterbug): Sure. But where's Trent?
(Private Message from Looker): Doesn't matter, just call me! But first I have to send Bishamon a message. Then I'll log off and you call me, okay?
(Private Message from Shutterbug): NO! LOG OFF! DON'T WRITE TO HIM!!!
(Private Message from Looker): But why?
(Private Message from Shutterbug): LOG OFF NOW, DAMN IT! I'M CALLING YOU RIGHT NOW!!!

Patricia's hand was shaking as she turned off the computer. Her phone rang almost immediately.

"Hi, sweetheart!" she said excitedly.

"Hi there, you bitch."

"What? Who is this?!"

"You heard me," replied a man with a strange nasal voice.

"Who is this?" she demanded.

"I know who you are, Looker."

"Phillip? Is that you?"

"No, this isn't Phillip. Why, was he supposed to call you? Is that why you left so quickly? Such a rude bitch you are. And I've been so nice to you, too."

Patricia slammed down the phone. Her heart was in her throat. She was desperately trying to figure out what to do, when the phone rang again. She was afraid to answer it. The ringing stopped, but started again about a minute later. This time, she picked it up, but didn't say anything.

"Hello Patricia? Trish, you there, babe? Trish??"

"Oh, Phillip...yes!"

"Hi, babe. I missed you."

"I've missed you, too, Phillip. Oh god, Phil, I just had a very strange call!"

"Tell me about it."

"Someone called me up. Someone from the room. He called me Looker, so I'm sure he must have been from the room."

"He called you just now?"

"Yes, a minute ago."

"That's why your line was busy then."

"Phillip it wasn't you playing some kind of joke on me, was it?"

"No, of course not! Did you give someone in the room your phone number?"

"No. I don't think so. Maybe a while ago. I might have given my number to one of the girls in the room, but I don't remember."

"Well this guy couldn't have gotten your number without knowing your name and where you lived, unless you gave it to him or…"

There was a long silence.

"Phillip?"

"Yes, babe, I'm here. Just thinking."

"God, you're scaring me, Phillip!."

"I was just thinking this guy who called you could have gotten your number from someone else in the room. Like one of the other people who knows you and you gave the number to."

"But who? I don't really remember ever giving anyone my number. And if I did, it was a long time ago and it would have been to one of the other women in the room. I don't think they would've given it to someone else."

Phillip thought for a moment. "Well, unless this person knows your real name, he had to have gotten it from someone in the room or from you."

"But you're the only one who knows who I am, Phillip!"

"You sure about that? I mean, when you first got to the room, you weren't real careful about things, you know."

"I don't know, Phillip. I guess I could have mentioned it to someone, but not to any of the guys, and this was definitely a man who called me."

"Well, it's probably nothing." Phillip was trying to sound convincing.

"I'm glad you think so," Patricia said with a sigh .

"You logged off and didn't go back in the room just now did you?" Phillip said.

"No, I logged off and then I got that strange phone call, Phillip. I didn't talk to Bishamon."

"Bishamon! I sent you an e-mail about him this morning." Phillip said.

"You did?"

"Yes, Bishamon has been acting weird in the room a couple of times, like he knows all kinds of stuff about other folks in the room. He's been really rude, and it made me wonder whether or not Nasty might be playing some stupid game by coming in under Bishamon's nick when he knew he wasn't likely to be in the room. Now, I'm not sure. I think it really is

Bishamon. I don't mean to frighten you too much or anything, but whoever this Bishamon is, he's a real jerk."

"What happened?" Patricia asked.

"Oh, he started sending me private messages earlier today when I was the room hoping you would show up. Anyway, I ignored him. That got him real pissed off. He started yelling and screaming about how he doesn't like to be ignored. He said he'd been watching several people in the room and he said he knew I really liked Looker, and that he kind of liked Looker himself. Then he asked me if I had seen ManInBlue..."

"Okay, go on," Patricia urged.

"I told him I didn't know who he was, and if he wanted to talk to me then he had better identify himself."

"And did he?"

"He said he went by many names and he knows a lot about the people in the room, that he could easily trace anyone in the room, that it was easy to do if you knew just a little about computers."

"Oh, my!"

Phillip continued, "I wasn't sure how true that was, but it made me more than a little nervous. I mean, I wonder if there *is* a way to trace people who are in the room, like you would someone who called you on the phone, you know with star 69 or whatever."

"Well, is there?" Patricia was afraid she didn't want to hear the answer.

"I did some research on that, and I wouldn't say that it's all that easy, but people have hacked into the system before and gotten people's e-mail addresses and accessed peoples private files and credit card numbers and stuff. I suppose someone could find out more, if they wanted."

"You mean people can hack into your home computers?" she asked.

"Yeah, if they know what they're doing. It seems to be possible."

"That's scary, Phillip. That's really pretty scary, if you think about it."

"Well, I've been thinking about it, Trish, and about a lot of other things, too."

"Go on."

"I don't have anything definite to add right now, except to tell you to be really careful, especially when you're on-line. I mean, Bishamon might not be someone you have to worry about; but then again, he might be."

"I understand, Phillip."

"Oh, and one more thing..."

"What's that?"

"I love you."

"I love you, too, of course. You make me smile in spite of everything."

"It's time for us to meet, you know."

Although her answer was obvious, his question stunned her into momentary silence. Finally, she whispered, "I know, Phillip. I want that so much."

"Are you sure?" His voice had an uncharacteristic tremble.

"Of course, I'm sure, silly. But are you sure you want to meet me?"

"What's that supposed to mean?"

"Well, I'm not some skinny young model, you know."

"What makes you think I want some skinny young model?"

"Well, of course, you do. Every man does."

"Well, I'm not every man," Phillip said with a chuckle.

"I love you, you silly, wonderful man. I know I say that a lot, but I have to."

"And you can say it as much as you want, baby. I love you, too."

Patricia remembered that she'd wanted to tell Phillip something important. She was in such a nice relaxed mood now, though. But she would soon be angry with herself if she didn't tell him.

"There's something else, Phillip."

"What is it?"

"I meant to tell you for a while now, but... Well, it's not something I was looking forward to doing."

"I have no idea what you mean, Patricia," Phillip laughed.

"No listen. This is kind of awkward for me, but I have to tell you this. When I first came into the chatroom, I was there to check things out for a friend mine. I was checking out somebody in the room for Alma. I didn't come into the room simply because I was curious."

"What are you talking about?"

"I was spying in the room for her, Phillip, that's what I was doing."

"Spying?!"

"Yes. She was worried about her husband and what was going on with her marriage. She thought he might be seeing someone else on the side."

"Who were you spying on?"

"I wasn't quite sure. I mean, in the beginning, I had no idea if Alma's husband was in the room or not."

"Frank, you mean?"

"Yes."

"You know who it is?"

"I almost positive Frank is ManInBlue, Phillip."

"Your sheriff, you mean. That's Alma's husband? The one you think is ManInBlue?"

"Yes."

"Whoa! You mean ManInBlue, this cop who everyone thinks is hot and heavy with Silky and the guy Bishamon was asking us about today...he's Alma's husband?"

"Yes, Phillip."

"Patricia, I am really not trying to play the paranoid type here, but..." Phillip stopped.

"I'm pretty sure we're thinking the same thing, Phillip. But it's like I don't want to say out loud what I'm thinking, you know what I mean?"

"I know exactly what you mean. It's like if you say what you're thinking, it might actually come true and you don't want it to."

"Yes, that's it exactly."

"Okay," Phillip said, "I think the best thing to do right now is to take a break."

"Okay," Patricia said.

"We need to think things through."

"You all right, Phillip?"

"I'm fine," he said. "I just don't like what I'm thinking."

"Yeah, I know what you mean," Patricia said weakly. "You okay about me?"

"About you?"

"You aren't mad at me, are you?

"Mad at you?" Phillip laughed. "No babe I'm not mad at you at all. Really!"

"I'm so glad. That's absolutely the last thing in the world I need right now is for you to be upset with me."

"Patricia, I love you so much. Don't worry. We'll find a way to get through all of this. I promise."

"Thank you, Phillip. I needed that," she said softly. "Well, I'd better get going."

"Yeah, me, too. I hate saying goodbye."

"I know. Me, too."

"I mean we shouldn't be ever saying goodbye to each other," Phillip added.

"Don't wait too long to talk to me, okay, Phil?"

"I won't."

"Hang up now," she said quietly.

"Okay. Talk to you soon."

PART II

The hearts of gold have all been sold

And buried in their fate.

A thousand friends with words to lend,

But always come too late

So please excuse me while I die, I've just run out of life.

Paradise

At such a price

Wasn't all that nice.

Chapter Nineteen

Talking over an omelet and some coffee in Catalano's Diner with Sheriff Frank Garrett and Bill Conner was a hell of a lot better than being interrogated at their station. Still, Phillip was uncomfortable being in an unfamiliar city and talking with people he'd previously only known through Patricia.

Where was Patricia anyway? Was she in some room still being questioned at the Sheriff's Office, or was she back over at her bookshop?

"Phil, we get all kinds of folks through here, as you might imagine," Frank said. "I mean, we aren't exactly a stomping ground for the rich and famous like Aspen or Vail." He slurped his coffee noisily and put the cup down before continuing, "But we see some of 'em come through here every so often, isn't that right, Bill?"

"Right. We do. Half the time we don't even know they are famous 'til Amy or someone asks us if we knew that the person we were just talking to was so and so."

"Well, a lot of people have discovered this beautiful place," Phillip said. "I know some people who came down here to work for a couple of weeks and ended up spending six months to a year. And believe me, I can see why! It's not just because it's a beautiful place. It's the light, in my opinion. The light here is what photographers call the 'magic hour.' In most places, this kind of light exists on certain days, and then only at sunrise or sunset for about an hour. But here? Wow, here it exists nearly the whole day!"

"Yeah, it's a pretty place all right," Bill replied. "Lots of people come here just to take photographs. I think it's one of the most photographed areas in the country."

"In the world, I think, Bill," Frank boasted.

"Is it the world?" Bill asked him.

"Yup. At least I think so." Frank was a little less sure now.

The three of them ate in silence for a few minutes before Frank spoke again. "You and Patricia have known each other for how long now?"

"Oh, about a year," answered Phillip.

Frank glanced nervously at Bill.

"Um...have you met, Trent, Phil?" Frank asked quickly and with some difficulty.

"Yes. Yes, I have. We met briefly yesterday, as a matter fact."

"Phil, I've known Trent a long time and he's real good people, you know."

"Frank, I think maybe we should talk about something else."

"No, I don't think so, Bill," countered Frank. "I've been through a lot the last few months, and it might not be the best thing to talk about right now, but goddamn it, I've gotta talk about it, okay?"

Bill glanced over at Phillip. He had already developed a liking for him and the confident way he conducted himself. He hated to see him placed under the microscope like this.

"That okay with you, Mr. Craven?" Frank asked. The edge to his voice was unmistakable.

"Yes, Frank, it's fine." Phillip said surprisingly warmly.

"She's married, Phil."

"I know that, Frank. And I've thought a lot about that in the last few months and so has she. This is not something either one of us has taken lightly."

"Glad to hear that." After staring at his plate for a moment and pushing his eggs around with his fork, Frank looked directly at Phillip. "Now I'll admit that I'm the last person in the world who should be talking about morals, you know? I mean, you must think I'm some kind of hypocrite right?" he asked.

"No, Frank, I understand completely."

"No. No, you don't, Phil. You don't know what I've been through and what I'm still dealing with. Hell, Phil, half the people in this goddamned town think I killed my wife! You know that?"

Bill looked nervously at the old couple seated a few tables away to see if they were listening.

"Yes, Frank, I *do* know that. I know a lot about the case and what happened, actually."

The silence that followed was heavy with the tension all three of the men felt.

"Frank, I'm Diabolique." Phillip watched Frank's eyes as his words sank in. He truly felt sorry for the man.

Bill looked quizzically from Phillip to Frank and back to Phillip. He had no way of knowing the importance of what had just been said. But there was no mistaking the look of shock and disbelief on his friend's' face.

"Repeat what you just said," Frank demanded.

"You know me as Diabolique, Frank."

Frank closed his eyes and sat back.

"Um…I'm definitely missing something here, guys." Bill interjected.

"It's a long story," Phil said quietly.

"It's really not that long of a story, Bill," Frank said. "And you should be a little more familiar with it actually. You remember that chatroom I was playing around in for a while?"

Bill nodded.

"Well, it appears that Phil here goes to the same place to chat."

"You mean you two have talked to each other before in that room?" Bill asked.

"Without him having any idea who I was," Phillip quickly added.

"But you knew who *he* was?"

Startled by Bill's question, Frank looked directly at Phillip. "You *knew* who I was?"

"Yes, Frank, I did. I mean…not right away I didn't. But, yes, Patricia and I figured out who you were a few months ago, just about the time Alma was killed."

Bill and Frank together, in total disbelief said, "Patricia?"

Phillip smiled. "Well I guess that answers that question."

"What question?" Frank's voice was shaking noticeably.

"I was going to ask if Patricia had told you about any of this and why I was coming into town to help out on this."

"No. Well, she explained to us that you were a photographer and a journalist who wrote a lot about the Internet and she pretty much convinced us that you could help us out," Bill said. "And she told us that you could be trusted to do things quietly and not involve anyone we didn't want involved."

"Our resources are limited, as you know," said Frank.

"Yes, I know."

Bill looked lost. "So, wait now…I'm not sure I understand this completely." It was an act, of course, and he was doing a masterful job.

"The chatroom I was going to, and Phil was going to, well…we knew each other in there. We joked a lot with each other, we talked."

Bill shook his head. "I had no idea. So that's how you and Patricia met, Phil? In the chatroom?"

"Yeah, we met in the chatroom and we just started talking." Phillip knew that Bill was well aware of at least that much. But who was he to blow Bill's cover?

Frank looked at Phillip. "Damn, it's a small world."

"Yeah, it sure is."

"I don't know what to say, Phil."

"You don't have to say anything, Frank."

"Yeah, I do. I've acted like an asshole, Phil. I mean I treated you like a suspect a couple of hours ago and then I was judging you and Patricia, and I've got no right to do that. No one has the right to do that really, but me of all people? Shit!"

No one said anything for a moment. The waitress began refilling their coffee cups.

"Everything taste all right, Sheriff? Bill? You?" she asked pleasantly, looking at Phillip.

"Phillip. Hi, my name's Phillip Craven."

"Hi, Phil. Everything okay here?"

"Yeah, Carla we're fine, thanks." Frank was getting impatient.

"Okay. Just holler if you need anything," Carla said over her shoulder as she walked away.

"I'm pretty sure who we are dealing with here," said Phillip. He was more than just pretty sure who was involved. He had suspected that he and Frank and Patricia had crossed paths with an individual who came across as very unstable several months earlier. Still, when he'd first become suspicious of the person they all knew only as Bishamon, he'd had no way of knowing how their lives would ultimately be shattered forever.

He still wasn't sure exactly who Bishamon was nor what his connection was to another chatroom personality named Silky. And how he was going to prove they were somehow involved in the murder of Frank's wife Alma was still a mystery to him. But it had become increasingly clear that Bishamon, Silky, and ManInBlue were somehow connected.

Several weeks ago, Phillip knew it was time to arrange a meeting with Patricia. There was no denying how deeply he felt for her, how his feelings for a woman he had never met had grown stronger and stronger over the previous ten months. There was no way of logically explaining how this could have happened. He hadn't been looking for love or companionship when he first struck up a friendship with Patricia. And even as their feelings for each other grew, he still didn't believe the relationship would be anything more than a playful diversion. He felt it would eventually fade away without permanently disrupting or altering their lives.

Phillip had been amazed at himself for taking this relationship with a woman he'd never met further and further. This simply wasn't like him. He was hardly a conservative prude, but neither was he one to abandon principles or to venture into territories he considered sophomoric and rather selfish. Surrendering to one's desires was not something Phillip was against on any kind of religious grounds. It was just something he chose to exercise restraint over. He just felt there were usually more important things to do with one's life. He'd witnessed in others, and many times in his own life, how frequently relationships based solely on lust ultimately created jealousies, problems, heartaches, and regrets. Regardless, he'd found himself becoming increasingly attracted to Patricia.

Since he believed in most instances it was important for him to experience things firsthand in order for him to accurately write about them, Phillip didn't resist all of his temptations. He experimented, giving in to his impulses on occasion. Part of what he was doing was writing about how people were utilizing the Internet, satisfying their curiosities in fairly anonymous ways.

Phillip didn't believe he was completely in control, but he felt he was remaining sufficiently aware so that he would realize when he was in danger of losing his perspective. Some temptations, particularly sexual ones, were tricky and a bit more dangerous than most (but that is exactly what makes them so attractive and compelling in the first place). A slice of the forbidden fruit could be so sweet. It was overindulgence that created problems. Phillip believed he was smart enough to control himself so as not to get himself or someone else into a truly compromising position.

When Phillip first discovered chatrooms, it was for some articles he was writing. The first chatrooms he observed seemed to be comprised mostly of teenagers who gossiped about their interests for hours at a time. Some tried to be disruptive and rude. Others appeared to be looking for romance and companionship. Phillip realized this and had written articles about the dangers of such places. There were people who preyed on the naïve and weak and these chatrooms afforded people the opportunity to manipulate others, if one was not careful to maintain his anonymity and distance. But with a little guidance and some common sense, these chatrooms were actually pretty safe.

Phillip then ran across some chatrooms where adult sexuality was discussed openly. Some chatrooms were informational, but most were completely interactive and were a place to not only discusses fantasies, but to participate in them—mentally, of course. This was a fairly safe and anonymous way to act out one's innermost fantasies and desires. Or it gave you a chance to act in the most immature ways imaginable, providing a needed and perhaps healthy release of stress and tension.

Phillip at times experienced some revulsion at the behavior and fantasies that chatroom participants participated in. He soon realized, however, what a fascinating phenomenon this was and that it could also be both quite beneficial and quite healthy to its participants. In moderation, there was no problem with people acting out on their fantasies through the Internet. Of course, some people overindulged and ended up avoiding their real life responsibilities in order to spend more time in the fantasy world of the chatrooms.

Then there were people who, after meeting in a chatroom, decided to meet each other in real life. From what he could learn, some of these meetings remained completely platonic, while others turned into brief affairs. And there were a few, he discovered, that had evolved into real-life romances from which even some marriages had resulted. Some of these cyber affairs led to divorce. There were some instances he knew of where chatroom dalliances led to bitter disillusionment, people using each other and then discarding each other with little emotional feeling. On a few occasions, this had led to violence. What most fascinated Phillip was how people typing messages to each other, engaging in cybersex, could end up in love. Internet chatrooms were becoming the singles bars of the new millennium. He wrote about what he observed—the good, the bad and the ugly. Although he had actively participated in cybersex himself, it was not something he regularly engaged in or desired to.

Perhaps if he were not writing about it on a regular basis, Phillip would have lost interest in the chatrooms a long time ago and moved on to other things. But he'd gotten to know some of the personalities in one of the chatrooms quite well, and the experience was like his own personal soap opera. He had managed to keep himself emotionally distant from nearly everyone, but he did offer useful advice and tried to be compassionate with the chatroom acquaintances he made.

And then there was Patricia, a woman who had stumbled into the chatroom seemingly by accident and whom Phillip guided through the pitfalls of participating in the room. Remain anonymous, he'd cautioned her. Don't tell people too much personal information about yourself, always be aware of what you are doing, and who you are talking to. And be careful. Use common sense was the basic advice Phillip gave Patricia.

An honest, flirtatious relationship developed between them. Phillip began their relationship as a protective guide to enable her to safely be as adventurous as she desired to be. However, Phillip found himself genuinely liking Patricia and wishing to explore their possible mutual desires. Their relationship slowly grew more intimate. They shared an intensely satisfying fantasy in which they sometimes pretended to be lovers meeting romantically in a fictitious hotel room in Big Sur overlooking the Pacific Ocean, and other times sitting by a quiet lake high in the New Mexico mountains.

Phillip's interest in Patricia continued to increase. And the attraction was mutual. There was no question that they were falling in love. Neither of them had been looking for love, but now they found themselves undeniably and deeply in love with one another. She was convinced this was no accidental meeting of two people, but was rather something much deeper. They were alike in so many fundamental ways. What motivated them, their inner selves and their spiritual selves?

All seemed to be identical. They often knew what the other was thinking, and they quite often typed the same phrases and expressions at the same time. They were miles apart, they had never met, and yet their minds and their hearts were synchronous.

How could this possibly be, they both wondered? What kind of spell were they under? And was it real or fantasy? As they tested each other in subtle and covert ways, their attraction to each other continued to grow and their love increased and matured.

Yet Phillip knew he could not let this go any further. Patricia was married and had a happy and good life, and he could not ever have her in real life as completely as he desired. This was a relationship that had gone way too far and it was one where very real boundaries existed for very good reasons.

Phillip discovered that Patricia also shared these feelings. This wonderful relationship of theirs was a beautiful thing, but it couldn't blossom into reality. Could it? Actually, they both knew it had to. So strong was their love and desire, it simply had to be. And as it became clearer to them exactly what this could mean, it became very frightening. They had lost their balance and they had lost their control.

Patricia told Phillip that she, not so unlike him, had wandered into the chatroom not simply out of boredom or curiosity, but to help out a friend of hers. Actually, she had come to the chatroom to spy on her friend's husband who had been carrying on a suspected cyber affair. And now she was involved in a cyber affair herself. How does one fully reconcile that? There was no denying the obvious truth. The mature thing to do, the right thing to do, was to end it. Stop it before there were regrets.

Phillip knew that a part of him also believed this is what they should do. They were, after all, too intelligent to allow themselves to be swept away like teenagers in love. There were very real consequences at stake, which would affect their lives and the lives of so many others if they were to continue. In a surprising moment of strength, Phillip wrote: *We are addicted to each other and must now work together to end our addiction.*

This seemed like a very reasonable and mature approach. They could get through this, get on with their lives and responsibilities, and possibly even remain friends.

A side benefit of this relationship was that Phillip had once again begun writing poems and truly enjoying his work as a photographer. His appreciation for life and for living had been renewed because of Patricia and the love he had for her. It would be possible to continue loving her, but he must simply shift the way in which he loved her into a more conventional friendship. Yes, he told himself, it was possible to do that.

Patricia was having similar thoughts. Phillip had gotten to the point where his life did not have many complications, and he was finally able to do what he needed to do without an inordinate amount of minor responsibilities. He didn't need her in his life.

The connection they had, however, was undeniable. Together they had rediscovered the joys of living. Their lives were new, colorful, and exciting again. Parts of them they had long ago shut down were opening up again.

Should they really deny themselves the very thing they had been looking for all their lives? Should they deny themselves each other after discovering how good for each other they could be, simply because the timing wasn't perfect, simply because there were complications? Were they denying themselves what they both wanted because of fear or guilt? In ten years, would they look back with sadness at what they had let slip from each other's hands?

"Are you sure, Patricia?" Phillip asked her over the phone not so long ago.

"Sweetheart, I've never been so sure of anything in my life."

"We can't turn back if we keep going, Patricia. It will be hard to...well, to stop what this is. But right now, it might be possible, Patricia." Phillip tried to remain logical as he talked to her.

"Is it possible for you?"

"I don't know," Phillip said honestly, wondering if it was time now to lie and tell her that they have to do the right thing. But if he had said that, Patricia would know he was lying and what purpose would be served by lying to both Patricia and himself?

"Phillip, I know you will always be a part of me. And I don't have the strength or desire to let you go, because I know it would be wrong to do so."

"Yes," Phillip said softly, his body trembling.

"We have been together before, Phil, and we have found each other again."

"I know, Patricia. I believe that, too. I'm fighting this, Patricia, because..."

"Because you're trying to protect me and because you are scared," she said finishing the sentence for him.

"Yes."

"I know," she said.

And then there was a silence during which they both felt themselves being drawn helplessly even closer to each other.

"Trisha, I have to tell you. I won't have the strength to stop this in the future."

"And you think you do now?"

"Probably not."

"What do *you* want, Phillip?"

"It's what you want, Patricia."

"Do you mean I can get what I want?"

"Yes," Phillip said. "You know you can."

"Then I want you, Phillip Craven. I've never been so sure of anything in my entire life."

Phillip felt overwhelmed with emotion and tried to force himself to say something but he couldn't. He was certain she could hear him crying.

"I love you so much, baby," Patricia said, her voice trembling.

"I love you, Patricia."

"You'd better," she said with a laugh.

"Oh, I do, baby, I love you so very, very much." As Phillip said those words that seemed so inadequate for the emotions and feelings he wanted to express to her, he felt a sense of great relief. He knew he was doing the right thing. It was the only thing that made sense. He loved the woman he knew he should love.

A little later, a new poem flowed out of Phillip.

As Long As…

As long as I can share my loneliness
I don't mind being alone.
As long as I can tell you
Things I can't quite say.

As long as you understand
What I don't quite grasp.

As long as I can hold you close
So I won't slip away.

As long as I can make you smile
And hide my pain.

As long as I can care about you
When I forget about myself

As long as I can keep you strong
And ignore my self-doubts

As long as the candy is sweet
The bitterness is swallowed.

As long as the future is bright
The past can stay dark

As long as I can feel the passion
Then hope is never lost

As long as I have you to love
Then I shall keep on trying.

To Patricia
from
Phillip
...always

Chapter Twenty

CONNECTION ESTABLISHED
Welcome to LoveMining.com
The Ultimate Adult Chatroom!

LOOKER HAS ENTERED THE ROOM

Dribbles: Hi Looker
NastyOlGeezer: Wow, you're here awfully late, Looker. Too horny to sleep? Wanna lick my ass, baby?
GUINNEVIERE: Are you always this disgusting?
SirLotsOfLance: Always, hey Looker.
Mrs.Robinson: Hey Looker, welcome back.
Looker: Hi there, Dribbles, Nasty, Gwen, Lance, and Mrs. Robinson, everyone else in private chats?
YoungandHung: I'm here too. Hi Looker.
NastyOlGeezer: Yeah I'll bet you are pervert.
Dribbles: Shut the hell up Nasty.
NastyOlGeezer: You didn't answer my question earlier, Dribble butt, you a fag or what?
Mrs.Robinson: Pc me Hung one.
NastyOlGeezer: Mmm...if you insist, you naughty little whore.
YoungandHung: Yes ma'am. Give me a couple of minutes.
NastyOlGeezer: THAT'S ALL YOU NEED IS A COUPLE OF MINUTES? YOU NEED TO GET A REAL MAN, Mrs. Robinson.
FANNY: LOL. You're on a roll tonight Nasty.
NastyOlGeezer: Like me to give you a roll, Wouldn't you FANNY?

DRIBBLES HAS LEFT THE ROOM

FANNY: Try me Nasty. Hey Looker, isn't it late for you?
LOOKER: Yes, I couldn't sleep.
NastyOlGeezer: aw, scared dribbles away, again. That pussy.
FANNY: Be nice Nasty.

NastyOlGeezer: I am being nice, stupid bitch.

FANNY: Yes I can see that.

NastyOlGeezer: Where's Romeo, Look. Desert you? Broke your heart?

LOOKER: Not at all Nasty.

NastyOlGeezer: You know I could rock your world baby.

LOOKER: I'll bet you could Nasty.

NastyOlGeezer: Oh you know I could baby. Rock it, roll it, leave you so satisfied you wouldn't think of anyone else for a week.

FANNY: Wow, you promise a lot Nasty.

NastyOlGeezer: Looker should take me up on it.

LOOKER: I'm flattered Nasty....You're such a stud.

FANNY: Oh oh.

NastyOlGeezer: You makin' fun of me Looker?

FANNY: Come to Fanny baby, I'll make it all better for you.

NastyOlGeezer: nah, you're too easy, fanny slut...

FANNY: Not that easy...

NastyOlGeezer : Well I'm off to bed... ALONE...as if anyone could give a rat's ass.

LOOKER: Bye Nasty.

NASTYOLGEEZER HAS LEFT THE ROOM

GUINNEVIERE: God that guy's gross.

FANNY: Yeah... but he's okay.

GUINNEVIERE: Glad you think so...

LOOKER: I'm sure he's a pretty nice fellow in real life.

FANNY: Well he sure ain't a nice fellow in here.... But sometimes that's fun too.

LOOKER: Boy it's quiet in here today.....

FANNY: Well most folks around here are busy talking one on one, Looker.

LOOKER: Don't blame them.

FANNY: How's Di?

LOOKER: Oh he's great, he was here earlier.

FANNY: Oh I'm sorry I missed him, did he mention how his trip went?

LOOKER: Said it went really well.

FANNY: Oh glad to hear it.

GUINNEVIERE: My knight needs me, ta ta.

FANNY: LOL take good care of lance.
LOOKER: Have fun Gwen.
GUINNEVIERE: You too, it you can.
FANNY: I'd love to. I'm feeling frisky tonight....
LOOKER: Are you?
FANNY: Ever cyber'd with a woman, Looker?
LOOKER: No, have you?
FANNY: Oh sure, it can be very nice.
LOOKER: I'll take your word for it.
FANNY: Have gone to bed with a few women in real life too.
LOOKER: Have you?
FANNY: You ever do that?
LOOKER: Me? No. lol. I don't think so.
FANNY: Not too adventurous huh?
LOOKER: Nope... pretty dull girl I am.
FANNY: 'sigh'......

DIABOLIQUE HAS ENTERED THE ROOM

FANNY: Well speak of the devil...
LOOKER: hey stranger.
Diabolique: Hey there! Hi Looker, Hi Fanny, HI room.
FANNY: Most folks are busy if you know what I mean.
Diabolique: I believe I do.
LOOKER: What brings you here?
Diabolique: Couldn't sleep.
(Private Message from Diabolique): Actually wrote you a poem.
LOOKER: me neither.
(Private Message from Looker): Hi baby...
Diabolique: Must be the moon.
LOOKER: Blue Moon?
Diabolique: Moon over Miami?
FANNY: When the Moon hit's your eye like a big pizza Pie....
Diabolique: Hey....you mooning us?
LOOKER: lol
FANNY: Hey I am Fanny you know.
Diabolique: Lol...
LOOKER: You all right, Di
Diabolique: Real good now?
FANNY: Oh you two...
LOOKER: What?

FANNY: oh I can tell you two like each other so much.
LOOKER: You can?
Diabolique: Wow, you're quite perceptive.
FANNY: Well maybe someday I'll find mr. Right, or mr. Cyber right...
LOOKER: You will, Fanny...
FANNY: maybe you'll loan me Di for a little while.
LOOKER: That's up to Di....
Diabolique: wink wink
FANNY: You flirt, you tease
Diabolique: Maybe we should have a threesome.
FANNY: oh don't even tease me... I'd gladly roll around with you two.
LOOKER: Hmm should I excuse myself?
FANNY: No way, Looker... I gotta get going.... Besides, he's just teasing.
LOOKER: Yeah he is a big tease.
FANNY: Well good night, you two.
Diabolique: Night Fanny...
LOOKER: Night Fanny.

FANNY HAS LEFT THE ROOM

(Private Message from Diabolique): Hi cutie... Glad you're here, love you.
(Private Message from Looker): Need you so bad. So you wrote a poem for me?
(Private Message from Diabolique): Yeah, maybe I'll send it to you.
(Private Message from Looker): You better.
(Private Message from Diabolique): You want me to?
(Private Message from Looker): Oh yes.
(Private Message from Diabolique): Well maybe if you are a good girl.
(Private Message from Looker): Or a bad girl.
(Private Message from Diabolique): Oh especially then.
(Private Message from Looker): You silly man.
(Private Message from Diabolique): How long you been here?
(Private Message from Looker): Oh maybe ten minutes not very long.
(Private Message from Diabolique): I see... been flirting with

anyone I should know about?
(Private Message from Looker): Hmm let me think now....
(Private Message from Diabolique): oh oh... have there been that many you can't keep them straight? I hate when that happens... can get you in a heap of trouble you know.
(Private Message from Looker): Oh brother...**NastyOlGeezer** and I already had a nice little chat while you were doing whatever you were doing...
(Private Message from Diabolique): Really?
(Private Message from Looker): oh sure
(Private Message from Diabolique): how fun.
(Private Message from Looker): Oh yes... laugh a minute LOL
(Private Message from Diabolique): Gosh he is such a warm wonderful human being.
(Private Message from Looker): yes he is......just like me...two of a kind ya know.
(Private Message from Diabolique): ah
(Private Message from Looker): Such a nice, shy man. He's so romantic once you get to know him, you know.
(Private Message from Diabolique): Is he now?
(Private Message from Looker): Yes, he is darling. You just have to get through that rough and tough exterior of his you know.
(Private Message from Diabolique): Yes, I see, I guess that is obvious.
(Private Message from Looker): What is obvious?
(Private Message from Diabolique): oh hush. you.
(Private Message from Looker): OH
(Private Message from Diabolique): So have I interrupted another fine romantic evening between you and **NastyOlGeezer**
(Private Message from Looker): Nasty ? Who is Nasty? I've forgotten everything now.
(Private Message from Diabolique): Oh have I spoiled you?
(Private Message from Looker): I HAVE LOST ALL MY CYBER LOVERS BECAUSE OF YOU
(Private Message from Diabolique): And I am reduced to merely an occasional hot and heavy flirt...all because of you...
(Private Message from Looker): So its just me...huh...no Fanny? No **Boobalicious**?
(Private Message from Diabolique): The sacrifices I've endured for you. You've ruined me, you know.

(Private Message from Looker): GRRRR.......don't you hate that?
(Private Message from Diabolique): No
(Private Message from Looker): Can I do anything to get you back in the girl's good graces??
(Private Message from Diabolique): Oh good graces I'm in... I'm sure... just not much else... I'm just not moved to accept imitations.....I suppose you might say...
(Private Message from Looker): Oh my...hmmm...what shall we do to correct this problem you find yourself faced with?
(Private Message from Diabolique): Well I suggest a steady diet of meetings like this..... a weekend alone with you...... oh let's see... and then I suppose repeat with even more frequency for the next... oh um...25 or so years...
(Private Message from Looker): LOL.....sounds like a wiener...as "they" say!!
(Private Message from Diabolique): They say, The Joneses or the Van Pattens?
(Private Message from Looker): yeah
(Private Message from Diabolique): Oh no... 'they' won't say anything..... they wouldn't understand... they'd grumble maybe... and look the other way... denying such a thing as us even exists... Nice of them huh?
(Private Message from Looker): I think so. Oh, I forgot: I LOVE YOU
(Private Message from Diabolique): And I didn't forget...I love you.....too...
(Private Message from Looker): Well you already told me that, didn't you? YOU ARE MUCH MORE EFFICIENT
(Private Message from Diabolique): I did?
(Private Message from Looker): oh I bet that was **NastyOlGeezer**...SORRY
(Private Message from Diabolique): Could have been if he were impersonating someone else, otherwise he would only say it like this...I love you, bitch, or whore... or worse?
(Private Message from Looker): HMMM.....He wouldn't dare..!!
(Private Message from Diabolique): Course he would, He's Nasty.
(Private Message from Looker): Then I must not talk to him anymore...
(Private Message from Diabolique): Okay...So enough about these foolish people in this stupid room...
(Private Message from Looker): HEHHEHE Hey now don't insult the

Neanderthals... Remember we met in the room and spend entirely too much time amongst them.

(Private Message from Diabolique): I was merely shortcutting you misunderstood... I would never disparage this fine establishment that afforded us the opportunity to meet and get to know each other. What do you think I am? A Neanderthal?

(Private Message from Looker): I don't know --let me hear you grunt......

(Private Message from Diabolique): oh hush... you...

(Private Message to Diabolique): That's hear, not here. Though you could come here.

(Private Message from Diabolique): When tomorrow? Ahem...
So...... .

(Private Message from Looker): So....besides the fact that you are the most INCREDIBLE human being I have met in a lifetime or so...and barring the fact that I love you and would give the world to be talking to you or holding your face in my hands or kissing you RIGHT NOW. Talk to me.

(Private Message from Diabolique): Mmm!

(Private Message from Looker): How can I send you a double-decker hug?

(Private Message from Diabolique): yes I need a hug from you here...For you ((((((great big bear hug))))))

(Private Message from Looker): oh my...you sure know my weakness...

(Private Message from Diabolique): yeah I guess I do...

(Private Message from Looker): I guess you know many of my weaknesses...since we are being honest with one another tonight......

(Private Message from Diabolique): You doing okay baby? Not too sad?

(Private Message from Looker): I'm okay babe. You make everything okay.

(Private Message from Diabolique): I wish that were true.

(Private Message from Looker): It is true.

(Private Message from Diabolique): but I know I have to be alone with you soon too...

(Private Message from Looker): I know, baby.

(Private Message from Diabolique): whew... okay... moving right along.....

(Private Message from Looker): Whoa! Not so fast...you heard

what I said
(Private Message from Diabolique): sorry what did you say... uh...
(Private Message from Looker): you can read my thoughts can't you. The feelings I kept having today in the misty dream sleep I was in...oh I do it a lot, mind you...but it was very strong today
(Private Message from Diabolique): yeah... of course...
(Private Message from Looker): sometimes I ache to put my real arms around you and hold you
(Private Message from Diabolique): Are you that scared of meeting me still?
(Private Message from Looker): NO
(Private Message from Diabolique): good...
(Private Message from Looker): not for the reasons that you would think...no
(Private Message from Diabolique): okay... explain... now! Oh, you of many words...
(Private Message from Looker): LOL.....NO. IT'S JUST ME.....
(Private Message from Diabolique): and I love you... so saying it's just me... is not getting you out of explaining...this to me. You mean to tell me you are nervous... for the well... typical reasons any one would be nervous about such meetings?
(Private Message from Looker): LOL...I dunno...such as??
(Private Message from Diabolique): Oh none of that playing dumb......
(Private Message from Looker): OH SURE
(Private Message from Diabolique): You're still nervous about appearances? How you look?
(Private Message from Looker): and you think I wouldn't be?
(Private Message from Diabolique): Of course you would be...and you think I care much about that?
(Private Message from Looker): Dang, Phillip...you come from the world of the beautiful people. You spent so much time in Los Angeles with all those perfect models and beach bunnies. You write wonderful words, poems, take pictures of beautiful things
(Private Message from Diabolique): Oh please... I ran screaming from those people
(Private Message from Looker): Well you might have...but you have expectations from where you have been...you can't deny that.

(Private Message from Diabolique): Expectations about..... no
(Private Message from Looker): and yes you care much about that...you're a man, very visual. It does too matter.
(Private Message from Diabolique): not when it comes to you... honestly... not when it comes to you..... It's... its not on that level at all...
(Private Message from Looker): I'm glad of that...although I'm not really sure I believe it. But the getting over is the hard part...so that is good.
(Private Message from Diabolique): I got over most of the bullshit... a long time ago... Not completely immune to it of course... but completely over it... You are nervous about it. You aren't too afraid are you?...
(Private Message from Looker): but no...I am not nervous to meet you or be alone with you or any of the things you might think other than I just worry...
(Private Message from Diabolique): good...
(Private Message from Looker): not afraid at all...well...in the beginning perhaps afraid a bit...
(Private Message from Diabolique): why do you worry.....
(Private Message from Looker): I have told you why I worry and you keep reassuring me...and I keep worrying.
(Private Message from Diabolique): okay...
(Private Message from Looker): You aren't really scared or worried, but you are something.....
(Private Message from Diabolique): I'm nervous...of course...but no I'm not scared, or worried...
(Private Message from Looker): lol.....
(Private Message from Looker): then tell me....really.....what are you the most nervous of? 'cause maybe I should be too and don't know it...LOL
(Private Message from Diabolique): Little things...I don't know... Nothing important.
(Private Message from Looker): I'm trying not to laugh...
(Private Message from Diabolique): you can laugh...
(Private Message from Looker): I failed
(Private Message from Diabolique): it's very silly...but ...
(Private Message from Looker): thanks...no was finishing .... "little things" go on and be serious.......please!
(Private Message from Diabolique): lol...
(Private Message from Looker): ((((((BIG HUG.....NOT LETTING

GO))))))))
(Private Message from Diabolique): Never?
(Private Message from Looker): nope!
(Private Message from Diabolique): I want ... oh I don't know...
(Private Message from Looker): its ok...
(Private Message from Diabolique): I want to hold you... make love to you... make you crazy, make you happy, make you laugh... all of it... so...
(Private Message from Looker): so???? Where's the downside?????
(Private Message from Diabolique): there is none... so.....
(Private Message from Looker): so.........surely you aren't afraid...or (excuse me) ... nervous...that you won't do all those things?
(Private Message from Diabolique): No... just nervous
(Private Message from Looker): Please don't be
(Private Message from Diabolique): a few minutes after being with you... I won't be I don't think...I can't imagine I would be
(Private Message from Looker): now you wouldn't be at all...and I can't imagine how you could be either
(Private Message from Diabolique): good...now hush you
(Private Message from Looker): but ------- you keep making me shut up!!!! ----------but you have to understand that I will never feel physically comfortable with you
(Private Message from Diabolique): I will make sure you will be.....but I understand the pre-meeting jitters... of course... hell, I have them too as I'm trying to tell you... I'm not really all that great ya know
(Private Message from Looker): NO...I AM AFRAID I DONT KNOW. What I do know is great beyond words so I have NO idea what you're talking about
(Private Message from Diabolique): and you are beyond words as well... so we worry for no reason at all... or for the silliest of reasons... Oh the glitch is a logical one...
(Private Message from Looker): probably so......maybe one day we will look back at this little glitch
(Private Message from Diabolique): but that's rather silly ... in our case
(Private Message from Looker): and laugh our fool heads off. go on

(Private Message from Diabolique): Yes.
(Private Message from Looker): GO ON
(Private Message from Diabolique): I'm hugging you in my brain
(Private Message from Looker): I was just recalling a conversation I had with you in my head today.........I recall something very much like that we said to one another... What are you thinking, sweetie?
(Private Message from Diabolique): Imagining I can see your reflection somehow on the other side... your eyes...looking deep into them...smiling at you...stroking your cheek with the back of my hand...telling you how I feel so much less lost than I've felt... probably ever before.
(Private Message from Looker): mmmm....I was just staring at the screen again
(Private Message from Diabolique): I love you Patricia.
(Private Message from Looker): Oh Phillip.......we love one another SO much...I know......and I have done nothing to make you feel less lost.........and it makes me cry to hear you say that......except to just love you as naturally as can be. No flowering explanation...I just love you so much that you know how sometimes you tell someone you could just squeeze them to death? Well, that's how I feel......like if I ever got you in my arms that I would never ever want to let go of you or let you let go of me
(Private Message from Diabolique): you mean when your arms are around me and mine are around you... I know.
(Private Message from Looker): yes of course...you do
(Private Message from Diabolique): I hope I know... I'd better know
(Private Message from Looker): have you ever really thought about the first time we meet??
(Private Message from Diabolique): a lot...
(Private Message from Looker): ME TOO
(Private Message from Diabolique): lol!
(Private Message from Looker): tell me what you think or it will be like--not what we want it to be like.
(Private Message from Diabolique): We will nearly die the moment before.....
(Private Message from Looker): LOL
(Private Message from Diabolique): and then...our eyes will meet. Panic will completely and utterly dissolve... we'll

become..... well each other for a moment or two... I'll smile, you will too... you'll try to look away, I won't let you, that will make you a little nervous...and I'll kiss you... and our arms will go around each other...and that's all she wrote

(Private Message from Looker): YEP

(Private Message from Diabolique): If we meet and we aren't alone.....now that will be a little awkward.

(Private Message from Looker): but wonderful as well

(Private Message from Diabolique): the hug... the polite kiss...the whisper...(I love you so much).....and... the drawing into each other... the looking away before too much trouble is caused... dance... will play out for a while. I'll suggest a walk or some way to get you alone for a few minutes.....And after your lipstick is already gone, or messed up ...(how convenient...).....And we'll go for a walk...to hug, and kiss and compose each other... and return...and plot how the hell we can be alone... for a while. Silly?

(Private Message from Looker): SILLY? NO!!! it's very much the dream I have for the two of us...only my greatest desire is to be able to show you how wonderful you are...and also to show you that I am not as inept as I appear...but then what if I fail?

(Private Message from Diabolique): You are not inept at all... and I know that. And you won't fail...and I won't fail you...

(Private Message from Looker): I know you won't.......you never have

(Private Message from Diabolique): And it won't be absolutely perfect... and it shouldn't be... because if it was it wouldn't be real

(Private Message from Looker): What???? You're not perfect?????

(Private Message from Diabolique): ah but yes...I am a legend in my own mind! lol

(Private Message from Looker): LOL! At least he's GOT a mind...lol!

(Private Message from Diabolique): you make me laugh!

(Private Message from Looker): that's what will make it fun...and amid all the love we have and all the joy and all the PLEASURE...we will always have fun and make each other laugh and find the real joy in one another that we have misplaced sometimes.

(Private Message from Diabolique): of course...wonderfully

stated...god that was it exactly... Patricia, of course
(Private Message from Looker): Then we can do that..........can't we?
(Private Message from Diabolique): yes of course we can... I love you more than I can ever tell you on a screen with blue letters... or white letters or polka dotted letters...and I want to create with you..... I want to be with you, I want to work with you and we will... The hardest part is right now... knowing what's around the corner and having to hold on right now... for a few more months...
(Private Message from Looker): we will...we have to accomplish all we want to
(Private Message from Diabolique): Yes sharing ourselves with others may be a little difficult... but we'll do okay with that.
(Private Message from Looker): oh sure...lord, no one knows better than we do how multi-faceted we are
(Private Message from Diabolique): indeed
(Private Message from Looker): I had a very pitiful but necessary talk with myself today...about what has happened and about being depressed and feeling alone and all that...I tossed it out somewhere in the desert! We need to plan on meeting in the near future ...... you game?
(Private Message from Diabolique): Yes... and probably in season too...
(Private Message from Looker): oh sheesh...when are you NOT in season? JEJEJE oops damm HEHEHEHE......LOL I can't type.
(Private Message from Diabolique): when am I not in season? for you? never
(Private Message from Looker): speaking of which
(Private Message from Diabolique): yes???
(Private Message from Looker): I found myself feeling fairly uncomfortable a couple of times (probably more) these past few days.
(Private Message from Diabolique): Why were you uncomfortable?
(Private Message from Looker): well, Mr. Intuitive...I figured you'd know why!..
(Private Message from Diabolique): well I love making you say things out loud you know...imagine the expression on your face as you do...the one underneath rolling your eyes... yes...
(Private Message from Looker): I have many expressions...as I'm sure you do, too.

(Private Message from Diabolique): You think?
(Private Message from Looker): Yeah!
(Private Message from Diabolique): lol...
(Private Message from Looker): I don't have funny voices though
(Private Message from Diabolique): good... I'll do the voices
(Private Message from Looker): oh thank god...for a minute there, I thought you might expect that from me!
(Private Message from Diabolique): no... you operate the puppet in my pocket... I'll do the voices.....lol
(Private Message from Looker): ROFL......you think I can do that? I mean properly?
(Private Message from Diabolique): probably with no training whatsoever...
(Private Message from Looker): you hate it when your mind drifts, huh?
(Private Message from Diabolique): mmmm
(Private Message from Looker): oh Phillip, how can I love you more than this moment? leaning up toward you... waiting for the kiss you owe me........
(Private Message from Diabolique): leaning toward you pressing my lips against yours softly, tenderly at first, just glad to touch, and feel your lips against mine... savoring the touch, smell, my senses... my heart racing too fast... the need to do more. so much more...but for now... right now... the touching of our lips, focused on the feeling of that... and nothing else...until my tongue softly touches your upper lip. tickling both the tip of my tongue and your lip... tracing...to the corner of your mouth...and back...sucking gently your lip into my mouth slightly scratching your lip with my teeth...and my tongue licking just barely underneath...tracing...feeling your breath...warm...
(Private Message from Looker): mmmmm
(Private Message from Diabolique): and touching the tip of your tongue... holding our tongues barely touching, as if in a kiss... for a moment...and then retreating for the moment...ending this first kiss.....opening our eyes... looking into each other...I love you
(Private Message from Looker): I love you
(Private Message from Diabolique): and we kiss more passionately this time.....I hold your face in my hands...my hands moving to the back of your head, your neck, caressing, holding...as our

lips, kiss again...many baby kisses...faster and more passionate until our tongues touch our lips again..... and then each other's tongues... and then I explore your mouth... deeply...teasing, and just as we need to breathe... and have forgotten...in our passion, I separate our lips... as we both gulp air... not stopping... continuing... even more passionately...my hands now moving down your back...my arms squeezing you tightly... I can't get close enough to you...feeling you touching you...and rubbing against you...my kisses passionate... as I lead your tongue into my mouth...and then I suck hungrily at your tongue...

(Private Message from Looker): yes...oh yes ahhhh......oh baby.......I want to be lost in you so badly...but more than that, I want you lost in me so close we really can't tell where one of us stops and one of us starts... I love you Phillip.... I want to show you how much, somehow.

(Private Message from Diabolique): I love you too, Patricia.

(Private Message from Looker): This is so hard.......but so wonderful because we know what is in store...at least in a partial way.....the real way will blow us away, I am afraid.

(Private Message from Diabolique): it will blow us together...and we won't be afraid...at all...I hold you so tight against me ,Patricia, and my kisses...your mouth, your cheek... down your neck your shoulder...hugging you... snuggling... now... squeezing you too tight and my hands holding your ass, mmm never too tight I am sure

(Private Message from Looker): mmm no...not too tight...no never.....pushing myself against you as hard as I can...feeling you against me...rubbing my open hands along your back and hips and ass and then back to your shoulders...feeling you press tighter to me

(Private Message from Diabolique): and finding your lips again... kissing them over and over again....hungrily...then more.....oh yes!

(Private Message from Looker): yes........pushing our tongues as deep as we can, as if we can't get deep enough

(Private Message from Diabolique): yes..... my hands moving all over your body...on your back, your ass, caressing and traveling and exploring and massaging and lightly scratching and moving between the front of us... and cupping your breasts and feeling your nipples... and pinching them lightly...running my hands down your stomach and rubbing between your legs and feeling the heat pouring through your jeans...and moving my hands around in back of you again...rubbing and pulling you tighter into me...as our wild kissing continues never stopping, making noises, moaning and gasping for air and finally..... we pause...and look deeply into each other's eyes...smile

(Private Message from Looker): ah......yes ...not too bad, huh?

(Private Message from Diabolique): not bad Patricia... for beginners, that is... yes it is...good and I breathe softly into your ear...

(Private Message from Looker): and when you pause you move away from me slightly and I slip my hand down your chest, your stomach and under your waistband.....moving lower and touching you slightly and feel you hard and erect pushing against your pants...I put my hand around it.....easily at first and begin to glide it up and down.....slowly

(Private Message from Diabolique): oh god I suck on your earlobe scratching it with my teeth...my hands unbuttoning your blouse...oh yesyes...off they go...as I can't wait to get them the hell off

(Private Message from Looker): I smile as you hurry clumsily...now I giggle and tickle the head of your cock with my thumb.....mmmmm

(Private Message from Diabolique): oh and I moan and pause for a moment and then finish pulling off the pants

(Private Message from Looker): and when you do the pit of my stomach hardens.....holding your cock harder now.....a tight ring with my hand and my fingers.....pumping my hand faster ......pumping......I can no longer be quiet and begin to moan and move .....pumping a little faster. I let my head fall back and move away from you...your cock still in my hand but I pull it a little harder and you moan loudly.......easily

(Private Message from Diabolique): now pulling off your blouse.....undoing your bra...

(Private Message from Looker): ooh

(Private Message from Diabolique): mmmm and I can't help but to kiss my way onto your breasts... trying to tease you a little between my moans

(Private Message from Looker): yes!

(Private Message from Diabolique): and finding your nipples... licking them... pulling them into my mouth...hard... and then biting your nipples.....pulling them through my teeth... flicking them with my tongue...pushing your breasts together..... rubbing my thumb over your nipples!

(Private Message from Looker): ahhhhhhh...I reach up with my free hand and push my breast deeper into your mouth..... massaging it.....my hand on your cock moving frantically now...down and cupping your hard balls......your cock red and throbbing......pushing against my stomach.

(Private Message from Diabolique): and I push my leg into you a little harder... rubbing it against you, both of us on fire

(Private Message from Looker): oh god Phillip!

(Private Message from Diabolique): as I lick your nipples with my tongue... and suck both of them at the same time into my mouth...playing with the nipples with my tongue...and moving them against my teeth in the back of my mouth...until I can gently bite both of them...and then a little harder...sucking...mmmmm

(Private Message from Looker): we slide to the floor.......never separating......and you reach down and begin to loosen your pants and kick them off with your feet.

(Private Message from Diabolique): I moan loudly..... and kiss my way down...moving awkwardly so you can continue to touch me...as I unsnap and slide your jeans and panties off at the same time

(Private Message from Looker): Using my feet I kick them down my legs.....but as I do I slide lower and lower.....away from your grasp and your lips.......and pushing your legs apart..... I slide between them...and move my mouth down onto your cock.....not teasing or sucking but gently taking your whole cock deep into my mouth and holding it there......not sucking or moving my tongue.......just enveloping it...... deeply...... very still.....listening to you moan softly at first...then louder

(Private Message from Diabolique): oh god ohhhhhhhhhhh yesssssssss

(Private Message from Looker): your hands falling away and resting on the floor.....your heart beating fast..... your breathing is jerky.....stopping sometimes..... then easily I begin to move my mouth up and down the length of your cock..... till only the tip is in my mouth...my tongue rolled tight and playing against it.....sucking easily.....quietly...slowly.....then easing back down the length of you......sucking as I go......till you are deep in my mouth.....my fingers scratching lightly the insides of your thighs...your own movements cause your cock to move inside my mouth.

(Private Message from Diabolique): yessssssssss

(Private Message from Looker): so I take my hands and cup your balls.....and begin to suck you up and down very fast.....all the way out to the tip.....holding my lips tight around you.....my tongue playing with the tip of your cock.....pushing into you...moving round and round...then licking you...enjoying you. your moans.....the way your eyes are only half open..... yes.....I glance up and watch you as I move down your cock again.....with deliberate ease.....slowly.....but not teasingly...sucking a little harder as I go...stopping... sucking.....deeper.....deeper...then I hold you there and stop sucking and just hold your cock tightly in my mouth

(Private Message from Diabolique): ohhhh

(Private Message from Looker): I feel your cock move in my mouth and I caress it with my lips again...carefully I let the tip of my finger move around your ass.....

(Private Message from Diabolique): Yes... looking for a moment then my head falling back down .....allowing myself to feel helpless...

(Private Message from Looker): sucking a little harder on your cock...moving it in and out of my mouth getting you very wet...

(Private Message from Diabolique): you are soooo good

(Private Message from Looker): now...faster.....faster.....my finger rubbing against you

(Private Message from Diabolique): uhhhhhh

(Private Message from Looker): and drinking your cock as far down my throat as I can.....sucking hard...too hard

(Private Message from Diabolique): ohhhhh

(Private Message from Looker): come on baby.....sucking you hard...

(Private Message from Diabolique): oh yessssss

(Private Message from Looker): I move my head and let you fuck my mouth...

(Private Message from Diabolique): Gonna make me ... ohhhhh.....

(Private Message from Looker): My fingers moving...pressing against the soft skin.....pushing a little ...... sucking you..... You push in and out of my mouth and I almost gag, but let you....want to make you feel so good

(Private Message from Diabolique): I stop you before it's too late and pull you up to me, finding your lips and kissing you deeply, so deeply, our mouths hot and open with desire... gasping for breath I break our kiss, to kiss my way over to your cheeks. Kissing my way down to your neck.

(Private Message from Looker): Oh my, Phillip! I can't be still

(Private Message from Diabolique): and I kiss you between your breasts, sucking some skin gently, scratching your skin lightly with my teeth, and driving you crazy.

(Private Message from Looker): You are DEFINITELY driving me crazy...

(Private Message from Diabolique): As I kiss your breasts, I get closer to your hard nipples that are waiting expectantly for my kiss. And as I get closer, as you feel my hot breath, I raise my head away from you.

(Private Message from Looker): No!

(Private Message from Diabolique): Looking into your half open eyes. Smiling gently at you, for a moment, teasing you. And then I take my tongue and lightly, too lightly touch the tip of your nipple. And then again. And then I flick your nipple as you arch your back wanting me to suck your breast, needing me to suck your breast.

(Private Message from Looker): Yes, baby.

(Private Message from Diabolique): ... licking your nipples, alternately sucking them deeper into my mouth..................

(Private Message from Looker): Oh god, Phillip, you're driving me insane!!!

(Private Message from Diabolique): I look up at you and see you are looking at me and I smile at you.....I kiss my way lower... kissing lower. You raise your hips and open up for me. I can feel your heat, smell your aroma....I breathe warmly on you between your legs without touching you...my tongue reaches out and barely touches your pussy lips. My fingers open you up, expose you to me.

(Private Message from Looker): Oh baby, I'm touching myself

(Private Message from Diabolique): Yes, touch yourself and imagine it is my tongue, lightly touching your clitoris. Teasing you again. Driving you crazy. Enjoy yourself as my words somehow become real...you find it impossible to lie still.

And then I push my face into you... tasting you. Sucking your clitoris gently into my mouth... my tongue going crazy on it

(Private Message from Looker): Ohhhhhhh...

(Private Message from Diabolique): I enjoy driving you crazy, baby... My tongue finds you so wet, and you taste SO good!!! I hold your ass in my hands so you don't move too much and then I pull you onto my face.

(Private Message from Looker): Uh my hands holding the back of your head, my fingers playing with your hair, rubbing myself against you

(Private Message from Diabolique): My tongue moving in and out and all around and oh you feel me, baby, you feel me! My tongue so deep inside of you...

(Private Message from Looker): mmmm!!!!

(Private Message from Diabolique): I gently insert a finger...and then two...in and out, all the while I keep licking and sucking and fucking you with my tongue. Faster and faster and you move against me wanting it, wanting me...

(Private Message from Looker): Ohhhh yessssssssss...and whatever you do, don't stop!!!

(Private Message from Diabolique): I can feel your orgasm building and building and building...your pussy squeezing my fingers...you're even wetter than before...you scream and push yourself up off the bed my...fingers buried deep inside of you.... And then move more slowly... letting you catch your breath

(Private Message from Looker): Oh Phillip......I love you so much Phillip.

(Private Message from Diabolique): And I love you, Patricia.

(Private Message to Diabolique): I pull you up to me. Wanting to hold you, kiss you. Our mouths open, licking kissing, tasting myself on your lips. My arms and legs wrapped around you, wanting to get closer to you... Wanting you inside of me, needing to feel you inside of me, now.

(Private Message from Diabolique): And I push myself into you, sliding easily inside of you.

(Private Message from Looker): Yes, and my hands move down your back and push your ass into me, I want all of you inside of me....filling me up, slowly and easily moving inside my hot, wet pussy.

(Private Message from Diabolique): I move with you as we create

a rhythm. Our bodies rubbing against each other. Our skin, hot, moist rubbing and holding each other.
(Private Message from Looker): You're so hard, so big, filling me up so completely... Moving in and out of me as I squeeze you, baby. Squeeze your wonderful hot throbbing cock. I want you so much...I am needing you soooo much!
(Private Message from Diabolique): yes, baby
(Private Message from Looker): Fuck me, Phillip, don't just make love to me, but fuck me!!! I need you now!!! I need you to thrust your hard cock in and out as hard as you can...I want you to think of yourself now. Let me make you feel so good. Thrust yourself in and out of my pussy as my legs wrap around you...and lick your face...and moan for you....
(Private Message from Diabolique): Oh gawd oh yes!!! Faster and faster
(Private Message from Looker): Yes baby, faster, come on baby. I need you. I want you, faster... harder... you're making me cum again!!! Cum with me please my love...explode into me
(Private Message from Diabolique): ohyesohyesohyes...I'm cummmmingggggg!!!
(Private Message from Looker): yes, baby... oh yes....
(Private Message from Diabolique): Oh Patricia.
(Private Message from Looker): Mmmmm that was wonderful Phillip.....
(Private Message from Diabolique): YOU were wonderful.
(Private Message from Looker): Mmmm, Oh you make me feel so good.
(Private Message from Diabolique): It takes two
(Private Message from Looker): Yes... it does...You okay?.
(Private Message from Diabolique): I'm great.
(Private Message from Looker): now I want you to sleep baby. Get in your bed, pretend I'm with you, holding you, and fall asleep in my arms...
(Private Message from Diabolique): Yes, I'd like that...I love you
(Private Message from Looker): And I love you, Phillip.

CONNECTION CLOSED

Chapter Twenty-one

Frank was typing frantically on his keyboard, his fingers moving faster than they ever had. His heart was racing, his mouth was dry. The colors on the monitor were as bright and vibrant as a neon sign.

"No, damn it! No!" he typed. "Listen to me, it cannot be this way. It is not going to be this way. Do you hear me?!" Frank gasped for breath. "This has gone too far and it has to stop right now. Do you understand?"

It was as if his computer monitor were alive. It seemed to be expanding and contracting, mocking him as his own chest rose and fell with each labored breath. He was shaking now, and the sweat dropped quickly from his brow. He stopped typing and waited for an answer.

He froze as the screen in front of him became like a pool of colored, swirling fog. He watched helplessly as a hand emerged from the mist and pointed a gun at him. He saw the finger press against the trigger. He saw the flash explode from the muzzle…

"No!" Frank was sitting up in bed. His T-shirt was soaked with sweat. He was out of breath. It had been so real. Again, the nightmare.

It had been several weeks, but he believed he would somehow cope with everything that had happened and find some way to forgive himself. Besides, maybe he wasn't really responsible.

He cried for the first time since Alma's funeral. How he longed for her embrace, to have her cradle his head against her breasts as she told him quietly that everything would be all right, that they would work together and get through this, that somehow she would find it within herself to forgive him his indiscretion.

He had promised her that he would change and be the loving man she'd fallen in love with. They had been the most extraordinarily passionate lovers only to see their love grow too familiar, then cold, and finally lead to resentment. It could spark and burn hot again. He knew that. He wanted that. They could once again be the lovers who had risked everything for each other. And they could watch as that excitement blossomed and matured over the years into quieter and even more complete love that would protect them both against the outside world.

So why then did Frank have doubts? Why could he not understand that the loss of the babies was not a punishment. He'd started thinking that he was wrong; that perhaps their love wasn't meant to be. Why did he let the resentment build inside of him? Why did he believe that Alma blamed him for what had happened and that she felt this was their punishment for defying their families and falling in love?

He regretted waiting so long before talking to her about it. He regretted even more that he'd been less than totally honest when he did talk about it. He hadn't realized how depressed she'd become, that she believed she'd somehow failed him by not producing a child. All he saw was that she had grown cold, distant. She'd rejected his admittedly feeble attempts to bridge the gap between them, and he took these rejections as proof she no longer loved him rather than the signs of her feelings of inadequacy.

Frank had interpreted her silence as anger at the fact he'd taken her away from her family and her culture. It was their illicit love that now demanded payment. The price was that they would never have the child they had wanted so badly.

Alma hated Frank for that and of course would never forgive him for the curse he had put on them, or so Frank had allowed himself to believe. Alma had been depressed, feeling she had failed her husband and there was no way she could make it up to him. She didn't want him to forgive her. What was there to forgive? She had failed him. She had failed them both. She would make it easy for him. She would not let him waste any more time with her. She was not worthy of his love and affections.

When Alma finally began to recover from her depression and realize she was not to blame, they had already grown far apart. Perhaps they could adopt a child, she thought, and that way repair the damage that had been done to their marriage.

But the space between them had grown too wide. They didn't talk about it. Both believed the other resented and hated them for bringing on the curse. Neither spoke of it, neither dared. Had this been a true love, they would been drawn closer together rather than being driven apart. If this was the test, they had failed.

A few years ago, however, there had been a change. They had reached out for each other again and begun to renew their love and passion. They came to realize that they still had each other. Whether their union was a blessing or a curse, they still had each other.

Then there was the vacation to Mexico, and a friend's beach house they would use for two weeks. It was to be a second honeymoon for them. Almost immediately in this foreign place, a passion seemed to be reborn. It was as if they'd been given permission to forget the past and to rediscover each other anew. They made love with an intensity unknown to them for the past three years.

It was while making love, however, that something again changed. Frank wanted to show Alma how much he still loved and desired her. He wanted to please her. On this night, he wanted her to reach heights of pleasure she perhaps had never experienced before. And so he began to make love to her by kissing her all over her body.

She resisted him when he gently pushed her legs apart and began kissing her as intimately as is possible. He continued, believing she would soon relax and give herself over to the sensations of pleasure. Instead, she began to cry. He stopped—confused, hurt, rejected. She was ashamed of herself. She couldn't let him do that to her. Certainly not that. She had no right to feel such pleasure when she was not even capable of producing a child. When he tried to hold her and comfort her, she pushed him away and ran from the bed and locked herself in the bathroom where she remained for several hours, crying softly in shame and embarrassment.

Their love changed forever that night. She had rejected him. There was no denying that in his mind. Still, when she came out of the bathroom, they hugged and then fell asleep in each other's arms. Eventually, their relationship changed into one of close friendship. They remained supportive of each other, devoted to each other, and respectful of one another. And it seemed to be enough.

Over time, Alma became close friends with Patricia Ridgeway, a coworker at the library. Patricia's Native American heritage seemed to give Alma something in common with her own Spanish-Indian background. Patricia and Trent and Alma and Frank saw each other frequently, enjoying dinners at each other's houses or at a local restaurant, going out to listen to blues or jazz or country singers at a local nightclub, and attending the occasional community theater performance. Alma would sometimes accompany Patricia and her friend, Sylvia Mondragon, on a girls' night out. Frank would take advantage of these occasions to put in a few extra hours of work or to spend time with his own friends. It was easy for Frank and for Alma to forget how completely dedicated to one another they once had been. They now had interests and activities apart from each other, and they enjoyed the times they had alone.

Frank Garrett had known almost nothing about computers, so he signed up to take a beginner's course at the community college. Soon, he bought himself a home computer and learned how to type better, how to operate a word processing program, and even how to do his household accounts on the computer. He found himself preferring the computer to watching television at night, while Alma put herself to sleep reading a book. He signed up for Internet access and enjoyed learning how to find and explore the endless websites, particularly those set up by other law enforcement agencies around the country.

And he discovered and was quickly fascinated by the adult websites. He was both shocked and titillated at how explicit many of the sites were with their pornographic pictures, erotic stories, and promises of free and unbridled sex. He was aroused by a lot of it, although there was still part of him that was disgusted by what he saw.

He eventually explored the world of adult chatrooms where he found that people from all over the world were able to talk to each other about anything they wanted. Rarely did he get involved in any conversations in these chatrooms. He remained a lurker, a watcher. He turned down or ignored offers of cybersex, until one evening when he decided it was time to be adventurous.

He'd logged into a chatroom under his usual nickname of ManInBlue, and almost immediately a woman who claimed to be a large-busted blonde college student with a weakness for police officers began flirting with him. She introduced him to the world of "private messages" with which two people could communicate without the others in the chatroom knowing what they were saying. It was in such a private message that she wanted him to masturbate while she gave him a cyber-blow job. Frank was too uncomfortable to actually do that, but he did find himself quite obviously aroused as the woman graphically typed out what she desired to do to him.

A few nights later, he flirted with someone else. She'd even asked him to call her on the phone and talk dirty to her while she masturbated; Frank again declined, but they did have cybersex. Frank was surprised he was able to type such graphically erotic things and send them over the Internet. He was also more than a bit self-conscious, aware that Alma could wake up and discover him sitting in front of his computer simulating sex with some stranger.

His concerns couldn't diminish his excitement, however, and after the cybersex encounter, he went into the bathroom and masturbated as he fantasized about having a wild, passionate, and anonymous sexual encounter. When he'd finished, a flood of guilt immediately washed over him. What kind of sick perverted animal was he? This was wrong, very wrong.

As a result, Frank resisted the urge to chat on the Internet for several nights after that. Even when he began visiting the chatrooms again, he resisted the urge to have cybersex encounters. He began to frequent a chatroom called LoveMining. He enjoyed teasing and flirting with many of the people he encountered there and he returned night after night for several weeks, getting to know the personalities behind many of the names listed there. He created a somewhat truthful identity for himself, that of a police officer in the southwest who had separated from his wife and was looking for a new and exciting relationship. The experience in that chatroom, he realized, was very much like becoming a regular in a bar. It was as if he were dropping by for a few drinks, chatting, and flirting with people who were slowly becoming friends.

Occasionally, there were new people in the chatroom, but usually it was the same twenty or thirty or so who entered, greeted each other, chatted, and then left. Frank was becoming relaxed and enjoying the experience more and more.

A couple of personalities intrigued him. One in particular was a somewhat quiet woman named Silky who attracted him enough that he'd had several private talks with her in which he told her a lot of personal (and truthful) things about himself. Although Silky had not gone into great detail about herself, she did seem to be genuinely interested in him. The rumor in the room that they were carrying on a hot affair was a bit premature, but the relationship did move rather quickly in that direction.

After many weeks of private conversations, ManInBlue and Silky consummated their friendship with cybersex. Frank tried to be less crude than he had been in his only other cybersex encounters, and Silky seemed to enjoy giving him great pleasure. She told him that she wanted to please him in absolutely any way he desired. She even suggested that she could use Frank's handcuffs to render him helpless while she drove him crazy for hours. Their cybersex trysts continued for weeks, frequently incorporating light sadomasochism. Frank found it oddly exhilarating when Silky would describe handcuffing him or tying him up. Frank might have gone too far one night when he suggested that Silky might please him even more by bringing another woman into their relationship.

(Private Message from Silky): I can't believe you could even suggest such a thing.

(Private Message from ManInBlue): I didn't mean to upset you, my love...

(Private Message from Silky): You disappoint me, Frank. I thought you were different from most men, but I see you're just like all the rest of them.

(Private Message from ManInBlue): I thought it might be something you would enjoy also. I wasn't being merely selfish.

(Private Message from Silky): I want you to be selfish -- but

selfish about just me.
(Private Message from ManInBlue): I'm sorry
(Private Message from Silky): I am willing to do anything for you, to give you pleasure, but not to share you with another woman. I want to be completely and utterly devoted to you mind, body and soul. And I want that from you.
(Private Message from ManInBlue): Okay, I understand and I'm sorry. I hope you will forgive me, I love you so much the last thing in the world I want to do is hurt you my love.
(Private Message from Silky): When we meet, which I hope will be soon, we must be completely honest with each other.
(Private Message from ManInBlue): Yes. Absolutely.
(Private Message from Silky): You told me that the love you have for me is more real and more powerful than anything you've ever felt before in your entire life.
(Private Message from ManInBlue): I said that and I meant it. I think about you all the time and I can hardly wait till I can hold you in my arms.
(Private Message from Silky): Somehow, I'm not convinced you love me as truly or passionately as you say you do...what if I don't look like you expect me to look? What if I am not what you think I am?
(Private Message from ManInBlue): I've grown to know you pretty well, Silky, and I love what I know about you.
(Private Message from Silky): If you know me so well why do you still hurt my feelings and suggest horrible things to me?
(Private Message from ManInBlue): Damn it! I told you I was sorry. Please forgive me. I love you so much and I'm more than ready to meet you, and I will love you no matter what.
(Private Message from Silky): No matter what? What if I was 90 years old? Or 15 years old? What if I was fat? Or skinny? Or if I was...other than what you expect... you think you would still love me?
(Private Message from ManInBlue): I know I would still love you, Silky. I don't care what you look like, I only know that I love you...
(Private Message from Silky): Words are easy. Why should I believe you.
(Private Message from ManInBlue): Why are you acting like this?
(Private Message from Silky): Why am I acting like a bitch ... that what you mean?

(Private Message from ManInBlue): No that's not what I meant.
(Private Message from Silky): It isn't?
(Private Message from ManInBlue): No, it isn't. I got you upset and you have a right to be mad at me. I'm sorry.
(Private Message from Silky): You think you know me, you think you know how to treat me but you don't. You don't know too much at all.
(Private Message from ManInBlue): Teach me, then.
(Private Message from Silky): I'm not your teacher, I'm not your mother. I'm the one you say you love.
(Private Message from ManInBlue): Yes, I love you.
(Private Message from Silky): I know you think you do.
(Private Message from ManInBlue): I don't think I do, I know I do.
(Private Message from Silky): You know you do? Really?
(Private Message from ManInBlue): Yes. Absolutely.
(Private Message from Silky): You have not put your love to the test.
(Private Message from ManInBlue): What do you mean...
(Private Message from Silky): We are just people on a screen in a computer chatroom. You haven't risked anything.
(Private Message from ManInBlue): What do you mean?
(Private Message from Silky): Would you meet me?
(Private Message from ManInBlue): I told you I would. Whenever you're ready.
(Private Message from Silky): Maybe I'm ready now.
(Private Message from ManInBlue): Then let's make plans to meet. I want you so bad.
(Private Message from Silky): Are you sure?
(Private Message from ManInBlue): Yes, I am sure.
(Private Message from Silky): Be careful what you wish for, it may come true.
(Private Message from ManInBlue): I hope you and I are able to be together for a long time.
(Private Message from Silky): You better mean that, Frank. Would you leave your wife for me?
(Private Message from ManInBlue): What do you want me to say?
(Private Message from Silky): The truth.
(Private Message from ManInBlue): I probably would leave her for you, yes.
(Private Message from Silky): PROBABLY??!!!

(Private Message from ManInBlue): I mean I would leave her, but it would take time.
(Private Message from Silky): Time yes... I think I understand.
(Private Message from ManInBlue): You will need to understand this because it's very complicated with my position and everything.
(Private Message from Silky): Yes, your position. A police officer.
(Private Message from ManInBlue): A sheriff actually.
(Private Message from Silky): Oh, you're a sheriff now are you?
(Private Message from ManInBlue): As a matter of fact, yes.
(Private Message from Silky): Why didn't you tell me that before?
(Private Message from ManInBlue): I'm not sure. But I do want you to know everything about me because I really do love you and need you.
(Private Message from Silky): And you must tell me everything, the truth if our love is to be real.
(Private Message from ManInBlue): Yes, I know I must and you must also.
(Private Message from Silky): I will meet you, show you and tell you everything you need to know about me. Perhaps I will come to visit you. You're in Taos, right?
(Private Message from ManInBlue): Yes, Taos.
(Private Message from Silky): I have a friend who's gone to college near there.
(Private Message from ManInBlue): You know a lot about me, more than I know about you.
(Private Message from Silky): True, but you will get to know a lot about me, Frank. A lot. And I'm not sure that you will love me when you know everything.
(Private Message from ManInBlue): Would you please quit talking like that. Please tell me anything you need to tell me. I won't judge you.
(Private Message from Silky): You're a sheriff...of course you judge. You always judge
(Private Message from ManInBlue): But not you
(Private Message from Silky): How do I know you won't?
(Private Message from ManInBlue): Because I love you and I tell you I won't.
(Private Message from Silky): Easy to say.

(Private Message from ManInBlue): Stop this...
(Private Message from Silky): Stop what?
(Private Message from ManInBlue): Playing this game.
(Private Message from Silky): I'm not playing a game, Frank. I'm reaching out to you and I'm trying to make you understand that I don't think we are just two people who are having a little fun in a chatroom.
(Private Message from ManInBlue): I don't think that either.
(Private Message from Silky): But sometimes you say things that make me wonder.
(Private Message from ManInBlue): I've already said I was sorry about that.
(Private Message from Silky): You will have to prove yourself to me, Frank.
(Private Message from ManInBlue): What can I do?
(Private Message from Silky): I don't know yet. I don't even know if there's anything you can do that will make me feel more comfortable or not.
(Private Message from ManInBlue): What do you mean you don't know?
(Private Message from Silky): I don't know, Frank. I don't know if you love me enough. Enough.
(Private Message from ManInBlue): Silky stop this, I told you how much I love you...
(Private Message from Silky): I know and I love you, Frank. But sometimes that is not enough...
(Private Message from ManInBlue): I believe it is always enough.
(Private Message from Silky): Enough to overcome anything?
(Private Message from ManInBlue): Yes.
(Private Message from Silky): Do you really believe you can love someone enough to overcome anything?
(Private Message from ManInBlue): Yes of course.
(Private Message from Silky): What if I was lying to you about everything?
(Private Message from ManInBlue): I don't believe you have lied to me. But I suppose if you have, then I would be in love with the lie... of course
(Private Message from Silky): How much would you forgive? Could you forgive?
(Private Message from ManInBlue): What do you mean?

(Private Message from Silky): I'm not sure what I mean. But if you love someone enough you can forgive them just about anything couldn't you?
(Private Message from ManInBlue): Of course. And people in love do that all the time.
(Private Message from Silky): Yes, but could you do that? Could you forgive someone almost anything?
(Private Message from ManInBlue): I could forgive you, almost anything...
(Private Message from Silky): Oh, you think so?
(Private Message from ManInBlue): Yes I think so... what do I need to forgive?
(Private Message from Silky): There are always things to forgive.
(Private Message from ManInBlue): Then, will you forgive me?
(Private Message from Silky): I will and already have.
(Private Message from ManInBlue): I love you.
(Private Message from Silky): Is it a love that exists apart from this place?
(Private Message from ManInBlue): Yes, I told you it was.
(Private Message from Silky): I have been hurt in the past.
(Private Message from ManInBlue): I won't hurt you.
(Private Message from Silky): Of course you will, you already have...
(Private Message from ManInBlue): I meant I wouldn't hurt you badly.
(Private Message from Silky): I don't know that.
(Private Message from ManInBlue): Is there a way I can possibly prove it to you?
(Private Message from Silky): Maybe... Maybe many ways.
(Private Message from ManInBlue): Then I shall.
(Private Message from Silky): We shall see.
(Private Message from ManInBlue): What do you mean?
(Private Message from Silky): We shall see how important our love is to you. How far you are willing to go!
(Private Message from ManInBlue): Why are you playing games with me?
(Private Message from Silky): I'm not playing games with you. What I'm trying to do is to be sure you're not playing games with me. Don't you understand that?
(Private Message from ManInBlue): I'm trying to.

(Private Message from Silky): Good. Now let's think and talk about something more pleasant. Let's think about how things will be when we are able to be together.
(Private Message from ManInBlue): Yes, I would like that.
(Private Message from Silky): When I am able to hold you in my arms, to kiss you.
(Private Message from ManInBlue): Yes to kiss your lips and feel your body against mine.
(Private Message from Silky): I feel your hard, strong muscular body against mine.
(Private Message from ManInBlue): Oh yes I would like that a lot.
(Private Message from Silky): But now I step back from you, push you away. You have made me upset and I think you must be punished for making me upset.
(Private Message from ManInBlue): Punished? You're teasing me now.
(Private Message from Silky): As a matter of fact, I am. I think I want to spank you.
(Private Message from ManInBlue): Spank me?
(Private Message from Silky): Why, hasn't anyone ever spanked you?
(Private Message from ManInBlue): Not since I was a kid, no.
(Private Message from Silky): Well, I think I would like to do that. Do you mind?
(Private Message from ManInBlue): I don't know.
(Private Message from Silky): Well, I want to spank you...
(Private Message from ManInBlue): Well, if that's what you want...then I want you spank me. To punish me for making you upset with me.
(Private Message from Silky): LOL!
(Private Message from ManInBlue): Now you're laughing? You're teasing me too much.
(Private Message from Silky): Then I shall make you feel better. I shall drive you insane with pleasure and be and do anything you want me to do, just love me completely, accept me completely, and never judge me.
(Private Message from ManInBlue): I Love you so much Silky, I want to love you, hold you, take care of you, and make you happy.
(Private Message from Silky): Someday soon we will possess each

other completely but for now I will be content to tease you, excite you, make you crazy with lust and passion and make you want me more than you have ever wanted someone before in your life.

Frank's desire for Silky grew stronger with each passing day. He couldn't wait to log into the chatroom and talk with the woman he now thought of constantly. He was barely talking to Alma now. She was usually in bed by eight-thirty each evening, reading herself to sleep while Frank flirted and often made love to Silky in the chatroom.

The strained peace of their relationship began to crumble when Alma logged onto the Internet one day while Frank was at work. She discovered some e-mail containing some explicit and terribly personal messages that Frank had exchanged with someone named Silky. She even saw the bookmarks Frank had saved and discovered several adult sites. She was surprised to learn that Frank was curious about such things. She quickly concluded that she didn't really even know her husband anymore.

Alma sensed they had drifted further apart in the last few months, and now she knew why. She knew she had to confront her husband, no matter how ugly it might turn out to be. She didn't want to lose him. That much she knew. She was still willing to fight for him. She believed these Internet meetings and flirtations, however embarrassing they might be, were not all that serious.

"What do you mean?" Frank asked.

"You've been talking to people on the Internet, Frank, flirting with them, visiting porno sites..."

"It's a case I've been working on, Alma, you don't understand." He said it in such a bored manner that he hoped he would convince her.

"A case? You're going undercover now on the Internet? You're working some special Internet sting operation for the government now, Frank? Is that what you're doing?" Alma spat out the words.

Frank smiled and sighed.

"Don't even try to lie to me, Frank. Give me at least enough respect that I'm not so stupid as to fall for something that lame..." Frank cut her off.

"I'm sorry, Alma, you're right." He proceeded to tell her how lonely he'd been for the last several months and how he had found some friends on the Internet to help pass the time with. He even told her how surprisingly exciting and erotic it was. "And now I'm ashamed of myself," Frank said.

"I'm glad you are. I hope you've gotten it out of your system and you're ready to work on our marriage again."

Frank looked at Alma. He knew how right she was. Maybe they weren't so far apart after all. Maybe their marriage could be put back together. And even he could see that spending all that time in the chatrooms was becoming more of an obsession than a diversion. He needed to face up to the fact that he owed Alma more attention than he was giving her.

Silky wasn't an obsession. She was an addiction. Frank knew about addiction. He had seen people addicted to drugs, perversions, and alcohol. He was once addicted to cigarettes himself. He'd broken that habit cold turkey. Now he would somehow have to find the strength and willpower to do the same thing with the chatrooms and with Silky.

(Private Message from Silky): And you think you can just discard me now?

(Private Message from ManInBlue): I'm sorry I have to do the right thing. I owe my wife that much, Silky. I owe her another chance.

(Private Message from Silky): Let me get this straight... The right thing is to break my heart? To hurt me? To turn your back on everything we have become?

(Private Message from ManInBlue): You told me to always be honest with you. Well, I'm being honest...

(Private Message from Silky): Oh fuck you, and your honesty, Frank. You've hurt me more than you can ever know.

(Private Message from ManInBlue): I'm sorry. I truly am. The last thing in the world I want to do is hurt you Silky

(Private Message from Silky): Is it really, Frank? The last thing you want to do is hurt me but as soon as it is time to stand up to your wife and tell her you have real feelings for someone else you cave in and deny everything that we are to each other?

(Private Message from ManInBlue): Damn it, Silky I know you are upset...

(Private Message from Silky): Oh you have no idea how upset I am, Frank. How hurt and betrayed I feel. How devastated I am at your lies and deceit. You are such a fucking coward! I believed you, Frank. I believed everything you said to me and I won't lose you. I am NOT going to lose you, Frank. I've lost too many things in my life and I won't just let this happen and let you go out of my life.

(Private Message from ManInBlue): Silky, please calm down.
(Private Message from Silky): Don't you tell me to calm down. I won't ever calm down until I have you for myself. I deserve you and you deserve me. We deserve each other. You made so many promises to me about loving me and how strongly you love me and how little things don't matter. How we will work them out... how we will be together soon and together forever.
(Private Message from ManInBlue): I know...and I'm sorry.
(Private Message from Silky): Sorry? Sorry is not good enough. Sorry that you have hurt me? That you have ripped me wide open and ripped out my heart? That you have made me vulnerable and completely exposed and then rejected me?
(Private Message from ManInBlue): Silky please.
(Private Message from Silky): Fuck you. I am too upset to talk to you now...
(Private Message from ManInBlue): Silky please let's talk about this... I don't want you to feel like this.

SILKY HAS LEFT THE ROOM

Frank was admittedly confused. Did he owe as much to Alma as he thought he did? Was his guilt clouding his own true feelings? Wasn't he allowed to be selfish? Had he not dedicated his life to the needs of others while ignoring his own?

He needed to get away from everything, yet there was no practical way he could do that. His was a life filled with responsibility and duty. His discipline would not allow him to set things aside and merely take some time for himself to consider what he was doing. Besides, he didn't dare do that.

He wished he could somehow start all over again with a fresh, clean slate. But how? Even if he could run away and start all over again, how long would it be until he realized he was simply running away from confrontation, the truth, the pain and the unpleasantness? No, he had to be strong. This was his own doing. He had started something he shouldn't have. Now, he must finish it as honestly and as truthfully as he possibly could.

Several hours later, he logged back into the chatroom, hoping to find Silky there so he could try and explain to her the way things had to be. There were several people in the chatroom, and Frank knew almost all of them. Silky, however, wasn't there. Bishamon was there, but he didn't know him very well at all. He knew that Silky sometimes talked to Bishamon and from Bishamon's conversations in the chatroom, Frank figured he was an Asian male possibly in his forties. He decided to take a chance.

(Private Message from ManInBlue): Have you seen Silky in the last couple of hours?
(Private Message from Bishamon): I talked to her about an hour ago. She was upset.
(Private Message from ManInBlue): Upset?
(Private Message from Bishamon): She loves you very much.
(Private Message from ManInBlue): I know.
(Private Message from Bishamon): She told me she had been very close to you for many months and that she has grown to love you very much. She told me you are married and you now want to end your relationship with her.
(Private Message from ManInBlue): She told you that?
(Private Message from Bishamon): Yes. Is that true?
(Private Message from ManInBlue): I don't know.
(Private Message from Bishamon): You don't know if it's true?
(Private Message from ManInBlue): Look, I'm not comfortable talking to you about this.
(Private Message from Bishamon): I understand.
(Private Message from ManInBlue): Thanks.
(Private Message from Bishamon): She's a wonderful young lady, you know.
(Private Message from ManInBlue): Yes, I do know that.
(Private Message from Bishamon): And I hope you realize what a lucky man you are to have won her heart.
(Private Message from ManInBlue): I do realize that yes.
(Private Message from Bishamon): She is someone I care a lot about and I don't want to see anyone hurt her, you realize.
(Private Message from ManInBlue): Then you are a good friend to her?
(Private Message from Bishamon): Yes, I think so. Enough of a friend, that I won't let someone get away with hurting her anyway.
(Private Message from ManInBlue): Do you know her in real life?
(Private Message from Bishamon): In real life?
(Private Message from ManInBlue): Outside of this room?
(Private Message from Bishamon): Oh, I see. Yes, outside of this room, I understand.
(Private Message from ManInBlue): So you do know her?
(Private Message from Bishamon): Maybe.
(Private Message from ManInBlue): Does that mean you do know her in real life or not?

(Private Message from Bishamon): It doesn't matter, does it?
(Private Message from ManInBlue): Well, no, I guess it doesn't matter.
(Private Message from Bishamon): I have to go now.
(Private Message from ManInBlue): Okay. If you see her and I'm not here, would you tell her I was looking for her?
(Private Message from Bishamon): She told me she'd be back in a couple of hours.
(Private Message from ManInBlue): She told you that?
(Private Message from Bishamon): Yes, she asked me to talk to you if I saw you.
(Private Message from ManInBlue): Oh I see.
(Private Message from Bishamon): She wanted me to tell you that she is sorry she acted so badly before, but you hurt her.
(Private Message from ManInBlue): Yes, I also wasn't on my best behavior.
(Private Message from Bishamon): She's very sensitive you know. Seeing her so upset, well got me upset and angry with you, to be honest. I don't like to see her upset.
(Private Message from ManInBlue): Yes, I'm sorry, I don't want to hurt her or get you upset.
(Private Message from Bishamon): I hope you don't.
(Private Message from ManInBlue): You like her a lot yourself don't you?
(Private Message from Bishamon): I do. Not as a lover you understand, but as a friend.
(Private Message from ManInBlue): Then you aren't interested in her?
(Private Message from Bishamon): No, I have someone...
(Private Message from ManInBlue): I see.
(Private Message from Bishamon): As I said, I'm a good friend to her.
(Private Message from ManInBlue): Yes, it's important to have friends.
(Private Message from Bishamon): I must go now. Be good to her.
(Private Message from ManInBlue): I will.
(Private Message from Bishamon): Good, take care.
(Private Message from ManInBlue): Thank you.
(Private Message from Bishamon): Of course. Goodbye.

Frank left the chatroom and went to a website where he could send a personalized e-mail greeting card to Silky. He chose one he thought she would like and composed a message to her. He didn't send it. He knew it wouldn't be appropriate to do that right now. He waited for a while and went back to the chatroom. Silky was there. He ignored the greetings of everyone in the room and began a private conversation with Silky immediately.

(Private Message from Silky): You weren't completely honest with me. I know that now.
(Private Message from ManInBlue): I was not being honest with you, that is true.
(Private Message from Silky): But you thought I didn't know that?
(Private Message from ManInBlue): Then you must realize that I can't desert my wife and turn my back on her.
(Private Message from Silky): I know you are very scared and you have much guilt. And I know if you try to turn your back on me, you will hate yourself for it.
(Private Message from ManInBlue): No you don't understand.
(Private Message from Silky): Oh I understand more than you realize.
(Private Message from ManInBlue): Please, Silky, I know how much this hurts you.
(Private Message from Silky): It more than hurts me, Frank. It goes so deep inside of me ... My mother was destroyed by a love she had for someone other than my father. She turned her back on her desire and passion and it destroyed her and our family.
(Private Message from ManInBlue): I didn't know.
(Private Message from Silky): I know that. And I didn't see how close this was to what happened to my own mother. I beg you to not turn your back on me. I need you, Frank. You made promises to me and I took them seriously. I believed you completely and I will be destroyed if you turn your back on me...
(Private Message from ManInBlue): I need time, Silky and I can't make you promises.
(Private Message from Silky): You've already made me promises. You've already pledged your love to me and you have already made me believe that we can overcome all obstacles. You have fallen in love with me completely and now you are frightened of what that means for both of us.
(Private Message from ManInBlue): Yes, I am.

(Private Message from Silky): And I won't let you run away from me. I won't let you destroy what we have. You can't betray me. You can't play with my emotions like this and then simply forget about everything.
(Private Message from ManInBlue): I know I can't.
(Private Message from Silky): Do you? Do you know that, Frank? Do you understand the game you're playing?
(Private Message from ManInBlue): I wasn't playing a game, Silky. Please believe me.
(Private Message from Silky): Oh you don't want to admit you were playing a game... but you are. A game where the rules change.
(Private Message from ManInBlue): I'm not sure I understand what you mean.
(Private Message from Silky): I'm not sure I understand what I mean, either, but I have had some time to think and I know what I must do.
(Private Message from ManInBlue): What are talking about?
(Private Message from Silky): I'm not sure I owe you an explanation or even can give you one. I can't let this destroy me though.
(Private Message from ManInBlue): No I don't want it to hurt you like this, Silky.
(Private Message from Silky): I will use my hurt to make me stronger and stop being a child about this.
(Private Message from ManInBlue): I'm confused.
(Private Message from Silky): Yes, you are very confused. You are very vulnerable now. Completely vulnerable in many ways and because you are scared you want to stop it. You want to run away. You are scared... too scared...
(Private Message from ManInBlue): I don't understand.
(Private Message from Silky): I'm sure you don't. But I do. I know what kind of a person you are. How you can need and use people and how you can hurt someone more than you ever realize.
(Private Message from ManInBlue): I'm sorry for your pain. I'm sorry I've hurt you, Silky, but please understand I didn't mean to hurt you. I wasn't trying to use you or hurt you or hurt anyone
(Private Message from Silky): No, of course not. You didn't even realize what you were doing and now that you do, you want to pretend you didn't mean to do it, and that it's okay.

(Private Message from ManInBlue): No that's not what I mean.
(Private Message from Silky): No? Think about it. Think hard about it, Frank. You can't tell me all the things you did and then take them back because things are getting complicated. You can't shut me out of your life simply because I was too naive to trust you and believe you. You can't do that to other people... and I sure as hell won't let you do that to me. I won't let anyone do that to me. It's what destroyed my family and I will not allow it to destroy me.
(Private Message from ManInBlue): Please, Silky I know you are upset and I'm sorry, I just have to think things through...
(Private Message from Silky): No, you've thought too much already, Frank. You've stopped feeling, and you've begun to think. And none of this makes sense, none of this is logical...It never was and it was never meant to be. A long time ago we talked about how far we were taking this. You remember that? You remember that, Frank?
(Private Message from ManInBlue): Yes.
(Private Message from Silky): You do? Do you remember when you asked me to be sure that I loved you. And I told you I was and I asked you if this was really what you wanted. If this was that important to you that you would keep going even if it meant that our love would become stronger. Remember that?
(Private Message from ManInBlue): Yes... I remember that.
(Private Message from Silky): We told each other that if we kept going, we would never be able to stop. And yet we kept going. It's too late to stop now, Frank. Too late.
(Private Message from ManInBlue): Silky, listen to me, I'm not sure what I want right now, but I have to take some time. I mean I don't know that I will stay with Alma, but I don't want to be unfair to you and promise you something that I shouldn't have.
(Private Message from Silky): You've made promises to me already and now you are frightened. I know you are trying to run away from me and I won't let you, Frank.
(Private Message from ManInBlue): What do you mean?
(Private Message from Silky): I mean I won't go away quietly.
(Private Message from ManInBlue): Explain please.
(Private Message from Silky): I promise you I won't let you do this to us, Frank. I won't let you do this.
(Private Message from ManInBlue): Are you trying to scare me?

(Private Message from Silky): You should be scared, Frank. If you hurt me, I can hurt you back, Frank. I want to show you that you can't treat people like this. Not even someone like me.
(Private Message from ManInBlue): Wait a minute, please. I'm not sure what you mean.
(Private Message from Silky): I don't know what I mean, Frank. And neither do you. I do know I wasn't thinking clearly about this either. I didn't see what this was and I too was very vulnerable and not as careful as I should have been.
(Private Message from ManInBlue): Let's stop this, Silky.
(Private Message from Silky): I've already told you, it's too late to stop, Frank.
(Private Message from ManInBlue): No?
(Private Message from Silky): No. I'm not stopping anything. I have friends, Frank. I have friends and I will
(Private Message from ManInBlue): Silky...
(Private Message from Silky): I'm crying, Frank. I don't know what I'm saying and I don't know what I'm doing...
(Private Message from ManInBlue): Oh Silky, I'm sorry, I'm so sorry. Goddamn it! I didn't want to hurt you...I don't ever want to hurt you. That's the last thing I wanted to do. And before I hurt you anymore, I wanted to stop this from going too far if I could
(Private Message from Silky): How many times do I have to tell you? Are you listening to me, Frank? It's already gone too far...much too far...and there's nothing you can do to stop it.
(Private Message from ManInBlue): Please, Silky, let me sort these things out....
(Private Message from Silky): Yes, yes, sort out your life... Frank. Sort out your life and figure things out. Yes. Yes take your time.
(Private Message from ManInBlue): Silky, I care for you so much, I really do.
(Private Message from Silky): I have to go.
(Private Message from ManInBlue): Wait Silky...

SILKY HAS LEFT THE ROOM

Frank looked over at the desk where the computer had been. After waking from the awful nightmare, he had made himself a hot pot of tea and without realizing it, had wandered into the den. That was the first time he'd had that nightmare in over a week. He had believed—or at least he had hoped—that he'd seen the last of it.

The computer had been seized several weeks ago as evidence. The desk looked naked without it. Several days ago in his office, he had nearly logged into the chatroom, but stopped. If the computer were on his desk at home, maybe he wouldn't have been so strong. It didn't matter. They had taken both the computer and the monitor, leaving only the small bubblejet printer/fax sitting on the small table next to his desk.

He recalled how they had questioned him about what he did with his computer, about some of the e-mail messages he'd received, and about the chatrooms and adult sites they knew he'd visited. He remembered the anger in Brenda Riley's face as she yelled at him.

"How could you do this to your wife, you bastard?" Brenda shouted, her nose just inches from Frank's.

"I did nothing!" Frank yelled back at her.

"You were having an affair, weren't you Frank?"

"I was *not* having an affair!"

"Bullshit! We know you were having an affair with someone you met on the Internet."

"That's not true."

"You're a fuckin' liar, you know that? You killed your wife or had her killed and I'm gonna make sure you don't get away with this!" Brenda yelled angrily.

"I did not kill my wife." His voice was firm but amazingly calm.

"You're not above the law, Garrett. I promise you, you won't get away with this."

"That's enough, Sergeant," said Detective Bud Richards as soon as he entered the room. Actually, he was quite pleased with the way Sgt. Riley was playing bad cop. She was so convincing, she almost had him believing that she was losing control. She grunted something unintelligible as she turned angrily away from Frank and glared at Bud Richards.

"Riley, that's enough. Appreciate your help, but we'll take it from here," Richards said in a low voice.

"Okay, if you say so. It's your show," Brenda said angrily as she left the interrogations room and slammed the door.

Detective Richards walked up to Frank and stuck out his hand. "Hi, Frank, got yourself in a bit of hot water, I see." He almost seemed to enjoy that Frank was in trouble. "Can't say I'm too shocked."

Frank looked at his hand and then at Bud's face whose skin had the leathery look of a man who'd spent too much time in the hot desert sun.

"I didn't kill my wife, Bud," Frank stated quietly.

"I want to believe that, Frank."

"Well, I for one don't think you do. You've already got Riley convinced I'm guilty."

"Brenda's a good cop. A bit overly anxious perhaps, but a good cop. She's been working on this thing without much sleep. I shouldn't have let her talk to you just now, but she wanted to start things off." Bud sighed. "Wasn't one of my better ideas, and I apologize that things started off on such a bad foot. Need anything? Coffee? Soda? Water?"

"No. I'm all right."

"Okay. Let's go over it again then."

Frank didn't want to remember anything anymore. He'd replayed all the details so many times already, realizing where he had overreacted, how he could have said things differently. In his first meeting with Bud Richards, he'd almost believed Richards wasn't there to try and bury him. But before long, Richards was up to his old tricks. Frank was sure he knew why Richards held a grudge against him, and quite frankly he didn't care about Richards' petty grievances. Old grudges die hard with ex-Texas lawmen and so it was with Bud Richards and Frank Garrett.

Frank had been through hell—accused of murdering his wife, relieved of his duty as sheriff, and immediately judged and convicted guilty by most of the people in town. Finally, the worst of it was over, and Bill had allowed him to return to some limited duties as his deputy until the matter was completely cleared up. The case was never the responsibility of his Department. The New Mexico State Police and Bud Richards were in charge of the investigation from the beginning.

Frank sipped his tea, aware now that he had been staring at nothing in particular, lost in his thoughts. There was a draft in the house. Frank could feel it very distinctly now. It was much colder than usual for this time of year. This place that had once been his home had lost its warmth. It no longer felt safe or comfortable. He paced back and forth as he tried to make sense of how things had changed, and why.

The house was filled with things he and Alma had purchased. The wood carving they had purchased on their second honeymoon in Mexico, the apron Alma wore when she cooked, the book Alma would never finish now lying on the coffee table beneath a growing layer of dust. Although it was still the same house Frank and Alma had bought, repaired, decorated, and lived in for more than twenty years, it had lost its soul. Alma was gone.

Frank could change neither what had happened nor the mistakes he had made. He knew he had to find the balance that would allow him to be strong again. And he would make sure that Alma's killer was brought to justice if even in the process it caused him more guilt. When that was accomplished, he would find some peace, though he knew there would still be a great emptiness within him that would mean everything would always be a little colder, a little quieter, a little sadder.

He owed all he was to Alma. He realized that now. Their love had a passion so strong that it had managed to run on mere fumes for nearly ten years. Frank realized he loved her as passionately now as he remembered loving her many years ago.

Chapter Twenty-two

Patricia found the large, unfamiliar bed terribly uncomfortable. She'd spent most of the night tossing and turning and she was wondering why she just didn't get up. It was after 7:00 A.M. and only minutes earlier, Trent had sat on the edge of the antique bed, rubbing her back and talking to her. He filled her in on his day and then bent down and kissed her quickly before leaving for his breakfast meeting. Conveniently, it was being held downstairs in the main dining room of the old Stratten Hotel. Early June is a beautiful time in Colorado's high country, and Trent had insisted that Patricia join him on this three-day trip to Durango for an advanced real estate seminar.

He had recently taken on a partner, Emily Abeyta, a middle-aged woman who'd moved to Taos from Cuba, New Mexico, following the death of her husband. The Abeytas had owned their own real estate agency for several years, but Emily was originally from the Taos area and felt the need to be near her family now. Trent had never worked with a partner before. As his business grew, however, he was constantly reminded that he would benefit by having a well qualified, bilingual partner on board. He was quite comfortable with having Emily run the business while he was out of town.

Patricia had only met Emily a time or two, but she already knew that she liked her a great deal. Emily was a petite woman, blonde and very attractive. She had quickly proven to be an asset to Trent's business and Patricia could see a definite improvement in his temperament in the last few months. Unfortunately, Patricia had never had much to do with his business, primarily because she'd been consumed first with her own career, and now the bookstore. Nonetheless, she was extremely proud of Trent's success and wanted nothing more than for his agency to continue to prosper.

Emily had surprised them both in the Diamond Jewel Saloon the previous night. Something quite important had come up in the office and she needed to talk to Trent face-to-face. As soon as the conversation predictably turned to real estate, land prices, and interest rates, Patricia left the two of them talking shop and went to their room for the night. She never heard Trent come in and was secretly happy for the time alone.

Patricia had spent much of her youth in and around the southwestern corner of Colorado and coming back to Durango was always a bit nostalgic. Her grandparents and great-grandparents had been ranchers in the area for nearly three-quarters of a century. Although they were all gone now, there were still a few scattered cousins around, but no one she kept in contact with very much.

There was an old high school girlfriend she'd made a halfhearted effort to get in touch with after they'd checked in the night before. But when Darlene didn't answer her phone on the third ring, Patricia hung up. She didn't have any intention of trying her again. After all, what would they really have in common after all these years?

Would they talk about kids? Patricia knew that Darlene had a house full of children and most likely, grandchildren by now. She and Trent had never had any children, and she hardly enjoyed being reminded of it.

What about careers? The life of a librarian and a bookstore owner would probably hold little appeal for a busy mother consumed with the important issues of raising and managing a growing, active family. These were not things that Patricia knew how to talk about.

Husbands? Patricia almost smiled to herself as she recalled the gangly senior basketball player named Doug who Darlene had married the day after their high school graduation. Patricia had seen them at one of the few class reunions she'd attended. The years had been less than kind to Doug. Where there had once been a stock of mousy red hair, there was now a pink and freckled bald spot! Not to mention that at the time, Patricia had wondered if it were simply a lack of money, fear of dentists, or perhaps a devoted father's sacrifices for his children that kept Doug from having a couple of conspicuously missing teeth replaced. Whatever the case, Patricia smiled at her fond remembrance of the two and thought of how she now envied them their innocent and genuine happiness. She hadn't envied them at the time, however. Back then, she was more than grateful for her quiet but productive life, her ruggedly handsome and almost too devoted husband, and her career with books—the only other love of her life.

But now? Well, things were different for Patricia now. Once, many years ago, Patricia had suffered from what she could now recognize as a severe bout of depression. She'd tried to ignore it and with time, the symptoms mostly vanished and her life slowly became normal again. When the subject of depression became more openly discussed, she recognized the similarities between her recent behavior and those darks days of before. She wondered whether it wouldn't be wise to visit her doctor and get some expert advice and medication. This time, she didn't think it unusual that she might benefit from something to help her cope with the things that were unraveling around her now.

She continued to lie there in the hotel room, staring at the intricate designs of the stamped tin ceiling, marveling at the beauty of it and wondering why such things of beauty had been abandoned and replaced by so much plaster and plastic in our world today. The spacious room was furnished with turn of the century pieces and she was stretched out on the luxurious feather bed that was so high she'd had to use a three-step oak stool to get up into it. The two narrow windows directly across the room were covered with navy and gold velvet draperies. Beneath the drapes were ivory-colored lace panels gathered to a full, rich thickness that added a feminine elegance to the windows. From the bed, she could see into the black-and-white tiled bathroom. Near the center of the room was a white cast-iron bathtub perched elegantly on four ball and claw feet. It had been modernized, a shower having been added to its fixtures, with a gold shower curtain. The toilet sported an original water closet. Everywhere around the room were reminders of an elegant, bygone era.

Perhaps it was that ambiance that caused her to recall a movie she'd seen years ago. It was *Somewhere in Time* and featured a handsome gentleman, played by Christopher Reeve who found himself transported back a hundred years or so where he fell madly in love with a beautiful woman. Patricia couldn't recall all the details of the memory, but she remembered that he had to leave her behind as he crossed back over into the present where he eventually withered away and died of a broken heart. The most touching part of the movie, she felt, was at the moment of his death. The few people present watched his drawn face transform into one of pure joy and peace just moments before he drew his final breath. The following scene found his lover of along ago, her outstretched hand beckoning him to join her in the foggy mist. Hand in hand, they walked away.

Patricia wondered what had prompted her to recall the movie at this particular place and time. She pulled the soft cotton sheets, which smelled vaguely of lilacs, tightly under her chin. She looked around the room. The antiques did remind her of the movie set. She had been drawn in by the opulence of that era when life and love seemed to be so cherished. No, it was more than that. It was, she knew, that she was caught up in the middle of her own movie, except this time the handsome gentleman had a name. And Phillip lived, not in another place and time, but in the here and now. Or did he? She couldn't touch him or hold his face in her hands. She couldn't sit close beside him and hold his hand while he shared his life, his loves, his passions and fears and hurts with her. Until then, she had to admit that he was as much an illusion as the characters in the movie. He had to be. Patricia's tears fell gently on the smooth, white pillowcase. It had been exactly two weeks since Alma had been murdered. Why did it seem like such a long time ago already? Patricia felt as though she'd aged a hundred years in that time.

She sat up slowly and dangled her feet over the side of the bed. She stared down at the worn, rose-patterned rug and traced the faded reds and pinks with her eyes as she ran through her options for the day. Breakfast, then some shopping, and maybe some sightseeing, she thought. She reconsidered making that phone call to Darlene, or perhaps she would drive up the Animas River to her grandparents' old farm. She hadn't done that in many years; the last time was shortly after her grandmother's death. The farm had since been sold. The buyers were intruders, interlopers, and people who couldn't possibly begin to appreciate all joy and sorrow she'd experienced there. And they'd had the audacity to repaint the house! The once federal blue clapboard home now stood there, a yellow and white embarrassment. Gone was the enchanted cottage she remembered by the side of the road. Gone too were the gigantic haystacks and the beautiful horses in the field south of the house. Maybe she wouldn't go and see the farm after all. Some memories—perhaps most—are better left as such.

She thought again of Phillip. She could not understand why she was feeling so guilty over an innocent flirtation in the make-believe world of a chatroom. It was as if she had somehow cheated on Phillip. How ridiculous, she thought. She hadn't really cheated on him. Still, she felt that overwhelming pain that comes from "almost" hurting someone you love. She also realized that, on the other hand, she felt virtually no remorse whatsoever where Trent was concerned. Patricia loved Trent very much. More than that, she admired and respected him, and she knew he loved her very much in his own way. She wrestled daily with her profound attraction to Phillip. Where was the logic in all this? She realized that there was none.

He had woven an enchanting spell with his words. Words. Simple black-and-white text that had appeared on her monitor. Could she hear his voice? Of course, and could feel his touch as well. And she was able through his magic to inhale his fresh, earthy scent, and to melt under his soft, tender lips that teased her body everywhere. She sensed the warmth, the passion, the emotion, and even the unspoken words of the man without a face. Patricia was able to gaze into eyes she'd never seen.

And now she felt guilty because someone else was also attempting to charm her? How ridiculous. She knew she'd never given Bishamon any reason to think that she'd be interested in pursuing a "relationship" with him. He'd gotten angry, somehow convincing her that she was "dirty and spiteful" for "leading him on."

How ludicrous the whole thing was. Patricia had to do something about it soon. First, she had to tell Phillip. Somehow this seemed more ominous to her than the thought of telling Trent about Phillip. That would also have to be done soon. Patricia rolled over again and willed herself to doze back off. As Trent had a luncheon to attend that day, she would not be bothered until near dinnertime. She drifted into a dream...

It was the early morning hours of that day late in May. Patricia awoke and felt an urgent need to talk to Phillip. She couldn't pick up the phone and call him. Trent was home. Besides, one glance at the clock told her it was barely after two o'clock in the morning in Cle Elum. Still, she had to try and reach Phillip.

The house was quiet as she crept into her office and turned on her computer. Many times in the past, uncannily it seemed, Patricia could go into the chatroom and if Phillip weren't already there, he would almost always materialize shortly thereafter as if summoned by an unseen force. If there were other insomniacs in the room, they would always laugh and tease them a bit and then go on about their banter while Phillip and Patricia would retreat to a more "private" box within the chatroom. When they were finally alone, they would greet each other with long and lingering embraces, followed by soft kisses that allowed them to drift into a sense of one another. Sometimes, they would both talk frantically at the same time, each of them anxious to share some special thought or adventure. Most often, however, they just needed to express their love for one another, slip gently into their familiar, quiet talks that frequently ended with a lengthy session of cybersex. Afterwards, they'd vow to fall asleep with one another wrapped securely in their arms until the day brought them around to the "real world," as the chatroom residents called everyday life.

When she logged onto the chatroom, Patricia recognized only six or seven of the names listed there. She wondered if any of these people had a real life because it seemed that no matter what time of the day or night that she logged on, she'd see these same people. She chuckled to herself when she realized they were probably thinking the same thing about her. She was fully aware that she spent a great deal of time chatting with friends and even more with Phillip. She'd been able to convince herself so far that her "real life" had not suffered because of it. Besides, she reassured herself, Phillip was worth any sacrifice she had to make to assure their time together.

Patricia recognized the names ManInBlue, TooHOT, LazyDazy, Silky, and HugeHeifer. She'd only seen Huge once or twice before, but her onscreen nickname made her laugh out loud every time. She imagined her to be petite, wildly attractive, and yet painfully shy.

HugeHeifer: hi Looker, what are you doing here so late...or is it early where you are?
Looker: thanks and hi, Huge. It's early. I couldn't sleep very well. How are you today?
HugeHeifer: Good thanks. It's after breakfast here. I've been up for hours, actually.
Looker: That's right, you live in London, right? I lived near there when I was a child.
HugeHeifer: You are KIDDING?? Where did you live?
Looker: A little village to the south called Little Chalfont. Do you know it?
HugeHeifer: I've heard of it, but I have never been there, love. Was your dad a bloke?
Looker: heeheehee...yes, he was a "bloke" I guess if you mean an American soldier.
HugeHeifer: Yes. LOL! Did you live other places besides England?
Looker: oh a few, yes. My best recollections were of Japan, though.
HugeHeifer: How old were you when you lived there? Did you like it? How exciting that must have been. I've only been outside of London a few times my whole life!
Looker: Oh goodness...how old are you Huge?
HugeHeifer: I'm 19. I go to a university right here in London.
Looker: well, I have settled down quite a bit since my childhood days. I started school in Japan, actually, and returned stateside when I was 10 years old. And yes, I liked it a great deal. I've always wanted to go back, actually. It's a dream of mine.
HugeHeifer: Dreams are nice, aren't they? I have dreams too.
Looker: Yes. Dreams are very nice.
Silky: Well...girls...I had to come up for air. Couldn't help overhearing your "girl-talk"...good early morning to you, Looker!
Looker: Good morning, Silky. You and the Man had a late date didn't you? heeheehee
ManInBlue: don't confess to anything Silk...wait for your lawyer!
Looker: ROFL...Good morning, Blue. How are you?
ManInBlue: Exhausted, actually. I'm gone boys and girls. See you later. Goodnight, my sweet Silk...I'll see you after I recover a little!

Silky: Good bye, my darling. Be safe and return to me soon!!
HugeHeifer: oh yuck! I'm going to have to find a cyber boyfriend...this is getting to me!
Looker: ROFL Huge!

SILKY HAS LEFT THE ROOM

ManInBlue: Goodnight, girls. Don't be taoooo jealous!! If I weren't so tired, I'd take you both on, but I'm afraid I am all done in after Silky!!
Looker: Oh, spare us, Man....bye!!

MANINBLUE HAS LEFT THE ROOM

HugeHeifer: I've got to be running, love. Hope to see you later. We will have to talk about England sometime, when you have the time!
Looker: Good-bye, Huge. And I'd love to, but my knowledge is limited. I was very small and my memories are simply those of stories that have been told and retold or journals I have read. Talk to you later!
HugeHeifer: Bye Love!

HUGEHEIFER HAS LEFT THE ROOM

Patricia was just about to log off when another familiar person logged on. Bishamon had become a regular visitor to the room in the past few weeks, but he appeared to speak only to Looker or Diabolique. He had approached Looker first. He told her he was waiting for a good friend of his to enter the room and asked Patricia if she'd like to chat while he waited. She'd been eager to oblige when Phillip was either absent or late to meet her. It seemed like a harmless and fun way to pass the time.

Bishamon came across as a gentleman—well bred and intelligent. They'd had some enlightening and thought-provoking conversations. What she missed in her chats with Bishamon was his obvious lack of humor. It was odd how you could pick up someone's personality and demeanor after just a conversation or two by just reading their words. Of course, that interpretation might be blown away if you were able to meet them in person. Maybe not. Through the words he typed, Bishamon appeared to be a serious, older individual, one prone to bouts of depression, which he readily admitted. Patricia surmised that he might also have a drinking problem that contributed to his depression. He told her he was a computer analyst of some kind in California; she couldn't remember where. What struck her as surprisingly unique was the improbability of connecting to someone who was not only Japanese, but was also familiar with so many of the places that she'd visited and enjoyed as a child.

Rarely had Patricia discussed her childhood with anyone. Few people knew of her colorful background and most who did dismissed it, thinking that such a small child would not be touched or affected one way or the other by her circumstances. How ignorant some people could be, she thought. Bishamon made Patricia feel special, and he told her often that sharing her experiences in the Far East was a real joy to him. He never talked about his own childhood, however. All she'd been able to glean from him was that he was a second generation Japanese-American who had traveled extensively throughout Japan.

Patricia had once shared a story with him about Seiki, the little fishing village where she'd lived as a small child. She recalled that the streets were quite narrow and almost always congested, and that her home was located about three blocks from the wharf. She and her family lived in a traditional Japanese home, complete with movable walls made of wood and rice paper, floors covered with tatami mats, and a sunken fire pit over which a kettle with water for tea was always simmering. The eleven rooms of the home were heated with colorfully painted hibachis, and they ate all their meals sitting cross-legged on the floor in front of a low, carved monkey wood table. The beds were slightly elevated soft mattresses placed on the floors. Each room had a small alcove in the wall very near the floor where a shrine could be erected. Her mother kept elegantly simple flower arrangements in each of these niches.

To the left of the home was a Japanese bottling works that ran noisily twenty-four hours a day. The din from the operation simply became a part of her consciousness and she was rarely aware of the machinery as it droned on endlessly. Across the narrow, dirt street was a soy sauce factory and to the right of the house lay the meticulously maintained grounds of a small Shinto shrine. Every day, there was a continual procession of mamasans, papasans and "sofubo" (grandparents) who visited the shrine. Patricia recalled that when they slid open the doors, she could see the statue of Buddha, so large it seemed to occupy almost the whole interior of the small room. She would watch as they knelt and chanted and tossed sacrifices of rice at the base the statue.

Directly across the street from the shrine was a large home surrounded by acres of mulberry trees. Three generations of a family lived together there. The youngest member of the family happened to be a small boy by the name of Batta. Patricia later learned that his name was Hoshida and that Batta was the equivalent of a nickname that meant grasshopper. Batta and his family owned a silkworm farm within the perimeters of their estate. Batta and Patricia became inseparable friends, Batta unconsciously teaching her the intricate art of the Japanese language while Patricia taught him children's English. The two youngsters became fixtures around the village and rarely was one seen without the other. Batta and Patricia were allowed, on occasion, to harvest fresh mulberry leaves and go down the rows and rows of silkworms and replace their eaten leaves with fresh new ones so that their cycle of life could continue as it had for century upon century.

Patricia loved to watched Batta's grandmother, whom he called Sobosan, sit for endless hours spinning silk from the fragile cocoons, the remnants of which were thrown into a large flat basket. Over time, the basket would become so full that she and Batta could roll and play in it almost buried from sight. What glorious memories she had of that brief time in her life.

How intricately woven our lives sometimes appear to be, she thought. Before moving to Japan with her family, Patricia had spent hours talking with her Cherokee grandmother who had told her stories of watching and helping her own mother when she herself was a small child. Her mother would shear sheep, card and dye the wool, and then spin it into yarn so the women could weave blankets and coats for the winter and for trading. Her grandmother had died shortly before they'd sailed for Japan and now, only a few months later, Patricia would sometimes sit quietly and unnoticed watching Sobosan spin, and imagine her to be her very own grandmother. Sobosan would glance sidelong at her occasionally, as if to say, *Yes, child, this too is how your grandmother would spin her wools.* Patricia loved Sobosan and lavished her with hugs whenever they greeted or before she went running home at the end of the day. Those hugs were magical and brought her own grandmother to her and sometimes the warmth from Sobosan almost had a life to it.

Bishamon had gotten quite excited when she told him of the village and her childhood memories there. He told her that he'd worked at a local Japanese botanical garden where his duties included taking care of one of its major attractions—the silk farm. He'd gone on for at least thirty minutes giving her every detail about the care and feeding of silkworms. Just as Patricia was going to talk to Bishamon about the significance of pet crickets, Diabolique logged on.

Diabolique: Wow! I thought I might find you here!

Looker: Oh, sweetie! How are you? I can't really believe you are here!

Diabolique: You can't? Do you want me to leave? I will.

Looker: NO NO....DON'T YOU DARE, YOU!!

Bishamon: Hi Di...good to see you my friend. I have enjoyed your Princess while you were taking your time arriving. Thank you for sharing, Looker. I'll talk to you later. I enjoyed this a great deal. Thank you for your time.

BISHAMON HAS LEFT THE ROOM

Diabolique: Huh? What was that all about?

Looker: Oh, nothing, sweetie. Oh, don't tell me you are jealous!!

Diabolique: NO. Not jealous. You been here long?

Looker: Not long at all, no.

Patricia woke with a start, her heart pounding and her body bathed in sweat.

"Maid service!" called the voice from beyond the door. Patricia smoothed her hair as she walked quickly toward the door and opened it just a crack.

"I'm sorry, I was sleeping in and didn't hear you. It's not necessary to clean our room today. We'll be staying another night. Thank you." With that, she closed the door and leaned against it. She was afraid to close her eyes, but they seemed to have a will of their own and she suddenly felt her head spinning. She reached down and put her hand on the table next to the door to steady herself, then crawled back up into the luxurious bed, where the dream continued.

When Patricia checked her e-mail that day, she saw a message from someone she didn't know. Out of curiosity, she ignored all the rest of the e-mails and clicked on the one from someone whose address was listed as taisho@metwest.net. What she read stunned her. Whoever had written it obviously knew a great deal about her, but she couldn't think of anyone she knew who would dare talk to her in such a manner.

The letter started out friendly enough, but then immediately turned to obvious rage. She realized that this was exactly the sort of thing Phillip had warned her about. How did she let herself get in this position? There was only one other person in the chatroom—besides Phillip, of course—to whom she'd given her e-mail address and she'd even been hesitant when she gave it to Silky. But Silky had seemed like such a nice woman. They'd chatted a great deal in the past and Silky seemed like someone who needed a friend, a shoulder to lean on now and again. Silky was in love with ManInBlue, but the possibility of anything ever coming of that relationship had begun looking bleaker and bleaker. It had crossed Patricia's mind that Silky might be capable of doing something she'd regret. Patricia had even asked her once if she might be suicidal. Silky had assured her that she wasn't and told Patricia that she had an extremely supportive husband and that she'd somehow get though this rough time with ManInBlue. Patricia had other motives where Silky was concerned, and reluctantly used their friendship to try and gain information about ManInBlue. Up to now, what she'd learned was sketchy and she had chosen not to share anything with Alma yet.

Even though she had Patricia's e-mail address, Silky had never written her. In many ways, Patricia was relieved that she hadn't. She had too much to do now to spend any extra time counseling someone she didn't even know, even though pursuing a "friendship" with Silky had been the basis for her involvement in the chatroom in the first place.

Patricia stared at the e-mail message for a long time, trying to comprehend its meaning. The signature on the letter didn't match anything on the e-mail address. This man, after his lengthy and childish tantrum, had signed his letter simply: *You'll Give Your Best, Crane.*

Whoever had written it knew way too much about her. Phillip had cautioned her not to be so free and open with personal information. But there was more to it than that. Whoever it was seemed to have something very personal against her, something apparently based on a sexual advance that she'd rejected. That, she knew, had never happened. For one thing, it was obvious to everyone in the chatroom that she and Diabolique were an "item." And no one had ever approached her besides NastyOlGeezer, and he was harmless and all hot air anyway. In fact, once when she'd felt particularly ornery, Nasty had teasingly made a dirty remark to her and she'd sent him a private message inviting him to join her in her "boudoir." Not only had he not answered her, he logged off almost immediately. She'd told Phillip about it and they both chuckled.

The e-mail alluded to things that had never taken place, accusing her of acts that were untrue, and naming specific people, including Phillip. A good guess on the author's part? She was certain Phillip would never divulge his real name. He had too much at stake. It briefly crossed her mind that perhaps Phillip had written the letter. But not even Phillip, who had more than a bit of the Irish devil in him, would ever have written something like this, calling her lurid and vile names and threatening her with vividly described acts of violence. There was certainly no humor in that! No, Phillip would never do that.

He often told Patricia that he would sometimes just break down and cry when he thought of her being so far away, vulnerable and hurting. He knew that she wanted him with her so badly, and yet she never pressured him. She never asked him to go against his morals or his better judgment. And she never gave him an opportunity to compromise hers. He told her time and again how he admired her and appreciated her for that. Their relationship was built on love and practicality.

"Love and practicality"—even saying those words together made her think of how they would not mix together, rather like oil and water. Patricia wished she were a scientist who discovered a formula that would change everything so that "love and practicality" could mesh perfectly without disrupting the environment around them. "Love and practicality." It didn't have the same happy-go-lucky, lyrical sound to it as that old tune "Love & Marriage." She'd come to accept that there would never be a perfect union between love and practicality.

Patricia's thoughts turned back to the e-mail many times over the next few days. She didn't respond to it, of course. And she didn't receive another one either. At least not right away. She decided against forwarding a copy of the letter to Phillip.

Patricia awoke on Memorial Day refreshed and rested following her night out with the girls. She loved summers in Taos. She needed to go into the store early, but instead took the time to check her e-mail from home. She hoped that Phillip might have access to a computer while he was down in Seattle and would drop her a quick note about his gallery show before he left to go backpacking. She only had two messages. One was addressed from taisho@metwest.net. Her instincts told her to delete it without opening it, but her curiosity won out. It didn't seem possible, yet it was even worse than the first one. It, too, contained references to the same lurid things she hadn't understood in the first letter. She shook as she read it.

She glanced nervously at the clock. She knew she had to go. She quickly clicked on the first such e-mail she'd received and forwarded it to Phillip. She cursed herself when she realized, too late of course, that she'd not written any explanation. She decided to forward this latest e-mail as well and added: *Phillip…I am so sorry to send these to you right now. But I got the one a few days ago, as you can see. The other one came today. I didn't worry you with the first one because I thought it was just a harmless prank of some kind. Then this one came today. I am uncomfortable about this, sweetheart. Forgive me for not telling you about this earlier. I am scared! What does he mean by all the things he said? I don't understand this at all. And you have to believe me, no matter what these letters say, there has NEVER been anything between me and anyone else in that room! I know you believe that, Phillip, or I wouldn't be forwarding these to you. I have to go to the store now. I will talk to you tonight, baby. OXOXOXOX PR*

Patricia woke with a start and looked at her watch. She had just enough time to wash her face, comb her hair, and run downtown. She would use one of the computers at the Durango Public Library to check her e-mail. She'd told Phillip that she wouldn't bother him while she was gone. She knew he needed time alone as much as she did. But she had to find out if he'd ever received the e-mails. If he had, she wanted to know why he hadn't responded. She tried to remember how long ago she'd sent them. Every day seemed to melt into the others without separation. It couldn't have been that long ago. A couple of weeks, maybe three at the most. *I remember now! It was Memorial Day*! Even though a great deal had happened in that time, those letters were not something that Phillip would soon forget. She was sure of that. If for no other reason, he would have confronted her about this supposed relationship. She'd seen his temper and fear once when that had accidentally happened. She never wanted to see him upset like that again. She had to send him an e-mail immediately.

She wished she could just call him. But he had told her that he'd invited his old friend Mark Murphy to join him on a combination backpacking/photography trip to Mt. Rainier. They didn't have a firm itinerary, but he'd assured her that he'd be back by the time she got home.

Patricia walked hurriedly down the rear staircase out of the hotel and across the parking lot. She started her truck and was adjusting her sunglasses when she spotted them. A man and woman were crossing the street just north of her. She watched as they walked slowly toward the front door of the Stratten Hotel. It was Trent! He had his arm draped casually over Emily's shoulder. They were laughing and smiling at one another. When they reached the double glass doors, he placed a slow kiss squarely on Emily's lips. They kissed again, quickly this time, and then he opened the door for her and they both disappeared inside the hotel.

Patricia just sat there. Was she shocked? Did she really have the right to be? She backed her truck of the parking space and turned east on the main road that ran parallel to the river. Once through town and well beyond the city limits, Patricia watched for the familiar mile marker; once she found it, she then turned north, several yards beyond it, and proceeded up the wide gravel road. There was a street sign now that had never been there before. Animas Valley Rd. Maybe, by now, the interlopers had a haystack. She couldn't imagine a farm without a haystack.

Chapter Twenty-three

Phillip knew he should be in the darkroom making the prints for the gallery opening. Instead, his mind was filled with other thoughts. He ached to hold Patricia in his arms, to be there for her, helping her deal with the pain and sadness she was experiencing following Alma's death. He also wanted to tell her what he had begun to figure out. He didn't want to worry her though, not until he was sure. Perhaps waiting was the wrong thing to do. He had no way of knowing for certain if Patricia was in any real danger.

Phillip had some suspicions that made him sound like some kind of conspiracy nut—how this was connected to that and how it proved beyond any doubt that there were people out there who were plotting and playing games with the lives of others. *Others. What if other people were in danger as well?* The more he considered the possibilities, the more it all made sense.

Maybe Alma hadn't been the victim of some random act of brutal violence, he thought. *Perhaps it was possible that she wasn't simply in the wrong place at the wrong time. What if her death had been carefully planned out in advance? Maybe I even know the person who did it? Who in the world would believe me? Patricia might believe me, of course. But if I told her, it would frighten her. Isn't it worse, though, if I don't tell her? On the other hand, what if I'm wrong about all this? What if I'm not?* He knew that even if he was only partly right in his suspicions, there was a distinct possibility that someone close to Patricia could be in danger, as well as Patricia.

He should talk to someone about it, to run his thoughts by someone else and get their take on things. Keeping them inside like this was driving him more than a little crazy. He considered talking to Mark about his fears. Mark would be able to advise him about what, if anything, he should do. Mark was that kind of friend. But to do so meant telling him all about Patricia. He wasn't sure he was ready to tell anyone that he was in love with someone he'd never met. He realized there was too much at risk. He called Mark's number and left a hurried message for him to return the call.

Phillip had seen Bishamon's name in the chatroom on several occasions. They'd been cordial to one other and even had a few brief conversations about some of the various personalities in the room. They were more comments and brief critiques than conversations, plus a little good-natured ribbing about some of the more colorful characters. Most of it was done in the open chatroom with others joining in on the fun; but sometimes it was through private messages back and forth between them. Phillip remembered distinctly one such time when Bishamon had said something about Looker, Patricia's nickname in the chatroom.

"She's a librarian or something in New Mexico, isn't she?" he'd inquired innocently enough.

Phillip recalled acknowledging that she was. Then it dawned on him—how did he even know enough to guess something like that? Had Bishamon spoken with Patricia before? Phillip couldn't be certain. Perhaps it was nothing. He had to admit that he himself was naturally curious about people. He remembered all kinds of trivial information about the people in the room. Some of this he barely disguised when he wrote his "Internet Phil" columns. There wasn't necessarily anything evil or wrong in having information like that on anyone. Phillip concluded that he was probably just being overly suspicious and paranoid. Still, he was more than just a little jealous.

Patricia had obviously been communicating with Bishamon, perhaps even flirting, or worse. *Jealous! That was kind of humorous.* And kind of normal, he supposed, as if any of this could be called normal. Phillip, however, didn't completely discard the matter because he remembered that Bishamon had once told him how people were not as safe as they thought they were in the chatrooms. He also told him that it was not that difficult to trace people to where they lived.

Phillip had asked him about this and Bishamon only mentioned that he had been on the Internet a long time and that he knew many hackers and had heard stories about people getting information on others from their personal files. He went on to tell him about hackers who were supposedly able to look at people's private e-mails and even change e-mail messages. No system was secure, he had said.

Because it would make a good column or two, Phillip had asked him a few more questions, but Bishamon became evasive. He had concluded that Bishamon actually didn't know very much about what he was talking about.

Phillip observed Bishamon for quite some time. He realized that Bishamon could very well be gathering little bits of information on everyone in the room. There were enough pieces of information freely exchanged that someone, if they were so inclined, could piece together a kind of dossier on anybody. Some of the information might be false or misleading, but a lot of it would be true. There might even be enough information to determine where someone lived and what he or she did for a living.

As a matter of fact, Phillip had done that himself when he'd helped a district attorney's task force discover that a Level Two-sex offender was violating his parole by trading pictures of young boys over the Internet. He had also taken part in a journalistic effort to prove how many predators there were on the Internet. Posing as a young schoolgirl, Phillip was inundated with propositions and offers. His part in the operation was very small, but Phillip also realized it was vital. Information is knowledge and knowledge is power that can be used either positively or negatively.

Because of the columns he'd written, a research company who wanted him to help them gather information on people and organizations for their clients had approached Phillip. Phillip learned a lot about how the Internet was used to target consumers for companies, sometimes by recruiting others to "advertise" their products. He discovered, for example, that there were literally thousands of people who regularly went into chatrooms and talked about a company's product. In exchange, these people could get such things as free T-shirts, free CD's, and free videos. There were also people who gathered information about people for other types of firms. As a result, no one really knows who is chatting and flirting and who is there gathering information for some other purpose. He learned that marketing companies gather as much personal data about Internet users as possible. The more they know, the easier it is for them to target potential buyers.

He realized that Bishamon could very well be a savvy independent operator who was trading information with marketers for money. Or he might merely be curious, a writer perhaps, or maybe he was just lonely. It was also possible the he might be a hacker gathering information to somehow use later on to break into a company's database and steal information to sell to others. Or he also might be an anarchist whose purpose is to disrupt and create chaos through viruses or some other means. In other words, Phillip knew, anything was possible. Phillip was still pondering all this when he checked in on the chatroom and Bishamon requested a private conversation and Phillip decided to answer.

(Private Message from Diabolique): So what's up?

(Private Message from Bishamon): Oh just trying to help out a friend of mine actually.

(Private Message from Diabolique): That's nice of you.

(Private Message from Bishamon): I'm not always an asshole you know.

(Private Message from Diabolique): Didn't think you were.

(Private Message from Bishamon): Some do.

(Private Message from Diabolique): Not me.
(Private Message from Bishamon): That's good to know.
(Private Message from Diabolique): What did you want to know?
(Private Message from Bishamon): Thinking.
(Private Message from Diabolique): Thinking?
(Private Message from Bishamon): Yes.
(Private Message from Diabolique): Okay...is this going to take a while? Should I go build a deck or something and come back later?
(Private Message from Bishamon): Very funny.
(Private Message from Diabolique): You said you wanted to ask me something, so ask.
(Private Message from Bishamon): You know ManInBlue?
(Private Message from Diabolique): I've seen him around, but I don't know him.
(Private Message from Bishamon): He lives real close to your girlfriend.
(Private Message from Diabolique): I don't know what you mean.
(Private Message from Bishamon): You know what I mean.
(Private Message from Diabolique): Okay. I might know what you mean.
(Private Message from Bishamon): Yeah. Look, I know a lot of stuff about a lot of people because I'm a nosy sonofabitch and I've been around a while okay?
(Private Message from Diabolique): I've noticed.
(Private Message from Bishamon): I'm not going to tell you everything, but I really don't like it when amateurs don't bother to understand what this is all about.
(Private Message from Diabolique): Not sure I understand.
(Private Message from Bishamon): I know who you are.
(Private Message from Diabolique): You do, huh?
(Private Message from Bishamon): Yes.
(Private Message from Diabolique): Well that's wonderful.
(Private Message from Bishamon): Internet Phil.
(Private Message from Diabolique): Internet Phil? I'm supposed to know what that means?
(Private Message from Bishamon): Cut the bullshit.
(Private Message from Diabolique): I've heard the name Internet Phil...
(Private Message from Bishamon): Of course you have. I'm fully aware that you write a syndicated column under the name

Internet Phil.
(Private Message from Diabolique): Why would you think that?
(Private Message from Bishamon): Maybe because it's the truth.
(Private Message from Diabolique): This conversation is over if you don't tell me why you think that is true.
(Private Message from Bishamon): You mean how I know that? Let's just say I'm a hacker. And I don't think you are a hacker, but you could be.
(Private Message from Diabolique): Well, I'm not.
(Private Message from Bishamon): I'm not so sure. Part of me thinks maybe you're a very clever hacker. I think you've been around the Internet a long time.
(Private Message from Diabolique): You don't know as much as you think you do.
(Private Message from Bishamon): Okay, maybe you're as new to the Internet as you claim in your columns.
(Private Message from Diabolique): My columns?
(Private Message from Bishamon): Look, I'm not trying to trick you into telling me you're Internet Phil because I already know you are.
(Private Message from Diabolique): And just what are you basing that on?
(Private Message from Bishamon): Easy. I've gone in and gotten people's e-mail addresses and passwords and even traced a few people further than that.
(Private Message from Diabolique): Maybe you have and maybe you haven't.
(Private Message from Bishamon): Oh I have. And why? Because maybe I'm just a little paranoid about who I talk with.
(Private Message from Diabolique): You're nervous about people here? Why? Got something to hide?
(Private Message from Bishamon): We all have things to hide now, don't we? I try to be careful. If I know more about someone than they know about me, then I feel a little safer and in control because I can pretty much guess if they're going to cause me trouble or not.
(Private Message from Diabolique): Why would someone want to cause you trouble?
(Private Message from Bishamon): Let's just say that it's possible I've done some questionable things as a hacker, and I was nervous about you.

(Private Message from Diabolique): And why was that?
(Private Message from Bishamon): Well, for starters, you've written some pretty interesting articles and you've cooperated with law enforcement folks in the past.
(Private Message from Diabolique): I see.
(Private Message from Bishamon): But I guess that if you were here to cause me problems, you would have done so already. And if you were working something with ManInBlue, then I would have known about it already, too.
(Private Message from Diabolique): What do you mean working something? I don't understand what you mean.
(Private Message from Bishamon): Let's just say that I've been onto you from the start. I'm pretty sure you're not after me. And you're smart. Very smart.
(Private Message from Diabolique): Let me get this straight...are you saying you thought I was here to spy on you?
(Private Message from Bishamon): I always presume someone is spying on me. It's healthier for me that way.
(Private Message from Diabolique): So you're selling secrets to the Russians?
(Private Message from Bishamon): lol!
(Private Message from Diabolique): You're not? Damn! I'll have to let the CIA know we were wrong about you.
(Private Message from Bishamon): I appreciate that. Sorry to disappoint you. I'm just a low-grade hacker who's caused some mischief in the past when I was a little younger. I'm not so stupid now.
(Private Message from Diabolique): Oh, got bigger fish to fry?
(Private Message from Bishamon): I've not spread any viruses for a long time and I haven't been too mean to the phone company lately either.
(Private Message from Diabolique): That's nice of you.
(Private Message from Bishamon): So do you know much about ManInBlue?
(Private Message from Diabolique): Guess you better tell me why you are asking.
(Private Message from Bishamon): He's a good friend of a friend of mine.
(Private Message from Diabolique): That's a very revealing statement.
(Private Message from Bishamon): You know who he's hooked up

with?
(Private Message from Diabolique): I think I do, yes.
(Private Message from Bishamon): Who do you think that is?
(Private Message from Diabolique): You tell me first.
(Private Message from Bishamon): You don't trust me, huh?
(Private Message from Diabolique): LOL
(Private Message from Bishamon): Okay, fair enough. ManInBlue and Silky are a couple, right? Well, Silky is a friend of mine.
(Private Message from Diabolique): Silky seems like a pretty nice lady.
(Private Message from Bishamon): Indeed. And I want to make sure she's not going to get hurt by this ManInBlue.
(Private Message from Diabolique): I guess that's very nice of you.
(Private Message from Bishamon): It IS nice of me. He's a policeman or something in New Mexico you know.
(Private Message from Diabolique): That's what he claims.
(Private Message from Bishamon): I know even more than that. I know who he is and where he lives. He's in the same town as your girlfriend, by the way.
(Private Message from Diabolique): ???
(Private Message from Bishamon): Don't play games with me. I'm fully aware that Looker is your girlfriend.
(Private Message from Diabolique): I'll admit that Looker and I are friends, good friends.
(Private Message from Bishamon): Cut the crap, Phil. Look, I'm going to tell you something so you know I'm not full of shit okay?
(Private Message from Diabolique): Go for it.
(Private Message from Bishamon): And when I'm done, I want you to answer a couple of questions for me.
(Private Message from Diabolique): Maybe I will, maybe I won't.
(Private Message from Bishamon): I guess I don't know if I should continue this conversation with you.
(Private Message from Diabolique): Then don't.
(Private Message from Bishamon): But I'd still like you to answer a question.
(Private Message from Diabolique): What might that be?
(Private Message from Bishamon): I want to know more about ManInBlue. Verify who I believe he is.
(Private Message from Diabolique): Why don't you just hack your

way in and find out for yourself?
(Private Message from Bishamon): I could do that. However, that has certain risks involved in it. And you can verify the information I think I know.
(Private Message from Diabolique): What makes you think I can verify anything about ManInBlue?
(Private Message from Bishamon): Because I think your lady friend works in the bookstore very close to his office.
(Private Message from Diabolique): So you've been talking to Looker, I see.
(Private Message from Bishamon): I have talked to her, yes, but she didn't tell me everything I know about her, and she sure as hell didn't tell me anything about you. I told you, it isn't that difficult to find out information about people, if you really want to. People think they're safe in a place like this chatroom, but they're really not.
(Private Message from Diabolique): Okay, so what is it you want to know?
(Private Message from Bishamon): I first wondered if ManInBlue was in the chatroom on some kind of official business.
(Private Message from Diabolique): Checking on something you might have been involved in?
(Private Message from Bishamon): No, nothing like that. I cover my tracks pretty well and I'd know right away if someone were trying to get information from me. I'm very careful.
(Private Message from Diabolique): You're not being careful now.
(Private Message from Bishamon): That's true. I'm not being very careful now, but I'm pretty sure you're in this chatroom mainly for recreation.
(Private Message from Diabolique): That's true.
(Private Message from Bishamon): I know I'm making you nervous and I apologize for that. I don't want to cause you any problems.
(Private Message from Diabolique): Glad to hear that.
(Private Message from Bishamon): Anyway, I'm going to assume that ManInBlue is the sheriff in Taos, New Mexico, and that he's married and shouldn't be having a cyber affair with my friend Silky. May I ask you for some advice? I think you are someone who understands people quite well. Probably lots better than I do.
(Private Message from Diabolique): I don't know how well anyone

understands anyone else.
(Private Message from Bishamon): I don't think ManInBlue is going to be leaving his wife anytime in the near future. How would you tell a good friend that the person they think they're in love with will wind up hurting them?
(Private Message from Diabolique): If you really feel it's necessary to tell them, then be honest with them. Tell them you care very much for them and then say that you believe the relationship has limited potential. Something, which you believe, probably won't continue outside of the chatroom.
(Private Message from Bishamon): Yes, I understand.
(Private Message from Diabolique): People say many things to each other in the chatroom (as they do in real life) that they won't follow through on.
(Private Message from Bishamon): Which is why Silky is going to wind up being very hurt.
(Private Message from Diabolique): And that happens all the time on the Internet. A lot of people have had their hearts broken in this chatroom and in others.
(Private Message from Bishamon): Have you?
(Private Message from Diabolique): No, but I understand how and why it happens.
(Private Message from Bishamon): It isn't very fair.
(Private Message from Diabolique): A lot of things in life aren't fair. And I'm not being flip about it either.
(Private Message from Bishamon): Glad to hear that. I am very serious about this. Silky is a very good friend and I would be very upset if someone played around with her and hurt her.
(Private Message from Diabolique): I understand, and I think it's wonderful that she has a good friend like you. Do you know her in real life?
(Private Message from Bishamon): I don't think I should answer that.
(Private Message from Diabolique): Okay. I guess it isn't important. I mean if you know her in real life, then you could talk to her about this in person and explain to her that there is value in having caring and loving relationships, but when the lines aren't clearly drawn, well that's when people can get hurt. And the lines, especially in a chatroom, become blurred... the lines between reality and fantasy, between real life and so-called "life" in the chatrooms... they all become

blurred, and it becomes a potentially dangerous game.

(Private Message from Bishamon): But a person who lies, is still lying isn't he?

(Private Message from Diabolique): Yes. But his intent probably isn't to hurt anyone.

(Private Message from Bishamon): That doesn't make any difference. If he hurts someone intentionally or unintentionally, that person's hurt either way.

(Private Message from Diabolique): I'm not saying it's ever okay to hurt someone else, but it happens. There are conflicts and circumstances that put everyone in situations where they could be hurt. We are sometimes at odds with ourselves when we try to control certain aspects of our lives. When we try to force ourselves to do things we shouldn't really be doing.

(Private Message from Bishamon): Wow.

(Private Message from Diabolique): Wow?

(Private Message from Bishamon): You are a very smart man.

(Private Message from Diabolique): Well, I don't know about that.

(Private Message from Bishamon): Oh yes, you are very smart. I can take what you said in a few ways.

(Private Message from Diabolique): I meant it that way. I'm glad you caught on. Anyway, you should let Silky know that you're aware she's having some difficult times and you want to listen to her and help if you can. Listening is more important to her than simply giving her advice or telling her what she really has to find out for herself.

(Private Message from Bishamon): I have done something like that already, but somehow she believes that love will triumph over logic and circumstance.

(Private Message from Diabolique): It has happened in the past.

(Private Message from Bishamon): Not very often.

(Private Message from Diabolique): No, you're right. And it does sound like she will be hurt. When you allow yourself to be vulnerable, you also allow yourself to be hurt.

(Private Message from Bishamon): I try not to be too vulnerable.

(Private Message from Diabolique): Then you're missing out on a lot of what life has to offer.

(Private Message from Bishamon): I guess I am.

(Private Message from Diabolique): Now tell me something about yourself that most people don't know.

(Private Message from Bishamon): Why?

(Private Message from Diabolique): So I don't feel like you know too much about me and some other people without me knowing very much about you.

(Private Message from Bishamon): Like what?

(Private Message from Diabolique): What's your name?

(Private Message from Bishamon): Gordon.

(Private Message from Diabolique): Gordon?

(Private Message from Bishamon): Yeah. My real name is Gordon and I'm 32 years old and I work in the M.I.S. department of a school district outside of Olympia, Washington. Not too far from you.

(Private Message from Diabolique): I thought you were in California for some reason.

(Private Message from Bishamon): Nope, we're practically neighbors.

Phillip paced back and forth after the conversation ended. He was waiting for Mark to call him back. Phillip was eager to share some of his thoughts with the Seattle police detective. He was pretty sure he knew what was going on, and he didn't like it one bit. He could only hope that Patricia was not in as much danger as he thought she might be.

Chapter Twenty-four

"Butch, this will be very difficult for me to do. You know that, don't you?"

"I know."

The two had been discussing the message that Butch's wife Angela had left for Patricia to read at her graveside service. She turned away from him when she heard someone on the wooden staircase that led to her office on the second level of the bookstore.

"Mrs. Ridgeway?" Chad's familiar voice spoke quietly from the top step. "There's a call for you on line one. I told him you were in a meeting, but he insisted on talking to you."

"That's all right, Chad. Thanks. I'll get it in a second."

"Go ahead and take that call," Butch offered. "I need get back downstairs and finish putting away some books that I never finished with the other day, before I…" Patricia knew he was recalling the day earlier in the week when Angela had called the shop and asked him to come home right away. Angela had died peacefully later that same night. She died exactly how she wanted to die—she simply fell asleep in the arms of the only man she had ever loved.

"Butch, please. You don't have to worry with those magazines now, really." Patricia placed her hand on his arm.

"No. I want to. Take your call and maybe we can go for some lunch when you're done. That is, if you have time."

Patricia smiled and nodded as she picked up the phone. "This is Patricia."

"Trish. It's me! I'm sorry to call you at work."

"Phillip!" Patricia was so excited to hear his voice that she momentarily forgot the heaviness in her heart. Phillip had never called her at the store before and it took her a second to adjust her thoughts. "Phil, is anything wrong?"

"No. I was afraid you'd think that. That's why I almost decided not to call. Everything is fine." He paused. "I got your e-mail this morning about Mrs. Killen. I just wanted to tell you how sorry I am."

"Oh, Phil, how thoughtful of you. You just got it this morning? I sent it to you a few days ago."

"I could see that. I had an unexpected opportunity to see Mark and I met him for a few drinks the other night and then I ended up staying in town. I was late getting home last night and when I logged into the room, someone told me I'd just missed you. I'm sorry, sweetie!"

"It's okay, really. Please don't apologize. I just took a chance that you might be there, anyway. Truth? I just needed you to hold me for a minute. It's so sad about Angela."

"I know, baby," he whispered. "How is her husband doing?"

"Good, actually. Much better than I would ever have thought. But it's early still. He'll feel it later on, I'm sure. Right now he's busy with matters that he has to take care of. Arrangements and things. I think he's just functioning on automatic pilot. In fact, he's here right now working! Can you believe that?"

"Sure, I can," replied Phillip. "I'd probably be doing the same thing if I were in his shoes. Besides, he probably doesn't know what else to do right now."

"That's true, I guess. He and I are going to go to lunch together in a little while. That will be good for him, I think. I don't know where to go, though. I'm afraid that every place around here is going to remind him of Angela."

"I'm sure it is, Trish. But don't worry about that. Go where you think he'd be the most comfortable. Even if it's somewhere they went together, he'll have to do it sometime, sweetie. Maybe it will be easier if you are with him."

"You're right. It probably would be. You sure you weren't a psychologist in another life?"

Phillip chuckled but quickly turned serious. "Trish, I need to ask you a question. I don't want you to take this wrong, okay?"

Patricia was momentarily startled by the tone of his voice. "Sure. What is it, Phillip? Is something wrong? Have I upset you?"

"Oh, god no, baby. It's nothing like that. I just need to know a couple of things… for my column." He hated lying to her. "Patricia, have you ever talked at length with Bishamon—Bishamon in the chatroom?"

"Well…yes, actually, I have. But I hope you aren't asking what I think you're asking, Phillip. We've just talked about some things that we have in common, really."

"What things? What kind of things have you talked about?"

"I have to tell you, Phillip, you're acting strange. Why are you asking me this?"

"Trust me, Patricia. I have a reason. Well, that's not true. I *think* I have a reason. I just need to know a couple of things from you. I'm not accusing you of anything, if that's what you're thinking. Honestly!"

"I hope not. That would be most unfair."

"I know it would be and believe me, I'm not. I love you with all my heart and know you love me just as much. Nothing will ever change that!"

"Okay then. Well, you know that he's Japanese, don't you?"

"Yeah. Well, I kinda surmised that. Is he from Japan or was he born here?"

"He was born here, but travels there from what I gather. Anyway, he's just fun to talk to about places and things that I remember from when I was a kid living in Japan. We talk about things I'd almost forgotten all about. I think he's lonesome and just talks to me when he knows you aren't around. Why the questions?"

"You've never told him anything personal about yourself, have you? Like where you live, what you do, who you know? Stuff like that?" Phillip could feel his chest tightening as he waited for her to answer.

"I might have told him a few little things, but nothing specific though. I've *never* told him anything about you or us, sweetie! Is that what you're worried about?"

"No, no, no. I didn't think you'd do anything like that. So you don't think you ever told him anything personal? Something that you might be afraid to tell me?"

Patricia's heart stopped when she realized what Phillip must be thinking. "Phillip, no! In fact, I even made up a story once when someone in the chatroom asked me what I did for a living. I told them I was a librarian in Minnesota! I'd have died if they'd asked me anything about Minnesota! If he'd ever asked me anything personal, which I don't remember him ever doing, that's what I'd have told him."

"I believe you. I'm just doing a little research on how people can trace other people on the Internet and just how little information it takes to do that, if some fairly savvy guy knows what he's doing. I didn't mean to make you think there was anything else to it, baby. I really didn't."

"That's okay. You said you had a couple of questions? Was there something else?"

He really didn't have any other questions which he felt were appropriate right now, then he thought of something he'd almost forgotten. "I do have another question, Trish. Do you know if Bishamon is a Japanese word?"

"I'm not sure. It's not a word I recognize. But gosh, I've forgotten almost all the Japanese I ever knew. But I've got a translation dictionary right here. Hang on a minute." Patricia flipped through the book but didn't find anything that even remotely resembled the word.

"I don't see anything here. Let me look in another little book I have. It's a book called *Enjoying Japan and Its People* and it has oodles of obscure things in it. Wait while I look in the index. While I'm looking, *I* have a question for *you*. Have you told me you love me today? I'm just curious, that's all."

Phillip felt the smile in her voice and was glad he could do that for her. "You know I love you."

"Good. I thought you did. Just checking, you understand. Oh, here it is, Phil. Yes! Bishamon. Oh, for pity sakes, it says here that Bishamon is a god of some sort. Oh sheesh! Wouldn't you just know it. A god no less! What kind of an ego does this guy have, I wonder?"

Phillip chuckled, but not because he found any humor in her words.

"This is interesting."

"What's that, Trish?"

"Well, it say's here that Bishamon is one of Japan's seven gods of good fortune. Oh, brother. Bishamon is the god of war!"

"Read me what all it says there. Do you mind?"

"No, I don't mind. Is this important? This name thing?"

"Well, yes actually. It's just another article I'm writing. About how chatroom visitors arrive at the names they give themselves. It's a pretty interesting study, really. Now read me what it says and I'll let you get back to work, sweetie."

"Work? You think I can concentrate on work? Well, I mean your call still has me trembling just a little bit! But here ya go. It says here that, "Bishamon is an armor-clad lady protector. A spear-carrier. Fierce looking but not warlike. He carries a sword in one hand and a pagoda in another, which portrays him not only as a warrior, but also as a missionary of virtue. Bishamon has his own private messenger, a centipede." She stopped.

"Is that it?"

"That's all it says, Phil. The end."

"Well, you have just been a wealth of information today, Miss Book Lady! How much do I owe you for your time and trouble?"

"Owe me? Oh, honey, you wouldn't have enough money if you were Midas himself to pay me for talking to you!"

"Really? Hmm. If you weren't at work and if I weren't expected somewhere in a few minutes, we might have to discuss this at length! Lucky for both of us that we aren't free right this instant."

"Phil, I'm glad you called. I didn't know how much I needed to hear your voice today. I got another surprise today, too."

"What?"

"Don't worry. Nothing bad. Actually, something very good, but I don't know if I can do it or not. Butch brought me something that Angela wrote and asked me if I'd read it at her funeral. She was going to ask me herself but she didn't get the chance."

"She wanted *you* to read it? What? A eulogy?"

"No, not exactly a eulogy. More like a farewell of sorts. To be honest, I've only just glanced at it because it took me so by surprise."

"When is the service?"

"Monday. Monday at eleven. Butch doesn't expect too many people there, but I think he'll be surprised." Phillip didn't respond to her answer. They just let the quietness lay between them until she spoke again. "You there, Phil?"

"Yes, I'm here, baby. Just holding you tight, thinking how much I love you. Say, sweetie?

"What baby?"

"You've never told anyone that I was Internet Phil, have you?"

"Heavens no, Phillip. I wouldn't do that. I'm not sure I like all your questions today, though. You're making me nervous."

"Trish, I'm sorry. I'm being rude and thoughtless. I'm going to hang up before I stick my foot in my mouth any more than I already have!"

"No, don't! It's all right. I'm just on edge, I think. I'm sorry too, baby." She had to catch herself before she burst into tears.

After the call, she looked at the crumpled paper on her desk. It reminded her once again how precious and fragile love really is. Then she remembered. She *had* mentioned "Internet Phil" to someone. But she reassured herself that the answer she'd given Phillip was okay. He was talking about telling people in the chatroom. It certainly wouldn't make any difference to Phillip that she'd told Alma all about him.

Exactly one week after Angela was memorialized and the final good-byes were said, Alma Garrett's mutilated body was found in a campground not far from Taos. Alma and Patricia had gone to that same area hundreds of times in the past to walk and talk and simply to enjoy the changing seasons together. Patricia felt alone and adrift in a world she didn't recognize and never dreamed existed. Her protective cocoon had been a strong and solid shelter for most of her life. She never dreamed that it could start unraveling like this with absolutely no warning.

There was Phillip, of course. But right now Phillip remained no more than an illusion with a voice, a faceless name in the glass cocoon of her computer monitor. *God, Phillip. Will you ever know how badly I need you?*

Unlike Angela's memorial service, Patricia remembers very little of either the events leading up to or the actual funeral for Alma when hundreds of people filled the courtyards on either side of the old mission in Arroyo Seco and filled its small chapel to overflowing. Those in attendance ranged from her rather large extended family, to nearly every resident in the close-knit community, to hundreds of law enforcement officers from around the state. Frank had been a sheriff's deputy for many years prior to actually becoming the Taos County Sheriff and was well known and widely respected.

Alma would have hated this, Patricia thought to herself as she sat in a pew near the back. The funeral mass, performed first in Spanish and then in English, seemed interminable. She reached for Trent's hand a couple of times, hoping for a reassuring squeeze, hoping perhaps that he'd place a comforting arm around her shoulders to help steady her. He didn't. Once though, he patted her hand affectionately. He offered very little physical support beyond that. He and his partner, Emily, excused themselves immediately following the service, explaining that they had a luncheon meeting with a potential buyer and were already late.

As was tradition in the strong Spanish community, an elaborate luncheon was planned following the graveside service in the adjoining cemetery. Alma's uncle, Jose Trujillo, had devoted much of his life to caring for and tending to the ancient cemetery. Oddly, his aged and bent figure was the only one that Patricia recalled seeing there as she stood alone by the rusted wrought iron gate. There were so many flower arrangements that they spilled over onto several of the adjoining graves. The graves of Alma's father and her mother, as well as her brother Rico surrounded hers. Rico had died, barely a year before from AIDS. Dozens of other graves and markers, which chronicled over a century of life and death in the Trujillo family, were nearby.

Patricia wanted to approach Jose and offer him her condolences, but she hesitated. The old man was mumbling to himself, talking to whomever it is an old man sees at times like these. He needed his solitude. He'd lived through nearly a hundred years of suffering and loss himself, watching almost everyone he loved vanish from his life. Heavy hearts often need the solace that only a silent cemetery can offer. Patricia found a bench near a large tree. She sat down and buried her face in her hands. And she cried, weeping for so many things in her life. She mourned more for herself than for Alma. And she was not ashamed. Alma would have understood.

Almost before the words were even out of her mouth, Patricia deeply regretted her emotional outburst at Frank that day at the station right after she'd learned of Alma's death. Some things once said, can never be rescinded nor forgotten. She had accused Frank of being somehow responsible for Alma's death. One person in particular would delight in reminding her of that when she questioned his authority when he literally "invaded" the Garrett home. And then again at the pre-trial hearing following the formal charges for murder which were lodged against Frank.

The day after Alma's funeral, Patricia had gone over to the Garretts' house to tidy up after all of the activity of the previous few days. The condition of the house astounded her! It had been ages since she'd actually visited Alma in her home. They were together almost every day at the bookshop and always ate lunch downtown or up in her office. Sometimes as couples or occasionally as a trio if Bill and Sylvia had the opportunity to join them, they'd have dinner and drinks at one of the local restaurants. But the appearance of the house now completely shocked her. Alma had been a tidy and organized woman, caring deeply for her husband and her home. Even those last months prior to her death, when she had suspicions about Frank's fidelity, she maintained an air of total commitment and trust in Frank.

After repeated soft knocks, Frank finally unlocked the front door and immediately apologized for the mess. Then he invited her in and offered her a seat. He had to move several days worth of old newspapers, fast food wrappers, and mail from the chair before she could sit down.

"Frank? What's happened here?"

"What? Oh, you mean, this?" said Frank, waving his hands around the room.

When Patricia didn't answer, Frank started rambling, trying somehow to explain. He told her about some recent developments in his life. Apparently the thought never occurred to him that Alma had probably shared many of the same things with Patricia. In fact, she hadn't. At least not in the same sense or to the degree Frank was doing now.

"She just gave up I think, Patricia. She wasn't strong in a lot of ways, and I think she just gave up caring about anything where we were concerned. Well, where I was concerned anyway."

Patricia was mentally preparing herself to tell Frank about Alma's suspicions and maybe even about her own involvement in their situation when the doorbell rang. The curtains were drawn against the light and it was impossible to see who was at the door.

"You want me to get that, Frank?" Patricia asked as she automatically rose and moved toward the door.

"No, I don't. But I guess we have to. Sure, go ahead." His face was in his hands as Patricia opened the door.

"Hello. Is Frank Garrett here?" An unfamiliar gentleman wearing a rumpled suit stood directly in front of the door. Several uniformed officers were behind him on the sidewalk.

"Yes. Yes, he is. May I ask your name?"

"You may." He reached slowly into his left breast pocket and produced a leather-encased gold badge and an identification card. He flipped it open for her inspection.

"My name is Bud Richards. I'm a detective with the New Mexico State Patrol, Ms…?"

"Ridgeway. Won't you come in, please?" Patricia reached for the handle on the screen door but Bud Richards had already pulled it open and was motioning for several of the men behind him to accompany him into the house. Frank stood up. The detective took three long strides toward him and offered an outstretched hand.

"Bud Richards, Sheriff Garrett. Sorry about your loss, sir." His manner and words seemed insincere.

"Excuse me, Frank," Patricia said, "I'm going to go tidy up the kitchen a bit. Would you like me to fix some coffee or anything?" Frank didn't have an opportunity to answer before Richards spoke up and told her that coffee would be fine. Then added, "Make it strong, please. We might be here a little while."

Patricia went into the kitchen and cleared enough dishes from the sink so she could fit the glass carafe under the tap. After locating the coffee, she put in a scoop less than she would normally have used. She didn't like Bud Richards.

Without thinking, Patricia began gathering up soiled linens and food-encrusted dishes and piling them on the already cluttered counter. She could hear the voices from the other room, but she couldn't make out the words. She wasn't really paying any attention. She was overwhelmed by the enormous job ahead of her and secretly warned Alma that she'd get even for this someday. She almost smiled as she fondly recalled her friend's face. Patricia was totally startled when a uniformed officer asked rather loudly from behind her, "That coffee ready yet?"

She glanced quickly at the still dripping pot and snapped, "No. No, it's not!" Her glare spoke for itself, and the officer turned and left the room without a word. In the next moment, she heard Richards' voice.

"Christ! She and Juan Valdez pickin' those damned coffee beans or what?"

Patricia walked over and yanked the coffeepot's plug from the wall and searched in the dishwasher for clean cups. There was one clean mug. Looking over the array of dirty dishes, she found a soiled cup with the words

ALBUQUERQUE BALLOON FESTIVAL 1994 boldly printed around the top. She leaned over the sink to turn the faucet on and rinse it out, then changed her mind and sat the dirty mug on the counter. After pouring the cups nearly full, she spun and walked hastily into the living room and handed the balloon mug to Richards and the clean one to Frank. Patricia turned to the uniformed officer standing near the door and said in a sarcastic tone, which even surprised her, "There's a McDonald's up on the main highway that I hear makes pretty good coffee. You might want to go get you and your friends some."

Only minutes into the heated confrontation that then took place in the Garrett living room, Patricia went into the kitchen and called 911 and asked the operator to send someone over to Sheriff Garrett's home immediately. She didn't wait for any follow-up questions. Instead, she hung up the receiver and walked back into the main part of the house. The group had moved from the living room and their voices were clearly audible from down the hall. A state trooper stepped in front of her as she proceeded toward the men.

"Excuse me, ma'am. I don't think your assistance is needed back there. Perhaps if you just have a seat." Before she could respond, the first of several local officers arrived at the door and stepped in. Patricia's heart sank when she saw that Bill was not among them.

"What's the trouble here, sergeant?" One of the newcomers directed his question to the state patrolman who had detained Patricia. She recognized his face, but didn't know his name.

"No problem, officer. We have a warrant to search the premises and confiscate any and all items which we feel might be pertinent as evidence in the investigation of the murder of Alma Garrett."

"May I see a copy of the warrant, sergeant?" The young man remained calm, looking from the state patrolman to Patricia and then in the direction of the raised voices down the hall. He turned and motioned to the other officers to go check it out. The state patrolman turned as if in an attempt to stop them and then seemed to think better of it. He returned his attention to the officer in front of him and handed him a letter-sized document.

"Now, do you want to tell me what this is all about, sergeant?" Patricia was impressed. She thought that he couldn't be more than twenty-five years of age. She wondered if that air of confidence was a quality that was innate rather than learned. Either way, she wished she possessed some of it.

At that moment, several men emerged from the back of the house carrying various computer components and file boxes. One of them, who was balancing several notebooks, dropped some loose papers as he proceeded through the front door. The officer who had detained Patricia reached down and retrieved the strewn papers and dropped them into the top of a box being carried by the last man to leave the back of the house. Richards and Frank could be heard arguing now. The local officer handed the paper back to the state patrolman and pushed passed him.

The two men emerged from the back room, almost scuffling. Frank's hands were behind his back and Patricia suddenly realized that he was handcuffed. Richards had a gun drawn and was aiming it toward the ceiling.

"What the hell is going on here?!" Patricia's words aimed at Bud Richards were demanding and indignant.

"I think it's quite obvious what's going on here, Ms. Ridgeway. Now, if you don't mind, I need to get through that doorway. Would you move, please." It was a demand, not a request. Patricia never flinched and stared at the two of them.

"No. I'm afraid it is *not* obvious to me what is going on here! The only thing *obvious* to me is that *you* have a gun drawn against an unarmed man and I find that extremely unnecessary and offensive."

Richards' face flushed and he shoved Frank away from him, lowered his gun, and holstered it beneath his jacket.

"Let's get something straight here, Ms. Ridgeway. I don't know exactly who you are and just what you have to do with Garrett here. But I have a feeling we are going to learn a lot about you before this is all over. And probably sooner than I'd care to, from what I know of you already. It's my advice to you that you step aside quietly before *I* get cranky and arrest *you* for obstructing justice. It doesn't take much to make me cranky, Ms. Ridgeway."

Frank's young deputy quickly moved beside Patricia and guided her to one side while Richards pushed Frank toward the door.

"I'm sorry, Patricia. Please...just tell everyone I am so sorry." Frank's eyes were brimming with tears and for an instant Patricia thought her heart would break completely in half as she watched him stumble toward the patrol car. When she turned back toward the deputy who still had his hand around her upper arm, she smiled through her tears as she watched him wipe away his own tears with the back of his other hand and smile at her.

The days that followed the confrontation at Frank's home were filled with several taped visits with Bud Richards, Bill Conner, and a new female deputy by the name of Brenda Riley whom Bill had requested in Frank's absence. Frank had been released only hours after Bud Richards' arrogant show of force. He'd lacked sufficient evidence to hold him. Richards had blown his credibility with the attorney general's office when he acted without the proper authority and evidence in actually placing Frank Garrett under arrest.

Two weeks after Alma's murder, an informal hearing was held in the Second District Court in Santa Fe, and all of the various trumped-up charges lodged against Frank were hastily dropped. The judge presiding over the hearing shook his head in stunned disbelief as he heard the purported evidence presented by Detective Bud Richards and others who were working under his direction. The courtroom was packed to capacity with Frank's local supporters who had voluntarily appeared as character witness and others who were there to substantiate his obvious alibi at the time of the murder.

Patricia and several other people were called to speak and within hours, all charges were dropped against Frank Garrett. The attorney general did, however, insist that Frank take a mandatory leave of absence until such time as the case was either solved or formally closed. A livid Bud Richards narrowly escaped being cited with contempt of court when he loudly pleaded with the judge to reconsider the case and, at the very least, lower the charges to conspiracy to commit murder.

Not surprisingly, when the court was dismissed, Richards and a group of other state patrol officers hastily exited the building and were immediately confronted by several radio and television reporters. As a result, a physical confrontation initiated by Richards was caught on tape in which he'd begun to verbally attack Frank Garrett, vowing to prove that he was indeed involved in the brutal slaying of his wife. Richards was later placed on two weeks' probation himself.

Chapter Twenty-five

Phillip didn't want to lie to Patricia, but he had no choice. There was no hiking trip on Mount Rainier with his police buddy from Seattle. Instead, he'd met Mark at a Thai food restaurant where he'd tried to explain all that had been happening in this life the last few months and what he now suspected to be reasons for very valid concerns about Patricia's safety and his own.

"No, I don't think you're crazy," Mark reassured him.

Phillip was relieved. "I don't think we're dealing with some casual, part-time Internet stalker here, Mark. This is someone who enjoys whatever sick game he is playing, and he's very good at it."

"I agree he enjoys the game, Phil, because he believes he's smarter than just about anyone else. But it appears he's already made a big mistake incriminating himself with the e-mail notes. And to me, that looks like a very clumsy mistake for someone who is trying to pass himself off as being pretty smart. He's either some sick jerk-off who doesn't have anything to do with what's going on and is just being a real asshole about it, or he's not nearly as smart and clever as he thinks he is."

"Still," Phillip added, "the information in these notes contains more than just stuff that someone playing a casual joke would know."

"Okay, then we have a very disturbed son of a bitch who's smarter than some, but somebody who's still about to be caught." Mark was obviously more confident about this than Phillip.

Just yesterday, Phillip had been at his home in Cle Elum, momentarily escaping into the sounds of the river rushing by and watching a hawk circle overhead. He'd spotted the fawn, which had grown a great deal this summer, remaining partially hidden in the brush. He sat on his deck and wrote some lines of a new poem in the journal Patricia had given him for his birthday, lines he had hoped would be calm and romantic. What emerged instead was quite different. He would certainly never send it to Patricia.

Wide

Zoos are loose
On the radio

The beasts are running
Free.
The freaks acting out
On the Internet
Why aren't you here with
Me?

Don't you know it's crazy out there?
Someone could get hurt
Don't you know it's crazy out there?
Someone could get burnt.

They're buying bigger wheels
To sit in traffic,
Still.
Drinking coffee,
Tea and health juice
Preparing for a
Kill.

Don't you know it's
Crazy out there?
Come and
stay with me.
Don't you know it's
Crazy out there?
Too scary to be free.

It's all about these
Measurements
And having to own
More.
Possessing things without
A soul
That you've never had
Before.

Don't you know it's
crazy out there?
I can be crazy too
Don't you know it's crazy out there?

I'll be crazy for you.

Buy on sale,
park for free
Count the quarters,
And the dime.
Put the mask on
Thick and cold
You're running
Out of time.

Yeah, it's crazy out there
All bought and most sold
Yeah it's crazy out there
Let's put it all on hold.

Don't you know it's crazy out there?
Someone could get hurt
Don't you know it's crazy out there?
Someone could get burnt.

He'd not been able to rid his mind of the demons. Ever since Patricia had told him about Alma and ManInBlue and Silky and Frank and Bishamon and now Crane, everything was getting complicated, out of hand. Over-the-line dangerous. Phillip had a bad gut feeling that Alma's death was no random act. He suspected Bishamon was somehow involved. None of the pieces fit. What he needed was Hercules Poirot to gather everyone together and then explain how this person was related to that one which led to this and how it made it plainly clear who was guilty. Life, however, is seldom an Agatha Christie novel.

Phillip was actually relieved when Patricia told to him she was going on a business trip to Colorado with Trent. Perhaps now she would be out of harm's way, at least for the time being, and he'd be free to sort through his thoughts and suspicions. He desperately wanted to know which ones were based on insecurities and paranoia, and which ones might be based on fact. Perhaps he should have been jealous that Patricia and Trent might be renewing their romance or working out some of the problems that had caused them to drift too far apart from each other. But he wasn't. The marriage was not unsteady or loveless, just without passion, he reasoned. The important thing was that she was safer in Colorado than in New Mexico. Only yesterday, she had forwarded a very disturbing e-mail message:

Subject: To everything Turn Turn Turn
From: "crane" <Taisho@metwest.net>
To: "Patricia Ridgeway" <PatriciaRidge@earthangel.net>

I thought you liked me. I really did. You've hurt me. And I'm tired of being hurt. Tired of people pretending to be my friend and then just treating me like some worthless piece of shit. You fucking bitch.

But now I know about you. I know all kinds of things about you. I know your e-mail address. I know where you live. I know where you work.

Maybe It's time that I do something. Stop letting people walk all over me. Stop letting people hurt me without hurting them back.

Maybe I'll come visit you; maybe I'll call a friend of mine to visit you. I have friends that will do almost anything I ask.

Maybe I'll give you another chance, maybe I won't.

CRANE

The header was the only indication that Phillip had that the note had been forwarded to him by Patricia. He was trying to understand what it meant, why it had been written to her, and why she'd forwarded it to him. The next message explained things:

Subject: Oops let me explain
From: "Patricia Ridgeway" <PatriciaRidge@earthangel.net>
To: "Phillip Craven" <PhilCraven@foxnet.com>

PHILLIP...I AM SORRY TO SEND THESE TO YOU RIGHT NOW. BUT I GOT THE ONE A FEW DAYS AGO, AS YOU CAN SEE. THE OTHER ONE CAME TODAY. I DIDN'T WORRY YOU WITH THE FIRST ONE BECAUSE I THOUGHT IT WAS HARMLESS. A MEAN PRANK. THEN THIS ONE WAS IN MY MAIL TODAY. I AM UNCOMFORTABLE ABOUT THIS, SWEETHEART. FORGIVE ME FOR NOT TELLING YOU ABOUT THE FIRST LETTER. NOW I AM NERVOUS. WHAT DOES HE MEAN

BY ALL THE THINGS HE SAID TODAY? I DON'T UNDERSTAND IT AT ALL. OH...AND NO MATTER WHAT THIS LETTER ALLUDES TO, THERE HAS NEVER BEEN ANYTHING BETWEEN ME AND "ANYONE" ELSE IN THAT ROOM! I KNOW YOU BELIEVE THAT, PHILLIP, OR I WOULDN'T FORWARD THESE TO YOU. I HAVE TO LEAVE NOW. TRENT IS WAITING. I WILL MISS YOU, BABY, BUT I WILL CONTACT YOU THE INSTANT WE GET BACK!!! OXOXOXOO PR

Subject: Remember
Date: Thursday, 02 June 2000 15:43:42 -0500
Subject: It's Time
From: "crane" <Taisho@metwest.net>
To: "Patricia Ridgeway" <PatriciaRidge@earthangel.com>

I waited as long as I intend to. It's time for you to pay for what you did to me. For hurting me. For making me think you liked me and wanted me. You were nice to me and I thought you cared about me. You led me on, Looker… or should I say Patricia… and then you just toss me aside like I'm nothing.

Well like I told you before, bitch, I am not going to let you get away with it. I know where you live in Taos, New Mexico and I know about your Take Another Look bookstore on the plaza. I know all about you. I've been finding out all kinds of things about you. I know about you and your cop friend, too. Does your husband know about that? Maybe your husband is too busy with his own affairs to notice what you are up to. You have been so busy, so deceitful, you bitch. I think you should go on that business trip with your husband and meet his partner. My friend has told me interesting things about your husband and his partner. Interesting things about you and your friends, too.

Does Phillip know about any of this? Are you lying to him about it? Do you even care about him or are you leading him on the way you led me on? Oh yes, I know all about him, too. He had a pretty successful showing of his work recently didn't he? Made a lot of money. Maybe it's all a game to you. But if it is a game, well then, I am prepared to win and I don't care about following any rules. Rules are for suckers and fools. Rules are to keep people in their place. Rules are for school children. And school is out.

I can hurt you. I can strike close to you any time I want now. I can get to you in ways you don't even understand.

You heartless bitch. Maybe I'll show up some day in your bookstore and make you come with me. Tie you up and do anything I want to you. Hurt you. Cut you. Burn you. Torture you. Laugh at you as you beg for mercy.

You've no idea who you are dealing with. Maybe I'll get my friend to hurt you. Then again, why let him have all the fun?

It's time you and all the other fucking whores out there pay for hurting me and people like me.

CRANE

Phillip felt the hair on his neck bristle. He still wanted to believe he was mistaken. But he knew he was right. That's why he had called Linda at the Gallery.

"Do you have his card handy?".

"Sure, Phillip. Hold on." She returned a few minutes later.

"Taisho Hum…blah blah blah."

He looked at the computer screen hoping he'd only imagined it. But there they were. The e-mails Patricia had gotten signed by Crane and addressed from Taisho@metwest.net.

Taisho, the strange looking Japanese man who had bid an incredible $12,000 for one of his photographs at the gallery just a few weeks before. It was obviously no mere coincidence. And he was just as certain there was some connection between Taisho and Bishamon.

"Is that all you wanted, Phillip?"

"Yes, thank you, Linda. I was going crazy trying to remember what his name was. I've almost got the print ready. I might want to deliver it to him myself."

"Oh, there's no need for that. I can have it done."

"No, Linda. I want to do this. I really would like to do it this way."

"So, when will you be coming into town?" Linda asked.

"Maybe tomorrow. Maybe the day after that." There was no advantage in being specific at this point.

"Is he incriminating himself with these notes or does he want us to know about him?" Phillip asked Mark after showing him the e-mails.

"Both probably. If you are right that Taisho is the same person as this Bishamon character, then it's clear he wants to terrorize you guys."

"But why?" asked Phillip. Mark, however, didn't appear as though he'd even heard the question. Phillip waited a moment and then asked, "Okay, what are you thinking about?"

"A case I was involved with," Mark said quietly. "I may have mentioned it to you. Colombian named Marco, from a couple of years ago, who stalked his ex-girlfriend. He decided he wanted to get back at her for hurting him."

"Yeah, I remember you telling me about that. Didn't I take some pictures?"

"That's right, you did. It happened outside the Stock Market Grocery Store on Rainier, a QFC now, if I remember correctly. This girl's brother was shot twice in the head as he was putting his groceries in the trunk of his car."

"Right. And there were people around that thought they saw something." Phillip interjected.

"But of course, people see and remember different things, as you know." Mark paused while the waitress filled their water glasses and left. "We tied Marco into all kinds of things later on. He had some guy follow his ex-girlfriend; her name was Deidre but she went by DeeDee. Well, Marco had someone follow DeeDee and her new boyfriend when they went out one night and then picked a fight with the boyfriend. Messed him up pretty bad and put him in the hospital."

"Didn't he try to get someone to kill her in a drive-by shooting?"

"No, no, Phillip. You're getting your facts mixed up. Anyway, Marco stole, or had someone steal, DeeDee's car. The car was used in a drive-by shooting down in the Hilltop area of Tacoma. So DeeDee was called and questioned about her car being stolen. She told us about a note she'd gotten from Marco. A note she didn't have, which supposedly said Marco was going to hurt her for hurting him. She cooperated with us and set up a date with the scum. She stood him up and he got very upset with that and tried to get to her."

Phillip nodded.

"Sorry, I didn't mean to bring this all up. It's just that in the e-mail this guy sent to your girlfriend, about I'm going to hurt you because you hurt me type of thing, well, it just reminded me a lot about this other thing."

"I understand."

"You need to be very careful."

"I think something has already happened, Mark. I think Taisho, or whatever his name is, already killed someone or arranged for someone to be killed."

"You're not kidding, are you? When? And who, for god sakes?"

"A few days ago. Memorial Day. A friend of Patricia's was found decapitated outside of Taos."

"Good lord, Phillip."

"I'm putting the pieces together myself, Mark. That's why I'm talking to you about this."

"But you really think this murder is somehow related to this Taisho freak?"

"I'm very sure, although I can't exactly tell you why I am. But yes."

"Now, you said this Bishamon character is in Olympia, right?"

"That's what he said, but I think he was lying. Taisho, though, lives in Kirkland. Caroline Point, I think. Anyway, Linda from the gallery has his card."

"Phil, I'm trying to follow you, but you've got to help me out here. Patricia is the lady you met on the Internet, right?"

Phillip smiled weakly and shook his head. "I'm not sure you'll ever be able to understand this. Hell, I'm not so sure I understand it myself!"

"Gee, that's a big help, buddy. Anyway, you love her, huh…this Patricia. Right?"

"Yes, I love her very much."

Mark studied his friend closely. "This is a woman you met on the Internet and you've never actually met her, right?"

"I know what it sounds like…" Phillip started defensively.

"I'm not judging you."

"Of course, you are," Phillip snapped.

"Okay, maybe a little."

"It isn't logical, it sounds crazy, and…"

"And you love her." Mark finished.

"Yeah, and I love her."

"And you've never met her, at least not in person?"

"No, I've never met her in person, but I feel like I've known her all my life. I feel like I've known her before, I don't know, in another life. I'm not sure how strongly I even believe in that stuff, Mark but I…"

"I'm glad you've found someone, Phil."

"Trust me, I wasn't even looking."

"I believe you."

"If someone were telling all of this to me right now, Mark, I don't know what I would think. I mean it all sounds… I don't know, it just doesn't sound like anything I would have imagined myself ever getting involved with. I've been writing about this Internet stuff for a couple of years now, and I'm not some desperate lonely person reaching out for some companionship. I'm not sure I understand how it happened, but it just seemed so absolutely perfect. I let it continue like some wonderful little fantasy and I thought that it would basically remain some sort of part real/part make-believe relationship. It was fun that's all. Something different. It was a little…I don't know…" Phillip searched for the right word. "Not dangerous, but forbidden. You know what I mean?"

"Sure, I do," said Mark half-jokingly. "The dark side of Phillip Craven."

"It's not funny, Mark. I mean, what we have together isn't sordid. I know out of context it might seem sleazy. I don't know that I can explain it."

"I think you already have. You told me you loved her. Love comes in all shapes, sizes, and ways. I've looked at people who have stayed married for sixty years and there doesn't seem to be anything to connect them at all, and I've seen people who have just met and seem to have been together for years, intuitively knowing things about each other."

"Yes," Phillip said, "that's what it's like. Beyond judgments."

"Beyond judgments?" Mark repeated the question, trying to understand.

"If I were to sit back and judge this," Phillip explained, "I mean judge Patricia and me, it's easy to say it's wrong—wrong on more than a few levels. But I know how I feel about her deep inside, and I know without question that it's right." Phillip sighed. "I know how that sounds, Mark, I really do."

"It's okay," he said. "I can accept the fact that you love her very much. And, quite frankly, that's all I need to know."

"Good."

"If you were in love with a crack addict, I'd try and talk you out of it. But that's not the case."

"And I'm not drooling after a twenty-two-year-old either."

"You're not? Why the hell not?"

They laughed, letting some of the tension of the conversation dissipate.

"Hey, the fact that you're in love with a woman. A married woman. A woman you've never met. I mean, that's not such a big deal, ya know." Mark shook his head and sighed. "On second thought, maybe I *should* talk you out of this!"

"You wouldn't be able to."

"You're probably right. And besides, who am I to judge? I mean, look at my life of lust!"

"True."

"And that stuff is coming to an end for me now, too, Phil."

"I'm glad you found someone, Mark."

"Anyway, so how does this involve these other people you were telling me about?"

"I can't be sure, but Bishamon is a good friend of another lady who is part of this chatroom. She goes by the name of Silky."

"And Silky is this woman who is involved with a cop, right?"

"The sheriff, yes."

"You know he's a sheriff?"

"Yes, he's the sheriff in Taos, where Patricia is."

"Your Patricia?"

"Yeah, my Patricia. Patricia Ridgeway, owner of Take Another Look Bookstore in…"

"Okay, okay. Damn, Phil, this is a little confusing, and in some ways just a little too coincidental, if you ask me."

"That's why I think there's a connection. Frank Garrett is the sheriff's name. He was married to Alma, the friend of Patricia's who worked for her at the bookshop."

"Alma?" Mark blurted out. "You mean the woman that was just…"

"The one who was just murdered. Yes."

"Jesus Christ, Phil."

"You're confused?"

"I am, yes, but I'm also thinking. Back up to what you told me earlier."

"What was that?" Phillip asked.

"About Silky and the Sheriff."

"Silky and ManInBlue, as they are known in the chatroom."

"But ManInBlue is this sheriff, Frank Garrett, who is Alma's husband, am I right?"

"Right."

"You realize we sound like we're talking about freakin' daytime soap operas, don't you?"

Phillip smiled.

"Well, I think I know what we might do next," Mark continued. "It's just that I'm not sure how's the best way to go about it."

"What's that?"

"If Taisho had anything to do with this, he would have had to make a trip to New Mexico."

"Right."

"That shouldn't be too hard to trace. "

"If we get lucky and he flew from Seattle to Albuquerque you mean?" Phillip asked quickly.

"Right. If he was little tricky, he might have paid for the trip with cash."

"But you can trace his credit card pretty easily, can't you?"

"If I bend the rules a little bit, I could. Maybe."

"Maybe?"

"Well, you let me worry about following up on it, okay?"

"That's why I'm talking to you," Phillip said. "Oh, and I forgot to tell you one thing. I've got a delivery to make to Taisho tomorrow."

"You what?"

"Yeah, and I thought you might want to go along when I deliver the print that Taisho ordered from the gallery."

"So you think I'm just gonna go along with you when you make this delivery?

"Think?" Phillip said, barely suppressing his smile. "I know you wouldn't miss being there for anything."

Chapter Twenty-six

One of Patricia's favorite haunts had always been the historic old Fontana Hotel in Santa Fe, so the invitation to attend the New Mexico State Women's Entrepreneurial Conference there had just been an added bonus. Most of all, however, she just wanted some time away from home in order to try and sort things out.

After meeting a couple of her friends for cocktails in the lounge the first night, Patricia returned to her room and found a phone message from Bill Conner. He was asking that she meet him the following day for lunch. There was no further explanation, but that fact didn't surprise Patricia. Bill wasn't one to waste words. Besides, he knew her well enough to know that she'd be there. She got ready for bed and then lay on top of the covers, her mind too preoccupied to even consider giving her over to the sleep she needed.

In addition to all the devastating losses, she'd discovered the affair that Trent was apparently having with Emily Abeyta. She couldn't decide when it was that she'd actually lost Trent. Or perhaps more to the point, when Trent lost her. Maybe it was that day in early May as she dozed by the banks of the river where she'd been sitting and watching Trent fly-fishing. She should have been better prepared with a ready answer when she woke up, startled to find him standing over her with a bewildered look on his face. She simply wasn't ready when he asked her point-blank who Phillip was. It was at that moment that she completely lost the sense of balance in her life she'd been struggling for so long to maintain.

Bill's intrusion now would undoubtedly snap her back into the reality which she'd foolishly hoped to forget as much as possible while she was at the conference. Patricia had an inkling why he wanted to meet with her. Plagued with a little too much guilt, Patricia was tempted to call Bill and tell him she'd not be able to meet him. She couldn't do that, she reasoned, because deceit was simply not a part of her normal behavior pattern. She found that a bit ironic when she realized that she was now seemingly caught up in a whole new world of practically nothing other than deceit—that, and love and sadness and guilt and regrets. The pressure she felt was affecting every aspect of her life.

Patricia stepped out of the elevator and into the lobby. They caught sight of one another immediately and embraced.

"Hey, there, Patricia! Thanks for seeing me." Bill gave her a quick kiss on the cheek, which she lightheartedly returned. It was good to see him.

"Well, sir, I *did* have to cancel a luncheon date with the governor and rearrange my audience with the Pope. But hell, I can *always* do those things another time!" They both laughed and Patricia was glad that Bill was there. She quickly forgot about the misgivings she'd had the night before.

"So, Marshall, wanna eat here or did you have someplace else in mind?"

"Honest? I was hoping you'd suggest here."

"You were, were you?" She winked playfully and hooked her arm into his. "I was hoping *you'd* say that! You know this is one of my favorite restaurants in the entire world? Well, maybe not the *whole* entire world."

They made their way down the wide hallway toward the dining room. The five star restaurant was understandably crowded with the usual array of local and colorful business people, grinning honeymooners, and wealthy summer tourists. A handsome and exceedingly pleasant gentleman, who would serve as their host, met them just inside the arched portal and escorted them to a secluded table. Patricia recognized his distinct accent from talking with him earlier that day when she called the dining room and made reservations for lunch. He introduced himself as Juan, and then led them to their table.

As soon as they both were seated and their drink orders taken, Bill leaned forward and rested his elbows on the table. After glancing around the room, he reached across the table and took Patricia's hand in his. The simple gesture brought a lump to her throat, which she couldn't quite explain. She hoped he'd speak first, and he obliged.

"Patricia. How are you doing? Really?"

She didn't have to look up to know that the concern in his question was genuine and that he was implying nothing more than what he'd asked. "*Really*, Bill? Or do you want the 'Patricia the Pollyanna' version?"

"I want the real Patricia Ridgeway version, if you don't mind."

She looked at him, her confidence beginning to return. "Bill, I know that I've never told you how much your friendship has meant to me. I should have. I know that."

When she lowered her eyes, Bill reached across the small table and placed a finger under her chin and gently raised her head. "Patricia, some things don't need to be said between friends. Some things are just felt, okay?"

There was a long pause.

"No. Not okay. I'm sorry, Bill, but I have to disagree with you this time.

Allow me that for today, okay? And please don't hold it against me forever." She smiled, although they both knew that she meant what she'd said. Bill picked up his water glass, leaned back in his chair, and waited for her to continue.

Whatever energy Bill had transferred to her in those few moments was enough for her to release all of the pent-up confessions, fears, worries, and suspicions that she'd been harboring for such a long time. Everything about the last incredible year of her life began to flow out of her in a flood of words, some of them cascading so fast that she knew Bill was struggling to keep all the various scenarios straight. For the most part, Patricia was honest with what she told him. She felt more than a little guilt when she described Phillip and her feelings for him, the things that had transpired between them, and how he had changed her life in so many ways. She certainly didn't elaborate on their personal relationship, and she also told Bill that Phillip was a salesman from Milwaukee named John Altman. The longer she sipped her drink, the harder she had to concentrate to remember the name she'd just plucked out of the air. Above all else, no matter how badly she needed to talk to someone, she would never jeopardize Phillip in any way by divulging his true identity.

After lunch they retired to the small, intimate lounge across the hall. Four hours and possibly one too many cocktails later, Patricia's emotions were finally spent, but her heart was blessedly lighter and less encumbered. Bill leaned back in the booth, took a deep breath, and closed his eyes for several moments before speaking.

"Patricia. C'mon. Let's go up and get your things gathered up. I'm going to take you home, okay? You need to be home."

Patricia nodded wearily and waited as Bill walked around the table and helped her to her feet. He paused at the registration desk, while Patricia proceeded on to her room. After satisfying her bill, he made a phone call to the room of the woman Patricia said had driven down to Santa Fe with her and made arrangements for her to drive Patricia's truck back to Taos when the conference was over. When the elevator door finally opened into the lobby, the two of them nearly collided as a giggling Patricia stumbled out with her bags.

"Whoa, lady! Need some help there?" They both laughed, and Bill quickly grabbed her two bags and headed for the parking lot. It was almost dark when they left Santa Fe for the two-hour ride up the mountain to Taos.

"You okay to drive, Bill?" Patricia was leaning back in the seat, her eyes already closed. She was quickly losing the battle against the overwhelming urge to fall asleep.

"Me? Oh, you mean the drinks? I've been drinking coffee for the last three hours! I sort of anticipated this, you know." He glanced over when she didn't respond and saw that she had already fallen asleep.

In the darkness, Bill carefully watched the winding road and shook his head from side to side, not quite sure if the mindless gesture was to clear his own mind or an attempt to erase some of the things that Patricia had shared with him. Perhaps it was because he was just beginning to comprehend what the last few months had been like for her. Her story had unfolded much like a Shakespearean tragedy, yet it lacked any of the attendant pomp and circumstance. He couldn't fathom how she'd allowed this to happen, letting things go this far undetected.

Perhaps Patricia, Bill thought, had actually suspected something long before now only to ignore it in some form of denial, perhaps in order to protect her own conscience. He continued to wind his way northward through the canyon, enjoying the fresh, cool air as they made the ascent. As Patricia slept, obviously fitfully, Bill continued trying to fill in some of the blanks from their earlier conversation with things he knew as fact. His misgivings at that moment fell somewhere between not telling Patricia why he'd really come to Santa Fe to talk to her and actually telling her everything he knew and then seeking her advice on how to proceed. He had to admit to himself that he had no idea what to do.

Sometimes being the strong, silent type had its disadvantages. People regularly sought Bill out as someone they felt comfortable confiding in. For the most part, Bill was glad that his friends trusted him enough to share things with him, knowing that he would never violate a confidence. However, he had been wrestling with his conscience on this since before Alma had died. There was too much at stake here. This wasn't some childish game, even if it had started out as such. In addition to everything that had transpired, Sylvia's concern for Patricia and her odd behavior had prompted Bill to call Patricia. The day was nearly over and he hadn't even broached any of the issues with her. He was afraid he was going to lose his nerve. Still, he knew that his decision to break a trust was the right one. Bill leaned across the seat and touched Patricia's shoulder.

"Patricia? Patricia, are you awake?"

She opened her eyes. "Yes. I'm awake now. Is something wrong, Bill?"

"No, nothing's wrong. But we are almost to Ranchos and I was hoping to talk to you for a few more minutes before I took you home. Do you feel up to it, or would another time be better?" As soon as he'd said it, he was sorry he'd given her that option. He knew he had to talk to her now.

"Well, of course I do. I'm sorry, Bill. I did all the talking and then had the audacity to fall asleep! I feel terrible."

"Hey, quit that! I enjoyed today more than you will ever know, and obviously you needed to talk about that stuff. You feel okay about it now, don't you?"

"Yes, I do. I really do. I'm still amazed that I told you all those things. But I do feel better. I had to tell someone I trusted about this whole sordid mess! I'm surprised that you're not afraid to be alone in the car with me!"

"Who said I wasn't?" Bill answered laughing.

Bill slowed the car to a near stop and pulled into the gravel parking lot of the St. Francis of Assisi Church in Ranchos de Taos. It was only slightly illuminated from a light on a post near the road. A pile of buckets could be seen near the front door of the church.

"I almost forgot. It's the annual mudding for the church. Have you come down to help at all, Bill?" Every year, members of the community came together to replaster the old church, one of the most famous old missions of its type in the country.

"Actually, I haven't had time yet, but I'm going to bring Sylvia's boy down on Saturday. I heard they are expecting over a hundred volunteers and there's going to be a mariachi band, too. How 'bout you?"

"No. I should, I know. We sell a lot of books about the church and its history. But this year, I think I'll go up to Arroyo Seco and help with plastering up there. Alma and I did that two or three years back when they initially restored the old mission, and I've sort of committed to helping them out again. This year, it seems even more important that I go up there." She looked across the parking lot at the church. "They must be nearly done. They've repainted the crosses already."

Bill looked at her a moment before speaking. "Patricia, I have to ask you some questions and I hope you'll feel comfortable enough to answer them, or at least help me out a little. I also want to tell you that whatever you tell me, I won't repeat unless you tell me it's okay. Before I'm through, you'll wonder if you can trust me with your confidence or not, and I won't blame you one bit. But I'm giving you my solemn vow that I will honor anything you ask me to, okay?"

Patricia nodded hesitantly.

"There are so many places to start. I know that this is going to get all jumbled up, so please bear with me, okay? There is a reason for all my questions, but even I'm not really certain what it is at this point." Bill rested his hands casually over the top of the steering wheel as he talked.

"Do you work personally with students and instructors out at the Taos Art Institute. Do they frequent the bookstore much?"

"Gosh, Bill, let me think. I'm sure a lot of them come into the store. I offer the students and faculty both discounts on art-related books and supplies, yes. Why?"

"I'm not exactly sure why at this point, but I have a strong suspicion. If it's okay with you, I'll get to that in a few minutes. I wish I knew my Taos history better. I'm learning, but somehow I missed a very well publicized and unsolved murder that took place here around the 4th of July, in the late 1920s, I think. Do you know anything about that?"

"You mean the Manby murder?" She was rubbing her hands together nervously and that did not go unnoticed.

"Yes, I believe that's the one. Can you tell me what you know about it? I heard some rather bizarre stories when I asked around."

"Well, sure. I'll tell you what I know, but I'm afraid I don't know a whole lot. It's interesting that you ask me about this, Bill. I assume there is a reason. Would you share that with me?"

"Yes, but not right now. Actually, I'm not even sure myself why I'm asking. I just have a hunch that in some way there is a link to everything else that has happened."

"Well, I know that there have been a dozen or so stories circulated around about it and about the Manby character. There's even a western novel based it. There is only one publication that I'm aware of, however, that seems to present the facts, limited as they are." Patricia paused as she tried to recall whatever bits and pieces she could of the story of Arthur Manby. "The Manby Murder of Taos, as it's called, was never solved, as far as I know," Patricia continued. "From what I've been told, Author Manby himself was a suspected murderer, but I don't think any charges were ever filed against him."

"Do you know how he was killed?"

"Uh, yes. He was beheaded." Her words hung heavily in thin air.

"I thought so. Is there anything else you can recall?"

"Well, some people believe that he wasn't killed at all, that the body that was found was somebody else. There are rumors that Manby has been spotted in and around the area and as far away as Europe. Another story is that the ghost of Arthur Manby still haunts the area. "As a matter of fact," she chuckled, "there's a famous saying about God and Taos that circulates periodically, especially around election time."

"Really? What saying?"

"I'm not sure if I'm telling this exactly right or not, but I read it in a book about Arthur Manby. It seems that a newspaper reporter from back east somewhere called the local doctor who attended to Manby's body. He wanted some information on the case, and he asked the doctor if there was a police commissioner in Taos. Apparently the doctor told him that there wasn't. Then the reporter asked who the police chief was. Again, the doctor told him that Taos didn't have one. So the reporter finally asked who was in charge here then and the doctor told him that 'God's in charge up here. God's in charge of everything that happens in Taos.'"

They both laughed when they realized that things really hadn't changed all that much in Taos in the past eighty years.

"Is that all you know about the case?"

"Almost," Patricia answered. "It was grizzly enough by itself, but by the time his body was found, his dog had apparently dragged his head into another area of the house and eaten most of it. That was where the identity problem came in. There wasn't anything left but a skull."

"Yuck, Patricia! That's gross!"

"I *know*! Why in the world did you ask me about that anyway? Whoever killed Arthur Manby would hardly be around to kill again."

"I know. It's just another piece of this I'm trying to put together. Brenda Riley came across an anonymous letter that the department received about three days before Alma's death. Nobody thought anything of it at the time because it didn't seem to have any bearing on anything that we could tell. Then, with all that happened so soon after receiving it, somehow it was just shoved aside until she ran across it a couple of days ago."

"A letter about Arthur Manby?"

"Well, we thought it was about Manby at the time. But now I think it might have some bearing on Alma's murder."

"And you don't have any idea who sent it?"

"No. I'm not at liberty to reveal its contents, but I can tell you that we were able to trace where the stationery came from. So we feel confident that the range of our investigation can narrow to that area."

"Well, where did it come from?" she asked, hardly expecting Bill to answer her.

"It came from the Taos Art Institute. That much we are sure of." After another few tension-filled seconds, Bill finally continued, "Patricia, now tell me the truth about Phillip Craven."

The question took Patricia's breath away. She looked at him for a long time before answering, "I already have, Bill."

"John Altman is Phillip Craven? Is that what you mean?"

"Yes. Would I have fooled you had you not already known?"

"Probably, yes. But if I hadn't already known, I wouldn't have had any reason to question it one way or the other. I might have had an opinion, but I would have kept it to myself unless you asked me for it." That was precisely the type of statement she expected from Bill.

"How did you find out, Bill?" At this point, it was difficult to keep her voice from giving away her deepest fears. If Bill knew about Phillip, what would keep Trent from knowing about him as well?

"He called me a few days ago, and then again yesterday."

"*He* called you? What do you mean *he* called you? I don't understand Bill. Why on earth would he do that?"

"The first time he called was to ask me for some advice, share some suspicions, and...well, to introduce himself, I guess you might say." Patricia watched him carefully.

"I'm sorry, I don't have any idea what's happening here, Bill."

Instinctively, he put his hand on her shoulder. "I know you don't. At first, I didn't understand either, Patricia. The first time he called, he presented himself as a concerned citizen who thought he might have a lead on who might have killed Alma Garrett and why."

"What! What do you mean, he might know who killed Alma? Bill, this isn't funny. You're not making any sense!"

Bill gripped her shoulder a little tighter now. This was going to get complicated and he wasn't sure how she'd react.

"Well, this is a rather long and complicated story. After tonight, Phillip is going to explain everything to you as best he can. You were gone when he realized that his suspicions might have some validity, so he called me and told me enough so that I'd take him seriously and come down to Santa Fe and get you and bring you home."

Patricia stared at Bill in utter disbelief. She had no idea where he was going with this story. And Trent...what about Trent? Did he know, too? She was beginning to shake uncontrollably.

"What Phillip didn't tell me about the two of you, Patricia, you filled in the blanks for me. That certainly helped me see this whole thing from a completely different perspective. What I don't know now, however, is where to go next."

So Bill began by telling Patricia that he'd known for some time about Frank's participation in an Internet chatroom. Frank had not been truthful about how deeply he was involved. There really hadn't been a reason to, he'd explained to Bill, other than to justify some of his prolonged computer time and try to assure Bill that it was just sort of a childish, though admittedly erotic, fascination that he planned to end quickly. He had actually confided to Bill that he had become "involved" with a woman and that the relationship had created some tension for him at home, as well as some uneasiness as far as the woman was concerned. What had started out as an immature sexual adventure had escalated into a full-blown "cyber romance" and Frank had just recently become aware of what an ugly turn these situations can sometimes take. He'd told Bill that he'd gotten some very uncomfortable feelings about the whole thing. Basically, he had sought Bill's advice, and Bill had told him in no uncertain terms that he should end the relationship as quickly as possible and get what he considered to be an unhealthy addiction under control.

Now it was Bill's turn to be nervous. If what he suspected were indeed true, he'd given Patricia every opportunity to provide the last few remaining bits of information he needed, but she hadn't made any type of move in that direction. The two of them sat in silence for quite a long time before Bill continued.

"Does the name Caesar ring a bell with you?"

Patricia folded her hands and rested her chin on them. "Caesar? Yes, but I'm trying to think why. There must be a reason for asking me that, Bill. Perhaps if I knew that, I could place him." For some reason, she'd decided to find out why Bill was asking all these questions before telling him about Caesar.

"That's the problem. I am running on speculation here and I can't risk making an assumption unless I have some way to verify my facts."

Bill decided to come at this from a different approach, hoping it would jolt Patricia enough to tell him what he hoped she knew. He was rubbing his forehead and realized he was subconsciously trying to erase the first few twinges of a migraine headache that he'd hardly felt developing until now. He leaned across the seat and opened the glove compartment. He fumbled around and eventually produced a small prescription drug bottle and shook two of the blue tablets into his hand and swallowed them with a backward toss of his head. He recapped the bottle and put it away. He saw that Patricia was not the least bit cognizant of what he had just done. Little by little, he'd begun to realize that Patricia, the compassionate woman who'd been such a wonderful friend, had suddenly become a stranger. He'd sensed earlier in the day when they sat together in the Fontana Lounge, that she was just as aware of that fact as he was. Bill had one last idea. He hoped that it would work.

"While you're trying to place Caesar, Patricia. Let me ask you another question. Does the name NastyOlGeezer mean anything to you?" That was obviously the switch he should have flipped earlier.

Patricia leaned back in the seat and began to tell Bill about Alma's suspicions and how she'd originally begun going into the Internet chatroom as a "spy" of sorts on Alma's behalf. She'd hoped to find out one way or the other whether Frank was indeed one of the frequent visitors and if he was having some kind of a cyber relationship with someone in the room.

It took Patricia over an hour to tell Bill everything she knew. She told him that Frank had actually kept a pretty low profile in the room, but that it hadn't taken her long to determine that ManInBlue and Frank were one and the same. She had suspected that a graphically sensual woman in the room, who went by the nickname of Silky, was the person with whom Frank was involved. Along the way, Patricia told Bill that she had become involved with Phillip rather early on, and in many ways had developed empathy for Frank's position. She'd begun to avoid Alma's questions. More to the point, Patricia admitted to Bill, she'd lied to Alma and simply told her that she didn't have the time nor the patience to continue their little Sherlock Holmes adventure, and that she never did determine anything that she could substantiate and had ceased going into the chatroom. Alma's disappointment had been evident, and Patricia was somewhat shocked at her ability to lie to her so easily. She admitted to Bill that she was more shocked, however, to realize that lying to Alma affected her conscience far more than any guilt she felt about her relationship with Phillip. She told him that she'd convinced herself that she could and would end this affair as quickly and painlessly as she could. It was impossible though. She was hopelessly in love with Phillip.

"I hope you understand how hard this is for me to comprehend, Patricia. I'm trying. I'm honestly trying; but I'll have to be frank with you, it's difficult for me to even begin to understand what can trigger these sorts of emotions and affect lives to the degree that I've seen it affect you and Frank. Damn, Patricia!"

"I know."

She knew it would be futile to try to explain that she'd occasionally logged into the chatroom as someone else in order to continue her vigilance of Frank. She couldn't even remember who now, because she'd just pluck names out of the blue—a word on a tissue box or phrase on a hand cream jar on her desk. Once, she'd even opened the phone book and chose the first name that her finger landed on. It was a man's name. That posed a whole new set of rather comical disasters as she tried to anonymously converse in the room, always keenly aware of the exchange between Silky and ManInBlue and of the long lapses into silence as they disappeared into their own private chatroom.

Though Patricia and Frank were not necessarily close friends, she did have a certain respect for him. He'd always behaved and talked like a perfect gentleman whenever she'd been around him. His demeanor belied his physical appearance. He was a brute of a man who, she presumed, could easily become threatening. But in all the years that they'd been acquainted, Patricia had never witnessed this side of him, nor had Alma ever indicated that he was anything but loving, gentle, and considerate. In the chatroom, however, he would frequently engage in disturbing, lewd, and degrading conversations with the character known as NastyOlGeezer.

Several times, Patricia had to engage ManInBlue in a private conversation in the room. She'd try to get him to stop what he was saying, asking him why he felt like he had to say the things he did. She once told him that behind the personalities in the chatroom were living, breathing individuals with hearts and feelings, and what gave him the right to trample on them like he did. He'd blast her in the open room, calling her one of a hundred of the ugly names he liked to use. Patricia could feel her pulse race and her face flush from the sheer embarrassment for herself and the rage and despair that she felt it must be causing the other people who had to endure it.

Of course, therein lies an even stranger chatroom phenomenon. Why would anyone in their right mind choose to stay in an atmosphere such as that? There was no answer to that question that Bill could possibly understand. Patricia, on the other hand, knew she would put up with practically anything if it meant she could spend time with Phillip. She tried to explain this to Bill as intelligently as possible, underscoring that perhaps much of the allure of this medium was that it afforded the opportunity to be completely anonymous and free to express your emotions in any way you chose.

Patricia wondered if her explanation had crossed that fine line where Bill drew the line between rational and irrational behavior. But he had asked, and it had to be said. She then realized that she had run out of words. Her explanation had stopped abruptly, and the two of them sat in a kind of stunned silence until a dark-colored diesel pickup pulled into the walled parking lot, circled it once, and then roared back out onto the main highway, leaving in its wake a choking cloud of dust and a shower of pebbles.

"Damned kids!" Bill grumbled as he reached to quickly roll up the window before they both started coughing.

"Oh, Bill," she said with a smile, "they're just kids looking for a place to go parking, you old grouch!".

"They better not be, or they'll sure as heck be candidates for curfew violation!" He tried to sound gruff and official, but when he realized it wasn't working, they both began to chuckle.

"Curfew violation, my hind leg! What time is it anyway?"

Bill turned on the dash light. The clock read 2:37.

"No way!" they shouted in unison. The sudden realization of how much time had passed, coupled with their joint reaction to it, caused them both to break into hysterical laughter. Laughter came easily to Patricia and once she got started, it was sometimes hard for her to stop. She personally hated it because once she got going, she would eventually embarrass herself with a few uncontrolled snorts, which in turn created more infectious laughter. Once the cycle was finally broken, she normally had tears in her eyes and the start of a frontal headache. That was the case tonight. Once they finally settled down, Bill said, "God, it's been a long time since I've done that!" They looked at one another and smiled and Bill took Patricia's hand in his.

"Thank you for talking to me tonight, Patricia. I know that couldn't have been easy for you."

"I really haven't the faintest idea what all I said, actually. But we have been at this for over fourteen hours, and I don't see where we are any further along than we were when we started this at lunch."

"Oh, but we are. How far, though, I'm not sure yet. But I'm convinced that somehow all of this is going to fit together in a nice little complicated package. Someone holds the key, and that's what I've got to find, Patricia. Frank's hearing is in just a few weeks and we have to come up with more than we have now or we are going to have a heck of a time getting a postponement until we can."

"They still want to charge Frank with this somehow, don't they?"

"Sure they do. And why not? Often times a conspiracy theory is hard to prove, but with all the evidence stacked against him that they were able to salvage from his computer's hard drive, it's practically a case built in heaven for Richards. Everything is there except the actual discussion of the plot. All the evidence links Frank and Silky. All of the threatening e-mails from her to Frank, and then those final conversations when Frank apparently conceded that he couldn't live without her and would do anything she asked of him, have convinced the powers that be that he knew that something was going to happen. There are some mighty big loopholes and gaps in the whole thing, but these federal hackers know what they're doing and it's just a matter of time before they find all the missing links."

"Missing links? Such as?"

"Such as why the experts can't trace the origin of Silky's computer. Apparently, that's a fairly simple thing to do. In fact, there are three or four of your so-called friends from that chatroom who haven't been traced—or can't be traced—I'm not sure which."

"What do you mean traced, Bill? Like they can tell from Frank's computer who was talking, who they really are, and where they're located?"

"I wasn't aware of that either, Patricia. I knew that an expert could hack into a chat in progress and easily find out the points of origin of each one involved, but I was as surprised as you to learn they can find that stored somewhere on the hard drive. Had Frank been more familiar with computers, he might have been able to erase it. But for whatever reason, Frank chose to save the conversations he had with Silky. That's pretty incriminating stuff, Patricia."

"Oh, Bill, I had no idea." Her voice was barely above a whisper.

"I know. Phillip said you wouldn't."

"I know more than Phillip might think, Bill. Maybe not about this, but I know about a lot of other things."

"That's why he wanted the two of us to talk before he spoke with you. I had no reason to doubt him when he began unfolding his suspicions, and I assure you that he never told me the two of you were romantically linked in any way. It didn't take me long to figure that out, but he didn't tell me."

"I know he didn't. He wouldn't."

Bill started to say something, but Patricia kept talking. She was ready to tell him what she knew. "Caesar is a student at the Taos Art Institute. He started coming into the store a few months ago, and found every excuse he could to be with Alma. I didn't like the kid. He was cocky and arrogant and he demanded her attention even if she were busy with other customers. We talked about it a few times and she was just as annoyed as I was. But she didn't know how to handle him. I think he came onto Alma a few times and, well…in light of the situation between Frank and her…she was flattered. Hell, I can't blame her! She's not as old as I am, but that kid can't be over eighteen or nineteen." Patricia paused, evaluated whether she wanted to continue or not, and then decided to go ahead.

"This does need to stay between the two of us, Bill, okay?" She paused and Bill nodded. All of what Patricia was telling him about Caeser and Alma came as a complete surprise. Everything except the fact that Bill knew very well who Caeser was.

"I don't know for sure, but I think the two of them met a few times. What happened between them, I couldn't tell you, but Trent told me that he was up appraising some land north of Arroyo Hondo and passed her Mustang pulled off to the side of the road. He said when he came back by, Alma and some kid were just coming across the clearing toward her car. He said he honked at her, but she ignored him. When he told me about it, I asked him who the kid was and he said he didn't know. He described him, and I knew immediately that it was Caesar. Well, you must know him. He's pretty distinctive looking in an odd sort of way.

This was the part Bill knew he might eventually regret. "No, I haven't met him. I just started putting two and two together yesterday, actually." That was a lie. Caesar Abeyta was a student in his martial arts class. His best student, actually.

"Put *what* two and two together?"

This was the first time Patricia could actually feel the energy vibrating in the air surrounding them. Her skin tingled as she waited for Bill to answer. He rolled the window down slightly, and the first rush of cool air made them both shiver.

"Patricia, Caesar is NastyOlGeezer in your chatroom."

Chapter Twenty-seven

Phillip wished he had told Patricia more, but he didn't know how much of what he was speculating might actually be true. There was no need to make her more paranoid than she already was. Besides, there were enough facts for her to really worry about. And it was entirely possible that he was mistaken. Unfortunately, it was beginning to seem less and less likely that he was. He now wished he had simply dropped everything and hopped on a plane to go see her. Everything else seemed to be excuses for avoiding the inevitable.

He began writing some poetry while he waited for Mark. The title, he decided, would be simply "Three Dots"—as in a continuation,

...

The lights are on
Someone is home
It is I
After all.
Never alone.

An Angel,
Not of mercy,
Born of desire and need
Grows into a partnership.
As my locked-away demons
Are freed.
The demons learn to fly
No longer crawling and lurking,
Fears faced.
Transformed.
Two Angels
In the sky.
Embraced.

Destiny faced.
Together two.
Destiny is an angel
It's you
And it's me.

Angels of passion
And compassion;
Of bitches
And riches;
Of giving
and living;
Of believing
And receiving;
Of faking
And taking;
Of being
And seeing;
Of light
And sight;
Of imperfection
And sweet confection

Of comedy
And tragedy
Of might
And right;
Of ruthlessness
And truthfulness;
Of doing
And renewing;
Of duality
And spirituality;
Of schemes
And dreams;
Of stories
And everlasting glories.
Finally free
Destiny is an Angel
It's you
And

Its
Me
. . .

It was funny, that feeling that came over him sometimes, that his thoughts were somehow connected to hers. He sensed perhaps she was discovering at this very moment that he'd talked with Bill Conner about what was going on. Maybe that was why he was thinking about all of this right now. Maybe he could actually feel Patricia's emotional thoughts. She would most likely feel hurt that he had not told her everything that was going on, but he knew that she would eventually understand that he was only protecting her.

They had talked often about spiritual lives and about how souls travel throughout time learning, teaching, absorbing, searching, understanding, and healing—healing others and themselves until arriving at the point where they could truly enjoy life the most. You could easily dismiss it as a mortal's need to feel that life has more meaning than what it appears to, and that one human life is not all that is given to us. Not that one human life is an insignificant thing by any means, but rather a part of a much larger puzzle that one can never really comprehend. One individual life is but part of a continuous thread woven back and forth into a complete blanket of existence. Phillip believed that at the end of a life begins a journey taken by the soul across the River Styx or the Sanzu River separating this life from the afterlife as it wends its way inexorably toward the next existence.

If each person lived his or her life as though their contributions were the seeds to create an abundance of knowledge and understanding and love, then the entire perspective with which one views everyday existence would change dramatically. If at the end of the day, we knew—truly knew—that we have lived that day in a manner which was better than the day before and that what was done that day will lead to an even better tomorrow, then we have lived a near perfect day.

How many times do we excuse ourselves from living an almost perfect day, Phillip wondered. Perhaps it is not such a terrible thing if we don't realize we have the capacity for creating those kinds of days. But if we do realize that and then we do not have perfect days, we deny ourselves a life as good and as meaningful as it should be. We end up trading it for one less satisfying or rewarding. Patricia would agree and say, "*It is the way of things.*"

* * * * *

"Been waiting long?" Mark asked. Phillip smiled and shook his head, trying to emerge from his haze of thoughts about spirituality and Patricia.

"You okay, Phillip?"

"Perfect," Phillip said unconvincingly as he took a seat across the table from him in the restaurant.

"Glad to hear it!" Mark laughed. "You ready to make your delivery? I've only taken half a day off."

"I'm ready."

"You sure you know what we are getting ourselves into?"

"I think we're dealing with someone who's only dangerous when he's operating in secrecy."

Mark replied, "But if he thinks he is being discovered, do we have any idea how he will act?"

Phillip chose not to answer.

"I know you can't possibly answer that question. I just hope we don't make this guy nervous. But if we do, I just hope he doesn't have a lot of weapons around!"

Phillip smiled wickedly.

"Oh, *that's* a good reaction," Mark said sarcastically.

"Hey, I'm simply delivering my extraordinary work of art to the man who bought it for oodles of money!"

"Yeah, but if he's been stalking you, then to have his prey surprise him with an appearance may prove to be quite unsettling to him."

"Which is exactly why I have *you* along!"

"Cripes, how do I let you talk me into these things?"

"Hey, do you want to order something?" Phillip asked.

"Have they got sanity pie?"

"No," Phillip chuckled, "but you must be mad to even suggest such a thing."

"I must be."

"Coffee?"

"Yeah, a cup of coffee is the least you can buy me."

After the waitress brought them their coffee, Mark asked, "So, is Toto actually expecting this delivery?"

"Toji," Phillip laughed. "Toji Taisho is his name. He's expecting us at eleven, actually."

"Toji Taisho? Shit, you think I'm gonna remember that?"

"He lives in a condo in Kirkland by Caroline Point."

"Guy's got the bucks."

"Yep. He does okay for himself, I'm sure."

"And this guy Toe Jay…" Mark began.

"Toji! As in gee-whiz," Phillip corrected.

"*Toe Gee*… yeah. This is the one who calls himself Silky *and* Bishamon in the chatroom world?"

"Yes. And Bishamon is the name of the Japanese god of war."

"Oh, that's nice. Imaginative fellow, isn't he?"

Phillip chuckled.

"Oh, stop laughing at me! It's a lot of shit to try and remember for my poor dumb cop brain, you know!"

"Okay, I'll take it slower this time," Phillip replied with a smirk. "Silky is the cyber girlfriend of Frank, the Taos County Sheriff."

"The one whose wife was killed."

"Yeah."

"And you think Silky is really Toji Cashew?"

"Taisho, right."

"And the reason he is doing this, Mr. Holmes?" Mark asked Phillip.

"I'm not exactly sure why. Maybe because he's not comfortable with the feelings he has for another guy, or maybe it's some kind of a game to him."

"And he's also this god of war, too?"

"Bishamon? Yes, I think so," Phillip said hesitantly.

"And this Bishamon guy is the one who is very upset with this woman you know? Patricia?"

"Right. Those were the e-mails I sent you."

"Which aren't the most rational things I've ever read, by the way."

"That's why it occurred to me that I needed your help," Phillip added.

"Lucky me," Mark muttered.

"You really hate this as much as you're pretending to?"

"Yeah, I hate this. I never like going into situations without having a sense of control, and I like it even less when I'm going into a situation with an untrained civilian friend of mine. Not to mention that I know almost nothing about this guy. And then I'm in this because you're in love with a woman you've never met, an invisible someone you bumped into on the Internet. And there's some sheriff's wife who's been decapitated in Taos, which is just a little bit out of my jurisdiction. What's there to hate?"

"You realize nothing's likely to happen, don't you?"

"Yeah, right. Listen, if I get killed, I'm really going to be upset for letting you talk me into this."

"You really can be an asshole, you know that?"

"I'm a fuckin' cop," Mark said. "It's what folks expect. People would be worried if I didn't act this way."

"You do it so naturally though.".

"Fuck you, asshole!" Mark said with a fake snarl.

Mark and Phillip walked up the stairs toward Toji Taisho's second floor condo. Under his arm, Phillip carried the gallery piece entitled *First Autumn Storm* wrapped in white paper.

The three-story building sat on the banks of Lake Washington and overlooked a marina where dozens of million-dollar yachts were moored. Across Lake Washington was an impressive view of the Seattle skyline. Kirkland was a squeaky clean area, just a short drive from Microsoft's Redmond campus.

Phillip pushed the doorbell and a short, well-dressed Japanese man in his mid-forties soon greeted them.

"Ah, I am so honored you are here," he said as he invited the two inside his home.

"Well, I'm glad I was able to meet you again," Phillip said. "This is a friend of mine, Mark Murphy."

Toji bowed slightly. Unsure whether he should return the bow or not, Mark nodded his head slightly.

"Come in, please."

In the entrance hallway, Phillip noticed seven extraordinary pieces of art. The first, fourth and seventh were beautiful figurines carved in jade. The others were watercolors, intricately painted figures on silk and rice paper scrolls. When they turned the corner, Phillip paused and looked at a small, black lacquered table upon which sat a vase with three fresh flowers comprising a simple arrangement. The table was inlaid with mother-of-pearl in a design he thought to be a palace and gardens.

"This is beautiful, Mr. Taisho."

"Thank you, Phillip. But please, call me Toji." He bowed again.

"It is a traditional arrangement signifying Shin, Soe, and Haiku? Am I correct?"

"Very close!" Toji answered as he gently touched the petals of the Asian lilies.

"They are actually called Shin, Soe, and Hikae—Heaven, Man, and Earth. Haiku is a form of Japanese poetry, my friend! I'm impressed, however!" Toji's delight seemed genuine. "You have studied the Japanese culture?"

"Not really, no. But I try to learn as much as I can from listening and reading a little."

Toji smiled and then led them into the living room where Phillip noticed several things immediately. First, in the corner was a nearly life-sized bronze figure of what appeared to be a seventeenth century Samurai. Over the fireplace were several antique swords and daggers. On another wall were three gold picture frames. In the largest one, in the middle, was a color photograph of Emperor Hirohito. To the left of that picture was a framed collection of gold coins, and on the right was a painting of beautiful cherry trees laden with blossoms and overlooking a lake.

"I'm sorry, tea would be wonderful," Phillip said, quickly realizing that Toji was waiting for a response to his offer.

Toji bowed and looked at the painting of the lake that seemed to have captured Phillip's attention. "That is Lake Biwa, the largest lake in Japan, near Kyoto where some of my family still lives."

"It's very beautiful."

"Thank you, Phillip. Perhaps some day you will visit there and take some wonderful photographs."

"I'd love to."

Mark came over to Phillip as soon as Toji left the room to get the tea. "Is that Hirohito?"

"Yes. It's very common for Japanese families to have his picture."

"Isn't he dead?"

"Yes," Phillip answered quietly, "but Hirohito was and still is very much admired and respected for a variety of reasons. He created a great deal of controversy after World War II when he proclaimed that, though he was from was an unbroken line of rulers, he was *not* divine, as so many of the Japanese people believed."

Phillip was going to say more, but Toji came back carrying the tea service. He placed the tray on the table and turned to Phillip. "You seem to know quite a lot about my home, Phillip-Sama."

Phillip smiled. "No, not very much at all."

"I see." Toji said. "The emperor who preceded Hirohito was Emperor Taisho."

"Taisho?" asked Mark. "Your name is Taisho, isn't it?"

"Yes."

"So you're related to an Emperor?"

"Oji-San. A great uncle," Toji said.

"So you're part of the royal family?"

"Part of my family was part of the royal family, I suppose. But that was many years ago and before the war." Toji motioned for his guests to sit on the cushions scattered around the low teakwood table. Mark first watched Toji and then Phillip, before dropping cross-legged onto the silk cushion. Toji poured the tea.

After a few moments, Phillip asked, "Perhaps you will tell us about those wonderful pieces on the wall as we entered. I'd be most interested to hear about the impressive collection of swords on the wall there, too. I couldn't help but notice that you have what I would call a Seppuku blade."

Toji smiled slightly. "It may have been used in Seppuku, but I do not know. It is from a collection that has been in the family a long time. The sword on the top there may have belonged to Munenori himself."

Phillip was very impressed. He had studied martial arts several years before and knew who Munenori was. He glanced at Mark and could see that his friend had no idea what they were talking about.

"You are familiar with Munenori?" Toji asked.

"I believe so, but I don't think Mark is."

"One of the most respected teachers of Samurai customs and techniques was Yagyu Muneyoshi," explained Toji. "Muneyoshi developed the Shinkage-ryuu style often called New Shadow. One of his sons was Munenori. Munenori taught the first three Tokugawa shoguns swordsmanship in the sixteenth and early seventeenth centuries."

"In other words, Mark, it's three hundred years old, famous, and worth a lot of money," Phillip clarified.

"Yes, that is true," Toji smiled. He liked this photographer Phillip very much. "The Tokugawa, or Edo period in Japan, is named for the fifteen generations of the Tokugawa Shoguns, or the military overlords, who ruled Japan for over 250 years. It was a feudal system then. But during this period our modern culture developed. Everything from Haiku to puppet theater was created and refined, but still we remained isolated from the Western world until the mid-1850s. That particular sword could be from the 1500s or even before then. And those two swords are from a well-respected Samurai, who was one of Jubei Mitsukoshi's mentors and are probably from about the mid-1600s. The owner of those swords was a very rich Samurai who was in charge of a large rice paddy, had several horses, and those two swords and dagger."

"Jubei Misuyoshi is one of Munenori's sons I believe," Phillip said, not completely sure that he was correct.

"Yes, that is true," Toji nodded.

"Misuyoshi is a famous samurai character who is used in many films and even is in a few video games," Phillip explained to Mark.

"I am quite impressed," Toji remarked.

"Well, don't be too impressed. The real reason I know any of this is because I absolutely adored Samurai films when I was going to college. And there was a group of us that used to go and see the Lone Wolf and Cub films and the Baby Cart movies which were shown at the midnight shows."

"He's a real movie nut," explained Mark.

Toji smiled. "Yes, but that is how most of us learned about the history of the Samurai. From the Lone Wolf comic books. They were most popular in Japan in the sixties and seventies."

Phillip took another sip of his tea. "Are you going to hang my piece in here?"

Toji pointed to the other side of the fireplace where a poster from a Japanese art exhibit was hanging. The poster reproduced a watercolor that seemed to be of a strong young man surrounded by several wild animals.

"My piece is replacing Kintaro?"

Toji smiled. "You know Kintaro too, I see. That is a nice poster from an exhibit that traveled around the country a while ago now. I will move it to my son's room."

"Oh, you're married?" Mark asked quickly.

"I am no longer married, no," Toji said quietly.

"Well I've been divorced twice," Mark said. "Can't live with them, can't live without them.

Toji nodded several times. "That is very true, yes." He paused while he refilled everyone's cup. "It was my son who first heard of you, actually. Then I heard that some people at my office were going to your exhibition and I invited myself along."

"I wish I could have sold you the piece you originally wanted."

"But you had promised it to someone already. I understand and respect that."

"I was honored by your generous offer for it."

"Now I am honored that I am able to own this piece and I am overwhelmed you are here visiting me in my home." Toji bowed his head.

Phillip was almost admiring the masterful way Toji was pretending to be a quiet traditional Japanese man and how well he was hiding his "other self." There must be a way to bring his other personality out into the open.

"Those coins..." Phillip began.

"Kobans. From the early seventeen hundreds," Toji answered quickly.

"May I?" Phillip asked as he started to get up.

"Please."

Mark watched Phillip as he studied the gold coins in the frame.

"These must be worth a fortune!" Mark said.

"They are probably worth several thousand dollars. But they are of sentimental value, too. My grandfather gave them to my brother and me many years ago."

"You've done pretty good for yourself, I guess," Mark said.

"Yes, thank you."

"Your wife was American?" Phillip asked.

"Yes, that is correct."

"How long have you been divorced?"

"About five years now." Phillip wasn't sure if the question bothered him or not.

"You met her here?"

"When I was in college, yes, Phillip. We were together twelve years," Toji answered. "Are you married, Mr. Craven?"

"No, I'm not."

"So you are also no longer married?"

"That's right."

"But you understand things so well," Toji said.

"He does?" questioned Mark.

"Have you seen his work?" Toji asked.

"Yes, I have. He's very talented."

"But it is more than just talent, there is much that lies beneath the surface of what he does. He captures much more than colors or beautiful things. He captures spirits…"

"I hope my work does reflect spirits, thank you." If it were someone else saying this to him, he would have been flattered. But since it was Toji, he felt they were playing some extremely elaborate game of chess. "You are very perceptive to see the layers of my work."

"People are made up of many layers, but to capture more than one or two at a time is a rare ability," Toji continued.

"We all hide a great deal, don't we?" Phillip said with a slight smile.

There was a long and awkward silence.

"Pain and disappointments are not things which should be shared openly, although it seems as though this is more commonly done in Western cultures," Toji finally said quietly.

"Very true. But keeping such things inside manifests them into something else. Perhaps it metamorphoses into something else." Phillip let his words hang there. He wasn't as careful with his words as he would have liked, but he was glad he got them out.

"Would you mind if I use the rest room?" Mark asked.

"Certainly not." Toji bowed slightly and motioned down the hall.

After Mark left the room, Phillip moved over to the fireplace and looked at the photographs on the mantle. There was one of a beautiful American woman holding a toddler of maybe two years old in front of a large Buddhist temple.

"Your wife and son?"

"Yes," Toji nodded.

Phillip saw a young man with a very old Japanese man standing in front of some bushes.

"My son again," Toji explained, "with his friend who works with the Parks Department in Seattle."

"I see," Phillip said. "Looks like a fine boy."

Another picture showed a younger Toji, his American wife, and their son at Disneyland. There were black-and-white photographs of an elderly Japanese couple and of several other Japanese people at what appeared to be a wedding party.

"Your parents and relatives perhaps?"

"Yes."

"You have a wonderful home," Phillip said, glancing toward the large picture window that looked out over the lake toward Seattle in the distance.

"You are a very kind man."

"We'll have to be going in a few minutes," Phillip said when Mark reentered the room.

"And I must be going also," Toji said.

"If I may use your rest room, too, before we go?" Phillip excused himself and went down the hall toward the bathroom, pausing in front of a display case. Behind the glass were what appeared to be the various stages in the life of an insect, including a butterfly emerging from its cocoon. Phillip then realized that it was showing how silk was created, beginning with the silkworm.

When Phillip returned to the living room, he found Mark talking to Toji about a boat out on the water.

"So do you get a discount if you want to moor your boat at the marina?"

"I don't know. I don't own a boat. I barely know how to swim," Toji laughed.

"Well, Mark, we should get going," Phillip interrupted.

"Yes, I have to get to work."

"As do I," Toji said as he began to lead them out of the living room.

"You asked about these seven pieces," Toji said when they reached the hallway. "The scrolls were part of a set owned by my great grandfather. The jade carvings I had commissioned about ten years ago when I moved into this place."

"And these are the gods of good fortune?" Phillip asked.

"Yes. The first one is Evisu, the god of fishermen and tradesmen. Daikoku is the god of wealth and considered to be the patron saint of farmers. Benten is the god of art, music, and eloquence."

"A lady," Mark noted.

"Yes, a female. And this...this is Bishamon, the god of war." Phillip glanced quickly at Mark who cocked his eyebrow slightly.

"Fukurokuju is the god of wisdom."

"Easy for you to say," joked Mark.

Toji smiled, but Phillip wasn't sure if he'd understood the joke or not.

This is Jurojin, the god of longevity, and this is the happy and generous beggar god known as Hotei."

"They are wonderful," Mark said.

"Thank you. I'm obviously quite proud of my culture, but I am also very honored to be part of this country."

Mark smiled. "And we're glad you've made our country a little more interesting by bringing part of your culture here with you."

"Kind of you to say so."

"It was a pleasure meeting you again, Toji," Phillip said extending his hand.

"Shit!" Phillip said loudly once they were back in the car.

"Seemed like a pretty normal fellow to me, Phillip."

"Did he? Did you notice the display case outside the bathroom?"

"The one that looked like a science project? Sure. I figured it was probably his son's."

"Silkworms," said Phillip.

"Silkworms?"

"Silky and Bishamon."

"I see…I think" Mark said, cocking his eyebrow at Phillip.

"And did you find it interesting how he shook your hand?"

"How he shook my hand?" Mark looked over at Phillip to see if he was kidding.

"Oh fine, look at me like you think I'm crazy."

"I *know* you're crazy."

"Not about this."

"Hey, I'll go along with you that there's a reason to have suspicions about the guy."

"Well, *thank you*."

"You're quite welcome," Mark replied. "Now why the hell did the way this guy shake your hand upset you?"

"He seemed very Japanese most of the time, didn't he? Very traditionally Japanese. Not speaking perfect English, using a few Japanese terms here and there."

"Yeah, okay. So?"

"Yet he shook our hands, just like any American would, without hesitation. Not too soft or awkward."

"Phil, he's been here all of his life and he married an American for chrissakes. That's not all that unusual!"

"Then why the traditional Japanese act during most of our visit?"

Mark shrugged. "I don't know, Phillip."

"I do. I managed to look in his wallet. It was on his bedroom dresser and copied down his credit card numbers for you to trace."

Mark was smiling. "Now if this guy took a trip to Albuquerque, it certainly will make him a person of interest. I should have an answer for you in a few hours."

"And I'll get hold of the authorities in Taos, if you tell me what I think you will."

"Which is that he took a trip to Albuquerque and rented a car?"

"Yeah," replied Phillip. "I'm sure this son of a bitch is guilty as hell."

"You got a hunch, a strong feeling?" asked Mark who started laughing at his friend.

"I know what I must sound like."

"I sure hope so!" exclaimed Mark.

Phillip enjoyed the next ten minutes of near quiet as he replayed the visit with Toji in his mind. Suddenly Mark said, "You know you should go and visit this woman right away. Patricia, right?"

Phillip shrugged.

"I don't know why you've waited this long."

"I don't either," Phillip said softly.

Chapter Twenty-eight

Patricia slowly began to realize what the past fourteen plus hours had been all about. She probably should have been more surprised, but she wasn't. She was surprised, however, that Phillip had not shown more faith in her by talking this over with her before taking it upon himself to contact Bill. She began to wonder if he'd talked to anybody else. She also wondered if he'd perhaps told Bill some things that Bill was too much of a gentleman to repeat. She couldn't decide if she should be grateful or embarrassed.

Embarrassed? Should I really be embarrassed about my relationship with Phillip? Well, for pity sakes, of course I should be embarrassed! Was this normal behavior for someone my age? Hell, I don't even know what's considered normal anymore.

Actually, the whole thing with Phillip seemed normal. Why, for over a year now, she'd been getting up every morning, making her way sleepy-eyed into her office, logging onto her computer, and sending Phillip "good morning" notes saying how much she loved him, how much she missed him, and how she'd held him all night long, which must account for why she always awoke with a smile on her face.

"Patricia, considering the hour, would you like me to take you to Sylvia's for what's left of the night?" She and Bill were still sitting in his car in the parking lot of the old mission. He had let her absorb his last startling statement concerning NastyOlGeezer and was hoping for some feedback. He wouldn't get any. He was neither surprised nor amused. Instead, he was getting nervous and impatient. He wanted some concrete answers and she wasn't supplying them.

"No, thanks. I'll just go home."

"How will you explain this to Trent?"

"I won't have to explain, Bill. Trent's not there. He moved out the day after we got home from Durango."

Bill was surprised but not shocked. "You told him about Phillip then?"

"No. As far as I know, he knows nothing about Phil. Well, hardly anything..." She seemed to leave the sentence dangling, and Bill wasn't sure where to go next.

"It's that serious between this Emily woman and him? Damn, Patricia, I had no idea."

"Neither did I. I confronted him about it on the way home from Colorado and he damned near exploded. He told me that I was a fine one to be accusing *him* of improprieties and reminded me about a time or two I'd accidentally mentioned Phillip's name. I told him he was being an ass and to drop it for the time being. After we unloaded from the trip, I went to the grocery store and to the bookshop for an hour or so. When I got home, he was gone. Most of his clothing was gone, too, and he didn't leave a note."

"Patricia, I don't..."

"Don't say anything, Bill. I asked for it, really. Even you have to admit that. He'll be back, though. It's a tantrum. He deserves that much, don't you think?" Bill didn't answer. He just started the Trooper, exited the parking lot, and turned north.

As he carried her bags into the house, he struggled with a way to express his feelings about what had transpired between them. As usual, Patricia filled in the blanks and let his discomfort go presumably unnoticed. She walked up behind him and gave him a warm, reassuring hug.

"Hey, Marshall, you look like you are about four hours late with your daily dose of Metamucil! Lighten up, okay? We have an awful lot to absorb and think about here. But I want to thank you for telling me about all of this and trusting me to understand your intentions. You know that anything that has been said between us will stay there—except for what we shared about Phillip. I'll contact him right away. He should be home from his hiking trip by now."

"Hiking trip?"

"He and a friend of his took a few days to hike a local mountain. He didn't mention that?" She visualized Phillip and Mark acting like two overgrown Boy Scouts.

"Phillip isn't hiking, Patricia. I've talked to him. Don't worry, though, I'm not betraying him. He'll tell you all of this himself as soon as you reach him."

Patricia wondered at just what point one more surprise would be one too many. She didn't want to know the answer. She said good-bye to Bill and started brewing a fresh pot of coffee and began sorting through the mail. Most of it was the usual junk mail—ads, a couple of clothing catalogues—but there was one envelope that caught her eye. Nicely watermarked with a beautifully scripted initial logo bearing a local return address: LSL/Attorneys at Law, 137 -J North Pueblo Road, Taos, NM 87571.

Patricia opened it and read through the brief contents and then placed the divorce papers back in the envelope and tossed it on the counter. *Dammit, Trent, get over yourself.*

She poured herself an oversized mug of coffee, added powdered creamer, and made her way through the quiet house to her bedroom. Kitty Gato was at her heels the entire time and when she flipped on the light, Kitty beat her to the closet door and sat rubbing her face against the molding. Patricia stepped into the closet and stripped off her clothes. Tossing what needed to go to the cleaners in one basket and the rest in the hamper, she kicked off her shoes and gave them an uncustomary fling and grabbed a peach silk robe from a hook on the back of the door. By this time, Kitty was playfully rolling in the cleaning basket and purring quietly. Patricia smiled, thinking that some constants in life are good. She hardly remembered life before Miss Kitty. She couldn't imagine life without her. She barely remembered life without Trent either, for that matter. She reached down and scratched the contented cat's tummy. *At least the cat is here when I get home.*

Even now, the uneven oxblood floor was cool on her feet as she walked down the hall to her office at the rear of the house. She always left a radio playing so that Miss Gato wasn't entirely alone, and she could hear Frank Sinatra crooning "In the Still of the Night" when she walked in and flipped on the overhead light. She'd always liked that song. Tonight the house did seem oddly still. There was an additional stack of new mail on her desk. *Well, either Trent has been here since she'd left or Sylvia was over to check on things.* More junk mail, nothing significant.

She turned on her computer and while it booted up, she listened to her phone messages. The first one was from the morning she'd left for the conference. It was Trent telling her that if she needed him or if there were an emergency, he could be reached at the office. He said he'd be staying there for the time being. *Yeah, right.*

The next two calls were hang-ups.

Then Sylvia had called to say she'd wanted to come over and check on things but for some reason she couldn't find the key to Patricia's house. *For as long as she could remember, it had hung on a small brass hook at Sylvia's back door.* She'd get her a new one, and jotted a note to remind herself.

Another hang up.

The next message made her smile. It was Butch Killen asking her to call him after she got back to town and they'd do lunch. He also told her that everything was fine at the store. *What would she do without Butch?*

Trent again. The message had been left around eight o'clock that night to say that he was sorry he'd left like he had. He hoped she was okay. *Jerk. It's been five months and NOW you call to apologize?* He'd wanted to come by, but couldn't bring himself to and maybe he'd see her on Thursday. *So he hadn't been by. Sylvia must have found the key, after all.*

Another hang-up. End of messages.

She looked at her computer monitor and cringed at the number of e-mails she needed to attend to. Only one person was important now, and she checked to see if Phillip had written. He had. Only once. He'd sent it less than three hours before. Just as Patricia clicked to open the mail, she was startled out of her wits by the ringing phone. "Good god almighty!" she exclaimed out loud. She glanced at the clock. 3:54 A.M. She picked up the phone.

"Trisha, it's me baby." At the sound of Phillip's voice, she burst into tears. After some gentle coaxing and shushing from him, she finally regained her composure. "I'm sorry, sweetheart, I don't know why that happened."

"It's okay. Did you get my e-mail?"

"No. I mean *yes*. Just now, but I haven't read it yet. I just got home a few minutes ago."

"Yes, I know."

"You know? How do you know?"

"Bill just called. He filled me in on the past day. You must be exhausted and confused, baby. I'm not sure where to begin."

"Just hold me, Phillip. God, I just need someone to hold me." There was almost a childlike pleading in her voice. He'd expected everything but that from her. Tears filled his eyes.

"You still there?" asked Patricia.

"Yes, of course I am. Why?"

"I heard a funny click. I guess it was nothing. Just typical Taos phone service, I guess."

"Baby, it's going to be okay. I promise you. Are you alone?"

"Yes."

"Okay…shhh…just lie here in my arms, close your eyes, baby, and let me hold you for a few minutes. You don't need to talk, okay?"

"Uh-huh."

For the next half-hour, Phillip related the rather intricate details of his deductions and suspicions. Very little of what he said surprised her, and now she was doubly grateful for the time that she and Bill had shared.

"What are we going to do, Phillip?" Her voice was stronger now.

"I told Bill that I'd be flying to New Mexico on Saturday."

There was a long pause. Patricia wasn't sure she'd heard him correctly. *He was coming…on Saturday. Did he really just say that?*

She knew she should say something. Phillip was waiting for a reaction.

"Oh," she said finally, feeling foolish as soon as she did.

"Trisha, we can do this without meeting. If that's what you want, I will understand."

Patricia swallowed hard. "You don't want to see me, Phil? Is that what you mean?"

"No, silly! You know better than that! Why did you say that?" His tone was almost angry and she started to cry again, although she assumed he didn't know that.

"I don't know, Phillip. I don't know. Please don't do that, okay?"

"Don't do what? Come to Taos? I have to, Trisha."

"No! I mean don't you dare come here and not see me. We have to do this. You know that as well as I do." She was shaking now. She wanted so badly to see him, but part of her was terrified at the same time. There would be that moment when he would judge her looks, she was certain of that. That moment when she would feel every one of her imperfections magnified a hundred, maybe a thousand times.

"I don't think I could stop myself from seeing you, Patricia."

"You sure as hell better have said that."

"I know it's complicated, Trisha, and it's maybe bad timing and I'd understand if..."

"Stop it!" Patricia snapped. "I can't wait to see you, Phillip. I'm going to be a stark raving mad lunatic now. You know that, don't you?"

Phillip chuckled. She loved that. It showed her he was nearly as nervous as she was.

He didn't seem to know about Trent. She'd have to thank Bill for that. She decided not to tell him yet.

"Saturday? Do you know what time yet?" she asked.

"Well, my flight arrives in Albuquerque at eleven-thirty Saturday morning. By the time I rent a car and get up there, I'd say it would be around two-thirty or three. Does that sound about right?" He didn't tell her that he was actually leaving in less than five hours.

"That sounds about right, yes. Will you come to the bookstore first, Phil?" Her voice had dropped in volume to where he could hardly hear her.

"If you want me to, yes, I will."

Patricia was crying softly, the tears a mixture of happiness, fear, longing, and the realization that the fantasy would soon become reality.

"Yes. I love you, Phillip. I do."

"I know, baby, I know. I love you, too. Now, can you get some sleep? I know you must be tired. Please?" His concern sounded genuine and she could almost feel his strong arms holding her, giving her strength.

"Yes. I can. I'm already in my robe and it's not long 'til I have to be at the shop."

"You'll be going to work then?"

"Of course, I will."

"All day?"

"Yes, all day," she said with a smile. "It will no doubt be a busy day, and Butch and I will probably have lunch together. Why?"

"No reason. Just makes it easier for me to call you, if I know where you are, you know?"

"Yes, I know. By the way, did you call several times the past few days and hang up?"

"No. Why? I was camping, remember?"

So Bill hadn't shared everything with him and he wasn't going to confess just yet, either.

"I just had some hang-ups on the answering machine, that's all."

"Don't you have caller ID?"

"No. Never saw a need for it, I guess. Anyway, it's not important."

"You gonna be okay?"

"Of course. Kitty and I have planned a two-hour slumber party!" She laughed out loud.

"Two hours?"

"I don't think I'll be sleeping much tonight."

"I know what you mean, but we should both get some sleep. It's going to be a very busy weekend."

"Mmm, promise?" Patricia said softly, for a moment surprised at herself.

"Oh, yes, I promise, baby."

"I can hardly wait. I wish you could be here tomorrow, Phillip."

"Well, better look for a shooting star then!"

"Oh, there's dozens of them tonight," Patricia said. "I could have any number of wishes come true."

"Make them good ones then! Listen, I'm going to let you go, Trisha. You sleep tight okay? I'll be out and about real early tomorrow, so I probably won't talk to you till after lunch or so."

After they said their goodnights, Patricia sat back in her chair recalling their conversation. A subtle noise somewhere in the house brought her out of her reverie. The mail could wait. She shivered and shut down the computer. Kissing the tips of her fingers and pressing them to the screen as she bade goodnight to the fading name on the screen.

After a less than enthusiastic attempt to wash some of the grime and makeup from her face, she turned on CNN on the bedroom TV and fell onto the bed. When she reached over to scratch Miss Gato's ears, she was surprised to find the cat wasn't curled there. Patricia rolled over to get comfortable but remembered the odd noise earlier and decided she'd best go investigate what that damned cat had gotten into and bring her back to bed. Patricia smiled as she listened to herself groan when she hoisted herself from the bed. *Damn, it's hell getting old.*

A walk thorough the house produced nothing out of order nor Kitty Gato. Usually very visible during the night, till it was time for bed, Patricia found this highly unusual and annoying. She was dog-tired and resented the intrusion on the time she could be sleeping. *To hell with her, I'm going to bed.*

It was only when she turned off the light next to the bed that she realized the closet light was still on. If she'd been under the covers, she would have ignored it. She walked across the room to turn it off. The door was slightly ajar and she heard an odd noise. "Ah, so that's where you are, you stupid thing! I should leave you there!"

Patricia tried to open the door, but it was jammed against something. With some effort, she forced it open wide enough for her to step into the closet. She screamed when she saw Kitty Gato on the floor, struggling to breathe. Her cat's eyes were barely open, but Patricia was sure she saw relief and recognition in them. She fell to her knees and scooped the almost lifeless old cat into her arms, rocking and pleading with her not to die. *No! No! No! Don't you do this to me! Don't you dare do this to me! Please...please... please!*

The sun was up, though the morning was still eerily quiet, as Patricia put the last shovel of dirt over the shallow grave she'd dug beside the garage. *She's hardly ever been outside before. Fourteen years old and she's never been outside alone. She'll be scared. I just know she'll be scared. Goddamn it, Kitty. Damn you!* Patricia stooped over the shovel handle and sobbed.

She was unaware that Sylvia was next door standing at her kitchen sink, her arms wrapped around her son Carlos. They were watching her through the window. Sylvia gently answered Carlos' question.

"It's Miss Kitty, sweetheart. She must have died." Sylvia's heart was in her throat, remembering her inability to get into Patricia's house, wondering if somehow this was her fault. She cursed the misplaced key.

"Mom, what should we do? We have to do something for Aunt Patricia. We have to! Should I try to find her a new cat today after school?" He was crying and had turned to see his mother wiping away her own tears.

"No. Not yet, honey. This will take Aunt Patricia some time. Remember when Daddy left?" Carlos nodded. "Having a new father wouldn't have taken the hurt away, would it?" He shook his head.

"But there *has* to be something we can do, Mom. There must be." He was crying openly now, watching the woman he had grown up with, kneeling on the ground, her face in her hands. Sylvia had turned away now and was staring at the back door, her hands over her mouth. On the hook next to the door was the key to Patricia's house.

Chapter Twenty-nine

It didn't bother Phillip at all that he'd lied once again to Patricia. He felt quite good about it actually. Besides, he was looking forward with excitement to later that afternoon when he would just casually wander into her bookstore and surprise her. Perhaps she wouldn't even recognize him. That possibility made him smile like a schoolboy involved in some devilish prank.

He had sent her a couple of pictures about three months ago. One was a shot of a large group of people. He'd written on the back that he was seventh from the left in the seventh row of people from the bottom. It was almost impossible to tell where the seventh row was, let alone who the seventh person in the seventh row could have been. It didn't make any difference because whoever it was, it wasn't Phillip. He wasn't even in the picture. He'd tucked the other photograph inside a poem he'd written. This one really was of him and had been taken a few years ago. In this picture, he was standing in the shadows some distance away and wearing a baseball cap.

Patricia had sent him a picture as well. Hers was also from a few years ago. In the inscription on the back, she'd explained that it had been taken when she'd gone cross-country skiing near Taos. What features were discernible were washed out because of the contrast between the bright sunlight on the snow and her dark parka.

Phillip wasn't sure he would recognize Patricia, but he was confident that he would know her. She was not a woman of perfect figure. *Not by a long shot*, she had said. Nor would she be mistaken for a twenty-three-year-old starlet. Absent knowledge of her physical looks, Phillip had fallen in love with her inner spirit. It really didn't matter to him what she looked like.

Okay, it did matter, some. But not like it would have when he was younger. He was really in love this time. A passionate love, he would have to call it. And not a blind love, but a deeply spiritual and the "way-it-was-supposed-to-be" kind of love. He sometimes longed for her in a way that made him physically ache. This was the kind of love so many believe they have, only to find later that it wasn't reciprocal. Theirs was not a love of delusion. To both of them, theirs was an old love, a very old love, perhaps even ancient. At the same time, however, it was also an excitingly new kind of love—one that neither poetry nor music nor art could ever capture. And it wasn't a love that made him worry about controlling or possessing, because he knew instinctively that it couldn't be. His whole life had changed because of it, making everything old and faded seem new and bright again.

Phillip wasn't being foolish about it, however. He knew full well there were dark days ahead for them, and that it wasn't an absolute given that he would be able to give himself over completely to this love. But he would give it everything he had so that he could sip of this love. As long as he refused to be afraid of it or build walls around it to protect himself from the honesty of it, then he could luxuriate in a strength and happiness that few men ever realize.

Subject: LIGHTING
From: "Phillip Craven" <PhilCraven@foxnet.com>
To: "Patricia Ridgeway" <PatriciaRidge@earthangel.net>

Hey you!
Did I tell you that I wouldn't be around in the morning? I can't remember if I did or not. So now I will. I have a very early appointment. I promised my friend, Mary (have I mentioned Mary to you before?) that I would do some sunrise shots for the Chamber of Commerce directory she is putting together. Well, I'll probably be back and have a chance to talk with you sometime about mid-afternoon. Until then hugs and kisses!!!!!! I love you. So much. And just because…

Lighting

A flock of golden lit seagulls
Flying by,
As the setting sun casts its
Magic warm light;
Reflecting.

Reflecting

These words hoping to capture
A moment,
Of tranquility and peace.

Seen by stranger's
Eyes searching.

Searching

For a way to make a difference.
To grasp
A feeling and share a truth
Touch a cold heart;
Sharing.

Sharing
Some words simply to
Communicate,
A common peace
To connect beyond the words;
Enlighten.

After sending the message, Phillip continued to stare at the screen for several long moments before deciding to go to bed. He tried to sleep, but it was impossible. Too many persistent thoughts grabbed hold of his imagination and refused to let go. He was still staring at the alarm clock when it went off.

As he showered, he made a mental list of the things he wanted to take with him. He'd stuff his clothes into one duffel bag and in the other, his camera gear, his daily journal, and a book to read on the flight. In twenty minutes, he was dressed, packed, and running the brush one more time through his thinning hair. He glanced at the clock and realized he had time for a cup of coffee.

As Phillip stepped out onto the deck, he felt the mixture of cool morning breeze and already warm sun. He breathed deeply, savoring the fresh air, haughty with a hint of old growth rot, and sipped his coffee and thought about the e-mail to Patricia. He'd mentioned Mary on purpose, knowing that he had never said anything about her before. He would have no secrets from Patricia and he would tell her about Mary if she asked—and she probably would—and then he would tell her a little too much. Patricia would understand. There was little doubt.

He had a certain passion for Mary, and he always had a helluva good time with her. But he didn't love her. Not in the special way he now knew existed. Not in the way she needed him to. He would end the relationship, and they would hopefully remain friends. It wasn't likely, however. He'd hoped that with Sarah, too.

Everything was different now. No longer would he have even the slightest doubt about the importance and strength of love. No longer would he be the compromised Phillip who built walls around his broken heart. For too many years, he now realized, he'd kept the hope alive that Sarah might somehow walk back into his life. It was hard to forgive himself for not feeling guilty as he let go of the hope and the need for the hope to be there. He looked at his watch. It was time to go.

As he hit the I-90 freeway on his way to SeaTac airport, "While You See a Chance," a most appropriate Steve Winwood song began playing on the radio:

Stand up in a clear blue morning until you see what can be
Alone in a cold day dawning, are you still free? Can you be?
When some cold tomorrow finds you, when some sad old dream reminds you
How the endless road unwinds you
While you see a chance take it, find romance fake it
Because it's all on you

Phillip managed to beat most of the traffic and pulled into one of the off-airport parking facilities a little ahead of schedule. A short shuttle bus ride later, he was inside the terminal, through security, and checking the monitor for the number of his gate.

Phillip was fascinated by airports. Always had been. They were places with so many people with so many agendas and with so many different ways of expressing their varied emotions. There was a certain cruel coldness to them, too. Concrete, steel, and glass boxes where the joy and laughter of reunions played out next to the sorrow and tears of separations, all watched by the thousands of strangers streaming by, day after endless day. It was a cross-cultural experience that never ceased to amaze him.

Phillip stepped up to the counter to request a window seat. The gate agent, a pretty young woman, smiled at him. Phillip convinced himself that she'd winked at him, if for no other reason than to indicate her approval of the very special journey he was about to take.

He put his boarding pass in his shirt pocket and took a seat near the ticket counter. He was not impatient about the wait. He was enjoying the moment actually, watching all sorts and shapes of people walking or running past him on their way to wherever. Occasionally, children noticed him watching, some even smiled at him. How interesting, he thought, that it's the children who are most aware of their surroundings and unembarrassed to look at you and to smile. Adults too often retreat so far into themselves that they are nearly invisible.

The flight was only half full. When he eventually settled in, he was relieved to find that the two other seats beside him remained unoccupied. He enjoyed the feeling of being somewhat isolated from everyone else. Throughout the flight, he drifted in and out of random thoughts as he watched the land formations and clouds drift steadily by beneath him. As the plane began its gradual descent toward Albuquerque Sunport, Phillip could feel his heart beating a little faster. Soon, Patricia would be no more than a few hours away.

When he stepped off the air-conditioned shuttle bus at the car rental office, the heat felt like he'd just entered a blast furnace in comparison to Cle Elum. How quickly he'd become accustomed to the temperate climate of the Northwest. Summertime temperatures in Cle Elum occasionally rose to ninety degrees, but quickly dipped below seventy again after sunset. Phillip could also tell right away that the New Mexico air was a lot drier. It almost felt as though he were in California again. *And this is early fall!*

Phillip rented a mid-sized car and stowed his gear in the back seat. He was thirsty. Maybe he'd stop in a couple of hours and buy a bottle of water. Maybe sooner than that. He didn't have a specific agenda.

The airport seemed to be located near the outskirts of Albuquerque. That was good. It meant he wouldn't have to find his way through the city. Then he saw a sign pointing the way to Kirkland Air Force Base. He hadn't been aware that there was a base here. Funny how little things like that trigger certain memories. He visualized his older brother who had been killed in Vietnam. Phillip was a pre-teen when his brother had died. From that moment on, his family rarely ever spoke of him. He'd told Patricia all about him one evening. She did that to him, made him open up like that, and he couldn't understand why exactly. Sarah never knew about his brother.

Phillip was appreciative of the beauty around him now—the sparsely populated little villages and towns, the landscape a mosaic of colors and contrasts. The last time he'd seen such endless miles of high desert grassland, juniper, and sagebrush was on a trip through Mexico many years earlier. In the distance loomed the magnificent Sangre de Cristo Mountains. The colors turned to deepening red in the soil and in the canyon walls as he drove past signs designating turnoffs to San Juan Pueblo, and Santa Clara Pueblo. He remembered Patricia telling him that they were some of the oldest settlements in North America. He couldn't recall which one was where her friend Sylvia was from. Later on, he caught glimpses of magnificent old homes along the road through Santa Fe. Someday, he'd like to return and see what lay behind the carved gates and thick walls.

The gas station with the red tiled roof blended in so well with the buildings in the area that he almost missed it. Even its modest sign was low to the ground and made to look antique. He paid for the gas, some bottled water, and a few packages of corn nuts. He was on his way again just minutes later.

Outside Santa Fe, Phillip exited onto State Road 285 and then later onto U.S. 64 for the final climb into Taos. He was traveling through the very soul of one of the most stunningly beautiful places in the world that has inspired countless artists such as Georgia O'Keefe, James Fields, and R. C. Gorman who have captured on canvas the magic of Taos and its people. His ears popped several times as he continued to climb higher and higher. He slowed to navigate the rather treacherous curves in the road. And whenever he dared, he glanced down at the beauty of the Rio Grand River far below.

The sunlight began to dance in and out as he drove among the high canyon walls and he had to swallow hard every time his ears popped. He continued along the twisting road upward and upward until it leveled out into the shadowy, fertile land studded with orchards. The narrow roadside was dotted with small fruit stands draped with assorted deep red chili ristras and wreaths. He took the opportunity to stop at one of the stands and buy a sack of assorted apples. When Phillip stepped from the car, he was startled by the cooler temperatures and the strong, pungent smell of drying chilis mingled with the unmistakable aroma of fresh apples. While he was paying the young boy for the apples, a small girl, perhaps barely seven or eight years old, offered him a tiny plastic glass of homemade apple cider. She smiled at him when he took it from her and her grin broadened when he winked, smacked his lips together exaggeratedly and asked the boy to add a quart of the cider to his bill. Everything about this trip, both physically and emotionally, was an entirely new experience for him. Phillip continued up through the canyon until soon, there before him on the high mesa, lay the ancient town of Taos. Patricia's world. Like nowhere else in the world she had told him when they'd first met.

It did indeed appear, as she had claimed, to be unaffected by the outside world. It's was almost as if that last rise up out of the steep canyon had magically deposited him in a world all its own. He recalled her words...*herein lies the magic of this world all its own, unique in its beauty, its changing moody sky...so captivating in its many cultures.*

He remembered how she'd written him describing the deep oranges, vermillions, and purples of the mountains, of Taos as the "Place of the Magic Light," and of the incredible, ancient world that existed within the walls of the pueblo. He was surprised once when she asked him if he knew that the Manson family had once had a commune in the forests just outside of town. He was going to research that, but had never gotten around to it.

He drove slowly through the narrow road as he made his way through Ranchos de Taos. Ranchos, as it was known locally, was a suburb of Taos, but somehow that word seemed inappropriate in this rustic world. On his right, he recognized the old mission, San Francisco de Assisi, she had told him about. Phillip glanced at a street sign and saw he was passing Lower Ranchitos Road. Patricia's house was nearby. With a yellow highlighter pen, he had marked on a map the clearest route to her house. That hadn't been necessary. From their endless conversations, he had memorized all the unique street names and everything about the place she called home. His heart began to beat faster now. Phillip glanced nervously at his watch. It read 3:35. He could swear he heard his heart pounding. *Quit this, Craven. Don't do it! Don't panic now. Not now!*

He took a deep breath and let it out slowly. The light that he never remembered stopping for turned green and he accelerated slowly through the intersection. Phillip was somewhat saddened to see the garish signs, architecturally altered but nonetheless unattractive reminders of the all-too-familiar fast food chains and super stores. They assaulted his sense of the charm and beauty of the area. A few blocks later, he entered a more historic part of Taos, which thankfully eschewed the trappings of modern America.

A few moments later and he was at the plaza he'd heard so much about. He spotted the blanket-clad Indian men milling about. Patricia had told him that the old men walked the several miles to the plaza every day from the pueblo. As he looked at them, he remembered some of the leathery old faces he'd photographed in Mexico. Had it not been a different time and a different place, he would have sworn he was looking into those same wise eyes from so many years before; back before he accepted the reality of time before time.

Phillip found a parking space next to a very dusty old Lincoln. Patricia had told him that people in Taos were famous for their eccentricity and their dirty cars. He looked around. She was right! He turned off the engine and just sat there. He was here. *God, now what?*

A few yards in front of him, he saw the small sign, which clearly marked the back door of Patricia's bookstore. He couldn't move. He tried, but he couldn't. He was terrified. *This isn't fair to Patricia at all! What if I'm putting her in a compromising position?* He concentrated on breathing slowly and deeply, and the fear gradually began to disappear. Cleansing breaths. Calming breaths.

There was a dark blue pickup truck parked a couple of spaces away to his left. Maybe it was hers. It sure looked like the one she'd described to him. It wasn't dirty like most of the other cars he'd seen in town. There was some odd, arty thing hanging from the rearview mirror. That surprised him. About her, that is. It was a round spiderweb-like thing. He'd tease her about it later. *What would I say if she'd had velvet dice hanging from the mirror?* He chuckled to himself. *You're stalling, Phillip boy. Get out of the car. It's time.*

He got out of the car and looked at the back of the adobe building and saw a small passageway that seemed to lead around to the front. He walked through that passageway and into another world. Tall oaks lined the plaza on three sides. The buildings could easily have been mistaken for residences, not businesses. They probably had been homes at one time before succumbing to the needs of expanding commerce. Pots filled with colorful flowers—petunias and geraniums mostly—and plants hung from the wooden vigas that protruded from the rooflines of the buildings.

In the center of the plaza were several rough wood benches. He watched with interest as a tourist got up from one of the benches and walked toward a group of the blanketed Indian men standing near the outer wall on the street side of the plaza. A passerby, a local probably, stopped the tourist just as he raised his camera. The two exchanged a few words, and then the tourist lowered his camera and returned to the bench. He had witnessed an education—the passing on of the reverence for the sacredness of custom and culture.

He walked slowly toward the bookstore, stopping only to look in the window of Anasazi Parchment and Pens, a shop Patricia had told him about. The store specialized in writing paper colored with the dyes made of the dirt and clays of the area and inlaid with dried wildflowers, leaves, and even weeds. He spotted some leather-bound journals in the window, much like the one she'd sent him and that he now carried everywhere with him. The store also carried antique fountain pens. Patricia had told him she collected fountain pens. *What hadn't they shared this past year?*

The shop next door bore a sign whose letters were done in a sweeping script as though written with a quill. It was the Take Another Look Bookstore. He wasn't quite ready yet. He stuffed his hands deep in his pockets and began nervously jiggling his car keys. He looked past the bookstore to the Blue Corn Gallery. Patricia loved the gallery and famous Taos resident who owned it. They had been fast friends for years, though she missed him now that he spent most of the year traveling through the United States and Europe. *Who'd have thought it, she had told him one evening*? Only a few short years ago he used to come and sit for hours in the library, poring over children's books. He couldn't read! He'd spent his youth roaming free and helping his family with their crafts. Then he began painting and used to sit on the wall of the plaza, along with the old men and sell his paintings. Only in America, Phillip had remarked. "No, only in Taos," Patricia had corrected him. *He was beginning to understand what she meant.* Finally, he approached the entrance to the bookshop.

The large oak door was opened wide and latched against the exterior wall. He slowly opened the screen door and stepped inside. One of the first things he noticed was the floor. It was an oxblood floor she had told him. It was dark, almost ebony, and shiny. It's a dirt floor just like the one she had at her home, she had said. It was sealed with a modern resin-type liquid to capture the look of what originally was a dirt floor sealed with actual oxblood. They were uneven and extremely cold in the wintertime, she'd told him.

The store had an old, sort of dusty leather scent to it. Mixed in were the more delicate aromas of herbs and spices and what he recognized as Earl Grey tea. *Patricia was always brewing tea for her customers. He was getting warm.*

It was quite dark for a bookshop. There were very few windows. Phillip wondered if that could be traced to the old days when windows were very small and heavily shuttered to protect the inhabitants against the bullets and arrows of marauding banditos and renegade Indians?

He looked to his left and saw a small room partially enclosed by a three-foot wall. In the center of the room, was a worn Navajo rug, about three small wooden tables and chair sets, and some old-fashioned wooden toys. Patricia had told him that Angela often conducted "reading hour" for the youngsters. There was even a pint-sized version of a ladder that rolled along the bookshelves.

Directly in front of him were shelves with small, handwritten signs identifying the various genres. A large section of the shelves at eye level were devoted to "coffee table" style books. The bookshop did not seem to cater to all tastes, as did the commercial chain bookstores. Instead, it specialized in titles that were related to the area. You had to look hard to find the few volumes of *The New York Times* best-seller list books here. Most of the books on display were about the Southwest or written by Southwestern or Native American authors and poets. Lying near the center of the table were three of his own books. *Would other people notice they were out of place here? He was getting warmer.*

To his right was a long wooden counter covered with pocket-sized daily journals, handmade bookmarks, and some other handcrafted items. Perhaps the most unique item on the counter lay right in the middle of everything. A large, dozing Calico cat. A little girl, who Phillip guessed was about eleven years old, walked past the cat, tickled its ear, and continued on her way. *There was that warm feeling again.*

At the far end of the counter was an antique register and on the floor, directly in front of the register, was a rather unkempt sheepdog...sound asleep. An attractive, older woman was leaning a bit uncomfortably over the sleeping dog in an attempt to pay the elderly gentleman behind the register for her items. Phillip assumed the man to be Butch Killen.

Phillip smiled. This was certainly Patricia's shop. *Could things be any more perfect?* It even had an old potbellied woodstove and two worn, overstuffed chairs near a window. A man, vaguely resembling Burl Ives, slouched comfortably in one of the chairs intently looking through a magazine, a non-lit pipe clenched in his teeth.

As Phillip looked around almost in amazement of what was before him, he heard what he presumed to be Butch Killen's voice. "I'll be with you in a moment, sir." He turned to see if he was talking to him. He was, and Phillip replied with a nod and a smile.

All along the walls were small little nooks and crannies, some with chairs and tables, reading materials, odd pieces of scratch paper, pens, and pencils. There were a few more of the small windows with wooden shutters on the inside, each of them pulled open and beneath each one a table with a planter on it. Lush green, trailing plants were growing up and enveloping the shutters. On closer inspection, Phillip discovered to his delight that the plants were actually sweet potatoes floating in water-filled mason jars. He chuckled at the absurdity of it all. It was culturally worlds apart from anyplace he'd seen before, but one with which he was completely comfortable.

There was the same voice asking Phillip if he would like some tea. He hesitated only momentarily before saying, "Tea. Yes, tea would be nice. Is that Earl Grey I smell?"

"That and all these damned herbs," the man said, pointing toward the ceiling. Phillip looked up and saw that the entire ceiling was covered with little bundles of hanging herbs and dried flowers.

Phillip was handed a small teacup and saucer. "If you'd like anything in it, fixins are over there," he said, pointing to a shelf.

Phillip thanked him. "By the way, is Patricia in?"

"What was that?"

"Patricia? Is she here? I'm an old friend. I'd like to surprise her."

The man studied him for a moment, then nodded and looked toward a small staircase just behind Phillip.

"Well, she's in her office, but I'm not sure this is a good time."

"Oh?"

"Bad day, I'm afraid. She lost her cat this morning, you see."

"Kitty Gato?" Phillip blurted out in utter surprise.

"You knew her? Then you know how much that damned cat meant

to her."

"Yeah, I do."

Phillip bent down, mostly to conceal his surprise and emotion; carefully balancing the tea in one hand, and patted the sleeping sheepdog with the other. "That's a good girl Abby." *Oh god, what's wrong with me? How do I handle this? Get a grip, man!*

The man looked at Phillip suspiciously now. He didn't know who this man was, but he obviously knew about Patricia and Kitty Gato and surprisingly about his dog Abby.

"Reminds me of a dog my best friend had...named Abby," Phillip lied.

Butch nodded. "Well, her name is Abby, too."

"Really?" Phillip said in feigned surprise.

"Yeah, I wondered how the hell you knew her name. You're an old friend of Patricia's, you say?"

"Yeah," Phillip said. "I think I might be able to cheer her up little."

"I suppose there's no harm in trying. Though it'll be pretty difficult."

"She's not expecting me," Phillip said. "Are you sure it'll be all right?"

"Well, you might be just what she needs right now. Go surprise her then," Butch said pointing toward the stairs.

As Phillip started slowly up the stairs, he saw even more shelves built into the wall. And among the collectible historic journals and first editions, he noticed the leather-bound collection of Zane Grey novels and the Braille books that Patricia had told him about a long time ago.

On the third step, the stairs creaked loudly. Phillip froze. He looked up toward the landing. He waited for a brief moment and then began to climb even more carefully now on up the staircase. When he emerged into the room at the top of the stairs, Phillip saw that he was in a large loft area. It was like a cozy den. It seemed as if he were entering an entirely different world from the bookstore below. *I'll bet the Mad Hatter's even hiding around here someplace!*

Fluffy large pillows were scattered on the long floral-patterned couch. There were three doors along the left wall. The first one, he could see, looked like an office. That was where Patricia most likely was, just a few feet from him now.

Phillip began to move very slowly toward the open door. He didn't want to make a sound and give himself away. Despite the unbearable anxiousness and excitement he felt, he was breathing evenly and almost silently. He moved to the doorway and saw her at a desk. She was wearing a colorful Navajo print jacket and was sitting ramrod straight in front of a computer screen. The table next to her desk was cluttered with books and papers.

He wanted to remember every detail of this moment. Her long black hair was tied into a simple ponytail falling almost to her waist. He could only see a small part of her neck, but he could tell her skin had an olive tone.

He thought of everything from tugging at her ponytail to gently caressing her shoulders. He could almost hear himself saying hello to her, in a voice barely above a whisper, so as not to startle her. But he waited. This was a moment to savor. There would be just one moment exactly like this, and he had to cherish it.

She was typing something. From where he stood, he couldn't quite see the screen well enough to make out the words. Phillip took a small step forward, hoping the floor would not creak. The room remained silent. She was writing an e-mail, he could see that. But to whom? Wouldn't it be perfect if she was at this very moment writing to him? It was time to say something, or make a little noise or…

"Whatcha need, Butch?" Patricia said suddenly.

Phillip paused. And then took a breath. It was time.

Chapter Thirty

"I hope I'm not disturbing you."

Patricia turned around very slowly and faced him.

"Excuse me?" She sounded a bit angry. Obviously, she thought, some customer had made his way upstairs to her private office. She barely looked at the man. This intrusion, especially today, was most untimely. She could feel her patience nearing its end.

Phillip smiled. There she was. She was different, yet just as he'd expected her to be. Her eyes were indeed dark brown, perhaps even black. Her face was round, slightly masculine and her lips full.

"Can I help you?" she asked sharply.

"Yes, you can."

"I'm sorry, there should have been someone downstairs who could assist you." She rose from her chair.

"Patricia."

She froze at the sound of his voice this time. She looked straight at Phillip and removed her glasses. She had been crying a lot today and knew she looked horrible.

"What did you..." Her voice trailed off.

She searched his eyes. Then the moment of recognition came. He watched her fear fall away.

"You know." Not necessarily brilliant. But under the circumstances, it was all he could think of to say. He instinctively started to reach out for her, but he stopped himself.

"Phillip..."

"I'm sorry about Kitty, baby." He said this so quietly he wasn't even sure it hadn't been merely a thought.

Her knees suddenly went weak. She dropped her glasses just as she caught herself on the arm of the old leather chair.

He stepped forward quickly and steadied her without thinking. Even through the heavy cotton fabric of her jacket, he could feel her warmth and it filled him.

"I wanted to surprise you."

"Oh god, Phillip. Phillip. Well, you sure surprised me all right. I mean, I knew you were coming. I just wasn't sure when you'd get here." She was self-consciously brushing back the hair from her face, knowing that she looked just about as opposite as she'd have liked to look at this particular moment. This moment was supposed to be perfect.

As he searched for the right words, she stepped toward him, encircling his waist with her arms. Without another thought, nor the slightest hesitation, he pulled her to him, squeezing her perhaps a little too hard, stretching out his hands to feel her back, as if to convince himself he was honestly holding her. He boldly pressed his cheek against hers, their skin touching for the very first time..

"Hey you!" She forced a smile that automatically turned to a slight giggle. Then she repeated herself, "Hey you."

Phillip was hugging her tightly and warmly, as he would an old friend. A best friend, actually. A friend he was returning to, someone he belonged with, a friend with whom he could feel at home.

"It's been a long time, hasn't it?" He paused, studying her face, then continued in a breathy whisper, "Oh, Patricia, you feel so good."

This was easy. All those fears. This was way too easy. It felt so right. These and a thousand other thoughts raced through his head.

"It really is you, isn't it?"

"It's me, baby," he said. "It's me."

He leaned forward and gave her a gentle kiss, his lips barely touching hers. For a long time, they said nothing, holding each other tightly in an embrace neither wanted to end.

"So, how come I've been looking forward to this moment for so long and now that it's here, I have absolutely no idea what to say?" laughed Phillip.

"I know. I'm sort of nervous here too. I've created a million scenarios about this very moment, intricately detailed dreams to make this as special as possible. And look at me! I'm a mess!" A nervous laugh of embarrassment escaped her lips. She let his hand drop from hers, stepped past him, and quietly closed the door to her small office. She stood there with her back to him.

"So, this is the central nervous system of the best little bookstore in the Southwest, huh?"

"And the oldest, if you will recall, sir." She turned with that half smile and walked toward him, her hands outstretched invitingly.

"Ah, yes, the oldest. Certainly, I recall that." He took her hands in his. He looked at her eyes watching him. He kissed her hand as she took that last step into him, leaned forward, and rubbed his nose playfully against hers.

"How did you know about Miss Kitty?" she asked softly, avoiding his eyes.

"I forced Butch to tell me," he quipped, intentionally trying to hide his sadness. "Um, that is Butch downstairs, isn't it?"

"Yes, that's Butch. But I don't believe for an instant that he told you anything!"

"Oh, no? If you must know, he was behind this whole thing." Phillip said, waving his hands theatrically in a sweeping circular motion around the room. "Oh, yeah. That Butch, he's quite the matchmaker extraordinaire."

"Oh, he is no such thing. Stop that!" she giggled.

"No lie! He called me and said I should get over here right away, that I should surprise you even! He told me you'd love it!"

"Liar. Liar!"

"Oh, he didn't, huh? You think I would just show up here on my own?"

She was laughing. That was a good thing, he thought. He knew she was on the verge of breaking down only seconds before, and that would be something that they'd both regret later. Neither would want to recall that as their first memory of this long-awaited day.

"Yes, actually, you *would* come on your own. I told you I knew you were coming."

"Oh, right! You're just using that old...what's it called...that old feminine instinct thing."

"Intuition. Its called intuition."

"Yeah, yeah, that's it. Institution. Women's institution."

"*Intuition*, you silly! And, no, that's not what I'm using."

Patricia pulled him by the hand toward a boldly floral love seat, using her other hand to clear away several books and magazines.

"Since you're such a psychic, what do you think I'm going to do now?" he asked teasingly.

"I'm *not* a psychic! It's just that *you* blew it this morning on the phone. Any idiot could have read right through your little charade, and quite frankly..." She was starting to appear a little pale, "Personally, I don't plan to do *anything*, right now except sit down before I fall down. How about you?" Phillip sat down next to her, and Patricia moved shakily toward him.

Without hesitation, Phillip pressed his lips passionately to hers, holding her face in his hands as he did. He felt her first resist and then melt into him. He was relieved, for he too wanted things to go perfectly. Still, he abruptly ended the kiss.

"I'm sorry, Trisha. Something just came over me. I knew I'd find you irresistible!"

"I'm sorry, too…I think," she whispered rather plaintively. "Did you have this all planned out in your head…I mean, how all this would happen, what you would say to me, what I would say back, how we would look and feel? Like a perfect setting. You know, like with perfect clothes, perfect makeup, and all that? Like in some romantic movie?"

"Oh, yes, of course," he laughed. "And I see you were as brilliantly well prepared as I was!"

They laughed together and fell into a wonderful embrace.

"You'll have to excuse me for breaking every rule of protocol…" He stopped mid-sentence and began placing small kisses on her cheek and then pressed his lips onto hers. He could feel her lips part slightly as he lightly traced her upper lip with the tip of his tongue. He was inescapably aware of how it was making him feel.

Patricia realized how this had become so easy and natural on the computer. And so it was here. It was just how they both knew they'd feel, how they would instinctively react to one another. It made her forget all about the things that surrounded them. Right now it was just as it should be—just the two of them finally together. They had waited such a long time.

She caressed Phillip's face as he began kissing her more deeply. The passion was building faster and faster until she had to push herself away from him. She let her hands drop to his chest and as he watched, she stared into his eyes.

"Oh…" She tried to take a deep breath. "Oh, my…"

"*I'm* feeling much better now, thank you," Phillip said.

She smiled and poked him in the stomach.

"I realize I may have gotten carried away there. But, hey, it had to be done!"

"No it didn't. Not here, anyway!" She winked. "So, are you satisfied now? Ready to go back to Seattle?"

"Oh, sure! You bet. Absolutely. That's all I needed. Every five or ten years or so, all I'll drop in for is a quick kiss and then, hell, I'm good to go. How about you? Work for you?"

"Great for me, sure! Well, whew, that was easy. Ya wanna ride back to the airport?" She stood up and looked at him as he leaned comfortably against the back of the love seat. He smiled. This was the "them" that they'd become comfortable with over the past year. His eyes moved slowly up her body.

"Did anyone ever tell you that you are a *very* sexy lady?"

Patricia blushed. "I thought you promised not to go there. Don't, okay? Please?"

"No," Phillip answered with a devilish smile. "I would make no such promises. Whatever do you take me for, madam? A gentleman?"

"Grrr! I'm going to get you for this! Just you wait!" She couldn't help but giggle. She always did that when she was nervous and hadn't a clue what to say or do next. She purposely ignored his question and averted his eyes by glancing at the clock.

"Scared as I am, huh?"

"No! I'm not scared at all. It's just… Well, I might be something, but I'm not scared. At least, I don't think I am. Are you? Really scared, I mean?" She had a look of real concern.

"Of course not. *Real* men don't get scared. Not of girls, anyway. Hell, what's to be scared of? I read where doctors cured cooties a long time ago, ya know."

"You are *impossible*!" She reached out and pinched him this time

"Oh, fine! Abuse me. Take advantage of me, why don't you?"

Quite a few witty but acerbic comebacks flashed through her mind, but she chose to say nothing.

"Ah, restraint. I see that the fair lady shows restraint. You are quite wise, my dear."

She glanced at the clock again. Phillip noticed.

"Have I told you how much I love you lately?"

For the first time, Phillip could actually see the effect his words had on her. Her color deepened and her eyes filled with tears. He rose quickly and tried to take her in his arms, but she resisted.

"Damn! Why do I always do that, Phillip? I even do that when we're typing!" She shook her head and stared down at her feet.

"Hey, baby, it's okay. Look at me." He placed his hand beneath her chin and raised her face to him.

"It's *not* okay…it's not."

"Sure it is." She let him hold her now, softly and with the tenderness he felt and knew she needed. He looked over her shoulder at the computer screen. He could see that the letter she was writing was to him:

Subject: Surprises?
From: "Patricia Ridgeway" <PatriciaRidge@earthangel.net>
To: "Phillip Craven" <PhilCraven@foxnet.com>

You know of course you don't have to do this, you don't have to surprise me, and you don't have to actually sweep me off my feet. Why am I typing this? I suppose because there is a slight chance I am wrong and you aren't on your way here, about to show up here in Taos. You've already done that and more…

"Look at me." Phillip waited until she reluctantly gazed directly into his eyes. "I love you, Patricia. I have loved you for a long, long time. And there's not a damned thing you can do about it." He touched the tip of her nose with his finger.

"I know." She smiled as he'd hoped she would. "Say, wanna go for a ride?" She said this rather animatedly, something he really hadn't expected at that moment.

"Wow, you're full of surprises! Sure, but do I get to know where we're going?"

"No. But it won't come as a surprise, and you'll know right away."

She turned off the computer and said, "Okay. All set. Just let me make a quick phone call, clear some things with Butch and Chad, and then I think we can blow this newsstand."

He listened as she made her phone call. From what she was saying, he presumed she was talking to Trent. Phillip wondered to himself how all this was going to play out. Then he realized, somewhat relieved, that it wasn't Trent. She was making up some sort of imaginary excuse to a friend to get out of something they must have had planned. He was still stunned to be actually sitting there in her office, watching her do what he knew she did day after day, week after week. Everything looked just as he expected it might.

"There! Now, let me go down and talk to Butch, okay? I'll be back in a minute. Make yourself at home." She wanted a moment to talk to Butch alone.

"I saw what you were writing to me, you know."

"I know."

"Hurry back or I'll start rearranging everything in here, and then you'll be sorry!"

"Gad, I wish you would. This place is a sty. It's driving me nuts!" She bent down and without thought touched the telltale dent in the cushion where Kitty Gato had no doubt spent many a lazy afternoon napping. Phillip stepped toward Patricia and she was in his arms before she knew it. He let her cry for a long time without saying anything. Patricia was comfortable in his arms, grateful to be there. It was so wonderful to finally have someone to cry with.

Patricia leaned back in his arms and looked at his shirt. She tried unsuccessfully to brush away the wet mascara marks.

"It's okay. I figured you'd do that, so I wore an old one."

She slapped playfully at his arm. "I knew you didn't have a sensitive bone in your body, you old fool. Jeez! Okay. I really do have to go talk to Butch now and tell him I'm leaving the store again."

"Again? You leave often? You leave him in charge so you can go meet your secret lovers, do you?

"Hey! Be nice, you! Secret lovers, indeed. Well...um...he does know about all the others, you see. That's what I have to explain to him. I have to tell him you're a new face on the scene!" She was trying to look everywhere but at him to keep from laughing.

"Is this okay, babe? I mean, that I'm here? That I've barged in on you like this? I don't want to make things uncomfortable for you."

"You silly! Of course, it's okay. It's just that I've been gone from the store a lot lately and I've been feeling pretty guilty about that. I'm glad Butch needs this store as much as I need him. That's the only thing that eases my conscience a little. Now, you stay put while I'm gone. Make yourself at home. And stay right where you are, hear me?"

"Yes ma'am!" said Phillip, snapping to attention and saluting her as she disappeared down the staircase.

He began looking around the office and noticed a framed photograph on the wall. It was a picture of Patricia and several other women posing in front of the bookstore with champagne glasses in their hands. *I'll bet that was taken during the grand opening. And those two must be Sylvia and Alma. And maybe that's Angela.*

Then he spotted a photograph resting on a stack of what appeared to be legal documents. Feeling more than a little nosy, Phillip picked up the photograph and stared at it. A man in his late forties, dressed in hunting gear, holding a rifle, and with his foot resting on the body of a bull elk. *Trent?* He glanced at the legal papers. On top was a letter from a law firm and addressed to Patricia Ridgeway. Phillip saw the word "divorce" and didn't read any further. He replaced the paper exactly as he had found it. Patricia had never mentioned anything about this to him. He looked at the paper again and tried to read it without touching it. *Trent was filing for a divorce from Patricia? What could he possibly be thinking? Stupid fool.*

Patricia found Phillip still standing where she'd left him.

"Oh, I'm so sorry. Did I forget to tell you that you could sit down?

Phillip feigned exhaustion by exhaling loudly and letting his arms dangle limply. "You mean I can move now?"

"Oh, brother! That's what 'make yourself at home' means in these parts! Lord, what does it mean where you come from?" She was laughing and he could tell that she was feeling much better.

"Everything okay?" he asked, embracing her as he spoke.

"Yep. Everything's okay. You? You okay?"

He pulled her toward him and kissed her forehead. "Oh, they are awfully good right now."

"They?" she asked quizzically.

"They. You know...things. As in you and...we... they, us, and them."

"Ah, things. Yes. Things. I think they're okay, too," answered Patricia.

"Well, actually, they're more than okay. Of course, it would help if I knew what I was talking about. Why don't I just say a bunch a words and you pick and choose the good ones and throw away the ones you don't want, and see if you can make sense of any of them?"

"Don't throw anything except yourself at me, understand?" She poked him in the ribs. She thought he seemed a little more tense since she'd come back upstairs.

"Hey! Do I look like the Pillsbury Doughboy to you?"

"No, goofus! I just wanted to see that smile of yours. So, you ready to rock 'n roll?"

"Where we going?"

"Can't you guess?"

"Not a clue."

"Oh, c'mon." She dropped her cell phone in her purse and turned off the light on her desk. "Ready?"

"Take me away, Calgon"

The instant he started to say "take me away," she expected the "Calgon" to follow. Their relationship had always been one where they often knew each other's moods, humor, and the words they would use. *I know this happens between lovers. But it's never happened to me before. This is so special, so different, wonderful, and strange!* She wished she could stop thinking so much about everything and just enjoy the moment.

"C'mon, let's go."

Once downstairs, Phillip started for the door.

"Wait. I want you to meet Butch, okay?"

Butch didn't even look up when they approached. Phillip wondered if perhaps he was hard of hearing. Patricia tapped her fingers on the counter, and Butch looked up at her.

"Butch, I'd like you to meet my friend Phillip. Phillip Craven. Phil, this is Butch Killen. You've heard me speak of him, I'm sure."

Phillip stuck out his hand. "Glad to meet you, again, Butch. Patricia has, indeed, said many things about you. Most of them were almost nice."

"Hey, there! Cut that out," she said, trying to look shocked.

"And she's warned me about you, Mr. Craven," Butch said dryly.

"Okay, this is a conspiracy! I'm sorry I even considered being mannerly and introducing the two of you. I'll rue this day, I'm sure."

"Do you have to help her get up on this high horse of hers, Butch, or does she get up there all by herself?"

"Excuse me for not answering that. I have to work here, remember?" Butch winked at Phillip.

"Oh, right! I'm sorry. Gosh, I sure didn't mean to put you on the spot. You have to keep the peace. I understand. We'll talk later, okay? Compare notes, trade stories, and all that?"

"Oh, no you won't," Patricia interrupted. "Say 'it's been nice Phil.' Say it!" Patricia tapped her foot while she waited for him to obey.

"It's...been...nice...Phil," Butch said with a laugh. Patricia burst out laughing.

"S'cuse me, Butch. I'm gonna get her some air. Nice meetin' ya."

Butch laughed for the first time in quite a while.

"Okay, Butch. We're gone. Are you sure you'll be all right? Oh, heck, there's no one here. I'm gonna turn the sign. You close up and get outta here, okay? Get now, okay?" She walked to the front of the store, pulled the oak doors in and latched them. Phillip watched as she hung the "Cerrado" sign in the window. He noticed that it said "Abierto at 10:15."

"You don't open until ten-fifteen?" Phillip was a little astonished.

"Oh, sometimes," she replied. "This *is* Taos, remember. We open when we open. God, it drives the tourists crazy!"

"We're pretty good at keeping to a schedule, really," Butch quickly broke in.

"Oh, so you're in on this conspiracy, too, huh?" Phillip asked.

"Hell yes! I used to own this joint!"

"It's a wonderful place, Butch. I can feel it, you know what I mean?"

'Thank you. Yes, it is. And you take wonderful pictures."

That caught Phillip by surprise. "Well...thank you!" he stammered

"Actually, I have your book."

"Well, you better let me autograph it for you." Sensing that he might have sounded a little egotistical, Phillip quickly added, "It would be an honor if you'd let me, Butch."

Butch looked at Phillip closely. He liked him. "Now, you two get out of here and let me close up." He said, shooing them away from the desk.

Butch watched as Phillip casually put his arm around Patricia's waist and the two of them walked out of the store. He'd never really liked Trent. But he'd never approved of something like this before either. *Damned, life is sure complicated.*

"Trisha?" Phillip stopped her in the middle of the parking lot.

"What?"

"I'm not sure how to say this carefully, but...uh...well, it's about Trent."

"What about Trent?"

"I don't know, Patricia. I just don't want this to be...well, too complicated for you."

"It's okay, Phillip, really. Trent's..." She stopped. It wasn't time to tell him about Trent moving out and filing for divorce. Not yet. "Well, Trent's away for a few days. This is perfect timing, actually." She felt he was seeing right through her poorly crafted attempt at a cover-up.

Phillip sensed that she was uncomfortable telling him about what was going on between Trent and her, but he was certain she was even more uncomfortable about lying to him.

"So, the coast is clear then?" Phillip asked.

"Coast is clear, matey."

"So, what's the plan here, Stan?"

"Well, the plan, man, is this. You just hop in old blue here," They'd stopped beside the blue pickup he'd assumed earlier was hers. "and I'll just take you for a little scenic drive, okay? We aren't going far, I promise. And it won't take long."

"Do you think my rental car will be safe in this part of town? I hear it's pretty seedy in these parts. I mean used bookstores and all."

"Oh, shut up! Get in and shut up."

He opened the door for her and waited for her to get in.

"Why, thank you, kind sir!" She couldn't remember the last time someone had done that for her.

"My pleasure, ma'am."

Patricia watched as he went over to his rental car, opened the door, and reached across the seat for something. He unzipped his duffel bag and pulled out a camera and a well-worn leather World War II bomber jacket. Patricia smiled. She knew that he'd probably come prepared. *And he likes leather, too!* She rubbed her hands against the soft seat of the truck.

"Patricia, I think it's time I introduced you to someone," Phillip said as he climbed into the truck and shut the door. "Miss Piggy, meet Patricia. Patricia, meet Miss Piggy." He held his camera up for her to see.

Patricia realized that the old Pentax did somewhat resemble a pig's snout. "So nice to meet you, Miss Piggy!".

"Hey now, don't be too nice to Piggy! You'll spoil her."

"Okay, just a minute." She began again, this time pretending but failing to look serious, "Why, it's nice to meet you, Miss Piggy. I've heard so much about you, you know. Most of it not very good, I'm afraid."

"Sh! Don't you listen to her, Miss. She's just trying to annoy me. And if you want to know the truth, I think she might be a little jealous of you, too."

Patricia reached over and patted the old worn case and then touched

Phillip's jacket.

"Nice," she said, her hand moving slowly over the soft leather.

"Thanks. It's the real thing. A gift."

"She loved you very much...in her own way, Phil. I'm glad you kept the jacket." Patricia watched his eyes for a moment, and then leaned forward and started the truck. *Had he told her that Sarah had given it to him? Of course not...he'd never told anyone.*

"I need you to meet someone very special, too, okay?" Then Patricia added, "Don't say no. It will be okay."

"As long as these aren't people I'll be meeting on Monday, then it's fine with me." Phillip answered. "I'm here now to be with you as much as I can."

"The traffic is horrible here in the fall. We all have a love/hate relationship with it." She waved at the driver of a car with out-of-state plates who'd allowed her to merge. The radio was playing softly and Phillip could distinguish a rock-and-roll beat but couldn't identify the song. "Lost in the fifties..."

"Huh?" Patricia glanced over at him.

"The fifties. That's what you said once when we were talking about music. That you were lost in the fifties."

"I don't know. I probably did though..."

Patricia drove north. Sooner than he expected, Phillip saw the sign proclaiming the Arroyo Seco town limits. Beside a small adobe mission, Patricia pulled the truck off the road and into a gravel parking lot. Behind the lot, he could see the tiny, well kept cemetery.

"I have to do this, Phillip. It'll be okay. Really. If it weren't for Alma, we wouldn't be here today. You know that as well as I do. Of all the things about Alma and I... The one thing I will always regret is never telling her everything about you."

"I understand," Phillip said quietly. He came around the front of the truck and opened her door. She took his hand and jumped to the ground.

"Let's walk a minute, all right?" She squeezed his hand to let him know she was okay.

They wandered among the rows of grave markers. Some of them new, some military markers from various wars, some so old the inscriptions were illegible. Many were sitting at an angle, and more than a few had toppled over.

"Can I tell you something?"

"Of course, Phillip. Go ahead."

"Cemeteries mean a lot to me. I found a lot of peace in old cemeteries when I was growing up, and I took a lot of pictures of them when I was a kid. I don't know how to explain it exactly, but I know I don't have to either."

"No, you don't. Please, go on."

"There were a couple of really old cemeteries in upstate New York where I grew up. I used to spend hours there reading the tombstones and trying to envision the lives those people had led. I loved the tombstones and reading what people had engraved on them." He shrugged his shoulders. "I don't find cemeteries morbid or even all that sad."

"It's funny you should say that about cemeteries. One night a while back—and no, I don't expect you to believe me, but it's true. It was the night when you and I were talking about Washington, D.C., for some reason…and I can't explain this, but I was going to tell you about a unique photo I took. I just never got around to it. I got sidetracked or something, I guess. I was going to tell you about a time I'd gone to Harper's Ferry and was wandering around the old graveyard alone. Everyone thought I was a crazy old fool, of course. Anyway, when I got the film back, the cemetery photos were extraordinary! Have you been to Harper's Ferry?"

"Nope. But you can take me there someday," he said. "I'd like that."

"Well, as you will see when we go there…" She paused purposely for effect before continuing, "…the cemetery rambles up and down a steep hill and stops at a ledge overlooking the confluence of the Potomac and the Shenandoah rivers. It's an incredible place!

"Anyway, I took several photos from the very top of the hill looking down through the tombstones. When I got the pictures back—and I know that you can logically explain this and spoil my story—but all of the tombstones looked like little ghosts running down the hill! They were almost cute and comical because they were all slightly out of focus and hazy looking. The extraordinary part was that there were people in the photo and they weren't out of focus at all. Oh, and you know what else? The date on the picture was October thirty-first! Halloween!" She waited for a reaction. She wanted to hear an "Oh, wow" or something like that from him.

Phillip tried to have a zombie-like look on his face. "Hmm," he said looking directly into her eyes, "it's all quite pitiful." He chuckled and then tried to explain that it was most likely an effect caused by the contrasting lights. "Or maybe, just maybe, it was something else entirely. Something eerie. Something that could never be explained." He was teasing her, although he was not altogether sure she realized that.

"Oh, quit that! You don't believe me, do you?"

"Of course, I believe you, Trish! Honestly! Who do you think you're talking to? Seriously, these types of things happen to us all the time, don't they? At first, we're surprised, and then we kind of forget about them. Sort of like the old cemetery in Rhinebeck, New York, I went to. Want to hear about it?" She nodded enthusiastically. "Well, it dated back to the

Revolutionary War times. And the…not the morgue…the… Oh, what's the word I'm looking for? It's where they…"

"Mausoleum?"

"Yes, that's it! Mausoleum. Where they keep families. Well, there was one I tried to open. It had a stone door. I wasn't real strong, you know, but I managed to open the thing and I went inside. There really wasn't much to see. It sort of looked like a corner of a basement or something. There were plaques attached to the wall. About fifteen of them, I think. Well, after a few minutes, I left and pushed the door closed."

Phillip stopped them in the gravel pathway and turned to her as if he was just coming out of a daze, "Is this okay? Me talking like this, I mean?"

"Of course, it's okay! Why wouldn't it be? This is so perfect, don't you see, Phillip? It's so perfect." He looked at her with the most unusual look, and then surprised her by kissing the end of her nose.

"Okay, I'll go on. Well, about three months later, I went back, and there was a priest who was from the nearby church there, so we talked. I don't remember too much about our conversation. But then I told him that I'd gone inside one of the mausoleums, and I pointed it out to him. He looked at me like I was some kind of a ghost or something! He mumbled something to me about how I must be mistaken. I told him I didn't think I was. Anyway, we went over to it and, yep, you guessed it. It was sealed shut and obviously had been for a long, long time." Phillip stopped, a faraway look in his eyes. Patricia waited for him to continue.

"I told him I wasn't crazy. I told him that I really was inside it. I even described what I'd seen. Well, he just shook his head and said something like it's one of those things we'll never understand, I guess."

"The same thing happened to me about two years ago in Tivoli, New York. This time, though, I was in a graveyard behind a church that dated back to before the Civil War. It was almost exactly the same thing except this time, the supposedly sealed mausoleum wasn't sealed up at all. I came back later with some people and it was still unsealed so a bunch of us went inside and looked around. I found out that just a few weeks after that, the place was sealed up. I don't know if it was resealed, but I do know something was very odd about that because I made a connection. Am I talking too much, Trisha?"

"Oh no, baby. Not at all."

"I know I'm going on, but I've never told anyone these stories before. Not in this much detail, anyway. You sure I'm not boring you?"

Her almost annoyed looked answered his question.

"This next story is kind of interesting," Phillip said, "but a very long one." He glanced at her again and she raised an eyebrow and he dove quickly into the story.

"Well, it's about this place I was at—a sort of commune—and it was once the home of a general in the Civil War. Well, I didn't know anything about the history of the place, but I looked up at the tower that was there and I knew beyond any doubt that something tragic had happened there. Did a child fall from there? Did someone…" Phillip stopped. "Am I scaring you?"

"No, not at all. But you'll take me there one day, won't you? To Reinhope and Tripoli, I mean?"

Phillip laughed at her mispronunciations. "That I probably can't do. Rhine*beck*…ahem. Yes, I could take you there, perhaps. But…ahem…*Tivoli*, the place with the tall tower, was sold sometime back and is privately owned now. I don't know if the original buildings are even still standing or not. But it was owned by a Civil War general at one time and then it became part of the Underground Railroad. I discovered a lot of things about this place, some of which I was able to verify later. I guess I was led down this path to discover some kind of awareness or ability that I can't explain to you. But because of these things that happened in the cemeteries, I became very aware of things like spirits and souls and I guess you would say ghosts."

"I know, baby."

"Oh, I know you're aware of some of this," he reassured her. "But I know you're wondering what started all of this. And I don't blame you! I'm inspired by this place, Patricia. This cemetery. I can't explain it."

"This is a good place, Phillip."

"I can feel that it is. And I know your friend Alma belongs here." He noticed a look of surprise on Patricia's face. "I'm sorry, honey. I don't know exactly what made me say that. What I meant to say was that it's a comfortable, peaceful, good place for Alma."

Phillip hadn't realized they were standing exactly where Patricia meant for them to be. And he hadn't been looking at the tombstones when he'd mentioned Alma.

"Yes. Yes, it is, Phillip," she said pulling him down onto the stone bench beside the path.

In front of them was a newly engraved pink granite headstone. Inscribed were a few simple words: *Alma Trujillo Garrett. Go well.*

Phillip looked at Patricia and then at the tombstone. "I'm sorry, Trisha. I didn't do that on purpose, you know. Really, I didn't." Then he added rather weakly, "I haven't done this in a long time." He looked at her. Did she understand that this was yet another sign of how they were meant to be together?

"It's okay, Phillip." She remained purposely still for a few seconds, knowing that he needed this moment as much as she did. Then she added, "Phillip, I need you to make me a promise, and this is the place to make it, okay?" She waited for him to look at her. And when he did, she saw his eyes sparkle.

"I just love it when people want you to promise something before they even tell you what the request is," he said with a chuckle. "But for you, of course, the answer is yes. What is it you want me to promise?"

"Promise me that you'll stop apologizing for things you don't need to apologize for. In fact, don't apologize for anything to me again, okay?"

He thought about it for a while before responding, "I'm sorry. Really! I apologize! I didn't mean to be doing that. Of course, I promise."

"Grrr! You are impossible!"

She turned and looked at the tombstone. "See? See why I didn't tell you about him? He's a rogue and a scoundrel, and I should never have gotten mixed up with the likes of him!"

Chapter Thirty-one

His lips were once again on hers, the embrace long and passionate.

"So, do you do this often?" she asked. "Kiss strange women in cemeteries, I mean?"

"You got a problem with that?"

"Listen you..."

"Yes?"

"You're bad! So listen, hotshot, wanna go for another ride?"

"Good idea," he said. "If we sit here much longer, I'll just get us in all kinds of trouble."

"True," she smiled.

"So where you taking me this time?"

"How about a burger joint for some milkshakes and fries?"

"I don't know. I thought maybe you were going to surprise me by taking me someplace to watch one of your famous sunsets. Now *that* would have been a big surprise." He faked a cough.

"As a matter of fact, smarty, you *can* see the sunset from the Sonic. There's just one problem. I like root beer floats with chocolate chips and they've discontinued them," she pouted.

"Why, those rotten bastards! Then, we just won't go. It's not right to support a business that makes dumb decisions like that! Maybe we should organize a boycott and picket the place."

"That's right!" She pulled him to his feet and they started walking back toward the truck. "We can hold underground meetings to plan our boycott at the store."

Phillip tickled her a bit, and she playfully overreacted briefly, then stopped and threw her arms around him. "You drive me crazy, Mister Craven."

As they drove north toward the village of Taos Ski Valley, Phillip studied the decoration hanging down from the rear view mirror. It was round and consisted of a frame wrapped with dark green leather and woven into the web was a brilliantly polished stone of some kind. It was very similar to something he had seen before.

"Pardon my ignorance here," Phillip said, "but what is this thing? Is this a New Mexican version of furry dice? Some New Age thingy that's supposed to capture lost souls?"

Patricia raised an eyebrow as she stared at him.

"Was this perhaps something you found on the...*web*?" Phillip burst out laughing at his own cleverness. "Perhaps a 'web' special?" He just didn't know when to quit.

"You'd better stop that before my ancestors put a curse on you!" She laughed, too. "They'll do that, you know! So hush before they hear you!"

"Well, I guess I'd prefer to be cursed by family than by a bunch of strangers. Makes it more personal that way, don't you think?" He waited until she stopped giggling. "So, come on, what is it really?"

"It's the Native American version of a bug zapper."

"Oh, so now *you're* a comedian, too, huh?" Phillip said, lightly squeezing her thigh. She'd been fully aware of his hand on her leg, but when he squeezed it just then, her heart skipped a beat.

"Is it like a rabbit's foot or something?"

"No, wise guy, it's not like a rabbit's foot. We discussed luck once, remember? We don't believe in it. Take another guess."

"Is it supposed to be a spiderweb to catch something?"

"Very good! Do you know what it catches, Einstein?"

"Aha! It's designed to catch the spirits of really big horseflies!"

"Oh, damn your sorry ol' soul! Who needs ancestors? I'm going to get you myself! No, not horseflies. Actually, it's funny how close you really are. And it's not spirits either. But that's pretty close, too. It's a dream catcher. Wanna know what it's for?"

"I think I heard about this once, but I don't remember how it goes."

Patricia slowed the truck almost to a stop. They turned right off of the main highway onto an unmarked dirt road. He tightened his grip on her leg as they bounced over a cattle guard. The rather roughly bladed road then began a steep incline.

"A lot of people think that it's just a gizmo sort of thing. Some whimsical sort of touristy trash. I'll admit that some of them are, I guess. But this one happens to be the real thing. See the polished stone in the middle of the web? That's a tigereye stone. Some of the New Agers, as you called them, like to put things like crystals and beads in the center. That's when you know that they're just junk. There are other ways to tell, too, like the most obvious. If a Native American didn't craft it especially for you and then bless it especially for you..." Patricia stopped. "Are you really interested in this? Are you sorry you asked?"

"Of course, I'm interested in it. Even if it weren't hanging from *your* rearview mirror, I'd be interested. So, c'mon! Tell me. Or do I have to torture you until you spill the truth about this, dream catcher lady."

"Hmm, torture, huh? Now, there's a... Never mind!" She reached down and put her hand over his and left it there.

"Well, all right then. Most people mistakenly think that a dream catcher is supposed to capture your most wonderful dreams and hold them for you. Keep them safe and within reach so that if the time ever comes when you can use them, all you have to do is reach out and pluck it from the web. That's a great belief, don't get me wrong! But it's not entirely correct.

"And it's not very believable that Native Americans would actually believe they can control or alter the natural order of things," Phillip interjected. "Or something like that."

"That's exactly right. Although, someone wiser than myself would have to explain why this logic would be more believable. But the true duty of the dream catcher is to catch—or stop, I'd guess you'd say—the bad dreams or the spells or curses that may be sent to you, before they have a chance to inhabit your being. That's why a dream catcher is always placed near where you might sleep. I have a habit of just needing to get away from the shop now and again, so I often go out to the truck because it's usually warm and quiet. Sometimes, I eat lunch or read or whatever, and then I usually fall asleep. So anyway, a friend made that for me a long time ago. You still awake?"

"Yeah, I'm wide awake. So tell me what the tigereye means."

"As a matter of fact, I am not positive which stones stand for which animals...well, sometimes not always animals, but I won't freak you out at this point with that. Anyway, the tigereye does, in fact, stand for the tiger. It's a rather fierce protector, you might say."

"That's fascinating, Patricia. And so is being here with you."

"Uh-oh! Hold on! Another cattle guard!" She was going a little too fast that time and they bounced, hitting their heads on the ceiling of the truck.

"Yikes, woman! Watch what you're doing! If you're trying to knock some sense into me, forget it. I got it all knocked out of me a long time ago."

"*You*? Hell, I was trying to knock some sense into *me*! But you're right, it's pretty senseless, huh?" She was obviously changing the subject.

"You're suggesting that what we're doing is senseless?" Phillip asked teasingly.

"I didn't say that, exactly. But it's..." She had to brake in order to negotiate another tight turn in the rough road. "But, do *you* still think it's right, Phillip?" She didn't look at him.

"Would I be here, risking serious injury to my head, if I didn't?"

"No, I s'pose not." She tried to sound convincing, but was sure she failed.

"Stop the car a moment, Miss Ridgeway. Please."

"Now? Here?" She shot a look his way, but then rolled to a stop in the middle of the deserted road.

"I just wanted to look into your eyes a moment, Patricia,"

She had turned toward him, but averted her eyes.

"Look at me, Patricia," he commanded. And as he looked into her eyes, she felt self-conscious and tried to look away. He touched her chin. This was not what she'd expected. She acquiesced and looked directly into his breathtakingly blue eyes. He waited until she finally began to relax and a slight smile appeared on her face.

"It's time for us to relax with each other, Patricia," he said. "I mean to not worry so much." He stopped again. "I mean, *please* don't worry so much. Look at me, baby. Look in my eyes. Look in there and see now how much I love you."

"I know. God, I know Phillip." She wanted so desperately to believe the wonderful things he was telling her. She looked at him for a long time. She knew it was true.

"I'm just feeling differently than I ever thought I would," she said. "I can't really explain it exactly. I'm not really nervous. And for a time, back in the cemetery, I was totally relaxed. Totally. Like we had sat there and talked like that a thousand times before. I can't explain it, Phillip. Can you?"

"It defies explanation, I think," he said. "But you know what? Let's get going, huh? I haven't got all day you know!"

"Oh, I am so sorry. Of course. I'm sure you have a dinner date or something. What was I thinking? Selfish me!" she said, putting the truck in gear.

As they reached the top of the ridge, she heard Phillip sigh. She was pretty sure he would. The view was simply amazing. The crystal blue lake shimmered in the late afternoon sun. She was glad that he was seeing her "secret spot" in almost its full glory, although she wished he'd be able to see it in the first full grip of fall, just after the first heavy frost when the aspens are in their golden splendor. They watched as three or four of the resident chipmunks skittered about, noticeably annoyed at this intrusion into their world. Her secret place was now theirs. She couldn't have been happier. In a sense, they'd come home. She could see in his face that he was probably feeling that way as well. He knew exactly what this place was and what it meant to Patricia and why. He, too, felt it was a place where you could go to be recharged, renewed, and reborn.

"I need to get out a minute," he said quietly. She nodded. Together they walked to the edge of the tree line and stood back from the shore of the lake. Arms around each other's waist, they felt not the slightest need to say anything at all to one another. The moments melted together as the heavy air of evening began to envelop them. The only thing that passed between them was unspoken words of recognition and reassurance, discovery and remembrance. Any need they might have felt for justification or explanation was past.

Patricia leaned her head against Phillip's shoulder. "You like?" she finally said in a whisper.

"Oh, my yes. But like isn't the right word."

She waited for him to say what she expected him to say, but he remained silent. She removed her arm from around him and slid her hand into his. Together they walked to the edge of the water. The sun had begun to slip below the treetops and the once azure blue lake had magically become the color of spun gold, turning to shades of copper in some spots.

"Did you not have an answer to my question a minute ago, Phillip?" He stood silently, as though trying to figure out how to answer.

"Mitla," he finally said in a quiet voice. He felt Patricia must have understood what he had said. *No, she couldn't have.* He looked back at the lake, almost expecting to see the three familiar pyramids, the tallest one in the middle. He felt inexplicably exhilarated. A lightness, a warmth, an awareness of all his senses being opened at once. He wanted to hold onto the feeling for as long as he could.

"You know how they say that every person in the world has a twin or a double somewhere else in the world?" She didn't wait for an answer. "Well, we Indians believe that every magical place in the world has another place equally as magical somewhere else in the world, too. Science would explain it by telling us that it happens because the sun and the sky and the clouds absorb the energy of that place and transfer it somewhere else. Not unlike a mirage, I suppose. Does that make sense to you, Phillip?"

"Yes, it does."

Patricia sat down on the ground and invited him to join her. "One night, you told me about Mitla and about climbing to the top of the pyramid when you were a young man on a great and glorious adventure. You also told me about the feeling you got there, and about the spirits you thought you felt there. Do you remember that, sweetie?"

"Yes, I remember. I thought you'd understand. I'm glad you remembered it, too, Trisha." His voice had a kind of strange, unattached tone to it, and it surprised her. She decided to let it pass.

"As you were describing your experience to me, it was almost as if you were exactly reflecting the feelings I have when I come here to this lake.

You never mentioned a lake though. I think it was just the feelings that I related to, I'm not sure, really. But if I'd been telling you about this lake, I would have told you in almost the same way as you described the pyramid."

She paused until she was sure he wasn't going to speak, and then continued. "So, bright and early the very next morning, I drove up here, just to be sure of my feelings. It was amazing, Phillip! Even knowing what I'd see, I was still almost stunned."

"This place has nearly the same energy, the same feeling, though it's still different somehow," Phillip said slowly.

"Exactly! It's the feeling. The energy."

"Is it coincidence that we both know that?" he asked. "Or is it…how it should be? Yes," he answered himself. "It's exactly as it should be."

Patricia fell back onto the ground laughing. "If you hadn't finished that sentence, I was going to tease you unmercifully. Remarkable, indeed! No, it's not remarkable at all, is it?"

He didn't answer. Then, it was as if time and space had together skipped a beat for he found himself with his lips pressed against hers, kissing her alternately tenderly and passionately. He felt her lips hungrily kissing him back, wanting to share in the passion that was passing between them. They kissed deeply, but not in the desperate and hurried ways of some lovers, but rather as two lovers who were destined for one another. They were lovers who needed and wanted each other equally.

Their kissing became even more intense until Phillip withdrew slightly to allow them both to draw a breath. But Patricia followed his tongue, lifting her head slightly in an effort to continue the intensity of the kiss. Their bodies began to burn now with a desire-demanding fulfillment. Finally it was Phillip who broke the kiss, gasping for air as he continued to hold Patricia tightly.

"Phil…" She meant to continue, but the words weren't there. *Say something, you idiot. Say something!*

She couldn't. If she wanted to ask if he were feeling the same emotions, she didn't need to. Phillip delicately traced her eyebrow with his finger and tickled the soft, smooth skin down her nose and then traced her lips. She sighed and nuzzled her face toward his hand. He bent down and barely touched her eyelids with his lips. He leaned close to her and fluttered his eyelashes against her cheek.

"Butterfly kisses," he said softly, "for my angel…"

"I thought this moment would never happen, Phillip." Her eyes were filled with tears.

"You knew it would," he said softly. "I certainly did."

"How? How did you know? I wanted it to happen so badly, but I never really thought it would. Maybe I tried to think it never would. I don't know."

"I love you so much, Patricia." He leaned back and removed his jacket and placed it on the ground beside them. "We might need that later," he said with a slightly wicked smile.

He came closer to her face, which was turned up to meet his. She began to close her eyes in anticipation of his kiss; her arms circled him and pulled him tightly to her. To Phillip, the way her arms opened and then folded around him reminded him of a tulip closing its petals for the evening, protecting itself from the elements of the night. Was he ready to be her protector? No, the two of them were equals, for she was protecting him as well.

Their lips finally met in a kiss that was at first tender, then yielding quickly to the hunger they both felt. Patricia kept running her fingers through his hair, not daring to move to another part of his body. Surely her heart had ceased beating. Phillip's kisses grew more urgent as his hands rubbed her back, though not nearly as tenderly as just moments before. They roamed lower, squeezing her, pulling her even closer to him. He couldn't get enough of her, and he wanted her to feel the effect she was having on him. She placed her hands on his chest and pushed herself away.

"Oh god, Phillip, what are we doing? This is real, baby. You and me. I mean really you are here with me. We're together, touching and holding each other. This is really real."

Phillip put his finger on her lips. "Sh, I know, baby." Without looking, he felt her eyes on him seeking an answer. She was beginning to realize that her life was about to change forever, going in a direction she had only fantasized about.

"I don't know all the answers," he whispered. "I wish I did. All I know is that I'm here, Trisha, and you're here. And it's real. It isn't a dream. I just know how right this feels, or why would I be here right now? Why would you be here? Look at the odds against our ever even knowing each other, and yet here we are. Together."

"So..." Patricia stopped, but then decided to continue. "So, you aren't sorry? That you came, I mean. Or disappointed?"

She saw the anger in his eyes almost immediately, and wished she could have pulled the words back before he'd heard them.

"Sorry? Disappointed? What the hell are you talking about, Trisha? Sorry I came? Why?" He didn't allow her any chance to respond. "Are *you* sorry I came? Is that what it is? Is all this too much for you? Damn it, Patricia!"

She had never seen his temper before. Quite frankly, it scared her. And he wasn't finished.

"Is that what you think? Is that the kind of person you think I am? Is that what you think of us? That we existed on the Internet because that's the only place we could be perfect together? Did you hope that we'd never really meet? Were you happier when it was just an illusory affair on a computer screen?"

His voice noticeably softer when he added, "Have I somehow disappointed you, Patricia? Tell me, have I done something wrong?" She didn't give him time to go on this time.

"No!" Her voice began to crack. She began again. "No, Phillip. Good god, *no*! You didn't disappoint me. How could you? I just know that I was never entirely truthful with you. I didn't lie to you, really. I just never prepared you. I was..."

"You were what?"

"I was writing a letter to you this afternoon when you came. I knew that you'd be gone, at least I thought you'd be gone. But...well, I don't know for sure. I guess somehow I thought that if I told you the truth, even if you didn't see it before you saw me, that somehow it would make things easier. Clear my conscience, I guess. Oh hell, Phillip, I don't know what I'm trying to say. I'm sorry."

Phillip chuckled.

"What? Don't do that! Don't laugh at me, okay? Please?"

"I'm not laughing at you. Really, I'm not. Well now, how do I put this?"

"Gently, okay? Put it gently," she pleaded.

"Okay. Gentle is good." He knew basically what he was trying to say; it was just getting the words out in a way that would make sense. "I guess all I have to tell you is that to me... To me, Patricia Ridgeway, you're perfect exactly the way you are. I wish you weren't. I mean, I wish you didn't even have this feeling that you need to be more... more glamorous...or whatever the hell it is that's bugging you." Phillip chuckled at his own ineptness in describing his thoughts. "I fucked that up. Or did you understand what I was trying to say, even as badly as I messed it up?" He was anything but prepared for the burst of laughter that came at him full force.

"*Glamorous*? *Glamorous!* Oh, that's too funny, Phillip. No, I don't want to be glamorous. I just want to be what I am. It's just that I'm not what you are used to. I am not your stereotypical woman that is sought after by younger, handsome men like you. Now don't say anything. Let me finish, okay?"

"Sure, it's your shovel!"

"Oh, never mind! Never you mind!"

He felt her melt into his embrace. "Then may I continue to ravage your body?" he laughed.

"No, you may not."

Her answer was unexpected. And not only to Phillip. She desperately wanted to be anywhere but here right now.

"It's not dark, Phillip." Her voice was hardly above a whisper.

"But if it were dark, I wouldn't be able to see you, and I very much want to see you. I love you, Patricia, and I don't want it to be dark. And I don't want you to be perfect. I just want to get you naked as quickly as possible so you can't think about it anymore, and then I want to hold you and tell you how wonderful you make me feel. And then I want to try and make you feel as wonderful as you make me feel." Phillip looked at her and added, "Now, do you have any objection that you think I would listen to?"

She didn't know what to say. Well, that's not entirely true. She *knew* what she wanted and needed to say, but somehow she almost believed what he'd just told her. She tried to rise up on her elbows, but he was making it impossible. She suddenly felt almost trapped.

All he wanted to do was kiss her and tell her she was being foolish and more self-conscious than she needed to be. But instead, he merely moved against her, making it difficult for her to struggle. Then he felt the awkwardness of the situation, and he sighed.

"Trisha, I need you as much or more than you think you need me. You might not want to believe that, but it's the truth, and I may not ever admit that to you again—unless, of course, you're tickling me in just the right spot."

She collapsed back into his arms. "You aren't just saying that, are you? Not just saying it because you are here and for the moment you have no way out of this? You really meant what you said?"

"I meant it."

Her eyes were getting brighter and more playful, the muscles in her back relaxing. The warmth was again exuding from her body. Phillip rolled them on their sides so that their hands and arms could rub and caress each other as they kissed.

"Oh, Phil…" She was breathless, her face appeared flushed. The sky above them had turned crimson and its magic seemed to enfold them. She rolled away from him, lying flatly on the cool, damp ground. The look on her face was unmistakable, and his body responded. He moved on top of her, rubbing against her as he did and kissing her lips, her cheeks. She moved her face slightly, letting him kiss her and sweep her off into the cinnabar sky with his caresses as their bodies moved against one another.

With a deftness that she appreciated, his hands were on her blouse, tenderly squeezing her breasts a moment and then fumbling with her buttons. Patricia's hand found his and began helping him unbutton her blouse. She sat up and let it fall open as Phillip reached around her and unhooked the lacy bra. He reached up and his hands held her warm, soft, and ample breasts. His thumbs brushed past her nipples which quickly responded to his touch. Urgently, his mouth wetly kissed down her neck and between her breasts, his tongue alternately teasing her nipples. The intensity of her reaction startled him a bit. She arched her back, moaning louder than he expected, causing a reaction within him for which he was somewhat unprepared.

Her moans understandably made him want to give her even more pleasure. He quickly pressed his lips over his teeth and pinched her nipple gently with his mouth and then sucked her breast hungrily into his mouth. Her back arched again. Her hands pulled his head more tightly to her, wanting him to suck harder. Her hands moved down his body, rubbing him and causing more arousal than he wanted at that moment. Their senses were on overload.

He watched with anticipation as she removed his shirt from his body. When she started to fumble with his belt, he reached down to help her. They quickly rid themselves of the rest of their clothing. They were both totally naked, and it was only the heat of their passion that shielded them from the cool evening air. Slowly, she lowered herself onto his soft leather jacket and watched dreamily as he slid on top of her, feeling for the first time all of his flesh against hers. His hands explored the body he'd only dreamed about before now, and they touched, kissed, and tasted each other, guiding each other in and out of ever-heightening states of pleasure.

Their dance of desire was at times less than perfect, but utterly human and all the better for it. Soon their bodies overwhelmingly demanded more than the pleasure only kisses and erotic caresses could bring them. She opened herself up and Phillip was soon inside of her warm body. She moved and squeezed and responded in ways she hadn't known possible, and it was all as perfect as it was meant to be. Rising up, curling, and then crashing back into each other again as waves against the shore. And again. And again.

Patricia gave herself over to the moment in ways she had never done. Her moans were neither forced nor reserved, but rose from some deep, hidden part of her she'd never explored before. Her body began to shake with the explosion of pleasure that was running through her and she could feel his need past any point of control. Finally, it all rushed over their bodies at exactly the same time, rendering them faint with the intensity of pleasure that neither of them had ever felt before. Afterwards, they lay quietly in each other's arms, listening to their heartbeats.

"You know what, Phillip?"

"What, darling?"

"It's cold. I mean, it's fucking cold!" She giggled at her own boldness.

"That's a good way to describe it!" he laughed.

"Are you going to hand me my clothes, or just let me lie here and freeze to death?" She pushed him away from her body and stood up, clutching the leather jacket over herself.

"Well, if it was a little warmer, I don't think I'd ever let you get dressed!" Phillip wiggled his eyebrows and pretended to be flicking a cigar. "But considering that we're both about to die from frostbite, let's find a warmer place where we can play some more."

"Oh my gosh, I forgot to tell you about the infamous Taos Mountain rattlesnake that lives around this sacred lake. Dang, baby, you'd better watch your…ah, well, your…you know!" She giggled and let her eyes dance down his naked body.

"I love you, Phillip Craven"

"I love you Patricia Ridgeway."

"I know you do." *Perhaps as much as I love you.*

Chapter Thirty-two

"Do you people have radio stations in these parts, or do you just prefer being isolated from the rest of the world?" He seemed to have been sleeping since shortly after they left the lake. But now he was leaning forward and spinning the dial on the radio.

"Sweetheart, if that wasn't so close to the truth I'd laugh! I'm afraid the local stations don't have enough power to get those little air-wavy things over the mountain. We can't even pick up many of the major cities, although late at night we can actually get KOKA, a fantastic station out of Oklahoma City. Trent told me once that he thought people could get KOKA in Hong Kong on a clear night!"

Damn! Not now, you idiot! What did you have to go and mention his name for?

Patricia realized that's one of the beauties of the chatroom. She thought back on how many times she'd typed something inappropriate and then had the foresight to hit the "delete" button before sending it. *What would my life be like if I'd ever slipped up and sent some of those messages? I sure as hell wouldn't be sitting here now with Phillip. That's for sure!*

There had been many times that she thought, for her own sake as well as for Phillip's that she should end their relationship. It sometimes felt to her as though it was her responsibility to let the two of them get back to the real world. She'd lost track of the number of times she'd typed something to Phillip trying to initiate the right conversation, and then by some miracle the next words to pop on her screen would be his, bringing her to her senses.

"There is no way for me to tell you how happy I am that I'm here, Trisha." His voice was strong and he didn't hesitate nor stumble over his words.

Good. He didn't say anything. Maybe he didn't hear me say Trent's name after all.

"Me, too, sweetie. But you'll have to forget about radio stations though. Here, listen to this. I think you'll like it." She reached over and put in a CD and the unmistakable voice of Tony Bennett surrounded them, and

Phillip leaned back and smiled.

"Mmm, yeah. That's nice."

There was a ten-year difference in their ages. To some, that would be an inconsequential difference. To others, it was a chasm nearly a full generation wide. There were probably lots of reasons. For one, the 1960s "baby boomer" generation somehow stepped out of synch and became a sort of a struggling generation at best. Then sometime in the 1980s, the merry-go-round stopped just long enough to let them back on. Those who did found little there that they recognized. In defense of that, many of them fell quietly back into a time frame of comfort and stability. Content with the reliability and assurance that it was all right to have taken a vacation from the life for a little while.

The 1960s, of course, had been a complicated time of dramatic changes and international conflict that rocked the entire world. The Vietnam War stole many of the best our country had to offer, sending home plastic bags filled with shattered watches and blood-spattered dog tags as tragic reminders of lost potential. And standing proudly beside the flag draped caskets, were the parents of World War II who tried to convince themselves that war is honor, duty, and sacrifice. The price of freedom.

The new generation needed drugs to cope. The lost and struggling generation needed Tony Bennett.

"Patricia?"

"What, baby?"

"I never told you I liked Tony Bennett, did I?"

"No. But you didn't have to."

Because of you, my life is now worthwhile and I can smile because of you... The orchestra continued playing for several seconds after his last words faded into nothingness.

When the flickering lights of town came into view, Phillip said to Patricia, "I didn't know where to make a room reservation. I thought I could do that after I got here and I'm afraid I...uh...forgot about it. You see, there was this woman, and..."

"I don't suppose it ever occurred to you that this is a famous tourist haunt and perhaps there just might not *be* any rooms available this time of year? Hmm? Ever think of that?" she asked, interrupting him with a smile.

"Yep."

"Well, when in doubt, Phillip, go have a root beer float with chocolate chips! Let's go to the Sonic drive-in. I lied. They *do* still have Root Beer floats with chocolate chips!"

"I'd appreciate it, you know, if you'd stop lying to me."

"Yeah? So?" she laughed as they pulled into the drive-in.

"You like it?" she asked.

"I can't taste it."

"Oh, brother. And *why* can't you taste it?"

"There's a chocolate chip stuck in my straw."

"Oh jeez!" She put her head on the steering wheel in mock exasperation. "You are impossible, Mr. Craven. Truly impossible."

"Why, thank you, Mrs. Ridgeway." He made a loud slurping sound and started choking. "There! That's better! Oh, this is...uh...almost good. Yeah! Almost good." He put his face down on the top of the cup and stared. "Are you *sure* these are chocolate chips?"

"Okay. Okay! That's it! I've had enough! Just let me get some gas, and I can have you back down the mountain to Albuquerque and at the airport in time to catch the last flight to Whogivesadamnsville."

"Really? You think you can get rid of me that easily?" His eyes were sparkling.

"I certainly hope not."

"Good. Because you can't."

Phillip began watching the young carhops on rollerblades zipping in and around the parked cars.

"They're cute, huh?"

"Oh, yeah. They're cute all right. Mmmmm. Nice tight little asses, firm perky breasts, long smooth legs."

"I'm afraid I'll have to kill them all now." She was looking away from him, staring out of the window.

"Sheesh, Patricia, I was just teasing," he said with a laugh.

"I know."

He saw the look on her face. He wanted to know who and what had done this to her. He sat quietly waiting for her to speak first. Several minutes passed between them before she finally did.

"I just wish I hadn't missed my childhood. It makes me sad sometimes."

Her words failed to startle him. "Yeah, I missed that part of me, too," he said. "It *is* sad, isn't it."

"Yes, it truly is."

"Hey! Listen to the song that's playing on the jukebox." He rolled the window the rest of the way down.

It's my party and I'll cry if I want to...cry if I want to, cry if I want to. You would cry too if it happened to you...

PART III

Paper brothers return as lovers

Embrace you in their thrills

And through the action of slight distraction

Cripples my will.

But I just had to touch the face to find out if I'm real.

I've learned to cry

I will not die

For the face and I

Chapter Thirty-three

"Where's Phillip?" demanded Patricia as she glared at Sgt. Riley. This was the third time Patricia had pressed her for an answer and Riley was getting noticeably annoyed. *Damned dyke!*

"It's not important right now *where* Mr. Craven is, Ms. Ridgeway. What I am trying to do here, well... More specifically, what I am *required* to do here is talk to you so I can try to understand a few things."

"Such as?" Patricia's sarcasm was not lost on the sergeant.

"Such as, *Ms. Ridgeway*, what involvement Mr. Craven has in the death of Alma Garrett, and why the Sheriff's Office is questioning him and not the State Police. I have a feeling you know the answers."

"Questioning him? What do you mean, *questioning* him? Phillip has come here voluntarily to offer you people some information that will help you find Alma's killer! He is *not* here to be questioned!" Patricia's incredulity fell on deaf ears.

"To satisfy my own curiosity, I would also like to know," Sgt. Riley continued, "why Sheriff Garrett didn't contact the State Police when this little meeting between all of you was cooked up. And then I want to know what else you and this Craven know. And, since the two of you seem to know a helluva lot more about all this than I do, I want to know why you two conveniently chose not to come to us earlier in this game.

Game? My best friend is dead and she's calling this a game? Fuck you. Fuck you!

"It seems more than just a little odd to me why Garrett and Conner agreed to talk to your friend at all! What the hell were they thinking? They both had to know how that would look! Let's be honest here, shall we? Now Garrett...well, I can understand his stupidity. But I gave Conner more credit than this!"

"Detective Richards, of the homicide investigation team, is on his way here from Albuquerque right now. I called him as soon as I got wind of this little soirée. I have to tell you, Ms. Ridgeway, that I was not the least bit amused. I thought you and I understood each other. And you know what? I really liked and respected how you handled yourself through that whole nasty mess. I know that Alma Garrett was your friend and worked for you. I can appreciate the feelings you must have had and how hard it must have been to stand up and defend Frank Garrett like you did. Considering how you felt about him, I mean." Brenda paused, hoping for a reaction from Patricia, but was met with a steely gaze. Riley was getting frustrated, and perhaps a bit careless.

"Of course, I thought you were a damned fool. Frank Garrett killed his wife, or had her killed, and you and I both know it! But somehow, you stood your ground and made what at least appeared to be some fairly valid points. What I can't figure out is why the hell you would do that. Damn! I'm glad *I* don't have friends like *you*. Alma Garrett must have been as big a fool as her husband is."

"Anyway, my point through all of this is that I respected you for your guts. But that respect has long since been replaced by my mighty serious doubts. Especially after learning that there were a few fundamental facts omitted from that hearing. That, and now a witness of some sort has miraculously materialized who claims he's put two and two together. I'm guessing here that you knew this shit all along and frankly, it pisses the hell out of me!"

Patricia couldn't stop herself from staring at the two dark circles of sweat that had begun to grow under Sgt. Riley's armpits. *Getting a bit uncomfortable, are we?* Patricia didn't feel at all bad that she was causing her this much anxiety. There was nothing about her Patricia could find to like. In all honesty, she hated her. She'd have to be careful how she conducted herself around her in the future. Patricia watched as Riley began flipping through a file marked "Garrett" that must have been five or six inches thick.

She was relieved that Sgt. Riley didn't seem to know that Patricia had gotten a telephone call four days ago from Detective Bud Richards of the New Mexico State Police. The conversation with Richards had started out pleasantly enough. He'd introduced himself and then asked about Trent and about how the bookstore was doing and if she was coping all right with the loss of her friend, Alma. Patricia answered all of his questions except the last one. She resented his intrusion into her emotions, and didn't feel he really cared one way or another. *Hell, no, she wasn't coping with Alma's death. I probably won't ever be able to!* Something soon told her this was not a social call.

"Ms. Ridgeway, I'm quite certain that you are not nearly as stupid as you would like me led to believe you are. I'm not sure if it's intentional on your part or if you have been advised to act the fool for one reason or another. But, well...I'm getting pretty sick of your little act. I'd sincerely appreciate it if you'd just cut the fuckin' crap and be square with me for once here!"

"Sgt. Richards..."

"*Detective.* It's *Detective* Richards, Ms. Ridgeway."

"*Mrs.* It's *Mrs.* Ridgeway, *Detective* Richards."

Despite the tension of the moment, Patricia had to smile at the silence from the other end of the dead line. She'd always thought that adolescents were more prone to slam down a phone than adults were. *Wrong again!*

Bill Conner called Patricia and asked her if he could drop by her house later in the evening. He didn't explain the nature of his intended visit. He only said that Frank had planned to talk to her, but he'd been unexpectedly summoned to Santa Fe to testify and wouldn't be home for a day or two. When Bill arrived at the Ridgeways, he was surprised to find Patricia home alone.

"Trent out of town again, Patricia? Sylvia told me that she thought he'd moved home. I guess she's seen his truck here a time or two."

"No. He drops by for his mail and things, usually when I'm not here. I'm afraid it's over between the two of us, Bill."

Bill liked Patricia and he enjoyed Trent's company, as well. He'd never thought Trent appreciated Patricia the way *he* would have if she were *his* wife. But, hell, most men think that about husbands they're envious of.

"I'm sure this will pass, Patricia. Hell, things like this just happen sometimes. And besides, you guys have had a lot of stress these past few months. Frankly, I don't know how you've been able to deal with all this stuff. I'm sure Trent will be okay. Just give him some time."

He gave her a reassuring hug. Not an intimate embrace, by any means. Just a hug between friends. He remembered how, after he'd first moved to Taos, Patricia had sensed his loneliness and frustration over his divorce and not having his children with him. She'd been a good listener. He owed her his strength and a lot more right now.

Although he was hesitant to talk to her about why he'd stopped by, he had to find a way. He was a little annoyed that Trent wasn't there. Bill felt like what he had to say was something the two of them needed to digest together and make some decisions.

"Would you happen to have any coffee made, Patricia?"

"Bill, I can't honestly believe you asked me that. Of course, I have coffee made! I found this incredible site on the Internet where I can order gourmet coffee and it's on my doorstep in three days. No shipping, no tax, and a pound of coffee is actually a pound of coffee! Isn't that's a novel approach to modern math?"

"What?"

"Modern math, silly! In the coffee world, a pound is eleven ounces or something like that." She was laughing as she held his hand tightly, like a wayward kid. She led him to a chair in front of the thick butcher-block table and playfully pushed him into it.

"Take a load off and tell me to what I owe the pleasure of this dishonor? Oh lord… I hope Sylvia doesn't have those opera glasses of hers aimed in this direction. She might not approve of that wonderful hug I just got!"

Before Bill could say anything, Patricia put her hand on his shoulder for a moment and then stepped toward the stove. "I approved though, Bill. I guess I didn't realize how badly I needed that right now."

"You know, I needed that hug, too, I guess. Therapy for both of us, huh?" He watched her from across the kitchen. He was going to make it a point to drop by Trent's office. He hoped that they were good enough friends that Trent would talk to him. This had gone beyond a "mid-life crisis" as far as Bill was concerned. Did he blame Patricia for the path that her life had taken lately? It went against everything he trusted and believed in, yet he was trying desperately to see things from her perspective. Oddly enough, it was getting easier and easier to do.

Patricia brought two steaming mugs of coffee and placed them on the table.

"This smells mighty good, Patricia. What kind is it?"

"Its called Emerald City Blend, actually. In honor of a friend of mine, you might say." She pulled out a chair and sat down beside him. "But you didn't come here to talk about coffee. So, do you want to tell me, or am I supposed to guess?"

"I'll tell you what I know, Patricia. It's not much. And I wish Frank could have told you himself, but I'll do my best."

For the next two hours, he tried to summarize the entire series of events, which had taken place over the past several weeks. Everything that he shared with her was in addition to the many surprises they'd shared in Santa Fe and on the drive home. Patricia found it astounding that Bill had kept the two incidents separate, then realized that much of what he was sharing now had happened in the short time since that visit. Well, part of it anyway. The other part of it was ancient history.

The first pot of coffee was soon gone. After Patricia brewed another, they moved into the den where Bill continued to talk while he built a fire. Bill was becoming more comfortable, and Patricia was seeing a side of him she'd seldom seen in the past. He exuded an air of confidence that he rarely showed anyone.

Bill had begun the conversation by reminiscing about the "old days" with Frank. Patricia found herself enjoying his stories, and through them developed a new appreciation of the deep friendship between the two men and what it had endured through the years. She certainly admired Bill's commitment to Frank, but had to contain her surprise at one particular story for which she was quite unprepared.

Bill paced slowly in front of the fireplace as he recounted Frank's embarrassment—and his role as Frank's defender—when Frank was brought before their college dean and questioned about some absurd homosexual charges that had been levied against him by another member of their university football team. Patricia laughed, but she could clearly see that Bill was still incredulous regarding the allegations.

Throughout their conversations that evening, Patricia occasionally had to struggle to maintain her attention. Her thoughts persisted in drifting to times when she and Alma had shared "girl talk" times. Patricia had never heard Alma make any reference to anything that remotely alluded to the time Frank had been accused of being homosexual. *Maybe this was something Alma had never known.*

"What is it that makes me want to talk to you, Patricia?"

Neither spoke for a few moments.

"You've always been easy to talk to," he began again, "Forgive me, will you? Like you, I suddenly seem to be losing everything that means anything to me. I guess I was just trying to hold on to a little bit of my past before it slipped away, too. Most of that didn't have anything to do with what I came here for tonight. Well, some of it did, I guess. Oh, hell, Patricia. This is all so damned hard."

Even though she was uncertain what he meant, she admired his rather clumsy attempts at candor. "Bill, I'm glad you talked to me. You know Alma meant the world to me, and I knew her better than I know myself. But I really don't know Frank very well at all, and his past is important in making him what he is today. Well, I suppose that's true of all of us, isn't it?"

"Yes, I suppose it is." He watched as she placed her empty cup on the coffee table. "Want some more coffee?"

"Sure. That would be nice. Thank you." She curled up in the corner of the couch and gathered a gray cashmere throw around her shoulders.

"Frank's a fighter, Patricia. He fought Alma's family to make her his wife. He fought the odds and prejudices to become Sheriff of Taos County. He fought those same prejudices to bring me here as his Deputy Sheriff. And he fought to clear his name when they tried to accuse him of killing Alma."

The color suddenly drained from his face.

"What's wrong, Bill? Has something new happened?"

"I'm not sure. Well, that's not exactly true. Yes, something has happened, but I don't know exactly what it is. It has to do with Frank and Brenda. Brenda Riley. You remember her, don't you?"

Patricia shifted uncomfortably on the sofa. "Oh, yes. I have to admit, I took an immediate dislike to her."

"You're not alone. I don't think many people like her. And I suppose you know that I'm responsible for her being here, right?"

Patricia shook her head no.

"That's surprising. I just figured you would. Anyway, I felt like I wasn't qualified to step up and take over the department when they put Frank on probation. So I actively sought another, more street savvy officer. Hell, Patricia, I never dreamed that I'd just be *sent* someone without being allowed any say-so in the matter. Frank says I was railroaded by the big guns in Santa Fe. I don't know if that's true or not, and he hasn't been back long enough to have had time to investigate it for us. But the point is, Sgt. Riley has been making Frank's life miserable and that's why he's in Santa Fe right now."

Patricia listened as Bill filled her in on the intricate workings of the appointments and hiring, transferring and promotion policies of the Sheriff's Office. Admittedly she was growing a bit weary of trying to understand where this had any connection to her and why she was being made privy to all of this information. But she attempted to remain attentive and cordial, even though she offered little to the conversation. Bill went on to tell her a few of the problems that had arisen because of some questionable behavior by Sgt. Riley. Suddenly things started making sense. She stared at Bill in disbelief as he related some shocking revelations.

"So, now you know why Frank is in Santa Fe. He has to present his case to the State Attorney General before Riley and Richards get the last pieces of their little puzzle all together and beat him to the punch."

"So, Bill, you're telling me that Brenda Riley was a plant? Sent here by whom? Bud Richards?"

"Yes. At least, that's what we think. From what we understand, Richards hates Frank because apparently Richards has a brother-in-law that he'd been grooming for Deputy Sheriff up here. So when Frank hired me, I guess Richards was livid. Apparently, he didn't get any help or cooperation from the guys at the state capitol, and when he found out that there was a way he could infiltrate the system up here...well, he jumped on it. Hell, Patricia, he knew I wasn't in any position to do anything but accept anyone they sent up here. And he also knew that if a woman was on the list, she stood a damned good chance of getting the job. He was right."

"So according to Riley, Bud Richards had been told *prior* to arriving here the day that Alma was killed that Frank was a closet homosexual and had killed his wife because she had discovered this out about him?" Patricia asked. "How did you find all of this out, Bill? Who told Richards that and why? He could have made that all up, couldn't he?"

"I was afraid you'd ask me that, Patricia. Now here is where I lose all credibility. I don't know how the hell Frank found all this out. And as far as I know, Richards claims he got an anonymous tip early the morning of Alma's death. Some guy called him and told him that he was Frank's lover and that he had reason to believe that Alma was in grave danger."

"In danger? Then why the hell wasn't someone watching her? She wasn't warned, Bill! She would have told me something like that! Where were the police if this was true?" Patricia slid to the edge of the couch and angrily threw the shawl from her shoulders.

"For some reason, Patricia, Richards didn't act on the tip. Hell, cops get those kinds of threats all the time. Richards claims he made a few inquiries and didn't find anything to indicate the slightest possibility that the caller was credible at all. He ran a check on the number from where the call was placed and said it turned out to be a pay phone at the airport. Would you have believed some jerk if he'd called *you* with the same allegations? Hell, no, you wouldn't. Well, neither did Richards, I guess."

"But Richards is a cop, Bill! Cops are *supposed* to take those things seriously!."

When she began to cry, Bill turned and stood silently staring into the fire.

"So, how did you and Frank find all of this out, Bill?"

"I think you know."

"Yes. I think I do. Phillip's coming here, isn't he?"

"On Saturday. He'll fly into Albuquerque, rent a car, and drive up. We expect him about mid-afternoon."

Patricia could still feel the flush in her cheeks as she spoke. "How much more do you know about any of this, Bill?"

"Truthfully? Not much. And I don't think Frank does either. He knows the guy's name. And he knows that he's a friend of yours. Frank said the guy told him that you'd vouch for him and verify his credentials or something. When Frank asked him how he knew you, he was told that it was a long story he'd rather explain face-to-face."

"And you know the story and you didn't tell Frank, did you?"

"No, I didn't." He looked at the floor and traced the pattern of the Navajo rug with the tip of his boot. "No, I didn't. And I won't, Patricia."

"So, Phillip is coming on Saturday? And am I supposed to know this, Bill?" She was still sitting on the edge of the couch, but watching him closely now.

"He's going to tell you, yes. If he hasn't all ready."

"He has, Bill. He told me late last night. But he didn't tell me much else. Am I in for any more surprises? Anything that I need to be prepared for?"

"If you are, then so am I. Hell, there has been one surprise after another around here, so why should that change? But as far as I know, no, there shouldn't be any more surprises. Since they've had to allow Frank back on the force, we'll be able to talk to Phillip together and see what all he has to tell us. Then we'll talk to you, okay?

"I'm sure you'd be more comfortable—and frankly I would be, too—if the two of you could just come in together. But with Sgt. Riley around, neither Frank nor I want to bend any rules here. I think she reports to Richards every time we make a move!"

"As if things aren't bad enough for Frank...well, and for you...she has to be part of the equation. What do you really think she's up to?"

"That's puzzling both of us. You can bet there's a reason she's here. We just don't know what it is yet. Frank's smart, Patricia...really smart...and Riley's taking him for a real dope. That's working to our advantage right now. Maybe if he can keep her thinking that, maybe we'll be able to figure out the answer and find out who it is that keeps trying to finger Frank. There's more to this than just Bud Richards."

"How much access does she have to any of the files and things that were confiscated from Alma and Frank's house?"

"Well, she didn't have any until a few weeks ago. Everything was in the DA's office in Santa Fe until the charges were dropped against Frank. When he asked for all this stuff back, they had to give it to him. Why?"

"Just curious."

* * * * *

It would have been very easy for Patricia to escalate the discussion with Sgt. Riley into a full-scale war, but she kept reminding herself that it would be the very worst thing she could do right now. She also knew that the other very best thing she could do was to get her ass out of that office and away from anymore questions as quickly as she could.

"Are you quite through with me, Sgt. Riley?" She had wanted her tone to be a bit more conciliatory.

"You have a date, *Mrs.* Ridgeway?"

"I have a business to run. And I'd like to get back to it. Now, if you will excuse me. It's been a pleasure." She pushed her chair away from the inexcusably grimy table.

"You aren't leaving town again any time soon, are you, Mrs. Ridgeway?"

"Is that honestly any of your business, Sgt. Riley? And what makes you conclude that I might have been out of town? Am I under surveillance for some reason?"

"No. You are not under surveillance."

Patricia turned to leave.

"Should you be?"

It took a few seconds for that question to fully sink in. When it did, Patricia's response was a knee-jerk reaction.

"YOU BITCH! YOU FUCKING QUEER BITCH!" she yelled with more malice than she'd have thought she was capable of. Patricia walked past Brenda Riley, went through the door, and never looked back.

Chapter Thirty-four

"I'm pretty sure I know who we're dealing with here," Phillip began.

He watched as Bill took a sip of his coffee. Phillip was continuing to pretend quite convincingly that he didn't know as much as he actually did about the case. He did wonder why Bill hadn't stopped the interrogation at the station house. Phillip reasoned Bill knew Frank better than most. *He must have had his reasons. Anyway, I won't blow his cover by mentioning that he and Patricia had brunch at Dylan's with Bill and Sylvia on Sunday.*

"Who's that?" Bill asked.

"He goes by the name of Silky." Phillip stopped and watched as the color drained from Frank's face.

"I'm sorry, Frank. Silky isn't who you think," Phillip continued.

It was obvious that Frank now wished he were any place but sitting here in the coffee shop and having this conversation.

"I apologize for putting you on the spot here, Frank," Phillip said. "I know you a little better than you realize."

Having just learned that Phillip was the person he knew as Diabolique from the chatroom, Frank couldn't possibly imagine what else he might know about him since he was obviously aware of his secret life.

Phillip tried carefully to pick just the right words. "Bill, what I'm trying to say is that Frank and Silky are…well, they're friends…on the Internet. He waited for those words to sink in before continuing, "Like Patricia and I are."

"Jesus Christ, Phil!"

"It's okay, Frank," Bill said.

"Oh, it is, is it?" said Frank glaring at Bill.

"Frank, it's okay. We're friends, aren't we?" Bill said.

"Yeah, we're friends." Frank wished again that he could just disappear.

"I understand how you feel, Frank," Phillip said. "And if there was anyway to turn back the clock and not have any of this happen, I know you wouldn't hesitate to do it. Things got out of control and you followed your passions with your heart rather than your head. I know how that can happen. No one is blaming you or judging you for that."

"Well, I am," Frank said without looking up.

Phillip continued, "Frank, I understand what happened between you and Silky. It happens to people on the Internet every day. I write about it in my columns. And thousands of these people feel guilty about it because they normally wouldn't let their fantasies run out of control. And yet in chatrooms, they can share their fantasies with others in a way they presume is safe and private."

Frank was clearly looking very embarrassed.

"We're not saints, Frank." Phillip said. "None of us are. It's just that when you think things are completely private...well, you say things you would never allow yourself to say in real life. It's almost as if an alternate reality, a secret life, takes over. And it can become almost addictive."

"Look, we all know what I did was sleazy and wrong. I'm sorry, okay? I don't have any excuses" Frank said defensively.

"You were just being human, Frank," Phillip said.

"Bullshit! I've got no excuse, and I'm not going to pretend that I do. I betrayed Alma and everyone else I know. I'm supposed to be more responsible about things like this than most folks are, right?"

"Maybe, Frank, but that doesn't make you perfect," Phillip replied. "And I'm not judging you either."

"I judge people all the time and if you're telling me you aren't judging me, then you're fucking lying!" Frank snapped.

"Frank, relax," Bill said trying to defuse the situation.

"Relax? You want me to relax, Bill? I got caught being a sleazy, horny bastard and now our mysterious friend here is telling me that it might have something to do with my wife's death!"

Frank turned away from Bill and looked directly at Phillip. "You're pretty sure Silky had something to do with Alma's murder?"

"Yes, I am, Frank. And I know who Silky is. I believe I met him a couple of days ago."

"Him?" Frank asked incredulously.

"Silky is not who you think."

"You said *him*?" Frank repeated.

"Yeah."

"You're trying to tell me that the woman I thought I was playing with is a man?"

"Yes, Frank."

"I can't fuckin' believe this! I suspected something several months ago and I decided I was crazy to even think that," Frank admitted. "Fuck, if this gets out... How the hell do you know this?"

Phillip went on to explain how he had enlisted the help of his friend, a Seattle police detective, to follow up on his suspicions and how that had led to the discovery of Toji, a forty-six-year-old divorced, Japanese-born man who lived in an expensive condo on Lake Washington.

"You didn't know any of this, Frank," Bill said again, trying to be reassuring.

"Shit," Frank said loudly. He stopped to see if anyone else was sitting close enough to hear him. "I shouldn't have done it at all, and I goddamned well should have known better than to let any of this happen." Frank's started to slam his fist down on the table, but stopped at the last moment, not wanting to draw more attention to himself.

"I had doubts about her…or him. God, it makes me sick to even think about it. She was always asking me questions to find out things about me, and sometimes she…or *he*, I mean…seemed to know things that I didn't remember telling him. I began wondering if he was talking to other people about me." Frank stopped talking, seemingly lost in thought.

"What is it, Frank?" Bill asked.

"You were going to meet Silky, weren't you?" asked Phillip.

"How the fuck do you know that?

"Because people in these situations often toy with the idea of actually meeting in person. Some people do meet each other, but a lot of them just talk about it."

"Yeah, well," Frank said, "We talked about it, and I decided I didn't want to do that. I knew that what I had been doing with Silky was bad enough. I tried to rationalize that it wasn't really the same thing as cheating, but it was sure damned close."

"So you weren't interested in meeting Silky?"

"Oh, I was interested, all right! I was very interested, if you want to know the truth. But I realized I couldn't. I knew I had to end it."

"And did you?"

"Yeah. I basically did break things off."

"And then she…*he* started threatening me."

"Threatening you?" asked Bill.

"Yeah. Silky let me know that she/he knew a lot about me. He knew who I was, where I lived, and he wasn't going to let me walk away or forget about him. He even said he knew how he could find me and hurt me."

"So he obviously wasn't going to let you end it?" asked Bill.

"No," Frank said, "Silky didn't want it to be over. But if I'd ever had any doubts, the threats sure cleared those away."

Bill put his hand on Frank's shoulder. "We'll get through this, buddy."

"Yeah, like back in college, right?"

"It's nothing. Really," Bill said quickly.

The three of them sat there in silence for a few moments before Frank spoke. "I suppose Bill's told you that some people think I murdered my wife, right, Phil?"

"Yeah, I'm aware."

"Then do you have any idea how angry I am at this point?" he said through clenched teeth. "I am about to fucking explode! You have any evidence on this fucking bastard you think did it?"

"My friend Mark is trying to verify some things."

"Why the hell are you doing this anyway?" Frank asked.

"Alma was a very good friend of Patricia's," Bill explained.

"I got involved in this because of Patricia," Phillip joined in, "and because I do a lot of writing about the Internet and thought it was an interesting story."

"Speaking of Patricia, I wonder if that bitch Riley is still questioning her," Bill said.

"Call over there, Bill, and find out!" Frank ordered.

Bill pulled out his walkie-talkie, but stopped, realizing that it would probably be better to use his cell phone.

"Brenda Riley and Bud Richards don't like me very much," Frank explained to Phillip while Bill talked to someone quietly on his cell phone. "Goes back many years. They really didn't like it when I got Bill assigned to work with me over Richards' worthless kid brother a couple of years ago. Richards had some plan to have the state take over this area rather than the county, and getting Riley up here was somehow going to help him. Brenda's uncle is a state politician and Richards thinks he's got some weight to throw around, but really doesn't."

"Okay, thanks for the heads up," Bill said, winding up the call.

"So what's the word?" Frank asked.

"Patricia left about ten minutes after we did. Amy thinks she's over at her bookstore."

"Good for her," Frank said. "Patricia ain't no pushover.

"Uh, hold on. I think we've got a problem. Amy said that right after Patricia walked out, Richards showed up and went ballistic. He and Riley both headed out, but not together. Anyway, before Riley left, Amy heard her on the phone saying something about an arrest warrant."

"For Patricia?" Phillip asked excitedly.

"No, not for Patricia. For Frank," Bill said. "Amy told me she heard Riley say something about the fact that they'd found something on your property."

"Oh, shit! Now what?" Frank groaned. "Okay, Phillip, you said you might be able to prove this guy Toji was involved?"

"Yeah. Mark, the police detective in Seattle... He's checking to see if he took any trips recently."

"Has he got a warrant?"

"Huh-uh. He's cheating."

"If he turns anything up, then he'll have to go by the book, and that will take a few days," Frank muttered.

"And Riley and Richards might have their warrant within a couple hours," said Bill.

"You really think they are going to arrest you again?" Phillip asked.

"I wouldn't put it past them." Then he turned to Bill. "What the hell could they have?"

"I don't know," answered his friend. "I'm not sure what Riley's up to, to tell you the truth. When this all started, she'd come into my office and she'd have nothing good to say about you, that's for sure. I finally just told her to keep her opinions to herself. In the past few days though, I've gotten some different vibes. All of a sudden, now, she's actually been saying some rather decent things about you. I thought it was because she must have realized that she'd judged you prematurely. Guess I was wrong, though, huh?"

"Hey, Frank, if you think it would any good for me to talk Richards, just let me know," offered Phillip.

"I really appreciate that, Phil," Frank said, "but at this point, Richards only wants to put my ass under a magnifying glass and burn the hell out of me. He got reprimanded for arresting me in June, and that only made him madder."

"Okay, whatever you say. Just know I'm perfectly willing to do that, if you think it would help," Phillip said.

"We'll see how everything shakes out, Phil. Thanks," Frank replied. "You know, you sure seem to know a lot about quite a few things," Frank said slowly. "I suppose we are just going to have to trust you."

"That would be nice," Phillip said flatly.

"Okay. Say, Phil, I think Bill and I need to talk for a bit. Do you mind?"

"No problem. I'd like to run over to the bookstore anyway and make sure Patricia's okay."

"Good idea," Bill agreed. "Hey, how long are you in town for?"

"Until Wednesday afternoon."

"Then we'll be talking again," Bill assured him.

"We got this," Frank said when he saw Phil pull his wallet out of his pocket.

"Thanks. I appreciate that." And then tossing a few dollar bills on the table, "Let me at least get the tip."

"Go see Patricia, Phil. And call Bill in a little while and let us know what went on between her and Riley, okay?"

"I planned on doing that anyway."

As Phillip got up, Frank grabbed his wrist. "Patricia's good people," he said softly.

"I know."

The two stared at each other for a moment, and then Frank shook Phillip's hand warmly.

"Thanks again for your help. I'm sure I owe you more than I realize."

"Sure thing."

Chapter Thirty-five

After Patricia stormed out of the interrogation room, Brenda Riley sat tapping her pencil on the metal table. She wasn't happy with herself. *Sometimes Brenda, you're just going to have to be a little quicker on the uptake and figure out who your friends are and who they aren't.*

She'd been excited—flattered, really—when Bud Richards had contacted her earlier in June and asked if she'd take a temporary reassignment in Taos. The agency, he said, needed someone to fill the Deputy Sheriff's position that had become vacant when Bill Conner had taken over as acting Sheriff of Taos County, and she qualified. She'd heard about the arrest of Sheriff Frank Garrett for the murder of his wife. *Hell yes, she wanted the job!*

It had been a tremendous ego boost. She was beginning to have some nagging doubts, however. Something told her that Richards zeal to see a fellow cop brought down had a really sour ring to it.

She had met Richards three years earlier, when she was in the Academy. He'd taught a couple of the firearms classes and had spoken at the graduation ceremony. She'd learned that his younger half brother, Lucas, was also in the Academy. Lucas Tafoya was an A-number one goofball who, in her opinion, had no business there. She found him to be a hotheaded, immature slacker. She figured Richards must have been using his clout at the school to see if it might somehow get little brother on a department somewhere and moved out of his house. She never knew how Lucas ever managed to make it through the Academy. She had her suspicions, but no proof.

Brenda heard through the grapevine that after a dozen or so failed attempts to land a job in law enforcement, that Lucas had gone to work for the City Manager in Taos as a legal assistant or something.

The second day on the job, Tafoya was waiting by her car for her when she got off duty. He'd seemed surprisingly genuine in his inquiry about what and how she'd been doing since graduating from the Academy. When she first saw him standing there, she had to do a double take. She hardly recognized him, and the difference was not altogether unpleasant. He'd definitely cleaned up his act, and the move to the job in the City Manager's office seemed to be agreeing with him. He told her that his brother had called him when she was selected for the fill-in position. They chatted for a few minutes before she had to leave. They had agreed to meet for lunch or dinner sometime soon. They never had, although he'd asked her several times.

Patricia Ridgeway had been one of the first people that Brenda had spoken with after arriving in Taos. She'd tried to make it as casual as possible, so they met for a quiet lunch. She might have been a cop, but she understood feelings. Brenda had felt that the Academy had done little to train the officers for adequately dealing with the emotions and heartaches they would encounter. One of Brenda's crusades while working in Santa Fe had been to lobby for more funding for training in the way law enforcement personnel treat the families of victims. She was fully aware, however, that given the situations and potential behind-the-scenes scenarios that officers might not know are being played out, their first obligation was always to the immediate victim and the situation at hand. She knew that officers must conduct themselves and their investigations so as not to say or do anything that might possibly alter the outcome.

Patricia had made Brenda's job easy. She was straightforward and articulate, and her attention to detail filled in a few of the blanks that were left by some of the others Brenda had already interviewed. She was impressed by Patricia's objective observations of everything that had transpired. Even before Brenda had arrived in Taos, Bud Richards had given her his evaluation of the situation and the people involved. For whatever reason, Richards clearly did not like Patricia Ridgeway. He never came right out and said that. For that matter, he'd never directly said he hated Frank Garrett, either. But the implications were there.

Rehashing what had taken place during the past hour she'd been questioning Patricia, Brenda was mentally beating herself up over how she'd handled things. She knew from the start that she was letting Richards have too much influence over how she performed her job. He was always after her to bend the rules if necessary in order to keep digging. For example, when she accidentally stumbled onto the memo on Bill's desk regarding Phillip Craven and then overheard a phone conversation between the two, she immediately called Richards. This was definitely something she knew she was going to regret.

He'd advised her to eavesdrop, bug the vehicles belonging to both Conner and Garrett, and basically pull every dirty cop trick in the book to find out what they were up to. He had her requisition the department's phone records and see what else she could learn. It wasn't hard to find out that this Phillip Craven lived in Cle Elum, Washington, and that he was a freelance forensic photographer for the local law enforcement agencies and the King County coroner's office. He also had made a name for himself writing columns under the pseudonym of Internet Phil. There was some other background information on him, but nothing noteworthy as far as she could see. Richards was baffled by the information Brenda had prepared. Nowhere had this guy's name cropped up during the investigation, and for the life of him he couldn't make any connection.

What Brenda Riley hadn't told Richards is that during the conversation between Conner and Craven, she'd heard Patricia Ridgeway's name come up often enough that a red flag went up in her mind. At the same time she'd requested the department's phone records, she'd also requested the records for the Ridgeway residence and for the Take Another Look Bookstore. For some reason, she was having trouble obtaining the residential records, but the business information was forwarded to her almost immediately.

There it was! A call placed to the Take Another Look Bookstore just a few days prior from the Washington number of Phillip Craven. Her hand was on the phone to call Richards the instant she got this. She stopped herself. She wouldn't be able to explain why she'd requested these records on her own and then kept the information to herself. She had to think this out some more. She knew how he wanted to take the credit for everything.

She'd really wanted to drop the bad cop crap and tell Patricia how she felt about the case, that her tough cop act was as phony as Bud Richards was corrupt. But she couldn't do that. First of all, Richards was likely to come strolling in here any second. Her palms were sweaty. She wanted to be anywhere but sitting right where she was when he showed up.

Maybe Patricia hadn't left the building, and just maybe she would still have time to fill her in on some things. Just as Brenda stepped into the hallway, she spotted Richards walking toward her, followed closely by Amy, the department's receptionist.

"Riley, where's Garrett and Conner?" he snorted. "I thought I told you to delay that meeting until I got here. Shit, Riley! Worst thing that ever happened to this outfit was they day they started allowing split-tails!"

"Fuck you, Richards! I've had Mrs. Ridgeway in here trying to talk to her. I couldn't stop that meeting, and you know it! You want it stopped? Stop it yourself!"

Brenda was glad Amy was there because if she ever had to testify that she saw Richards reach for a gun, even for a split second, she'd need her corroboration.

"Watch your mouth, Riley. I can get you suspended for that!" He turned to see what Brenda was looking at. There was the receptionist, taking everything in. *Fuck! She's just way too efficient for her own good.*

"So you don't know where those three are then?" he asked, trying to regain his composure, "is that what you're saying?"

"I'm not sure, no. They were in the building earlier."

Amy tried to help. "They didn't tell me where they were going. I'm sorry."

"All three of them, or just Garrett and Conner?" Richards barked.

"I'm sorry, I don't know." Amy said, her lower lip trembling.

"Okay then, it looks like I'll start with Mrs. Ridgeway." Richards pushed by Riley and stared into the empty room. "I thought you said you were talking to her?"

"I was. She's gone."

"Goddamn it, Riley, I can *see* she's gone! You're a piece of work, you know that?" Richards stared at her, words forming but never leaving his mouth. Careful to make certain no one but Brenda could hear him, he whispered, "I'm going to pin this murder on Garrett if it's the last thing I ever do. Do you understand me, Riley? And I will do it with or without your cooperation. Is that clear to you, too?"

She ignored both questions.

"And if you haven't got the balls to do this, then I'll get that little shit Lucas to do it. He owes me. I *will* win this, Riley. Just watch me. I *will* win."

She was humiliated. Not by what he'd said, but by the fact that she'd been part of Richard's plan to hang an innocent cop for a crime he didn't commit. *Lucas! Why hadn't she thought of Lucas?*

Her thoughts were suddenly shattered by an earsplitting alarm announcing an "unauthorized exit" from the building. Officers rushed to their assigned positions. Above the commotion and the shouting, a man's voice from the front of the building yelled, "All clear, entrance!" This was followed by another male voice that Brenda could barely hear, "All clear, west exit!"

The tires on Patricia's car squealed on the asphalt as she backed out of the tight parking space and sped toward Lower Ranchitos Road. Brenda spotted her just as she drove out of sight. "All clear, north exit!" she shouted. *Good! Maybe Patricia heard Richards and everything the pompous ass had said.*

Brenda knew at that precise moment that she was taking herself out of the game. She'd make it up to Patricia later; but right now, she had a few things to take care of. She had to make sure that Amy got word to Bill Conner that Richards was out for Frank Garrett's blood. Somewhere along the line, Richards had come to believe that, if at first you don't succeed, lie, cheat, and fight dirty.

Chapter Thirty-six

Patricia couldn't bring herself to roll over in the bed and look at the clock. Phillip had told her he'd need a couple of hours to get ready to leave town. He'd have to leave by 10:00 or so in order to get to the Albuquerque airport in time for his 3:30 P.M. flight. She'd called the rental agency and learned he could turn in his car here in Taos and she'd tried unsuccessfully to talk him into doing that. She desperately wanted to drive him back to Albuquerque, to spend those few additional hours together before he left to go back to Washington. They couldn't be sure when they'd see one another again, and the separation would be much more difficult now.

The alarm was set for 7:00 A.M., but she knew instinctively that it was much earlier than that now. There was a door, which led from her bedroom into the enclosed courtyard. Through the leaded glass window in the door, she could see the earliest rays of sunlight dancing on the flowers. She looked at Phillip who was still sound asleep next to her. She resisted the urge to reach over and touch him. She knew how badly he needed to sleep. This time together had been an incredible melange of events and emotions, but the nerve-wracking hours they'd spent with Brenda, Frank and Bill had drained them both.

At first, she'd wished that the circumstances under which they met could have been different. Then, she realized that had it not been for these circumstances, they might never have met. Who's to say, really? But they both knew that their lives had now changed forever.

Patricia couldn't speak for Phillip, of course, but she'd miss the innocence she'd once had. She hadn't given it up freely. Had she been given a choice, she would never have done so. Some would argue this, of course, such as the proponents of the philosophy that we, ourselves, are wholly and completely in charge of our own destinies, due primarily to the choices that we make for ourselves. Patricia, on the other hand, believed that some choices are already made for us, and nothing in our mental or physical power can do anything to change them or their outcome.

Patricia lay back on the pillow and rested her arm over Phillip's chest, and reflected on the past few days. She wondered whether meeting Phillip in person had been everything she'd hoped. And she wondered, too, about what he felt. Neither of them had ever put into tangible terms what they'd expected. Sure, they'd talked on the phone over the past several months, more times than she could count. But the phone calls were always light and friendly, touching on the past and present, but seldom on the future, except to remind one another that they'd meet one day if it were meant to be. They both knew it was.

Phillip mumbled in his sleep and rolled toward her. She reached over and covered his shoulder with the sheet, leaned over and kissed his forehead, and then quietly slid out of the bed. Patricia stood there a moment to make certain she'd not disturbed him, and then went into the bathroom and silently closed the door. She braced herself against the vanity and thought about the man who lay in her bed. She had an urge to crack the door open and look to make sure that he was really there, that he wasn't some phantom, some figment of her desperate imagination. For almost thirty years she'd shared a home with a man she'd loved and admired. They'd carved a comfortable life for one another. Still, she and Trent had not shared a bedroom in over ten years. Patricia thought of Emily and wondered if Trent offered her the same excuses that he'd given her so long ago.

She quickly showered, put on a little makeup, combed her hair, and reached for her robe, which was hanging on the porcelain hook behind the door. Next to it hung Phillip's bathrobe. She tried, but couldn't resist the need to touch it; to press it close to her face and lose herself in his scent. It reminded her of the smell of a river. It took her a second to become aware of the quiet tap on the door. "You okay, Trisha?"

"Sure. Of course, I'm okay. Did I wake you, sweetie?" She was scrambling for her robe, not realizing that Phillip had opened the door and was watching her in the mirror.

"No. I just woke up. You don't need that, you know." He stepped inside the warm, humid room and took her in his arms. They were both naked, his body felt warm against hers, yet she shivered.

"Mmm, you sure are warm." He nuzzled her neck and his hands caressed her shoulders and back. "You didn't dry off very well. Want me to do that for you?" His voice was barely a whisper, and Patricia reacted instantly to its sensuality.

"No. I want you to keep doing just what you're doing now.

An hour later they found themselves exhausted.

"I've got to go, Trisha."

"I know."

She watched him get out of bed and leave the room. Then she heard the shower running. Her first inclination was to pull the sheet over her head and pretend that this moment hadn't come. But it had. This moment and a dozen other things had to be dealt with intelligently, strongly, and courageously now. Everything that they meant to one another and everything that their future held in store depended upon what lay in the days to come. They each had their own kind of strength and confidence and together; they had the determination to see this through to the end.

She'd been keeping something from him, and she had to tell him before he left. She'd wanted to wait until she could try and fit the pieces together, but time was running out. She had to make a decision. The shower was still running when Patricia picked up the phone and dialed Trent's office. He answered it on the third ring.

"Trent, are you alone?"

"I am. Are you?"

When she didn't answer him right away, he wanted to kick himself. He really didn't want to know if she was alone or not.

"No. As a matter of fact, I'm not. Listen, can you get away today? Phillip is supposed to leave, but I have to somehow convince him to stay. I think I'm right about this, Trent. Are you still willing to help us?" Her voice was as strong as her suspicions. She desperately needed Trent's help.

"I can be available, one way or the other. Don't worry about that. Just let me know. Try and give me a little notice, if you can. If you can't, then I'll figure something out." He was doodling mindlessly on a scrap of paper, and then realized he'd written her name in several different scripts and was drawing circles around them. He picked up the paper and dropped it in the shredder.

"Okay. I've got to go. I'll call you as soon as I can." She paused. "Trent?"

"Yes?"

"Thanks."

"Right."

Phillip stayed in the warm comfort of the shower as long as he could, gathering his thoughts and trying to reassure himself that he was really ready to leave. He was ready to leave as far as Frank, Bill, and Alma's murder were concerned, but never as far as Patricia was concerned. He felt that the worst of this nightmare was behind them. Now they just needed to get the evidence together on Toji and get it presented to the proper authorities. Then, together with Mark, get a warrant issued for Toji's arrest. What would follow should be all that would be necessary to clear Frank's name and to see that justice was finally served in the murder of Alma Garrett.

He figured Bill would be all right. He had Sylvia and her son Carlos. Bill had confided to him that as soon as this was all over, he and Sylvia intended to get married. In fact, he was planning on asking her in the next few days, and had shown him the ring he'd bought for her. He and Patricia would be all right, too. Everything about them was so complicated now that neither of them had even begun to think about the future. He knew that it would all work out somehow. He was just pleased that they'd even gotten this far.

As soon as he stepped out of the shower, he glanced at his watch. He looked in the mirror and shook his head. *I can't do this. I'm not ready to go. Not yet. Just a few more hours. I have to have just a few more hours.* Phillip dried himself and fastened the towel around his waist and stepped out into the hall. He moved quietly into her office and picked up the phone.

When Patricia entered the kitchen, she was startled to see Phillip already there. "Goodness, don't you look handsome, Mr. Craven. Going somewhere special?"

"As a matter of fact, I was planning on it, yes. Would you care to join me for a very late breakfast this morning, my dear Ms. Ridgeway? Some little, out-of-the-way place downtown, perhaps?"

"Don't tease me, you! This is hard enough without you making light of it. You should already be gone, you know that?"

"Nope. I'm okay. I called and changed my flight to one later this evening. I just need to call Mark now and ask him to pick me up at midnight. I'm just not ready to go, Trisha."

They stood there in the middle of the kitchen, holding one another for a long time. "Trisha," whispered Phillip, "we both know what needs to be done and we both know that we have to use our heads so that this nightmare can be over and we can be together. This asshole has played all of his cards now. He's smart, but he's far from brilliant. He'd trip himself up if he tried anything else now, and he knows it. I think he wants us to stop him."

"No, Phillip, he doesn't want *us* to stop him. There is an ancient code of honor among these people. He will stop himself when the time is right."

"Maybe you're right. Anyway, let's go eat, want to?" He seemed more relaxed than she'd seen him since he arrived in town. He looked almost carefree. Just looking at him made her heart swell.

"Yep. I wanna!"

Phillip pulled into Patricia's parking place behind the plaza and turned off the engine. "The Cider Barrel, huh? Sounds like this could get dangerous."

"It's good! And they have the most scrumptious thing, too! Stuffed French toast! Have you ever had it?"

"No, can't say as I have. But if you say it's good, I might consider trying it. Do I get a full refund if I'm not satisfied?"

"Have I ever told you that you're impossible?"

"Yes, I believe you have."

"Well, mister, I'm telling you again!" she laughed.

They crossed the tree-lined street and entered The Cider Barrel. Like Patricia's bookstore and several other businesses in and around the plaza, The Cider Barrel had been someone's hacienda at one time. The entry was narrow and dark and broke off into several small rooms. The hostess led them to a table in the courtyard.

"Trisha, your world is wonderful. I'm glad I came. I'd have never envisioned it like this."

"It's hard to explain, isn't it? But now, don't forget, I want to go to your world, too, baby. I can't wait to sit on your deck, all wrapped up in a wool blanket and sip hot coffee with you while we watch the hawks fly up and down the river. And I promise to be really, really quiet and wait for your Dolly Doe to come out."

"Dolly Doe? Where did you ever come up with Dolly Doe?"

"Dolly Doe. Sure! Why, what did you name her?"

"Nothing. I never thought about it, I guess."

"Men!" she declared, her tone teasingly exasperated.

Phillip looked around the small courtyard at the others eating there under the vine-covered lattices. Only a few tables were empty. There were what he presumed to be local businessmen seated at the tables closest to them. A bit farther away, a woman, dressed rather eclectically, was writing in a journal. He watched as the waiter moved about silently. Phillip noticed that when the waiter spoke to the patrons, it was almost in a whisper. *That was it! It was quiet here. Not just any quiet, but a reverent quiet of some kind.* He understood all that this place evoked in Patricia and now in him. He could better understand now her heartbreak and her anger at having someone enter her sheltered world and stealing that sanctity. This misplaced town lost in time had been stripped of a certain respect. Phillip reached across the table and touched her face.

"I love you so much, Patricia."

"I know."

When he was finished eating, he put his napkin on the table and leaned back with a groan. He admitted that the French toast was the best he'd ever eaten.

"Told ya! One of these days you'll listen to me, Mr. Big Shot Know-it-all."

"Do I really seem that way to you? Really? Because I don't mean to."

"No, silly. I didn't mean that the way it must have sounded. I'm sorry. I just meant that…well, you just always seem so much surer of yourself than I do. Sometimes it makes me think that I'm not as smart as you are or as…oh, I don't know…as astute as you. I'm not sure what I'm trying to say. But I meant it as a compliment anyway, okay?"

"I'll accept that," he said with a smile.

"There's something I have to say, Phillip. I'm afraid to say it."

"For heavens sakes, Trisha, what?"

"It's just that you have so much proof, Phillip, and can come up with answers and evidence, and I have nothing concrete to base my assumptions on. So, I know it would be better to just keep my mouth shut and let you handle things. I'm liable to really muck up things when we are so close on this."

"I'm not quite following you, Trisha. What feelings? What evidence and answers? If you're talking about Frank and Alma and Silky, I thought we arrived at all of these conclusions together. What feelings can you possibly be talking about?"

They interrupted their conversation while they waited for the waiter to finish clearing away their dishes. He placed a fresh carafe of coffee next to Phillip and left.

"I can't put my finger on anything specific, Phillip, but…"

She'd paused too long and Phillip was uncomfortable with the frown on her face.

"But what?"

"I just don't think its Toji. I can't make myself believe, by what you've told me about him, that he's capable of duping Frank like he did. And I don't think he is capable of being Silky and convincing Frank to fall in love with him. And further, I can't believe that he could be capable of writing those things that were in those e-mails I got. I just can't see him as Bishamon, Phillip. And most of all, I can't imagine him coming here and knowing how to find Alma, luring her into that campground, murdering her, and then calmly going back to Seattle and resuming a normal life. It just doesn't figure right for me, Phillip. I can't tell you exactly why, though. It's a feeling mostly, and a couple of other things that you don't know about."

"What things, for crying out loud? Why are you waiting until the last minute to spring all this on me, Trisha? I thought you agreed with everything we'd talked about. Granted, there are more holes in this whole thing than there are stars in the heavens, but I think that we just all assumed that once we got Toji into custody, he'd fill in those holes for us. I guess I'm a little confused." He hadn't meant to be so confrontational. He could see that Patricia's face had become flushed.

"Excuse me for just a minute, okay? I'll be right back." Patricia pushed her chair away from the table, stood up, and walked back into the restaurant. All of the other late morning diners had gone by now and he found himself alone in the courtyard. He got up from the table and walked slowly across the flagstone patio. In the corner was a large concrete fountain he'd not noticed earlier—a statue of a patron saint, no doubt St. Francis, held his hands out before him and a small, chipped concrete bird rested on them. Water trickled down the rocks behind the statue and splattered into an algae-lined basin. He ran his fingers through the water. It was colder than he expected. *What was she talking about? Of course, it was Toji. It made perfect sense. I've been to Toji's home, for chrissakes! I've seen everything, including all the weapons the guy had.*

"I'm sorry." Patricia had sneaked up behind him. He could tell she'd been crying.

Phillip jerked and spun around toward her. "Trisha, you scared me, baby!" He pulled her in his arms and could feel her heart racing. "I'm sorry I said that. You just startled me, that's all. You okay?" He leaned back and looked at her.

"No, I'm not okay, Phillip. None of us is okay. It's not Toji, Phil. I don't know who it is for sure, but I know it's not him."

"What the hell do we do now, Trisha?" He was convinced of her sincerity, but he already had all his ducks in a row. "Look, can we go over to the bookstore? Let me call Mark." The lunch crowd was beginning to filter in. Patricia took his elbow and led him back toward their table.

"Okay, let's go over to the store. But we need to talk before you make any calls." She looked at her watch. "What time is your flight tonight?"

"Nine thirty-five."

"We've got some time. C'mon."

Phillip tossed two twenties on the table and they smiled at the waiter and left the sunlit patio and walked back through the dark interior of the restaurant and out onto the street.

"On second thought, let's just go back to the house, Phil. It'll be easier to talk there."

"That's okay by me." He stopped when he realized she was no longer walking beside him. He turned and around and saw her standing there. "What? What is it?"

"I'm not sure, Phillip. I know this is going to sound funny, but trust me, okay? I'm going to go over to the store and touch base with Butch and Chad and tell them that you've gone back to Albuquerque to catch your plane. Then I'll tell Butch that I'm going home to work on the books. He won't question that at all. You can drop me at the end of my street and I'll walk on home and go in the front door without Sylvia seeing me. Then, you need to turn around and go back downtown and park your car behind the library. I'll come and get you in the truck. We need for everyone to think that you've left town. Do this for me, even if you don't understand, okay?"

"Patricia I've done a great many things in the last year without questioning why. I've got a feeling that this is not the time to start."

When they got back to Patricia's neighborhood, she could see that Sylvia's car was not in her carport. When he stopped at the bottom of the hill, Patricia got out. "You remember how to get to the library, don't you?" Phillip nodded. "Give me about fifteen minutes," she continued. "I'm going to make some calls. I want to let Bill know that you've left. Then I'm going to call Butch and tell him that I'm going to have the phone off the hook for a few hours. I'll call Sylvia, too, and leave her a message that I've gone for a drive. Then I'm going to call Trent and ask him to meet us somewhere."

"Trent?"

"It's okay. He'll help us. Honest."

Phillip was totally confused, but willing to hear her out. He wasn't sure he was ready for any of this. He considered trying to stop her.

"It's over between us, Phillip, and it was over long before either you or Emily came into our lives. He doesn't blame you any more than I blame her. But we have to put all of this aside right now. Just keep trusting me, baby. You have to."

"I'll be at the library," he said reluctantly. "But don't be too long, okay?" She saw the look of concern and winked at him before she closed the car door.

The house was quiet. It was the first time she'd come home alone in several days, and she felt oddly abandoned. Trent was gone. But he'd been gone for years. Kitty was gone, too, and that would take some getting used to. Phillip wasn't there, but everywhere around her she sensed his presence. In a lingering smell wafting down the hall, in the coffee cup still sitting on the table, to his jacket that was hanging just inside the kitchen door. When Trent walked out there was everything, yet nothing, to leave behind. When Phillip left, everything about him stayed behind. She walked back to her office and dialed the phone.

"Trent? Can you break away? Is this a good time?"

"This is a good time. Emily went up on the mesa to take some pictures of some chaparral lots. We could use any of a hundred photos we have and who'd know the difference, know what I mean? Anyway, where do you want to meet?"

"I've been thinking, but I don't know where. We have to be careful."

"Yeah, I know. Let's see, if it's okay, let me come by the house and pick you up. That will eliminate a parade of vehicles. Where is Phillip? With you?" He said this without reservation and Patricia admired him for that.

"No. He's waiting for us behind the library. I just told him to park back there because, with all the cars, no one will notice."

Seemingly out of nowhere, Trent blurted out, "I miss you, Patricia."

When she chose not to respond, he said, "Okay, let's pick him up and drive out toward the school. Then, if we decide I need to, I can go on up and talk to the administrator. There are some places where we can park and no one would ever see us."

"That sounds good to me. And Trent? Thanks. Before things get awkward, I just wanted to tell you that. This couldn't have been easy for you. And I know you've got a lot at stake here." She was sincere and Trent knew that. Another one of the things he'd forgotten to admire about her.

When Trent pulled around to the back of the house, Patricia was waiting. She stepped quickly into his Bronco.

"Hi."

"Hi, yourself. You look good, Patricia. Are you all right?" She wasn't and he knew it, but she nodded as she fastened her seat belt.

"We still going to the library?"

"Yes. He's waiting there. Trent, he doesn't have any idea why we are doing this. I hope you can help me explain this so he'll understand. I don't think you know what this means to me."

"Why do you think I wouldn't know? Where the hell do you think I've been the last twenty some odd years? Goddamn it, Patricia, Frank and Alma were friends of mine, too, you know. This isn't any easier for me than it is you. Hell, Garrett and I don't always see eye-to-eye, but the last thing in this world I ever wanted was for something like this to happen to him." His controlled rage was a comfort to her, odd as that might sound.

"I'm sorry I made it sound like that, Trent. You're right, I was being insensitive. How have you been?"

"Okay, I guess." He turned into the off-street parking lot behind the county library and approached the white sedan. Phillip got out of the car as soon as he saw them.

Patricia was looking at Trent. He chose to answer her unasked question.

"I saw his car at the house when I came by a couple of days ago. I didn't stop. That's what you were wondering, isn't it?" Patricia didn't answer. Instead, she got out of the car and took a seat in the back. She motioned for Phillip to get in the front seat. Trent extended his hand and Phillip shook it.

"Good to see you again, Phillip."

"Good to see you again, too, Trent. Although I have to admit that...well, this is a little awkward. I'm sure one of you is going to explain all of this to me, right?" Phillip saw Trent look into the rearview mirror.

"Right."

After that brief exchange, they drove in silence through town, turning east at a small, hand-carved wood sign that read: *Taos Art Institute*. A short while later, Trent eased the Bronco off to the side of the road and drove several hundred yards through the tall grass. He stopped behind what appeared to Phillip to be an old abandoned gas station. Part of the roof had caved in on the windowless structure, and only concrete rubble remained where the gas pumps had once stood.

"Nice office, Trent. Business must be going well," Phillip said with a laugh.

"As a matter of fact, it's really booming right now! You looking to invest?"

"You both think you're being real cute, don't you?" Patricia smiled in spite of herself.

Phillip quickly turned serious. "I'm starting to feel like everyone knows what's going on here but me. C'mon, somebody help me out here."

"That's the problem," Patricia answered, "nobody knows for certain what's going on."

"Until a couple of nights ago, I'll admit I was pretty clueless," Trent said. "You'd probably like to hit me for that answer, and I wouldn't blame you. I know I should have been more attentive these past few months. You're obviously aware of the situation between Patricia and me, and so I'm not going to offer any excuses. Anyway, Patricia told you that she called me after we ran into each other at Dylan's the other day, right?"

Phillip turned and looked directly at Patricia. "No, as a matter of fact, she didn't."

"Then you really are in the dark. Sorry about that. Anyway, after talking with Emily and Caesar, I sat back and started looking at this whole thing a little differently, and probably a lot more realistically than I had. Patricia and I have only touched on some of it. Maybe she should start. Patricia?"

The two men sat quietly while Patricia unwound the newest threads as carefully as possible. Everything she said took Phillip by complete surprise, although perhaps it shouldn't have. He listened, but he was not ready to accept everything she told him. He had to admit, however, that what she said was making perfect sense. Even so, there were still too many unanswered questions. Perhaps, he thought, they may never know the entire truth.

Patricia continued, "So until Sunday, when I realized that Caesar was Emily's son and a friend to Carlos, Sylvia's son, I couldn't be sure about

Caesar Abeyta. Once I was certain that he was the same boy who had been schmoozing with Alma in the shop, I had to talk to Trent about him, on the off chance that Carlos might have met other friends of Caesar's.

"You know that photo you scanned for me? The one you took from Toji's, the one of him and his son? I took a chance by showing it to Carlos, and he recognized him immediately from another picture that Caesar had of the two of them together at some Oriental swordsmanship thing they participate in. And guess where? In Seattle." Phillip was being attentive, but the expression on his face showed that he was getting lost.

"Oh, I'm sorry, Phillip. Emily's ex-husband, who is Caesar's father, is half-Japanese and lives in Seattle. And you'll love this! He works for the same company Toji does. They know each other from work, and that's how Caesar became friends with Toji's son, Jordan. Apparently, Caesar volunteers with Jordan at the Japanese Gardens there in Seattle, as well. They handle the silkworm exhibit, Phillip."

She waited for some sort of a reaction from him; but he remained quiet, waiting for her to continue. "Anyway, it seems that Jordan went a little nuts after Caesar told him that he was going to leave and move to Taos to attend the Art Institute. He had several choices, I guess, but when Emily told him that she was moving here he thought it would be a good opportunity to get reacquainted. Apparently this really angered Jordan. He hadn't recovered from his mother leaving him, and he certainly had not accepted her death."

"Her death?" Phillip looked at Patricia in astonishment. "When did she die and how? Do you know?"

"Well, no. I don't exactly. Trent, maybe you should take over from here."

"I'll tell you what I can," said Trent. "But to be perfectly honest, I've only known some of this stuff less than twenty-four hours myself. You're both free to believe whatever you want. But I gotta tell you, this whole thing is just way too weird for me. Anyway, after Patricia called me with her story, there was nothing left for me to do but tell Emily as little as possible and then ask her if we could talk to Caesar. Hell, I hardly know the kid. He boards out here at the school and is a strange acting sonofabitch, if you ask me. I've avoided him as much as possible. He was griping one night at the house about wanting to go back to Seattle, and I almost butted in and asked him if I could help him pack. I didn't, because at the time, I really thought I was in love with Emily and I didn't want to cause any more problems than we already had.

"Well, there really isn't much to tell. Emily got furious when I told her that Patricia had asked me to talk to Caesar. I thought she was pissed because I'd talked to Patricia. It didn't take me long to figure out that she didn't like the idea of me questioning Caesar—which I went ahead and did—and I can assure you that Caesar definitely didn't like it. I'll admit that I probably didn't handle it very diplomatically. That kid always acts like a worm on a hot rock anyway, but he really got defensive when I started asking him some of the questions Patricia told me to ask. But when I handed him that picture she had of that kid and his dad, well, he damned near exploded! He started yelling and telling Emily that I was some kind of a weirdo. Then he took off. I didn't really get anywhere with him. And damned if Emily didn't get on my case and ask me what I was asking all the questions about? Hell, I hardly asked him anything. I swear Emily knew more about what I was going to ask him than I did. Suddenly she started asking *me* questions. I could tell she was going to cover his butt."

Trent paused and asked if either of them had any questions. They didn't, and so he continued. "I figured that I'd pretty much pushed Caesar as much as I was going to and I doubted that he was going to come back to the house, not as long as I as there anyway. So I asked Emily if she knew why he took off like that. At first she blamed me for coming on too strong, but then backed off. What seemed to have upset him the most was when I asked him if he'd been seeing Alma Garrett before she was killed. If he hadn't have reacted like he had, I wouldn't have given it a second thought. But after thinking about it... Well, Trisha, remember when I told you I saw Alma's Mustang up near Arroyo Hondo that day and later when I drove back by I saw her coming across the meadow with some kid? Well, now I know it was Caesar. I hadn't met him at that point and when I did, of course, I didn't have any reason to make a connection. Then I pushed my luck a little too far, as far as Emily was concerned anyway, when I asked her why Caesar backed out of our Memorial Day picnic plans. Uh, okay... we'd planned a picnic that day, Patricia, because I knew you'd be busy at the shop. Anyhow, that's where I was when Bill got hold of me that day. I'm sorry." Trent was obviously quite nervous about having made that admission. He was relieved when she chose not to comment on it.

"Are you saying that Caesar didn't show up for the picnic," asked Phillip. "Did Emily have an explanation?"

"Oh, he showed. It wasn't that. He pulled up late at the house, just as Emily and I were leaving. Emily went over to his car and was talking to him for so long I was about to go see what the problem was. Finally, Emily came back to the truck and said he'd meet us up at the gorge. I wouldn't have thought much about it, since the kid is such a weird duck anyway, but Emily was acting funny and kept rubbing at this spot on her jeans with a Kleenex."

"What kind of spot?" Phillip asked.

"Well, that's what I finally asked her, and she was short and snappy and just said she got something on them from the kid's car. We were going out toward the Gorge for the picnic—that's about a fifty-minute drive west of here—and Emily hardly said a word the whole way. I told Patricia earlier that Emily and I were not getting along very well at this point, and I was figuring that she was thinking about our situation and honestly expected her to break up with me. So, even her attitude that day didn't seem all that out of the ordinary."

Phillip looked over his shoulder at Patricia in the back seat, staring out the window. "Trent, maybe we should get out of the truck and stretch our legs, okay with you?" Both Trent and Patricia agreed that was a good idea.

The three of them walked around to an old well over by a grove of cottonwoods. Trent and Phillip sat down on a large boulder, while Patricia took a seat on some old concrete steps that seemed to have sprouted up there for no good reason at all..

"So," Phillip said, picking up where they'd left of, "Emily's actions didn't seem out of the ordinary for the circumstances, and her kid was just acting like he always acted, right?"

"Yeah, I guess. I had a lot on my mind, too, and really wasn't paying too much attention. When we got out to the Gorge, there were a ton of people there, so we just sat in the truck for a while waiting to see if anyone left so we could have a table. We waited maybe ten or fifteen minutes before some folks did leave, and I asked her if she wanted me to go put our stuff over there. It was the first time I'd said anything since we'd driven up. I was starting to sense something was really wrong, but I just assumed it had to do with us and our relationship." Trent looked over at Patricia who was watching Phillip draw in the dirt with a stick.

Without looking up, she said, "Trent, maybe you should get to Caesar."

"Yeah. Well, anyway, we got our lunch out and fixed some sandwiches and by then, when Caesar hadn't showed up yet, I suggested we take a walk over to the edge of the Gorge. We were over there for, oh, I don't know, probably twenty or thirty minutes or so. We ran into the Hoppers, a couple we'd just sold some property to, and we talked for a while. Emily kept looking around and looking at her watch, so I finally told the Hoppers that we were getting hungry and we headed back to the table. Just as we got there, Caesar came roaring up like a bat outta hell, stirring up a whole cloud of dust. I just felt like strangling the little bastard. Emily sort of broke away from me and rushed over to his car, almost like she wanted to talk to him before he got out. I went on over to the table and started getting the plates out. Hell, it was about four o'clock by now, and I hadn't eaten since breakfast." Patricia laughed when he said that, and Phillip looked up just in time to see some private line of communication pass between them.

This story was dragging out, and Phillip didn't have any marks on the right-hand side of his diagram. He'd drawn a large cross in the dirt and over the left bar, he'd scratched the word "Toji" and a question mark over the right. As Trent talked, Phillip had been mentally racking up points and marking them in the dirt. So far he had thirteen for "Toji" and only two for the question mark. It wasn't looking good for Patricia's theory.

"Well," Trent continued, "I was just as surprised as Patricia seemed to be the other day at Dylan's when Carlos seemed to know Emily and Bill, and Sylvia obviously knew Caesar. After we got settled in at our table, I asked Caesar how they all knew one another. But before he could answer, Emily interrupted and started answering for him. The kid's a weasel and never looked up at either one of us. He just let his mother do all the talking. She went into some long story about how the two boys had met at Bill's martial arts class and had become friends. Hell, Carlos grew up under our noses and I was immediately put off by how Emily was describing their friendship. Caesar was a lot older than Carlos, not to mention the fact that the kid was a jerk. The first thing I thought was that I was going to tell Sylvia that I didn't think it was a great idea that the two hung out together. Well, then Emily just went on about how nice it was that Caesar had a friend in town because he was lonely since he'd gotten there and how he missed an old friend back in Seattle. I could tell that Caesar was edgy and finally, he basically told her to shut up. I wanted to smack him. He's got a smart mouth and it was obvious he hated me from the beginning."

Phillip drew two check marks in the dirt under the question mark.

"So, Carlos and this Caesar were karate buddies and hung out together?" asked Phillip. "Was Sylvia usually home when the two of them were over at her house?" He saw Trent look to Patricia for an answer.

"Sylvia is at the deli a great deal of the time, except at night," explained Patricia. "Sometimes in the mornings or on her day off, I'll go over for coffee; but Carlos is in school then, so no one else is there. I've never seen Caesar anywhere around. That's why it took me a minute to recognize him as the kid from the art school who'd been pestering Alma."

"I see. So what are you saying, Trent?" Phillip asked. "There's some connection between Carlos and Caesar that somehow ties into…what? I'm lost here."

"You and me, both, pal. That's basically all I really know. Oh, except for one more thing. Late that evening, after Caesar fouled up our outing, I got the call from Bill on my cell to get to the station and get Patricia. I suppose you know all about that, so we don't need to go over it again. So, anyway, after I felt like she was settled, I left the house for a while later that night…" He was noticeably uncomfortable proceeding but Patricia encouraged him to continue. "I told Patricia that I needed to run to the office for a minute, but actually I drove over to Emily's. Hell, it must have been ten or later, and Caesar was out washing and detailing his damned car! I didn't think anything about it much until I went in the back door. The door goes into Emily's utility room. She's got a big ol' soaker sink in there and the thing was full of wet clothes she was washing by hand when I walked in. The water was dirty, the color of red mud, and I remember saying something to her about something really fading and she just said 'yeah' or something and asked me what I was doing there."

"This was still Memorial Day, right? That night?" Phillip asked. When Trent said it was, Phillip drew another check beneath the question mark.

"Anyway," Trent continued, "I told her that I didn't have much time and hurriedly filled her in on Alma and what had happened."

"How did she react?" Phillip held his stick poised over his chart in the dirt.

"She didn't react at all. And I mentioned that to her. She just said she'd heard about it on her car radio earlier. That's when I told her that I was surprised at that because I didn't think she was going any place else after I dropped her off. That's when she told me that she hadn't left the house." Trent saw Phillip look up at him with a puzzled look on his face. "I know it sounds crazy, but she doesn't have a radio in her house. I knew there was only one way she could have heard about it and it had to have been on the car radio." The three of them exchanged glances.

Trent looked at what Phillip had drawn in the dirt. "You have a theory, don't you, Phillip?"

"I wish I did. I thought I did, but I don't now. Two hours ago, I had a pretty good theory. Now, thanks to the two of you, we have more suspects than I can shake this stick at." With that, he pushed himself up from the rock and tossed the stick on the ground. "*That* stick as a matter of fact."

Patricia sensed the tension building up in Phillip, but decided to go ahead anyway. "So, Trent, when I called you today, you suggested coming out here in case you thought you needed to go up to the Art Institute and talk to the director. What was that all about? Caesar?"

"Yes, I think so. Even though I haven't followed every step of this the way I should have, I have grasped enough to know that something isn't right with that kid. I hate to bring it up, Patricia, but remember when we took that business trip to Durango in June?"

She didn't want to be reminded, but she obviously had no choice. "Yes, I have a vague memory of that." She regretted the sarcasm and was glad that Trent let it pass.

"Well, Phillip, you need to hear this, too. Emily was also in Durango."

Trent shifted his position, propping himself against the remnants of the old well. "That was not intentional on my part, Patricia. I never got an opportunity to tell you that. Actually, the whole thing was a bit of a mess, if you want to know the truth. When Emily got the seminar information in the mail, she sent in the form and put her name and mine on it without asking me. I didn't know she'd done that, Patricia. I honestly didn't."

Trent knew that defending himself at this point was probably futile, but he obviously wanted to if for nothing else than his own self-respect. And for what it was worth, he wanted Phillip to know that he wasn't the asshole that he might have thought him to be.

"Anyway, after all that had happened, I thought the Durango trip would be a perfect chance to get Patricia away for a few days. We needed time by ourselves, I felt, to see if we could work out our obvious differences. Well, when she agreed, I mentioned to Emily in the office the next day that I was pleased Patricia was going with me to Durango. Well, that's when the shit hit the fan, let me tell you. Emily was furious! Man, the first thought I had was to just leave the office for a while and give her time to cool down. It was only then that I realized she'd planned on the two of us spending those three days together; whereas, I'd fully expected her to stay in town and keep the business open.

"I didn't start piecing some of this together until just recently, Patricia, so bear with me while I try to put things in the right order. I've actually never thought this all through completely. Let's see… There had never been any problems between Emily and me at all until that Memorial Day. At the time, that seemed insignificant enough. The part that stood out in my mind the most, of course, was how obnoxious that damned kid of hers was. I'm just not used to these arty kinds of guys, I guess. Emily had never even hinted to me that the sonofabitch was gay, so I probably didn't conduct myself in a very 'politically correct' manner, as they say. So, I just figured that was why she was so short with me when I went over later that night." He paused again and looked at his watch. "I'm taking too long here. What time do you need to get going, Phillip?"

"No time. Don't worry about it. Just go on."

Satisfied, Trent continued, "Okay, that was Memorial Day. Then we got through the funeral, which was a fiasco in itself. Emily clearly didn't want to attend, and I insisted on it. I told her it was not only out of respect for Alma and her family, but also out of respect for Patricia and me, too. I warned her that it would not look good if we weren't there. She relented, but made me promise that we would leave as soon as the mass was over."

Phillip stopped him at this point. "Was Caesar at the funeral? I mean, hadn't he been coming on to Alma right before her murder?"

"No, he wasn't at the funeral. And, yes, you're right about the timing, although I never mentioned that to Trent."

"Patricia, I didn't stop you when you said that earlier," Trent said. "But where you're going is ridiculous."

"What do you mean?"

"Caesar is queer! You know, gay?"

Phillip picked up his stick and scratched off one of the check marks from beneath Toji's name.

"When Patricia and I left town, absolutely the last thing I expected was for Emily to show up in Durango. Man, was I a fool! Patricia, you have no idea how I felt when she walked into the saloon that evening. I had wanted it to be a special time for us. I had planned to tell Emily as soon as I got back to Taos that our relationship just wasn't working out. Not our relationship, nor our partnership. I was fully prepared to give her back the money she'd invested, and rid myself of her. That's the truth, even if you don't believe me. And even if it doesn't really matter any more."

Patricia appeared to be bothered by the way Trent's explanation was unfolding. "Trent, just go on. We can talk about some of this other stuff later, if we have to. Right now though, we might have a loose grenade out there somewhere and we have no idea when or who is going to pull that pin. But I do believe what you are telling me, if that helps."

"Okay. Well, Emily became Princess Charming over those three days, confiding in me about some of her struggles and heartbreaks with Caesar and apologizing for her recent behavior. I think she sensed that I was going to break off our relationship, so she was trying every trick in the book in order to keep that from happening. Then she tried to convince me that she was out of money, money that was supposedly set aside by her husband for Caesar's education. She whined about how she needed me and needed her job. I guess this was supposed to convince me how much she loved me and how dedicated she was to the business. She promised that she wouldn't throw any more of those wild tantrums if I'd just try to understand Caesar and try to be more of a father to him. She told me that needing a father was Caesar's only problem." Trent was pacing nervously now.

"Can you imagine? Like what? I'm supposed to turn around a nineteen-year-old kid? I'm supposed to cure him like he's got a disease or something? I don't know what the hell she thought I could do, I really don't. It was crazy. I was crazy to have listened to it. I realize now that I was crazy to get involved with any of it. But I also knew that I couldn't do anything about it at the moment. So I had to play along with it while she was at the seminar. I sure as hell didn't want some wild scene going on while Patricia was there."

"I can imagine!" Phillip said. "You know, if this weren't so damned tragic, Trent, you have to admit it'd almost be funny!"

Trent managed a chuckle before continuing. "So basically I've been in a sort of limbo in this situation ever since. I'll spare you the unnecessary details, but Caesar has pulled a couple other pranks that have pissed me off. Like stealing my credit card number and using it to order some stuff off the Internet. I haven't even told Patricia about that yet. Actually I think it started happening last spring, but I didn't realize it. I just wasn't keeping up with things very well there for a while."

"What kind of things was he ordering?" Patricia wanted to know.

"Oh shit, for that karate class or whatever it is he takes. I guess he's advanced into another phase where he does that meditation stuff and ballet type exercises with long fancy sticks and swords and things. It's got a name but I don't know what it is."

Phillip was staring intently at Trent, not sure exactly what he was hearing. "So Caesar ordered some of these sticks and what, swords? Are you saying he ordered *weapons*, Trent?"

"Yeah, that's what I'm saying. He ordered a few things like special clothes and a couple of those stick things and some damned expensive sword or knife of some kind. I called American Express and they gave me the merchant and all the information, so I called and found out it was Caesar and that he'd had it shipped out here to the school."

Phillip drew another check mark.

"Trent, you know there are a lot of things you need to talk to that director about besides just the delivery of merchandise out here, right?" Phillip was watching Patricia who had gotten up from the steps and was brushing off the back of her skirt.

"Damn right. I've got several questions for him. Do you want to go up there and talk to him with me? I'm sure there are some questions you'd like to ask, too."

Patricia moved quickly to put herself between the two men. "No, Trent. He can't go with you. We jumped through a lot of hoops to make sure everyone thought he'd left town. Besides, the school director isn't likely to tell you very much. You're not Caesar's legal guardian or father. If he's going to tell you anything, it's because you used your sales ability to convince him he should, and having a stranger with you isn't going to help."

"She's right, Trent."

"Okay, okay. You're both right," conceded Trent.

Chapter Thirty-seven

Phillip walked Trent partway to his truck. After talking briefly to Trent, he made his way back through the tall, brittle grass, his hands pushed deep in his pockets. They'd agreed that the smartest thing for them to do was to get as much information as they could, and get back to town to meet with Bill as soon as possible. Patricia was standing over the marks he'd made in the dirt. She didn't bother to look up as he approached.

"Bishamon, Caesar, and Jordan. I might be wrong, Patricia, but I think that Emily is also involved."

"Emily? You've got to be kidding!"

"Yes. Emily. I think it's entirely possible that perhaps we have a regular Ma Barker on our hands; one with two very impressionable young men to do her command. Do you know if Emily got along with Alma?"

"Phillip, stop! I don't know what to think here. Give me a second, okay?"

"Sure, baby. Hey, I'm not sure about any of this either. Besides, this whole thing was your idea, you know!" He realized that he sounded almost too accusatory. He put his arm around her and drew her to his side.

"As far as I know, Emily didn't even know Alma," Patricia said. "And if Alma knew that Emily was Caesar's mother, she never told me.

"Perhaps, Emily didn't like what she thought might be going on with Alma and her son." Phillip sounded as though he was trying to convince himself.

"Gosh, well, that's entirely possible, I guess. I wonder if Trent would know the answer to that? I think he would have said something if that were the case, Phillip."

"Right now, I don't give a damn."

Patricia's mind had been wandering a bit, and when his somewhat flippant words finally sunk in, she exclaimed, "Well, I'm so sorry about that, Phillip. But I *do* give a damn! You think I'm crazy, don't you?"

"Honey, I *know* you're crazy. I know *I'm* crazy. But what's that got to do with the price of beans in…"

"Damn you, Phillip! I thought you were serious." Still, she felt like he wasn't convinced of her suspicions and was somehow making fun of her.

"Babe, I don't know what to believe, much less what to think, right now. What you and Trent are saying makes some sense actually."

Patricia withdrew from Phillip's embrace. "But if what you're saying is right, Phillip, then Trent could be in a lot of danger, couldn't he?"

"I honestly don't know, Trisha. It's possible. If I'm half right, then he's gonna be right in the middle of things." He knew he should stop himself at that point, but he couldn't. "So how much does that bother you, Trisha?"

"That's not fair, Phillip. And you know it." She stared directly at him.

"Hey, life's not fair. Until now." He let her wonder just how the hell she should interpret what he'd just said. He stepped closer to her. She looked at him for a long moment. He grabbed her around the waist and pulled her to him and kissed her passionately. She didn't resist.

After a few seconds, she removed his hands from her waist and pulled away. "Let's walk, Phillip."

"An excellent idea."

"Things simply aren't very fair, are they?" she asked.

"No, they aren't. They never are and never will be, especially if you expect them to be." He decided to say the remainder of what was on his mind. "Maybe we make our own fairness, Patricia. My idea of fairness right now is spending as much time with you as possible."

"That's what you meant when you said, 'life's not fair until now,' isn't it?"

"Yes," he whispered. "And we'll get through all this other stuff, too, baby. I'm not sure how, but I know in my own heart that we will get through it. I have no idea about Trent, or any of the other people, but I am sure about us. Now, Trisha, it's your turn to trust me, okay?"

"I've always trusted you, Phillip. Always. And I know that you're right. We *will* get through this somehow."

They stopped walking, and she invited him to join her on the ground. "You're a very observant man, Mr. Craven. But have you noticed recently that I love you?"

"Yeah, but I wasn't sure."

"What do you mean you weren't sure?"

"I mean, you're always playing so hard to get…"

"Oh, sheesh!" She pushed him to the ground and rolled over on top of him, pinning his shoulders in the soft dirt.

"See? This is exactly what I mean! Does this mean you like me, or you just want to wrestle?"

"It means neither." She paused, their lips barely inches apart. "It means…well, it just means I love you, I guess." She started to move away.

"And I love you, too, Patricia." He held her tightly and touched his lips to hers, letting her decide if she wanted this to be a passionate kiss or not.

Patricia returned his kiss lightly, then pulled away and laid her head on his shoulder. "Oh, Phillip. What's happening? I don't know what's happening to us. It's the unexpected things that keep surprising me, that's all."

"It's my guess," he said, "that you were just expecting things to not possibly work out the way you dreamed they might. So the fact they are working out, at least as far as you and I are concerned...well, it's something you're not used to. Am I right?"

"It's definitely something I'm not used to, Phillip. When I first knew I was falling in love with you, my life was a nice little neat package. Not too much seemed out of order. There was very little discord. Everything just flowed from day to day like I believe it's supposed to."

"In some sense though, I think you were living a little delusion, Trisha. I saw that the two of you had separate bedrooms, Patricia, and I'll bet it's been that way for a while. A passionate woman like you dies a slow death not being able to share a bed with someone she loves."

"There were a lot of reasons for that happening, Phillip. We used a lot of excuses we deluded ourselves into thinking were logical. I hardly remember any of them now. And, as for being a passionate woman, you are forgetting one very important thing. I didn't know I was passionate, Phillip. I'd never allowed myself to make that part of the equation." She kissed him again. "Do you want to know what is my very, very, *very* most wonderful memory of the two of us?"

"Yes, please. I'd like to know that."

"Maybe. But then again, maybe not."

"Okay, how much is it going to cost me?" sighed Phillip.

"Oh, it will cost you a great deal. However, it comes with a complete refund if you are not altogether satisfied!"

"That's a little dangerous, lady. Are you aware of what it takes to make me satisfied? You woman enough to make a guarantee like that?

"Yep! Think so. I'm feeling pretty darn lucky today. You gonna answer me or not, big boy?"

Phillip shook his head.

"So, you're not gonna try and guess, huh? Just gonna roll over and play dead, huh? And you say you want passion. Sheesh! Okay, my very best memory, and the time that I will remember as the best of the best..." Patricia stopped mid-sentence. "Oh, dear, this is going to sound so corny. Never mind. I should never have said anything."

"You know I could tickle you until you tell me."

"You could, but I don't think you'd want to tickle me after I tell you.

Actually, now that I think about it, somehow I'm afraid that you will take what I say as an insult."

"I'm sure I won't. So tell me."

"Okay then, here I go. The defining moment, the one which I will cherish forever, is the time when you took me to Big Sur." She closed her eyes, waiting for his reaction.

"And I cherish that very much, as well, Patricia."

"You do? But, it was make-believe."

"I disagree. I don't think it was make believe at all."

"You're right, Phillip. It wasn't make-believe for me either really. Not any less so than the past few days you've been here. Do you understand what I'm saying?"

"Yes, I do. And I don't mean to break this wonderful spell, but I really think we need to get going."

"No, not yet."

"Yes, baby. I don't want to go either, but we have to." He leaned over and kissed her. "Let's make ourselves look presentable and go see what Trent's found out, and then prepare ourselves to go tell Bill what we're thinking."

Chapter Thirty-eight

Phillip barely arrived in time to make his flight. Mark had said it was urgent that Phillip return to Seattle as soon as possible. As he got settled in his seat, he began to reflect on the incredible events of the last week. It was the first time in the past thirty-six hours that he could begin to relax. He wondered how long the guilt about leaving the way he did would haunt him. Bill had tried to assure him that Patricia would be safe staying with Sylvia. He wasn't convinced. And he worried that Patricia would become suspicious of why Sylvia had suddenly become so protective. Patricia would probably realize that he'd not told her something. All this made leaving her all the more difficult. There were several loose ends Phillip wished he'd been able to tie down.

He felt better when he realized that, in just a few hours, they would most likely have Caesar in custody and a warrant issued for the arrest of Emily Abeyta as an accessory in the murder of Alma Garrett. Perhaps there was enough evidence to arrest Toji, as well. And soon, Bud Richards would be exposed.

He leaned his head back against the seat and closed his eyes. It was hard to believe that it had only been nine hours since he and Patricia waited for Trent to return from his visit with the director of the Taos Art Institute.

As soon as Trent had pulled up in his Bronco, he motioned for them to get in. This time, Phillip got in the back, while Patricia sat next to Trent. Before she'd even closed the door, Trent sped off, barely missing the concrete steps hidden in the grass, and jerking the vehicle up onto the main gravel road which lead them back to the highway.

"Wow! I take it from the way you're driving that the meeting with Mr. Fabrique was less than successful?" Patricia asked.

"Actually, I think it was pretty helpful. He seemed to be as helpful as he could be."

"Is that all? Are you going to tell us what you found out?"

"Yes, there's more. Give me a second, okay? Man, I just needed to catch my breath! I'll tell you what, these guys are all weird, if you ask me. I swear, they're all limp-wristed weirdos." Trent didn't speak again until they'd turned onto the highway.

"At first, I thought Fabrique was annoyed at me for interrupting his class. But if he was, it didn't last long. Anyway, he had me follow him into his office. By the time we got there, he had a pretty good idea of who I was and why I'd come. He confirmed that Caesar had missed a lot of classes. He also told me that Caesar spends a lot of time with computers, and that the school was upset with him for having torn apart a couple of the computers in the library."

"That doesn't really surprise me," Phillip interjected. "What else?"

"I tell you what was really curious. He just sort of volunteered the fact that he happened to have Caesar's file out because someone else had been in asking about him. A woman, he told me. That's when he told me that it was a cop who said she was following up on a few things."

When Patricia said she thought it was probably Brenda Riley, Phillip agreed.

"Who?" asked Trent.

"The new deputy that was brought in after Frank was placed on leave," explained Patricia. "What else did you find out?"

"Well, Mr. Fancy Pants made a point of telling me that there were a couple of tuition payments that hadn't been paid. He gave me a bill and a late notice and said that he wanted me to give them to Emily. When I assured him that he would get his money, he seemed satisfied. He also told me that Caesar had a lot of talent but, like a lot of gifted students he'd seen over the years, he had some conflicts and issues and needed more guidance in his life."

"Did he mention any problems specifically?" Phillip asked.

"No." Then Trent thought for a moment. "You know, I had no idea how expensive the place was. It costs around ten thousand dollars a semester to go to that fairy school!"

Patricia sighed in obvious exasperation. "Trent, it's a highly regarded school. And considering what some schools charge these days, that isn't that out of line."

"Whatever! God, it costs an arm and a leg to send kids to school these days. I don't know how people afford kids. I really don't."

"You don't much care for kids, do you Trent?" Phillip asked, surprised at his own bluntness.

"Oh, it's not that I don't like them or anything like that. It's just that I've never been around kids too much. Well, except for Sylvia's. They were born and grew up next door, of course, and they are really swell kids. It's just that I've heard too many horror stories about raising kids, and I figure that life's hard enough at best without complicating it with something that's preventable. Know what I mean?"

Phillip declined an answer. For the first time since meeting Trent, he was seeing a side of him that could only be described as selfish and unpleasant.

Trent looked at Phillip. "You have kids, Phil?"

"No, I was never that fortunate." Phillip looked and saw the sadness in Patricia's eyes. She'd been unusually quiet during the drive back to town. He wished he could find a quick way to change the conversation. It was already too late.

"That's unfortunate, Phillip, especially if you wanted children. I'm sorry you missed that opportunity." Her eyes and the quietness of her voice told him everything that he needed to know. His heart was screaming at him to take control—to stop the car, grab her up, and transport both of them as far away from this place and time as possible. His mind reminded him that such a time was not yet theirs.

Trent was oblivious to the effect of his callousness, and instead had begun laughing out loud. "Oh, I found out another interesting thing while I was there. I'd thought this about the kid once or twice, but just thought it was me. You know how some people just act like they were born old? I used to think that, anyway. Well, Caesar always seemed old to me for some reason, you know what I mean? So when I was looking through his file, I was reading his application and under 'Nickname,' he'd written Geezer. I sort of laughed, I guess, and Frenchie Fabrique asked me why and I told him. He laughed, too, and then reached over and took the folder from me and flipped through to a page near the back where someone had made a bunch of notes. It took him a minute to find what he was looking for. And then he handed it back to me with his finger on a note in the margin."

"What did the note say?" Phillip asked the question for which he was certain he already knew the answer.

"The guy was laughing and said that Caesar actually called himself this! The handwriting was hard to read, but I finally saw that it said NastyOlGeezer. He told me that some of the girls had started calling Caesar that as soon as the semester started."

* * * * *

Was that only yesterday that Bill and Sylvia discovered that he'd arrived in town earlier than expected? On Friday, Bill had made his usual stop at the Take Another Look Bookstore and found that Patricia was not there. He asked Butch where she was, but received a rather obtuse answer. He sensed that perhaps he was covering up for her for some reason.

He wondered what Patricia was up to now, and decided to drive over to Sylvia's and see if she was there. He knew it was Sylvia's day off and that the two women often spent that time together. When he got there, he learned that Patricia hadn't been there. When Sylvia kidded him about suddenly being so concerned about her friend, he explained that he was genuinely concerned that she was up to something and he was going to find out what it was. This prompted Sylvia to go ahead and tell him the truth, that Phillip had arrived early and was spending some quiet time alone with Patricia.

Phillip's involvement with Patricia explained his interest in helping with the case. Early on, Frank Garrett had become suspicious of Phillip's motives and concluded that he knew more about what was going on than he was letting on. Though it seemed unlikely that Phillip had anything to do with the murder, Frank told Bill that he'd still have to be considered a suspect. Bill pondered the irony of Frank, himself considered a suspect by some, suspecting Phillip who was promising to provide some valuable information on the case.

After Bill left, Sylvia waited a few hours before calling Patricia and filling her in on what was happening. When she called, Phillip could only hear half the conversation. When she recounted the call for him, she was teasingly melodramatic..

"Uh-oh, sweetie. I'm afraid it looks like we've been discovered," Patricia said after she hung up the phone.

"Excuse me, but would you mind telling me what's going on?"

"Okay, I'll tell you. You obviously aren't in the mood to be teased! Well, you know Bill, our deputy sheriff?"

"Yes. What about him?"

"Well, seems he was next door at Sylvia's and she told him that you're in town. He knows that you're here with me."

"Is that all right?"

"It's fine, silly. It has to be fine now, doesn't it? I mean, there's not much we can do about it now anyway."

"Honestly, Trisha, tell me. Does me being here put you in an awkward position?"

"Mmm, an awkward position?" Patricia giggled devilishly. "We haven't tried that one yet."

Phillip tried not to laugh, but he couldn't stop it.

"Aha! Gotcha!"

"That you did, you stinker."

Patricia pulled the sheet around her and leaned back against the pillows. "Seriously, everything is fine, Phil. They're very good friends and there is nothing to worry about. I do have a confession to make though. While you were taking a shower earlier, I called Sylvia and told her a little bit about you. We're having brunch with them on Sunday, as a matter of fact, at this wonderful place in the plaza called Dylan's. I figure you'll go cabin crazy if I don't let you out of this bedroom soon!"

"Yes. Cabin fever. I think you should do something about that right now, if you don't mind?"

He began by kissing her softly again.

Patricia and Phillip were a few minutes late getting out of the house on Sunday morning. Bill, Sylvia, and her teenaged son Carlos were already at the restaurant waiting for them.

Phillip found Bill to be pretty much as he'd pictured him. He looked younger than his age, and reminded Phillip more of a high school science teacher than a cop. He was not a tall man, and he had slightly graying, sandy blonde hair and a well kept moustache. At first glance, he appeared a little stocky. But on closer inspection, Phillip could see that he was just very muscular. Bill had an air of confidence about him. Phillip liked him immediately, and was glad to finally be able to put a face to the voice he'd spoken to on the telephone.

Phillip got the impression that Sylvia was looking him over. The woman was smart, he could tell, and the last thing she was going to do was let him know whether she approved of him or not. That didn't worry him. He liked her, and was confident that she'd come to like him as well.

He looked at Carlos. The young man seemed oblivious to those seated around him as he read and reread every item on the menu. Phillip had actually met Carlos earlier that morning. While Patricia was showering, Phillip had stepped out onto the front porch with his coffee and encountered Carlos delivering the Sunday paper. Carlos brought it to the door and introduced himself. He seemed like a nice enough kid.

"Carlos, nice to see you again," Phillip said as he reached across the table and shook his hand.

"When did you arrive?" Bill asked hoping that he didn't sound as though he were prying.

"Friday..." Phillip started to say.

"Thursday," said Patricia at nearly the same time. They looked nervously at each other.

"Right! It was Thursday." Phillip corrected himself.

"Yes, Friday. That's right!" Patricia exclaimed at the same time again. They burst out laughing.

"I think perhaps you two should have rehearsed this a little more," Sylvia said with a devilish grin.

"Oh, is there a test later?" Phillip asked quickly.

"There always is with her," Bill said.

"Oh, my. What *is* today?" asked Patricia, batting her eyelashes.

When the waiter appeared and began taking orders, Carlos leaned over and whispered something to his mother. Sylvia seemed to be glaring at Phillip. When Phillip turned to see if she was looking at something else, he found himself nose to belt buckle with a tall young man.

"Hey, Carl, can I talk to you for a minute?" the kid asked in an almost demanding tone.

"Hey, Caesar," Bill said warmly.

"Morning, Mr. Conner."

"You going to start showing up to class again soon?"

"Yeah, sorry."

The lanky, fairly rude young man appeared to be part Asian and part Latino. His small nose looked out of proportion to the rest of his face, and his large, bushy eyebrows gave him an almost comical appearance. His eyes were small and beady, his jawline well defined. Phillip noticed that Caesar completely avoided any eye contact with the adults at the table. He immediately mistrusted him.

"You coming, Carlos?" Caesar asked impatiently.

"Sorry," Carlos said quickly to everyone at the table, "I'll be back soon."

Patricia leaned over and whispered in Phillip's ear, "That's the young man I saw in the bookstore. The one who was always bothering Alma." Sylvia overheard.

"Caesar? Caesar knew Alma?" Sylvia asked.

"Caesar Abeyta is his name. He's Emily's son." Bill explained in a hushed voice. "And, Patricia, Emily and Trent are sitting across the room behind you."

When Phillip heard Trent's name, he turned around to see who he was.

"Oh god," gasped Sylvia, "he's coming over!"

"It'll be okay," Bill said trying to reassure everyone.

For a brief moment, Patricia panicked. Then she stood up quickly, turned around, and greeted Trent brightly. Then Trent reached down to shake Bill's hand. Bill didn't stand as he had when Phillip and Patricia arrived. Southern manners were a pick-and-choose option, he figured.

"Say, I'm sorry about being here like this, I really am." He stopped and stared at Phillip, the stranger who was obviously escorting his wife. "Patricia, I had no idea you would be here, or I wouldn't have come."

"You're here with Emily?"

"Yes," Trent said. "I'm sorry Patricia."

"No, it's fine. You have to eat sometime, too, right?"

"Would you be more comfortable if we left?" Trent offered.

"Don't be ridiculous! Besides, there's someone I'd like you to meet. Trent, this is a friend of mine, Phillip Craven. Phil is from Seattle."

"Nice to meet you, Phil," Trent said politely, reaching toward him with a large, weathered hand.

"So, did Caesar and Carlos take off, Sylvia?" Trent asked. "I didn't realize they even knew each other," Trent said.

"They left for just a few minutes." Sylvia's bluntness did little to hide her disgust of Trent Ridgeway.

"Bill teaches the boys martial arts," Sylvia explained to Phillip.

"Well, I don't mean to keep you from your food," said Trent. It was nice to see you all." He started to leave, but stopped and looked at Patricia. "Have you been getting your mail all right?"

"Yes, I got the papers, Trent. And I will sign them, of course." Her composure did not go unnoticed by the trio politely trying to ignore the exchange. Trent, however, looked a bit embarrassed.

"That *is* what you were wondering about, isn't it?" Patricia asked.

"Well, I have to admit that it was, yes."

"You'd better not keep Emily waiting too long," Sylvia deadpanned.

Trent glanced over at Emily who appeared to be glaring at him. Trent said good-bye and walked slowly back over to his table.

"All right now, where were we?" Patricia said, pretending she was unaffected by the visit. Phillip watched her sip her now lukewarm coffee. He also noticed Trent steal a glance or two over at Patricia before he sat down across from Emily.

"I didn't realize that Emily had a son," Patricia said quietly.

"Oh yes," Bill said. "Apparently he was in a private school in the northwest, but there was trouble of some kind and...well, I guess she decided to bring him to Taos so he could attend the Art Institute."

"He's a bit odd, but he seems to get along with Carlos quite well." Sylvia added.

"This is Carlos and Caesar, right? Not Trent and Caesar?" Phillip was confused, but Bill straightened him out.

"Caesar doesn't have many friends in town," Bill said.

"He's quite an interesting looking young man," offered Phillip.

"Hey, Sylvia, want to go to the little girl's room with me?"

"Excellent idea, Patricia."

Patricia winked at Phillip and squeezed his shoulder as she and her friend excused themselves from the table. After they were gone, Bill surprised Phillip by saying, "Patricia positively glows, Phillip."

"What was that?"

"I mean she's never looked happier. I like Patricia very much and seeing her so, well so happy is… Sorry, I'm just making it worse."

"I love that woman, Bill, and I suspect we'll be part of each other's lives more and more."

Phillip caught Bill staring at Trent across the room. "Smooth, Bill. I hope you're better at being a cop then you are at this sorta thing!"

"Me, too!" They both burst out laughing. "You know, I don't care much for Caesar myself. He's an outsider. I think he might have some sexual identity issues and from working with him in class, I suspect he's quite high-strung. The martial arts stuff does seem to calm him quite a bit though."

The conversation was interrupted by the waiter offering more coffee. When he left, Bill continued. "I just realized something. I teach him different elements of the Martial Arts, you know?"

"Yes…and?"

"He's quite good…" Bill didn't finish his sentence. He was deep in thought, and Phillip watched him as he twisted his napkin into a tight coil.

"You okay, Bill?"

"Sure, it's just an awkward situation," Bill said quickly before launching into a completely different train of thought. "You're coming into the station what time tomorrow?"

"I might as well come in with Patricia. I suppose around nine or nine thirty."

"That'll be fine. Say, you got a place to stay while you're in town?" Bill asked. Then stopped himself and shook his head in disbelief. "Good grief, just ignore me okay?"

Phillip chuckled, "Oh, don't worry 'bout me. I'll be fine. This town has a spare park bench or two, doesn't it?"

"You're a real smart ass, you know that?" quipped Bill. "Look, Phil, I'm going to be straight with you." Bill's tone was suddenly somber.

"No reason not to be, Bill."

"We have some people from out of town that wouldn't mind seeing Frank hung for this murder."

"I'm assuming you are referring to this woman cop that Patricia has told me about, right?"

"Riley, yeah, and some others as well. I made a mistake letting her stay on here. Brenda's a good cop, but I didn't realize she was as close to Bud Richards as she is. Bud and Frank go way back and they've never liked each other very much along the whole way. Fact is, Bud didn't like it very much when I left Texas to come up here to work with Frank. He was planning some political move, and I messed up his plans when I showed up on the scene."

"So, you and Frank have also known each other for a long time?"

"Since college, back in Texas, yeah. He's two years older, but he was in the service before he started school, so we were freshmen together and ended up being roommates."

"I see. Is Bud the jerk who arrested Frank a few weeks ago?"

"He's the one, all right." The look on his face revealed a real disgust for the man.

"What's he got against your boss?"

"Oh, long story. And I probably don't know the half of it."

"You gonna tell me what you do know?" Phillip asked.

"Maybe."

"Maybe?"

"You seem like a good man, and Patricia's one of my favorite people on the planet, Phil, but I found out a few days ago that you disappear from Cle Elum and pop up here in Taos a few days earlier than you should have."

"These things happen, Bill," Phillip said quietly.

"Yeah, I know. A lot of things have happened in the past few months."

"I think we should wait till tomorrow to talk about this."

"Yeah, I suppose you're right. So how do you like Taos so far?"

They both laughed at the sudden shift in the topic of conversation just as Patricia and Sylvia to arrived back at the table. The two men quickly explained what they'd found so humorous.

"Whew! I thought I had toilet paper on my shoe or something," Sylvia said. "What's gotten into you?" she said, turning toward Bill and pinching his leg.

"This guy," he said, nodding toward Phillip.

"Yeah, he's something else isn't he?" Patricia commented.

"Ah, Patricia, you're going to make him blush," teased Sylvia.

"About time something made him blush!" Patricia declared.

Phillip laughed quietly to himself as he recalled that Sunday brunch at Dylan's. He shifted positions in the cramped seat as the plane rushed down the runway now toward takeoff. He turned to look out the window and watched as the plane became airborne. His mind wouldn't turn off. Several hours earlier, he had been talking with Trent.

"I'm glad Patricia isn't alone right now," Trent said. "I know it's an awkward situation for both of us, Phil, and part of me doesn't want you anywhere near her. But the other part of me knows that I blew it. I took her for granted for too long. It's my fault that we grew further and further apart."

Phillip wasn't sure what direction the conversation was taking, but he admired Trent's candor.

"I have to do the right thing," Trent said. "You just let me know how I can help, okay?"

"You can count it," Phillip assured him.

"I mean, going up to the school and asking some questions is the least I can do."

"It's not exactly putting you in a good position though," Phillip offered. "You be careful."

"Be careful?"

"With Emily and Caesar."

The plane had reached its cruising altitude, and Phillip watched the moonlit clouds slipping by beneath him. He thought about how much he loved Patricia, and how much he missed her now. The familiar lyrics of an old song ran through his mind and seemed to ease his sadness:.

Fly me to the moon
Let me play among the stars
Let me see what spring is like
On Jupiter and Mars
In other words:
Hold my hand
In other words:
Darling kiss me

For several minutes, Phillip just enjoyed the new way he felt, before once again going over everything in his mind.

At Patricia's suggestion, Phillip and Bill walked over to her house to continue their discussion. "Here, take the keys. I'll be over later."

"So *now* you don't believe it's connected to this guy in Seattle that you know?" Bill asked as they made their way across the footbridge.

"That's what I'm thinking, yeah. I mean, my mind still thinks it could be Toji, and there are certainly a lot of things that would implicate him; but in my gut, I know he isn't right for this."

"Bad cops talk about gut feelings, you know."

"I'm not a cop at all, so that rule doesn't apply!"

"You're a son of a bitch, is what you are."

"Can't help it," Phillip shrugged.

"What the fuck do I do now, Phil? Riley wants my goddamned head for letting Frank get away from me. And Bud Richards, of course, believes I know exactly where he is."

"Is Frank okay for a few more days?" Phillip asked.

"You really think I'm going to answer that?"

"Don't see why you shouldn't."

"I'm not supposed to have any idea where Frank is, remember?"

"I didn't ask you *where* he was. I asked *how* he was, and if he'd be okay for a few more days. I realize that you could be in contact with him without actually knowing where he is. But the way you're acting tells me you know exactly where he is."

Bill was obviously about to get extremely defensive.

"Stop worrying," Phillip said with an irresistible smoothness. You'd tell me if Frank *wasn't* going to be okay while we sort this out, wouldn't you?"

"Frank is fine," Bill said.

"And I know you'll do all you can to make sure he stays fine," said Phillip. "I know all about Caesar being in your classes. So did you teach him how to use a sword?"

"I can't fuckin' believe it, Phil."

"Nor should you, at least not yet," Phillip said. "It's just a possibility. And just because you taught someone how to use a sword, doesn't mean they go out and do something stupid with it either."

Phillip fumbled with the keys and then unlocked the door to Patricia's house. They went inside and Bill flipped on some lights.

"Let's raid the liquor cabinet for a drink, shall we?" Phillip suggested.

"Excellent idea."

When Phillip walked into the dining room, he had the odd feeling as if someone were watching him. He was about to dismiss it when he heard Bill whisper his name.

Phillip turned around and saw Bill motion to him and then begin moving cautiously down the hallway. Phillip watched as Bill reached down and removed his gun from the holster. Phillip walked behind him as they made their way down the still dark hall toward the bedrooms and Patricia's office. Phillip realized that the gut feeling he'd had just might have been genuine.

Before they reached the door to the office, they heard a sliding glass door being opened, followed by the sound of someone running away from the house. Bill took a quick look around Patricia's office and then bolted through the open door. When Phillip stepped outside, he saw Bill already several yards beyond him, looking in all directions in the darkness.

"I saw someone run down over that way!" Bill shouted, pointing in the direction of the tree-lined canal.

"Did you see who it was?"

Bill stood motionless, squinting through the darkness, looking for any sign of movement that would give him some idea where the intruder had gone.

"If he was smart, he went down the drainage ditch. It takes a sharp bend over there."

"Did you see who it was?" Phillip repeated.

"I'm not sure, but it could have been Caesar," Bill said. "It was the same height and build, but I just can't be sure."

"What the hell was he doing in her house?"

"He might have been looking for something."

"And he might have been waiting for her," Phillip said.

After several minutes, the two men returned to the house. The two of them walked through each room trying to determine if anything was missing. When they entered Patricia's office, they found several papers scattered across the floor and her chair overturned. Phillip suddenly thought of something and walked over to Patricia's desk. He sat down and turned on the monitor: *Drive C has been reformatted.* "Son of a bitch!"

"What is it? Bill asked.

"That bastard just erased Patricia's hard drive. Evidence we could have used was on this computer."

"Evidence?"

"There were some threats made against Patricia, and there's ways of recovering data from hard drives if we needed to do that to link Caesar and Toji and Emily together. But Patricia forwarded me the notes, so we might be able to trace it from that. I forwarded copies of the notes which were signed Crane, a name I think Bishamon was using, to Mark my detective friend."

"I'll admit it," Bill said, "I'm lost."

"The letters we need I've got on my computer and my friend Mark has them as well."

"But not Patricia?" Bill said.

"Nope. Everything on her computer is gone."

"When they arrested Frank, they seized his computer," Bill said.

"Yeah, but what were they looking for in Frank's computer? And did they find it?" Phillip asked, not really expecting an answer. "Patricia is going to need help getting her computer up and running again."

"Carlos is pretty good with computers," Bill offered.

"Can you get him to come over and help?"

"Yeah, no problem. Say, how about that drink?"

Phillip and Bill dug around in the liquor cabinet, found a half full bottle of Glen Fiddich, poured themselves two fingers over a couple of cubes of ice, and clinked their glasses together before taking that first slow sip.

"I think I'll go get Patricia. You want to stay here in case that jerk decides to come back?"

"Yeah, that's fine, so long as long as you leave that bottle behind."

Phillip had just left when Patricia's cell phone began to ring. Bill looked at it sitting on the kitchen table. He considered letting it ring, but walked over to see who the caller might be. Bill recognized that the area code was from Seattle. He decided to answer it. It was Mark.

Bill ran back over to Sylvia's and stood outside. He could see Phillip and the girls inside laughing. Apparently Phillip hadn't told them about the intruder yet. He motioned at Phillip to join him outside. Bill told him what Mark had said, and then discussed several different options for getting Phillip back to Seattle as quickly as possible.

"I know you don't want to go right now, Phillip, but you have to."

Phillip looked at his watch. "There's not much time if I'm going to catch that flight."

"I realize that," Bill said, "but I can get you on a commuter flight within the hour which will get you to Albuquerque in time. We'll return your rental car to the agency here and pick up the tab for you. See? There's a little bit of an upside in this."

"The car? Oh, yeah. That makes me feel a whole lot better."

"Least we can do for you after all your help." Bill was sincere.

"You sure Mark didn't tell you why he wanted me back?"

"No. He was on a cell phone and, I don't know, either he couldn't talk or didn't want to."

"I can't go, Bill." Phillip said, "not now."

"Patricia will be okay, Phil. I promise you, she'll be okay. You didn't tell her about the intruder, did you?"

"No. She needs to know though."

Bill added, "Computers do crash for no logical reason sometimes, you know. I'll have Carlos fix her computer as soon as he gets home. Patricia can stay with Sylvia. I won't lie to her, but she doesn't have to know anything about Caesar."

Phillip thought through his options, and finally relented. And soon, Bill and Sylvia and Patricia were driving Phillip to the airport. When they arrived, Bill turned to Phillip. "You and Patricia should be alone for a few minutes." Syl and I will wait over here.

Patricia tried to remain composed so that Phillip wouldn't know how much his leaving was affecting her. They kissed and held each other longer than they should have. "I knew it was going to be hard to let you go," Patricia said, fighting back the tears.

"I love you so much, Patricia."

"I love you, too."

He boarded the small plane without looking back at her.

Phillip kept his eyes closed in the darkened cabin. He wasn't going to sleep, he told himself, just rest. When he opened them again, his plane was landing at Los Angeles International Airport where he would soon catch another flight to Seattle.

Chapter Thirty-nine

On the drive back into town from the airport, Bill fiddled with the radio, trying to get the Oklahoma City station to come in, but the background static was irritating. Just as he was about to turn it down, Sylvia reached over and flipped the radio off. She found Bill's hand in the darkness and held it tightly. Patricia was in the back seat, her eyes closed. She wasn't even trying to fight back the tears. She was so emotionally exhausted that she simply couldn't think any more. Saying good-bye to Phillip was the hardest thing Patricia could remember ever doing in her life. Yet harder to deal with than her own feelings was seeing the sadness in Phillip's eyes as he kissed her quickly and then turned to board the plane. Her one wish in life would be to never have to do this again. And then she slept. Instinctively, Patricia woke up just as Bill turned onto Pond Street.

"Patricia? You awake?" Bill looked in the mirror but could only make out her silhouette. "You're going to spend the night with Sylvia, okay? Before you argue, I'll just tell you one thing. Phillip made me promise that I'd see that you did that. I promised him, all right?"

"That isn't necessary, really. I'll be fine! That's silly. Phillip is just being...well, he's just being Phillip. I have tons of work I need to do, and I know I won't sleep. This would be an excellent time to catch up on all I've let go this week. You understand, right, Syl?" Apparently, Phillip had not told Patricia about the intruder.

Bill pulled up in front of Sylvia's house and turned off the engine. He tried one more time. "Patricia, I assured Phil I'd do this for him. I don't want to have to explain why I didn't. Just don't act like a woman for a few hours and cooperate, will ya?" He smiled.

"I'll overlook that 'woman' comment if you'll make a deal," Patricia said as she leaned over the front seat.

"I tell *you* what," Bill interrupted, "let's *don't* and *say* we did! How's that, for a deal?" He laughed at Patricia's obvious aggravation with him.

"Okay, okay. I'll go in and we can talk about this over coffee."

When she got out of the car, Patricia looked up at the crystal clear night sky filled with flickering stars that danced before her eyes. She watched the lights of an airliner as it passed noiselessly overhead. "Nice night for flying, but those little commuter planes scare the beejezus outta me! I'm sure Phillip will get home fine on a night like this."

"You worry too much, girl!" Sylvia followed Patricia's eyes upward to see what she was looking at. "It *is* pretty, huh? I love this time of year." She'd barely said the words, when Bill slid between them and placed his arms around their waists.

"Hmm, you girls are warm! Whatcha lookin' at up there anyway?"

Bill smiled and thought of the diamond ring he had in his pocket and the dozen red roses he'd ordered to be delivered in the morning. Tomorrow was Sylvia's day off, and he only planned to work part of the day himself. "Patricia, can I talk to you a minute? Alone, that is?" He winked at Sylvia.

"Careful now, Bill. You know I'm the jealous type."

"You are? Even if I just want to talk to Patricia about you?" He led Patricia away from the car. He knew that Sylvia suspected that he was up to something. He was acting like a kid and enjoying every moment of it.

When they'd walked a short distance, Bill told her about his plans to come over in the morning and surprise Sylvia with the ring. Patricia was overjoyed and suggested that he give her the ring so she could hide it somewhere within the bouquet. *Men always needed a few nudges to remind them that game playing is a major part of courtship.* She assured him that, if in fact she stayed the night, she'd be gone long before he showed his bright, shining face. He thanked her, but told her that he had a little plan of his own all cooked up for presenting the ring. He reminded her one more time how important it was that she spend the night at Sylvia's.

"We'll see, Bill. Let's go inside and have some coffee. I'm really cold!"

Once inside, Bill set about starting a fire, and Sylvia put on a pot of decaf. "I wish I had some dessert or something to offer you guys, but I don't think I do."

"Okay, that does it! I'm not staying!" Patricia made a half-hearted attempt to leave through the back door, but stopped and started laughing when Bill ran around the corner to stop her. *Jeez, he acts like Phillip put the fear of God into him!*

"Okay, you got me!" Bill laughed. "So, what kind of dessert you girls interested in? I'll go get us something. I'm in the mood for something sweet myself. What would you like, Patricia?" He'd stepped behind Sylvia who was standing at the sink. He put his arms around her waist and was nuzzling her ear. Sylvia was uncomfortable with his affections in front of Patricia and was playfully pushing him away.

"Get away! Scram! Let me think!" Patricia laughed at them and was glad she was there.

"Sonic! I want something yummy from the Sonic!" Patricia exclaimed.

Carlos came bounding into the room, a broad smile on his face. "Sonic? Did I hear Sonic? Cool!"

Bill took Patricia's order last. "So, what will it be tonight, Miss Patricia? Pheasant under plastic or the Sonic's own creatively prepackaged crème brule?"

"Neither, thank you. I'd prefer a root beer float with chocolate chips."

He stopped writing on his hand with an imaginary pen and looked at her. He was aghast. "I'm sorry, what did you say? You say you want a *what*?"

"Oh god, Bill," Sylvia said, "she drinks those things all the time! Just get it for her so I don't have to hear her say it again."

"Oh, brother!" Patricia whined. "Carlos, help these two, will you, please?"

"For sure!" Carlos laughed as he and Bill headed out to get dessert.

Now Bill would have the perfect opportunity to explain to Carlos about Patricia's computer going down and ask him if he'd help get it back on track for her. Although, he had no intentions of mentioning that he and Phillip thought it might have had a little assistance from his friend, Caesar. He'd handle that some other way. He also thought he'd take this time to ask Carlos for his mother's hand in marriage. He didn't anticipate any flack about that, but he preferred to have Carlos' blessing.

The back door had barely closed behind the two before Patricia was standing next to Sylvia, pouring them both a fresh cup of coffee. "Just so you know, I'm not staying over here, and that's final."

"I knew you wouldn't. Now, let's make another deal. Don't tell Bill you have no intentions of staying. After he's gone, I'll walk you home, how's that sound?" Sylvia dried her hands on a towel and reached for her coffee.

"Perfect! Thanks!"

"And," Sylvia continued, "when we get to your house, I can spend the night over there! How's that for a deal?" She laughed, knowing full well how irritated this plan was making her dear friend.

"Oh, all right! You guys are being ridiculous, but I'm really too tired to argue anymore about it. It's a deal, but only if you'll promise to leave me alone early and come on back home. You need to get Carlos off to school and I really will need to dive into some work. Promise?"

"I promise," Sylvia said with a smile. "But don't let Bill find out, okay? I heard him talking to Phil, and they were dead serious about this."

"No problem, I promise." Patricia poured some more cream into her coffee, then said, "Let's go in by the fire! Wow, I can't believe how cold it feels tonight, can you? Brr!"

"Are you sure you're not coming down with something? I don't think it's all that chilly."

"Easy for you to say, Pocahontas. You've got Captain John Smith to keep you warm."

"I know, Patricia, but I've waited a long time for this." Sylvia reached out and touched Patricia's hand.

"Yes, you have. And you deserve Bill Conner and every wonderful thing that comes with the package, Syl."

"What about you, Patricia? How long have you waited?"

Patricia stared at their two hands together on the countertop, "Oh, for some things, at least a lifetime, maybe two, Sylvia. Who's to really know? We do what we do when it's time to do it. It's just the way of things, isn't it?"

"Yes, I believe so. Last year, when I went home to the Blessingway ceremony, I came back here knowing that there would be changes in store for me. I tried not to purposely act on anything and let the things just work. I think this union between Bill and me will be good. When we burned the logs at the ceremony and Nelson saw into the smoke, he told me of seeing the signs of great trial, great love, great tragedy, and ultimately a great peace. He was just learning the ways of the elders and was not yet a true medicine man, but his words were wise and the elders supported his truths. Perhaps it is time for you to go to the mountain, Patricia. Talk to the People, seek what you need, and let go. We both know where the power is, and where we must go for its strength. I'll never have the power that you have, because that is the way of things, too. But we all need the renewal. I think it's been far too long since you've done that, Patricia. Perhaps tomorrow would be a good day, before the winter snows come to the mountain. The herds have begun to move south already. It's early for them, which means an early winter. The owl has come, too. I heard him last night for the first time." She paused a moment while a soft shudder went through her body. "I'm sorry, Patricia, I'm not sure what got into me." Sylvia looked at her friend with a soft, rather bewildered look on her face, honestly not sure why she'd spoken about these things on this particular night.

"That's good advice. Indeed, it has been too long. Before I can go on this path that seems set for me, it is time to talk to Inner Form. There is so much about Phillip that he has told me, Sylvia, and he isn't even aware of it. He randomly speaks of rainbows, for instance. I am not sure if he even really knows that our Inner Form travels on the rainbow. He knows some things, Syl. Sometimes he knows way too much, yet he knows nothing of the People." The women had picked up their cups and moved into the family room. They sat now on the floor in front of the fire, facing one another.

"Does Phil know about Rainbow Tribe?"

"I don't think so. Like I was saying, there is so much that either he is not aware he is saying or he is aware and is just testing me. I'm not sure yet." Sylvia nodded, wanting Patricia to continue. "What has entered our world, Sylvia, is a black and evil force. I haven't been sleeping well for some time now. I contacted Nelson many weeks ago and asked for a Handtrembling. With all that's happened I just haven't been able to go meet with him, though. Then just last week, he called and said that he'd had a dream and was torn, not knowing which path to take. I asked him what he meant, and he said that a Handtrembling was not in his dream, but a different Chantway, perhaps two, and he'd sought the advice of an elder." Patricia paused, as if rethinking what Nelson Yazzie had shared with her that day.

"You mean he wanted to hold a different Blessingway ceremony? For what reason?" asked Sylvia.

"Oh, I could kick myself, Syl. I wasn't in a position where I felt like I could talk to him. Phillip had just arrived the day before and I'm afraid that my mind and my ability to concentrate were anywhere but on what Nelson had to say. But he did ask me to think over any reason why his Inner Form would direct him toward an Enemyway or a Ghostway chant. I knew right away, of course, but Phillip was sitting out in the courtyard and I didn't want to take any more time away from what little we had, so I told Nelson I'd get back with him."

Sylvia studied her friend for a moment. "I can understand perhaps his feelings about the Ghostway, but Enemyway is used so rarely that I am surprised by that."

"I was, too. The first chance I get I am going to get out some of my resource materials and see the various meanings behind the value of that particular Chantway. I was always under the impression that it was used for the purification of warriors, an ancient war ceremonial for their protection."

"Well, that's what I was always told. Hmm, maybe Nelson thinks you are going to join the Army or something!" Sylvia had finished her coffee and set the cup down on the hearth.

"Hark!" shouted Patricia, "I believe I detect the approach of the two Delivery Boys of Decadence bearing gifts of fizz and chocolate from the all-night soda fountain! All things of a serious nature must naturally give way to the more pressing matters of pure indulgence!" The two laughed easily together. Sylvia and Patricia understood one another like no one ever could. That was the wonderful way of things for them.

The foursome ate and drank and enjoyed their late night treats, and were all groaning by the time they'd finished.

"Aunt Patricia?"

"I'm sorry, Carlos, don't bother me. I'm dying, thank you." Patricia moaned and rolled over onto the floor.

"C'mon, Aunt Patricia, would you mind if I ran over and used your computer for a few minutes? I've got a project due for science class tomorrow and my whole system is down for some reason. I really shouldn't be very long."

"Goodness, I don't mind at all. I need to do some work later…" She stopped herself. "…um, tomorrow when I get home, so you are certainly free to help yourself to it tonight."

"Oh, thanks! I appreciate that. I just need to get my backpack first."

"Oh, I better get you a key."

Carlos laughed. "Aunt Patricia, we *have* a key, remember? Mom says that key is older than I am!"

"Oh, shut up, you little brat!" Patricia teased. She watched him move down the hall toward his room.

"Is that going to pose a problem, Patricia?" Sylvia asked.

"Carlos using the computer? Heavens no, not at all!"

Carlos stepped carefully over all the adults lying on the floor, still groaning over their sweet treats. "Jeez, you guys are pathetic! Be back in a few, Mom."

In less than thirty seconds, he was back. "Where's the key, Mom?"

"Isn't it on the hook?"

"Nope."

"That's odd. I'm sure it was there this morning. This happened the other day. Damn, Patricia, now even your key has a mind of its own."

Patricia struggled to her feet. "Oh, that's okay. Let me get you mine out of my purse." Patricia followed Carlos back into the kitchen, found her purse and keys, and tossed them to him. "Hang onto these, would you. You're mother's not very trustworthy. I don't have another set that I can think of."

"Okay! See you later." Carlos waved as he bounded out the door and down the back steps. Patricia stood at the window and watched him jump the ditch, completely ignoring the footbridge. *Hell, I never could jump that stupid ditch!* She waited until she saw the light come on in her den, and then she went back to join the others in the family room.

She came upon Sylvia and Bill in a tight embrace, kissing deeply in front of the fire. Either she'd been exceptionally quiet, or love somehow creates deafness, she thought to herself. She backed out the room and went back to the kitchen where she got down another mug and poured herself some coffee.

She turned off the kitchen light and sat there in the darkness looking out the window at the harvest moon that was growing brighter as the night wore on. She could see Carlos sitting at her computer and was surprised by that. In just the past week, many more leaves had fallen from the cottonwoods that separated her house from Sylvia's for much of the year. She never really realized that she was that visible at night in her secluded den. She could hear muffled voices now, and decided it was safe to attempt another entry into the family room. She put her cup on the counter and walked back through the dining room. She stopped when she heard Bill raise his voice.

"What did you say? Tell me that again."

"I just said that this is the second time I've needed Patricia's key and it hasn't been there. Last time, I know it wasn't there and then the next morning, I looked up and there it was on the hook! I am not crazy, Bill. I swear, one minute it was gone and the next minute it was there."

Bill thought for a minute. "Did you ask Carlos about it?"

"Sure, but he didn't know anything about it." Sylvia watched Bill's expression change. "What are you thinking? Talk to me, Bill."

"Does Caesar have free access to your house, sweetheart? I mean does he come and go when you or Carlos are not here?"

"My goodness, no! To be honest, I am a little distrustful of the kid. I haven't said anything to Carlos, but he knows the rules, and as far as I know, Caesar has never been here when we're gone."

"But what about when Carlos is here alone?"

"I can't be sure. He isn't supposed to be, but..."

Patricia decided to walk in at that point. She'd heard enough.

"So, Mr. Policeman, isn't it getting a little past your bedtime?" She feigned a sleepy stretch that actually materialized into a full-fledged killer of a yawn. She was wearier than she thought, and suddenly what little energy she was holding on to seemed to vanish.

"You're right. I do need to be going and let you girls get some sleep. You are going to behave, aren't you Patricia?"

"Yeah, yeah, yeah." She stuck out her tongue at the two of them and reached for her jacket. "While the two of you say your lingering good-byes, I'm going to run home while Carlos is there and get a few things for the night. You two take all the time you need and I'll be back in a few minutes. I might stay over there until Carlos is through."

Patricia waved as she rounded the corner and heard Bill holler once more, reminding her of her promise. *Men! So naïve. I had my fingers crossed all along!*

She called to Carlos when she started down the hall, to alert him that she was in the house. She waited until he answered, and then went into her bedroom. She saw something lying there on her pillow on the bed that made her weak at the knees and gave her the most wonderful, warm feeling.

"He didn't forget," she whispered to herself as she picked up the picture he'd left for her. It was the piece Phillip insisted she'd been responsible for. He'd told her that she, and no one else, should have the original *First Autumn Storm.*

It was beautiful, with the words written in a silvery text, wrapping around the picture of the raindrop. Most of the picture appeared in a strange sort of bleached sepia tone, but inside the raindrop that hung suspended from a porch railing, was a small very brightly colored rainbow.

Sleepless dreams
passing through like a cloudburst
in the desert,
flooding my mind
with images

Flashing
like
a lightning
bolt.

Striking.
Reality.

Stop making Sense.

Then,
when the storm
has passed…

The birds
sing praises
for
predictable
changes.

You notice
a single raindrop
clinging under

the porch
rail
like
hope.

Patricia enjoyed the picture, the words, but mostly the fact that Phillip had purposefully set it up on her bed to surprise her.

And then she saw the envelope. And inside the envelope, on several sheets of blue paper, was another poem.

Her Smile

Bracelets of blood.
hungry for tenderness,
needing adulation,
needing understanding,
craving a touch.
Adrift in a cold sea,
Afloat.
Reaching for a caress
a soft kind
word.
some hope.

She smiles
with lips
you want to kiss.
Lips
you long to someday
miss.

With a quiet sigh,
you look
into her eyes.
Pools
talking loudly
and they
need you.
Need you
too much.

She lets you,
but you can't
bear to see.
Yet you must
Persist
And drink in
all.
You can't possibly
Resist.
It scares you.
A chill
through your
soul.
Terrifies you
for it can never
be controlled
And you know
you'll try.
But as you
Attempt to possess it,
it will
possess
you.
Long after
you
die

And all the power
you ever felt.
All the words
you tried to
write.
And the few you
got right.
All of the flowers
you ever
smelled,
mean
nothing
if she
is not

next to you.

If you can't hold something
so fragile
and love
something
so beautiful…
If you can't mix the
delicate
with
iron and steel
you have
almost
nothing
And nothing
is real.

You glimpsed
but a
reflection
of the rainbow
but
turned away.

Except
you'll now
know,
as sure
as the sky
is blue,
how
powerless
you really
are…

You glimpsed
a reflection,
a rainbow,
but turned away…
afraid.
It's beauty

Would show
You too much
and
you would not
have enough
left
to still
see.

Turn up the music,
drown the voices
in your head.
The doubts
the longing in
your heart
the
dread.

It works for
a while.
Yes
it works
for
a long while.
Till she turns
and
you see
forever
that
smile.

She read the poem several times, feeling the emotions Phillip must have experienced as he wrote it. She loved the way he expressed things—simply, yet with phrases and combinations that reveal more complex meanings with every read.

Patricia realized she had been admiring the artwork and reading the poem for quite some time. She stood up and stretched. She was more tired than she thought. Even the idea of a shower seemed too overwhelming. She walked into her closet, took off her clothes, and slipped into a long gown. She didn't even bother to find her slippers, the thought of going to bed sounded so good. Before she crawled beneath the covers, she peeked her head around the corner to tell Carlos goodnight.

"Hey, I thought you were staying at our house tonight."

"Change of plans, my little friend. Woman's prerogative. Your Mom is going to spend the night here instead."

"Does Bill know that? Somehow, I think he's gonna be pissed!"

"*No*, he doesn't know. And you, dear one, are *not* going to tell him, either, capiche?"

"Capiche!" He shook his head and turned back to the computer. "This is taking me longer than I thought. Am I going to bother you?"

"Nope. An avalanche on Wheeler Peak wouldn't bother me tonight, cutie. Take your time and get your project done. Oh, and when your mom gets here, tell her to just bed down in the guest room, okay? Thanks!" She was asleep before her head hit the pillow.

Patricia forced her eyes open and looked at the clock. 2:37 A.M. She thought she'd just talked to Phillip. *Did I? Please tell me that wasn't a dream?* Very slowly she rose up to sit on the edge of her bed. She looked at the clock again. She saw Phillip's *First Autumn Storm* leaning against the wall where she'd left it. The mental cobwebs were clearing. She climbed out of bed and walked toward the door and opened it very slowly so it wouldn't make a sound. There were no lights from either her office or the guest room, though both doors were open. The night-light in the guest bathroom clearly reflected into the guest room. She could see Sylvia sleeping soundly. Patricia tiptoed down the hall and was startled by a strange noise. Then she realized it was Carlos asleep on the sofa in the den.

She wished she'd found her slippers. The floor was cold and she was shivering. Silently, she moved to the kitchen and poured herself a glass of milk and sat down at the table. She finally realized that it *had* been Phillip on the phone. He had called to let her know that he'd arrived home safely. She presumed he meant by "home" that he was staying with Mark in Seattle as he'd said he was going to. At least, when she told him that Sylvia was there, he wasn't *too* upset with her.

It had been barely a week since he'd surprised her in the bookshop. *A week? More like a lifetime, if you ask me!* The wee hours of the morning are hardly the time to analyze life-changing events. But the wee hours had presented themselves nonetheless, and she knew it was unlikely she'd go back to sleep. There was so much to think about at once. Never in her entire life had so many things bombarded her from so many different directions. Each one of them took a great deal of effort. There was just so much to think about. She laid her head on her arms, closed her eyes, and thought of Phillip.

"Patricia? Patricia?" Sylvia was gently shaking her shoulder and whispering in her ear. Patricia jumped with a shiver!

"Oh god, Syl, you startled me! What time is it?" She was freezing and her body was stiff as she tried to turn and look at the wall clock.

"It's early. Five-fifteen. I need to get Carlos home so he can get ready for school. I'll do a few things, shower, and then be back over, okay? What are you doing out here anyway?"

Sylvia got a cashmere afghan out of a basket and put it around Patricia's shoulders.

"Oh, thanks. That's much better! Did you hear the phone early this morning? It was Phillip just telling me that he'd gotten home safe and sound. I hardly remember talking to him, I was so tired. I thought it was a dream! Anyway, after that, I came in here and got some milk, and I guess I fell asleep."

"Okay, I'm going. I'll be back in an hour or so."

"Sylvia, please. That's not necessary, really. I am fine. I'll lock the house up. I'm still tired. I might just go back to bed. And if I can't sleep, I have tons of paperwork to do to keep me busy. Please. Don't come back, okay? You're not mad are you?"

"No, silly girl, I'm not mad. But damn it, Patricia, all these years you've helped me through so many things, you were just always there out of the blue and…well, hell, I didn't even know that you and Trent had split up 'til a couple of weeks ago! And then it was Bill who told me. That hurts, Patricia. The most you've shared with me in months was at dinner with Alma that night. I just wish you'd let someone in. I want to help. Bill wants to help. This is a bad time, and you just won't let anyone in. It's as if Phillip is the only thing you need in your life right now." Sylvia was now standing behind one of the ladder-back chairs, running her hands back and forth over the top rung. She was near tears.

"I had no idea! Sylvia, that's not it at all. It's not that Phillip has taken anyone's place or that I've shut you out. I've never been one to share very much of myself, with you or anyone else for that matter. So please don't take it personally. And please don't use Phillip as a whipping boy, okay? That's really not fair, Sylvia. Sweetie, its just been an incredible year long roller-coaster ride. Quite frankly, I'm ready to get the hell off, but no one will stop it so I can. It's not you, it's not personal, and it's not even me, Sylvia. Hell, I've spent a lifetime accumulating all these issues that I've always just shoved to the corners and under the rugs. But now, for about the last year, little by little, Phillip has pulled me out of myself. Then just as I was finally realizing, over halfway through my life, what I was all about, suddenly all this other stuff starts happening. Sylvia, please believe me. We didn't ask for this to happen. This is just one of those inexplicable things you and I have talked about so much in the past, Syl."

Patricia knew she'd hardly drawn a breath since the words started pouring out. She could only hope that her heartfelt words meant something to Sylvia.

"Oh, I know it *is* just you. And it's the *just you* that I know and love and I wouldn't want you any other way, I guess. I think I'm tired and confused and feeling a bit out of the loop with all this that's going on with you guys, and now with Phillip and Bill and Frank. I'm being selfish."

Patricia got up from the chair and gave Sylvia a tight hug. "You are not being selfish! Stop this right now! Get home. And thanks for spending the night! That will keep Phil and Bill at least half-happy. I'll see you later on today, okay? Cheer up! Things can't get any worse, can they?"

"Lord, I hope not! I look absolutely awful in black!" Sylvia regretted those words the instant they left her lips, but it was too late to take them back. "Oh, I'm sorry, Patricia. I don't have any idea why I said that. I honestly don't."

Patricia laughed. "I do that all the time. If there is something in your mind that you know isn't the right thing to say, you can count on it to pop out at the worst possible moment. In fact, let me tell you a funny true story!" She patted the table for Sylvia to sit down. Patricia stood by the counter, clutching the soft gray afghan around herself.

"I'm sure I never told you this, but... Oh, stop it!" Now Sylvia was making faces, as if to say, *see, this is exactly what I am talking about.*

"Anyway, so this is called *sharing*. I'm practicing, dang it! I have to learn sometime!" Both women laughed and Patricia pulled out another chair and sat down. Carlos came in and leaned against the kitchen door, rubbing the sleep from his eyes.

"Well, this has been a good many years ago now, but my mother's younger brother was shot to death by his drunk and jealous wife. When I got the call from my father, I was totally shocked. It was the sadness in his voice that got to me. He and my uncle were extremely close. They had hunted many winters together. Uncle Jim was a tracker and an elk guide, as well as a field surveyor. Anyway, Dad filled me in on a few details, and then Trent and I had to make quick arrangements to go to Colorado for the funeral. It was all handled very nicely, but we were all being very careful around my grandmother. It's an incredible blow to lose a child, no matter how old. And under these types of circumstances, it must be doubly hard. No one wanted to make anything worse for her than it already was. So while all the gals were sitting around chitchatting, the topic of buying expensive clothes came up. Now remember, my grandmother was right there in the thick of things, but we were pretty much treating her like one of the girls. Well, I can't remember exactly where the discussion had led, but someone said something about spending four hundred dollars for their outfit for the funeral. So what do you suppose I chimed in and spouted off in response to that? Oh, big as life itself, I tossed up my hands and shrieked, 'Good god! Trent would have shot me in the head if I'd done something like that!' My uncle had been shot in the back of the head, of course."

Sylvia burst out laughing, and even Carlos joined in.

"See what I mean?" Patricia said. "The oddest things come out at the strangest of times because of what your mind is trying so hard to tell you not to say or do. It's just a phenomenon of human nature, I suppose. "Why did I tell that story, anyway? Oh, I remember. You said you don't look good in black." The two women laughed again and hugged each other. Then Sylvia took Carlos home to get him ready for school.

Patricia stood at the door and watched the two of them run across the field, cross the footbridge, and disappear through Sylvia's back door. It was crisp and still outside, and a faint fog hovered just about the ground. She could see their footprints in the frost on the grass. It would be freezing soon, she thought. She and Sylvia always went up to Blue Lake in the late fall. She'd have to remind her that they needed to set aside a day for that. It always seemed to Patricia that smells often brought the neatest memories, and the aroma of roasting piñons in the fall was one of those extra special smells that cannot be forgotten, no matter how hard you try. Harvesting the nuts would be good therapy.

Several hours later, Patricia realized she hadn't heard back from Sylvia since she'd called earlier in the day telling her the coffee was ready. *I did hurt her feelings! Damn!*

She had always been one to get in the kitchen and futz around when she was nervous. After she told Phillip that she couldn't go over to Sylvia's until after Bill left, she tried in vain to get back into her books, but couldn't concentrate. *When in doubt, go into the kitchen and bake some pumpkin bread!* That would bring fall into the house. She hadn't eaten all day and thought she'd save her calories for when she could have some of the bread with Sylvia later in the afternoon. Bill hadn't mentioned it, but more than likely the two of them would go out for a nice evening together to celebrate.

* * * * *

What took place the rest of that day would take Patricia many years to fully recall. When she woke up, or at least when her brain woke up, she knew she was not in familiar surroundings, but she couldn't force her eyes to open.

There must have been buckets of cement sitting on them and she tried to move her hand to her face, but it wouldn't move either. *What's wrong with me? Where am I?*

Apparently her hand must have moved slightly, because the next thing she knew, someone was holding it and calling her name in the blackness. She wanted to go back to sleep. *Who is in my bedroom?* Whoever was trying to talk to her was persistent and she was getting annoyed. *Leave me alone!* Suddenly a woman's voice was talking to her. *Sylvia?*

"Mrs. Ridgeway? Patricia? Can you hear me? Wake up now, okay? There's someone here that is anxious to see you. Wake up. You are going to sleep your life away if you aren't careful." The voice was soft and nice, but it wasn't Sylvia. She managed to force her eyes open. She saw a form reach over her and turn off a bright light.

"There, that's better. I don't know why these dumb doctors come waltzing in here and turn these lights on and then just leave." *Was she talking to her?* She started to ask her what doctors was she talking about when she heard a man's voice answer.

"They have so much on their minds, I suppose," he said politely.

Patricia heard the female agree and then someone was squeezing her other hand. "Okay! Nap time's over! No more Romper Room for you, Patricia. Up and at 'em!" The woman was jostling her shoulder now. Someone was lifting the buckets from her eyes. This time, when she tried to open them, it was much easier and they began to focus after a few seconds. *I don't know this woman.*

"Goodness, that's quite a frown, Mrs. Ridgeway. Do I look *that* bad?" The woman laughed and adjusted the pillows under her head. She could hear a funny droning sound and felt the head of her bed rising. "There now. That's much better, isn't it? Of course, it is. Don't look now, but you have a very handsome visitor! If you don't start being cordial, I might have to ask him out to dinner or something. Then you could go back to sleep!" Patricia heard a man laugh. *Phillip's laugh!*

She tried to turn her head toward his direction and it seemed to take a lifetime. Her eyes still wouldn't focus. She was so relaxed. It would have been so easy for her to just close her eyes again.

She decided she really wanted to know what time it was and where she was exactly and if… She didn't want to think. There was no need to think, she was so relaxed and so tired, and so comfortable in this bed. She heard muffled voices again. *Were they talking to her? Was that Brenda Riley standing by a doorway? There's Phillip again! He was coming closer. It sure seemed like Phillip.*

"Hey, cutie. I thought you were never going to wake up." *It was Phillip.*

"Phillip?" She wasn't sure any sound came out of her mouth.

Oh, but he was hugging her now. Everything would be just fine now.

Chapter Forty

Phillip took another sip of single malt scotch, holding it in his mouth and savoring the flavor of smoke and fire before swallowing slowly.

"Good?" Mark inquired. He ordered another double shot of Glen Fiddich on the rocks for himself.

Phillip had been as patient as he was going to be with his friend. They had been at Daniel's Broiler on Lake Washington in Leschi for nearly an hour, and Mark still had not shared his news.

"You gonna tell me, or do I have to beat it out of you, Mark?"

"Toji is dead," Mark finally said matter-of-factly. "His body was found yesterday at the Botanical Gardens…in the silkworm exhibit."

"You're shitting me."

"I thought you would find that interesting."

"He was murdered, I presume?"

"Oh, yeah. Preliminary toxicology report showed some traces of drugs, alcohol, and some poison. They're not sure which one or if a combination of all three killed him, but they're definitely listing it as a homicide."

"Why are they so positive it wasn't suicide?"

"Not likely," Mark assured him. "It appears his body was placed in the exhibit on purpose. They're going to want to talk to you about it, Phil."

"They are?"

"Afraid so. Your friend from the gallery, Linda? Her business card was in Toji's wallet, and your name was written on the back of it. They've already talked to Linda and she told them that you delivered that *First Autumn Storm* print to him last week."

"What about you? Don't they know you were there with me?"

"Nope. If that has to come out, don't worry about it though. You should know that you are a suspect. That's just one more reason I wanted you to come back right away; so you could explain everything." Mark waited for Phillip to absorb that bit of news before continuing, "When they tried to get hold of you, you were missing in action. They asked Leo to look in on you. He didn't know you'd gone out of town. He knew that you sometimes go off on photo shoots for a week or two at a time, so he told the investigators that. You need to thank him for that first chance you get."

"But why the rush for me to get back here? A few days more wouldn't have made a difference, would they?"

"Well, after you e-mailed about how things were going in Taos, I figured your help here might get an arrest warrant issued a lot faster for you there," explained Mark. "Besides, there's more. Toji's son, Jordan, has disappeared, too, Phil. He lived with Toji and worked part-time at the Botanical Gardens. In fact, I found out that half of his college tuition is paid for because of his work there. And I found out Toji charged a few round-trip tickets to Albuquerque on his credit card, too," Mark added.

"I'll be a son of a bitch," Phillip whispered.

"Well, it was Toji's credit card, but Jordan could have made the charges. Fact is, Toji gave the kid his own credit card. Hell, I could've used a dad like that when I was growing up, how 'bout you?"

"A dad like Toji? No thanks."

"Listen, I'm going to go talk to the detectives tomorrow," Mark said, "and let them know what we know, or think we know anyway. You should be with me."

"That's okay by me," Phillip said. "You're the boss."

"I happen to know Hobart, one of the detectives assigned to the case. He's okay. With your help, I'm pretty certain that we can get things expedited and hopefully get this Garrett fella cleared pretty damned quick."

"That'd be a big help."

"So, you a little less pissed about having to come back now?"

"I'll let you know," Phillip said with the hint of a smile. "You know how old this Jordan is?" *Jordan? Jordan… Oh, my god… Jordan. Yes.*

"What? You think I've been sitting on my butt while you've been jetting around doing god knows what with your new lady friend? Hell, yes, I know how old he is. I know a lot of things about Toji and Jordan and some other folks you might find interesting."

"So, what you're telling me is that you really don't know how old he is," Phillip said sarcastically.

"Nineteen."

"Nineteen?"

"He's your Silky, isn't he?" Mark asked.

"It would certainly appear so." Phillip thought about that for a minute. "What other things have you found out?"

"Well, Toji became an American citizen when he married Jordan's mother, a woman named Melissa. Jordan's mom is half-Hispanic, half-English."

"And quite attractive from the pictures I saw of her at Toji's," Phillip added.

"It's also interesting that she has a stepsister who also married a Japanese man. Her stepsister has the same Hispanic father but different mom, I guess."

"Two sisters both marrying Japanese men. I'm supposed to find that interesting?"

"All right, wise ass, you want to make fun or let me finish? I'll tell you why it's interesting. The stepsister of Toji's wife is named Emily. The mother of some kid named Caesar. Caesar Abeyta. Ring any bells, jackass?"

"Caesar?"

"Yeah, Caesar. Appears Eduardo Abeyta adopted the kid and changed his last name."

Jesus!" Phillip exclaimed.

"Emily took his name after they married, naturally, so when Eduardo adopted the kid, they changed his name legally, too," explained Mark.

"And what happened to Eduardo?"

"Dropped dead of a heart attack about three years ago. Caesar, I guess, was pretty upset by it. Wound up in the care of some psychiatrist, got into a little bit of trouble. How bad, I don't know because his juvenile records are sealed now. There was some information not sealed about an investigation into child abuse, though. I couldn't find out much about it except I traced that he was in therapy for a few years. So was Jordan."

"Jordan?"

"In therapy, yeah. And a little checking told me he also was involved with an abuse case that might have involved his mother and another man."

"Hey, you're losing me."

"Figured I would. That's not that important right now. Back to our friend Caesar."

"Okay."

"He was sent to a very expensive private prep school. When the kid got into trouble, it was over there in some small town in New Mexico where they lived. Anyway, after the kid blew it there, Emily sent him to Seattle to live with his real dad. I guess he hated it here, hated the dad, and things really didn't get any better. That's when he got mixed up with Jordan."

"Man, you've been busy," Phillip said. "So what else have you found?"

"Bet you didn't know Caesar and Jordan went to the same private high school together, and that they were president and vice president of the computer club. They also took martial arts classes together, volunteered at the silkworm exhibit together, and went on a few trips together. They were pretty inseparable. They even hired a private detective to help find Jordan's mother after she left."

"What?"

"She didn't want to be found is what I hear. But the good news is she's not dead."

"Was Jordan told?" Phillip asked.

"He only knows that his mother is alive and wants to be left alone, according to the detective. There's a strange history there between Jordan and his mom as I was telling you. Lots of issues to clear up."

"And she wants to be left alone. That's gotta hurt."

"Yeah," Mark agreed, "it isn't exactly wonderful when your best friend, perhaps lover, moves half a country away from you either at the same time." Mark took another sip of his drink. "Did you manage to have a little fun on your trip, or was it all doom and gloom?"

"I had a lot of fun, Mark. Patricia turned out to be as wonderful as I thought she was."

"Glad to hear it."

"And you," Phillip asked, "did you propose yet?"

"I will. I'm gonna do it. Honest!"

Phillip just shook his head.

"Oh, don't you dare start with me."

"Wouldn't dream of it," Phillip laughed. "So, any idea where Jordan might be?"

"Hobart's had all kinds of folks looking for him the last twenty-four hours. Jordan didn't have a lot of friends, but he's got money. In addition to his father's credit cards, he's even got an offshore bank account. Transferred ten grand into an account just a few days ago."

"You're kidding!"

"Nope. And here's what else we know about him. He's extremely bright. He skipped a grade in school, started taking college courses when he was seventeen, carries a double major. He's also a third or fifth degree black belt in a couple of martial arts styles. After Caesar moved away, though, he became completely withdrawn."

"You planning to write a whole book on this guy?"

"I actually didn't spend all that much time finding this stuff out," explained Mark. "A few phone calls is all. This detective guy they hired told me he knew who Jordan was because he collects comic books."

"Of course, I follow that logic perfectly," Phillip said with a sigh.

"Apparently, when Jordan was twelve or thirteen, he created a comic book hero and someone paid him ten grand for the rights it."

"Wow!"

"Yep. The company put out ten or so comics in the series, but they went bust and folded. So this series of comics became very collectable and is worth a few bucks now. The series is called *Bishamon*."

"What was that?"

"You heard me right. Bishamon. Japanese god of war."

The two men looked at each other for a moment. "And that's everything I can tell you," Mark said.

"That's a lot. Listen, I've got to get some things off my computer."

"Tonight?"

"No time like the present. Right before I left Taos, Caesar broke into Patricia's house and erased her hard drive. I think Jordan and Caesar are working together, Mark. And Jordan goes by at least a few names I know of—Silky, Bishamon, Crane, and who knows what else. Patricia got a couple of very disturbing letters from Bishamon which she shared with me. I sent you copies of those. I'm going to print them out so we can talk to your friend Hobart about them. We figured out that Caesar has been hanging around the chatrooms using the name NastyOlGeezer and maybe even some other names, too, who knows."

"I'll tell you what, I'll see if I can't get Hobart to come with me out to your place tomorrow."

"That would be perfect. I'd like to get back to Taos as soon as possible."

"I understand."

Before he left, Phillip told Mark what a beautiful place Taos was, and how much in love he was.

"You've got it bad, pal!" Mark joked.

"And you don't?"

"Apparently not like that!"

An hour later, Phillip was driving through Snoqualmie Pass on I-90 on his way home, recalling the rest of that conversation: On the radio, Van Morrison was singing "Bright Side of the Road," whose lyrics seemed so appropriate:

From the dark end of the street
To the bright side of the road
We'll be lovers once again
On the bright side of the road

Little darling come with me
And help me share my load
From the dark end of the street
To the bright side of the road

When Phillip got home, he parked in front of the house instead of pulling all the way into the garage. He grabbed his bags and went inside. He'd lived alone for quite a while, yet it somehow felt emptier than when he'd left.

Phillip flipped on the lights and headed for his computer to check his e-mail. He could feel the hairs on the back of his neck stand straight up. He stayed perfectly still and listened for any sound that might reveal an intruder in his house. He jumped when he heard a noise to his right. *It's just the breeze, you jerk!* Phillip took several slow, quiet steps toward his computer. Across the keyboard lay a small branch of mulberry leaves.

He backed away and began moving cautiously from room to room, opening doors and searching as thoroughly as he could. He even pulled down the ceiling ladder and went into the attic to make absolutely certain that whoever had been in his home was now gone.

Then it hit him. Maybe whoever it was wanted only to do to his computer what had been done to Patricia's. He quickly returned to his office and turned on his computer, fully expecting to see that his hard drive had also been erased. When his computer booted up, however, he found everything seemed to be just as he had left it. On closer inspection, however, he discovered that the e-mail messages Patricia had forwarded to him from Bishamon were missing. And several other files had been erased as well.

Whoever it was had all the time in the world to go through every one of my damned files—and my whole fucking house, too! Phillip felt suddenly exposed, and very angry.

It was after midnight. Phil picked up his phone and quickly dialed Sylvia's number. After several rings produced no answer, he hung up and called Patricia. *I knew she would never stay...*

"Hello?" her tired voice answered.

"Shshshs," Phillip said. "I know it's very late, I just wanted to let you know that I got home safe and sound."

"Mmm, Phillip. I'm so glad you called." The sleepiness making her voice sound even warmer than usual.

"I wasn't sure if you would be at home or at Sylvia's."

"Sylvia's in the next room. She didn't want to leave me alone tonight," Patricia quickly reassured him.

He smiled. "Well, baby, you get back to sleep. I just wanted to tell you how much I love you and that we'll be together again very soon."

"Mmmm, I love you, too, baby."

"Good night, sweet dreams baby." Phillip quickly hung up the phone and sighed loudly. *Damn this is hard!*

There was another phone call he needed to make. He picked up the phone and dialed his friend's number.

"Mark, its Phil."

"Ah, I was just turning in. You got home okay then?"

"Yeah. My place was broken into, Mark." Phillip explained to his friend that he believed Jordan had broken into his house, found some files on his computer, and then erased them. "This took a little time to do Mark, so he either knew I wasn't home or he wasn't worried about me catching him in the act."

"How would he have known you were out of town?"

"Our friend Caesar, I would guess," Phillip said. "Caesar saw me on Sunday at a restaurant with Patricia. He knew exactly who I was and more than likely why I was there. My guess is that Caesar must have reported to Jordan."

"And this Caesar is the kid you think was tampering with Patricia's computer?"

"Yeah, that's right. Listen, I'm gonna turn in. I've checked all around and the place is safe.

"All right. I'll see you tomorrow afternoon."

"Sounds like a good plan, Mark. I'll talk to you tomorrow."

Phillip tried to relax. Tomorrow was going to be a busy day and he needed his wits about him. He was very tired and knew as soon as he could unwind a bit that he would sleep. So, he put one of his favorite CDs on—Joe Sample's *Rainbow Seeker*—and stretched out on the couch and closed his eyes. It didn't take long for him to get lost in the music. He drifted off while "Melodies of Love" was playing.

The next morning, he sat on his deck with his coffee and listening to the river tumble by. He was more than a little disappointed that he hadn't caught a glimpse of the small deer. He thought of Sarah and hoped that she was at peace. He thought of Mary and the conversation he had to have with her. As he went into the house to refill his coffee mug, the phone rang.

When he first picked it up there was no answer.

"Phillip Craven?" inquired the strange sounding nasal voice on the other end of the phone.

Within a few moments, Phillip realized that the strange voice, which still sounded like a very bad imitation of Peter Lorre, was most likely Jordan. Where was he calling from? The bastard was taunting him now. Phillip got him to agree to answer a few questions.

"Are you the person that was in my house recently?" Phillip asked. He waited and realized that his silence was verifying the answer.

"Where are you calling from? Seattle?"

"Oh, you ask too many questions," the caller stated rather tersely.

Phillip didn't want to show the caller how scared he actually was, so he forced himself to chuckle. It would be better to keep him on the line as long as possible, try and get him to say something and give Phillip an indication of where he might be or was he was planning on doing next.

"Well, you said I could ask you a question." The response was one Phillip would hear several times.

"I'm playing a funny sort of game with you, but it's not a joke, Phillip Craven." A moment later the phone went dead.

Phillip again felt very vulnerable. Jordan, he realized, might have murdered his own father, most likely broke into his house while he was out of town, and probably told Caesar to break into Patricia's house and erase the hard drive on her computer. Phillip had never owned a gun, nor kept one in his house, but he wished there were one nearby now!

The next call was from Sheriff Conway telling him that there had been a gruesome murder and he needed Phil to take the necessary pictures for him. Phil hadn't done any forensic photography work in a few months, but he was happy to oblige. Besides, it would give him a chance to talk a little to Leo about what had been occurring with Jordan and his friend Caesar.

"Prepare yourself for this one, Phil. It's bad," Leo said. He also told Phil that the victim had been decapitated. Phillip had agreed to meet Leo on one of the paved roads near where the murder had taken place.

He was sipping his coffee, about to go back out onto the deck for a few minutes, when the phone rang again! Three phone calls in rapid succession was a rarity, and Phil snatched up the phone, almost annoyed at the interruption.

"Hello," he managed to say in a normal tone of voice. In a moment, he realized that it was Patricia on the other end and she was upset and scared. She started in by trying to explain to him that Jordan was there! Phillip could hardly believe what he was hearing her say. He wanted to tell her that Jordan couldn't possibly be there because he had been at his house and had actually just called him a few minutes ago!

But...wait a minute! Jordan could have been in his house *yesterday*. Or the *day before* for that matter and he certainly could have called from practically anywhere!

"Trish, are you in any danger right this minute? Is he in the house?"

Patricia explained that she was sure she saw him outside, in the street. She had brought the flowers inside, flowers that she thought might possibly have been from him, but then she saw the mulberry branch and knew that the flowers weren't from him at all.

"What was that, sweetheart? What did you just say?" He'd heard exactly what she'd said, but wished he hadn't.

"The mulberry branch, Phil. We don't have mulberry trees around here, and nobody would put something like that in a nice arrangement.

Don't you see, Phillip?!" Her voice sounded like she might possibly be near hysteria.

Phillip swallowed hard. His eyes were shut and he was rubbing his knuckles against his forehead, waiting and hoping that this nightmare would come to an end. Of course, he knew what she was saying to him. Mulberry branches—just like the ones that were lying on his keyboard right now. Mulberry branches, like the ones used by silkworm breeders. Mulberry leaves were the silkworms' preferred cuisine. *Silk worms. Silky. Jordan. Gordon. Patricia needs me right now and I am completely helpless! Fuck!*

Patricia was about to read to him what was written on the card. She had not been able to read it earlier because she said she'd tossed her glasses down when she went to answer the door. He was trying to get this all straight. That was when she must have thought she'd seen Jordan.

"Go ahead, baby. It's okay. Just read it to me, Trisha." Phillip was demanding calmly, his mouth bone dry.

"It says: Remember the spoils of Sleepy Hollow. And it's signed: Ichabod Crane."

Phillip could barely breathe, and he had his hand over the receiver so Patricia couldn't hear him gasping for air. He hadn't told her about Caesar breaking into her house, or about the break-in at his own home, nor about his conversation with Mark, nor the fact that Toji was dead. God, there was so much happening way too fast! He was sure he couldn't tell her these things right now. Not while she was alone and in the state she was in. Not on the telephone anyway.

"He wants to scare us, baby. Frighten us." Somehow he managed to keep his voice sounding calm and collected for her. "We've got to be strong Patricia. You've got to hold yourself together, okay? We've got some time or he wouldn't have sent you those flowers. He's not going to do anything right now because he's enjoying all of this too much and if he tipped his hand now then his sick little game would be all over."

There was an uncomfortably long pause. "Trisha, did you hear me?"

"Yes." Her voice sounded weak and miles away.

"Patricia? Where's Bill or Sylvia right now?" He asked this with some annoyance. *She was not supposed to be alone, dammit*! Bill had promised him that she would be with one of them at all times whether she liked it or not!

"Oh, they just wouldn't leave me alone and I was tired and I finally kicked Sylvia out of the house this morning so I could get some work done. I'm really behind at the store, Phillip. You understand, don't you?" She was near tears and was certain she wasn't hiding it very well.

"Listen to me, Trisha. Please go over to Sylvia's. And after you get there, call Bill, okay?" Phillip chose his words carefully and requested this of her as tactfully as he dared.

"I will, Phillip. But not right this minute. Bill is over there right now, and I'm almost positive that he's proposing to her. I can't ruin this moment for them, baby. Bill told me about his plans last night after we got home from taking you to the plane."

Phillip could hear the excitement in her voice and that gave him some reassurance that she was okay. He didn't have much time to talk. He wanted Patricia out of her house as soon as possible and over with Sylvia. "Then promise me that you'll go over there as soon as Bill leaves, okay?"

"I will, baby. Trust me, I'm scared too."

He cursed himself for not disguising his fear very well. "Okay, I've got to go, Trisha. I'm running late. God, I hate to go now, baby." He didn't even try to conceal the desperation in his voice. His words were quick and choppy. He was thinking about Patricia, about all the things Mark had told him last night, about his conversation with Trent and the nasty business at hand now with Leo Conway. Phil needed to go out to his garage workroom and get a couple of lenses that he might need to take the photos of the body and the crime scene.

Patricia's voice broke through his thoughts. "I know Phillip. So on the count of three, I am going to hang up. I've got work to do and so do you. Life can't stand still while this lunatic plays games, baby. No matter how dangerous they are or how sick he is. You're right. He is just having his own sick fun now. We are going to be fine, just like you said. I am positive now that he fully intended for me to see him, just to make his game more fun for him. Now listen up, you cutie! I love you, I'm thinking about you every second and I know we will see one another soon. So, here goes. *One...two...three.*" The line went dead before Phil could say anything. He'd never been more relieved about anything in his life than the silence that greeted him at the end of the line.

The night before when he had come in so late, he'd left his car outside the house and hadn't noticed that the overhead garage door was open. *He* hadn't opened it, he was certain of that. Most of the time he used the small side door entrance to the garage to go in and out. It occurred to Phil that maybe Jordan decided he needed to get into the garage for some reason.

As he stepped into the darkness, his eyes were not yet used to the shadows. He could hear the buzzing sound of too many horseflies. There was a dank, musky animal smell which was almost overpowering. His eyes adjusted slowly as he scanned the windowless room.

Suddenly Phillip gasped and let out a short yell. There, in the middle of the floor where he normally would have parked his vehicle, was the body of a mutilated deer. Most likely the same deer he eagerly awaited each morning and late afternoon while he languished on his deck.

Phillip must have shut his eyes the instant that he saw the animal, for when he forced himself to look again he realized to his horror that it's head was missing. It had been decapitated.

When he stumbled into the darkroom to get his lenses he also instinctively picked up one of his backup cameras, loaded it with film and proceeded to take several photos of the animal. He wasn't exactly sure why he was doing it, but he reasoned that the killing of this deer was a crime and he would take photographs of the scene. It was purely instinct, he realized later.

By the time he pulled to the side of the road at the spot where he was supposed to meet Leo Conway, he was running a good fifteen minutes late. And a few minutes later, when Leo was leading him down the crushed gravel road, Phillip realized they were driving very near where Mary lived. Then, as if the nightmare of the last few hours were not horrific enough, they turned and were approaching her house.

Everything seemed to move in slow motion from there. Phillip's senses were alternating between over-keen and totally numb. As Leo's car turned off the road and crawled into the large clearing in front of Mary's modified A-frame, Phillip began to silently pray to God like he'd never prayed before. This couldn't be happening! Then he prayed that he didn't actually see the bright yellow crime scene tape stretched across Mary Foreston's front porch. He prayed that he was having a horrible nightmare and he would soon wake from it.

Somehow he managed to hold himself together, finding a way to disconnect from his emotions and fear and go through the motions of taking pictures of the grisly scene. The one thing he forced himself to believe was that Mary wasn't tortured and didn't suffer. Her head had been cleanly removed, possibly with a very sharp sword. *Bishamon. Martial Arts. Sword.*

Phillip tried to remember something from his experience with the martial arts. The master he had studied under for several years in California was Korean, but had studied with both Chinese monks and Japanese masters. Phillip remembered discussing the Samurai with him at great length. Phil's skill with the bow and the long wooden staff had impressed the master, and comments were frequently made that Phil would have made an excellent Samurai. This led to Phil's interest in the movie field and his love for Japanese Samurai movies and then to his love of the Tachi.

Tachi was the long, curved blade created hundreds of years ago by Japanese sword makers. It was worn proudly by the highest members of the Samurai class and royalty as symbols of status. Today, they are used purely for ceremonial purposes. Once they were forged out of the finest materials and in skilled hands Tachi were among the deadliest weapons ever made.

Phillip remembered seeing one of the finely crafted forty-inch Tachi swords hanging on the wall in Toji's condo. It was sheathed in a stunning rosewood scabbard with light blue braiding about the grip and mounts. It had a silver guard and was a remarkable showpiece.

Phillip doubted that it was authentic, since those would most likely be in museums, but he had seen reproductions of the swords being sold for thousands of dollars.

The Tachi, the Katana, the Wakizashi, and the Tanto were all swords of medieval Japan. Those were the dark ages of Japan, a time when few from the outside world were allowed into its closed and private feudal society. That type of society had existed far longer in Japan than in most of the rest of the world.

Remembering and thinking of anything but taking pictures of Mary Foreston had kept Phil somehow together and gratefully functioning. He nearly fell apart in front of Leo right afterward, however, but held on to his sanity and kept his emotions in check a little longer.

An hour later, Phillip stumbled back into his own house, ran to his kitchen sink, and splashed cold water in his face. *This was not happening! This could not be happening! First Alma…Mary…the deer. NO…oh god NO! Kitty didn't just get old.*

Phillip picked up the phone and called Patricia. The phone rang. No answer. His heart was racing. He couldn't stop thinking about the note Patricia had read to him just hours before, the one that had come with the flowers and said something about Sleepy Hollow and Ichabod Crane.

Why doesn't she answer? Then he took out his wallet and found Bill Conner's card and quickly dialed the number for the Taos County Sheriff's Office. Busy. *No fucking way!* He tried again. Still busy. His body was shaking, and he was slightly dizzy. He pushed the redial button. The call went through.

"Amy, is that you?!"

"This is Amy, yes."

"This is Phil Craven, Amy. I was with Patricia Ridgeway…"

"Yes, Mr. Craven. How may I help you?"

"I can't reach Patricia…"

"Patricia?" interrupted Amy."

"Yes! I need to know if she's all right. I need someone to check on her right away!"

"Patricia's fine, Mr. Craven. She's here right now with Deputy Sheriff Conner and Sergeant Riley."

"Oh, thank god!" Then he realized what she'd actually said. "She's there? At the station? What's she doing there, Amy? There's something wrong, isn't there?"

"I'm sorry, Mr. Craven. There's a lot going on here. If you'll give me a number, I'll have someone call you as soon as possible. Patricia's here and she's fine."

After he told Amy where he could be reached, Phillip hung up the phone and let himself slide down the cabinets to the kitchen floor. Thoughts he'd fought to keep at bay suddenly flooded his brain. Something was very wrong. Patricia was definitely in very grave danger since he now knew that Jordan was capable of anything. Jordan felt that life had been cold and unfair to him, and he was now taking out his anger on anyone or anything who stood in his way.

Dear God, Please keep Patricia safe. Please just keep her safe.

When he finally got up from the floor, he saw the flashing red light on his answering machine. He pushed the play button and listened: *Phil, it's me. I'm not sure if I told you that I loved you before we hung up. Sweetie, I just wanted that to be the first thing you heard when you got home, okay? Call me when you get back in. And don't worry about calling, Trent is at Emily's or who knows where. It doesn't matter how late it is. I love you. And I miss you so much.* There was a slight pause, and then she continued: *You mentioned you were on your way to an appointment. I realized I didn't ask where you were going. Call me soon and tell me, okay?*

Phillip closed his eyes. He thought about Patricia. He knew now that he had to tell Leo Conway about his relationship with Mary Foreston. Tell him about what he had discovered in the last few months, about the murder in Taos, several months earlier. Tell him about the strange relationship that Jordan was having with Frank Garrett and about his friend Caesar and about how being rejected again by Frank had unleashed something horrible within Jordan Taisho. And he would confess to him about his relationship with Patricia, how it had evolved and why, and then prepare himself to sit in the judgment seat that he knew was justified.

Maybe Jordan had an elaborate plan to somehow reunite with his friend Caesar through his deception with Frank Garrett. Maybe he'd genuinely fallen in love with Frank while he was masquerading as the female Silky. Phillip's head was throbbing. Thoughts, memories, worries, and trying to remember all the things he should be doing. It was time to call Leo Conway.

After he called Leo, he sat down to wait. The phone rang again. This time, it was Trent Ridgeway. He explained that Amy had found him as he was leaving the station to follow the ambulances to the hospital. She'd told him that Phillip had called. Trent knew that he should be the one to call him and let him know that Patricia was all right. She and Bill Conner had just been taken to the hospital as a precaution. Brenda Riley was with her, and would stay even after he got there.

"Hospital? What the hell is going on, Trent? Tell me now!" Phillip demanded.

"They just left with her for the hospital, but she's okay. That's the truth, Phil. She's not hurt."

Phillip felt suddenly drained of all energy and his weak voice reflected it. "What do you mean, she's not hurt? What's going on, Trent?"

"Phil... There was a long pause. Phillip could hear Trent breathing into the phone.

"Goddamn it, Trent, what is it?"

"Sylvia was murdered sometime this morning." Trent's voice was barely above a whisper.

"What?!"

"Sylvia has been killed, Phillip," Trent said. "Patricia found her body a few hours ago."

"Oh, my god!" Phillip's head was spinning. "Are you sure Trisha's okay?"

"Yes. Nothing happened to Patricia."

"Then why are they taking her to the hospital?" Phillip's voice was rising.

"For shock, they told me. The paramedic I talked to told me she'd be okay," Trent added quickly.

Phillip braced himself against the counter. His legs felt like rubber.

"You there, Phil?"

"Yeah, I'm here."

You gotta be strong, pal. Pull yourself together. C'mon now, don't panic.

"I'll call you as soon as I find out exactly what's going on and make sure that she's okay, Phil."

"Thanks, Trent, I really appreciate it. Actually, I don't really know what to say."

"It's the least I can do."

"I think I'm coming back to Taos as soon as I can get a flight," Phillip said. "Any chance you could pick me up?" Phillip asked. "I know I shouldn't really ask you..." He stopped mid-sentence. "Damn! I wasn't thinking, you said they were taking Bill to the hospital? What happened to him? Is he okay?"

"Bill was in shock, too. He wasn't hurt—physically, that is. Apparently he'd been at the house earlier in the day and then left. He walked in only minutes after Patricia did this evening. He's not hurt, no."

The space between Trent and Phillip was momentarily filled with silence.

"Of course, I can pick you up at the airport, Phil. Just let me know when and I'll be waiting. It would mean a lot to Patricia if you were here."

"Trent?" Phillip said. "Thank you."

"You're welcome, Phil."

"Let me have your number. I'm going to try and get a non-stop flight to Albuquerque, but I'll probably have to go through LAX or Burbank again."

"There's a flight that leaves SeaTac at eleven. It's not non-stop, but I can book you on that, if you'd like," an airline reservation agent was telling him. It was already nearly nine o'clock.

"I'll take it."

After booking the reservation, Phillip called Trent. "That means I'll be getting in at five in the morning your time. This is asking a great deal of you, Trent. Isn't there a shuttle or something I can take from Albuquerque to Taos at that hour?"

"Don't worry about. It's okay. I'll be waiting for you when you get off the plane."

"All right, if you're sure. Say, do you know how long they're keeping her in the hospital?"

"No, not yet. But I hope by the time you get here I can tell you a lot more."

"Me, too. Meanwhile, she'll be safer there than anywhere else," said Phillip.

"Safer? You think she's in danger, don't you Phil?"

"I honestly don't know. I mean, I don't think she is, Trent. I really don't think she is. But hell, I'm not a hundred percent sure about anything anymore. I'll fill you in on some more things when I get there. Meanwhile, just make sure they keep Patricia in the hospital until I get there. I'm sure she's a nervous wreck and it's a good place for her to be."

Phillip unzipped his duffel bag and replaced the dirty clothes with some clean ones. Then he marked the rolls of films he had taken earlier that day and put them on the kitchen counter, and called Leo to come pick them up. He was sure he was forgetting something, but reasoned there were probably going to be a lot of things he was forgetting under the circumstances.

Leo Conway saw the packed bags by the front door. "Christ, man, you going on another trip already?"

"Yeah, in just about two seconds. But first, I have a lot of things to tell you. And then I'm going to ask you to wait for Mark and a detective named Hobart that'll be with him and explain some things to them. "And before I forget it, the film I took is on the counter. If you would, drop them off at the paper and they'll develop them for you."

Leo blinked. "Man, slow down here! You been drinking that espresso stuff again?"

Phillip took a deep breath, and then proceeded to tell Leo everything that had happened in the past few months. As Leo absorbed all this information, it occurred to him that he shouldn't let Phillip go anywhere, and he told him that. Leo explained that there was enough circumstantial evidence here to make him a suspect in Mary Foreston's murder. For one thing, he was involved with another woman and Mary could have found out and created a scene. Leo told him candidly that he thought it odd that Phillip had never mentioned his involvement with Mary before.

"What are you talking about?" Phillip demanded to know.

"It's a good thing I trust you," Leo said.

"Jesus Christ, Leo, I don't have time for this!"

"*You* don't have time?"

"No, I don't!" Phillip could see that Leo was quite serious, and so he softened his tone. "I'm sorry, Leo. All I meant was that I have to make a flight. I need you to understand enough of what I've been telling you to explain this to Mark and the detective."

"And if they don't show, do I assume I've just let a deranged murder suspect get away?" Leo asked. He wasn't smiling.

Phillip glared at him. Leo couldn't hold a straight face any longer and tried to cover his smile by coughing.

"Fuck you. Leo! I'm glad you find something humorous in all this.

"Phil, you're gonna drive yourself over the edge if you don't relax a minute, ya know. You're no hero, Craven. You're only human like the rest of us."

"Hey, you've got a lot more experience being a hero than I do," Phillip countered.

"Maybe once I thought I was. But that was a long time ago."

"That's true. If heroes don't wind up dead, they end up getting sued by greedy lawyers anyway, don't they?"

"Boy, that's the truth."

"Leo, I'm sorry for having to take off like this and leave things in such a mess."

"Oh, shut the hell up. I'm used to picking up messes, especially yours!"

"You haven't seen the garage," Phil muttered.

"Oh Christ..."

When Phillip was at Los Angeles Airport waiting to catch his connecting flight to Albuquerque, he tried to remember if he had told Leo everything. *I know I told him about Caesar and Emily, but did I mention NastyOlGeezer and Silky and Bishamon? When we walked out to the garage and I showed him the deer, did I tell him about seeing the sword at Toji's condo? Shit!*

His mind was a maelstrom of facts and speculations. He was trying to do too much without having enough time to sort through everything. He had hit the pavement running, several days ago, and hadn't slowed down since. He looked at his watch. Mark should be arriving in Cle Elum about now, and Leo would fill him in on the latest developments. Hopefully, Mark would then explain to Detective Hobart what Phillip believed was going on. Regardless, it was out of his hands at this point.

"So, you are saying that Patricia didn't know that Caesar was in her home messing with the computer?" Trent asked as they made their way north to Taos.

"No, she didn't."

He was trying to understand what was going on. "Why was Sylvia killed then?"

"I don't know, Trent," Phillip said. "Maybe Jordan or Caesar was in Sylvia's house and she caught them there." It was possible, Phillip reasoned. He didn't know why Mary Foreston had been killed either. There may not even be particularly logical reason for their deaths.

Maybe that's why Agatha Christie is so entertaining to read. You can suspend your disbeliefs and enjoy the fictional exploits of Hercules Poirot as he figures out, in the last couple of chapters, who was guilty and why, and all the loose ends would be tied up. You enjoy it, because you know it's fiction.

"I'm trying to understand this," Trent said.

"I am, too."

"You mean that this Jordan and Caesar are related?"

Phillip nodded. "Half-cousins, I guess."

"Bizarre."

Phillip had to agree. The entire last year of his life could be summed up with that word. If he'd not gotten involved with Patricia, would things be worse or better than they were right now, he wondered?

The time passed quickly, and soon Trent was pulling into the parking lot of the Piñon Inn.

"Here we are," he said, as he turned off the truck. "I booked you a room here, too."

"I really appreciate everything you've done, Trent."

"Phil, I have something that belongs to you now." He reached inside his shirt and pulled something from around his neck. "It's a medicine bag. Patricia gave it to me when we married." Phillip took the small suede bag from Trent.

"I'm not sure if it's in the proper Indian tradition for me to pass this along to you like this," Trent continued, "or if it's the way it's supposed to be done. But if feels like the right thing for me to do. It's my choice," Trent said.

"I'm not sure I understand."

"Oh, I'm not sure I do either. It's a Native American thing. There are special stones, herbs, animal bones, fetishes and other things in here that represent Patricia. You basically have part of Patricia's soul in that bag. By taking it from me, you are accepting responsibility for it. And for her, actually."

Phillip swallowed hard. Regardless of how much he believed in what he was being told, the gesture was one of the most selfless things anyone had ever done for him. In essence, Trent was blessing Phillip's relationship with Patricia, sharing with him something intimate and very special.

"Patricia has no idea I'm doing this," Trent said. "You'll have to pick your moment to tell her you have this. And it might not be proper for me to give it to you at all. I'm not sure. But I do know that once it was given to me, it was my responsibility to treat it with the utmost respect. I failed at that, Phillip. I failed miserably." He was close to tears. "It's to be worn as close to the body as possible at all times. Legend has it that not to do so could result in severe punishment. You can bet I never tested it!" It was the first moment approaching levity in the two hours since Trent had picked him up at the airport.

"If I remember how this works," Trent continued, "you probably shouldn't open the bag on your own. You wait for her to open it with you and tell you what all the things mean. If I'm not mistaken, these have all been given to her specifically and blessed by the elders in a special ceremony. They are sort of like spirit guides, and she shares them so that those she loves can be protected and led along the same path that she is. She has an identical one, as well. Well, the bags are identical, but what's inside them isn't. These things are the guardians of her spirit. I am afraid I didn't take very good care of what was entrusted to me. You do a better job, okay?"

Phillip watched as Trent reached into the pocket of his leather vest and pulled out a small piece of paper. He held on to it for a few seconds, touching it like you might something very fragile, and then gave it to Phillip. "I was at the hospital all night," explained Trent. "I went in a few times and checked on Bill and had some coffee with Sergeant Riley. That reminds me. She's posted at the hospital, by the way. I meant to tell you that, I'm sorry." Phillip nodded. Obviously he was not the only one who thought she and Bill might need some protection.

"Anyway, while Patricia was sleeping, I opened the drawer in a cabinet next to her bed and saw that one of the nurses had put her medicine bag there. I don't know why, but I decided to open it. I guess just to compare it to mine, I don't know. In all these years I've never looked inside of it. I want you to read this, and then I'm going to put it back in her bag and put it back in the cabinet. I don't know when it was written; but by the yellowed paper, I'd say it was quite a while ago."

Trent watched as Phillip carefully unfolded the paper. Written, in faded script and in someone's hand other than hers were the following words:

Where is love?
At night when stars hang in the sky
My heart is so empty that I silently cry.
What did I do from where I last came,
To bring so much loneliness, sadness, and pain?

I reach out to others for
Answers or truth.
But they are so lost that their thoughts
Are misconstrued.

If only I could remember.
So I could search for the eyes,
Of the soul who knows what
I'm feeling inside.

I review my life from the day
I was born
What am I doing here,
I don't belong.

I need to smile! I need to laugh!
I need to bring back the
Beauty from somewhere in the past.

Oh, Great Spirit, I humbly beg,
Give me the strength to move
Straight ahead.

I need to find him, I know he is near.
I can feel his breath very
Close to my ear.

Oh, please let him come,
Let him come soon,
Before I wither and die in the
Dust and the gloom.

I need to laugh!
I need to sing!
I need to feel love
—Just once—
Then I'll go
On a wing.

"I don't know what to say, Trent."

"You don't need to say anything. Accepting this is all you need to do for now. It feels like the right thing for me to do. I've made a lot of mistakes, but this isn't one of them. It's the right thing to do. You are required to wear it, Phillip. She's going to be an important part of your life from now on."

"She already is."

Phillip placed the medicine bag around his neck.

"I know, but you must understand something else. She'll always be a part of my life, too. And now it's time to get you to your room so you can get a little sleep."

"I can't do that, Trent. I've got to go to the hospital. You were there all night, and then made that trip down to get me. You're the one who must be exhausted. If you'll let me borrow your truck and tell me how to get there, I'd be grateful."

Chapter Forty-one

"Here you go, Patricia, take a sip of this."

She guessed the woman to be in her early sixties. She had beautiful white hair, a soft face, and a light-up-the-room smile. She was dressed in a pale yellow uniform and a tag with a happy face next to her name—Maxine. *I like Maxine*, she thought to herself. She'd already forgotten that Phillip was there. She sucked some of the cold water up through the straw. Her eyes started closing again.

"Oh, no you don't! If I can't sleep, you can't sleep!"

Patricia could hear her clearly. She just didn't feel like paying any attention to her. *This is weird. Now there's a man's voice.*

"Patricia, it's Phillip. You need to wake up, okay? Come on, wake up."

He was standing beside the bed now, holding her hand. He leaned down and kissed her forehead. While he was bent over her, he whispered her name again and again. She began to stir.

He turned to watch Maxine walk out of the room and as she pulled the door closed behind her, he caught a brief glimpse of Brenda Riley walking down the hallway. When he turned back toward the bed, Patricia was sound asleep again. This time, he couldn't wake her.

He heard someone come in the room and turned around to see Brenda. "How's she doing?" she asked quietly.

"I don't know for sure. She's just having trouble waking up." He held Patricia's hand carefully so as not to touch the IV tube taped to the top of her hand.

"I imagine. They gave her some pretty high-powered stuff to knock her out for a while. Did you hear what happened? Why we brought her here?"

"All I know is what I got from Trent. You were there, right? You can fill me in, if you don't mind." Phillip motioned for her to sit down.

"No, that's okay. You sit. I need to stand for a while anyway."

Brenda watched as Patricia turned her head in the direction of Phillip's voice, though her eyes never opened.

"I want to be careful what I say. I'm not sure how much she can comprehend in this state, and I don't want to upset her more than she already is," Brenda whispered.

Oh wonderful, now they'll know I'm listening.

"That's true. I just want to know basically what happened." Patricia didn't have to open her eyes to know that Phillip was looking at her.

Who was that now? Oh it's that Riley, Brenda Riley talking again, sounding different, almost like a human being. Maybe I was wrong about her. Or was it the drugs? Everything was fine.

"We got the call at the station about five-thirty. It was Bill and he said to send an ambulance to the Mondragon house. Amy talked to him and said that he sounded upset, but certainly not hysterical. I think he was in deep shock right from the beginning. I don't know how Patricia held out so long. It was almost as if Bill waited for her permission, because the instant he realized that we'd lost Patricia, Bill went limp in a matter of seconds." Brenda paused. "I've seen a few people in shock in the past. You can't predict how it will affect them.

Patricia felt herself slipping away now. Going back to sleep. *Phillip's still here. Good. I can feel him holding my hand. I don't want to sleep. I can't help it.* Phillip felt Patricia's hand go limp.

"Well, Bill and Patricia managed to get back to her house from Sylvia's, and that's where he called from. No one knew that, of course. So when officers and the ambulance arrived at the Mondragon's and no one was there, you can imagine the shock when they walked in."

"I don't want to, Brenda, but I can."

"Well, they called for backup and everyone who possibly could responded. I'd been on a domestic call and had just gotten back into my patrol car when the second call came in. When I arrived on scene it looked like total chaos. No one seemed to know what to do or where to look. I figured Bill had to have been over at Patricia's. I didn't know until I talked to Bill a little later, that it was Patricia who had actually discovered Sylvia in the first place. What made it worse was that Bud Richards was in town. Damn, there is so much to this story!" She was physically and mentally exhausted, and then she looked at Phillip's weary face. She wasn't even sure whom to feel sorrier for right now.

"I know. Just tell me about Patricia, okay?" He'd dropped his eyes and Brenda Riley wasn't sure, but she sensed it was perhaps to hide his emotions.

"We talked for a long while at the house. The two of them answered questions from every direction. Richards was a total jerk, of course. I knew that she was going into shock. She got ice cold. I should have insisted that we call a doctor right then and there, but I didn't. Then I'll be damned if

Richards didn't insist on taking them both down to the station for additional questioning. He had some idea they'd cooperate more if they were in a 'neutral atmosphere,' he called it. I should have stopped him, Phil. I know that now. I'm really sorry about that."

"I understand. It's hard to know what to do when situations get out of control. I'm sure you did everything you could, and if I'm not mistaken, you're responsible for Patricia and Bill being here now, right?"

"Yeah, but it was going to happen anyway, I just reacted first." Brenda took a very deep breath, and then went on.

"We took them to the station in separate vehicles, but arrived at approximately the same time. I had Patricia in the car with me. I kept trying to keep her talking, but I was losing her. She started talking about Trent, and not ever having children, and something about her grandmother, and she wanted to know if I was aware Carlos snored. I was getting pretty desperate by the time we pulled up to the back door. Richards was there waiting. He opened the passenger side door, almost lifted her out, and was ushering her inside before I realized what was happening. He'd slammed the car door before I had time to tell him to call for medical attention. Of course, there were media people around, and I know he just wanted to get her inside. When I got inside, there seemed to be a hundred people crowded around them in the hall. She and Bill were standing near the door to the interrogation room, and I heard Bud Richards tell someone to take Patricia in there while he took Bill to another room. First of all, that may be a wonderful rule if you think you have suspects, but these two had just shared a terrible experience. They weren't murder suspects, damn it! The instant someone started to force Patricia into that room, she panicked and started fighting them. Bill, out of pure instinct, broke away from the officer who had him partially down the hall. And when he started toward the interrogation room, Richards strong-armed him and yelled at him to calm down and hold himself together and act like a cop. If I'd been close enough, I would have hit him, Phillip! Swear to God, I would have hit the bastard!" She had to stop for a moment. Phillip turned away and brushed Patricia's hair from her face.

"I can't believe I wasn't there!" He rested his forehead on the cold railing of the bed. Brenda watched him for a moment. He suddenly felt very weak.

"Please go on, Brenda. I'm sorry."

"Don't be sorry. Don't ever be sorry for loving someone, Phillip."

Phillip nodded and forced himself to stand up. As he did so, he felt dizzy and he half fell against the pale blue wall. Phillip tried to talk, but his mouth was dry and the words he was thinking in his head weren't going anywhere.

"Sit down, Phil! I'll be right back."

Brenda ran out into the hall and called for assistance from a nurse sitting at the station just outside Patricia's door.

"Here, drink this Mr. Craven." Someone was handing him something that looked like orange juice. A few seconds later, he was able to focus again. It was Maxine. "Okay, handsome! To the cafeteria with you two, right this minute! You both need something besides coffee, and they'll be closing the food service line in just a few minutes."

"No. I'm sorry, I don't want to leave her alone."

"You won't be leaving her alone. I'll be with her. Now scoot. Ms. Riley, remember what I said, okay?" Maxine winked as Brenda tugged at his sleeve and helped him from the room.

Over his objections, Brenda ordered eggs, bacon, hash browns, and toast for the two of them and paid for it when they got to the volunteer Candy Striper at the register. "I owe you," Phillip said.

"You sure do. Only thing cheap about a hospital is their food. I think this was about a buck ninety-five. I'll bill you later, how's that sound?" They carried their trays to an empty table in the far corner of the cafeteria. "Now where the hell was I?"

"The asshole had taken Patricia to the station house."

"Yeah, that's right. Well, what happened next is based purely on assumptions I made from talking to a few people, Phillip. So it's just my opinion, okay?" She waited until he responded.

"It must have been the room that triggered her. Apparently that was the same room they had her in when Alma Garrett was murdered. Anyway, the instant Richards got her in there, all hell broke loose. I yelled at Amy to call the paramedics before I even realized that Bill had collapsed. By the time I got back to Patricia, she was like a wild animal and even Richards had backed off. She'd gotten his gun somehow and was waving it around with one hand and demanding that someone get you. Hardly anyone, besides Richards, Amy, and me, had any idea who she was talking about. Everyone cleared out until someone could figure out how to get the gun away from her. Richards, conquering hero that he is, was in the hallway yelling at me to do something before someone got hurt! I have to tell you, I can't wait to file this report, Phillip." Brenda took a couple bites of her food and continued.

"I opened the door and started moving slowly toward her and calling her name. I kept asking her to please give me the gun. It was like she didn't even see me. All she kept doing was asking for you. Then all of a sudden, she just sat down in the middle of the floor and laid the gun beside her. In a matter of seconds, they had her on a gurney and out the door.

"Anyway, that's where I ran into Trent. He was begging to go with Patricia in the ambulance, but they wouldn't let him. So he asked me to go with her. That's pretty much it, in sort of a nutshell, Phil. I'm so sorry about all of this. I truly am."

Phillip understood. "It's all going to be all right, Brenda. Thank you for everything you did. If you hadn't been there, there's no way of knowing what might have happened to Patricia. As far as I'm concerned, you saved her life."

"Thanks, Phil, but there's one more thing I have to talk to you about before we get interrupted. I know you and Bill are trying to clear Frank. I don't know the whole story. And quite frankly, I'm not sure I really want to know any more. But I found out something yesterday that you should know about."

"I'm all ears, Brenda."

"I'll be the first one to admit that I came to Taos with a bit of an attitude. I figured that since I was Richard's handpicked 'chick cop' that I could waltz in here and do whatever I wanted. I had some preconceived notions about Frank that, even when they were proved wrong, I wasn't willing to let go. And I also did some things behind Bill's back that could have caused a great deal of trouble. I don't even have the right to make apologies for what I've done, Phil."

He had to agree with her up to this point. "Go on," he urged.

"Richards thinks he has an ironclad case against Frank now."

"Ironclad? Bullshit! He can't have anything, Brenda, because there *is* nothing. He's bluffing."

She looked around to make sure she wasn't being overheard. "Without a lot of unnecessary detail, I'll just tell you that there is a young man by the name of Lucas Tafoya who works in the City Manager's office. Lucas and I were in the Academy together. Although he made it through, he just didn't have what it took to make a cop. So he wound up here as the assistant to the City Manager."

"Go on."

"Well, it seems that Lucas has a stepbrother who's a cop. Still following me?"

"Richards?"

"Bingo," she confirmed.

"Shit."

"Right. Well, Lucas has been asking me out for dinner ever since I got here, and I just haven't been interested. The kid is a damned sight better now than he was three years ago, but he's still a real geek. Tries too hard, has a chip on his shoulder, and drinks too much—which, incidentally, I only found out night before last. This next part is a little confusing, so I'll just give you the highlights.

"So, anyway, Phil, Bill teaches a martial arts class, right? Right. Lucas, for some reason, is the person in charge of all the keys to all the rooms that are for public use in the city hall complex. The gym is one of those rooms. Lucas has a key to it. Follow? Sure you do."

Brenda looked at Phillip to make sure he didn't have any questions before continuing. "Well, funny thing about all of this Alma Garrett investigation is that a murder weapon has never been found. No trace of a weapon. They've gone through Frank's house more times than I can count. So guess what Richards does day before yesterday morning? Don't guess, I'll tell you. He had me go outside with him to his patrol car. He opens the trunk and shows me something wrapped up in what looks like some kind of exercise mat. It's a god awful looking ornamental sword! He told me it was the weapon that killed Alma Garrett. Still with me?"

"I'm afraid so. Go on."

"Now, mind you, there wasn't a drop of blood on it that I could see. It was just as shiny and clean as it could be. I asked him where the hell he'd found it. And with a totally straight face, he said that he'd just come from the campground where he'd found it buried not ten feet from where Alma's body was found. No shit, Phil. He pointed to this museum condition sword and told me he'd found it buried in the dirt, and said most likely it had been there since the murder."

"He was really planning on doing this, wasn't he, Brenda? Framing Frank for her murder?"

"Hold on, Phil, there's more. This is basically for your information, for when you present this entire thing to whomever you end up presenting it to. That was on Tuesday morning. I pretended to fall for the whole darn thing and was going to try to get a written report together and sit down with Bill before Richards had an opportunity to run to Santa Fe with this crock of shit. I ran into Lucas in the parking lot later that same day, and he made another valiant attempt to get me to go to dinner. I surprised the schmuck and said yes. Poor fool damned near wet all over himself!"

"Anyway, when I met Lucas after work, I lied and told him I'd left my purse in the gym a few nights before, and asked him if would he mind letting me in to get it. Hell, I'd never been in the gym before, so I had a heck of time acting like I knew where I was going. Of course, there was no purse in the gym, so then I told him that I bet it was locked up in an office or a security room or something. No problem, he tells me. He fumbled around until he found the key for the only room marked 'Private.' He opened the door and flipped on the light. It looked like an office for the coaches. And just as I suspected, hanging on the wall over a desk, were about eight or ten of these ornamental swords. They each had a special little rack. One rack was empty. That was all I needed to see."

"You can read the rest of the details in the report and save me the embarrassment of telling you. Basically, I got the bastard dead drunk on wine and...well, I sorta seduced him and then persuaded him to admit to me that he'd stolen the sword for Richards."

"You put all that in the report?"

"Well, not like that...no. I also didn't put in the report that I had a recorder running. For obvious reasons, I don't want to use that unless it's the only way to hang Richards. Then I don't mind hanging my ass out to dry. Literally." Brenda blushed slightly. "Lucas never did admit that he knew why Richards asked him to steal the sword," she continued, "and as stupid as the guy acts, it's possible he really didn't. A polygraph exam will determine if he's really that dumb. I am laying odds that once Richards produces this weapon out of thin air, it'll look like it's been buried for a long time. I have no idea how he plans to fake the other forensics that he'll need. It's my opinion that he's working on that as we speak."

"You've got this all down in a report, right? Written down, I mean?"

"Yeah, it's all there, Phil. Well, almost. There are a few details that I keep remembering. But for the most part, it's together, yes. There is one problem though that I can't handle and I don't know if you can either."

"What's that?"

"Frank Garrett. We now have another sensational murder case which is directly related to Frank. And no one has seen him in four days! It looks bad, Phil. If you know where he is, you need to have him materialize as soon as possible."

"I don't know where he is, Brenda, and that's the truth. But I might be able to find out."

"Bill knows, huh?" Brenda asked.

Phillip smiled. "I don't know if he does or not."

"You know, you're not very good at lying."

"I need to ask you a question, Brenda. I think I know the answer now, but I need to ask."

"Sure. What is it?"

"When you and Richards left the station and went to Santa Fe together, that wasn't to get an arrest warrant issued for Frank?"

"Whoa. Leave for Santa Fe together? I didn't go anywhere with Richards, Phil. I went to hand over my information to the head honchos at the state capitol. I wanted a warrant issued for Richards' arrest, not Frank's!

Richards was right on my ass, and what he handed over to them, I'm not sure. But no, Phil, I'll admit I'm slow—or just slow to admit a mistake maybe—but I knew beyond a shadow of a doubt that Frank was innocent by then. Why?"

Phillip pushed his chair away from the table. "No reason, really. Just renews my faith in mankind a little bit. I guess I've grown too cynical over the years, you might say. Oh, by the way, you ain't bad for a cop, you know that?" He winked and she started to blush.

He put his coffee cup down and stood up. "I'm sorry that I can't act more enthused about your information, Brenda. I hope you'll forgive me. You've done an incredible piece of police work, and there is so much that all of us owe you. But I can't even think about it right now. I've got to get back to Patricia."

Brenda stood up and gave him a quick, friendly hug. "Sure. Now get on up there! I'm going to peek in on Bill, and then I'll be right behind you."

When Phillip reentered Patricia's room, he could see that the nurse was sitting there, writing on some papers in her lap. Patricia was still sound asleep. "Hi there," the nurse greeted him. "You feel better?"

"Much, thank you. That was a good save."

"Hey, that's what I'm paid for." She smiled and walked over to check Patricia's pulse. "She's doing just fine. I think she'll be waking up here in a little while. Some people just have to sleep these drugs off, and she looks like she's one of them. I'll leave you two alone. Come and tell me if she wakes up, okay?" After Maxine left, he turned and saw Patricia looking at him.

"It's about time, sleepyhead. Welcome back! Did you have a nice trip?"

"Hi. When did you get here?" she asked groggily. Her eyes began to close and he was afraid he'd lose her again.

"Don't you dare go to sleep on me again! I've come a long way just to see you. Show a guy some respect, would ya?" He looked down at her and got tears in his eyes when he saw her smile at him. "Oh, baby, I've missed you!" He leaned down and gathered her in his arms and held her.

"Aha! I thought I heard voices behind this door!" Maxine poked her head in the room. "So, you must be Patricia! I'm Maxine and I'll be your nurse, until three that is. Then I get to lug this bag of bones home and some ol' ex-Marine drill sergeant will take my place. So I suggest you look alive and get your buns released from here as fast as you can!" She laughed heartily as she walked in carrying a tray of food.

"It's nice to meet you, Maxine. You were here earlier, weren't you? I sort of remember talking to you."

Bits and pieces of memory were just beginning to come back to her. Phillip had told her why she was here and, though she knew that what he said was true, she found it hard to believe. She watched Maxine remove lids from the dishes on the tray and stick a straw in a half-pint container of milk.

"I've been right here since you got all settled in yesterday, Mrs. Ridgeway. We're a bit shorthanded here this week, so I pulled a double shift. You own that bookstore down on the plaza don't you?" She raised Patricia's bed and fluffed her pillows.

"Yes, I do. I think I've seen you in there, haven't I? I apologize for not remembering you." Patricia's eyelids were getting heavy again, her words slow and deliberate.

"Uh-oh, keep those eyes open! Mr. Chippendale here is going to help you get this gourmet meal down, aren't you, handsome?" Maxine motioned for Phillip, but he was looking the other way. Brenda was standing in the doorway.

"Oops, waited too long. He's got another date! Run along and Mrs. Ridgeway and I will see how much of this whatever it is we can devour."

"I'll be right back. Brenda must need me for something. You be okay, baby?"

"Of course, she'll be okay! Scoot! But hurry back, I have real patients who need attending to." She laughed good-naturedly and Phillip kissed Patricia on the forehead and hurried out the door where Brenda explained to him that Bill wanted to see him. She led him to Bill's private room and let him go inside by himself.

"Hey there!" Phillip greeted him. "Say, you look pretty good." Under the circumstances, he really didn't know what else to say. Bill's eyes were sunken and he appeared to have aged twenty years in the past three days. Phillip thought of the plans that Bill had shared with him for his life with Sylvia. He had to clear a lump in his throat before he could go on.

"Of course, I do! I'm fine, shouldn't be here, don't want to be here!"

"I understand."

"There's too much to do for me to be lying around here like this, goddamn it!"

"And it will all get done," Phillip reassured him. "Let's use this time to think things through and not just react."

"I don't want to think right now. Bill suddenly had a look of incredible loneliness on his face and he was fighting back the tears. "Ah, shit!" Bill was embarrassed about the uncontrolled emotions pouring out of him. Phillip moved all the way into the room and closed the door.

"Sorry about this," Bill said, wiping his eyes.

"Nothing to be sorry about, Bill. Trust me, I'd be much worse off if I were in the same situation." Phillip watched as Bill collapsed back into his pillow and tears fell freely from his eyes.

"If you need to talk..." Phillip began.

"Shit." Bill wiped his eyes and tried to regain control of his emotions. "I need to talk with Frank. Did you tell Brenda that I know where he is?"

"No," Phillip said, "but she's not stupid."

"Damn!" Bill brushed yet more tears from his eyes.

"Bill, stop fighting this, will you?"

"I loved her so much, Phil."

Phillip handed him the box of tissues.

"Thanks. Patricia okay?"

"She's good," Phillip assured him.

"That's a relief! By the way, you know, Brenda somehow seemed different when I talked to her."

"You mean almost human?"

"That's it." Bill smiled.

"She's not only figured out that Bud Richards has a hair up his ass about Frank, but she's got proof that he's trying to fame Frank for Alma's murder."

"Are you serious?"

"Yeah. I had a long talk with her."

"Then I guess I wasn't such an ass for okaying her transfer here after all."

"We need to go pay Frank a visit and tell him what's been going on."

Phillip nodded. "You want to phone him?

"He doesn't have a phone. Talked to him yesterday for a few minutes though."

"After talking to Brenda, I don't think we have to worry about him being arrested."

"That's good." Bill sighed. "I really don't want to be here."

"Oh, I'm sure you don't," Phillip chuckled. "But it's a good place to be right now."

"You think?"

"We'll spring you from this joint as soon as we can."

While Phillip visited with Bill, Brenda Riley returned to Patricia's room.

"May I come in?" she asked.

"Sure, come on in," Patricia answered. "I've eaten about all of this wonderfully bland food that I can."

Maxine then handed Patricia several little white cups with a variety of tablets and capsules in them, and ordered her to swallow them down before she was allowed to have a "hen party."

"You sure look better than you did last night! Don't you think so, Maxine?"

"You two know one another?" Patricia was quickly becoming confused again.

"Oh, yes, Mrs. Ridgeway!" Maxine said as she picked up the meal tray. "We had a lovely night together watching you sleep."

"You were here last night, too?"

"Sure was! I'd have been hung if I hadn't been. Bill Conner kept telling me that it was his job to keep an eye on you, and since we didn't think it would be proper to let him roll his bed in here, I was appointed door monitor. He'd have been totally worthless, anyway. All he did was sleep, too! You two are the laziest folks I've run into in a long time!" Brenda Riley was trying to be light and casual, but she wanted to carefully nudge Patricia into remembering the events of yesterday that had led to her being in the hospital. The doctor had said that Patricia couldn't be released until she did. She and Maxine had devised a little test. Neither of them knew, however, that Phillip had already given Patricia some of the answers.

"I don't remember you being here, but I remember Trent. He was here, wasn't he?" Suddenly, Patricia felt as though the lights were dimming. "Maxine?" she moaned, her hand reaching out toward the yellow blur.

"Yes? What is it, love?" Maxine had already pressed the button to alert the nurses' station that she needed assistance.

"Will...you..." Her voice was fading. Maxine grabbed Patricia's wrist to take her pulse. Brenda stepped aside quickly as two other medical personal rushed in. One of them was pushing a cart with an array of electronic equipment.

"Will I what, Patricia? Talk to me, okay? What do you need? Don't you go to sleep on me here, okay?!" Maxine turned to Brenda and mouthed for her to go get Phillip. "Tell me what it is you want, Patricia," she continued. "Stay awake now. Phillip's on his way!"

Her eyes felt like they were wide open, but it was very dark. And although she could hear everyone talking, she had that floating sensation again. She was drifting. But she felt like she needed Maxine to open the door! *Can't anyone hear me?*

A doctor arrived from the emergency room and began issuing orders. Several more hospital personnel were going and coming quickly, and a lab tech was drawing several vials of blood. *Quit that! Somebody open the door, damn it. It's cold out there and my grandmother wants in.*

As Phillip raced down the corridor from Bill's room, he ran headlong into Trent, who was just arriving, flowers in hand, to visit Patricia. "Phil, whoa. You okay? What's wrong?" Then they turned the corner and saw hospital personnel running into Patricia's room.

"What's going on here?" Trent yelled at no one in particular. One of the nurses pushed them away from the door. Trent recognized the male nurses as having been on duty the night before. "What the hell is going on?" Trent demanded to know. "Please! I need to go in!"

Just as Phillip started to push on the door to go in, Brenda Riley stepped out into the hallway. Phillip grabbed her arm. "What happened? Is she all right? What's wrong?!" Phillip had felt just about as helpless as any human being can feel so many times in the last forty-eight hours, but this was the worst.

"I'm not sure what happened," Brenda started to explain. "I'd just walked back in from Bill's room. She seemed fine at first. We talked for a second, and the next thing I know, Maxine's calling for assistance. A doctor just came in and put something into her IV. That's all I know." Just then the doctor came out of the room with Maxine right behind him.

"Oh, Doctor Hudgins, this is Patricia's husband Mr. Ridgeway, and a friend, Mr. Craven."

"Gentlemen." He neither held out his hand nor smiled. "Mrs. Ridgeway is going to be just fine. She just had a relapse, that's all, and a slight reaction to some medication. It's just like in the case of the flu or pneumonia or anything of that nature, the relapse is oftentimes much worse than the original illness. I'm guessing that something once again triggered whatever it was that caused the original shock. It caused her brain to shut down part of her system to protect itself from harm. This is by no means unusual."

He turned toward Maxine. "Nurse, you gave her meds right before this episode, right?"

"Yes, sir."

"Did you or anyone else try to talk to her about what brought her here? Or did she start asking any questions about it?"

"No, sir. Sgt. Riley and I were just visiting with her. She'd just eaten some of her meal. That's all."

Phillip was growing uncomfortable. "Excuse me, Doctor Hudgins?"

"Yes? You've got something to add?"

"Just before I left her room a little while ago, she and I were talking. I'm afraid I might have said something without realizing what could happen. I feel I might be responsible for this."

"Before you go any further, no one is responsible for what happened. It was more than likely going to happen sometime anyway. The best part about the whole thing is that she was here when it did and being able to administer something for the drug reaction immediately was a blessing."

He handed Patricia's chart back to Maxine. "Now, gentlemen, if you will excuse me, I have a little boy in ER in need of a few stitches. Mrs. Ridgeway's regular physician should be around a little later for rounds. Any questions that you might have, I'm sure he'll be glad to answer for you." He smiled at the small group, stepped back into Patricia's room and looked at the various monitors, took her pulse, then flashed them a broad smile as he walked by them on his way out.

"You folks can go on in, but just for a moment, okay?" Maxine said as she held the door open for them.

"Trent, you go ahead. I'm going to run Brenda down to the cafeteria for some doughnuts and coffee. Cop stuff." Trent got a bewildered look on his face when Brenda started laughing.

"Never mind, Trent. The man just owes me, that's all! But I could use a Coke."

Trent went in to Patricia's room and began searching for something to put the flowers in. Finally, he just opened the lid on her blue plastic water pitcher and put the flowers in there. A nurse sitting on the far side of the bed appeared to be oblivious to his presence. She startled him when she said quietly, "They will look a lot prettier and last longer if you take the paper from around them."

Trent was in the process of removing the wet paper when Patricia slowly opened her eyes.

"Hi." Her voice was quite weak.

"Hi, yourself. I brought you some flowers." He sounded like a proud kid who'd just brought his mother a bunch of wildflowers.

"They're beautiful, Trent. That was sweet. You look tired. You okay?" She leaned over and smelled the flowers. "Oh, my, they smell good, too. Thanks, Trent."

She extended her hand and he took it, then leaned down and kissed her lightly on her forehead. He didn't know what to say. They'd known one another for thirty-five years, and he had no idea what to say to her.

"I'm glad you like them. Bought 'em myself!" Trent took a deep breath. "You look better than you did when I left early this morning. Do you feel any better?"

"I think so. I just keep having these weird dreams. I dreamed that Phillip was here and a beautiful lady all dressed in yellow and my grandmother! Oh, and I dreamed that we were having a party or something and tons of people were at our house and no one would open the door for my grandmother. How long ago did she die, Trent? I can't remember now."

Maxine came back in, her coat over her arm and purse in hand. "Hey there, just wanted to say bye before I left. Tomorrow is my day off, so most likely I won't see you again. They'll spring you tomorrow, I suspect!" She was by the side of the bed now as she added, "It was very nice to meet all of you, even if it was on my turf! Next time I see you, Mrs. Ridgeway, it better be at your bookstore!"

"I remember now, you bring your grandkids in, don't you?"

"I sure do. I've known Butch Killen for years, and I think the kids just come in to see that darn dog! I wish they came in because they liked to read!" She leaned down and hugged Patricia, then quickly scurried out the door.

"What a neat lady," said Patricia with a smile.

"The other nurse looked up and laughed. "That's exactly what she said about you, too!"

Right after Maxine left, Phillip came in the room.

Patricia's face came alive with a giant smile. "Oh, my gosh! Where did you come from?"

"Oh, a little bird told me I might find you here. How ya doing, cutie?"

"I'm good. But I want to go home!"

"Whoa! That's one thing you gotta watch about her, Phil." Trent was feeling uncomfortable. "Always wantin' something, this girl!"

"Hey, trade you Patricia's truck for mine," Trent said. "I drove hers to the hospital." Phillip dug Trent's Bronco keys out of his pocket and tossed them to him. Trent gave Patricia a quick peck on the cheek, shook Phillip's hand, tipped his hat at the nurse, and made an excuse for needing to leave. When he stepped out into the hall, Brenda Riley was just coming back with a soft drink in her hand.

"How long do you think you're going to stay down here, anyway, Brenda? You look exhausted!"

"I was just getting my things, actually. My replacement is here. I'm going to head for home and get some sleep. God, what I wouldn't give for some of whatever they gave her!" she said, cocking her head toward Patricia's room and laughing.

"Yeah, sounds good, huh? Say, you need a ride?"

"Yeah, I guess I do."

"Phillip, I am so glad you are here!" Patricia maneuvered herself to the side of the bed and Phillip sat beside her, holding her.

"God, me too, Trisha! I'm just so sorry that I ever left. I'm not sure if I'll ever forgive myself for that." Patricia touched her hand to his cheek.

"Don't let me ever hear you say anything like that again, okay? We don't control what happens in our lives, baby. You know that. This was a test. A trial. It couldn't have been any other way." She put her hands around his neck and they embraced fully for a very long time.

"What's this?" she said, tugging on the leather lace around his neck. Very slowly she pulled out the medicine bag. Phillip didn't know how to respond.

"When did he give it to you?"

"This morning. He picked me up at the airport and drove me back here. I was speechless, Trisha. I'm not sure what it means, but that doesn't matter."

"Trent is a very remarkable man, Phillip. We all have faults and shortcomings, but he has fewer than most." Patricia stopped for a moment.

"He's a wise man," she continued. "He knows things can happen in life that require you to step aside because something unseen and very powerful has manifested itself for some good and taken charge of a force that we might not have the strength to take control of ourselves. I do know one thing, this meant a great deal to him. To part with it took a lot of courage, as well as unselfishness, Phil. Do you know what's inside?"

"No. I haven't dared peek. Trent told me there were things in there that could bite if provoked! I'm not stupid, ya know!"

"Oh, give me that, you! Nothing bites. Sheesh!"

Phillip watched as she dumped the contents on the bed.

"Okay, let's see if I can remember all of this. First of all, do you know the significance of a medicine bag?"

"I think I do, but you'd better tell me." He watched as her fingers caressed each item.

"Well, different tribes believe a variety of things, but this is *The World According To Patricia* version. Most Indians believe that everything—not just living things, but inanimate things as well—have a life force or a spirit. And every life force of everything in the world is interconnected. Each and every person or animal or bird or fish. Even stones and plants and particular places have an influence on everything that is around them or comes in contact with it. To use the medicines that these totems provide is to use the forces of nature to influence you and help guide you on this life's path. Some people call the things in the bag totems or charms. They all mean essentially the same thing. When we are born, and even before we are born sometimes, a particular Elder often takes on the responsibility of carefully gathering and assembling the proper charms. In that way, that person thinks that they have had a very special hand in helping you choose your path."

Phillip interrupted her. "Do you have an Elder, or do you know who your Elder is?"

"Oh yes. My grandmother! Although she died when I was very young, that doesn't mean that her Spirit ever left me. And many times in my life, I know that she has manifested herself by becoming someone else's Inner Form in times of great trial or sadness. No one ever really leaves us, Phillip. No matter how alone or empty our feeling of loss is, they never truly leave us all alone. It's just the way of things."

She looked up and found him watching her as she talked, and she instinctively reached forward and touched his face, like she'd done so many times in her dreams of him.

"Go on. Tell me more." He touched his hand to hers before she reached to pick up a particular stone.

"Isn't this pretty? It's a perfect amethyst quartz. Quartz crystals are clear and generate warmth, strength, and vitality. Some people call them the light of the universe. That's why we are often prone to stargaze, because the stars remind us of the quartz. Some also say that they are a light balancer, which means that they offer stability. In other words, it prevents our path from being unusually bright or unusually dark. Just a proper mix, I suppose. My grandmother told me that by doing that it kept one humble and never boastful, and reminded us that for every very bright thing that happened to us, another dark thing might happen to balance the two. Am I making sense, sweetie?"

"Yes, you are making plenty of sense."

"You'll recognize this, I think. It's a polished tiger-eye. It was chosen to represent strength, much like the one within the dream catcher hanging from the rearview mirror in my truck, remember?" Phillip nodded.

"Now, this bone is deteriorating, I see. We will have to get a new one blessed for you and replace it. The bone represents the Spirit that blesses the hunt. When we hunt game, which you know I do, we can expect success because the hunt represents almost all of the necessities of life. That isn't true now, of course, but it certainly was long ago and because we all believe that we are still part of the long ago, we hunt, now, for the same reasons. For meat to sustain and nourish us. For hide to keep us warm in the winter and to build the lodges that the people needed when they followed the herds. For leather to clothe us and make moccasins and leggings to protect us from the elements and things of nature that might harm us, like brush and cactus and snakes, things of that nature. Oh, and this beautiful red stone is a jasper. See how it's in the shape of a heart? That is natural! Cool, huh? These are very rare to be found like this and, of course, it means the natural thing. The blessings of abundant love, honor, and respect. This little lizard carving, or fetish, teaches us inner strength and stillness. Oh, and it also represents survival and self-protection, it rather clarifies our primal needs, too. This particular fetish is carved from rose quartz, which is significant because rose quartz is a healing stone. Healing in many different senses of the word. If it's blessed and given to a girl or a woman, it might be blessed to bring with it a beautiful complexion or beautiful outer beauty, but in the same respect it can also bring beautiful inner beauty and personal self-acceptance. I'm not really sure what some of these herbs and leaves are anymore. Trent may have added these things himself."

When she paused, Phillip asked to hold some of the things and she dropped them carefully into his hand. He felt like he was very much holding the most valuable and priceless things that he might have ever held in his life. She hadn't handed him everything. He watched her finger touch an odd-looking stone.

"What's that rock, Trisha?"

"This one is called a Spirit Catcher. My grandfather gave it to me when I was about twelve years old. It had been my grandmother's, and instead of burying it with her, she'd asked him to save it and give it to me when I was older. He was getting very old and I think he felt he should do it, in case, as he used to say, 'I wake up dead tomorrow morning!' These were used by the ancient shamans and were objects of magnificent healing power. They are made of an element that reacts to your body much like a magnet. A shaman could move this stone over someone and it had the power to draw out and catch the negative spirits that made the people sick. Then in a secret ceremony, the shaman would take the stone and purge it so that it could not hurt anyone again."

"May I see it?" he asked.

"Sure. Feel how much it weighs for such a little thing."

"Yes, it does! It looks a lot like pewter, doesn't it? What are these tiny holes in it for?"

"It does, doesn't it? For as long as I can remember, which wasn't long, of course, my grandmother wore this around her neck. The cord must have disappeared some time ago. To be perfectly honest, I'm not sure why this was in Trent's bag. I'll have to think about that." She paused, leaned back against the pillows and watched Phillip's face in the dimming light as he studied the objects in his hand. "I really had to think to remember what I've just told you. I'm sure I've left many things out. I seem to be having a little trouble thinking clearly. That will go away, won't it?" She was looking at Phillip, realizing that she had suddenly become very tired.

Phillip rose from the bed, took the bag from her, and gently poured the items back inside and secured the top. She watched him, but never spoke. He eased the leather strap over his head and tucked the worn suede bag inside his shirt.

"You're sleepy again, aren't you, sweetheart?"

"I am. Did I tell you about everything in the bag? I can't remember." Her voice was fading, and some of her words were slurring again.

"Yes, you did, baby. You told me about everything." Phillip pulled the sheet and the thin blanket over her, then reached up and turned off the light attached to the bed.

"You aren't leaving are you?" she asked slowly. Her eyes were closed now.

"No baby, I'm not leaving. I'm never leaving again. Now go to sleep." When she didn't respond, Phillip kissed her lips softly.

A young nurse came in to check the monitors and to take Patricia's pulse. She stood quietly and wrote something on the chart, and then whispered, "She's doing just fine. A good night's sleep, and I bet she'll be able to go home tomorrow. One of the other nurses just made a fresh pot of coffee and you are welcome to help yourself."

"That's very nice of you. I'll be out in a few minutes. I want to make sure she's settled."

"Sure. But trust me, she's a goner 'til morning. But if you want, I'd be glad to bring you a cup."

"You wouldn't mind? I sort of made her a promise that I really don't want to break, if that's okay."

"I understand. And it's no trouble at all. Black, or cream and sugar?"

"A little milk, no sugar, thanks."

Phillip fingered the bag around his neck, then opened it and felt around until he found the Spirit Catcher. He opened the drawer in the bedside table and found the bag that Patricia always wore and dropped the pewter colored stone inside. Pushed neatly down into the bag was the folded paper with the poem that he'd read early that morning. The poem that answered so many of his questions. He started to slide the drawer closed, then decided against it and took the bag out. As carefully as he could he gently placed it over Patricia's head and tucked it under her hospital gown.

The nurse returned with his coffee. "There you go. Can I get you anything else?"

"No. Not at all. This is just great. Thank you so much, really."

"Make yourself comfortable. That chair folds out almost flat, and there's a blanket in the compartment on the side. You get some sleep, too. Be sure and call if you need anything. Goodnight."

Several hours later, Patricia opened her eyes and saw Phillip sleeping soundly next to her bed. She closed her eyes and drifted back to sleep, a smile on her lips.

Chapter Forty-two

Brenda was reaching out toward Bill. He finally allowed her to ease the gun from his hand. Then he turned and stared at Phillip. There was a look of profound sadness in Bill's eyes. Phillip could almost understand his inner conflict, the blinding rage that made it so easy for him to pull the trigger over and over and over again. But with the blood lust satisfied, he knew Bill would be left with nothing but regrets. What he'd done would never bring Sylvia back.

"Hey, you," Patricia whispered softly, snuggling next to him in the bed. "What are you thinking about?"

Phillip had his arm around Patricia's shoulders, enjoying the feel of her warm skin next to his. They had fallen into bed several hours before, drifted off to sleep, awakened, made love, and then Patricia had nearly fallen asleep in his arms once again.

"Talk to me, please, Mr. Craven," she said softly, placing her leg over his.

"Trisha, I can't forget the look on Bill's face."

"I know. You okay?"

It had been less than twenty-four hours since Phillip awakened in her hospital room. Startled from a nightmare. For a few moments, he hadn't known exactly where he was. He'd looked around and seen Patricia asleep in the bed next to him. And then he remembered that it wasn't a dream.

Phillip felt a bit stiff as he got up out of the recliner/bed. Patricia was sitting up in the narrow hospital bed by the time he reached her. They began to hug.

"Feel better?" he asked.

"Oh, I think so. I think I feel fine. Should I, though? Should I really feel fine? Somehow I don't think I have the right to feel this good, Phillip." There was a note of confused desperation in her voice. She let him hold her. She drew strength from his arms. "I'm so sad, Phillip."

They sat on Patricia's bed holding each other, saying little. After a while, he glanced at his watch. "Quarter to seven," he mumbled to himself.

"You going to be late for work?" she chuckled.

"I sure hope so."

Phillip stood up and stretched. Patricia started to do the same, but Phillip stopped her, reminding her that she was only to get up with the assistance of a nurse.

"I'll call for her, and then I'll go get us some coffee."

When he returned from the cafeteria with a banana nut muffin and coffee, she emerged from the bathroom, no longer tethered to her IV.

"Ooh, the muffin man is here!"

"Wanna nibble on my muffin, little girl?"

"Oh, yes, I'd love a bite of your muffin, sir!" she said teasingly.

When a nurse came in and announced that it was bath time, Phillip decided to check in on Bill.

"Please tell me you've come to break me outta here!" Bill was only half-smiling.

"Pretty soon, I think." Phillip said. "Patricia's feeling much better, and I can see you are, too. Getting a little antsy, are we?"

"No shit!" Bill said tersely.

A Dr. Morrison came into the room. Phillip had met him briefly the night before, when the aging doctor was making his rounds. He'd answered all of Phillip's questions and reassured him that he was not responsible for Patricia's setback.

"How's the patient, Doc?" Phillip asked.

"Everything looks good. Really good. I think you and Mrs. Ridgeway can both be released before lunch. But first, Mr. Conner, I do want you to arrange to talk with Dr. Walton. I can set up the appointment before you leave today. Also, I'm going to prescribe something to get you through the next several days. Mostly it will help with the anxiety. If you feel you need something stronger than that, you can certainly call my office. Any other questions?"

"No. I can't think of any. But I'm telling you I don't want to go get my head shrunk."

"I'll make the appointment, Mr. Conner. It's up to you to keep it." With that, he turned and left.

Almost immediately, Brenda Riley rushed into the room and crashed into Phillip who was standing by the door. She was excited and out of breath.

"Brenda! What's up with you?" Bill asked quickly.

"I've been arranging for that arrest warrant for Bud Richards!"

"I don't think you'll be too popular down in Santa Fe," Bill offered with a smile.

"I expect not. But that's okay. Being popular in Santa Fe wasn't high on my list anyway. Actually, there are a lot of people who won't be too upset about it."

"When this is all over, I'm hoping I can find a few dollars in the budget and convince you to stay on here, Brenda," said Bill.

"This'll probably come as a surprise to you, but I'd like that!"

"Glad to hear that."

Brenda sighed. "Bill, I haven't had an opportunity to tell you how sorry I am about Sylvia. Well, and about so many things, I'm afraid. But I can't begin to express to you how I feel about what has happened to you and to your family. I am just so terribly sorry, Bill. And I know that's such a feeble word. I'm no good with words, anyway." She was struggling with what to say next when Bill simply nodded and looked away.

"So, are you going to go talk to Frank soon?" she asked. "I hate to put that on you now, but we need him and need him bad."

"Yeah, goddamn it! I'm going to go see him as soon as I can get the hell out of here! He's up at the Trujillo summer line camp north of Blue Lake. Neither of you probably has clue where that is. Never mind. Anyway, I'd would like to see him alone for a little while, if that is all right."

"Sure, but you're going to need to finish your statement and…"

"Brenda, stop being a cop!" Bill said sharply, but then turned and winked at Phillip.

"I'm pretty sure Frank doesn't have a radio," Bill said, "and so he won't have any idea what's happened. I want to tell him alone. And, Phil, I think you and Patricia should meet me up at the camp this afternoon. If she feels up to it, that is."

"I'm pretty sure she'll insist," Phillip answered. "I probably wouldn't have a lot of say in it anyway."

"You too, Brenda. You can get away, can't you?"

"I'll sure find a way."

"So did you bring our car or yours, Brenda?" Bill asked quickly.

"Ours," she said, referring to the patrol car.

Bill got out of the bed. "Then I'm going to get the hell out of here."

"Wasn't the nurse going to check…" Brenda stopped mid-sentence. "Oh, never mind." She slipped the keys off her belt and tossed them to Bill.

An hour later Phillip, Patricia, and Brenda were pulling out of the hospital parking lot. "Should we drop you off at the office, Brenda?" Phillip asked.

She thought for a moment. Bud Richards was probably there by now.

And perhaps someone had already tipped him off that the state police were in the process of issuing a warrant for his arrest. And if the coroner had turned in his report, there would no doubt be media people crawling all over the place. "I think the last place I want to be right now is at the station."

"I think they'll do fine without you for a few hours, Brenda," Phillip laughed.

"We could go to my house for a bit," offered Patricia.

"Huh-uh. I'll bet there are reporters camped out there, too, Trish," Phillip warned her. "It's after ten, do you think the Sonic is open?"

"Oh, hell yeah! It's open twenty-four hours!" Patricia said happily. "I'll bet hamburgers, fries, and shakes would taste very good indeed." During the meal, it was Patricia who asked if Jordan had been arrested yet. Brenda damned near choked on a french fry when she tried to answer.

"No, but Emily was questioned yesterday," Brenda was finally able to say. "She either doesn't know or isn't saying where either Caesar or Jordan are."

"And she wasn't arrested?" Patricia asked, a little surprised.

Phillip began telling Patricia some of the things she'd not yet been told. Patricia became extremely quiet. It was obvious she was getting very angry.

"I'm sorry, Trisha. I can see you're upset," Phillip said.

"Upset? No, Phillip, I'm pissed as hell and well, just disappointed, I guess."

"At me?"

"Yes, at *you*!"

"What did I do?"

"Goddamn it, Phillip, that wasn't fair not tell me! I don't need you to protect me, Phillip!"

"I didn't know what to do Trish and..."

"Jesus, Phillip! Now you're telling me that Caesar was in my house. He could have come back anytime! He could've been there all along and nobody told me?" She didn't want to be angry with Phillip, she never wanted to be angry with him. But she felt betrayed by him.

"He was being chivalrous," Brenda said, attempting to come to his defense. It was the perfect word to use to describe Phillip's decision.

"Men," Patricia sighed.

"Can't live with them," Brenda chuckled.

"Oh, yes, you can. If you're hopelessly in love, that is," Patricia added. She kissed a now stunned and even more confused Phillip on the cheek.

"I don't want us to ever be so considerate and protective that we have to hide things from one another, Phillip."

"Um...okay," Phillip said weakly.

"What does *that* mean?" Patricia demanded.

Phillip averted his eyes from her. Patricia waited.

"It means that there's several more things that I have to tell you, Patricia."

"Then I suggest you start talking."

"I'm not sure this is a good time. You've been through a lot and..."

Patricia reached out, touched his chin and forced him to look at her. "What is it? Just tell me."

"I'm not sure exactly where to begin," Phillip said.

"Should I go for a walk?" Brenda asked uncomfortably.

"No, there's no need for that. This has to do with what's been going on. There's more than Caesar breaking into her house, tampering with her computer, and his friend Jordan possibly showing up."

For almost the next hour, Phillip explained what had happened when he got home to Cle Elum. He gave them sugarcoated details of Toji's apparent murder, the break-in at his house, the mutilated deer in his garage, and Mary Foreston. Phillip told Patricia everything about Mary Foreston. He had to. He fought hard against the tears but failed. Patricia held him close for several minutes.

It was during the time that she was holding Phillip close that more pieces of this extraordinary puzzle fell into place. *Her missing key from Sylvia's kitchen. The unusual noises that night. Kitty Gato.*

"I'm so sorry, Phillip," she said finally. "I'm so, so sorry, sweetheart."

"I wish none of this were happening." Phillip was pulling himself together.

"We all wish that," Brenda added.

"Whew! Anyway, we need to get up to Frank." Phillip pulled a piece of paper from his pocket. "Bill said you'd know where this place is." He gave the paper to Patricia.

Patricia squinted, trying hard to read it without her glasses. "Oh, yes, I know where this is! Alma, Sylvia, and I went up there every fall. I guess he's forgotten that. You'd better let me drive though. It's a little tricky, and I've done it before."

"I don't think that's wise, Trisha. I mean, you just got out of the..." He watched a furrow form between her eyebrows, and didn't say another word. He just passed her the keys.

Phillip recognized the road to Blue Lake, although it looked entirely different in the bright sunlight. He also noticed that many more leaves had fallen and the mountains and the riverbank were taking on a more ghostly appearance as bare branches revealed themselves. Dried leaves blew across the road and drifted on the wind. He recognized the gravel road that turned off to the lake as they sped past. He didn't say anything, but he was sure he could feel Patricia's eyes on him for an instant. Within a few hundred yards, she let up on the accelerator and slowed to make a right-hand turn onto a deeply rutted dirt road. They jerked and bumped over some large rocks in the road, and then Patricia slowed down. The thick vegetation was limiting the visibility.

"I'm sorry this is so rough, you guys. It's been a long time since I've been up here." She was quiet for a minute. "Have you ever robbed squirrel caches?"

Brenda leaned forward from the back. "Robbed what?"

"They're areas beneath these piñon trees where the squirrels gather up nuts and bury them for the winter. All you have to do is feel around for soft dirt, then dig down and find a treasure trove of nuts! Then you wash and roast them and they are yummy!"

"Isn't it rather inhumane to take their winter supply of nuts?" Brenda asked.

"I suppose it would be if we took everything they needed to survive, yes. But, in actuality, very few people do this and if someone has preceded you, then you just tell yourself to be quicker on the draw next year! Actually, there are normally three or four caches beneath each tree. You only rob one cache and leave the others untouched. There is more than an adequate supply for the winter, plus they harvest other things, too"

Patricia quickly brought the truck to a stop. "Look, there's a car up there." An abandoned sports car was on the side of the road, a few hundred yards ahead of them.

"That's very odd. You can see how bad this road is for a truck, let alone a car like that," said Patricia. "Maybe it's stuck."

Patricia pulled forward until they were even with the car. It was a mid-1980s, once bright red Camaro. Brenda got out first and discovered that the tire on the front passenger side was flat and partially off the rim. "They're lucky if that's the only damage. Must be kids with more money than brains. Are we close?"

"About a mile, maybe two at the most," said Patricia. "Then we'll have to walk in about a quarter of a mile or so. The line camp is just over that ridge up there."

Brenda walked around the car, looked inside, and tried to open the doors, but they were all locked. Patricia and Phillip were already in the truck waiting for her to get back in. A few minutes later, they pulled up behind Frank's Bronco and began hiking up the trail. Brenda spotted Bill coming toward them at a brisk walk. "Hey, stranger," she called out to him.

"Everything okay?" Phillip asked.

"Yeah, everything's good. Frank's up there waiting. I heard a truck and came down here to see if it was you guys or not. I thought I'd heard a truck behind me earlier, too. Never spotted it though."

"You think somebody might have followed you?

"Yeah, I thought so."

Brenda told him about the abandoned Camaro. "You didn't see it?"

"Nope."

"You couldn't have missed it," said Phillip, "so it must have come up after you did."

"Camaro, you say? Red?" The trio nodded and Bill's face was suddenly pale. "Did you notice if there was a Star Trek spaceship hanging from the rear view mirror?"

"As a matter of fact, there was," said a surprised Brenda.

"Caesar's car."

"You're shittin' me, Bill," Phillip exclaimed. "Caesar's car?!"

"I'm gonna head back up the trail," whispered Bill. "You guys wait a minute or so, give me a little head start, then follow me to the cabin. I'll signal you to let you know everything's okay." He was out of sight in a matter of seconds.

"That wasn't the car I saw outside my house, Phillip," Patricia said quietly.

They waited another minute or so, and then began walking quickly up the path. "There they are," Brenda said, slightly out of breath. Within a matter of minutes, they'd reached the edge of a clearing and could see Bill and Frank standing just outside the door of a cabin.

Brenda started to wave to them when suddenly Bill yelled out, "Down! Get down!" just as he threw himself on the ground and rolled away from the cabin. Phillip grabbed Patricia's arm and pulled her down behind a tree. The three of them lay there and watched as Bill pointed his gun at the cabin door.

"You've got nowhere to go!" he yelled.

Phillip saw someone grab Frank from behind and press a large knife against his neck.

Bill shouted back to them, "Stay down, he's got Frank!"

Phillip crawled forward a few feet trying to get a better look. Was it Jordan? He couldn't be sure. It looked like a young man, younger than Frank and quite a bit shorter.

"You're not going to get away," Bill yelled again. He felt helpless. He couldn't get a clear shot at him.

They all watched as Frank struggled briefly with the young man. When he twisted his head around, the polished knife blade reflected the sunlight and silver fire shot into the sky.

"No one has to get hurt." Bill yelled again, desperately trying to find some way to defuse the situation.

"Then let us walk out of here!"

Phillip instantly recognized the slightly nasal voice. *It's Jordan. The fucking bastard!*

"You know I can't do that," Bill shouted back.

"Sure you can. Frank goes with Caesar and me. Simple. We drive out of here, no one gets hurt, no one dies."

"Not going to happen that way!" Bill shouted. "Caesar, don't do this. Come on out of there."

"Stay where you are, Caesar!" Jordan ordered sharply.

"You don't seem to understand," Bill yelled back at him. "We've got a helluva lot more firepower out here than you two have. If you hurt Frank, you're goin' down, and you know it. Give yourselves up, and no one needs to get hurt." Bill was playing for time.

"No, *you* don't seem to understand. If you don't let us go, Frank is going to die. Simple as that. Jordan's voice had a calmness that was chilling.

"Then, simple as *that*, so will you," Bill yelled back.

Brenda looked at Patricia and Phillip. "You guys stay where you are," she said in a hushed voice. "I'm gonna try to get a little closer so I can be in a better position to take a shot if I need to."

"Caesar! Tell your friend to give this up!" Bill shouted. "This doesn't have to end this way. Killing someone else isn't going to solve anything. I'll do everything I can for you, Caesar, you know that! There's a good chance you won't even have to go to jail."

"We're not that stupid, ass wipe!" Jordan shouted back. "I said, let us walk out of here with Frank and no one dies. Are you deaf, or just fuckin' stupid?"

"You know I can't do that," Bill responded.

"Then I guess we don't have a lot of options here, do we?" Jordan said. "Just remember, freaky… Frank didn't have to die. You can live with that on your conscience from now on!"

"Bill," Brenda shouted, "maybe we should let them go. They can't get very far. Besides, we've got backup on the way!"

"No, I can't do that!"

"*Is* anyone else coming?" Patricia whispered hoarsely to Brenda. Brenda shook her head no.

There was a noise in the brush behind them and Phillip turned around.

"Don't move!" Caesar was standing, his gun aimed directly at Patricia's head.

Brenda looked over her shoulder and started to raise her gun.

"If you move, bitch, the lady dies." Caesar's voice was cold.

There wasn't anything Phillip could do. He knew that even if he made an attempt to throw himself on top of Patricia or towards Caesar, there was no guarantee he would succeed. He was too far away. And Caesar could see that he was unarmed. *Try and be a hero, and you'll get her killed,* Phillip warned himself as the adrenaline coursed through his body.

Caesar ordered Brenda to toss her gun out in front of her. She didn't move.

"*Now,* damn it!" Caesar said in a loud whisper. He didn't want to alert Bill to his presence. Brenda complied. Meanwhile, Bill's eyes remained trained on the front door of the cabin.

"Why are you doing this, Caesar?" Phillip asked, stalling for time. "Caesar, at least tell me why you're doing this?"

"Jordan and I need to get the fuck outta here. Can you make that happen, Mr. Craven?"

"Stop being NastyOlGeezer, Caesar," Patricia said suddenly. He looked surprised.

"Caesar, you and Jordan are going to wind up being killed, if you do it this way," Phillip said.

Caesar smiled. "We've been dead for a long time already," Caesar said flatly. "And we knew it was almost over when we realized that Alma knew way too much for her own good."

"Caesar, do you even *know* what you're doing?" Patricia asked, her voice steady and low. He glared back at her.

"Jordan, I'm in position!"

Bill jerked around and looked up the hill and saw Caesar. He assumed he had someone hostage, maybe all of them. He had no way of knowing.

"Throw your gun out in front of you where I can see it, Bill!" commanded Caesar.

Bill's mind raced through all the facts he had. Caesar had a gun and was obviously holding one or more of the others hostage. The gun. It was probably Frank's gun. Jordan appeared to have only a knife. No one else seemed to be in the cabin.

"Throw it down, Bill!"

"Caesar, don't do this!" Bill shouted.

"Fuck you!" Caesar shouted back. "Throw down your weapon! Right now! I mean it!"

Brenda looked at Caesar and then at Bill. "Bill! His safety is on, Bill!"

Bill sat up instantly, aimed, and shot. There was no hesitation. He prayed that everybody else would remain lying down. He fired again.

The first bullet hit Caesar's right shoulder. The sharp pain burned through his body and he jerked backwards and to the side. The second shot shattered his pelvic bone and caused him to scream out in pain as he fell to the ground.

Phillip grabbed Caesar's gun and held it on the young man who writhed in pain a few feet in front of him. At the same time, Brenda crawled forward and retrieved her weapon.

As soon as he saw Caesar fall to the ground, Bill turned around quickly toward the cabin. Frank and Jordan were no longer standing in the doorway. He scanned the bushes near the cabin. No sign of them. He looked back up the hill at the others. "You okay back there?"

"We're all okay, Bill," Brenda answered. "Caesar's down, but alive and…" She was just finishing her answer when she saw Bill suddenly jump up and rush the cabin.

"Stay down!" she ordered the others, "I've got to go help him. Don't move!"

Patricia ignored her command. Before Phillip could stop her, she'd moved over next to Caesar. She saw the blood soaking through his jeans and through his flannel shirt. He was staring up glassy-eyed.

"Hold your hand down hard right here," she was telling Caesar. "Try not to move."

"Hey cowboy," she said, "you know how to use that thing?"

Phillip looked at the gun, then back at Patricia. "I used to go target shooting when I was a kid." She smiled at him, then turned back to Caesar.

"You're gonna be okay, Caesar," she said reassuringly. She was pressing her hand hard into his shoulder, trying to halt the bleeding. He was obviously not only in pain, but also frightened.

"I'm so sorry." Caesar was crying now.

"Don't try to talk," she said quickly. Then with an edge to her voice, "Just tell me one thing, Caesar. Please. Did you kill Sylvia? Did you?" Her eyes were squeezed shut, as if doing so would prevent her from hearing his answer.

"No, Jordan did."

"You killed Alma then, didn't you? Why? Just tell me why! And it was you that killed my cat, wasn't it? Why? Goddammit, why?!" Patricia was screaming her words at him, shaking him and willing him to answer her. He didn't. He just laid there, his eyes open and staring directly into the sun. Patricia pulled her knees to her chest and buried her face in her legs. She didn't look up when Caesar began struggling to speak.

"Jordan wanted Frank. He hated me for leaving him." Caesar gasped for air and the strength to continue. "I just wanted someone to love me. I just wanted someone to love, and Alma didn't believe me when I told her about Frank that day. I tried to tell her, she wouldn't listen. I just needed her to love me, that's all…that's all I wanted."

A gunshot rang out, causing Phillip and Patricia to instinctively throw themselves on the ground again. Phillip grabbed onto Patricia's arm and looked at the cabin. He saw Bill appear from behind the building and run up the hill toward them. Brenda was right behind him.

"What's going on?" Phillip shouted to Brenda as she crashed by them through the brush.

"Frank's out cold," she said. "I think he's okay. Jordan slipped out the back somehow. We think he's probably got Frank's keys."

She stopped when they heard the sound of a car starting. Brenda ran over the ridge and down the path toward the vehicles.

"That son of a bitch…" Phillip started to say.

Patricia grabbed him by the arm and looked at him menacingly. "No, Phillip, don't even think about it! Don't you dare even think about that!" Phillip glared back at her. "Please! I don't need you to try and be a hero, okay? I can't lose anyone else. We can't lose one another now, Phillip. Not now, baby." Her eyes searched his. He nodded as they heard the car drive away. Gunshots rang out. The sound of the car's engine faded in the distance.

Brenda's voice screamed out. "Bill!" Phillip looked, but couldn't see anyone.

"Bill!" Brenda shouted again. "Stop, Bill! *No*! Stop!"

When Phillip first saw him Bill was walking fast up over the ridge toward them. He stopped and stood over Caesar and aimed his gun directly at the boy's head. Caesar lay motionlessly, staring helplessly up at Bill.

"Bill, for chrissakes don't do this!" Brenda yelled again, as she came up behind him.

"You son of a bitch!" Bill's voice was full of hatred. He fired several quick shots.

Patricia buried her face in Phillip's shoulder. He held her tightly, and squeezed his eyes shut against the sound of the gunfire. He prepared himself, and opened his eyes. He watched as Bill stood there and unloaded the rest of his rounds into the ground near Caesar's head. Patricia was screaming. She couldn't bring herself to look.

"Shshshsh, baby. It's okay. He didn't shoot him," he said quietly. She didn't raise her head. She just held onto Phillip and sobbed.

Brenda walked slowly over to Bill and held out her hand. Bill allowed her to take the gun from him. Then he turned and looked back over his shoulder at Phillip. There was a strange look in Bill's eyes, one of sadness and great emptiness. Bill realized how easy it would have been for him to have killed Caesar. But he knew that doing so would never have brought Sylvia back to him.

The soft, early evening breeze was suddenly very cold.

Chapter Forty-three

Patricia swiveled in her large leather chair away from Phillip and faced Butch. She removed her glasses and fidgeted with them in her lap. A storm had blown in, and they could hear the wind whistling around the old windows that looked out over the east side of the ancient plaza. Patricia watched a few errant snowflakes drift past their view. Abby had somehow managed to lumber up the stairs, and Butch was rubbing her back with his foot.

"I'm sorry, I just couldn't go to the hospital, Patricia,"

"Oh, stop it, Butch."

"I gotta tell you, because I feel bad about it."

"You don't have to explain. I was only there a minute, and it wasn't necessary, for pity sakes. I needed you here, anyway. Now, are you sure this is okay?" she asked again.

Butch looked at both of them. "Yes, 'cause you two need some time for yourselves. And quite frankly, I'm looking forward to running things here, Patricia. It would have been too hard a few months ago, but not now."

"You're sure then?"

"I couldn't be more sure. Now, stop asking, okay? I just needed to walk away from the store and be with Angela as much as I could last year. I did that, and I'll never regret a moment of it. But I can't tell you how much I miss the shop when I'm not here. It's part of me, just like it's part of you. It's not a favor you're asking of me, Patricia, it's an honor. The matter is settled. I'll be here for as long as you need me. Understand?"

"Understood." She started to lean over to give him a hug, when Abby growled without ever raising her head or opening an eye. "Oh, shut up, you cantankerous ol' mutt!"

Mutt. Funny how I use my father's nickname sometimes without even thinking about it. Truth was, she often thought of her father. Hardly a day went by that she didn't communicate with him on some level, and she'd shared much of her feelings about him with Butch through the years.

Butch knew what she was thinking. "He's always right here, Patricia, you know that. Just like Angela is. She gave me hell last night, as a matter of fact! I woke up at least a dozen times. And then, like a bolt out of the blue, I remembered that I'd forgotten to bring in her begonias from the back porch. They'd have been frostbitten by this morning for sure if I'd left them. They have their little ways, sweetheart. Don't forget that."

"I know. I won't." Patricia looked at Phillip for a moment. He continued to be a quiet sentinel of strength for her.

"Were you ever sorry that you never had children, Butch? I mean now? When you're alone?" She didn't phrase that right. The question seemed to come from nowhere and hang suspended in the herb-scented air.

"Nope. I love children, and they are meant for certain people to have and nurture and raise. They're sometimes meant for others to enjoy. There are people out there, Patricia, grown-up children who need a different kind of parent."

"Like me, huh?" she said with a laugh.

"Yeah, you're very much like a daughter to me, Patricia. I take a father's pride in you, and I'm glad for it. I'm glad for both of you."

"Thanks, Butch. I needed to hear that."

"No, you didn't, but I'm glad you want me to think you did!"

Patricia knew she was about to cry, so she quickly changed the subject to bookkeeping. "Do you understand how I do the accounts here? I really haven't changed too much from what you taught me. If anything, they're just much simpler and probably not as well done as when you handled them."

Phillip liked listening to their exchange, feeling somehow invisible and privy to some wonderful shared secrets. Oddly at that particular moment, he suddenly recalled some distant yet warm memories. He swore he could hear the crack of a wooden bat and see a high fly ball to center field and smell those Yankee Stadium hot dogs and the smell of cigars. He could see Pop-Pop watching him keep track of the score on a big form. "Good job." A "good job" from Pop-Pop was a wonderful thing to hear. Phillip then flashed forward to 1983. It was just after Christmas, and he knew Nana had just died. Nana—his grandmother—his favorite person in the world, was gone. It was several weeks before anybody told him officially that she had died. His father wrote him a long letter, and enclosed the memorial service card. He wrote how losing his mother had affected him. That letter contained feelings and emotions that Phillip had never heard his father express before. And there were regrets and apologies, but mostly love. Phillip and his father had never really been close, and they had drifted farther and farther apart as Phillip grew through his teen years. It took Nana's death to bring them back together.

After Phillip met Sarah, he was inspired to write a poem for Nana that he would share with his father and with Pop-Pop, as well. Pop Pop was a bit more complicated a person than he'd ever realized when he was a child, of course. Although he'd been by all accounts a pretty terrible father and not a very good husband, he somehow reinvented himself into the most wonderful grandfather a kid could have. He, too, would die, less than a year later and be laid to rest next to Nana.

Phillip later included the poem in a small book of poetry that he published himself. In the introduction to the poem, Phillip wrote: *My father's parents were called Nana and Pop-Pop (as in Pop's Pop); my mom's parents were called Grandma and Grandpa. Nana, as I grew older, become more and more of a friend to me. Nana was one of the few people that I felt ever listened and cared deeply about nearly everything I had to say. Nana died a few days after Christmas and this poem is for her.*

Prayer for Nana

Memories of a childhood in terror
Never feeling like I was heard
Or even slightly understood.
Perhaps that's why I write, so it isn't
all quite so absurd.
Through words written I could
Tell of my frustration,
The desperation,
And the dark, cold moments of fear.

But through it all there were
Moments of exoneration,
When under the praises of a wise
Old lady, I was able
To take a vacation
From my fears.

For in her eyes, I could do no wrong.
She was the libation
That made the little boy high.
She was my father's mother but
As sweet as a song.
She made me want to strive to be
That person I wanted to be
And I knew

I could be strong.

Be true to who you are.
I know you can get what you want.
To me you're already a star.
You can be whatever you want to be.
And with her words, giving me faith
When I lost all hope,
I've pushed on quite far.

In late December, I felt something
Let go inside
And I wondered why.
Two weeks later,
I learned she had died.
And tearful memories
Came forth into my head.
She was my sanity,
The push, the voice telling me to
Go forth, move ahead.
But now she won't share
any more successes,
Now she is dead.

But not to me.
To me she will always live on.
She'll always be the wise old lady
That gave me sound advice
In a quiet voice
With a smile and twinkle.
She instilled in me a sense of worth
And assured me I was more often right
She made me believe I was something important
And she made me see
I would win the important fight.

To fight with dignity
To stand up to her son,
My father,
and do what was
right you see.

It will not last
All that long
She promised me.
It will soon be the past.
He'll see much of it
Was wrong
And so will
You.

And she said,
Do you remember what you would say,
When you were just a little boy?
When we would watch a horror movie
On chiller theatre and I would turn away?
"Oh, Nana, you would say, it's okay,
It's only a movie!"
I've never forgotten that.

And now that she's gone, I say,
"Oh Nana, it's only a life
and inside my heart,
you're so very much alive."
Forever whispering positive words
Giving me strength
To cut more strings
And make a fresh start.

Everything old is new again,
Nana, I know somehow
You hear me.
For in my life you'll
Always be.
And I thank you
With every ounce of
Humility
And respect within me
For being the best grandma
And friend a young boy and young man
Could ever hope
To have.

And I thank Pop-Pop
For the Yankee games
For making you happy
For making my father with you
Who with my mother,
Made me,
Who brought us together,
So I could see
How beautiful you were
And still are
And always will be
To me.

And I'm happy
For you,
But a little sad
For me
though I'll try and
Rejoice
Now that you
Are
Free.

Sarah hadn't said much after she'd read the poem. She didn't seem to want to know much about Nana either. Sarah. Beautiful, brilliant, ambitious Sarah. Today, he might not even be all that attracted to her.

Phillip came out of his thoughts a moment and watched, and barely listened, as Butch and Patricia went over some papers, opened a dozen or so envelopes, and rummaged through a stack of files. Patricia's hair fell around her face and she absently tucked it behind her ear, giggling about something Butch was showing her. Butch fussed like all old men fuss who don't know what else to say. Then Abby rolled over with a groan, and Butch and Patricia laughed together. Phillip felt like he was somehow a little boy in a bubble, floating between his thoughts and hers, on an unseen current of wonderful familiarity.

I'd rarely ever seen her cry. That was it! Even when they were drifting apart, Sarah never cried. She never showed the emotion he would have expected. He remembered once telling Mark over one too many fingers of scotch that she was the Ice Princess. It had been one of those rare and unusual times when they'd reminisced over lost loves and lost wagers. He had shed more tears in the last year than he was sure he'd ever shed in his entire life. Oddly, so many of them were happy tears. None he could recall were ever over regrets or shattered memories. Patricia had taught him that love is a many-sided emotion.

Would he ever quit thinking about Sarah? Probably not. He'd also learned in the last remarkable eighteen months of his life that you can't forget or toss away a part of you. Just like you can never step into the same river twice, you can never throw away what you've been entrusted to hold dear.

"Phillip?" They were both looking at him. "Phillip?" How long had they been looking at him? He didn't have a clue.

"Yes? I'm sorry..."

"No, *I'm* sorry to disrupt your thoughts, honey. Butch was just asking you if you knew when we'd be leaving town. Do you know?"

"No. I guess right after the memorial service tomorrow, but it depends on what else the authorities need from us, I suppose."

"Tomorrow..." Butch looked at the calendar on Patricia's desk.

"Yes, but it's not necessary for you to go, Butch. I know it will be hard. It's going to be a brief service. It's for Bill's benefit mostly, and for her friends here in town. Her ex-husband will take her back to the pueblo for a traditional burial. He told me on the phone last night that I could go, but I'm not going to. I don't think I'd make it through it. She'll understand. Oh, by the way, did you hear where Bill is going to hold the memorial service? Up at Blue Lake."

Butch smiled. "That's wonderful. How is Bill? I saw him going into the deli earlier today. I thought he might drop over, but he didn't."

"He's doing pretty well. It will be difficult for him, but knowing that Carlos is going to stay with him has made all the difference in the world. They'll be good for one another. I think they've decided not to sell the house. That's probably just as well. Keeping things as normal as possible for Carlos is important. Bill is strong. He'll be okay. It'll just take time...lots of time."

"Trisha?" Phillip was hesitant to interrupt. "It's getting late, and you said you wanted to see Trent and Brenda. I'm afraid this snow is getting a little heavier. I hate to rush you."

She stood up and looked out the window at the long shadows that were cast now across the snow. "You're right. We should be going." Phillip held open her jacket for her.

"I'll talk to you tomorrow, Butch. If you think of anything else or need to tell me anything, we'll go over it then. It's not like I'm going to be gone forever, I promise." She hugged him again and asked him not to see them downstairs. From the bottom of the staircase, Patricia looked back up at her old friend who'd gotten up to stretch and watch them go. Patricia knew Butch really had given her his blessings, and it meant more than she could ever tell him it did.

"Are you sure you want to do this, Phillip? I can go alone."

Phillip pulled into the parking lot behind Ridgeway Realty. He saw Trent's bronco was already covered with snow. "I'm sure. But did you need to talk to him by yourself for a little while?"

"No, that's not what I meant," Patricia said with a soft smile.

"Well, *I* need to talk to him myself, Trisha."

"Oh, really?"

"He treated me with respect, which I never expected. A lesser man might just as easily have shot me." He unfastened his seat belt and opened his door. "Hold on, let me help you. This parking lot is slick."

Trent was on the phone when he saw them walk through the back door. He motioned for them to help themselves to coffee. He faked an excuse to return the call later, and was walking toward them before Trisha had the coffee poured.

"Want a cup, Trent?"

"Sure. I thought I'd see you earlier. I was afraid I'd missed you. And, Phil, good to see you again. How do you like this weather?"

"Well, it surprised me a little. It's kinda early for this kind of storm, I guess?"

"Oh, not really. And it won't last long. We'll be wearing shorts by the weekend." He took the cup that Patricia handed to him, then invited them into his office where they quickly settled into a friendly conversation. It was Trent who finally changed the subject.

"Your message said you were going away for a while." He watched Patricia move uncomfortably. "I think that's good, actually."

"Yes," Patricia replied, "for a little while, anyway. You know I won't stay gone long. This is my home, Trent. I could never leave all of this behind me." She looked to Phillip for some sort of reassurance. He smiled, and that was enough.

"I'm going with Phillip...to Washington. I don't expect you to understand, Trent. We hardly understand ourselves. I just want you to know that this is very hard for me to do, even as badly as I want to do it. Sometimes I want to be angry with you that you aren't making this harder for us. Does that make sense?"

"No," Trent chuckled, "but that's okay. It doesn't have to make sense to me. I sometimes screamed out to you in my mind for you to stop me from doing what I was doing with Emily. You were too easy on me, too, Patricia. Maybe it's a good thing. Who knows?"

Patricia waited a moment before asking, "Is that over now?"

"Oh, sure," Trent said. "Probably best that it is. Got some stuff I've got to pick up from her place, and that's all that's left."

"Trent, I'm sorry." She moved over and sat on the arm of his chair, her arm around his shoulders as he stared into his empty cup. Phillip got up and moved to the large picture window. It had stopped snowing and the clouds were beginning to break a little.

"We plan on leaving right after Sylvia's service tomorrow. So please, move back into the house, okay? I can't leave it empty this time of year anyway, just go back home. Please." He reluctantly but happily agreed.

Phillip found the silence that followed to be deafening, and it was he who finally spoke. "Trent, can we have a word alone? It'll only take a second."

Patricia watched them step outside and walk around to the side of the building to escape the chilling wind. She poured herself another cup of coffee. *I'll miss you, you know.* She decided to make a call.

"Amy, this is Patricia Ridgeway. Brenda wouldn't happen to be in, would she?" She listened as Amy told her that Brenda Riley had just left on an accident run south of town, but assured her that she'd have Brenda return the call as soon as she got back to the station.

"No, that's all right. I really don't know when I'll be back by a phone. I'll just touch base with her tomorrow." Amy asked her how she felt, and they talked for a few more minutes. She hung up the phone just as Trent and Phillip emerged from the side of the building and hurried inside, shivering for her benefit and acting like two fraternity brothers who had just pulled off a great prank.

They struggled with their good-byes to Trent for a minute or two. "You going to be okay?" she asked him.

"Me? Oh, sure! Actually, I'm having dinner with Frank a little later. He called this morning, sounded pretty good, actually. Just nursing a nasty lump on his head and a splitting headache that he thought a good T-bone would cure!" Patricia could see right through his banter, but it made it easier for her to leave.

"Trent. Take it easy. I'm sure I'll see you tomorrow." The two men shook hands, and then Trent gave Patricia a hug before walking them to the door. He watched as they drove away, then closed the door. He slammed his fist against it several times. After he'd paced around the office, Trent sat down and took the smooth, red stone from the inside breast pocket of his down vest and studied it, rolling it over and over in his hands. Red jasper. He had no reason to doubt anything that Phillip had just told him. And the more he got to know him, the more he trusted him.

Love. Honor. Respect. Phillip had asked him to take the stone back, with his blessing this time. Trent put the perfect heart-shaped stone to his lips.

Phillip had more insight than he'd have in a million lifetimes, he told himself. Trent tried to remember his exact words. *Love. Honor. Respect. These things cannot be given or taken freely. They must be earned.* Phillip told him that while Patricia slept, he had studied the contents of the medicine bag and looked for the hidden meanings behind the words that she'd said, as well as behind all the many words she didn't say. Phillip told him that he knew that Trent had earned this stone more than any other man he'd ever known. He assured him that one day he'd tell Patricia what he'd done. Just as soon as he felt like he had earned half of the love, honor, and respect from Patricia that Trent had.

He placed the stone back in his pocket and picked up the phone. "How's the headache? Whatta you say we move dinner up an hour or so? Suddenly I think a big, juicy steak is just what the doctor ordered for me, too!" Afterwards, he put the "closed" sign in the window. He stared at it for a minute or two and decided that taking a few days off sounded good to him, too. He'd wanted to go back to Texas and fish the Pecos again. He hadn't done that since college. Maybe Frank would like to come along.

"So, Mr. Craven, are you going to tell me what that was all about or not?" Patricia propped her elbow on the console between the seats and teasingly batted her eyelashes.

"Or not," he said. "So, you hungry?"

"A little, yes. What are you in the mood for?" She was momentarily lost again in her own thoughts. She hadn't noticed that he didn't answer her.

"I'll give you a penny, little girl." They were stopped at a light. The snow was beginning to fall again, only now the wind had stopped and the large flakes were drifting down slowly.

"Do you want to know how I finally mastered snow skiing?" The words were out of her mouth before she knew that she'd thought them. Phillip started laughing uproariously.

"Stop that! Don't you laugh at me!"

"I'm sorry, but where in the world did you come up with that?"

"What do you mean where did I come up with that? Where do you think? I was watching it snow and I thought of a song. That reminded me of when I was learning to ski. Right up there, actually!" She pointed through the windshield up toward Taos Ski Valley.

"Oh, that makes perfect sense. Of course, how silly of me! That's precisely how I learned to ski, too! Small world!"

"You don't ski, mister," she said in mock seriousness.

"My point exactly." He never flinched. She tried to poke him in the stomach, but he grabbed her hand, moved it to his lips, and tenderly kissed her fingers.

"Waltz Across Texas." She didn't even look at him when she said it.

"What?! Waltz across *what*?"

"That's how I learned to ski, silly. I sang 'Waltz Across Texas' over and over again. Skiing is very much a dance, like a waltz in the snow, you know!" She was dead serious. He knew that about her now. It had taken him a while to understand that about her. "Well, you asked how I learned to ski," she pouted.

"No I didn't."

"You didn't?"

"No."

"Oh, I thought you did. Well, you should have."

"You're right. I should have. I'll be more attentive after I've eaten," he deadpanned.

"I should hope so. By the way, where are we going?

"You just think about waltzing across the snows of Texas and let me worry about where we're going."

"Listen, wise guy, where are we going?"

"Up that hill yonder."

"Listen, are you gonna tell me, or not?"

"I heard there's a place up ahead that has some great chicken curry. Ever hear of such a thing?" He was holding his breath, hoping he hadn't made a wrong call.

"Oh, very good!" Patricia said. "You asked Trent where this place was, didn't you?"

"Yep."

"I didn't realize you liked chicken curry," she said.

"You didn't? I'm surprised. You know everything else about me."

"I do not."

"Yes, you do. Well, okay," he chuckled, "maybe not everything."

"What not everything. Try me," she said.

"I bet you don't know my favorite song in the whole world." He watched her out of the corner of his eye as he followed the signs to the Alpine Lodge.

"Hmm, favorite song in the whole wide world. Can I have a few minutes on this one?"

"I'll let you just this once. But don't ask again, though." He looked up at the Swiss chalet ski lodge. "This the joint?"

"This is the joint."

He came around and opened her door, and she stepped out and into his arms. The snow was much deeper up here and they stood in the dying light of evening, feeling the whisper soft flakes melt on their faces. *Snowflakes that stay on my nose and eyelashes, Silver-white winters that melt into springs. These are a few of my favorite things.*

"No," he said, holding her at arms length, and then suddenly licking a snowdrop from her forehead.

"No what?" she asked dreamily.

"It's not 'My Favorite Things' from *The Sound of Music*." He smiled as he watched her eyes grow wide. "You were humming it."

He laughed as he led her up the broad steps and into the magnificent old lodge. He requested a table near the massive stone fireplace. They ordered wine, and enjoyed a leisurely dinner. The snow continued to fall, and so they decided it would be best to spend the night at the lodge. It seemed like a wise decision, especially after their second bottle of wine.

Later the next morning, the weather had cleared and the sky was a brilliant blue. Bill stood among a group of uniformed officers. Some of them Patricia and Phillip knew and recognized, most they did not. Vehicles were still making their way slowly up the muddy road and parking in the clearing above the lake. While Phillip was talking to Brenda Riley, Patricia walked over to Trent and gave him a warm hug. He and Frank had arrived together.

"See you later, Trent," she said as he went over to greet some old friends. "Hi, Frank," she continued. "Your head feeling better?"

"Oh, it's fine now. Thank you. I hear you're leaving this afternoon. I'll miss you, Patricia." He looked surprisingly sad.

"I'll be back before you know it. You understand."

He nodded. "Is all of this my fault, Patricia?" He needed an answer, but didn't necessarily want to hear it. I didn't know he was a man. A boy, really. I swear to God I didn't." It was almost the truth.

"It's okay, Frank. You don't really owe me an explanation about that."

"Of course, I do." He fingered the brim of his hat nervously. " I think, I could have stopped it, if I'd wanted to."

Patricia didn't expect him to say that. She stood motionless.

"I loved Silky, Patricia. Perhaps you are the only one who can understand that." He was staring at the gathering crowd. People were in groups, talking in hushed voices. Some people were talking to Carlos and Bill. Patricia noticed that Carlos' dad wasn't among the people paying their respects.

"Maybe I can, Frank. I don't know. Are you saying you *still* love Silky?"

"I love what Silky represented. That won't change. I love how she made me feel and how she let me make her feel. We were both running to or running away from different things. It's hard to explain. It started with a need, Patricia. I needed Silky as a fantasy, then more. Then a craving, and then a compulsion, I guess. Isn't that how it happened with you and Phillip?"

"No, ours was much more elementary, Frank. Simplistic and idealistic, really. I think ours started, for me anyway, from curiosity. Then passion. Phil and I both sought a passion with one another, like the way we passionately embrace everything else in our lives. We were both searching for ourselves, and in the process found us in each other. It was a crapshoot, right? Thousands of chatrooms and millions of chatters, and we bumped into one another one cold February night. That's the long and short of it, Frank. There are no explanations for things beyond our control." She took his hand and then began walking toward the others. "As Phil has said," she continued, "we aren't going to understand everything, even within ourselves. And believing we have to understand it all will lead to a very frustrating life."

"Yeah, I heard him say that, but he said it much better," Frank chuckled.

"Oh, shut up."

"I want him to be okay," Frank said quietly.

"Who?"

"Jordan."

Patricia stopped and looked at Frank. People were dead because of Jordan. Good people, and Frank was hoping the monster was okay?

"I know how terrible that is, Patricia. I know what the son-of-a-bitch did and I feel like an ass for saying what I just did out loud."

"It's okay, Frank." She said it simply because she didn't know what else to say. She said it with no feeling at all.

"They'll find him soon and have him behind bars, Patricia."

"I hope so, Frank. I hope so..."

The law enforcement officers gathered in an area just to the left of the lake. Bill stood in front of them, his head bowed and his arm draped over Carlos' shoulders. The black armbands were the only outward reminders of why they were assembled. Bill looked up and scanned the crowd, thanked everyone for coming, and then caught Frank's eye. He hesitated, patted Carlos on the shoulder, whispered something, then stepped forward and walked directly across the snow-covered meadow to Frank. He stood for a very brief moment, then asked Frank to join him and his fellow officers. A few loud whispers passed through the crowd, and then several people started clapping quietly.

Brenda stood, directly behind Bill and Frank, her hat in her hands. She caught Patricia looking at her, and they exchanged smiles. Patricia was glad they'd talked yesterday. It's hard to be so terribly mistaken about people, harder yet to admit it, even more difficult to apologize. Brenda had made it easy for her to accomplish all of that, and yet maintain some dignity.

From somewhere behind her, Patricia heard the haunting notes of a native flute. Very slowly, the tom-tom talkers began to drum one by one. The sounds blended with the sky and rose on invisible wings. When Carlos sat on the ground and began to beat rhythms on his own cottonwood drum, Patricia began to weep. That which was old, that which had become as comfortable as her favorite pair of twenty-year-old moccasins, was gone now. All gone. In its place, the newly discovered. She was slowly understanding that it would soon encompass and embrace all that she had been and all that she was going to be. All about them The People wailed for their dead.

Bill made a point of talking to Phillip and they stood apart from the crowd of people slowly making their way back to where they had parked their cars.

"I don't think Jordan will be stupid enough to bother you or Patricia, but you have to be very careful, Phil." He nodded, trying to block some of the things he was trying not to think about.

"You bring Patricia back to us back real soon, okay?"

"I will, Bill. You take care of yourself, and remember Carlos needs you to be strong right now."

Bill was silent for a few moments. Phillip had this ability of saying things, even perhaps when he shouldn't, that were exactly the things that needed saying.

"Thanks, Phil, I appreciate that."

"Got everything, baby?" Phillip walked through each room of the quiet house with her. He glanced at his watch; they had plenty of time to catch the 9:35 P.M. flight.

"I think so. If I don't, then I don't need it, right?"

They had already loaded her things into the car before they'd driven up to the lake. After the short service, Brenda reminded her that she still needed to drop off the two letters from Bishamon that Phillip thought were lost when their computers had been tampered with. Patricia had printed copies of them and had filed them in her desk at home. She'd actually read them aloud to Brenda the day before. She'd forgotten how vile and ugly they were.

Phillip walked out onto the porch and was drinking in the early evening air while Patricia finished up inside. She was searching through the files, more slowly this time. It was gone. One more time, she told herself, and sat down and meticulously went through her entire desk. The one file, the one that she had cryptically labeled "Love Letters in the Sky," was gone.

She looked around the room for any other signs or feelings that Jordan or Caesar had been there. Nothing. She jotted a quick note to Brenda, put it in an envelope, sealed it, and addressed it to her at the station. Her heart was racing. *She'd had the file just yesterday!* She heard Phillip as he started down the hall.

"Ready?"

"Just about. I need to leave Trent a note, okay?"

"Sure. I'll be in the courtyard. Take your time." He started to say something else, but thought better of it.

Trent… Don't worry about me. I'm fine. I'll be back in time. Don't hesitate to call. Here's the number, okay? 287-778-8742. The papers are all signed and I dropped them off at your attorney's office this morning. Let me know if you need anything else. And yes, Trent. I will always love you, just as I always have. Love Patricia.

"All set, handsome. How about you?" She disguised her uneasiness.

"All set. God, as odd as this sounds, I hate to leave here, Trisha. I love something here, but I can't put my finger on it."

"I know. No one can. It's a mystery. But you can't be selfish, you must share, you know. Share your world, sweetheart. It's my turn now. You've been indulged quite enough." She tried to punch him in the stomach, but he grabbed her hand.

"Quit that before you poke a hole there, and I begin leaking every time I drink something." He shook his finger near her nose, then kissed her lightly.

They parked behind the municipal complex, and Patricia ran the envelope inside. Luckily, Amy was not at her desk and no other officers were in sight. She hated good-byes. She breathed a sigh of relief as she dashed back out to the car.

"That was fast!"

"I just left the letters on Amy's desk."

"You big chicken! Bokbokbokbok!"

"Stop that."

"Never."

"Never?"

"Not ever."

"Good."

She couldn't tell him about the missing file yet.

"I love you, Phillip Craven."
"You'd better, Patricia Ridgeway."

EPILOGUE

The Glass Cocoon
by Phillip Craven

Words flowing from somewhere
Sparked by a muse
Of the Spirit

Turning from text here
Into feelings there

From black and white
Into rich color.

The mind's eye?
No, the Spiritual eye.
Transforming a word
By itself so cold
Into something
Real
Warm
Bold
Meaningful

The words
On the page
Soon to be more
Like a caterpillar…
In a
Glass Cocoon.

So close to becoming
A splash of vividly bright
Color

To be more for a moment
Than just black and white.

To defy simple description
As the colors
Take flight.

Ah…if only it was true.
If the ego balloon
Was really not just hot air
Or platitudes
But…a
Living creature in
A
Glass Cocoon.

When Patricia finally forced herself to open her eyes, she was surprised how dark the room was. She looked around for the clock that she could hear ticking. She finally remembered where she was. Especially early in the mornings or when she got overly tired, her memory still played a few tricks on her. She'd paid Dr. Morrison a visit before they'd left Taos, and he had assured her that she was doing fine. Little by little, he said, her mind would allow her to remember.

She found herself alone in the small, dark room. On the pillow next to her, she found a note written on yellow paper. She sat on the edge of the bed for a moment, listening to the sounds of morning outside the window. Eventually she leaned over, turned on the bedside lamp, put on her glasses, and began to read: *Good morning! No, it's not Maureen McGovern's "The Morning After" either. I'm only doing this because I feel sorry for you, and you only have one guess left. I'm on the deck when you find the time to wake up. xoxo Phillip.*

Patricia smiled. She looked around the room. It was very much Phillip—a little cluttered, but neatly cluttered. The wooden floor looked worn beneath the scattered rugs. Above the dresser was a large framed mirror. She walked over to get a closer look at the variety of small snapshots, clippings, and ticket stubs tucked around the edge of the frame. Some of the photos looked very old. His family, perhaps. There were several pictures of an older woman in an apron, and she guessed that it was his Nana of whom he'd spoken so fondly. Others were obviously more recent photos, yet were taken in black-and-white. There was one of Mark sitting on the hood of his patrol car. He had a moustache.

Patricia thought about the evening that they'd spent with Mark and his fiancée Judy the night before. She'd met them very early that morning when Judy had accompanied Mark to the airport to pick them up when they arrived. No one is at their best at midnight; but even under the circumstances, she felt very comfortable with them and looked forward to sharing Phillip's friendship with the handsome couple. It was easy to see why Phillip allowed him to be his friend. She hoped that Phillip had felt as comfortable with her friends as she had with his. She sensed that this relationship with Judy might be a lasting one for Mark. Phillip had shared a little of Mark's previous marriages, and they both were in agreement that it just takes some men longer than others to "get it." After spending a relaxing and enjoyable evening watching Mark and Judy, if he wasn't getting it, he likely never would, she thought to herself. Judy was very beautiful, a bit bashfully alluring, and obviously well bred.

Men are unusual creatures, in comparison to women. She knew that they were certainly not from different planets, but sometimes their idea of communication differed dramatically from a woman's concept. Still, she knew that Phillip understood her like no one else did or ever would. *God, I love that man.* She removed an old photo and studied it. It must have been Phillip, she realized, probably around the age of six or seven, sitting on a wooden step with the attractive woman in the apron. She turned the picture over, and in a young child's hesitant print, it simply said "Nana and Me." In a frame, on the wall, was a very old photograph of a stunningly beautiful woman in a wedding gown. It looked to possibly have been from the 1920s. Next to it, at eye-level, was a black-and-white framed photograph of Mae West. It was signed: *To Phil, Best Wishes, Sin-cerely, Mae West.*

Patricia would certainly have to ask Phillip about this one. Did he meet Mae West? Then Patricia laughed. She realized she had misread the inscription. It now looked to her like it said: *To Phil, Bed Wishes, Sin-cerely, Mae West.*

There was also a picture of Groucho Marx. It was a publicity photo from the television show "You Bet Your Life" with the duck and the word "winner" on it. Probably from the late 1950s. It was signed: *Phil, Do I know you? Groucho Marx.*

There was a stack of oversized, professional looking photos lying on the dresser and various other odds and ends—loose change, keys, nail clippers, and a tube of cherry flavored ChapStick, and a lot of dust. She replaced the picture of Phillip and his grandmother as carefully as she could, then drew two interlocking hearts in the dust that covered the dark wood. Within the hearts she put "PR + PC." *Sheesh, how childish*! She smiled to herself and left it, of course.

Patricia walked over to a short bookcase and studied some of the titles there—photography books, computer manuals, a set of *National Geographic* wildlife books, and a few paperbacks of varied genres. There was also a trophy being used as book-end. Patricia realized it was an Emmy. "Best Documentary 1986." Phillip had won an Emmy award? What other surprises were in store?

There was a stack of outdoors and photography magazines on top of the television tucked into an armoire next to the bathroom door, and there were dozens of video movies, all very neatly arranged on the two shelves beneath the television. Patricia smiled when she saw that they were alphabetized by title. She should have suspected that.

There were stacks of mail and papers lying on a small desk near the only window, but she didn't look at them. Phillip shared what he wanted to with her when he wanted to, and he allowed her that same privilege. She respected that about him. Patricia walked over to the window and lifted the shade. Brilliant sunlight flooded the room. It was obviously much later in the day than she'd imagined.

She went into the bathroom where she found the source of the ticking. The old wind-up clock told her it was nearly noon. *Oh, my goodness!* Patricia looked at herself in the mirror and saw that she hadn't removed her make-up the night before. *Mercy, I look like an orphaned raccoon!* She quickly splashed cool water on her face and found a dark towel to dry with, erasing the black smudges and wishing she could erase the crows feet and dark circles as easily.

They hadn't brought much in from the car when they arrived late the night before, and it only took a second for her to realized that her overnight bag was nowhere to be found! *Yikes*! She opened a drawer and found a toothbrush in the back that almost looked new. She took a deep breath and ran it under hot water for a few seconds. As she tentatively brushed her teeth, she hoped that Phillip had never used it to clean the bottom of a bird-cage. She made herself smile.

After she ran Phillip's brush through her hair, she stepped back into the sun-drenched room and realized that the only clothes she had in the house lay scattered and crumpled on the floor. She had no desire to put the travel-worn jeans back on. Instead, she pulled the blue down comforter off the bed and wrapped it around herself, then slipped into a pair of Phillip's loafers that were on the floor at the foot of the bed. Her feet swam in them. She giggled out loud, curling her toes to keep them on as she walked.

The minute she stepped into the main living room of the house, she smelled fresh coffee and her senses suddenly came to life. The cozy little house was everything that she'd imagined and a thousand things more. Phillip was standing with his back to her, leaning against the low railing that enclosed his deck.

Maneuvering to keep the comforter around her, Patricia poured herself half a cup of coffee. Phillip had left the sliding door partially open, and she slipped through it and moved silently to his side. He knew she was there. Neither of them spoke. He just casually draped his arm over her shoulder. They sipped their coffee and shared what little bit was left of the morning.

"Nice outfit, by the way," he whispered after a few moments.

"Thanks. Made it myself."

"The shoes, too?"

"No. Just found the shoes." She stifled a giggle.

"I see," he said. "By the way, do you cook?"

"No."

"I was afraid of that." He set his cup on the railing, took her mug and set it next to his, then turned her toward him.

"You *sure* you don't cook?"

"Positive."

"Damn."

"I come with a money-back guarantee though. You can return me."

"Nope. Can't do that." He shook his head. "Lost the receipt, damn it."

"That's a shame. Pity, really. But why do you keep cussing?" She reached up and straightened his jacket collar.

"I'm not cussing."

"Where I come from, that's called cussing."

Phillip smiled and turned her toward the railing and pointed down toward the river.

"Where I come from, that's called a river," she said.

"Fancy that. That's what we call it here, too! Small world. Damn."

"You're cussing again."

"I'm not cussing, I say to you!" He drew his eyebrows together and squinted against the bright sunlight.

Patricia followed his gaze. It didn't take her long to spot them and she smiled broadly. *Ahhhh...how perfect.*

Turning more serious, Patricia asked him, "Is this the first time you've seen them, baby?" She slipped her arm around his waist.

"Yep."

"Is this something like that old saying—*when a door closes, a window opens*?" She watched his features soften as a shadow drifted over the deck.

"I think so. I'm not sure. Maybe. I've only had door after door close on me, Trisha. This is almost my first window." He didn't look melancholy or remorseful, just far away when she looked at him.

"In my world, those are called beavers. Let me guess. In your world, they're called beavers, too, right?" She had both hands resting on the railing now and Phillip pulled the warm blanket up around her neck.

"You are amazing! How did you know?"

"In my world, beavers build dams, too. I just took a leap of faith, hoping that the old small world theory held together. Damn! That was a close one, huh?" She laid her head against his shoulder.

Phillip rehearsed the words carefully in his mind before he spoke. The last thing he wanted to do was leave right now. *She couldn't know how frightened he was or how much danger they were most likely in.*

"Trisha, I have to go somewhere for just a little bit. I hope that's okay. I wouldn't do it if I didn't have to, honestly."

"Sweetie, why do you think it wouldn't be okay? I'm sure you have oodles of things you need to be doing. Of course, it's okay! Well, it's okay if I can talk you into bringing in my bags before you leave, that is."

Phillip stepped away from her, let his eyes travel slowly and provocatively up and down her body, stopping too long a couple of times. "Hmm…no…I don't think so." He watched her wheels turning and spoke up quickly. "What's it worth to you?" he said with a wink.

"Oh, it's not what it's worth it to *me*, dahling. It's what it's worth to *you*!"

"You win!" he laughed.

"But, of course!" She threw her head back and laughed.

After Phillip left, Patricia showered and washed her hair, rinsing it in lilac water. She lingered in the shower, enjoying the warm water cascading down her back. By the time she heard his Subaru pull up near the front porch, she'd gotten dressed, changed the bed linens, and cleaned up his tiny kitchen. She heard him take the steps, two at a time, and looked up as he pressed his face against the screen door, flattening his nose and wet lips into a sloppy kiss that lingered on the fabric of the screen even after he moved away.

"Hey, Mrs. Ridgeway, can you give a guy a hand? I've got a box I need to unpack out here. Second drawer, left of the sink, has knives. Mind bringing me one?"

She found a small paring knife, with the tip broken off, buried under an array of rubber bands and twist ties. She went outside and saw Phillip crouched over a large box at the base of the steps. There was something about him. His hair was partially in his face, and he looked casual and happy, like a full-grown little boy. *Oh, my! There's that feeling again.*

"So, what do you have there, Mr. Craven?"

"Dunno. Must be some equipment I ordered. Leo had it at his place." He looked up to see if that answer had flown. She looked clueless. He didn't believe that for an instant. Phillip took the knife from her and carefully cut the tape across the top of the box. "Oh, here!" he said feigning exasperation. "I know how women like surprises. *You* open it!"

"Oh goody! I hope it's a case of film! I haven't gotten a dozen rolls of fresh film in ages and ages!" She knelt down across from Phillip and lifted the four flaps back from the box. She stared into the semi-darkness, then up at Phillip, then back into the box.

Some Steller's jays loudly squawked their annoying bickering and other mountain birds taunted and teased them. There was the faintest breeze in their faces and Patricia could almost hear the river behind her over the pounding in her chest. "Oh, Phillip," she finally sighed. "Oh, my..."

"Say something, Trisha... please."

"Oh, she's beautiful, Phillip! Oh, my gosh!" Patricia was speechless. Her enormous smile awakened the woods around them as she lifted the furry puppy out of the box. "It's a Husky, isn't it?"

"Yes, officially I think she's called a Copper Siberian. She doesn't have papers or anything. I guess that's okay. Leo found her for me in the paper. The price was right, so I couldn't resist. You like her? Really?" He looked like he was afraid she was going to say something he didn't want to hear.

"It depends. You didn't pay a lot for her did you? I wouldn't want you to do that, Phillip." She was frowning at him as she rubbed the puppy against her cheek.

"I told you, the price was right."

"That's not an acceptable answer. Tell me how much she cost, and I'll tell you if I like her or not." The dog had managed to somehow nuzzle under Patricia's arm and was curled up and falling asleep as they argued.

"Well, I'll tell you if you promise not to get mad. I can work a few odd jobs around and pay for her in less than a year, I'm sure."

"A year!" she yelled, and Phillip burst out laughing.

"She was free, baby. Some folks down in Cle Elum just needed to get rid of her." He watched her cuddle the puppy closer to her.

"She's priceless. That's what you meant to say, isn't it?"

He smiled, watching Patricia rub noses and bury her face in the six-week-old ball of fuzz. When she looked up and saw him, she placed the pup back in the box and wrapped her arms around his neck. With one motion he slipped his arms under hers and lifted her to a standing position and held her tightly.

"Welcome home, baby," he whispered into her hair. "Welcome home."

"Oh Phillip, this is absolutely beautiful!" Patricia said, soon after she sat down in the window seat at Salty's, a well-known Seattle restaurant.

So far that day, Phillip had taken Patricia on a little mini-tourist adventure of Seattle. They'd been to Pike's Place Market and watched the energetic vendors throwing fish at each other to the amusement and amazement of the onlookers. They had wandered into dozens of shops, taken a walk on the pier, and driven to Seattle Center where they enjoyed a perfectly mediocre lunch atop the Space Needle. Phillip had been waiting a long time to take her up there to enjoy the view together. There was Puget Sound in one direction, Lake Union and Lake Washington and Mount Rainier in another direction, and downtown Seattle in yet another. The view changed slowly and magically as the restaurant turned. Afterwards, they took a stroll in Volunteer Park, walked through the greenhouse and admired the plants, and then climbed to the top of the water tower for another spectacular series of views. The weather was perfect. Somewhere in the low seventies and the sky was deep blue. Patricia was amazed at all the green there was, no matter where she looked.

"In case you ever wondered how many shades of green there might be..." Phillip smiled and gestured upward, as they drove down a street covered so thickly under a canopy of maple trees that it appeared to be dusk when it was only mid-afternoon.

Soon, they were sipping lattes in Starbuck's and holding hands like teenagers. Afterwards, he took her into Twice Told Tales, a used bookstore in the Capitol Hill neighborhood of Seattle. Phillip told her how much he'd always loved the store, but assured her that maybe in time, hers would grow on him. She punched him, of course.

Now it was a little past seven, and Mark Murphy was running late again. No doubt Judy would be showing up any moment, and Mark would be forced to struggle with lame excuses for his usual and expected tardiness.

Salty's sat right on the Sound, just south of Alki Beach, in west Seattle. Through the windows, Patricia and Phillip could see the entire Seattle skyline. By turning around, they could see Mount Rainier in the distance. From here, the Space Needle looked like a model from the old Jetson's cartoon show.

Clouds were moving in, covering the blue sky and changing the quality of the light inside the restaurant within just a few minutes. "Maybe a squall," Phillip said.

A few hundred yards away, Patricia could see a foggy mist. It became an ominous swirling cloud, dumping rain as it moved quickly up the channel closer to them. This was not a common sight. Food servers, customers, and busboys stopped and watched the fast moving storm system as it rushed toward them. Wind and rain blocked out nearly all of the daylight. As quickly as it had come, it was gone. The clouds were parting, blue sky and the fading light of day were beginning to reappear, creating a spectacular triple rainbow. Two of them seemed to rise out of the water itself and form an enormous bridge over the city. The third appeared to the south, framing a snow-peaked Mount Rainier.

At that moment, Mark appeared. "I'm real sorry I'm late." He had started to apologize, but the triple rainbow caught him speechless.

"Something else, huh pal?" Phillip said.

"Whoa. Gotta love it! Only in Seattle."

Mark was dressed in a camel-colored sport jacket, and looking very sharp. Patricia reminded herself to tell Phillip later that she thought Mark looked a lot like Harrison Ford when he was younger.

"The always punctual Judy is late?" Mark asked hopefully.

"Looks that way, unless she's standing you up," Phillip said.

"Phillip!" Patricia scolded.

"Quick!" Mark said. "Let's order some wine before she shows! Tell her I was on time, will you?" Mark looked around for a waitress.

"Too late! She's here!" Phillip announced, spotting Judy coming toward them.

Judy Baxter had been born with good skin, high cheek bones, and didn't have to work too hard to maintain her trim figure. She was in her mid-thirties, but could have passed for late twenties, and you would almost hate her for being too good looking if it weren't for the way she smiled that revealed she wasn't entirely comfortable with the good looks she was born with. She wasn't going to act like a spoiled princess. Maybe because not everything in her life had gone storybook perfect.

She apologized for being late, and soon they were eating, sipping wine, and conversing easily without having to work at it at all.

"Are we really going to try and go to this art museum opening?" asked Mark with a frown as he looked at his watch.

"What time is it?" asked Judy.

"Nearly nine," Mark answered.

"Do you mind terribly if we don't go?" asked Phillip.

"It's fine with me! I could stay here forever! This is wonderful." Patricia meant it. "I mean, if we hurry we could make it, but I would just rather have some dessert and keep talking."

"I'm sold!" Judy exclaimed.

"You sure?" Phillip asked. "I mean, I don't mind. I think Linda was kind of expecting me…"

Mark tossed Phillip his cell phone. "Call Linda, tell her we aren't going to make it, and let's just relax and enjoy ourselves."

"Hold on. Now wait a minute! The first one wasn't called *The Nutty Professor*?" Mark was asking again.

"No, that's *The Absent Minded Professor*. That was the first one!" Phillip repeated.

Where had she been? It didn't matter anymore. "In black-and-white, with Fred MacMurray?" asked Patricia.

"Right," Phillip said. "The sequel was called *Son of Flubber*."

"And they remade it with Robin Williams," Judy said.

"Right! It was called *Flubber*," Phillip said. "I thought it was pretty good."

"You're kidding!" exclaimed Judy.

"It was pretty dumb, but I laughed a lot!" confessed Phillip.

"This sounds promising," added Patricia.

"It might be a Three Stooges thing though," Mark warned.

"What's that mean?" Judy asked defiantly.

"Women tend to not like the Three Stooges very much," Phillip began to explain.

"Oh pleeeease…" Judy whined.

"Well, do *you* like the Three Stooges?"

"I could take them or leave them," she admitted.

"Well, I *like* them," Patricia said.

"So does Joe Friday have anything to share with us tonight?" Phillip asked, quickly changing the subject.

"She hasn't given me an answer yet," Mark said, a bit embarrassed.

Patricia and Phillip looked at Judy.

"Well, I gotta make him sweat, don't I? I mean, look how long he took to ask me!"

"Well…?" Mark leaned forward.

Judy looked at Mark and shook her head, and then looked over at Patricia. "He is so pitiful."

"Kinda cute though," Patricia smiled.

"Don't do it Judy! Save yourself while there's still time!" Phillip said quickly.

"Oh, fine! All right, fine," Judy said. "Yes. The answer is *yes*!"

Mark grabbed Judy and pulled her toward him and planted a big kiss on her lips.

"Oh, stop it!" she protested.

"She said yes!" Mark said proudly.

Phillip shook Mark's hand. "Congratulations! You should immediately buy some lotto tickets! You are one very lucky fella!"

"I said *yes*, but I didn't say *when*," Judy said with a smirk.

They spent an hour more having coffee and dessert before finally saying their good-byes and heading off in separate directions. They never once mentioned any of the events of the last several weeks, and it was wonderful.

"*Now* where are you taking me?" Patricia asked as they strolled toward Phillip's car.

"Home."

"I know where it is…" She smiled at him. "Somewhere Over the Rainbow."

"What?"

"Well?" Patricia demanded an answer.

"Yes, you're right. Finally! I'll admit it's not the most original song to have as a favorite, but yes, that's it."

"It suits you, sweetheart. And it suits me just fine, too."

"You're favorite, too?" Phillip asked, not a little surprised.

"Oh, sure. I wanted to grow up to be Judy Garland."

"I wanted to be Mickey Mantle. And then John Lennon. And then Woody Allen. And…"

"Wait! Wait! Woody Allen?" Patricia was more than a little surprised.

"Of course! I wanted to be able make a film every year or two, a small film that I felt like making, a film I get to make my very own way without interference from anyone."

"Oh, I see."

"Do you?" Phillip was looking up into the sky.

"An eagle?" Patricia looked up at the bird, circling far above them.

"Yep."

"Of course, I see," she said reassuringly. "Are you happy, Phillip?"

He just smiled.

"Answer me!"

"Of course, I'm happy," Phillip said. "Question is, are you?"

"Yes. I'm happy that I'm here with you, and I'm happy to love you, and I'm happy to be loved by you."

Phillip held Patricia for several minutes while they gently swayed, just enjoying being in each other's arms.

"What are you going to name her?" Patricia asked.

"The puppy's ours, baby. We both name her." Phillip said. "But not now."

"No?"

"No."

"Okay," she relented. She turned around and leaned back against him. He loved holding her, feeling her body pressed against his.

"Are we really standing here together, baby?" Phillip asked hesitantly.

"Yeah, we are," Patricia assured him.

"The last year has been so…" Phillip was not sure how to complete the sentence. He didn't need to. He just stood there holding Patricia like this was all that needed to be done. And it was.

"What was that?" Phillip asked after a few moments.

"I didn't say anything."

"Not out loud, but I thought I heard you thinking."

"Oh, it's a bit silly."

"Isn't it all a bit silly?" he asked.

"I hope so," she said.

Phillip pulled some folded paper from his back pocket. "So, what were you thinking, then? Tell me, please."

"That truth is stranger than fiction sometimes," she answered truthfully.

"Yes. You're right, that's very true." He handed the paper to her.

"What's this?" she asked.

"The best poem I've ever written. I started it years ago. I finished it this morning while you were sleeping. It's been a work in progress for more than twenty-five years. It's for you."

Patricia looked deeply into Phillip's eyes. "Whatever this is, baby, it's only the beginning. Just the beginning, my love."

Phillip smiled. He'd let her get the last word this time.

She unfolded the papers and began to read:

The Face and I

Faceless oceans still in motion
Drift before my eyes.
The stabbing sounds another's found
Briefly laughs then dies
How far must you go before you find out where you are?
The golden road
Its pleasures loathed
Memories explode.
The hearts of gold have all been sold
And buried in their fate.

A thousand friends with words to lend,
But always come too late.
So please excuse me while I die, I've just run out of life.

Paradise
At such a price
Wasn't all that nice.

Paper brothers return as lovers
Embrace you in their thrills
And through the action of slight distractions
Cripple my will.

The winds of discontent
Have been planted and soon must all be sown
They knock down the comfy house
And leave us all alone.
The words once deeply meant
Come rushing back
Forwarding address unknown.

Out of the lonely darkness
Through the frigid cold
Arrives a ray of warmth
Upon an almost felt caress.

A voice deceptively strong
And so unerringly bold
With another's whisper
Dares to celebrate
Two rainbows
Coloring the sky
Improbable and rare
An eagle circles
Way up high.

So cling a bit
To get some strength
Wipe that tear
From your eye
Have no fear.
Faceless oceans
Seas of emotions
Drift before my eyes
The stabbing sounds

Another's found
Briefly laughs
Then sighs.

But I just had to touch the face
To find out if I'm real
I've learned to cry
I will not die
For the face
And
I.

###

Acknowledgements

I was not sure when Serena and I began this project if it was something that we would be able to finish. It was a unique way to create a book, and it was one of the most fulfilling and satisfying experiences in my life. I will be forever grateful to Serena. Her writing inspired me to try a little harder, do a little better, and hope my writing was worthy enough to meld with hers. In fact, at times when she was writing circles around me, I wondered how I was going to possibly write well enough to avoid embarrassing her!

There are a lot of other people who made this book possible and I cannot possibly mention all of them. My family gave me the support and encouragement with which few are blessed. Thank you Azi, Natasha, Natalia, and Christina. Thanks also to my brother Bob, sisters Jackie and Jennifer, and parents Robert and Augusta. And I want to express my appreciation to my friends—some new, some old—who helped me believe in myself. Although at times I felt like I was working without a net, that wasn't at all true, thanks to their support.

Serena and I would also like to thank our publishing consultant, Linda Radke of Five Star Publications, and our editor, Paul M. Howey, who helped shape our raw and somewhat undisciplined material into the finished product you hold in your hands. We also want to thank graphic designer Kim Scott and illustrator supreme Jeff Yesh who created the cover as well as our Flibbertigibbet Platypus. We extend our appreciation to the proofreaders, typesetters, and the whole team of professionals (like Barbara Kordesh) Linda put together, people whose work is too often taken for granted.

Last but not least, we thank you, the reader, for spending some time on our words and making our dreams a reality—creating a book for others to enjoy. We hope that you will now go realize some of your own.

Christopher J. Jarmick

I want to thank the people in my life who *almost* patiently and with good humor remained supportive while Chris and I created this rather unorthodox novel. I will refrain from naming them here for two reasons. First, I'd live in fear that I might inadvertently forget someone. Secondly, due to some of the necessarily straightforward content of this book, there are many who would probably prefer their names not be linked with mine! Anyway, you know who you are and I send my love and thanks to each and every one of you. I also extend my boundless praise and admiration to my partner, Christopher Jarmick, without whom this book would not have been written.

Cle Elum is a real village in Washington, and there is a famous town in New Mexico called Taos. That, however, is where the connection between reality and this book ceases. This novel is a complete work of fiction. Its central theme, however, is very loosely based on personal experiences, research, and newspaper articles that captured our attention and led us to investigate and write about the intriguing phenomenon known as the Internet chatroom.

To quote author Robert James Waller: "As anyone who's been around will tell you, it gets strange out there."

Serena Holder

On the Creation of The Glass Cocoon

One might describe the evolution of *The Glass Cocoon* as a planned accident. Co-authors Serena Holder and Chris Jarmick first met in an Internet chatroom for writers of adult-oriented fiction. On a whim several days later, Serena e-mailed Chris and asked if he would consider collaborating on a book about the Internet chatroom experience. He accepted without hesitation.

They decided that the book should be a combination mystery/psychological thriller/love story that would explore the dark underbelly of the on-line chat world. It would also incorporate the "small world" phenomenon in which people reveal themselves to be connected by the simplest of things. Interestingly, both Chris and Serena found they shared many unique experiences in their own lives.

It was an interesting writing process, to say the least. Consider this, if you will: Chris and Serena are two complete strangers, living thousands of miles apart. They are of different genders and almost a generation removed in their thinking and life experiences. They are of different social, professional, and religious backgrounds. What they discovered, however, is that these differences had remarkably little bearing on how they both viewed life and love.

Since they took turns writing chapters, neither could do anything until they received the latest chapter from the other. They had absolutely no idea what turns the plot might have taken, or who was involved now or why, or whether any new characters might have been "born" while they were asleep! When something totally unexpected cropped up—which it frequently did—they would look at it as you would a stumbling block in life, and they would simply deal with it and move forward.

Most surprising perhaps is that they started (and ended) the project with no outline whatsoever. In fact, they had no idea how the plot would unfold. They didn't even know how it would end, until it did!

A year has come and gone since Serena and Chris embarked on this project, and they still have never met face to face. They actually worked for quite a while on the manuscript before they even spoke on the telephone.

Several noted authors have been quoted as saying that collaborating with another writer had been a nightmarish ordeal they would never try again. Maybe they should have worked with Chris and Serena, for they found the experience of writing *The Glass Cocoon* to be an immensely rewarding and life-changing adventure.

Chris and Serena have already started on their next novel. And who knows? They might even meet this time!

Additional Acknowledgements

Music Lyrics used or quoted in *The Glass Cocoon* include:

While You See a Chance
Written by Stephen Lawrence Winwood (BMI) & Will Jennings
Published by Blue Sky Rider Inc., dba Blue Sky Rider
Songs c/o Sussman and Associates
Irving Music
Warner-Tamerlane Publishing Company

Because of You
Written by Arthur Hammerstein, Dudley Wilkinson (ASCAP)
Publisher: Oliver Ditson Company

Fly Me To the Moon
Written by Howard Bart (ASCAP)
Publishers/Administrators: Hampshire House Pub. Corp.
c/o The Richmond Organization

That's Amoré
Written by Dr. Irvin Cooper (BMI & SOCAN)

Bright Side of the Road
Written by Van Morrison (BMI)
Essential Music c/o Stan Diamond
Universal Songs of Polygram Inc.

Somewhere Over There
Written by James Charles Olivero Jr. (ASCAP)
Publishers/Administrators: Oliverio Music Inc. (Collected Editions Ltd.)

It's My Party
Written by John R. Gluck, Wally Gold, Seymour Gottlieb, Herbert Wiener
Publishers/Administrators: World Song Publishing Inc./Spec. Acct.
c/o Warner/Chappell Music Inc.

Rainbow Seeker
Written by John Cameron
Publishers/Administrators: Bruton Music Division

Till
Written by Buisson Pierre Sananes Charles, Sigman Carl
Publishers/Administrators: Chappell & Co. Inc.
c/o Warner Chappell Music Inc.